THE TEARS
OF THE TIGER

Christie Dickason

CENTURY

LONDON SYDNEY AUCKLAND JOHANNESBURG

BY THE SAME AUTHOR

The Dragon Riders

Copyright © Christie Dickason 1990

All rights reserved

First published in Great Britain in 1990 by
Century Hutchinson Ltd
20, Vauxhall Bridge Road
London SW1V 2SA

Century Hutchinson South Africa (Pty) Ltd
PO Box 337, Bergvlei 2012, South Africa

Century Hutchinson Australia Pty Ltd
20 Alfred Street, Milsons Point, Sydney, NSW 2061
Australia

Century Hutchinson New Zealand Ltd
PO Box 40–086, Glenfield, Auckland 10
New Zealand

British Library Cataloguing in Publication Data

Dickason, Christie *1942–*
The tears of the tiger.
I. Title
813′.54 [F]

ISBN 0–7126–2424–4

Photoset by Deltatype Lecru, Ellesmere Port, Cheshire
Printed and bound in Great Britain by
Mackays of Chatham PLC, Chatham, Kent

For Patrick, Larry, Alan, Claude, Tom,
George, Stan, and Gerry, with thanks.

And for my own sons, Joshua and Thomas.

In addition to those named above, I would like to give special thanks for their help in researching this book to Theresa Cederholm of the Boston Public Library, John Cederholm, Mike Howard, Ed Giarusso, Frank E. Horack III, Chris Butchers, and several others who wish not to be named.

My thanks also to my editor Rosie Cheetham for faith beyond the call of duty, and to Robert and Wendy – my support system.

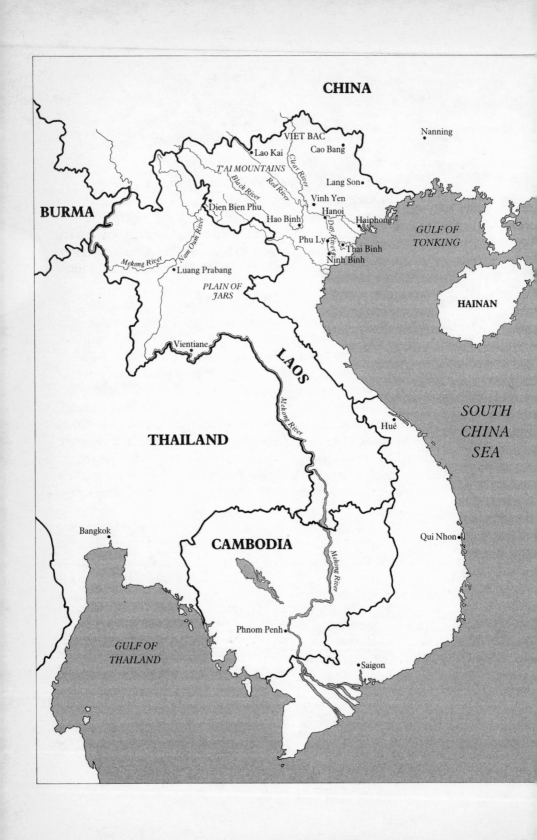

Preface

Saigon – 1966

A neighbour brought the warning.

'Madame is coming!'

The whispers spread like flood waters through a broken dike, along the shadowy corridors, through wicket windows, across a weed-filled courtyard which was dark beneath the leaves of an overhanging lime tree.

'She is coming here! Herself! Coming now!'

The voices soughed like the tree in the wind before a storm. The woman was coming. The woman, the *métisse* – half Round Eye, half Vietnamese – as unseen and powerful as the spirits to whom one made offerings. Like the spirits, she had power over men's lives.

The trappings of this power made anonymity impossible for her. The big Renault, which twisted through the alleyways of Cholon like a shark among coral reefs, was necessary. The fur stole, the high heeled shoes, the diamond studs in her ears, and the silk western-style dress were necessary. The two armed bodyguards and the driver were all necessary. These things defined and protected her. They created a fragile shield of awe. Among the ignorant, power lay where it was perceived to lie.

In the back seat, apparently nonchalant on the grey leather, she peered into the open fronts of shops and homes only a few feet from the car. She studied the passing minutiae of ordinary life: families eating their evening rice, lantern-lit card games, hand-cranked sewing machines clucking out a few more piastres of rice money, men in friendly drinking bouts, suckling children, caged songbirds, students bent over scratching ballpoint pens and notepads. Eyes lifted at the sound of the car, then were averted. Conversations stopped. Movements froze. The lives into which she peered were suspended until her car had moved on, from fear of drawing the attention of the passenger of such a machine. Only one curious toddler, naked except for a shirt, reached to touch the shiny metal flank, so big and so close in the narrow street, then his grandmother snatched him back.

The car paused by a gate in a high wall of brick and peeling stucco,

1

topped with broken bottles. One of the bodyguards spoke through a tiny window in the gate. The other opened the car door. The woman stepped out. The gateman bowed low. A small boy sprinted across the courtyard under the lime tree to tell the proprietress of the *fumeur*, but the whispers had already reached her.

'Madame. . . !' said the proprietress, bowing. She was a half-Chinese, half-Vietnamese woman in her early thirties, wearing a loose green rayon cheong-sam which flapped around her bony hips. Her bare feet had been shoved into rubber sandals and there were diamond studs in her ears. 'If I had only known that you were coming. . . .' She let silence conjure up the wonders of hospitality that she would have prepared.

She smiled to cover her panic. She was dead. Her licence would be taken away. They were going to smash all her pipes. Cut off her supplies of smoker's opium. Cut off her left hand. She would kowtow and confess immediately. Perhaps honesty would mitigate the punishment for her crime. She had revealed only a small piece of information to that other visitor, only the name of the agent from whom she bought her opium. Anyone could have told him that – and charged him more for it as well. But perhaps Madame wasn't sure of her guilt. The proprietress didn't know what to do.

'Will Madame do me the honour of coming in?' she asked with a dry mouth.

The woman from the car stepped past the proprietress into the dark, wood-panelled corridor. The air was hot, thick, and sweet-smelling. 'Where can I see without being seen?'

The proprietress swallowed. 'What do you mean, Madame?' See what? she wondered. Her own punishment? Her knees began to give way, to drop her to the floor to beg for mercy after all.

'I want to observe your clientele. You must have arranged that for yourself.'

'Oh, yes, of course.' The proprietress was now confused as well as frightened.

She led the woman and the two bodyguards along the dark corridor past a short row of closed doors, each inset with a carved wooden grille over a spyhole, like an elegant prison.

'The private rooms,' she explained. 'Not many people in those. This is where you can see the most.' As she opened the door to her office, she prayed that her assistant had had the sense to put everything away.

She held open the door to her office and felt a small quiver of relief in

2

the midst of her fear. Her assistant had heard the silent plea. The table in the modest room held only a lidded teacup, an open account book, and a telephone. The full cash box had been hidden, as had the tray holding the prepared pipe of opium to which the proprietress had been about to treat herself and the visitor who had just been bundled out of another door. She stepped back to a position near one wall and lowered her eyes respectfully.

Her visitor surveyed the room. The floor was bare wood polished only by feet. The walls were dirty whitewashed plaster. On one hung a crucifix adorned with pink and yellow plastic roses; a spyhole had been cut into the opposite wall and masked with a carved grille like those in the doors of the corridor.

The woman from the big car shrugged off her fur stole and one of the men darted forward to catch it. With her two guards watching her, she placed her face close to the grille. The smoke-filled room beyond it filled her nostrils with a heavy sweetness. A mosquito could be heard whining faintly from near the ceiling as she stood staring into the shadows on the other side of the fragrant cedarwood lace of the grille. The proprietress stole sideways glances, trying to read her own future in the set of the woman's red silk-clad back and smoothly-knotted head.

The room beyond the grille was dark as the hold of a slave ship. Bodies lay just visible on the floor and on wooden shelves around the wall, some tightly curled, some with limbs akimbo. Here and there, one had frozen with an arm raised in the air, or with a leg adrift from a supporting wooden shelf. Their eyes were all half-closed. The woman could see teeth, white in the shadows, in loose-lipped mouths, behind secret half-smiles. A body stirred and subsided. The smoky shadows stretched and thickened, revealing and then re-veiling other dreamers not visible at first. Tiny oil lamps burned under glass domes like the eyes of small supervising devils.

'They look dead,' the woman said aloud. Her voice was tight and vibrated with intense, bitter private meaning. Her face, as she turned away from the grille was younger than either her bearing or the expression in her large dark eyes.

She's younger than I am, thought the proprietress in surprise. In her position! Her eyes probed the woman's being for clues to her own best course of behaviour, her future.

And she's pregnant! thought the proprietress with a quiver of shock. I'm sure she's pregnant! She felt a sudden mix of nascent outrage and undefined relief.

3

The two men exchanged quick glances. This odd behaviour again! Everyone at the heart of the business knew their mistress was not herself . . . had not been for many weeks. Somebody was going to have to float the dangerous truth to the surface. To save all their necks.

The proprietress saw the glances and stared back down at the floor as if drilling a hole in which to hide. I'm not here, declared every angle of her body. I heard nothing. Observed nothing. Will say nothing. She was becoming more and more sure that her own small transgression was not the point of this visit after all. The tension she now felt in the office still put her in danger but in a different way. She began to feel anger as well as fright. How unjust that this woman had behaved so unexpectedly, coming here where only her agents had ever come before, and created this danger!

'Now show me a private room,' the woman ordered.

The bodyguards shifted their feet, trying to think of an excuse to remove their young mistress from the avid assessment they saw in the eyes of this bitch of a proprietress, who had not yet learned, so recent rumour had it, to keep her mouth sufficiently shut.

The two men knew for certain that the young woman was pregnant, as all her household servants also knew, though she had not yet told them. This was the reason, the servants reassured each other, that she was not quite herself. Some temporary derangement was normal, in these circumstances. It would pass.

Her maid, who had first deduced and spread the news, offered further clarification. 'The father,' she declared, 'Is that pointy-nosed, red-haired American who has been practically living here so shamelessly for the last seven months! What do you expect of her, even if she were Guan Yin herself, if the father then vanishes the way he did, without any warning? Naturally it has affected her state of mind.'

'No, you're quite wrong!' corrected the cook, who was seventy-four and did not fear contradiction from her juniors and inferiors. 'My nephew has seen Madame's cousin, the Colonel Thu, slipping away from the house much too early for an innocent man. On at least two occasions.'

'And what was your nephew doing at that time?' retorted the maid.

'Mowing while the day was still cool,' said the cook firmly. 'In any case, the Colonel is a far more suitable father, as they are already cousins and business partners. It's fitting! I'm certain the father is Colonel Thu!'

The Number One Boy, wash ayah, and cleaning maid all agreed with

4

the cook and her nephew the gardener that it was the Colonel. The two bodyguards, like most of the other business employees were less interested in the possible paternity of a future heir to the family business than the present behaviour of its mother-to-be.

'Show me a private room,' the young woman repeated tightly.

The proprietress led the little party into the dark hallway, trying frantically to remember whom she had put into which room that evening. She hesitated outside one door. Behind it lay a wealthy, elderly Chiu Chao widow, a client for many years, from the days of her visitor's father and her own mother. Best not risk angering her. Then the proprietress thought of a possible plus to set in her account against the tiny, and perhaps unknown, betrayal. She moved two doors further along the corridor.

'A new client, Madame,' she said proudly. New in his addiction, not yet dried up by the smoke like the bodies in the big room, who had, it seemed, displeased Madame by looking 'dead'.

The young woman stared through the carved grille. The man inside was fair. His pale, naked torso was covered with gold hairs and his drowsy face was burnt by the tropical sun.

'A Round Eye!' said the young woman, surprised.

'American!' said the proprietress proudly. 'Many are coming now. Like the old days with the French. Business is getting better all the time!'

'It depends on what you call better,' said the young woman quietly. 'And is it also an improvement to use children to serve? And for what services?'

'Oh . . .' said the proprietress. In her fear, she had forgotten that detail. 'She is only preparing the pipes, Madame! Nothing else, I swear! Only pipes! She is my own daughter!'

The young woman watched through the grille while the girl, a tiny fawn of about eight years, spun the ball of smoker's opium on the tip of a long needle over the flame in the glass-domed lamp. Then the child pushed the ball of opium into the tiny silver bowl of the bamboo pipe, re-heated it briefly over the lamp and placed the pipe into the hands of the blond man who lay half-naked on the low wooden platform bed.

The woman turned from the grille and studied the proprietress until the *fumeur* manager felt the marrow twist in her bones. Then the woman walked away down the corridor, out of the *fumeur*, into the lime-shaded courtyard. The proprietress bowed deeply, already beginning to shake with relief.

5

The two bodyguards marched grimly after their mistress, the taller one carrying her stole. Each knew the other's thoughts. The proprietress was now dangerous. Not only had she escaped punishment for her near-certain betrayal, but she had seen for herself the strange new weakness of the woman she should most fear. She had become another of the growing band of cobras which shifted and swayed in the shadows, waiting to strike – a small cobra, to be sure, but others, more dangerous, would observe and follow suit.

The problem with their mistress wasn't her pregnancy; that was women's talk. The truth was more serious, and more dangerous for all of them.

Once upon a time, seven years ago, they had all been persuaded that the Heavens had chosen her for special protection – how else could so young a girl have taken up the reins dropped by her father and then her brother? How else could she have survived the murder of her brother, and won and held the loyalty of the family's employees? She had been brave, and astute. She had her father's force and intelligence. She was lodged in the perceived hierarchy of power by her birth. With the protection of the Heavens, and the help of her father's friends, she had made the most of all these.

On the other hand, she had been very young to take up such power, and was still young. She was half Round Eye on her mother's side. And, though she had her father's energy and intellect, she did not burn, as he had done, with an internal fire fuelled by hate. She was not ruthless enough. She did not see the world in its true dark colours. Most alarming of all, she had recently fallen under the influence of that red-haired Round Eye devil whom she screwed; perversely, she had begun to question the favours the Heavens had granted, and they, in turn were becoming restless in their support. In short, she was losing her grip and the wrong people had begun to notice.

The two men knew that four of her agents had already begun secret talks with her cousin Thu who controlled the shipment of crude opium from the northern poppy fields to the refineries of Saigon. They had heard that he was happy enough to cut her out of her father's business, no matter what else gossip might have him doing with her. Two other agents had been seen talking openly with the Corsicans. As they ushered her back to the big Renault, each of the two bodyguards was wondering how much longer a prudent man could safely continue to serve her.

★

Nina knew what her two bodyguards were thinking, nearly enough. She had survived alone to the age of twenty-six by taking no one for granted. With finely tuned antennae, she constantly probed the unspoken reality behind the words of the men and women who surrounded her. She had not realized how lonely such constant suspicion made her, until she had met Will John Haines and, against her own better judgement, allowed herself to trust for the first time in her adult life.

Back in the bedroom of her big house in the former French quarter of Saigon, Cholon's Siamese twin city, she now dismissed her maid and sat on the edge of her carved and gilded wooden four-poster bed in her silk nightgown, which was the same rich cream as her skin. Her dark hair, freed from its chignon, fell like a shawl across her shoulders. Her hips stretched taut the pale pink mosquito netting draped from the canopy. She pulled her feet up and hugged her knees like a child, her wide soft mouth pressed hard against her kneecaps.

That her world was changing frightened her as much as it did her employees. However, she was not losing her grip as they thought, but, like a space-drunk climber on the brink of a precipice, was overwhelmed by a terrifying hunger to let go. Now, with lips pressed against the silk of her kneecaps, she stared at the Chinese carpet with dark hazel-flecked eyes. When she thought about what she had seen that night, and the night before and the other nights since she had first begun to see clearly, she felt as sad and slow and heavy as the tortoise which holds the world on its back.

I was only nineteen! she thought. And so ignorant!

The smoke of burning opium had coiled through her life like a dragon, both beautiful and terrifying, a force both good and evil. For many years, while it was a legal trade, opium had paid for her safe and privileged childhood, just as it had financed books and medicines under the French. But under the French rule, it had also paid for soldiers and informers, and protected the war lords. It soothed the hunger pangs of peasants and eased rainy season colds. But it also killed, either by design as it had her brother or by accident as with her mother, an unlucky bystander of the struggle to control the lucrative trade.

Poor, silly *maman*, she thought. Who couldn't read the signs . . . who wouldn't see the warnings. Like me. She swallowed against the old grief which had been overlaid by many more.

Maman! she begged. Be here! Be alive again to tell me once more about the wonderful cool breezes of Cap Ferret, about the wonders of the Paris Opera, about the gardens at Villandry and Versailles, which you wanted me to see one day. I need you to make some other world real enough to trust!

She turned her head and rested one cheek against her knee, resisting self-pity, trying to think straight.

I can't be imprisoned by a choice I made while barely more than a child! Restlessly, she pressed her other cheek against the damp silk of her knees.

The opium smoke had twined itself around her in the guise of filial duty, hiding its full import among other duties like the management of factories, a fleet of fishing sampans, and hotels. Even when she had finally learned the whole truth about her father, the purpose of her life, as explained by her father's followers, had seemed clear: to act as caretaker of his empire while he was in hiding from his enemies. She had made (she thought) a clear-sighted choice to carry on. Then the order of this world, of which she was custodian, had shifted.

Her father had died. The war against the French had brought a different foreign influence to the former French colony. The smoke began to blow far beyond the boundaries of her country. The American Sicilians who now vied with the Corsicans and Chinese to control its direction were terrifying aliens beyond her education or desire to understand. For months, she had carried a discomfort as uneasy as the shifting of broken glass. Then she herself had changed. Or buried parts of an earlier self had resurfaced.

She stood up and crossed on slim bare feet to the large, heavy-shuttered window, which had no glass, only metal mesh against mosquitoes. The big Renault stood in the circle of driveway below. A gaunt beige tomcat quivered with hungry intent under a bush, eyes on a grackle perched on the edge of the lily pool. A bougainvillaea lolled against the compound wall, waving its papery magenta bracts with careless extravagance above the precise dark green punctuation of a climbing fig. Nina inhaled the musty sweetness of the garden and swung restlessly away from this world she was thinking of leaving. The hands she wrapped across her bare arms were cold.

Safe in Will John's love, she thought, I stepped outside Father's world and looked with Will John's eyes.

She had been shocked and frightened by the evil she had seen. She saw how she could become evil herself . . . perhaps had been. . . . Then she learned she was pregnant with Will John's child. The woman she was afraid she might become could never be a mother. Her life seemed to hold its breath, waiting for her to do the unthinkable.

The climber had let go and begun to fall.

It's right! she thought, as she paced the formal Chinese cloud pattern that swirled around the edge of the rug. I know it's right! But, oh. . . ! Her breath was tight in her chest and her throat dry. Will John! . . . why aren't you here to tell me where I will land . . . and if it will kill me? I can't see without your eyes. The bottom is too distant and too strange!

She stopped walking suddenly. The silk hem of her nightgown settled like water breaking around her ankles. But I am going to do it. I have already begun to go, without admitting it. She looked down at the new tightness of her belly, the faintest curving of the cream silk. 'We must find a safe world for you,' she said softly. 'If such a thing can be found.' Her decision, so many months in the making, tilted from thought into deed.

She raised her head. 'Forgive me, Father,' she said, as if his spirit could hear her from the tomb in the northern mountains beyond the dead land of the De-militarized Zone. 'I know you understand. For the last seven years, I have lived only to please and honour you. But, whatever the risk, I can't go on. The disharmony inside me is too great. Different parts of me are living in separate houses.'

She listened as if for a response but heard only the burring of cicadas in the trees above the verandah and the rustling of the gecko behind her shutters. 'This is your last chance to protest,' she said with the dry humour that invaded even her most serious moments. She seemed to listen again. 'No? I suppose I must be satisfied with that.'

Her earlier heaviness shifted like the first shreds of a rising fog, but her fingertips were still icy cold. Swiftly, she turned and slid into the centre of her bed, pulling the netting closed behind her. She wrapped her arms protectively around the mystery that was growing beneath her ribs. How to carry out, and survive, her decision was tomorrow's problem. Like a child hiding from the dark, she dived for the fragile safety of sleep.

1

'Ooooohhhhh . . . we'll all go together, when we go,' sang Gabriel Simpson.

'. . . When . . . we . . . go,' James Putnam's voice echoed in a descending *basso*.

'And a one! . . . two! . . . threeee!' With an arm slung around his friend's shoulder, Simpson dragged him across the grass in a giant tango.

Other new graduates were still filtering with their parents out through the iron gates toward the Houses and sherry. Other voices sang and shouted different songs.

'We're out of our skulls,' said Gabriel, suddenly sober. He took off his black mortarboard and skimmed it at a tree in the centre of the quadrangle. 'Look at that . . . took his head right off!'

Both young men stood absolutely still, gazing at the unimpressed tree, and the black silk, moiré-covered bachelor's mortarboard on the ground beneath it.

'We're not the only ones to go,' said James Putnam.

'We're the only stupid bastards I know who volunteered!'

Gabriel Simpson was just under six feet, thin and wiry, with long dark blond hair, bright blue eyes and a sailor's tan. James Putnam was a little taller, a little heavier, and a little darker, with a smile of such sweetness that more undergraduate females than he could imagine had fought for seats beside him during four years of lectures and seminars.

Simpson's father was a professor at a nearby, competing university. Putnam's father was a structural engineer and the first black to run for public office in his particular southern California town. Simpson's mother was a professor, like her husband. Putnam's mother was a real estate agent. Neither set of parents was happy with either son's decision to enlist in the US Army, for service in Vietnam in a conflict which seemed to be growing into war.

Putnam and Simpson watched six other new graduates of both sexes, and noisy with alcohol and endings, trying to climb a tree. One of the young men finally lifted a happily shrieking girl onto a branch.

'My father is going berserk,' said Simpson.

'They get frightened when we start to take control of our own lives,' said Jimmy Putnam.

'Poor *pater*,' said Simpson with the lofty compassion of youth. 'Worried about reviews of his latest book about somebody else's book in a literary journal no one reads. Making his book required reading for his seminars to sell a few copies. Wanting me to flatter him by imitation. No thanks!' He walked over and picked up his mortarboard. 'All life is there . . . where we're going, James, my friend. Terror. Humour. Pathos. Loyalty. Death. . . .' He glanced sideways at his friend. 'Of course, you think it's the right thing to do.'

'Don't you? I never asked.' James Putnam met his friend's eyes with unaccustomed seriousness. In his four years at university, Putnam had learned to camouflage his natural capacity for sincere belief in order to enjoy Gabriel Simpson's irreverent mockery of nearly everything. Sharing it gave him a sense of mad, though temporary, freedom and a pleasure which was nearly illicit in intensity.

The ant and the grasshopper, he thought. How am I going to manage without Gabriel, the gifted, agile-minded grasshopper . . . and a fiercely protective friend?

Like the ant (which he in no way underestimated), Putnam had learned early how exigent life could be. Simpson mocked everything but saw no evil anywhere. Putnam worried about how Gabe would handle it when he began to learn about real life, outside the iron gates.

'Don't you think it's the right thing to do?' Putnam asked, trying to imagine other reasons for making such an enormous decision.

Simpson grinned. 'I just think it will be interesting.'

Saigon – 1966

On her last morning in Saigon, Nina woke before dawn, burned the last of her private papers in the white-tiled washroom and sluiced the ashes down the corner drain. She buckled a muslin money belt around her bare waist then slipped on a blue silk dress and high-heeled Italian shoes. She smoothed the silk of her dress against her stomach and looked in her full-length mirror at the faint swelling of her five-month-old pregnancy. Even enlarged by the money belt, it still did not appear obvious, even to her. Sometimes, as now, it did not even seem real. She might be a little short of breath. Her belts might need an extra hole or two. But the idea of an entire, separate person preparing to be alive sometimes seemed absurd to her, to be greeted with the same polite, smiling disbelief as a piece of wicked gossip or traveller's tall tale.

Then she met her own eyes in the mirror and disbelief swung to panic. The young woman in the mirror was a stranger, the host for a growing thing that was a force of change in a life already dizzy with change. Her skin seemed drawn too tightly over the high cheekbones. Her pointed chin seemed weak, her mouth tremulous. In the large dark eyes, Nina saw fear.

She turned away abruptly and began to brush viciously at her long black hair. After she had coiled it into a chignon on the nape of her slender neck, she made up, drawing on the public face she was leaving behind – polished, exquisite, all cracks carefully disguised.

Working fast, and trying to close out thought, she rolled a dark blue cotton tunic and loose trousers around five small bundles of currency notes – Vietnamese piastres, French francs, English pounds and US and Hong Kong dollars – and put the rolls in the bottom of a small leather carryall beside a pair of rubber-soled thonged sandals.

This early in her pregnancy, she still moved like a large cat, with the long relaxed strides of a hunter rather than a domestic tabby. Her French mother had given her an unusual length of bone and generosity of breast. From her father, she had, as well as intelligence, a fierce energy which could drop into total stillness.

Quickly, she threw back one corner of the Chinese rug and knelt by a small floor safe. As she bent forward, she felt the reality of the small hard lump beneath her navel. A little distracted, she took from the safe a scratched blue enamel tin labelled 'cinnamon sticks'. Inside were sapphires, zircons, and pearls in plastic bags, and eight gold rings – her small change for places where official coinage was valueless. She set the tin aside. She bent forward again above the small hard fist and lifted out four bars of perfumed French soap.

To the eye, they were ordinary soap – she inspected them carefully one last time – but each had a dark, cold heart the colour of good claret. A large part of her assets had been distilled into those four large rubies known as Burmese reds, which were her funds for true emergencies on her journey.

She put the soap and the blue enamelled tin into her make-up bag with the other imported fripperies expected of a wealthy, half-French, half-Vietnamese socialite and businesswoman. She put the make-up bag on top of the clothes and sandals in the carryall. Then she had to sit down on the edge of her bed. Her knees were shaking and her lungs sucked at the morning air.

Is it the baby? she wondered. Or just nerves? If the baby makes me feel like this, how much worse will it get? I wish I had gossiped more with other women! She took a deep breath and stood up again. With a growing sense of unreality, she laid on top of the make-up bag a silk blouse, a sweater, a nightdress, the latest fashionable French novel, and a three-month-old copy of 'Elle'. She inserted a hundred piastre note between the pages of the 'Elle', one edge just showing as insurance against a customs' search.

She unlocked her leather attaché case and lifted up the camouflage of business papers to re-check, yet again, the used brown manila envelope holding bearer bonds worth just under a quarter of a million US dollars. That was the heart of her child's future, and her own, as far as she could imagine it.

Will it be enough? she wondered. To shield the two of us – how strange to think of 'two' – from dangers that I don't yet know? Or, if I can get to Will John, is it too much? Another envelope held documents for modest bank accounts in Bangkok, Hong Kong, Lausanne and Los Angeles. More insurance. She knew the cost of the trappings of power, but not the costs of the new, unknown life she was choosing, with or without Will John Haines.

She inspected her passport one last time. Though the passport was genuine, its visa for Thailand was forged. She would put it right as soon as she felt safe from the official world of Saigon with its busy eyes and whispering mouths. And eventually arrange one for the child. Under what nationality? she wondered. And to live where?

She glanced at the stripes of faint light drawn across the closed shutters of her room. It was barely light. She still had time. She would be gone long before Thu came for her that evening. The thought of Thu arrested her with her passport open in her hands, balanced between rage and pain.

He was her father's cousin, from a village near her father's own, in the mountains of Tonkin in what was now North Vietnam. First her father's partner in the family business, now hers. Under the guerrilla colonel's uniform which he wore when not disguised in a suit as a southern city dweller, his back and arms had been scarred by the French managers of the Tonkin copper mines and the warders of Con Son prison. But his heart had been more damaged than either back or arms by the wars which had made up his life. This cousin imagined he loved her at the same time that he betrayed her. She had heard the same rumours as her bodyguards. Even while he was planning his fantasy of their future together in northern Laos, half of the opium her agents bought in the northern mountains was being stolen by his soldiers before it could reach Saigon.

Now she was betraying him in return. It made her feel as false and uncomfortable as the fraudulent bars of soap with their cold, sharp-edged centres. She replaced the passport in the attaché case, then stood for a moment, temporarily paralyzed, one hand locked for strength onto her father's carved ivory seal which hung around her neck on a gold chain.

Oh, Will John! Help me escape a world where acts like Thu's and mine can pass as love!

An unexamined train of thought took her back to her desk. She dug out an old photograph she had left buried among unwanted papers and studied the portrait of contrasting mother and child. As always, it chilled her.

The mother was a blonde smiling Madonna whose painted nails, black in the photograph, lay across the belly of her dark-haired child as casually as if along the arm of a chair. The little girl's three-year-old bean-belly was encased in hand-stitched ruffled silk, each ruffle edged in imported French lace. Her curled hair was nailed down by two huge bows. The woman's pale eyes flirted with the cameraman. The little girl lay back with childish sensuousness into the soft twin mountains of her mother's breasts, but her large, dark eyes were anxious, alert for what was to follow this moment of temporary softness and enclosure. The mother had the open expectancy of a child, while her daughter's face was already darkened by an adult suspicion of life.

Nina had been shocked when the photograph arrived from France, from her French grandfather's *pension* after his death, along with a pocket watch, bundled letters home from her mother to her parents, and bankbook for a small account in the *Crédit Lyonnaise*.

The picture had forced her to re-examine what she had always thought of as the golden days before the first disaster – the *plastique* explosion that had killed her mother and burned the family house when she was fifteen. Until the picture arrived, Nina had forgotten why that bleakness filled her own three-year-old eyes. Even now, at the age of twenty-six, her memory tried stubbornly to insist only on the value of what that child had lost – the bright picnics at Cap St Jacques, with cool blue octagonal shadows of umbrellas on the sand and tiny red steamed crabs which were a rare licence to make herself messy. Her pet gibbon Minou sliding down the folds of mosquito netting over the canopied bed to hide under Nina's silk nightdress, and tickling her naked skin with soft grey fur. The warm joys of the servants' quarters – the stories, the treats of sugar cane and bean cakes, the hugs and piggy-back rides, the games of *cache-cache* and secret expeditions to the cinema.

Her memory, protecting her, had tried to obscure the awful moment of rending, when her mother had insisted that she was too old to run wild with the servants any longer, and her once-beloved cook, gardener and *ayah* had seemed to agree. Instead, memory flaunted the grand pleasures of her parents' realm, which had filled her eight or nine-year- old heart with desperate pride and a hunger to belong. When the fifteen-year-old Nina had been sleeping in the rubble of mortared buildings and scavenging for food in the trash behind restaurants, her memory summoned up the noise and swirl of lost balls and parties which overflowed the big house like bright flood waters, her mother glamorous as a film star, and her father standing aloof and elegant in a tailed evening coat, as if in the centre of the world, wooed by his guests, politicians and businessmen alike, in spite of being a *jaune*.

Now, however, at twenty-six and about to become a mother, Nina could admit that her loneliness had begun as a tiny child who did not truly belong to either parent. Her father had wanted a son; her mother, distraction from her own desperate homesickness for France.

Nina had long ago accepted that the three-year-old in the photograph looked less like her mother than like the sober *ayah* who stood behind the two of them holding a paper sun umbrella above their heads. She now remembered her mother's overbright references to her daughter's 'fine eyes' and 'lovely creamy skin', as if disguising some truth too awful to admit. Nina had felt ashamed without understanding why, but because she had been so young, she had accepted her mother's version of the truth. Now, she knew she never wanted to see that expression in the eyes of her own child. But, chilling or not, the photograph was a guy rope to her past when she was casting off most of the rest. She slipped it into the carryall with the other essentials for her survival.

With a sense of disbelief at the meaning of her actions, she next took a small sandalwood box from among the silks and embroideries in a heavy chest of carved rosewood and brass at the foot of her bed and lifted out of it a pair of diamond studs which she screwed into her small earlobes. She slid five rings onto red-nailed fingers which seemed to belong to someone else, then slipped a single-strand pearl necklace and three gold chains over her head to lie hidden under the high front of her dress. How much was enough to buy off terror in an uncertain future?

16

She hesitated, then quickly added three gold bracelets to the gold wristwatch she already wore.

Enough, she instructed herself. Leave something for them to find. These things are not in the true kernel of your life. You are fortunate to have so much. Now let them go.

She began to walk aimlessly around her bedroom, touching familiar objects, trying to say goodbye, unable to believe in 'forever'. She touched the big carved bed with its bridal veil of mosquito netting where the swelling of her body had been conceived in unimagined peace and pleasure, the desk where she had worked, the bronze statue of Ganesha the Hindu elephant god which she had once used for self-defence. Will John's monkey. Will John, the father of her child.

She picked up the monkey and held it until the cool, carved jade became warm as her hand.

'I tried to find a gorilla,' he had said. 'I've learned enough Vietnamese to eavesdrop on your servants. I'm afraid this was the best I could do. From King Kong, with love.'

She had looked up and laughed, delighted and unbelieving that this warm, confident, reassuring red-blond giant was still in her life.

She put the monkey down quickly, suddenly uneasy. If she took an object as his understudy, she would not have him. She ran her fingers along a set of tiny, bronze, dragon-like birds – opium weights used by her father when opium was still a local cottage industry controlled by the colonial French in Indochina and their war lord allies. The man from Tampa, Florida, who had bought her father's labs, agents, sampan fleet, go-downs, safe-drops, and list of names, would see these working objects as mere curiosities. She picked up the tiniest weight, no bigger than her little fingernail and tucked it into the carryall with the photograph, not from sentiment but as a reminder that the world changes without prior consultation.

Then she looked at Will John's jade monkey again. In a rush of protectiveness toward the creature in her belly which was his child, and in spite of her earlier fear, she quickly added the little monkey to her bag.

For the child, she told herself.

At last, the shutters began to lay stripes of early light across the walls. She unbarred and pushed open the shutters of her front window, letting in the smell of jasmine, then leaned out into the still-cool morning air to imprint every detail on her memory: the pocked and mould-blotched cream stucco balustrade of the entrance staircase to the villa, the lime trees which shaded the high roof and the yellowing lawn as

17

other lime trees had shaded the lawn where she had learned to walk, tottering between her *ayah* and the gardener. She looked down on the leathery-leaved cannas in the garden, below her, with red-orange blossoms as blowsy as sat-upon Easter bonnets, and the weed-clogged lily pool where carp still flickered like gold coins in the murky water, miraculous survivors of years of neglect by her gardener.

Remember them all, she told herself. She closed her eyes and they vanished into blackness. With a dry mouth, she opened her eyes and made them real again.

Two sandbags had fallen from the ramparts built on the verandah against Viet Cong grenades and stray bullets of all nationalities and factions. They had split and spilled themselves across the weed-spotted gravel of the drive.

I must remind the gardener to weed the drive, she noted automatically, before she caught herself with a spasm of pain.

She inhaled the rich warm blend of sweet flowers, rot, mustiness, petrol fumes, and charcoal smoke from the servants' quarters. Her brain tried to record the early murmuring of the city, the scratchy static of a transistor radio outside the compound wall, the thud of a cleaver against a chopping block, and the solemn 'tonk, tonk' of a gold–beater bird in the neighbouring compound. She loved all these sights, smells and sounds with the intensity and anguish of a lover being told of the loved one's death.

'How can I choose to leave you?' she asked her world. 'Who will I be without you?'

In the circle of the driveway below her, Eight Hand Horse, an elderly Meo montagnard once her father's lieutenant and was now her own driver, advisor and self-appointed uncle, instructed the gardener on how to load into the Renault her big suitcase packed the day before by Nina's maid.

Directly beneath her, out of sight on the ground floor verandah, the taller of her two bodyguards also watched the old man and the gardener. After a few moments, the bodyguard went into the house to make a call from the telephone in the hallway.

At eight forty-five, when the maid had taken Nina her breakfast and the servants were in their quarters behind the house eating their own morning rice, Nina picked up her carryall and attaché case and joined the old man in the car. She felt numb, as if her heart knew that it would not survive knowledge. The big Renault crunched down the weed-spotted gravel of the driveway. She could not look back.

18

At Tan Son Nhut, Eight Hand Horse carried her big case to the Air
Vietnam check-in desk for the local flight to Dalat, the resort town on a
lake in the mountains north of Saigon, where wealthy Vietnamese now
fled from the wet heat of the monsoon season just as the colonial French
had once done.

'Still on schedule,' he said. 'No fighting today between here and
Dalat . . . so far.'

Nina accepted her boarding card for the Dalat flight from a female
check-in official who smiled brightly and seemed to talk nonsense. Nina
turned to Eight Hand Horse. She grasped his wrinkled hand and held
on for balance.

'Thank you,' she whispered. 'Thank you, Old Uncle. I'll see you
next in Bangkok.'

'The gods and my age willing,' he said. He touched her forearm
lightly with his free hand. She could not let go.

The old man's gaze swung across her shoulder and over the crowds.
'You are only going to Dalat,' he said quietly. 'Please!'

Their hands clung together a moment longer. Then, Nina forced
herself to open her fingers from around the dry, friendly warmth. He
bowed slightly, nodded, and vanished into the crowd.

Don't watch him go! . . . Only Dalat! she reminded herself. As if it
were only Dalat!

She feinted toward the local check-in, then stepped a little to one
side, to let the other passengers for Dalat move ahead of her. She put
away her Dalat ticket. Pulled out a ticket for Bangkok. Holding the
ticket for Bangkok and her passport, with its expensive, illegal Thai and
American visas, she began to walk quickly toward the Cathay Pacific
check-in for the flight to London with stops in Bangkok, Delhi and
Bahrain.

The muscles of her face arranged and rearranged themselves in a frenzy
of self-conscious terror. The rings on the hand holding her passport and
ticket felt like beacons, though the stones were tucked out of sight in
her palm. The knuckles of the hand clutching the attaché case were
white.

As she accepted her second boarding card, she scanned the crowd
around her.

I'm not the only one, she realized. Other rats see the water rising in
the bilges. Others are fleeing different changes . . . *coup* following *coup*,
leader following leader, and the numbers of both American soldiers and

refugees from the Delta still increasing. And we're all afraid of the ships' cats. I wish the old man had stayed until I board the Bangkok flight!

But anyone watching her would know him. If they saw him, they would look for her.

Passport control was still three metres away. She glanced around yet again. She was most vulnerable here in the crowded public area filled with travellers, vendors, cleaners, airline staff, porters, taxi-drivers, and watchers. On this side of the barrier no officials would need sweetening. A protesting young woman could be removed before anyone thought to ask why.

Nina slid into the current flowing through the narrow gap in the barrier, squeezed between two American uniforms and the shoulder of a red-haired, weary-looking nurse. A Japanese on her right bumped her with a clutch of shopping bags and apologized. Nina made herself sidle forward with the rest when she wanted to dart and slither toward the barrier like a terrified fish.

The weary nurse lost ground to an English woman who was simultaneously edging into the flow and giving her two small sons desperate last minute instructions for their next six months of life at boarding school. The two English boys went through, heads down, not looking back at their frantically waving mother. The pull of the current increased. Nina's heart raced. Her palms were damp. The nurse stepped forward with her passport which was no doubt genuine in every way. Nina took a deep breath and made herself unclench her teeth. The nurse reloaded herself with flight bag and plastic shopping bag, checked her camera and her sunhat and at last moved on into the departure area. Nina gave her passport to the tired young man in a dirty white uniform. She withdrew her hand quickly before he could see its shaking.

He flipped the passport open automatically. Consulted his clipboard. Closed the passport. Blinked. And looked back at the clipboard. He touched a pencilled scribble in the upper left corner of the printed page clipped to the board, and looked past her into the crowds behind.

'What's wrong?' Nina managed to say. Her lips were stiff. The smudged scribble smacked of an informal, private arrangement rather than the police. She almost wished it were the police. She began to calculate the young man's price for switching allegiance, but it was too late.

He stared down at his clipboard as a hand took her elbow. The hand belonged to an unfamiliar, heavy-set Vietnamese, wearing a Boston Marathon tee-shirt under a western-style sports jacket.

20

'Just one moment please, madame,' he said politely as he pulled her gently but irresistibly off course. A second man took her other arm. Nina planted her feet on the slippery floor but the two men moved her inexorably onward.

Her brain tried briefly to explain what was happening in an acceptable way. Then she acknowledged the truth. She tried to scream but produced only a dry croak. She clutched at a passing arm. It slipped from her grasp. The man, pink-faced, with a military crew-cut, turned in brief unfocussed irritation, then shoved past, briefcase held high like a plough between the shoulders of the crowd.

The two men rearranged their grip. Her elbow was pinned. If she struggled the joint would break. There was an infinitesimal pause, as if the three of them were waiting for something to happen. Syrup had been poured into her brain. She felt numb, as an animal about to be eaten by another is said to feel, tempted to relax almost pleasurably into the inevitable. But a few still-battling synapses insisted that to accept would be fatal. The end of her story. She wasn't ready for the end. She was about to begin a new life. Her child could not die before it had lived. Not yet! she protested silently. Not yet!

She felt a small pain in the back of her left hand. She opened her mouth again to scream. Someone in all that crowd must see what was happening!

Then her blood seemed to drain into her feet. Her head became too heavy to support and toppled backward. She tried to step back, to rebalance herself and found herself embracing the man in the tee-shirt. The weight of the attaché case unlocked itself from the white knuckles of her left hand. Then there was nothing.

2

Slowly, nothing became something again. Nina's first fogged awareness was a flare of satisfaction that there was something and that she was still in it. Death was not yet. She fought the fog, trying to give shape to the something. She tried to move, but her muscles were not yet reconnected to her brain. Her eyelids strained but would not open. Her lips parted, but the words remained trapped in silence inside her head.

She felt people on either side of her. Two people. Then she began to make out their shapes, dark against the light. She tried to sit up and was sick. A hand held her head and another wiped her mouth. She heard a man's voice and a woman's. Although she could not make sense of what they were saying, nor tell what language they were speaking, she knew the man's voice. Its deep male vibrations had first tightened the muscles above her knees at their first meeting when she had been only thirteen.

She tried again to open her eyes. Her first truly conscious moment was a sudden ice-cold clarity as she met her cousin's eyes, close above hers and opaque with anger.

Thu said something quickly in a language she didn't understand, and the woman, who had been kneeling by her head, scampered away carrying a basin and towel. 'This isn't the way I expected to welcome you,' he said to Nina.

Nina looked up at her cousin's face, its high, wide cheekbones and angry eyes half-shaded by the forelock of dark hair which curved away from his broad forehead. The icy coldness of that first conscious moment remained. He was waiting for her answer. She looked away, trying to think through the fog in her brain.

She had never seen the room where she was lying. Her hands explored. She was lying on a cotton pad on a wooden platform bed. She closed her eyes to buy time. She heard the brushing of the fabric of his black uniform as he moved impatiently. Now she could feel the warmth of his nearness and smell the leather and metal polish of his gunbelt.

'You're back now,' Thu said contemptuously. 'Don't try to hide behind closed eyes. Please look at me again!'

She obeyed. She had last seen that expression in his eyes when he had

22

caught one of his soldiers dealing with the enemy. The soldier had later been shot.

'Where were you going?' he demanded. 'When my men found you at Tan Son Nhut?' He waited, still as a tiger gauging its spring.

She beat at the last trailing wisps of the fog but could think of no safe answer.

Finally, he bent closer. 'Did it slip your mind that you were coming here, to live with me . . . with my son whom you carry? Was that so unimportant to you?'

'I would have been back,' she whispered. 'In time. . . .'

He hit her, with the cuff of a tiger's paw, holding his full strength in check but hard enough to stir the fog into rolling motion again. She closed her eyes to keep from being sick and turned her head away.

'Look at me!'

Dizzily, she tried to meet his eyes.

'I don't forgive lies,' he said. 'I don't forgive stupidity. And you are lying stupidly!'

'Cousin . . .' she whispered, in appeal. She could offer no excuses.

He placed a strong, scarred hand on her collarbone, his thumb in the hollow of her throat. 'While you were still asleep,' he said, 'it was very clear to me that I should kill you before you could speak again and confuse what I know that I know.'

He pressed lightly on her larynx with his thumb. The pressure increased her nausea, but her brain was beginning to clear.

She had never made excuses with him. 'Then do it,' she said, against the weight of his thumb. 'Now or not at all.' She held his eyes, giddy with chemicals and past caring. 'It has never been easier.'

The pressure of his thumb grew heavier.

From their first meeting, her only weapons against him had been daring and apparent indifference.

' "A speck of dust", remember, Cousin?' Speaking now hurt. ' "We blow away as easily as dust," you said, like the man you had killed in front of me at our first meeting, as my first lesson in your truths.'

His eyes studied hers.

Several months after they first met, she had learned that her young body was also a weapon of self-defence, but she had never dared test the limit of its power.

'Kill me now or not at all,' she said. 'And your son with me. That's my condition. I will not stay with you in fear.'

'You have no power to make conditions,' he said. 'I'm no longer skulking in the swamps and *paddis*, dependent on your chemists, your

23

couriers, your bookkeepers, your agents, and your politicians. We're in my country now.'

She closed her eyes against rising nausea.

'I was born on the other side of these mountains,' said Thu. 'A northerner, like your father . . . before he moved to Saigon and started wearing white Frenchmen's suits. And you are a foreigner from the city, dependent on *my* good will, a prisoner of my mountains and your own soft southern weakness and ignorance.' He lifted his hand. There was a knot in her throat where his thumb had been.

'I'm to live then?' she asked thickly.

'I haven't decided.' He pivoted away from her and turned to study her from a greater distance. 'I had expected to share my life with someone else. I must decide who you are, now that you're no longer Nina.'

She closed her eyes again, accepting defeat. A minute later, she felt him leave the room. She opened her eyes to survey the prison where she would await his sentence.

She was alone, lying on a soft quilted pad on a large wooden platform bed, naked under a yellow silk kimono she had never seen before. The large room was nearly dark. She turned her head carefully to the right. The opposite wall was made up of shutters which were folded back to show a lavender dusk outside. A small oil lamp was burning on a low table by the wall beyond the foot of the bed. The carved wooden beam of the ceiling immediately above her head wore a bandage of scarlet cloth to ward off the spirit of fire. In the shadows above the beam, she could just make out the undersides of split stone roof slates.

She turned her head to her left. The spinning had almost settled. On the wooden wall above the bed hung a scroll painting of a river plunging and twisting through a landscape of knotted boulders. Abruptly, she turned her head back to the right as something that she had seen registered fully in her brain.

Her carryall and attaché case stood side by side on the wooden plank floor, just beside the bed. She flung herself to the edge of the bed and pulled the bags to her. Both were empty. Everything had been removed – her passport, money, gemstones, bearer bonds, clothing, opium weight, photograph, Will John's monkey and the make-up bag with the four bars of soap. In spite of common sense, she searched each bag again. She pulled up their linings and felt deep into their folds and pockets. They were still empty, as she had known they would be the minute she saw the careful mockery of their placement by the bed.

24

Her hand moved to her throat. The necklaces were still there, beneath the kimono, and she still wore her rings and bracelets.

'I didn't strip the body,' said Thu's voice from the shadows beyond the bottom of the bed.

Shock jolted her to her feet. She pulled the kimono close around her nakedness.

'You still have your trinkets,' he said. 'I'm not a common bandit, in spite of what your new American friends in Saigon may say.'

'How dare you spy on me?' she demanded. 'How dare you frighten me like that?'

'I must observe my guest,' he said. 'How else can I learn the truth about her when she tells only lies?'

They faced each other in the growing darkness. The shadows now blurred the clean, elegant lines of his limbs. The silence grew and the shadows filled with ghosts of very different meetings.

'I don't know who you are either, any more,' she said at last.

'I haven't changed,' he said. He stepped onto the bed and stretched himself out on the cotton pad with careless grace. He touched the pad beside him with a scarred hand and looked up at her challengingly.

At the age of thirteen, Nina had lost her heart to the dark forelock that fell across his forehead and to the vibrations of his voice as he and her father talked quietly through the night on the verandah of the house above the lake among the pines of Dalat. Then he had disappeared from her life and she had more or less forgotten him in the normal preoccupations of an adolescent girl from a comfortable home – the swelling of her breasts, the size of her crinoline petticoats, the first attempts to define a self in a world confused by endless wars, declared or otherwise.

When the wars finally broke through even the thick walls of the family compound to take both her parents, he had reappeared – a distant cousin, the leader of one of Vietnam's many outlaw sects, and her terrifying ally in the family opium trade. First he had been her instructor in the trade, and then her partner, as he had been her father's partner.

'Are you afraid?' he asked, from the platform bed.

'No,' she said. But she was very, very afraid.

'Hungry, then?'

'No thank you, Cousin.' Her politeness matched his mocking solicitude.

25

'Then put out the lamp and come sleep.'

How can I sleep beside a tiger? she thought.

They had once reached for each other, as if with averted eyes, and found a physical passion which had shocked them both. Then she had taken a direct look and pulled back from a union which locked her into the world she was already beginning to question. She also saw that Thu imagined he loved her.

Will John, the American whom she had endowed with such virtue and strength, had then opened the shutters of her eyes onto a lighter world than the one she had inherited. Even if she did not totally believe in his world, the possibility that it might exist had given her the strength to leap from darkness toward the light. The child she carried was a hostage from Will John's bright world. Unfortunately for them all, Thu imagined that his child and his world inhabited her.

Slowly, she crossed the polished wooden floor and bent her head to blow out the little lamp on the low table by the end of the bed. The open wall admitted the faint glow of the early night sky. In the silence, she heard a lizard scuffling along a wall and a night bird cry above the roof. She crossed back to the bed and lay down beside him.

They lay side by side in the darkness. She felt the warmth of his arm, a few careful centimetres away from hers. Then he turned on his side to face her. She could hear the question in his silence.

I can't go back, she thought. I have made my choice!

She remembered other warnings to herself, when they had lain like this, side by side in the darkness. Never trust! she had told herself. Never trust either the heat or the ease that follows! Never trust the illusion of closeness! He is a tiger. A cobra. And now there is the child. If it is dark, like me, it will be a gaoler. If fair, like its father, it will be a sentence of death!

The narrow space between them seemed filled with clamour.

One of us must speak! she thought. But I don't know what to say. She listened for his breathing to settle, but sleep, and the remains of the drug, claimed her first. Her last awareness was of his fierce, silent watchfulness. When she woke the next morning, he was gone.

The shuttered wall was still folded back. A hen was exploring a crack in the wooden floor near the head of the bed. An old woman was arranging a small table of food on the platform beside Nina.

'Morning rice,' the woman said briskly. Her eyes watched Nina sideways from a net of wrinkles under her black turban. The folds of her aging neck nestled against a stack of fat silver necklaces. 'You better eat!' She eyed the gentle swelling of Nina's belly under the yellow silk kimono.

Experimentally, Nina swallowed a ball of sticky rice served in a small basket. Then sipped a little tea. The nausea of the night before had passed. She looked up to meet bright curious eyes.

'First baby?' asked the old woman.

Nina nodded.

'Where's your mother?'

Nina chewed another ball of sticky rice. 'She's dead,' she said finally.

'Never mind!' The briskness did not falter. 'Lots are. You can borrow me.'

Over the little porcelain cup of tea, Nina tried to assess just whom she was dealing with. Apparently not a servant, as she had first assumed.

The woman shifted the cud of betel which had stained her teeth black. 'I've had the most children up here.' She waved toward an outer room where Nina could now see two younger women pushing cloths around the floor with long sticks. 'Fourteen,' said the woman proudly. 'And ten still alive.'

Nina wasn't clear whether the two other women were daughters or less fecund unfortunates.

The woman craned her head to assess the dregs in Nina's cup. 'I'll make you a *tisane*. Don't worry. . . .' The eyes now studied Nina's face. 'We got a good *tay phap* and good midwife down in the valley. You got nothing to worry about here.' She left to brew the *tisane*, her bare feet brushing the floor like dry leaves blown by the wind.

As soon as she was gone, Nina pushed aside the tray of food, stepped past the empty carryall and attaché case and began her search. The room was shadowy and cool in spite of the growing heat of the light outside. Around its walls were stacks of baskets, carved boxes and small chests. She forced herself to work methodically, keeping one ear cocked for the return of the brushing feet. The two women with sticks and clothes had vanished.

Nothing to worry about, she repeated to herself with grim humour. Nothing to worry about!

The boxes in the stack by the head of the bed were all locked, with primitive hasp locks. She pulled at them in frustration, brushed her dark hair from her face and pulled again, without success. Later perhaps, they might yield to a patient knife blade. A shoal of baskets was next. Her black tunic and trousers, sweater and copy of 'Elle' were

27

in the first, though the piastre note was gone. The other baskets held clothing made of hand-woven cloth, Thu's uniform, a dozen Hong Kong-made business shirts, a set of French school books, fourteen unlabelled sealed pottery jars and a collection of belts and leather straps and buckles, grey-blue with powdery mould and smelling of must. Another carved box, unlocked, held five montagnard swords of carbon steel sheathed in rattan-bound bamboo. She looked at them thoughtfully for a moment; Thu still trusted her to that extent. Yet another box, beside the small table which held the lamp, was filled with tied-up scrolls. Nina hadn't really expected to find anything of importance. Dejectedly, she turned to the tier of lacquered boxes at the foot of the bed, each as round and full as a ripe gourd. Her make-up was in the top box. Her hands began to shake as she opened the second box in the tier. It held her hairbrush, and the four bars of soap.

Forgetting to breathe, she examined each bar for signs of having been tampered with, but each looked as it had before. She replaced them in the box and restacked the lacquer gourds. She remained on her knees before them, giving thanks to whatever deities claimed the mountains of northern Laos as their particular patch. The pressure of her elbows on her belly met the new hardness.

We may survive yet, you and I, she told it silently. Whatever you turn out to be – dark or fair. I still may have enough to buy our escape. Now I must test the limits of our cage.

Gabriel Simpson lay as still as a fallen tree. His long, thin body had settled into the ground. The leaf pattern of his camouflage uniform blended into the dried vegetation. He felt that his wet belly must be putting down roots, like the live branches of lavender and honeysuckle his mother nailed down into the earth with bent wires and old hairpins.

Once she used one of my croquet wickets, he remembered. I nearly killed her! I should get the ticks off, but I can't be bothered. Oh God, he thought. I'm so bored. Bored and terrified at the same time.

He had been watching the trees across the narrow dry rice field for two hours. Silent, motionless, boring trees. But at any time, those trees might kill him.

There was no wind. The line of trees was still. There was no rustling, sighing, or scraping of twigs, just silence, filled with the chirruping, whirring, rasping, buzzing, and clicking of insects. The racket from the grass that fringed the field made the silence of the trees seem emptier, more ominous.

Simpson stared at the closed face of the treeline. Like the dark windows of childhood nights, the half-open closet door, the space under the bed. Filled with devils of the imagination.

He glanced right and left. Boucher was on his right, a new guy named Doe on his left. Lieutenant Whittaker was beyond Boucher with Smith, the RTO, snuggled up like a duckling.

A jungle fowl crowed, just like a dawn rooster at home, from inside the trees. Simpson's headband, Boucher's captured NVA helmet with grass stuck in its netting, and Whittaker's tiger stripe boonie hat all turned toward the sudden, shocking sound.

The question is, thought Simpson, whether it came from the village behind those trees, that dot on Whittaker's map. And if it did, why did the damn bird get excited at exactly this moment?

The silence returned.

There is no war, thought Simpson. No enemies. Just trees. Trees that killed you, without warning. Like McMillan, who had been replaced by Doe.

McMillan had lived for twenty minutes after the sniper's bullet.

'You'll be fine, Mac,' Simpson had said, stroking McMillan's head, letting his own hand be crushed in a grasp of terror. 'You'll make it! You'll make it! You'll make it!' Over and over, he had chanted the magic spell, which had failed.

Dear Father and Mother, Simpson now improvised wildly to distract himself from the technicolour image of McMillan. Ignore what the papers tell you! We're at war with trees. The day before yesterday, I scored two bananas and a seedling eucalyptus. Unfortunately, a colleague was taken out by a banyan and three fish-tail palms. Be careful in the garden! Your loving son. . . .

There was movement on his right; he looked down the line at Whittaker. The lieutenant was making silent signs.

He's going to take us in, Simpson thought. Because he can't stand it either, lying here imagining what's over there. Nothing can be worse than what we're imagining.

Wrong! he contradicted himself. It can be worse. Let's stay right here until they lift us out . . . close the closet for another day.

Whittaker gave the signal. Simpson tore his roots out of the earth and began to run. Ran and ran without moving. His feet ploughed uselessly at the earth. Exposed in sunlit space as bright as a searchlight beam. A cartoon character trying to run on air beyond the cliff edge. The trees waited for him, silent and blank, saving their devils for the last minute.

Don't think, don't think, don't think, don't think!

They plunged into the trees and stopped. Silence surrounded them still. Then a leaf scraped. Simpson whirled, his heart beating against the back of his throat. The leaf scratched downward, caught on a branch, tilted, and fell again. Simpson saw nothing in the tree above the falling leaf.

Don't count on it, he warned himself. He kept watching that tree, all the time they were waiting, just inside the treeline.

They found the village a quarter of a mile away. Deserted. They went in slowly, checking for booby traps. Simpson stepped over a rubber sandal, like the ones he used to wear swimming. Then a broken rice-winnowing tray of woven bamboo.

'Trapdoors?' asked Whittaker.

Boucher shook his head.

Simpson turned around slowly. All around them were more trees.

As Nina was putting on her black tunic and trousers from the first basket, the old woman reappeared with a lidded basket in her arms.

'Not those clothes!' she cried, when she saw Nina. 'Those aren't suitable! Here. . . .' She lifted the lid from the basket to reveal a teapot in a quilted nest. 'Drink this while I get you something better to wear.' She called sharply into the outer room and in a few moments, one of the younger women appeared carrying a green silk *ao dai* and white silk trousers. The younger woman helped Nina dress, then the old woman brushed and braided her hair.

'Where is the Colonel?' asked Nina, having weighed possible loss of face through ignorance against the need to know.

'Gone away all day on business,' said the old woman. She tilted Nina's head gently but firmly forward, as if arranging a peony bloom, and coiled the braid on Nina's nape. 'You ask me for anything you need.'

'That's very kind,' said Nina. 'Thank you, I will.' She felt a final adjusting pat on her hair. She rose, smiled and walked out of the room, wearing the more suitable *ao dai*, feeling both pairs of eyes following her.

She stepped out into a broad, open verandah which ran the length of the main building where they had slept. In Saigon, when he talked of his plans to move to Laos, Thu's used of the word 'villa' had been misleading. 'Villa' had French colonial overtones of gracious white houses overlooking the combed pelts of rubber plantations. On the verandahs of 'villas', hand-wound gramophones scratched out Ravel and Josephine Baker while uniformed servants served *pastis* and beer to masters in tropical whites.

Below her, across a small parade ground of packed dirt, this villa compound descended the mountainside in uneven steps and terraces, clinging to the rock like a cliff swallow's nest. The *lalang* thatch or lichen-crusted slate roofs of the wood and stone huts seemed to have grown from the supporting earth. With the exception of a few green patches of vegetables tucked between the huts and one stand of banana trees, everything was the colour of dust. The dryness of winter was just ending; the drizzle of the *crachin* had not yet set in. A stand of bamboo at the corner of the main pavilion rattled like a *tay phap* shaking fortune sticks.

Here and there, she could see the sharper geometry of rectangular reservoir tanks and round rice storage pits. On the terrace below the parade ground, was a thatched stables in which the hindquarters of ponies or mules were twitching away flies. At the left end of the verandah, wooden steps led up to a ledge in the cliff above and behind the villa. Nina climbed them and looked down onto the moss and lichen of the main pavilion roof beneath which she had slept.

The villa had set its back against the natural protection of the sandstone cliff, within curved, enclosing wings of rock. An outward-leaning barricade of sharpened bamboo, each pole twenty feet high and thick as her waist, walled the rest of the compound's perimeter.

From the ledge above the roof, an ascending track, cut into the rock, climbed out of sight around the curve of the cliff. Nina inched carefully upward, not looking down the sheer rock face below her, to a flat lookout point high above the compound. With this rocky platform safely beneath her, Nina lifted her eyes.

The circle of her view into space was interrupted only by the peak whose cliff face backed the villa. She gazed out along folded ridges, through the receding wings of grey-green mountains toward the distant flatness of a hazy plateau. Far in the distance, the dots and dashes of a river flashed in and out of the jungle cover until it vanished in a wide, slack curve beyond the farthest mountain range.

Much nearer, to the east, across a valley as deep and sudden as a sharp intake of breath, lay a monstrous wrinkle of rock, thrown up by carboniferous folding that crushed soft sand and limestone against the granite heart of the central massif. The soft limestone of its ridge had been eroded into pinnacles which suggested objects distorted by dreams – a giant bird, a hat, the fingers of a gnarled hand.

Another ridge undulated northward from the peak on which the villa stood. Nina thought she could just make out the faint scratching of a trail rising and falling along the rocky spine. A few cleared fields scarred

31

the slopes just below the villa. There was no other mark of man on the landscape. The inhabitants of the villa seemed as alone as eagles.

She descended carefully back to the lower ledge and from there down the wooden steps to the verandah of the main pavilion. Apart from a haze of smoke around three of the huts, and the two women who were now at work in a little bathhouse behind the rattling bamboo, she saw no human life. A sway-backed sow dragged her dugs across the dust of the lower terrace and snuffled out of sight behind a hut. An invisible rooster crowed tentatively.

Nina went down the steps from the verandah. She crossed the parade ground, descended more steps to the lower terrace, then paused as if to gaze into a water tank. The surface of the water reflected a pewter sky. Her own image shattered and reformed as fingerling fish surfaced to gulp at gnats. She raised her head. The two women were watching her from the bathhouse on the terrace above. There was a gate in the palisade, on the terrace below the one she was on. Nina decided to give the bars of her cage a first gentle push.

She didn't look back. If the two women raised an alarm, she would know soon enough. The gate was unlocked. A track outside led under an arch of dry bamboo and dropped away through a fall of boulders. She lowered herself down the steep natural steps and let herself imagine for a moment that she was free to walk away.

The villa sat serenely above her, as quiet as the rocks from which it seemed to grow.

So, Nina thought, my cage is larger than the compound walls. But the bars are there. Don't fool yourself that they're not!

She descended carefully, feeling for her new centre of balance around the lump in her belly. The track she was following crossed another at right angles. Though she could see only a few yards through the brown scrub, this second track seemed to curve around the contour of the mountain parallel to the bamboo barricade. She noted it for exploration.

Then her track opened onto an outcrop of bare rock where she could get her bearings. She was headed down into the deep valley which was backed by the dream-object pinnacles of eroded limestone. At the far edge of the outcrop, just before the trail plunged downward again, one of Thu's soldiers lounged against a boulder, left leg bent up across his right, picking at the sole of his bare left foot.

Nina lifted her chin slightly and walked toward him.

He leapt to attention. 'Good morning,' he said, as she drew abreast.

32

'Good morning,' she replied with calm authority, and stepped past him onto the descending trail.

Is it possible? she wondered as she clambered and skidded downward, suddenly urgent in escape, expecting every second to hear him call her back. Instead, he gave a long, high-pitched whistle.

Out of the sentry's sight, Nina paused to listen. She tilted her head, scanning the medley of insects and gibbons and birds, and the differing *patois* of vegetation – scrapings, rustlings, whispers, and the crash of a falling branch or nut. An airplane hummed faintly above the canopy of scrub. The whistle was not repeated. Then her neck stiffened. She changed the tilt of her head slightly. She could hear running water, not a treble gurgling but a steady mumbling baritone.

She forgot caution and launched herself downward through a stand of sharp-edged, head-high *lalang* grass. As the track twisted and turned, the grumble and rush of the river below her surged and surfaced but grew steadily closer. Then she hit the bars of her cage.

'Please stop here.' He rubbed out with his foot his cigarette of home-grown tobacco in order to grasp his rifle with both hands. 'The Colonel's orders,' he explained politely but firmly. He took another step forward out of the green tunnel which had hidden him. He wore the black uniform and snarling Tiger badge of Thu's *Binh Xuyen*.

One of the River Pirates Thu brought with him to Laos, Nina thought. One of his own soldiers, fled with him from the new war which is invading their former stronghold in the swamps near Saigon. To make a new fortune here, closer to the poppy fields.

'I had hoped to swim on such a hot day,' she said mildly.

'I'm sorry, Madame.' He bent slightly as if with a stomach cramp of unease. 'I'm sorry,' he repeated.

I wonder if he knows that he once served me as well as Thu, thought Nina. Now, she would gain nothing by causing him embarrassment. She could not afford even small enemies. She nodded and turned back up the track.

Well, Cousin, she thought, I conclude that the river is a possible way out. She paused to catch her breath. She did not understand why she was so exhausted. The five and a half month pod of child-to-be wasn't yet such a burden. She gazed down at her stomach as she panted. How much worse would she feel when she was swollen like other women she had seen?'

She looked back down toward the river.

Even if it were not navigable, it could lead her like Ariadne's thread out of the maze of mountains, down to the Ou, the Seng or the Khan. If she survived the jungle that far, she could then float on any of those into the Mekong, which flowed for most of its upper length along the border between Laos and Thailand. Across the Mekong lay the pieces of what was left of her life.

Now she glared down at her belly. Alone and unencumbered, she just might survive. With this. . . .

She hauled herself back up a rock fall and leaned on her hands. Panting again, she stared at a column of ants and imagined following the river through mountain gorges.

Thu knows where I was going, she thought. He has my ticket for Bangkok, my passport with the fake visa.

She continued to climb. The sun was also climbing. It beat the moisture out of leaves and heated the rocks into griddles. By the time she reached the little side-gate again, she was dripping with sweat, the palms of her hands were seared red, and her knees trembled with tiredness.

Thu returned at sundown and summoned her to join him for the evening meal. He nodded curtly when she arrived and folded his slim legs under him to sit cross-legged on the floor of the wide wooden verandah. For a long time they ate silently. She watched him across the little table which sat like a barrier between them. His movements were as economical as an animal's.

He was still beautiful! she thought with surprise. Shaped by pain, solitude and war, he should appear ugly, in harmony with his actions, to warn the world of the state of his heart.

They reached at the same time for the red sea urchin of a lychee. Their hands touched. Both pulled back at the same time. Nina looked down at her own hand, then placed it on the carved edge of the little table.

We can't hide in this silence forever, she thought. No matter what happens when it is broken. Even as enemies, we know each other too well. She raised her eyes to meet his. The shutters of his anger were still down.

'You went sightseeing today?' he asked, with a dry edge to his voice. 'To see picturesque local rock formations? To tease your eyes with the mountains of Yunnan?'

To let her know that he knew.

'Are we so far north?' she asked casually.

He kept his gaze on her while he chewed his rice and vegetables. 'Does it matter?'

'I'm not planning to flee to China.' She looked back challengingly.

He shook his head in reproof. 'I don't like that joke.' He chewed a few more times, then looked away, out over the deep valley at the limestone pinnacles beyond.

'I would like to swim in the river,' she said. 'I can see no harm in that.'

Thu hissed slightly between closed teeth and put down his bowl. 'You are sometimes very stupid,' he said. 'Your father was right to call you a stampeding buffalo calf. Don't push for truth when it's better to leave it alone to see which way it will grow.' He drove his thumb deep into an orange. 'Do you really want the truth?'

She could see no safe route of retreat. 'Why not? I must live with it!'

He put down the orange carefully and leaned forward across the low table; his hands gripped its sides. 'I don't think you want to hear it, but listen carefully all the same. You ran away and humiliated me in front of my people. Nevertheless, I spared you because you carry my son. Please understand that I value the child, not your treacherous self. I did not trust you when we first met – when you were still a schoolgirl trying to play your father's part in the world. Then I came to trust you. Now, I won't ever trust you again. And you'd better not trust me!'

Coldness washed up through Nina's chest and tightened the roots of her hair. She swallowed, and lifted one hand in unconscious protest.

'You're right, Cousin,' she said after a silence. 'I didn't want to hear that. But it's still better to know what ground we are standing on.' She had not planned to be here, but she was, and she had to deal with that truth. Carefully, she said, 'I was running away from lies and corruption, among other things. However unwanted the truth may be, I won't sink back into lies.'

She studied the bleak anger in his eyes. Deliberately, she touched his hand again, to remind him of the one true connection they had shared. 'Don't rewrite too much of our past,' she begged. 'The good was true too. I ran away from you, but don't imagine other betrayals that never were!'

'Why did you run?' He was as intent as a crouching tiger.

She looked away briefly. 'Wheuuu.' She blew her breath lightly out between her lips. 'Do *you* want the truth? Have we reached the moment when we have no hope but to try to survive the truth?'

'I see no other choice. There are no more people between us to obscure the lies.'

Confession and accusation were equally dangerous. She looked at him across the chasm, then took her first step out onto the tightrope of truth which might or might not carry her across.

'I also ran from fear.' She felt the odd lightening of spirit that only real truth-telling brings. 'I was afraid of many things . . . of you. . . .' She smiled slightly. 'As you intended.' He nodded. His hands relaxed slightly on the sides of the table. She looked down at the strong tendons under their scarred, tanned skin and stepped a little farther out on the tightrope.

'I want out of our business . . . I have sold my part in it, as you will no doubt learn if you haven't already.'

Thu leaned back suddenly and looked away at the mountains. 'I knew,' he said.

She had wondered. 'And I, Cousin, knew where my lost opium was going.' The tightrope swung beneath her, offering her to the pull of gravity.

He continued to regard the mountains. In profile, when she could not see the lines around his eyes, he looked as young as the man who had talked with her father under the pines of Dalat.

'I could not . . . did not want to fight you,' she said, 'so I ran from that fight, even though it meant running from you as well.' She waited, but he said nothing.

She threw her words into the silence like a ballast too heavy to carry. 'But it was not just you – I could no longer do what I had to do to hold matters together from the top. I no longer had the stomach for the business. It was simple as that.' She looked down and arranged her spoon precisely parallel to the edge of the table. She wished he would move; he was too still. And she had the greatest betrayal still left to confess.

'My father knew,' she said. 'He knew, even before I myself was clear that I could not continue in the opium trade. He had started to make arrangements for me before he died. . . . When I learned that, I knew he had loved me.'

Thu still did not look at her. He said nothing for a very long time. 'I didn't know that,' he said at last, as if in wonder. 'I was both family and partner, and he didn't tell me!'

'I was his child,' said Nina, gently. 'Only a daughter, but still his child.' And he knew you too well, she thought.

Thu continued to study the peaks. 'So . . . our business was his life . . . but because you were his child, he gave his blessing to your desertion!'

She was balanced above the chasm. He turned his head suddenly back toward her. 'You had his authority for treason.' He shook his head in disbelief. 'I wonder if I could ever learn to weigh matters in the same way.' His eyes dropped to her belly.

36

She remained silent. She could not imagine this beast of prey as a father.

'Continue your truth-telling,' he said after a moment, 'now that you have finally begun. Let's look at the ground beneath our feet, as you suggest. What am I to you if no longer your business partner?' The question came as suddenly and casually as a sniper's bullet.

Nina fought for control of her breathing, the moisture on her forehead, the timbre of her voice, the flickering of her eyelids. 'That's for you to say as much as for me.' Her body rebelled against even evasion after its respite in truth. She could feel it denouncing her with every muscle.

'Could you live here with me?'

'As long as you let me,' she said. The next question was already growing in his eyes.

I can't answer it! she thought in panic. No matter what I say, he will feel out the truth! She fought to keep her arms from wrapping themselves protectively around her belly. She was going to fall to her death.

But he veered away unexpectedly. 'That's enough truth for one evening. It makes one tired.' He rose smoothly from the verandah floor and disappeared down the steps into the darkness of the parade ground. He was gone as quickly as a cat, not noticed until it moves, and by then nearly out of sight. He did not return before she fell asleep, nor was he there on the quilted pad on the platform bed when she woke in tears, early the next morning.

After obediently drinking her *tisane*, Nina left the villa by the same gate as the day before. The sun was just balanced on the wall of mountains to the east. Mist still lay in the cracks of valleys and trailed from pinnacles like tufts of sheep's wool caught on thorns. The scrub was still cool. She followed the track she had crossed the morning before. As she had thought, it swung around the flank of the mountain, across the top of a field of grey-green poppies, and ended at a gate in the western side of the villa wall. In the poppy field, three Meo women were checking the ripening of the pods, among the fallen petals which littered the ground like scattered firework casings. A fourth woman, bent nearly double under a bale of *lalang*, passed her on the trail. Nina saw no sentries until she reached the western gate.

After resting by the gate, she started up a narrow trail through the rocks on the back of the peak behind the villa. She abandoned the climb when it seemed to circle around toward the observation platform where she had climbed the day before. She walked a short way on the trail which led northward along the undulating spine of the ridge, but turned back. Small as it was, her belly seemed too heavy today to lug up and down hot rocks.

It will be harder tomorrow, she warned herself, and still harder the day after. In a few more weeks, you won't even be able to think of walking away! You'll be as heavy and awkward as a pregnant water buffalo cow.

But the growing heat was too much for her. She returned to the villa damp and red-faced.

The elderly Meo woman scolded her politely, fussed when she said she was too hot to eat, and insisted that she lie down for the afternoon. She lay in the shadows of the big room, listening to the lizards and sparrows among the beams, and for the sound of Thu's return from wherever he had gone.

The next morning, she lay on the sleeping mat groping for the trailing ends of a dream, but the images escaped her while a deep discomfort remained. Her head and body ached.

I'll rest today, she thought. Just today. She stretched in the still-cool shadows. Then a butterfly brushed its wing across her belly, on the inside.

Nina went very still. I imagined it, she thought. It was an air bubble in my gut. But she knew it had been something else. Then it brushed again, delicate as a lock of hair in the breeze, a moth. Something that was not her, inside her. The child was moving.

Nina sat up. She wanted to call out, to tell someone, to announce this amazing, unbelievable sensation.

The child is real! That absurd idea is real and it's tickling me on the inside. She rolled carefully onto her side and looked down. Hello, she thought. Whoever the hell you are! She lay for a long time, curled protectively around this new reality, with excitement quivering in her chest and pressing up into her throat.

The Meo woman pushed aside the shutters of the wall and came in with Nina's morning *tisane*. She looked at Nina. 'Are you all right?'

'Oh yes,' said Nina. She nearly told her that the child had just moved, then stopped herself. After meeting Will John, she had avoided Thu. He had surprised her only once, let into her house one night by one of her servants and in a dangerous mood. That night was six weeks before this child had been conceived. Thu in his male ignorance might be fooled into thinking the child was his, but a woman who had had fourteen children would surely know that Nina was behind schedule.

'Yes, I'm fine, thank you,' she repeated.

The woman busied herself in the shadows, sliding sideways glances at Nina. Finally she left.

Nina's earlier headache and lethargy had gone. The discomfort left by her dream had taken shape. It frightened her that Thu was keeping distance between them. She had that amazing butterfly to save as well as herself and did not know how much time she had left before it anchored her.

After her *tisane*, she left the compound by its main gate, beyond the main pavilion on the north-east side, where the bamboo palisade met the curving wing of rock. The track leading from the gate was wide and recently used. The fresh mule droppings on its surface heaved with flies but had not yet been dismantled by dung beetles. The powdery dirt was scuffed by many feet and dotted with cigarette butts. Nina nearly missed the fine accordion pleat of white paper among the chewed cheroots and dark brown, hand-rolled, local tobacco. She bent and picked it up from the dust. It was a Marlborough.

Thu smoked Chinese cigarettes. His men smoked the same, or local tobacco. In her first day and a half here, Nina had seen no one smoking any western cigarettes of any kind. Her breath grew short, this time with excitement. She searched the dust of the track until she found the dimpled print of a rubber-soled tennis shoe, distinct among the marks of the soldiers' boots and the tire-tread zigzags of their sandals. Coming and going.

The eagles had had at least one visitor from the lower world. She considered how he might have arrived and left. She reconsidered the geography she had seen from the observation platform the first morning and set off down the wide track to see what more she could learn.

The track curved downward between abandoned fields, which the Meos had slashed and burned out of the jungle, cropped with poppies and exhausted. The poppy farmers had then moved on to other fields, leaving the monsoon rains to carve gullies and ditches and sweep away what was left of the once-fertile topsoil. The next rains would scour these channels clean of any defiant tree seedlings trying to grow on powdered rock. *Lalang* tussocks were the only successful colonizers of the dead soil. Blackened stumps of the former trees, left by the burn-off, still bristled like dark beard stubble.

The poppy takes its toll everywhere, Nina thought. Even more than I thought, and that was bad enough.

Nevertheless, the gullies and ditches proved useful. She saw the sentry before he saw her, stepped off the track and crouched in the shelter of the nearest ditch. The sun burned the top of her head. A drop of sweat rolled into her eyes. As soon as she wiped it away, another trickled from her collar bone down the valley between her breasts. After a moment, she began to inch downhill through the erosion channel like a giant crab, the butterfly suspended safely beneath her. She looked back. The sentry was sitting on a boulder, surprisingly far above and behind her. She scuttled across seven feet of exposed, rocky dust into the shelter of a *lalang* tussock, where she squatted panting and brushing ants from her thighs.

A straight scramble from the tussock took her over a small ridge, out of the sentry's sight. She looked back to memorize landmarks for her return journey. Below her, the field ended in jungle.

Then she thought she heard voices, faintly in the jungle. She inched down a chalky bank into a wall of bamboo and listened again. The voices still seemed to be directly below her, farther down the mountain side. Two of Thu's black-uniformed *Binh Xuyen* rolled an oil drum across her line of vision while a third man, not visible, shouted instructions.

Two more men rolled a second oil drum after the first. Then the first men reappeared dragging what looked like a dead water buffalo. Nina sidled crabwise again, onto a rock outcrop, and peered over its lip into a long narrow clearing.

The clearing was a series of abandoned fields strung out along the ridge, older than the fields she had seen higher up. Scrub and weeds had taken hold here and there in the limestone and patched the ground with green around the black stumps. A long stripe of clear ground down their centre connected the fields like the string of a necklace. This stripe was stony and irregular in width but clear of stumps and large rocks. It was also very long. Nina could not see either end from her perch on the outcrop.

Three men began to pound blackened stakes into the clear central strip to her right. Two others did the same to her left. Four others were rolling a final pair of oil drums under cover of the jungle. The dead water buffalo was a bale of heavy camouflage netting which they spread over the barrels.

The eagles' visitor had come and gone on wings. She had found the landing strip where a pilot, who probably smoked Marlboroughs

40

probably landed a small plane to collect Thu's opium to fly it, most probably, to labs farther south in Laos, or in northern Thailand.

Nina sighed and rocked a little on her heels. We may be all right, after all! she told her stomach silently. Even together, you and I don't weigh more than two bales! And the rubies in my soap are even more rewarding . . . if I have a chance to speak to this pilot. The harvest is just beginning. He'll be back.

The climb back up the ditch was harder than the descent, but Nina was already making plans, allowing herself to imagine a future, to see herself ringing the number Will John had made her memorize before he left.

I must walk every day, she thought. So it's taken for granted. And to keep my strength!

Back on the trail, she brushed as much as possible of the chalky dust from her clothes. Two soldiers whom she passed eyed her but offered only polite greetings. Back in the villa, she changed into the yellow silk kimono and washed away the evidence of her crawl through the ditch in the thatched bath hut. The women would see the remaining dust on her clothes but that was a risk she had to take.

She was still awake that night when Thu's shadowy form came into the room. She pretended to be asleep while he stood beside the bed.

What have you decided about our new truths, Cousin? she wanted to ask. But now, with a real chance for escape, she couldn't risk a challenge.

Finally, he lay down beside her. She listened to his breathing for several minutes. Then he threw a slim arm abruptly across his forehead and turned his face away.

That night, Nina dreamed that Will John swooped down from the sky above the villa and lifted her by the arm. Together they rose high into the sky on a current of hot air, like a pair of eagles. Far below, Thu stared up from a miniature villa. He pulled and pulled at a thread from the hem of Nina's skirt, as if he could reel her back down like a kite. But with each tug, the thread unravelled neatly. As Thu pulled, Nina floated higher and higher, stripped progressively more naked by the unravelling fabric.

Thu called her name and she woke. He was watching her in the grey light just before dawn. His hand was a warm weight on her collarbone.

'You were on a strange journey,' he said. 'Welcome back.'

She stared at him, trying to see the face hanging over her as that tiny,

41

desperate man on the ground. She shivered. Thu pulled her body against his and returned to sleep with one arm thrown across her like an anchor or a prison bar.

For the next five days, Thu came and went irregularly, absent sometimes for six hours, sometimes for only half an hour. Nina half-suspected him of doing it only to thwart her own testing of the bars of her cage. On the surface, he ignored her presence entirely, except at the evening meal when they sat silently, separated by the little table, and at bedtime when he joined her without comment on the platform bed. He did not touch her again.

His pride is waiting for me to make a move, she thought. And I can't. Not since Will John. Not when I must run away again!

Though she walked every day, as she had decided to do, however hot and tired she felt, she could not continue her methodical explorations; Thu would have understood their pattern. Instead, whenever he left the villa, she searched it. Somewhere, he must have secreted the money with which he paid his men, bought his raw opium from the local farmers, and, perhaps, was paid in his turn by the man who smoked Marlboroughs. Wherever that money was hidden, she was sure she would also find her passport, currency and bonds.

One afternoon, as she was examining the padlock on a door in the back wall of the villa, into the rock face of the Tiger's Head – the peak behind the villa – she heard the clopping of mules and men's shouts. She reached the verandah just as Thu came up the steps from the parade ground.

'There you are!' he said. 'Go get me fresh clothes, then come wash me.' He wheeled away toward the bath house without meeting her eyes.

Slowly, Nina re-entered the cool shadows of the main pavilion and took a clean black cotton tunic and pair of trousers from one of the baskets by the wall. Then, with a sense of dread, she followed him to the bath hut.

Thu had stripped off his shirt and was stepping out of his trousers. He tossed them aside and stood with his back to her under the thatched roof, staring at the rock which formed the back wall of the hut. Her eyes slid away, then helplessly back to the nakedness he had offered her.

What am I going to do? she thought.

In the short period of their couplings, she had never grown used to the elegant symmetry of his outline, the fine balance between grace and power in the triangle of his shoulders and stem of his waist. It isn't right! she thought again. The surface should give more warning!

She had not seen him undressed for many months. That night he had come to her room in Saigon, he had barely unfastened his uniform. Now her eyes traced the angry, knotted, criss-crossing lines that ridged the skin of his back. These were the only clue to the scars on his heart.

'A gift from the French,' he had said when she had first tried to kiss away whatever ugliness had made them. 'A gift of clear sight – I know my enemies. Don't presume to pity it!'

She dug with the dipper into the waist-high jar and tipped the cool green water over his shoulders. The dipper shook slightly. She heard him sigh as the water ran along the conduits of the scars and spread out over the smooth brown slopes of his buttocks. She dipped again and again. He lifted his face and she poured the water over his head. He held out one scarred arm for her libations, then the other, then turned to face her. He was erect.

So? asked his eyes. And now? Finally.

And what shall I do now? thought Nina. She looked deep into the huge jar as she scooped out more water. Carefully, she poured it over his chest, not moving forward, not moving back. She stretched for more water and averted her eyes as it spread in a silver sheet across his belly. She heard it splatter on the rock floor and dipped into the water jar as if she could hide in it.

'Enough,' he said.

She stopped with the handle of the dipper resting on the lip of the jar, her eyes on the hollow of his brown throat.

After a long moment, he shook himself like a dog and put on the fresh trousers and shirt.

She waited to see which way he would go. If he returned to the pavilion, it would be a command. In their new mode of truth, she could not pretend to misunderstand. But after another moment, when she did not assist his pride, he stepped past her and disappeared across the parade ground.

He was not at the evening meal. Nina had no appetite. The elderly Meo appeared briefly to assess her and then vanished, clucking with disapproval at the full rice basket being returned to the cookhouse. When she had gone, Nina climbed to the look-out platform, but the sense of space did not ease the knot in her chest. She did not see Thu anywhere in the villa compound. When she finally went into the pavilion to try to sleep, she dreamed again.

She gave Will John a gift, a small flat parcel wrapped in banana leaf like a sticky rice and coconut sweet one buys from street vendors. Inside was a tiny golden child. Will John smiled, casually pleased.

'What's this?' he asked, as if she had offered him a strange fruit to taste. He raised the parcel to his mouth.

'No!' screamed Nina. 'It's your child!' But it was too late; he had swallowed it.

She woke up crying and holding her stomach.

Thu was there. 'Tell me. Is it a bad omen?' he asked. He placed his hand on her stomach. 'Is he all right?'

She stared at him in confusion, not yet fully awake, then curled onto her side to wait for the sense of horror to pass. The weight of Thu's hand and his warmth against her back were comforting.

'I don't know,' she said. 'I don't know what's happening. I just don't know!'

'I'll send in the morning for a *tay phap* from the valley,' he said.

'No!' She didn't believe in the magic of the *tay phap*, and yet was terrified that he might see the truth she wished to hide from Thu.

Thu sighed. 'This child has changed you,' he said. 'Not for the better.'

Nina fought down an urge to laugh. Tears were close behind.

'Do you regret bringing me here?' she asked.

'I don't know yet. The tale isn't finished.'

In the darkness, they both contemplated possible endings. After a beat of five seconds he asked, 'Why are you still hiding from me, now that we are telling the truth? Why are you still frightened?' He pulled her onto her back and leaned over her. 'Why?'

She turned her head away and pressed her mouth against the muscle of his left arm.

'I wish to trust you,' he whispered. 'But I can't. I wish to trust but I'm uneasy. Please tell me why. Sometimes I even wonder whether. . . .' He stopped.

He had never begged her for anything before. He had never before offered her so much truth. She wanted to cry, because she no longer had anything bearable to offer him in return.

This time, he was not going to veer away. He waited for her answer. She reached up with her hands and pulled his mouth down onto hers. He allowed it without responding, but she felt him begin to harden against her thigh. She slid one hand down his hard belly and pulled at the top of his loose trousers.

She could not prevent the moment when he would insist on the final truth, but she could postpone it. As she moved her mouth downward, biting first at the point of his shoulder, then at the smooth skin around his nipple, she felt treacherous and evil. She had never felt either before, in lovemaking.

44

Then, as his hands twined themselves into her hair, a quiver of remembered hunger shocked her with its strength and softened the coldness of her purpose. She cried later, when he slept, his arms locked around her as if fearful she would escape during the night.

The next day, he was icy and distant, as he had been in the past each time he became frightened by their closeness. But now he was right. She knew that he had heard her failure to answer his plea and was avoiding the final truth for his own reasons.

The beginning of the poppy harvest gave them both an outward reality on which to focus. Early every morning, Nina followed the women into the fields to learn more about the flower that had shaped her life. The women, joined by others from the Meo village on the far side of the northern ridge, scored the grey-green globes of the seed pods with triple-bladed knives. The next day, the women scraped off the sticky sap which had bled from the cuts, into containers they wore tied to their waists. In the villa, Nina watched the elderly Meo woman supervise the boiling of the 'dog' in a huge pot, with lime and water, to purify it into crude opium base.

A mountain of cloth-bound bales of crude opium was climbing the posts of the shelter near the stables. Now Nina recognized the sticky brown substance which had arrived by junk and mule train, via safe drops in the swamps and nearby countryside, at her father's laboratory in a confectionery factory in Saigon. She had tried to run from it and been brought to live at its source, trapped in its stickiness like a gnat.

In the meantime, her own pod continued to swell. The light brushing of a wing became firmer. Once, with delight, Nina looked down and saw her *panung* lift and fall just above one hip bone. Then the bulge shifted to the left as if a kitten were burrowing beneath the bedclothes. Then terror hit.

Who are you? Nina begged it silently. Can't you tell me what you will look like?

Mlle. Berthe, her French governess, had once tried to beat into Nina's head the genetic formulae which would have let her predict the odds that her child would be fair. She couldn't remember them.

Why didn't I pay attention? she raged now. She knew only that it was possible. She tried not to imagine Thu looking down at a son as golden as its true father. He would snatch up the newborn from between her thighs and impale it. Her sins would be beyond forgiving. This humiliation would not be bearable.

She must put her money on the airstrip and a pilot who smoked

Marlboroughs, but she was realistic about the odds, even with the bars of soap.

Or she could try simply walking away, toward the lowlands and the Mekong, which she would cross illegally, as many refugees from many wars had done. But the few trails through the mountains could be navigated only by the local montagnard tribesmen. The jungle thickened rapidly on the slopes below the villa. In this remoteness, it was still home to the occasional tiger, gaur, wild buffalo and poisonous snakes. Farther down the slopes, were armies – the Royal Lao, who were backed by the Americans, the Pathet Lao who had Communist Chinese and Russian backing, and the neutralist forces who could not find a steady ally. Worst of all, she had no idea where she was.

And she was now nearly seven months pregnant. Her belly seemed to grow as she watched it. The shadowy pool of her navel, which Will John had called 'the most beautiful and mysterious in Asia', first stretched flat and then bulged into a clumsy button. Her belly began to meet furniture and the edges of doorways before she herself had arrived. Its weight began to suck at the physical strength she had always taken for granted. Life in the villa felt as slow as a delta river, but the end was racing at her like a mountain river in flood.

One afternoon, while Thu was drilling his men on the parade ground, Nina went inside to lie down in the coolness. She lay listening to the shouts and staring up at the scroll above the bed. Horizontal rather than the more usual vertical. A river running through mountains, with Chinese characters beside some of the peaks and more beneath the river, as if a real river and real mountains were being named. She sat up and searched the painted peaks for a familiar shape. Even if, as seemed unlikely to her, she could walk to safety with a big belly and no breath, surviving wildlife, wars and the imminent monsoon rains, it would be suicide to launch herself at random into the maze of the northern ranges. She had seen paintings which were, in fact, stylized maps. However, the scroll remained the portrait of an unhelpful, alien landscape.

The shouts from the parade ground had been replaced by the grinding of steel on stone from the verandah. Thu was sharpening his knife. She closed her eyes and forced her mind deep into the centre of her dilemma.

To get away, she needed food and water, and the means to carry them. She needed money and she needed her passport – if she survived long enough to need legal proof of life. Thu had hidden money and passport, and the women in the villa watched her with the careless attention of cats. To get away, therefore, she needed help from a stranger and time she didn't have.

She heard the floor of the verandah creak under Thu's weight, then silence.

On the other hand, she had the four bars of soap. She had surprising energy, in spite of her growing bulk. And she had no other choice.

3

Laos – 1966

High in the same mountain wilderness of northern Laos, at the other end of the thread of trail which Nina could see snaking northward from the Tiger's Head, where even military maps showed only craggy desolation without the fine red lines of roads or black full stops of villages and towns, on a limestone shoulder between two shark's tooth peaks, lay an astonishing village. From the air, to American and Russian Intelligence overflights, it looked rather like the French royal gardens at Versailles – a hand, with a palm and radiating fingers.

The palm of the hand was a dusty rectangular *place*, scarred by formal flower beds and edged by three solid buildings: the so-called Palace, the prison and the Museum of Local History. The Palace, apart from the architectural whimsy of Moorish turrets on each corner, was whitewashed stucco, and bleak. Inspired by the Palace of the former French Governor General in Saigon, it proclaimed status with a red tile roof, now raddled with lichen, mosses, grasses and the odd seedling tree. Though also built of stuccoed brick, the other two buildings – the prison and the museum – rated only thatch.

Eight dust-paved streets fanned out from the *place* in a formal *patte d'oie*. Sign-posted in both French and Lao, they were the Avenues Marie Antoinette, de la Chapelle, Maréchal Foch, Deux Magots, Bonaparte, Descartes, Prudhon, and St. Cyr. The huts and sheds of thatch and woven bamboo which lined them almost disappeared when seen from the air, being dust-coloured and made from the same stuff as the surrounding jungle. Much more visible were the sharp circles of water tanks, squares of rice stores, the breast-like mound of the pagoda stupa, and the stone missile, ready for launching, aka the Cenotaph, at the end of the Avenue Marie Antoinette.

This incongruous settlement, like Thu's very different encampment, was walled by a palisade of sharpened bamboo trunks which effectively protected buffalo, chickens and babies from night predators. The wall also gave slight pause to random guerrillas, whether American, Vietnamese or Pathet Lao. It would be no use at all against either Chinese artillery or the American Phantom jets amassing on Pacific islands to the east.

On the slopes above the hamlet, twelve women in black cotton trousers, black turbans, loose jackets, and heavy silver necklaces slashed at the green tangles with machetes to clear land for the next year's crop of opium poppies. Below the hamlet, a small crowd had gathered to watch previously cleared land being plowed for maize.

Major Lucky, the Tonkinese founder and ruler of this secret kingdom, stood in solar topee and tropical whites under an oiled paper parasol held by a girl of about ten. Backing him at a respectful distance were his chief *aide*, his bodyguard, and wives Numbers Two and Three, both under 20 years of age. Besides him, at a distance which had more to do with distaste than respect, stood a thin, brown-haired, middle-aged Russian wearing a pale grey American drip-dry suit. Old women, children and a stray pig made up the fringes of the gathering.

Three ploughs were in action, two pulled by dirt-crusted water buffalo with back-swept horns like an ocean liner's anchor. The third was pulled by a yoked pair of American males. Their bare, bleeding feet slipped and scraped on loose clods as they leaned into their brow straps and against the wooden yoke which crossed their chests. Their clothing was opalescent with sweat and plastered to their bodies. As they strained, the curved plough blade jerked through the dry heavy soil, stuck, then jerked forward a few more inches.

Major Lucky snapped his fingers without taking his eyes from the two Americans. Number Two Wife leaned forward like bamboo in a wind to proffer a Gitane light it with a solid gold antique Bambu lighter.

'You're doing well,' Lucky called to the Americans in French. 'The buffalo have overtaken you only twice!'

The taller American, brown-haired, gaunt and bearded, a former football full-back, held the Major's eye. His teenage years of milk, vitamins and steak had long been worn off his skeleton leaving only a thin coating of spare muscle on the long bones. He glanced at his smaller yoke mate.

Jeff's going under, he thought in panic. He's giving up!

'Fuck the fat little bastard!' he murmured. 'Let's die doing it!'

The two Americans strained against the yoke; the blade sliced smoothly and rolled over a clean eighteen inch long shoulder of soil before it stuck again.

Major Lucky inclined his pear-shaped head toward the Russian. 'Trying prove their manhood ploughs my fields all the faster.'

49

Mihailo Rogov took no pleasure in the humiliation of his fellow man, American or not. If the truth were told, he felt more in common with the prisoners out there with the buffalo in the dry rice *paddi* than with his host. He and Lucky were locked professionally into an arranged marriage, and Rogov pined for divorce. He looked away from the two sweating Americans, toward the Major, silver-haired and still vigorous at sixty-two – as he had called on his wives to attest to Rogov more than once.

The Major was short with a torso like a half-filled bean bag, all weight at the bottom. His head was also a bean bag, narrow of cranium and wide of jaw, with small quick eyes and full, heavy lips. Rogov had observed that the Major, though ponderous looking, was lightly balanced when moved, like a weighted doll that instantly springs back up when pushed over.

'Where did you get these two?' Rogov asked. 'Did you send a kidnap squad into Vietnam?'

Lucky snorted, then made the Russian wait while he inhaled his cigarette. 'They're terrorists,' he said, gazing down his exhaled plume of smoke. 'Trespassing where they have no right to be. Taken by some Khmu montagnards – lower down the mountains, in Laos.' Lucky smiled. 'The ignorant *moi* were frightened of getting into trouble with the Pathet Lao if they handed the Round Eye bandits over to the Royal Lao Forces and of getting into trouble with the Royal Lao if they gave them to the Pathet Communists. So they gave them to me. No dilemma. No one the wiser. Also, I pay a little premium as inducement. They are of no interest to you.'

You might let me judge that, thought Rogov. Smugness was high on his list of Lucky's crimes. Though the Major's nose was scarred from a badly healed dagger slit, he claimed to be delighted because his eyes had been spared. Two teeth had been knocked out, the Major claimed, by interrogating Yankee Green Berets. Lucky seized on the chance to display his wealth by replacing the teeth with gold. He even congratulated himself on having lost two of his fingers to, he said, a recalcitrant gun-elevator.

'First of all,' he had told Rogov, 'it was not my trigger hand. Secondly, it left me with the lucky number eight in fingers.'

Rogov's eyes slid to the three enormous Burmese reds in gold settings which celebrated this lucky chance on the remaining two fingers and thumb of Lucky's left hand. He knew he should approve of such positive thinking. He wished he were not convinced that it was mere self-satisfaction. That Lucky always sprang back made Rogov want to

50

knock him down again. Rogov was ashamed of the urge, but it was real. He recognized, with some irony, his own jealous wish that he could feel so pleased with the course of his own life.

At thirty-eight, a member of the Soviet Trade Mission and GRU, Bangkok, Rogov knew he should consider his role in the growing Southeast Asian conflict as an honoured mission. But, as a northerner, he hated heat. He hated mosquitoes, ants, midges, leeches and snakes. He hated highly spiced food and Tiger, Black Cat and Sam Sen beer. Most of all, he hated having to pay court to jumped-up brigands who thought they were princes in a world where, to Rogov, princes had long ceased to have any significance whatsoever.

He did have colleagues who, unlike himself, would have been excited by stalking the titbit of information which Lucky was clutching to his chest like a child with a Christmas secret. There were colleagues who would enjoy being forced, as it were, to consume sticky rice, Suntory whisky, and child virgins in the line of duty. Rogov was repulsed by all three in ascending order. He preferred beefsteak (a taste acquired in England), Campari (which had been available to him as a privileged party member) and his young wife who was, unfortunately, living at the moment with her parents in Leningrad. Rogov did his best. In his lucid moments, he knew that he could not risk professional demotion, or worse, for what amounted only to being a bad sport.

Full of hope and vision, he had studied mathematics at Leningrad (where he also married Sophia), mastered basic English, French and German, then been sent as a mature exchange student to Reading University in England to become a computer expert. He had then expected a cosy berth in a Trade Mission, somewhere in the West, preferably at Friedrich-Engels-Strasse 3, in Cologne, as an authority on cracking into western computers for information both commercial and military. From Cologne, visits home would have been easy. He would have had everything a man could reasonably ask – a comfortable life and a sense of mission. Instead, through the inevitable, bureaucratic bungling, as he saw it, he had ended up in Bangkok, the stewpot of Asia, sweating in a non-airconditioned villa between field trips to assess, then pass on or not, information from a stable of varyingly reliable sources, about what he referred to as the Americans' refusal to stay home and mind their own business.

Today, he was feeling like a worse sport than usual. The Major had demanded his presence here instead of meeting at the normal rendez-vous in a hamlet on a navigable stretch of the Ou River. Rogov had therefore suffered a 5 a.m. start, a hideous ride on a forty-year-old cargo

51

plane to a jungle landing strip, then one and a half hours of indignity on muleback. He suspected from Lucky's solicitous enquiries about his well-being that a montagnard had reported the small accident en route – Rogov had slipped off the back of his mule as they lurched up over some particularly steep rocks.

'Are those two men the special treat you promised me?' he asked Lucky rather sharply. He watched the time lag between the flesh of Lucky's jowls and the sharp bone of his chin as the major shook his head emphatically.

'I wouldn't bring you here just for this,' said Lucky with mock reproach. 'You know me. Value for your money.'

Rogov watched the smaller American stumble and fall across the wooden yoke, pulling his teammate down with him. The man was gaunt with dysentery.

'Why don't you let them stop?' he asked. 'I'm sufficiently impressed with your two new buffalo.'

All playfulness left Lucky's small eyes. 'You did not lose a sixteen-year-old son to a pack of American terrorists on the wrong side of the Laos border. Our side. I am a little harder to impress, my friend.' He turned to his *aide*. 'Get that man up. Come,' he ordered Rogov, disdaining to watch the execution of his command.

Back inside the bamboo palisade, the two men strolled along the Avenue St. Cyr toward Lucky's palace. Rogov noticed that the usual village tapestry of footprints in the dust had been replaced by the snake trails of sweeping palm fronds. From the Catholic chapel at one end of the cross street, Rue Moulin Rouge, to the Buddhist pagoda at the other, the vista was clear of all careless ox carts, looms or rakes. A wreath of some sort had been propped against the Cenotaph at the far end of the Avenue Marie Antoinette. The hamlet's population, arranged decoratively in doorways and porches, marked their progress with a ground swell of bows.

As they entered the Place Louis Pasteur – the palm of the hand – the direct route to the wooden steps of the Palace was blockaded by a statue-in-progress. Major Lucky's face, slightly startled, had emerged from the limestone block like a swimmer from an unexpected wave, along with his left hand and lower left forearm. The rest of him was still immured in stone. A garland of freesias hung as best it could over what was available of the limestone ruler. All mason's tools and limestone chips had been cleared away for the occasion.

'How splendid,' murmured Rogov.

'I'm delighted that you approve,' said Lucky cheerfully.

Rogov considered the tone of this reply. There was a disturbing shadow of intelligence in Lucky's small eyes and a suggestion of constant humour. Lucky seemed to have no idea how ridiculous he appeared to the Russian, with his aping of a French world known only through books, and the fairy tales of a francophile war lord father. At the same time, he managed to suggest that perhaps – just perhaps – he found the Russian amusing. Rogov found this possibility unforgiveable. He might be able to laugh at himself, but gave others less licence.

Unfortunately, ruminated Rogov, Major Lucky was officially defined as a valuable human intelligence resource, or HUMINT source as the Yanks would say. After his warlord father had been executed by the Viet Minh in 1955 for helping the French at Dien Bien Phu, Lucky had escaped with enough jewels, money and family mercenaries to rebuild the family's empire on this remote, fertile limestone upland, where opium poppies grew like bindweed. His little kingdom also happened to be astride the very top of the loose skein of tracks and roads whose lower reaches, where they infiltrated South Vietnam, were to be known as the Ho Chi Minh Trail. Major Lucky had made a double fortune – from opium and espionage.

The poppies had kept him in contact with his father's old cronies in the Alliance Corse who had dug in their feet and stayed after the French defeat at Dien Bien Phu. His private army of Meo montagnards was invaluable as eyes and ears in impossible terrain. He seemed to have made, or bought, a private peace with most of the country's warring factions: the Communist Pathet Lao, the pro-West Royal Lao, the neutralist Free Lao, the Meo, who had fought on several sides, and the ethnic Chinese known as Hoa, who were being anxiously watched by all the others. It was a paradox that Lucky's titbits of information were the main reason the Russian remained so firmly anchored as a valuable agent in Southeast Asia.

They're probably the reason for the success of several American, French, German, English, and Chinese agents as well, Rogov reflected sourly as he watched the Major graciously receiving homage from his bowing subjects. And if you sleep with everyone, you're bound to catch the clap. Rogov abandoned his metaphor at this point. The clap was contagious. He himself would be vulnerable to any political infection Lucky might thus carry. In the meantime, however, the Major had promised something out of the ordinary; it was Rogov's duty to learn what it was. He followed his host past two octagonal flower beds, rehearsing phrases of indifference in their common language of French.

Rogov mopped his damp forehead before raising his wine glass to the Major, perforce and yet again. He glanced with distaste at the twin fourteen-year-old girls cowering on a pair of stools near the wall, both of them frosted and decorated for the occasion like a pair of Easter gingerbreads. Dessert, no doubt. He did not approve of abusing children. In any case, if the Major made him drink any more, he would also be incapable. He could see the man eyeing him slyly as he waved for the attendant to pour yet another glass. A cage of thrushes was rustling and twittering in the corner.

Rogov wished the Major would get on with whatever he had planned. Rogov was disconcerted by the uneasy blend of East and West which Lucky brewed as his style of life. They were sitting on chairs at a full-height table, eating from Limoges porcelain with US Army stainless steel cutlery, drinking Chinese wine from Waterford crystal. Their attendant wore a white jacket like a servant in any officers' mess. Lucky had changed for dinner into a velvet *smoking* with a silk foulard at his throat. On Rogov's plate were what appeared to be *quenelles*.

On the other hand, there were those girls, and the thrushes, and the constant flicks of movement in the corner of his eye which were lizards and mice. The occasional bat sliced through the air above his head in pursuit of the gnats which wrapped the paraffin chandelier in an uneasy, shifting fog. The *quenelles* had the firmness of Chinese fish balls and tasted of the local mud.

Rogov was a Ukrainian, more European even than the ethnic Russians. He had no romantic dreams of grandparental yurts, or high-cheeked warriors riding pell-mell without harness across the vastness of the Mongolian steppes. He considered himself to be a man of intelligence and moderation, with little need for the exotic. Not for the first or last time, he reflected that he was in the wrong place. After they had finished their fresh fruit, he accepted a hot wet towel from the white-jacketed attendant and gratefully wiped his sweating face. He imagined strangling the thrushes.

Lucky wiped his face and hands vigorously and tossed the towel back onto the servant's tray. '*Enfin,*' he said, in their common tongue. He snapped his fingers. The servant proffered a manila envelope which had been set conspicuously on a nearby table. Lucky inserted one plump hand slowly into the envelope.

A second-rate magician milking his timings, thought Rogov.

'*Voilà!*' said Lucky.

Rogov flinched internally from the banality of these theatrics and reached for the fogged and grainy photographs in Lucky's hand.

At first he could see only a tossed salad of high and low lights, and grainy greys. He tried to read the prints as bad copies of low-resolution aerial shots. Then their scale suddenly leapt into true proportion and he began to make out the shape of a piece of electronic equipment. His eye and brain began to work together. He began, at last, to enjoy himself. He was expert at navigating the under-stated geography of high-technology, where continents are contained inside a micro-chip. Now, his pulse accelerated slightly with the special excitement of the expert or connoisseur confronting an unfamiliar specimen in his field of expertise.

Lucky tabled another print, immediately recognizable. A crashed aircraft. Fusilage and broken wing. Almost certainly an American RF-4 Phantom jet used for both high and low level reconnaissance over-flights.

'Are you implying that both photos were taken at the same spot?' Rogov asked in a voice filled with ennui.

The Major beamed at him silently across folded arms which he had propped on his belly.

'Is this. . . .' Rogov pointed to the picture of the equipment, '. . . in this?' He indicated the crashed plane. His hand was steady but a tremor in his voice betrayed him.

Lucky stretched and squeezed his jowls like a concertina.

This bastard is about to produce another one of his unfortunately invaluable tit-bits, Rogov thought. He's having too much fun. He frowned sceptically at the photos and sat back in his chair.

'It's not far,' said Lucky. 'With the right guides, even you might be able to find it.'

He's always rude in proportion to the value, thought Rogov. He shifted his thin buttocks on the hard carved wood dining chair and prepared to open negotiations.

'The photos are bad,' he said. He was fairly certain that Lucky had taken them himself. 'And we have plenty of Phantom RF-4s to examine.'

'And the computer?' asked Lucky gently.

'Who knows what the weather may have done.' Rogov pretended to be interested in a final lychee. '. . . Even if it should be something new.'

Lucky beamed like Father Christmas. 'Hanoi would be interested, bad photos or not.'

'Hanoi hasn't the technology to know what to do with that instrument, interesting or not,' retorted Rogov. 'They would have to ask us . . . and I'd no doubt be the lucky man sent to investigate. Why don't you save yourself any illusions, and both of us time?'

Lucky's smile remained as wide as before but his eyes darkened like the sky before a sudden storm. 'No illusions,' he said, through the slice of his smile. 'Hanoi could do just as well as you with the rest of what I'm offering . . . perhaps better.'

He waited.

'All right,' conceded Rogov. 'Show me.'

Rogov knew, as soon as the Major began to lead him across the Place Louis Pasteur to the prison. Inside the main gate of the prison, was an unroofed compound. In one corner of the compound, inside a bamboo and wire enclosure like an oversized chicken run, squatted the two Americans Rogov had seen yoked to the plough, cooking rice over a small fire.

The larger American jumped to his feet when he saw Rogov and the Major. 'William R. Johnston, with a tee' he said quickly. 'If you understand English, please tell someone! I'm William R. Johnston, First serg. . . .'

Their guard began to shout loudly, over the American's words. He brandished his automatic rifle. Lucky pulled Rogov toward an iron door in the far wall.

'TELL someone!' the American shouted. 'Johnston with a tee! And Philip Macr. . . .'

The guard hit him with the butt of his gun. Rogov heard the thud as he followed Lucky through the iron door. The American was silent.

'You trust your beast to slight cages,' said Rogov.

'The mountains are bars enough,' said Lucky.

'Where did you say they were captured?' asked Rogov.

'I didn't,' said Lucky. 'Not for free. This way, please.'

Beyond the iron door, a double row of heavy wooden doors locked by old-fashioned steel padlocks lined a short passageway. Some stood ajar showing tiny cubicles behind. In the last of the cubicles, a man lay on the ground, strapped to a litter, blinking at the sudden light of their lantern.

Lucky took his Mauser pistol from its holster. 'The pilot,' he said. 'Please do not attempt to speak to him in English or I will shoot him.'

The man struggled briefly as if trying to sit up. Then Rogov saw that he was strapped to the litter not to hold him down but to keep him from falling off. His back had been broken. Rogov peered in the wavering lantern light. Both of the man's legs were in rough splints.

The man stared at Rogov, then at Lucky's Mauser. His hair and eyes were light but undefinable in the shadows of the lantern. 'Do you speak English?' he asked.

Even while Rogov hesitated, Lucky hauled him from the cell, slammed the door and marched down the passageway.

'Why should I believe he's the pilot of that plane?' demanded Rogov, following. 'You have shown me no evidence and refuse to let me verify your claim by interrogating him.'

'I also have his parachute,' said Lucky. 'His back was broken when he ejected.' He stalked angrily through the outer compound and into the Place Louis Pasteur, where he deigned to wait for Rogov. 'Monsieur,' he said. 'I have nothing to gain by lying to you. You, on the other hand, are in danger of seriously offending *me*!'

Rogov smoothed the sleeve of his suit where Lucky had pulled him from the cell. He disliked rough handling of any kind. In his opinion, the only men who praised the efficacy of physical violence were the ones who enjoyed wreaking it. On the other hand, any offence against his own dignity was irrelevant – if that man on the litter really were the pilot of the drowned RF-4, with the security clearance and training to operate a new prototype navigational computer. Or even, possibly, the rumoured real-time imaging system. Rogov very seldom stumbled onto intelligence that interested him personally as much as this might turn out to do. His superiors in the GRU would fall over themselves to interrogate the man . . . after Rogov passed him on. He began to let himself believe in what seemed to be happening. It would be a coup! Not that he was much concerned with individual success, beyond the desire to serve, he reminded himself. On the other hand, such success, worthless for its own sake, might earn him the right to request leave to see Sophia. Or even, depending on what came out of the interrogation of the pilot, the right to suggest, in a most gentle way, reposting to the West in order to develop what had been learned.

Back in the Palace, the white-coated servant poured both men a glass of cognac-coloured liquor from a bottle whose label was long eaten away by damp. Lucky sat with his sharp-pointed chin bone pulled back into the fleshy parallel curves below his jaw, watching the Russian trying to pretend indifference. Rogov could control his shortness of breath but not the brightness of his eye. The thrushes, the cowering children by the wall, the mosquitoes, and his host's complacency had become irrelevant. He was a collector, a connoisseur, about to take possession of an object of desire. Rogov lifted his glass one more time.

'To *entente cordiale*,' he said. Now to feel delicately for the extent of the Major's greed.

Lucky raised his glass in return. 'Men can sometimes be even more valuable than poppies, don't you agree?'

As Rogov surmised, Major Lucky did have other friends than the Russians and played the rural bumpkin with Rogov for his own reasons. Unknown to any of the major intelligence services, under the name of Charles Loan, he had attended La Rosay, an elite boarding school for privileged Catholic boys near Lausanne, in the French-speaking Swiss canton of Vaud. His mountain fantasia on a colonial past was not, as Rogov assumed, built from faded illustrations in old French textbooks and the memories of a war lord father fallen from grace along with the French. It was based on personal memories acquired between ages nine and thirteen.

Lucky had found much in French-speaking Switzerland to be alien – skiing, for example. The experience was cold and nasty, and, by the age of ten, he was already the wrong shape. He was appalled by the horrid food and freezing, spartan rooms of the school. The apparent aim of deliberately inflicting maximum suffering on the children of the privileged seemed to him completely mad – in total contradiction to his own background where one chief purpose of privilege was to increase your right to ease.

However, certain images lodged themselves deep in his adolescent brain: white steamers gliding in and out of clouds which floated on Lac Leman like huge ghostly seabirds. Sunlight on the ruins of the Castle of Chillon above the lake in a blue-and-diamond phase. School visits to France arranged during holidays for the boys who were too far from home to return easily, or whose homes were in dangerous political disarray. On these visits, Lucky (then Charles) perceived another form of antiquity, as old, as deep, and more organized than the one he claimed for himself.

He had long forgotten the name of the chateau, but not the awe he had felt, standing at the top of an avenue of ancient chestnuts, contemplating the cream-coloured broken pediments and arches of Baroque arrogance. The building stood above its vineyards in absolute sureness of physical permanence. To Lucky, far from home and busily shaping his own future world, it made even the Royal Palace in Bangkok, which he had found marvellous as a child, seem flimsy and light-weight, a confection of gilt and stucco built on a reclaimed swamp with the sea never far away.

Though nominally Catholic like many in the former French colonies in Southeast Asia, Lucky did not see himself, western-fashion, as a unique soul struggling toward its individual reward. He secretly believed what his grandparents had believed – that he was only the way station, so to speak, of a soul on a longer journey through many lives toward enlightenment. Nevertheless, he felt powerfully drawn to the men, like the one who had built that chateau, who proclaimed through their monuments, 'Me! I, myself have done this, left this testimony of my life. Remember *me!*'

When he finished La Rosay and returned to North Vietnam, he carried this paradox with him. When the aftermath of Dien Bien Phu, May 1954, shattered what had been his future, he rebuilt his kingdom in the image of vanished power. The avenues with French names, the Catholic chapel, the imitation of the Presidential Palace in Saigon (itself an imitation) were a form of sympathetic magic, tokens of the strengths of another culture which was both ally and foe. The fact that the French had been defeated by his own people merely proved his right to annex what he could of their puissance.

His years at La Rosay also left him with friends. One of these had been Grégoire Ince, another boy wrongly shaped for skiing and *futbol*. Like Lucky, Ince had grown up seeking other, less physical ways to exert power. He had done a stint as a junior officer with the SDEC in Saigon. Until Dien Bien Phu, he and Lucky had met regularly at Ince's club for Pernod, gossip and the occasional shared whore. After the French withdrawal in 1955, Ince flitted in and out of Indochina, paused occasionally in Bangkok, and sent Lucky postcards from Hong Kong.

Lucky lost track of Ince after the murder of his father by the North Vietnamese and during his own flight into Laos, until a chance meeting in Vientiane five years later in 1961. Ince was dining in public with an American openly known to be CIA. Lucky did not interrupt but later followed Ince to his hotel.

'You old wart hog!' Ince had cried when Lucky tapped his arm *en route* to the hotel bar. 'I can't believe you haven't been bumped off! Wonderful to see you!'

They had embraced strenuously, each half-consciously noting how much flesh the other had added since their last meeting five years earlier.

'And you're still not in gaol!' retorted Lucky. 'The gods are looking after us. Why aren't you in Paris, "the centre of the Universe", as you used to say far too often?'

'Yellow fever,' said Ince cheerfully. Unlike Lucky, he carried his weight high, in a wide rounded skull, heavy-rimmed glasses, and thick neck and chest. 'Chronic.' He looked Lucky up and down and performed a second dumbshow of delighted disbelief. 'Let me buy you a drink. The bar's not bad here.'

Lucky asked for a single malt whisky. 'I see you're snuggling up to the Yanks.'

Ince dropped his round fleshy chin to peer with raised brows over the tops of his glasses. 'You do, do you? And where do you see this taking place?'

Lucky shrugged.

'Testing the water,' conceded Ince. 'Passing the odd bit of gossip about their man. Diem . . . anyway, we never really stopped snuggling up, did we?'

'Did you ever stop cutting each other's throats?' rejoined Lucky. 'I seem to remember the odd shot being exchanged across the Rue Catinat between Deuxième Bureau and certain American "advisers" back in 1955.'

'Purely as back-up to the main contestants,' said Ince, unperturbed. 'It was nothing personal . . . Where are you now, anyway?'

When Lucky told him, he pursed his pink lips. 'I could introduce you to someone who'd love to hear all the local gossip from up there. Interested?'

'What language would we be speaking?'

'Do you care?'

Lucky decided not to bother pretending indignation. He made a *comme-ci, comme-ça* waggle of his hand.

'Not English,' said Ince, 'in spite of what you claim to see.'

And so it had begun.

As Major Lucky returned Rogov's reluctant toast, he enjoyed the sheen of excitement on that normally dour, permanently petulant face. Monsieur Rogov could carry that bony nose of his as high as he liked; the Russians would pay Lucky's price. When the bank in Vientiane confirmed the deposit, and the Lisu headman confirmed the arrival of the crated guns, flame-throwers and grenade launchers, with their respective munitions, then – and only then – would Lucky deliver into Rogov's eager hands the pilot with the broken back and American security clearance for Top Secret and also, undoubtedly, for one or more of the above-Top Secret Sensitive-Compartmented Information categories with codeword designation. Money for old rope, as the English would say.

Two hours later, however, after sending Rogov off to bed with a cheerful order to have sweet dreams, Lucky felt the strange dissatisfaction that had recently begun to poison his life. It both puzzled and outraged him. He was a man who had always made the most of what the fates sent him and never complained.

'Don't whine, take action!' he had always adjured his son. The memory of his son darkened his mood still further. He could not accommodate the boy's death in his positive scheme of things. For some reason, Lucky then remembered the two *moi* girls who, for all he knew, were still sitting on their stools by the wall. Both he and Rogov had had more interesting things to do that night. He called a servant to send them away. They could hang onto their maidenheads for another guest who would appreciate the treat.

Lucky let himself out of the gate at the end of the Avenue St. Cyr. A private from his personal army carried a paraffin lantern to illuminate his master's path down a series of rock falls, now organized into rough steps, onto a track along a small stream. Above the track, a multitude of caves, eaten out of the soft limestone by water and weather, showed dark against the pale face of the chalk cliff. After a ten minute walk, Lucky turned and began a short scramble up toward one of the dark cave mouths. The two men entered the cave.

The cave was no darker by night than by day. In the thin light of the lantern, a heavy grille could just be seen, blocking the way deeper into the earth. Lucky thrust his face against the grille and motioned the soldier to hold the lantern close.

'Are you still alive?' he demanded in French. Stretched out on the rocky floor lay one of the killers of his son. Not one of the Americans, unfortunately, but the Meo lackey who had led them across the mountains into Laos, where they were not at war . . . where they killed a teenage boy they imagined to be a Pathet Lao sniper. The man lay still, a dark bundle in the shadows.

'You are alive,' Lucky said. 'I won't let death find you so easily.'

Lucky had made certain the man had enough water to survive, and just enough food. When he refused to eat, he was force fed. He was kept in darkness, as Lucky's son had been sent into darkness.

The man did not answer. He did not stir on the rocky floor.

'*Merde!*' said Lucky. He sniffed the air. 'Unlock the gate!' He gave the soldier his keys and took the lantern himself.

The gate cried like a tormented spirit as the soldier swung it open. Lucky advanced and kicked the man on the ground lightly in the ribs he himself had broken. Still no movement.

'Give me my keys and turn him over,' said Lucky. One could never trust the mountain savages. They could bite your throat out before you knew it.

The soldier obeyed, and stepped back hastily. The man's face was a dark, shifting mass. Lucky held the lantern closer. Ants. Lucky sniffed again; the stink of the man's ordure had masked the early scent of death.

Lucky swore. 'Let him lie there. He can be company for the next guest.' His blackness settled firmly. He was awash in it.

'Lock the gate again,' he ordered the private. 'So his family can't find him and bury him. Let him wander! He can do no more damage than the living.'

He lowered his bulk cautiously back down to the main trail. He felt dark and empty and restless, as if a woman had denied him satisfaction at the last moment. But it was worse than that.

'I want. . . ,' he said.

'Sir?' said the private.

Lucky looked through the young soldier into the night. He didn't know what he wanted. More. Of something. Just more. Of whatever would restore the brutal clarity of his early life.

'I'll find it,' he assured himself. He let the private lead the way back up the treacherous path to the villa.

4

Not long after Lucky's meeting with Rogov, Nina saw Thu crossing the
parade ground toward the main pavilion beside a silver-haired, pear-
shaped man wearing a tiger-stripe camouflage uniform. She stepped
forward to greet them.

Is this my Marlboro smoker, the dark horse who might carry me
to safety? she wondered.

'Oho! What have we here?' Major Lucky's small eyes travelled over
Nina's geography, pausing on her gently swelling breasts and stomach.
'Making heirs, are we, Colonel? Or am I mistaken?'

'My concubine,' said Thu shortly as the two men marched up the
wooden steps to the verandah. Nina moved forward to be introduced
but Thu stepped past her as if she were a servant.

'Marry her if it's a son, my boy,' said Lucky, still eying the goods.
'Found a new dynasty for your poppy fields. She looks strong enough
for a dozen sons.'

Thu's eyes warned her. Nina glared back. She hoped Thu had good
reason for helping this gorilla humiliate her. And for denying her his
name.

'But then you have always been a lucky man,' went on the major. A
shadow flickered across his eyes as he remembered the son he no
longer had. 'On the wrong side from time to time, of course. But
which of us hasn't picked the wrong card occasionally? One can
always try again . . . pick safer or more profitable allies. . . .' He sat
cross-legged on the seating platform to which Thu had waved him.
His eyes flicked to Nina again. 'Your family life seems in good order.
How are politics?'

Thu stood very still, as if puzzled by some half-heard sound. Then,
without answering, he brushed an imaginary gnat from his arm,
delicately with his little finger.

Major Lucky flushed slightly around the jowls.

'Major Lucky, will you honour us with your company for the evening
meal?' asked Thu. 'Or must you hurry home?'

Nina had never heard the name before.

'No time to linger,' said Lucky with convincing regret. 'Perhaps a quick whisky, if you have any, while I say what I came to say.'

Thu looked at Nina. She bowed her head but raged with frustration at missing whatever business this odd pair might have together. As Thu no doubt intended!

She found the elderly Meo woman and sent her to dig out a bottle of ancient Suntory from Thu's natural *cave* beneath the cook house. The woman returned, dusting the bottle. While Nina quivered with impatience, the woman polished two glasses and arranged them on a tray. She put a handful of groundnuts into a bowl, then piled lychees in a little basket.

'I'll take it!' Nina said. She seized the tray from the old woman's hands and rattled hastily back to the verandah. Once there, she knelt by the sitting platform with modestly lowered eyes. Deferentially, she poured out two measures. If Thu wished to cast her as the maid in his farce, she would play the part to the hilt.

Both men paused and watched her fill their glasses. Her task performed, Nina shuffled away to stand by the wall, eyes down, hands folded across her bulge, waiting to serve again. Thu would now have to make a point of sending her away.

Lucky accepted her as both invisible and deaf. 'You could regret your decision,' he resumed. 'Whatever our differences, we both know that our Meo are running out of mountains.'

She had missed the crux of the meeting, as she had feared she would. They had not wasted time on the usual polite preliminaries. She looked at Thu under her lashes.

He smiled lazily. Nina wondered if Lucky recognized the rage behind the smile. 'Do I hear a threat?' asked Thu.

'Heavens no!' cried Lucky, chins awobble with indignation. 'I respect you far too much!' He blinked involuntarily at the recollection of how he had gained that respect. 'I merely wish to share my thoughts with you . . . We must be honest in hours of trouble, *n'est-ce-pas?*'

'*Mais oui!*' murmured Thu, countering the casual slip into French. 'Of course.'

Lucky now looked at Nina. He leaned forward and continued in French with a topic not meant for her ears or understanding. 'It's the new way, Colonel! And nothing at all like slavery, as you would have it. I believe the future of this commodity will be brighter even than the poppy's . . . opium is dwindling now that the Pathet Lao and North Vietnamese are driving the Meo south with such vigour, and the Royal Lao are squeezing them northward. But my new venture requires cooperation and mutual trust.' He sipped his whisky. 'Excellent!' he proclaimed with the air of a satisfied connoisseur.

Thu sat relaxed but ready, a watchful predator.

'I've been abroad,' explained Lucky. 'I have observed. I have connections . . . *suis plus à la coule*. I dare think I may therefore have a sense of smell for developments denied to someone who, however fortunate and able, is perhaps blinkered by provincialism . . . a lack of understanding of the Round Eye and his values.' He finished his whisky as final punctuation for his speech and took out a pack of Gitanes.

Nina hardly heard Thu's reply. This then was a second visitor to the eagles' eyrie. She had not heard an airplane or helicopter. Carrying that sagging weight, this man had not trekked overland much farther than from the gate of the villa. There was another way in, which did not require wings and which a larger belly than hers could negotiate.

'How generous of you to offer to share your wisdom!' said Thu, still without moving. 'Unfortunately, my provincialism, as you call it, blinds me to its value.'

Lucky blinked again. He replaced the unlit cigarette in the packet. The conversation had been stretched to its limits.

'Alas,' he said. 'Time presses. I must be back by lunchtime tomorrow. So, with regret. . . .'

Very carefully, both men stood in unison. Each begged the other to descend first from the platform. Neither spoke to Nina or to the other as they went down the wooden steps and vanished into the dusk at the edge of the parade ground.

Nina bent over to light the little oil lamp on the table. She tried four times to make her hands fit the glass shade back within its restraining crown of wire.

'By lunchtime tomorrow'. She put that astonishing new information away with the rest of the evening's revelations. She heard the sound of metal shoes on rock and the sound of voices and composed herself to deal with Thu.

'So?' demanded Thu, on his return a few minutes later. 'As you were clearly so interested in observing.'

'A clown,' said Nina shortly. 'With no manners . . . Are you going to offer me a drink now?'

'A dangerous clown,' said Thu, ignoring her dig. '. . . Who likes to juggle with live grenades. One of which is the ambition to corner the Burmese opium trade . . . thinks he can take on the Kuomintang bandits.' He grinned unexpectedly. 'It's not like you to let a fit of pique cloud your sense of smell.'

'He would be happy to slit your throat,' said Nina. 'Even pique couldn't obscure that. Nor your own desire to return the favour.'

Does Major Lucky dislike Thu enough to help me? she wondered.

Thu became serious again. 'Last harvest, his men attacked one of my mule trains and stole 26 kilos of raw opium. The following week, I took back my opium and shot 26 of his mules. That was the last I heard of him.'

'Why now?' prompted Nina. 'Does he want an ally against the Kuomintang?'

'You don't want to know these things any longer,' he said. 'You have chosen to make them not your business. Nevertheless, I would rather he hadn't seen you.'

'Is he so near?' she asked. 'How far from the villa must I begin to watch out for him?'

Thu considered the exact tone of her question. 'He's far enough,' he said. 'You needn't watch out for him.'

It had grown too dark for her to have seen the expression in his eyes. However, his tone was softer than it had been for the last twelve days. When he went to stand beside one of the verandah pillars, she joined him. Together, they looked out at the spine of the eroded limestone ridge.

'Do you find it very dreadful here?' he asked suddenly, in one of his lurches into directness which, when they had been lovers, had always disarmed her. Even now, she was flattered, as when an animal drops its guard and admits a human to a private moment.

'No,' she replied slowly, 'but its beauty is frightening.'

'The Dragon's Teeth,' he said, gazing at the distant pinnacles which were now only a dark silhouette against the lighter blue-grey of the night sky. 'I find them awesome but not frightening. Like the Tiger's Head above us. It protects us from the evils that always blow from the north.' He turned his head toward a faint sound, like distant thunder. Then it faded and the night continued its usual concerto. Bats and swifts danced in half-seen, half-sensed arcs of shadow above the dust of the parade ground.

'One day it may be safe for us to go back into the softer lands of the deltas,' he said. 'But not yet.' He repeated his words thoughtfully as if testing them. '. . . one day . . .'

She felt his head turn toward her in the darkness.

'I have never thought in terms of "one day",' he said. 'But with a

66

child coming. . . .' He looked back out toward the dark silhouette of the limestone ridge.

He had decided that she would live. She had been tried and acquitted. She didn't dare try to speak.

Laughter came from one of the huts on the lower terrace. She could hear the mules and ponies shifting and stamping in the stables. Then she heard the distant thunder again, from the north-east. The series of low-pitched explosions almost eluded the ear. 'That's not thunder,' she said.

'Artillery,' said Thu. 'One of the Major's worries. We're all running out of mountains.' His hand touched her arm, then slid upward to lock itself on the nape of her neck beneath her hair. They stood frozen, linked by his arm, looking out at the dark teeth of the dragon. His hand fell from her neck, brushing her spine as it did. He turned and walked into the back chamber of the pavilion. This was the order he had not given her in the bathhouse. She picked up the little lamp and followed, unsure whether remembered hunger or the evil of cold-blooded deceit would triumph.

He undressed her as slowly and reflectively as he had searched for their future in the shadows of the pinnacles across the valley. He tasted her warm skin with total concentration. When he finally reached the curve of her belly, he paused in curiosity and wonder, and exclaimed with astonished joy when the child inside slipped sideways under his cheek.

'I must not disturb him?'

She shook her head, fighting tears at what might have been, if only the other, public Thu were more like this private one.

'Then you must make love to me,' he said.

She woke the next morning with the heaviness of someone who has given a gift she must steal back. Thu was already working in the shed near the stables where the first bales of crude opium were being stacked. When Nina went out onto the verandah, his head lifted and followed her toward the bathhouse.

She did not dare search for Lucky's exit route while Thu was in the villa. He would understand exactly what she was doing. She bathed slowly, dressed with care, to fill the time, then sat on the verandah with her *tisane*, watching chinchook lizards scoot in inexplicable zig-zags across the wooden planking. When Thu showed no signs of leaving the stable area, she dug into a basket for one of his old school books. She rejected a history of France and *Le francais vivant*, in favour of *Lettres de*

mon Moulin by Daudet, to see whether she enjoyed the book any more
now than when Mlle. Berthe had force-fed her with French culture in a
previous life.

But she couldn't concentrate on reading. Her eyes and ears
constantly checked Thu's whereabouts. At last, he disappeared in a
clutch of Meos, and the compound became silent with the heavy
somnolence of a hot mid-morning. Nina abandoned Daudet and began
her search with the small gate which led onto the track to the river. But
the dirt had been disturbed by only a barefoot child and the same or
another fugitive hen.

The dust outside the main gate was an unhelpful wilderness of
sandalprints, bare foot prints, boot prints, arcs of lizards and snakes,
dots and dashes of rodents, and tiny craters where dew had fallen from
the overhanging stand of bamboo. The metal shoes of Lucky's pony
had left their crisp prints outside the western gate in the cleft of the
rock. She traced them just far enough to confirm that they followed the
track toward the bumpy ridge to the north.

She stood on a crumbling promontory below the Tiger's Head and
stared toward the Chinese border. As far as she could see in the
shimmering light, a trail followed the crest of the ridge, above the
tangles of the jungle, exposed to the eagle's eye. She placed both hands
absently together against her lips.

It was just possible – physically possible – that she could ask that
awful man, who wanted to slit Thu's throat, to be her saviour, if he
would. All other things being equal, which they weren't. Then the
momentum of the opium pulled her a different way.

Two days after Major Lucky's visit to the villa, Nina was following a
small track through the now-harvested poppy fields below the villa
when she heard the plane land. She scrambled frantically back up
through the flattened, withering stalks.

Inside the villa, a line of Meos, burdened like ants, was carrying the
opium bales up across the terraces toward the main gate. Soldiers were
lashing more bales onto the mules. A sunburnt man stood in the
parade ground with Thu – a Round Eye like Will John, but with
brown hair and hazel eyes. Next, Nina noticed the revolver in the
shoulder holster over his short-sleeved sport shirt. Then that he wore
tennis shoes. Then the pack of Marlborough cigarettes in the breast
pocket of his shirt. This, at last, was the visitor on whom she had put
her money.

★

68

Thu had his back half-turned toward her. Nina unleashed on the sunburnt Round Eye the full force of her smile. He grinned back.

'I'm Cassidy,' he said in Vietnamese. 'What's your name?'

Thu shot Nina a warning look of anger and alarm.

'I'd love to get acquainted,' said Cassidy, 'but this son of a bitch thinks he wants me to fly a plane instead.' He looked at Thu and his smile vanished. 'Sorry, chum. I didn't know she was yours.' He offered Nina a shrug of regret.

Nina dropped her eyes. Thu can't know what I'm planning! she assured herself. He can't! Even if he suspects, he doesn't know about the bars of soap.

The two men walked away toward the main gate, beside the line of opium-carrying ants.

A Vietnamese-speaking American, thought Nina. Flying opium. Not in uniform, though that meant nothing. He could be Air America or a private mercenary. CIA supporting the cottage industry of the local tribes on whom they depended for support in the area. Or a rogue. She hoped he was a rogue, in the game for fun and for money.

She climbed to the lookout platform. Soldiers were positioned thirty feet apart along the track down to the airstrip. Major Lucky, or others like him, were clearly being kept in mind, even this close to the villa. Thu and the Round Eye had vanished.

How? Nina asked herself. How can I talk to him alone?

Thu and Cassidy returned to the villa for a quick evening meal, during which, though he didn't send Nina away, Thu never left the American's side.

I must speak to him! thought Nina. Somehow! Urgency paralyzed her brain. She made polite, desperate conversation, and avoided Thu's eyes.

The man's name was Cassidy. He wore a star sapphire ring, smoked while he ate, and spoke a few words of Meo to the two women serving them. During the meal, Nina learned neither his identity nor the degree of either his greed or his loyalty to Thu, if any.

Fate was teasing her – offering her a chance, not letting her grasp it.

The two men left. As the Meo women began to clear away the debris of the meal, Nina suddenly stood and walked quickly down the steps and across the parade ground to the thatched shelter by the stables. Almost half the opium remained. The line of ants had disappeared. She sat on the wall of the reservoir, studying her dark reflection and watching the shelter. No one came to remove more bales.

69

Then she heard the sound of an engine in the night sky. Cassidy's plane, not showing lights, rose from the valley below, skimmed over the mountain flank below the villa and vanished to the south. She looked at the dark ridge of the remaining bales. He would be back.

He *must* come back! she thought. By next year's harvest, I will be dead.

Two days later, near dusk, Nina heard the plane again. She didn't bother watching the last bales being carried through the gate. She went straight to the pavilion and took the four bars of soap from their nest in the lacquered gourd. She wrapped three of them into the sash around her waist. Then with a bayonet from Thu's basket of knives and swords, she carved away the fourth to expose its cold red shining heart. Carefully, she brushed up every soft, crumbling chip of soap into a twist of paper which she tucked deep under some clothes in one of the large baskets.

She excused herself from the evening meal, pleading the weariness of pregnancy. She did not dare be near Thu. He would read her agitation like a seismograph. From the platform bed in the back room, she listened to the rumble of Thu's voice and Cassidy's. For a few seconds, she slipped back to the night when she had listened to Thu and her father talking on the verandah of the family's big house above the lake in Dalat. If that girl had known what lay ahead, she would have stayed hidden forever behind that hammock.

Then, miraculously, she heard a third man's voice, then Thu's, and then silence on the verandah. She rose and walked quietly to the door. Cassidy was alone, except for a Meo woman clearing the debris of the meal onto a tray. At last, the woman disappeared down the steps into the darkness of the parade ground. Cassidy was alone, but it would not be for long. Nina was on the cliff edge and it was time to jump.

'Mr Cassidy,' she whispered.

He was on his feet, with his gun in his hand before he recognized her.

'Jesus!' He replaced his gun in its holster. 'Don't do that kind of thing to me.'

'Please sit down again,' Nina said in English. 'Or someone will wonder what we're doing.' She had no time to do it right. 'Take me with you tonight,' she said. 'Please! I'll meet you at the airstrip.' A beating in her ears muffled the sound of her own voice.

Cassidy stared in brief assessment of her sanity, then shook his head. 'Sorry sweetheart, I don't get an offer like that every night, but. . . .'

'Thu is going to kill me and my baby,' she interrupted. 'I can pay my fare.' She held out the Burmese red in her cupped hand. It looked like a gout of bright blood on her palm. Her eyes tracked the shadows crossing and recrossing the parade ground below the verandah.

'Are you really serious?' he asked. But he was looking at the ruby.

Her eyes were wide and dark; the hand holding the ruby trembled visibly. 'Oh yes! I'm serious! . . . Please!'

'But I thought Thu was your *feen*. . . .'

'But not the father of my baby.' She glanced past him at the parade ground again for Thu's return. 'The father is American! I'm supposed to join him.'

'Jesus!' said Cassidy. He picked up the ruby. 'Lady, you're in deep shit!'

'Please, Mr Cassidy!' she begged. The woman would be coming back any minute with fruit.

'Do you know what could happen if he found out?' asked Cassidy. 'Do you have *any* idea?'

Nina recognized the shift. 'I have a second stone like that,' she said. 'Fly me out and you can have that one too.'

Cassidy stared at the stone, then at her face. 'Can you get down to the strip without anybody seeing you?'

She nodded, too short of breath to speak.

Cassidy wavered one short moment more. Then he said, 'Get one thing clear! If anything goes wrong . . . Thu sees you . . . I don't know what's going on. I'll dump you right in it . . . I have to, after last time when you gave me the full treatment and I thought you just thought I was cute!' He tucked the ruby into a flapped pouch on his belt. 'You got ten minutes to get to the plane. Then we'll be coming down to load up. Wait on the far side behind the landing gear.' He buttoned down the flap. 'Scram!'

Nina ran down the steps into the parade ground. The serving woman was crossing from the cookhouse, silhouetted against the light from its door. Nina slowed to a walk. Thu was on the terrace below by the stables. Three of his soldiers were walking toward the main gate, heads down over their first cut of the sale proceeds. She dropped in behind and followed them out the main gate.

The sentry just outside, at the top of the track to the air strip, was distracted by raised voices farther down the track. Two of the soldiers' wives squatted near the gate, smoking mango leaf cheroots and commenting on the evening's hubbub. They raised their eyes and watched Nina walk past, but it was none of their business if the Colonel's breeding concubine took one of her crazy *promenades* at night.

71

'Good evening,' Nina said, astonished to find that her voice still worked.

'Good evening,' they murmured.

The old woman will doubtless hear, thought Nina. But not too soon, please God! Not too soon!

Drunk with daring, she walked down the track and out of sight of the gate, around a concealing curve. Twenty-five metres farther on, after waiting for three small boys to run past her toward the excitement of the airstrip, she lowered her new weight carefully into the erosion ditch in the abandoned field.

From the edge of the clearing, she couldn't see the plane in the darkness.

Oh God! What now?

Then she swore at her stupidity and turned left, toward the end of the field where the track emerged from the trees. She saw a lantern and movement at the side of the clearing near the end of the track, where the bales of crude opium waited to be loaded onto the plane. She panted in the hot night air and peered into the shadows for the plane itself. Followed by a haze of gnats already drunk on her sweat, she began to cross the central open strip toward the far treeline. Then she froze. A little to her right loomed the solid darkness of an oil drum. Beyond it stood the fainter darkness of a man.

Her own breathing sounded raucous in the night air. She turned left, moving slowly as the moon. Dry grasses rasped across her shins like saws on mahogany. The soft cotton of her *panung* rustled like new taffeta. A small red spot glowed in the darkness ahead of her. She crept closer and saw the silhouette of a sentry who was sitting on an oil drum, smoking a cheroot. Beyond him was the dark bulk of the plane.

Nina retreated and circled, steering by the glow of the cheroot. The two-propeller plane was smaller than she had imagined. She bent her neck to stand against the undercarriage, beneath the wing on the far side from the opium bales at the bottom of the track.

All lights and movement remained centred on the bales. Nina slipped to the other side of the plane and tried the handle of the door. It was locked. As she released the handle, a tiny metal part struck another. The red glow of the cheroot dropped two feet through the air.

'Who's there?'

Nina froze.

'Is someone there?' the sentry repeated, a little less urgently.

'What's going on?' called another voice less than fifty feet away, on the other side of the plane.

'Did you hear anything?' asked the sentry.

'Nothing this side,' replied the second voice. 'Did you?'

'I guess not.' The cheroot rose again.

Nina went carefully back to her position under the wing.

Then the lights and men's legs approached the plane.

You'll be seen! You're sure to be seen! Nina's hands clung to the sash around her waist, which held the rubies, the rest of her jewellery and Will John's jade monkey. Then she reached out for the plane as if to hold herself back from bolting into the darkness.

It's now or never. The words echoed strangely in her head. Now. Or never. The cliché took on absolute meaning. She forced herself to remain still, pressed against the undercarriage. The baby kicked and turned inside her, sharing her adrenaline and agitated by the pounding of her heart.

She heard metallic sounds; the plane moved slightly against her shoulder. Someone had climbed on board.

'Chuck it here,' ordered Cassidy's voice from inside the fusillage. Nina listened for Thu.

The lantern-lit men's legs came and went, and came and went again. The plane shook slightly with Cassidy's movements as he stowed the bales. Still the legs came and went.

'Is that it?' asked Cassidy's voice at last. 'OK, go tell the boss to turn the lights on.'

The lanterns moved away, leaving the plane in darkness except for the glow from the cockpit. The plane heaved.

'Where the fuck are you?' Cassidy whispered urgently from the ground on the far side of the plane.

'Here.' She bent to cross under the plane.

'Get the hell on board and go right to the back. I left you a place. Move your ass – they're going to light up!'

As Nina stepped up into the door, the first two barrels flared in the darkness. Then another ignited. Then a third.

'*Move!*' said Cassidy from the ground behind her. He coughed. Then he farted. Obscenely.

She turned in the doorway. Cassidy was still on the ground, leaning back as if drunk, supported by Thu.

Thu and Nina stared at each other over Cassidy's shoulder. All three faces were now clearly lit by the double row of oil drums flaming eight feet into the night sky. Thu pulled his knife from Cassidy's body and let the man fall heavily to the ground. He moved toward the plane.

It's now, said Nina to herself. She stepped down onto the ground to

73

meet him. Now. She felt a spasm of grief for the unborn child but pushed it away. Now. She could feel all the small internal movements of her own life, as well as the child's life, and imagine the end, calmly.

'Please don't make me wait,' she whispered.

He stood close to her. She heard him breathing, harshly in and out. And her own heartbeat in her ears. And the roar of flames and the night noises beyond the airstrip. She tried to close her ears against the world that would continue without her. She tried to hold off protest and fear.

His face was half-reddened by flames, half in shadow.

'Dear God, don't make me wait!' Her ears were still filled by the sound of his breathing, and the surging of her own blood.

'Cousin,' she begged, 'if you ever loved me, do it before I start to fear!'

She felt his arm, and heard cloth brush against cloth. He was trembling. She felt the tip of his knife search delicately along the back of her ribs, slipping over the bone, catching lightly at the fabric of her jacket, sliding along the grooves of her skin.

I have already gone, she told herself. I am merely waiting for my body to catch up. Please! she begged him silently. Please, now! While it is happening to a mere body, to something else. While our wills are still in harmony!

Then the terror began, filling her like flood waters, tumbling, churning. She fought and gasped to stay afloat. Please, God, I can't wait any longer! Her legs were beginning to buckle. She no longer knew if she were speaking aloud or not. Please! Her body had waited too long; her soul was coming back.

She stood in his embrace, drowning in her own terror and in the terror of the child caught between them, who would never be born.

'Cousin,' she whispered, 'if you wanted to punish me, you have done as much as you can. You gain nothing by waiting any longer.'

He dropped her as he had dropped Cassidy. She staggered back against the plane. She saw the glint of his knife again but didn't think she had felt it being jerked from her body, not like Cassidy's body. Thu's face was turned away from her, looking down the illuminated air strip.

'Put out the fires,' he called hoarsely.

The drums were snuffed like candles, leaving only the smell of burning oil and smoke in the jungle night.

She huddled on the ground and hugged her shaking legs, unsure whether her body and soul were together or apart. The apparatus of flesh and bone which was her body had now begun to shake. Her soul observed, still a little distant and a little confused.

74

She still heard breathing near her in the darkness. Jerky and full of long-held silences.

A voice somewhere called, 'When is the flight, sir?'

Thu's voice answered, after a pause, 'There will be no flight.' He paused again. 'Go to bed. Dismiss.'

In her confusion, Nina thought he was crying.

5

Know thy enemy! thought Gabriel Simpson, staring at Lieutenant Whittaker's wet, olive drab back in front of him, which was all he could see. *Tectona grandis*. Teak. Rare but a tough cookie. His mother's kitchen on the Cape was made of teak. Resisted damp, she had said. Then there were the rattans – the wait-a-minute vines with fishhooks under their leaves that could pull your pants off. But enemy number one was bamboo. The vegetable guerrilla. Secondary growth where man had killed off the big boys. Give bamboo an inch and it would take over the world!

They were following a track through a heavy stand of bamboo. Simpson tried to see past the sweating back in front of him. Boucher's damp, leaf-patterned back swung out of sight around a mass of giant fishing poles and gardening canes. First Whittaker and then Simpson stepped carefully around a pile of dirt that looked like a bamboo rat's mound. In case it wasn't.

They were trapped between walls of tall, green, arthritic fingers, with an eighteen inch field of vision. The air rustled and creaked and scratched as if alive. Otherwise the afternoon was peaceful. Not even a jungle fowl this time. But behind those green walls was the dark closet.

A spring in Simpson's chest wound tighter and tighter, waiting for the peace to be broken.

There was light between the shoulders of the bamboo clusters. A clump of bright, shiny green, tattered fringes hung limply from lumpy stems. Bananas. Getting closer to the village. Boucher was walking point. Doe behind Simpson.

We're too close together, thought Simpson. He ducked slowly and carefully under a broken bamboo wand that bowed into his path, even though he couldn't see a wire.

Boucher signalled. The village. Simpson waited. Silence. He and Doe followed Whittaker forward along the track; there was no other way they could move. Simpson heard a baby crying. He stepped out of the mouth of the track into the clearing. Four huts, open and deserted except for the baby, crying in one of them. The men waited, looking at the huts and into the trees and bamboo clumps around the little village. The baby's screams were the only human sound.

Boucher peered cautiously into the hut. 'Nobody else here!' he said. 'Poor little bastard. Who the fuck'd leave a baby behind?'

They took their chickens, thought Simpson with alarm.

'Leave it!' shouted Simpson and Whittaker together.

Boucher entered the hut.

'LEAVE IT!' screamed Simpson.

The air was filled with pieces of Boucher, the hut and the baby.

I didn't warn him in time! thought Simpson, while fragments still pattered down around him. I didn't shout soon enough! Oh God! I didn't warn him in time!

Then he heard Doe behind him, with a bamboo sliver through his eye.

After Cassidy's murder, Nina lived in the void between two thunder-clouds, while electrical charges built toward the explosion across space that would burn everything in the way. The calmness of her straight look into the eyes of death had deserted her. She lived with the constant cold ache of terror.

Thu did not deign to lock her up. He did not set any extra perceivable watch on her movements. At first this puzzled her, then she realized that he would never publicly admit to the need. Instead, he moved to a great distance. If he could not kill her, he was nevertheless not going to forgive her for living through his weakness. He stopped using the main pavilion to sleep and eat. He looked through her if they met by accident on one of the terraces. He had begun, for his own protection, to transform her back into a mere thing, into the insignificant, disposable speck of dust he felt most of his other fellow men to be. Even the coming child would no longer protect her. Her only question was how long her transformation would take.

Nina walked every day, as she had always done. She mapped the position of sentries on all the tracks and printed them firmly on her mind. Every day, she tested her readiness simply to bypass the sentries and continue walking until she reached safety, died of heat and thirst, or Thu caught up with her and ended the whole story.

The child in her belly had become a tyrant. It now woke her with kicks. Then it kept her lying awake in the cold certainty that the sudden following stillness meant that it had died. Her stomach continued to inflate, and her breasts as well. She felt herself begin to lean backwards against the forward weight. To land heavily on her heels. Stop to rest

77

more often. Craftily, she exaggerated some complaints and omitted others. She puffed and panted noisily at the slightest effort and slept every afternoon, partly to establish pre-maternal fragility, partly to store up strength. She ate every nourishing titbit the elderly Meo offered her, like a temperate bear preparing for winter hibernation.

Women carry heavy loads and work in the fields, Nina reassured herself, and their babies are born alive! I wish I dared ask the mother-of-fourteen for advice on whether I can run away without killing mine!

Of all the women in the villa, only the old Meo seemd to know that something dreadful had taken place. Though she continued to nurse Nina, her manner changed. She offered but no longer cajoled. She avoided Nina's eyes and dropped her manner of jovial bullying.

One by one, Nina smuggled out of the villa the three remaining bars of soap, the black trousers and tunic, a sweater, a half coconut shell for drinking, a length of cloth for carrying rice and fruit, and Will John's little jade monkey. She hid everything in a rocky hollow on the northern back of the Tiger's Head.

One afternoon, she remembered the basket of swords and bayonets. But when she knelt to remove one to add to her cache outside the villa, they were gone. The empty basket shocked her. It was the first tangible proof that the events on the airstrip the night Cassidy died . . . that Thu killed Cassidy . . . had been real and not just a nightmare in which she sometimes persuaded herself she was indulging. She stayed on her knees, rocking gently, trying to rearrange the accidents of her life which had not been accidents at all.

A shadow fell across the floor from the door onto the verandah. The elderly Meo woman hesitated, then came into the room. Nina stood to face her, feeling suddenly on trial.

The old woman looked at the empty basket, then at Nina's face. She shook her head in a gesture of disgust, or disbelief.

'My nephew is a good man,' she said. Her hands made three small, helpless circles in the air.

'Thu?' asked Nina.

The woman nodded. 'He looks after those who are loyal to him . . . a good man.'

'I know,' said Nina. In a way, she did know what the woman meant.

'Then. . . ?' The woman shook her head again. She hesitated. 'He gave me those swords to hide,' she said angrily. 'Why should he have to do that?' She took a fierce step forward. 'Why should he fear you when. . . .' She stopped herself.

Nina felt the thought strike the woman and heard her exhalation of breath.

'He didn't need to hide the swords,' said Nina. 'Unless he feared himself.'

'And why would he do that?' asked the woman, almost reluctantly.

Now Nina shook her head. But the old woman held her gaze.

She knows, thought Nina. Somehow, she knows.

The woman shook her head again, like a mountain pony bothered by a gadfly. She sighed. 'Lie down,' she said to Nina. 'Rest. I'll make you a cool drink.'

As she lay on the bed pretending to rest, Nina stared up at the scroll painting, the illusion of a map, a taunting impersonator of reality. She would never know how real it was. She stretched and rolled her new bulk onto its other side. She stared out into the sky beyond the verandah. She was weary with effort, with struggling, with watching for openings, with fighting despair. She wanted only to sink into lassitude and let her fate overwhelm her. She wanted to lie, fat and thoughtless in the sun, like a cat or a lizard on a rock. Then the child turned and stretched inside her. The reality behind her wish sank its teeth into her mind, and Nina recovered her need for both of them to survive.

The next morning, she woke up knowing that she could no longer live waiting for the lightning to leap between the clouds. She lay on the bed with her heart thudding from terror. Then the terror became exhilaration.

Yes! she told the excitement of kicking in her belly. Today! I run for our lives.

She tried to eat but could not. Instead, she wrapped the rice and fruit in a handkerchief. She did not ask where Thu had gone. She preferred not to know. She had thrown the fortune sticks and would not question their answer. If he had left for the day, fine. If he had only gone down to the airstrip for an hour, *soit*. The Heavens, or the Blessed Virgin, or whoever was running the affairs of fate up here these days would arrange it.

Conscious of the usual watching eyes, Nina washed away the night's sweat with water from the jar in the bath house and coiled her hair neatly on her nape. She wrapped a dark green and gold *panung* around her hips and tucked in the pleats firmly above her child's head. Back in the shadows of the room, she put on her necklace and rings and bracelets.

79

In some ways, it's not so hard, this time, she thought. I've had practice. And have less to take.

And this time, her child felt real.

She left by the small gate which led down toward the forbidden river. Two old women were squatting by the reservoir.

'Good morning,' she called back to them.

'Good morning,' they echoed and watched her close the gate behind her.

A short way down the trail, she hunkered down to watch the gate, supporting the hammock of her belly on the tops of her thighs, waiting for death to call them both back. Sweat ran down the shallow channels on either side of her spine. She waited for half an hour. No one followed her.

She took the track to the right, around the mountain slope toward the northern side of the villa, and waited again, not far from her hidden cache. So far, pursuers could accuse her of nothing. After ten more minutes, she stood and strolled casually toward the rocky hollow where she had hidden her trousers and tunic, drinking shell, Will John's monkey and the bars of soap.

She leaned beside it, with a dry mouth and shaking knees, listening, imagining Thu stepping around the curve of rock. Then she quickly pulled away the concealing stones, wrapped her cache in the cloth and tied it clumsily around her swollen waist. She began to clamber down toward the ridge that ran north. Now there was only the lower sentry to avoid.

The circle around him took her two hours. At last, she reached the faint scratching of the trail along the spine of the ridge. She began to walk toward Major Lucky and the Chinese border, toward the north, 'from which all evils blow'.

For the next hour, until the sun drove her into shelter, Nina floated on her own recklessness. If anyone were watching the trail from the lookout platform, they would see a speck moving away.

It all depends, she thought, looking behind her at the distant back of the Tiger's Head, on whether Thu is ready to kill me yet, or whether it is simpler for him to let me go.

But as she rested in the shade of a chalky overhang, she began to imagine that the heat and effort would bring the baby early. She saw it clearly, beached like a small fish, suffocating in air it was not ready to breath. And she would be helpless . . . have to watch it die in the dust and rock of the track! She swallowed and felt disproportionately comforted when it heaved beneath her folded arms.

I'll get you there! she promised it, not sure where 'there' might be.

She set off again when the sun eased its attack and began to slide toward the horizon beyond the mountains, toward the Mekong River and Thailand. She still saw no signs of pursuit.

Don't feel safe yet! she warned herself. You could never feel safe when you were with him. Don't expect mercy now!

The sun vanished. The light lingered only a little longer on the ridge than in the valleys. Then darkness wrapped itself around her.

She kept walking. From time to time, she napped beside the trail, dazed with exhaustion but unable to sleep among the screams and grunts and rustlings of the night. Once she wandered off the trail but scrambled back up again. The weight of each heel seemed to break through the rock, but she kept walking. Her promise to the child propelled her through breathlessness, thirst, hunger, and weariness as seductive as death. She clung to it the next day like a drowning swimmer clutching at a slippery liferaft.

She slept during the hottest hours under some scrub below the trail. When she set off again, she talked aloud to the child, to distract herself from the impossibility of taking one more step. The very last force of her promise delivered her, white and shaking with exhaustion, to the first of Major Lucky's sentries, in the evening of the second day.

'The Colonel's concubine!' exclaimed Lucky. 'I'm flattered that you've gone to such lengths for us to meet again.'

'I'm grateful that you exist, monsieur,' said Nina in her best French. Her legs were about to give way.

'Isn't the Colonel with you?' asked Lucky. He looked at her dust-covered feet and grimy face but had already begun to readjust his assessment. He beamed. 'Have you run away? You don't want to help him found a dynasty?'

Nina closed her eyes briefly and imagined herself once again as the Saigon business woman and hostess. That other woman found the right words. 'I would be eternally grateful,' she said sweetly but firmly, 'for a cool drink, a change of clothes and something to eat. *Then* I would be delighted to answer all your questions.'

'You're no *moi* savage,' said Lucky.

Even in her exhaustion, Nina had registered the names of the avenues as the soldier brought her in. She recognized the inspiration for the design of the Palace. She had noted Lucky's smoking jacket and silk foulard, and the glass of *pastis* he was holding.

'Nor are you merely an ignorant local brigand . . . like some.' She smiled into his small eyes. 'What is a man of culture and sophistication doing so far from Saigon or Vientiane? Or Paris, for that matter?'

'Madame,' said Lucky, recovering his balance and beginning to enjoy this bizarre act of chance, 'I suspect we have quite a lot we could discuss . . . But I'm being rude. We must find you your refreshment and clean clothes. Forgive me. After you. . . .' He spread his short arms to usher her from the entrance hall of the Palace into what he referred to as the drawing room.

'In short,' said Nina, 'I'm throwing myself on your mercy.' She was too tired to eat.

They were dining at the same table where Lucky had entertained Rogov. The fish course, once again, was *quenelles*. Gnats still shimmered around the paraffin chandelier. The cage of thrushes still rustled and twittered in the corner of the room. There were, however, no local virgins sitting on stools by the wall.

Nina looked into the Major's small cold eyes and privately qualified her use of the word mercy.

Lucky had several options. He could truss her up, send her back in one piece and hope the bastard Thu would be grateful. But Lucky didn't want Thu's gratitude, he wanted his capitulation. His humiliation.

He could chop her up and send the pieces back as an expression of the regard in which he held her lover. But though it was gratifying to imagine Thu's reaction to an insult of such magnitude, the precedent of the twenty-six dead mules made Lucky question the wisdom of that choice. He was quite fond of both Number Two and Number Three Wife.

He could keep her himself. It wouldn't be long before she dropped the baby and became useful again. Lucky looked at the set of her small head on the slender neck, and the neat ears whose small lobes were set off by the glitter of diamond studs. He looked at the large, long-lashed, dark eyes flecked with hazel and listened to the education of her voice. She was a beauty, even with a bloated belly. And she was half-French. They would share that affinity. She would be far more interesting to him than the *moi* peasants who were his main source of entertainment.

'More wine?' he asked solicitously.

'Thank you.' She lifted her refilled glass with a hand which was graceful, even if badly in need of a manicure. The two rather fine rings she wore spoke as eloquently as her accent of her elevated past.

On the other hand, reflected Lucky, raising his own glass gallantly,

Thu was a dangerous lunatic with an unfortunate degree of influence and power in the region. If she lived here, Thu would certainly learn where she was. He might blame Lucky for her defection. If forced, Lucky was willing to exchange shots with Thu, but not over a woman.

That left him the option of helping her as she asked. At least as far as getting her out of Thu's reach. He owed her nothing beyond that.

'I have a caravan going south tomorrow night,' he said, his decision made. 'The transport won't be elegant, but you would have an armed escort.' Now that he had decided, he liked his choice very much. He could imagine Thu's fury, his suspicions which could never be proved. He, Lucky, could hint mysteriously, could tease and suggest, then always deny. Thu would never be sure one way or the other.

'How far?' Nina watched him deliberate before answering.

'Down to the Plain of Jars,' said Lucky. 'My men would have to drop you off there, I'm afraid.'

'Aren't they going to Long Tien?' asked Nina.

'I'm afraid that's not your business,' said Lucky. 'I've made the best offer I can. Take it or leave it.'

By 10:00 the following night, the caravan had been waiting an hour and a half for the local Meo guide to arrive. Nina sat impatiently on the plinth of Major Lucky's statue, listening, and watching the aimless energy in the Palace. The mules stamped and snapped at each other. the men paced or squatted to smoke and chat. A villainous-looking man in tiger-stripe uniform with a sergeant's silver stars on his collar tab kept checking and re-checking the cargo of opium bales, fiddling with girths, or vanishing on yet another remembered last-minute task. A pile of unloaded bales stood at one edge of the place. Six of Lucky's soldiers sat on it, armed and alert.

'I don't like this waiting,' muttered a soldier perched around the corner from Nina on his leader's stone feet.

A Vietnamese, Nina noted. Lucky brought these men with him from North Vietnam. And I don't like this waiting either!

Since she had arrived the night before, Nina had been expecting the shouts which announced the arrival of Thu to claim her back. She still didn't feel safe – he was too imaginative in his revenges.

'Go without the guide, then!' said another man whom Nina couldn't see. 'But I'm waiting.'

'I don't trust the Meos,' said the first. 'Those *moi* will betray us to the Chinese, sooner or later . . . they're the same race, after all . . . northern invaders!'

'Don't be stupid. They're only savages, and we don't want their mountain tops.' The voice paused. 'It's in the Meos' own interest to move the stuff for us instead of letting the Kuomintang do it still. The Chinese Army has had its turn! The Major's right – it's time we took control . . . sold to the markets *we* choose! The Meo chiefs know an opportunity when they see it!'

'Then why isn't our guide here taking this wonderful opportunity?'

'He'll come, he'll come.' The second soldier moved into Nina's line of vision and bent to tighten the thong holding a square of padding around the back hoof of a tethered mule.

The Meo guide arrived around 11:00, wearing a black baseball cap and carrying a French folding-butt rifle. He was accompanied by twelve armed men in black clothing and a dozen mountain ponies.

'Where the hell have you been?' demanded the sergeant in tiger-stripe uniform.

The Meo looked at him levelly from under the baseball cap. 'You're not going anywhere without us, so mind your manners.' He turned to his own men. 'Load the ponies.'

Lucky heard this exchange from the steps of the Palace. He was bothered by more than just his own man's loss of face. The *moi* would never have dared insult his own father like that, even indirectly, unless he had a powerful protector in the background. When Grégoire Ince had first suggested that the Meos were snuggling up to the Americans, Lucky had allowed for Ince's own bias and had reserved judgement. He knew that the Americans had trained certain Meo tribes as guerrillas in the last World War, to fight the Japanese . . . there were rumours of American training camps for the Meos, even now, in Vietnam. And Laos. But Lucky also knew that the Americans had now turned against other protegees of the same period, like Ho Chi Minh. The Meos were essentially Chinese, a nomadic tribe which had moved south only a century ago. Lucky did not believe that the Americans would trust any Chinese, anywhere, whatever they might call themselves.

On the other hand, Ince had sworn that the Americans were backing Vang Pao, a Meo general who controlled a large area in the centre of Northern Laos. Ince had even suggested that the Americans were flying Vang Pao's opium for him, in place of the ousted Corsican French. This opium of Lucky's was going to Vang Pao. Lucky had challenged the monpoly of the KMT bandits partly from ambition and partly as a gesture of solidarity toward the People's Republic of China which was practically peering over his village wall. Adept as he was at political balancing, he found the present situation complex.

He watched the leader of the Meo escort snapping orders at both Lucky's men and his own. Such arrogance confirmed Ince's information and insinuations. Unfortunately, like everyone who tried to operate in the mountain wilderness, Lucky needed the Meos. He and the Americans both needed the Meos, it seemed. It was really rather amusing.

He called his own sergeant aside. 'Space yourselves well along the caravan,' he said. 'Be sure to keep one or more of them at the front – let them be targets for an ambush. And. . . .' He glanced around. 'Remind your men to behave with the dignity of superiors. I don't want brawls!'

'Sir!'

The creaking of harness was the loudest sound they made. The men's weapons and equipment had been taped. The muffled hoofs of the mules and ponies raised faint puffs of silent dust and rasped quietly against rocks. The trail dropped abruptly off the spine of the ridge which Nina had followed from the Tiger's Head. Under the low roof of trees, the darkness was absolute except for the occasional disorienting beacon of a firefly. The mules lurched and felt their way down an invisible obstacle course.

Dependent on Major Lucky's good will, ignored by his men as if she were another opium bale, and jolted uncontrollably on her mule, Nina felt as helpless as a leaf caught in rapids. For the first hour of the journey, she waited for Thu to ambush the mule train. Wrapped in a dark shawl she had been given, she clung to the mule, braced against voices and shots from the darkness. The mule swayed and slipped; the baby kicked and protested. Nina's spine was shaken and battered from without and within. After several hours of numbing, jolting darkness, she forgot why she was travelling. She wanted only to get off the mule and to sleep without fear. But the awful rocking and jarring continued. Leaves continued to scrape across her face. The shadowy men ahead and behind continued to urge their pack animals onward in hoarse whispered oaths.

Shortly before sunrise, they came to a Meo village where they spent the day under cover. Nina slept gratefully for most of the day on a bamboo mat given to her by a teenage Meo girl in a black turban. That evening, they set off again with a different guide. In the early hours of the second morning, they stopped.

'What's wrong?' whispered Nina to the mule driver ahead of her.

'Too dangerous to go on,' he murmured back.

'Why?' she demanded, suddenly cold. 'Soldiers?'

'You'll see,' the man replied and led his mule off the trail into the dark, dry scrub. The mule behind her also vanished. Nina could hear the animals crunching in the darkness around her. She sat for a few moments, then slid to the ground. Her mule moved a few steps away to nose among the shadows of dusty rocks. Nina brushed carefully at a rock and prodded at its crevices with a stick, then sat, listening for whatever the unknown danger might be, until the sun rose.

When the light came, she saw why they had paused. Just ahead, the track entered a river gorge, etched into the side of a cliff along a narrow shelf of crumbling rock. It narrowed in places to one metre or less. Far below, still in shadow, the river twisted and plunged, carving the gorge even deeper into the core of the earth. Nina looked down and decided to lead her mule.

She edged forward with her right hand against the solid safety of the cliff face, the other hand holding the bridle. The track seemed barely wide enough for her mule to place all four feet. She could not look down into the gorge. She was still too much the dream-climber who had let go and given in to falling. These rocks pounding water into the mist were far more real than the unknown place where she hoped to land with her life and her child and a future.

A man shouted, ahead of her. The sound was shocking after two nights and a day of silence. A mule had missed its footing. Nina watched it slide over the edge in a small landslide of shale and boulders, then fall free, its lead rope snapping in the air like a whip. It thudded onto a narrow ledge about thirty feet below the track, where it lay screaming like an hysterical demon. Nina braced herself for the gunshot that would end both the animal's agony and its hideous, dangerous noise. But one of the Meos slid over the side on a rope and cut its throat.

When they moved on, the soldiers and Meos were tense and watchful. There was no way to retreat if enemies had been alerted by the mule's screams. It was impossible to turn the animals on the narrow track. They kept moving all day without another stop. Nina began to limp from rock bruises on her soles.

At the end of that afternoon, the track began to drop to meet the river. Nina remounted and kept her eyes closed. They picked their way downward until dusk, stopped for evening rice among a fall of rocks near the bottom of the gorge, and continued along the river by the light of the moon. The roaring of the water covered their noise. It would also cover the approach of enemies.

The mules were tired and snatched desperately at the green vegetation that grew by the water. The Meos shouted and slapped to keep them moving. Nina kicked at hers and hauled at the bridle. The saddle was rubbing raw patches on the backs of her thighs, and her head ached from the day's sun. Mosquitoes and gnats squeezed through the weave of her shawl wrapped around her head and shoulders, to attack her eyelids and throat. When rest was finally called, she fell from the mule without thought, cleared a space on a rocky shelf and slept as if on a feather bed, in spite of the mosquitoes.

When she woke early the next morning, the fourth day of the journey, her *panung* had stuck to weeping sores on the backs of her legs. It was not possible to ride.

'I prefer to walk,' she told the Meo escort. But by noon, she had to remount her mule to keep from passing out on the trail. The sides of the gorge trapped and reflected heat like an oven. The air was still. The rocks were too hot even for lizards. By mid-afternoon, Nina was numb in both body and mind.

As she jolted and swayed on top of her mule, with the shawl across her head to keep off the sun, balancing sidesaddle to stave off the searing pain in her thighs, she tried to call up images of Will John to cheer her. She tried to imagine the two of them playing with their baby on the verandah of the big house he had described to her, above the wide, cool, grey waters of Narraganssett Bay. She tried to imagine the telephone call she would make, when she reached Bangkok, to the number he had made her memorize before he left. She tried to imagine the shocked delight in his voice and tried to imagine their meeting . . . showing him his child . . . But the uncertainty of her immediate future was a fog through which she could not see her way. Finally, she put away these talismans of the future before she wore them down to powerless shadows. She gave in to numbness, too weary for the moment even to worry that the child seemed quiet.

The caravan finally left the gorge. A few minutes later it stopped.

Nina raised her head, in alarm. A surge of fear washed through her numbness. 'What is it?' she asked the soldier in front of her.

He ignored her and stretched to see for himself.

'North Vietnamese patrol!' hissed the man in front of him.

'Here?' asked Nina, suddenly alert. 'In Laos?' No one answered her.

It's Thu! she thought wildly. It would amuse him to wait so long. To let me think I had escaped!

Then she saw the soldiers in dark olive drab, Chinese-style uniforms, who stood beside the trail watching the caravan pass. On a rise, a little way back from the trail was a machine-gun emplacement.

That's why we can now travel by day, thought Nina, as her pulse steadied again. We've moved into a new sphere of influence. The Kuomintang don't reach south of the gorge.

She tried to find another inch of unscarred skin to sit on. Perhaps Thu really will let me go, she thought. Perhaps he really doesn't care any more. . . . The thought brought both relief and an odd sense of hollowness.

Her mule plodded past the perforated muzzle of the machine gun behind a wall of rice sacks filled with dirt and sand. Like the sandbags on her own verandah, at the house she would probably never see again. Like the sandbags in the street during the five days in 1955 when Vietnamese had fought each other in the streets of Saigon, one side backed by the French, the other by the Americans.

Everywhere, thought Nina. Even here in the wilderness. In spite of herself, she stared, hypnotized, at the dark eye of the gun which was more alert than the eyes of the man behind it.

A half an hour later, they changed guides.

Nina had run out of places to sit which were not already rubbed raw. Her back ached from the constant jolting. She dismounted to walk again beside the mule, but her head ached and the skin on the insides of her thighs rubbed away like damp paper. Mosquito bites on her neck and eyelids itched and stung from the salt of her sweat.

The caravan continued downward, sometimes along hot, rocky ridges, sometimes through dry, rattling scrub and secondary jungle. In some places where the trail nearly vanished the mules and ponies had to be cajoled and pulled up or down falls of rock. At night they slept in tribal villages, either Ahka or Meo.

Two days later, within sight of a distant lake of flatness which lay beyond the mountains, the caravan was stopped by a squad of Pathet Lao guerrillas. There was a long parley, money exchanged hands, and they were allowed to depart.

That night, Nina heard distant thuds, as if huge rocks were being thrown from the heavens. By day, they skirted the lake of flatness, staying high along the mountain ridges. From time to time, through openings in the scrub and jungle, Nina saw clouds of dust on the plain, as if herds of elephants were travelling. More rocks thudded down from the heavens by daylight and during the next night as well. That day, also, a jet plane screamed low across the flatness to the west, a demon from an alien world. Then others followed. On the sixth day, a sudden rattling of small arms fire opened up close below on the slopes. Like a conjuror's trick, the caravan stopped and disappeared under cover, where it stayed for three hot, tense hours until the battle ended. Nina accepted all these things dully. She was too lost in immediate physical torment.

Then, on the eighth day, as the mules and ponies were being pulled, protesting, from their lunch-time grazing, and Nina was preparing to haul her weight back up onto her mount, Lucky's sergeant spoke his first words to her.

'No more,' he said. 'You get off here.'

Nina looked at him, unbelieving. No landmark, village, road or side track suggested a destination of any kind. They had seen no one since the morning before when they had picked up yet another guide. They were leaving her to die.

'I'm coming to Long Tien,' she said firmly. She turned back to the mule and gripped her saddle with both hands. She wouldn't agree, not now. Not after coming so far at such a cost! Her brain, rusty from eight days of disuse, began to shuffle her choices. Bluff – nothing to back it. Pleading – irrelevant. Threats – ludicrous even to consider. Bribery. . . .

She heard a rifle bolt click behind her and lifted her hands from the saddle. She stepped back from the mule. Maybe Lucky had simply told them to shoot her and be done with it!

'You stop here!' repeated the sergeant.

Nina took off the single ring which she had not hidden in her sash and offered it to the sergeant. 'Then, thank you for your protection on my journey . . . a mere token. . . .' Her hand shook, betraying the steadiness of her voice.

The sergeant considered the ring. He glanced past Nina at the man with the rifle whose bolt had been drawn.

'And those. . . .' He pointed at her diamond studs.

She looked over her shoulder at the rifle. With trembling fingers, she fumbled at the studs, watching the sergeant's impatient eyes. At last, she unscrewed the second diamond from her ear lobe. The sergeant slipped ring and studs into a pouch on his ammunition belt.

Was the price high enough? She still had three bars of soap to trade for her life and her child's.

The sergeant turned and walked after the departing caravan. The soldier with the rifle followed, leading her mule.

Nina drew a breath. The sergeant had not yet given her her life, only postponed death. 'Would you be kind enough,' she called humbly, 'to leave me just a little water and rice?'

The sergeant kept walking.

'Which way must I go? Tell me that at least!'

The soldier with the rifle paused and half-turned back to her. 'Who do you want to meet? Vietnamese that way.' He pointed back the way they had come. 'Pathet Lao that way.' He pointed north. 'Royal Lao Army that way.' He pointed west and south-west. 'And up there . . .' He laughed and pointed to the sky. '. . . a long, long way – Americans.' He slapped her mule on the rump and ambled away beside it.

With rage and despair, Nina watched the two men and the mule vanish into the scrub. She and her child would have had a better death at Thu's hands. Faster, at least, than thirst and starvation.

She turned slowly, without hope. Rocks, baked earth and dry trees whose leaves hung limp as rags. Thirst would take them first. She took two steps after the vanished caravan, then stopped. What was the point? If she caught up with them, she would be shot. She squatted down on the track and leaned her head on her folded arms.

I'm sorry! she told her child. I'm so sorry!

The small life in her belly heaved, shifting position, but to Nina its force was a reproof. Too alive, too real to be denied its place in the world, even by the mercenaries of an opium warlord in collusion with wilderness.

A sound on the trail lifted her head abruptly. Two Meos from the caravan were watching her. She hadn't heard them return.

So, the end could arrive silently, like a snake in the dust. Well, she had been here before . . . had used up her fear.

'Couldn't the sergeant do it himself?' she asked them flatly. 'I'd have thought he would like pulling the trigger. . . !'

'He's nothing to do with us,' said one with contempt. He held out a water canteen. 'Best to go that way.' He waved the canteen.

West, back up into the mountains between Vietnam and Laos.

'Eight, nine kilometres,' he said. 'The People's Army are looking for porters . . . maybe even big-bellied ones. Anyway, there's a secret camp . . . my cousin has seen it.'

Nina didn't move. He came close enough to give her the canteen. She stood up, still trying to comprehend this new shift of fate. She looked into his face but couldn't think of words to say, in any language.

'Follow the caravan,' he said. 'Two, three kilos to next river. Then go upstream. You'll find them alright.' The two Meos vanished.

Nina shook her head. She took a thoughtful drink from the canteen, hooked it on her sash, and began to walk again, following the delicate stabs of hoofs, waffled grids of boot soles, and printed foot-shaped fragments of rubber tires.

It seems, she thought in bewilderment, that I am now looking for the entire People's Army of Vietnam.

The People's Army of Vietnam found her first.

The river bed was nearly dry. Nina stood among the boulders and peered up through the uncertain light of dusk into the cleft of the gorge above her. Reason told her that a wrecked suspension bridge, thirty-five or so metres long, and wide enough to carry a Saigon bus, was unlikely in this wildnerness without roads, without towns, without cars, busses or tracks. A primitive airstrip, perhaps. A fully engineered suspension bridge stretched credibility.

She climbed through the boulders of the stream bed. Any minute she would see that the bridge was only one of those spider's threads spun across gullies by the mountain tribes, slight webs of copra and narrow planks which swung and juddered beneath the weight of a single man.

Before she could satisfy her reason on that point, a stone slid down the riverbank. She whirled, saw two armed men in uniform, guns aimed at her. Felt another man close behind her. Then a black bag was pulled over her head.

She screamed. It was the long, full-throated cry for help that had eluded her at Tan Son Nhut, but this time there was no one who might help.

'No!' Someone hauled her elbows closer to each other than the muscles of her chest would allow, and tied them together. She would split apart down the front. She began to scream again, then she controlled her panic.

The Meos had given her both water and directions. They had sent her this way. She did not believe they had deliberately sent her toward certain rape or death.

'Please,' she begged more quietly. 'Please let me see. Untie my arms. I'll come. I was looking for you!'

Silently, hands shoved her forward over the rocks. She stumbled and lurched to keep from falling forward onto her stomach, with no arms to break the fall.

The hands heaved and pushed her up a steep bank onto what felt like a trail to her hesitant feet. A narrow trail. Leaves brushed the black bag and her clothes. Wait-a-minute vines clawed at her shoulders and legs. Insects chattered close to her head. Then they seemed to move into a more open space. The ground felt smooth and cleared of stones and fallen branches. Nina thought she heard other voices. Strong hands on her shoulders pushed her down into a squat.

'Please. . . !' she begged again.

'Wait there!' It was a young voice, speaking Vietnamese.

The cloth over her head muffled any sounds. She imagined a gun somewhere in the blackness around her, pointed at her. Anything could be there!

'Is someone there?' she begged. She tried to shift her weight on her feet. Her thighs ached and her arms were numb.

The dark, terrifying silence grew.

'What is your name?' He was only four feet away.

Reality lurched and took on a new shape.

'What is your name?' the voice repeated. North Vietnamese.

How long had he been there, watching her blind and hunched on the ground? What name was the right one for him? She ran a dry tongue over her cracked lips and gave her Vietnamese name, last used by her father a year ago, before he died. 'Luoc Le Thuyet.'

'All right, Miss Thuyet, please tell me who asked you to spy on our bridge.' He coughed.

Nina hadn't thought of that danger, among all her other culpabilities. 'Spy . . .' she repeated helplessly. Darkness was scrambling her thoughts. She needed to see her interrogator's face, and to let him see hers. 'I wasn't spying. I had been told to go upstream and find you . . .to find a camp. . . .'

'Told by whom?' His tone was neutral.

How much of the truth was safe? 'A Meo.' She decided to stick to the truth as much as possible. She would never be able to remember lies.

'Why did you need his directions?'

'I was lost.'

There was a long pause.

'Why were you spying?' he repeated.

'I tell you, I was not spying!' She drew a deep breath. 'Please, please untie me or I will fall over and hurt my baby!'

She felt him behind her, tugging. She twisted to fall sideways; her arms were free but deadened and useless. He picked up her right hand. His fingers on her palm seemed to be exploring dead flesh.

92

'You're not a peasant,' he said. 'Who are you? Who sent you?' He dropped her hand and coughed again, a moist jungle cough.

Awkwardly, she propped herself up into a sitting position, thinking as fast as exhaustion, shock, fear and darkness would allow.

'I was born in Saigon,' she said. 'But my father was from the north.' Like water, reality could take many shapes, according to the vessel or circumstances containing it at the time.

'From what village?'

'Ba Nam,' she said, 'North of the Red River.' In her head she tried to see every detail of the hamlet where she had buried him the year before.

'And you?'

What shape vessel did he hold, to receive her reality?

Stick with the truth when you can, she reminded herself. 'He left me in Saigon when he returned north in 1955.'

'After the Partition?' asked the man's voice.

Nina nodded. She did not need to tell the whole truth – that her father had fled from enemies in the opium trade. She hoped this unseen questioner would assume that her father had gone north like many others, as part of the two-way flow between north and south, after the defeat of the French at Dien Bien Phu and their withdrawal from the northern half of Vietnam.

'What did you do in Saigon?'

'Looked after his affairs,' she said truthfully. 'Until I could join him.'

'And your mother?'

'She was killed.' Again the truth, but only part. She saw no reason to volunteer that her mother had been one of the French colonialist oppressors. Her poor silly mother had not even realized that such a role existed, let alone that she might have been cast in it. Ariane Luoc had drifted on in Vietnam instead of listening to the warnings and going home to safety, all because of an infatuation with one of General LeClerc's officers. She had lost her life because of an affair.

'What are you doing here, such a long way from Saigon . . . on the wrong side of the mountains?'

Nina licked her dry lips again with an even drier tongue and skated gently across the thin crust of partial truth. 'My father died. . . .' Remember what you have said! '. . . I buried him and was trying to fly to live with a cousin in Laos, north of Vientiane.' She paused, but he made no small noise of encouragement or otherwise. 'The pilot put me down in the wrong place,' she offered. 'I ran out of money. And I have been lost ever since.'

'You're lying.' He gave an apologetic cough.

'Why should I lie?'

'Because you're an agent of the pseudo-colonial government in Saigon, sent to learn what you can of the PAVN's irresistible march to the South.'

'I don't know how to answer you,' Nina said, after a moment. 'I can only keep denying what you say, and that would be impolite.'

'What are you doing then, here on the wrong side of the mountains?'

'What I just told you.' Her tongue seemed made of parchment. 'My father died,' she repeated desperately. 'My mother was killed. My world has gone. Saigon is full of strangers. I left to look for a safe home for my child, and became lost! There's nothing more I can say!'

He sighed. Then he removed the cloth from her head.

She blinked. Set free from the cage of darkness, she felt one second of pure joy. Then she saw the other two men and reality lurched once again.

She was kneeling in the centre of the dirt floor of a one-room thatched hut with open walls. There were three men with her, not one – her interrogator, wearing black, and two other men in dark olive green uniforms.

'I still think she's lying,' said a grey-haired man with thick-lensed spectacles. Red tabs on his collar carried single gold stars. He left his position by one of the hut posts and stood over her. 'I'll give you one more chance before I have you shot. What are you doing here with your soft hands and Saigon accent? Who sent you?'

She looked up at him in despair. 'A Meo took pity on me and told me to go up the river. I came looking for you to ask for food and water and shelter. I have lost everything I have.' She thrust out her hands with their incriminating palms. 'I confess that I am not a peasant. I confess that I speak French and was raised a Catholic. And if any of that is a crime, punish it however you like. I'm past caring!' The last was nearly true.

The three men gazed at her almost absently.

'The story's too common to be worth making up,' said the grey-haired man with the single gold stars.

'She's pregnant,' said the third man, speaking for the first time. 'And a *métisse*. The other porters won't like it. Shoot her and save the rice ration.'

'Are you past earning your keep?' asked the grey-haired man.

'She can't carry!' said the third man. 'She's useless!'

'Would you object if she could carry only one bowl of rice but it was for you?' asked the grey-haired man wearily.

James Putnam stretched, yawned, rolled over, looked at his watch. Great! A few more minutes to sleep in a real bed, safe at the rear. He pulled up his lean, runner's legs and tucked his elbows happily into his flat belly. Then he smelled the flowers.

They were on his locker, stuck into a beer can with its top cut out. Freesias. A strong sweet smell. Reminded him of California . . . home. His mom liked them. He had written to his father asking him to buy her a big bunch from him for her birthday last month. Hadn't heard from her about them yet.

He lifted his head from the hard grey pillow and stared at the beer can. Who the hell left those there? He looked up and down the row of bunks at the sleeping landscapes. He reached for the can, then pulled his hand back.

Slowly he sat up and leaned forward to look closely at the innocent, fluted, honey-smelling tubes of gold, cream and lavender in the cut-off Budweiser can. He opened his locker and looked under the top. No wires. No taped package of explosive. He pushed the can gently one inch to the side, already shaking his head and mocking his own caution. This was the rear, not the jungle. Vietnam was making him paranoid.

The folded paper which had been leaning against the far side of the can hit the top of the locker like a falling leaf. He picked it up, still shaking his head in amusement at himself.

Wonder who it's from. Maybe, one of the maids. Hope it's that little one who irons my shirts . . . Vung.

'Dear Brother,' said the note in hand-printed English. 'Stop murdering your brothers and sisters. Throw down your arms and stop the killings. You owe nothing to the white slave owners who send you here to our country to die. Throw down your arms and we will welcome you with our own arms wide open and smiling hearts. You know it is right.'

Jimmy turned the note over. It was written on the back of a bar check and was signed, 'Your brothers and sisters in Freedom.' He read it again. His hand began to shake. He had felt safe in that bed last night, for the first time in four months. He watched the boy of about eleven who was sweeping just outside the door.

Who had put that note beside his bed while he was asleep? Which of the men and women who moved almost invisibly around the base, freely enough to approach a man vulnerable in sleep? Which of them belonged to the other side? Who had brought that gentle sweetness of flowers and razorblade of words?

Nina's interrogator led her out of the hut where she had been questioned. It was one of half a dozen scattered through a thinning in the jungle, each surrounded by a patch of bare dirt to lessen the danger from the little stick-coloured *kraits*.

Nina was unsure which of the men had won the argument about her fate. She followed her interrogator unsteadily. There were too many people here. She would never be able to bolt. And if she did, she would be back where she had been on the trail, gazing after the caravan. She looked for the execution posts.

They stopped at a large thatched shelter where thirty or forty men and women in peasants' clothes were eating evening rice. Some were old, some no more than children. A few eyes watched Nina and her escort approach. Most people simply ate, incurious from exhaustion.

Under the thatch of the cooking shelter a huge rice kettle steamed over a fire. The long hump of a buried chimney carried the smoke away to ooze out invisibly under the jungle canopy. By the front of the cookhouse stood a young soldier of nineteen or twenty in a dirty beige uniform tabbed with single silver stars on a yellow felt stripe. He was scowling at a sheaf of papers clipped to a board in his hand.

'Corporal!' said Nina's escort. 'Another back and pair of hands for you . . . of sorts.'

'As many as you can find!' said the young corporal. He looked up from his papers, saw Nina and his scowl deepened. 'Sir, she can't come with us! She's carrying too much already!'

'We need the supplies from the trucks,' replied the interrogator.

The corporal glanced at Nina. 'Some of the porters will refuse to go,' he retorted. 'Bad luck to travel after seeing a pregnant woman . . . Sir.'

'There's no question of "after",' said the other man evenly. 'As she is coming too. You need everyone you can get. We can't wait for another convoy to reach us this far south.'

The corporal stared back down at his papers, his young mouth thin as a knife.

'How many days would you be willing to fight in the Parrot's Beak with an empty stomach?' asked the other. 'Use her! That's what the general says!' He turned and went back to the interrogation hut at the far end of the settlement.

The corporal flipped over a sheet of paper on his clip board. Ignoring Nina, he walked away into what looked like impenetrable jungle, making notes at the same time with a ballpoint pen in the margins of the offending documents in his hand.

96

★

The officer with the gold stars had won. Now Nina had to earn her rice ration, to prove that she was too useful to shoot. She stood trying to get her bearings in this new shift of fate. She could smell the sweat of heavy work on the people around her and felt how desperately weary she was.

I wonder if I can do what will be asked of me, she thought.

'Here,' called a woman from the cooking shelter, offering a ladle of rice. 'Take it while it lasts.'

Nina accepted the rice into her cupped hands, swallowed it almost without chewing and licked the last of the sticky grains from her fingers. She wondered what she should do next, and how to find out without attracting the attention of the angry young corporal.

'You're in fine shape for this job!' observed another woman in her late fifties, with grey hair cropped in lowland peasant fashion. Her small beady eyes peered up as she crouched against one of the cook house posts finishing her rice. 'Make them give you some dried fish in the morning or you'll never last.' She snapped closed her underslung jaw, rose and disappeared into another thatched shelter. For lack of a better idea, Nina followed.

Under the thatched roof, hammocks were tied two deep, one above another, to the supporting posts of the shelter.

'Take that one,' said the woman with the cropped hair and strong jaw. 'Very low rent, hee, hee.' She pointed to the lower of a nearby pair, complete with mosquito net. 'I'm Auntie Eel. If you need to know anything, just ask me.' She bent her head and examined a sore on her arm.

The hammock still cradled the ghostly shape of its previous owner.

Did he or she die of exhaustion? wondered Nina. Or of snakebite? Or get shot for being useless? Her legs had begun to shake. Or die in childbirth? she thought suddenly. She sat on the ghost in the hammock, no longer caring, and sighed deeply at the possibility of sleep. She lay back, balanced her weight, pulled the tiny tent of mosquito netting around her and lost consciousness.

It was still dark under the jungle canopy when someone shook her hammock. Nina's eyelids felt weighted with stones. For a moment, she just lay watching this new world whose rules she must learn fast enough to satisfy the two men, at the least, who would prefer to put a bullet through her head. Many of the other porters were already untying their hammocks and bundling up their belongings.

'Take your hammock and net,' ordered Auntie Eel. 'For tonight . . . or are you leaving us already, again?'

97

Nina heaved herself out of her hammock, untied it, rolled the mosquito netting inside it, and looped it around her shoulder like a bandolier, as the others were doing.

Auntie Eel looked at her with curled lip. 'Don't forget to collect your rice before we leave. And fish.' She tied her own bundled hammock onto a bamboo pack frame, on top of another bundle wrapped in a shawl, and hung a dented US Army World War II water canteen from the top of the frame. She slung the frame over one shoulder and trotted away along a dark, narrow footpath. Nina followed her once again.

Early though it was, the jungle floor seemed unnaturally dark. Nina looked up. The tent of jungle canopy had been artificially thickened. She could just make out regular squares of bamboo trellis and rope netting across which live lianas had been trained. As she trotted heavily after Auntie Eel below this living roof, through successive thinnings of the jungle, she saw with surprise how many men and women were gathered in the shadows: besides the porters, at least a hundred soldiers or more, some in olive uniforms, some in black guerrilla pyjamas. Everyone was quiet. None of the murmurs were loud or clear enough to identify the soldiers as either North Vietnamese or South Vietnamese regroupees from 1955 moving south again.

Auntie Eel slipped quickly through the bodies, leaving Nina's bulk behind.

'Auntie Eel!' Nina called softly, and the old woman half-turned to wait. Nina followed her long thin back to the shadows beneath another spider's web roof, which held fourteen trucks. Some were olive-green Chinese vehicles. Some had once been civilian transports painted brightly as fairground rides. Others had been cobbled together from four wheels and an engine, and scrap metal, wood, or heavy rattan woven into giant baskets. Tarpaulins hid their contents.

The young corporal, in a state of quiet frenzy, was directing the transfer of bags of rice from one truck, which still trailed garlands of plastic flowers from its grille, onto the backs of the assembling porters. Nina and Auntie Eel joined the line of porters by the truck. Auntie Eel accepted a twenty-five kilo half-bag and staggered aside to tie it to her pack frame. Nina braced herself to stay upright under such a weight.

The corporal scowled at Nina. 'You! Big Belly! Get a bicycle! If you can!'

Nina stared around her in bewilderment.

Auntie Eel pointed across the clearing to a jam of heavy-framed bicycles with seats removed and bamboo poles lashed across their rusting handlebars like water buffalo horns. Awkwardly, Nina untangled one of the bicycles and steered it back through the crowded clearing to the rice truck.

A soldier on the truck dropped two rice bags across the frame of the bicycle. Nina staggered but held the bicycle upright. Carefully, she wheeled her load away from the truck, searching for the balance points on the buffalo horns, avoiding the eyes of the young corporal.

'That way! That way!' shouted the corporal impatiently. He pointed to a faint path into the jungle.

As Nina pushed through the undergrowth, her steering pole jammed in the branches and hanging rattans. She swore at the bicycle, the rice bags, which kept slipping, and her belly which got in the way of her reach. But difficult as the bicycle was to steer, fast as her heart was pounding, and short as her breath might be, she began to think that her story might yet, just possibly, have a chance to end well.

Suddenly the little track met the main trail.

'Please join the unit,' a man in khaki shorts told her. 'Over there, with the route liaison officer.'

Nina leaned against the bamboo steering pole and heaved her bicycle toward eight other bicycles and porters waiting fifty feet to her right. The main track was wide and smooth enough for the hidden trucks. Progress was much easier without shrubs and vines snatching at the water buffalo horns. Nina found a reasonably comfortable angle for her body and a rhythm for her walk.

Why not use the trucks? she wondered when she was finally able to think about anything at all except moving her load.

Though she was still under a section of artificial roof, the light was growing stronger and the soldiers more visible. Most were very young. Some looked tired and ill. They wore pouched vests and mine bags and a wide variety of scarves, canteens, knives, grenades, first aid kits, machetes, and hats. A few were in tee-shirts or sleeveless vests but most of them wore long-sleeved black shirts without cuffs, black trousers, and rubber thong sandals. Their backpacks bulged with cooking vessels, hammocks, mosquito nets, spare clothing and ammunition. Most of them also wore 'elephant guts', long tubes of rolled black cloth filled with rice. They carried old French carbines, and modern automatic weapons with curved magazines. They were talking quietly, as if content to be pausing. A few smoked cigarettes or chewed on pieces of vine.

Which was the route liaison officer? Auntie Eel had disappeared and couldn't help. Nina felt a moment of panic. Then she saw three other

99

bicycles laden like hers, and pushed over to join them. She leaned on her bicycle like a buttress. A man with a clipboard like the corporal's glanced at her and made a mark on his paper. Half an hour later, he sent the bicycles off. Nina was fourth in the line.

For the first two hours the trail continued wide and relatively flat, under low jungle canopy. When she had the energy to look up, Nina saw more of the artificial spiderweb canopy she had seen over the camp. In other places, branches of trees had been pulled over the track and lashed together.

'Where are we?' Nina asked a fellow porter during a brief stop which no one explained. She panted gratefully and leaned on the bicycle to relieve her leg muscles. The baby was churning as if excited by the speed of Nina's heartbeat.

'How should I know?' Her question seemed to make the man uneasy. 'Too far from home, that's all I do know.' He frowned slightly. 'The less you know, the better for you it is. Just keep your head down and stay on your feet.' He turned away.

After two hours, the track ended abruptly at a river gorge. Huge teeth had bitten a chunk from its lip. Trees and scrub on both sides had been scythed down and the charred cuttings tossed at random through the remaining jungle. The ragged ends of a suspension bridge swung out into the void.

Nina dropped her bicycle against some black, shattered bamboo stubs, forced her way through a cluster of porters and looked unhappily over the edge at what lay ahead of her.

The gorge was deeper than it was wide. Amid a tangle of pilings and lashing ropes tossed into the ravine like a giant game of jackstraws, swarms of men and women were at work with saws and machetes. Pickaxes and shovels clinked on the raw rock of the wound. Pairs of Siamese twins joined by baskets of debris scuttled up and down the sides of the streambed. One man clung half-way up a splintered piling, wearing a strap harness like a boy gathering coconuts, looking down, holding a rope, waiting patiently for something else, not yet apparent, to happen.

Auntie Eel appeared. 'Blown up!' she announced unnecessarily. 'Trucks no good!'

To Nina's horror, the corporal also arrived. 'Unload your cycles!' he cried.

Head down, Nina let her rice bags fall to the ground and watched the other porters hide their bicycles at the side of the trail. They loaded their rice bags onto their backs, then began to climb down into the gorge. Two soldiers cut branches to camouflage the bicycles.

'You too, Big Belly!' shouted the corporal. 'Get going!'

Nina dragged one of the 25 kilo rice bags onto the trail and left it there. Grimly, she hugged the other one in her arms. She lurched ten feet to the edge of the gorge, wavered, staggered sideways, dropped the bag, and tipped it over the edge. She kicked and pushed the bag, slipping and sliding down after it through the loose rocks and dirt. At the deep central river channel at the bottom, she stopped in despair.

The other porters were wading out through side channels to a tree which had been felled as a bridge across the deepest part. After balancing across it, they waded and clambered to the far shore. Nina looked back. The corporal was clambering and sliding down the side of the gorge toward her. She had no choice. She clutched at the fabric of the rice sack, twisted, trying to throw it across her shoulder as the others had done. Miraculously, it lightened. Another porter was behind her, lifting the sack.

'Quickly,' he urged her. 'To the log.'

Together they splashed across the side channel, climbed onto the log and reached the far side.

'Don't let it get wet! Don't let it get wet!' screamed the corporal from half-way down the gorge. 'You there! That's her job! Get back to your own load!'

'Just keep moving, however slowly,' muttered the man behind her before he turned back.

Terror and rage fuelled Nina up the far side. She swore at gravity, now her enemy instead of reluctant ally. Her arms were being pulled from their sockets. Step by grim step, she mounted the steep slope. Placed one foot. Shifted the weight up onto it. Sucked at the hot, still air. Waited as long as she dared, under the corporal's eyes, for her heart to stop trying to shatter her ribs. Then she lifted the other foot to begin again. She was shocked to find that it was already late afternoon when she arrived at the top. The other porters were huddled in the shade of the jungle, eating whatever cold rations they had carried with them. The corporal was still in the gorge, out of sight. Nina lay down to die.

'Hurry up!' urged the corporal's voice. 'The next station is still a long way!'

To her own surprise, Nina was able to stand up again. 'Auntie Eel!' she whispered urgently, as the corporal was kicking others to their feet.

Auntie Eel helped improvise shoulder straps for the rice bag from strips of cloth tied to its corners. The straps bit into Nina's shoulders but she could just carry on her back the weight that her arms would not support. She felt the corporal watching her set off and lengthened her stride defiantly.

They reached the next camp by midnight. No huts, no cook house, only a clearing beneath thickened canopy. The porters tied large sheets of plastic between trees, to catch falling insects, ticks, and pieces of leaf and bark, then slung their hammocks beneath the plastic. Nina tied her own hammock between two small trees and sank into it in exhaustion. Auntie Eel and the man with whom she had walked during the day both squatted eating plain boiled rice.

'Where did you get that?' asked Nina.

'I brought it with me. Didn't you?' The old lady looked surprised.

'I ate it all at midday,' said Nina.

'Don't you know anything?' demanded Auntie Eel. 'Here, then!' She offered Nina some of her rice.

'Thank you,' said Nina. 'But that's yours.'

'Come on!' Auntie Eel jerked her head peremptorily. 'What are we going to do with you?' She clucked her tongue. 'I don't know!'

Nina prised herself from her hammock and squatted beside them to eat a little of the offered rice. For the child.

'How did they get you?' asked Auntie Eel.

'I was lost and they found me. How about you?'

The old woman shrugged as if discussing a minor detail of her life. 'They came to my village for *corvée* labour. All the men were dead or hiding, so they took me. I'm old but strong. And they want to move as far as they can before the rains come.'

Nina looked at Auntie Eel's companion. She thought he was the man who had helped in the gorge but could not be sure.

He looked away. 'It's better than being shot,' he said to the trees. Then he stared back at the dirt between his feet. 'I will lose my rice harvest.'

'Iron Man argues with fate,' explained Auntie Eel. 'I tell him that maybe his village will be bombed and his life will be saved because he's here instead of there.'

'Is there much bombing?' Nina asked. 'Who is bombing whom?'

'If you're underneath,' asked the old woman, 'does it matter?'

Nina slept deeply. In the morning, Auntie Eel and Iron Man shared their breakfast of fruit with her. Then the corporal sent all three of them, with twenty other porters, back to the broken bridge across the gorge, to the first camp. The soldiers continued marching south.

Nina's body was at first immobilized with pain. She hobbled away from the camp, and the corporal, by will alone. Then, without a load, her stiffened muscles began to stretch and ease themselves as she walked with Auntie Eel and Iron Man along the flat, relatively open trail. She was a strong, resilient young animal with more years of eating well behind her than most of the other porters had. And as she walked, she gloried more and more that she had survived this far.

A small suspension bridge for pedestrians had been half-spun across the gorge beside the larger broken span. The remaining climb, though it still left Nina breathless, was far easier than the day before.

The second rice bag was gone. Nina found her bicycle and pushed it along the track through the burnt and twisted jungle, still savouring the relative ease of walking without a load.

'Quick!' hissed Auntie Eel as soon as they had arrived back at the first night's camp. 'Go get some rice and fish, before you load up again! This way!' She darted back along the little track through the soldiers' camp to the porters' huts and cook house.

With rice and dried fish tied into her bandolier of cloth, Nina presented herself at the trucks.

There was no sign of the corporal. Nina collected her ricebags and headed back toward the broken bridge. Her muscles soon remembered their former pain. And she had a new worry. Her belly felt oddly heavier than it had the day before.

However, the pedestrian bridge was now complete. Though she had to wrestle first the two bags and then the unwieldy bicycle down twelve feet of sliding rock to the beginning of the bridge, she could wheel her load across, safely above the two fords and log bridge of the day before. Iron Man helped her up the slope on the far side to the track.

'It was you yesterday, wasn't it?' she asked.

He nodded.

'How can I thank. . . ?' she began.

He held up a silencing hand. 'We have two choices,' he said. 'To die alone, or die together.' He walked away under his own load with his head down.

Their group reached the second camp by dusk. Nina kept her eyes down as the corporal checked off her sack. As long as she remained useful, she was fairly sure he dared not harm her.

'Up! Up!' Nina's hammock shook violently.

'Quick!' said Auntie Eel. 'Air attack coming!'

In darkness, porters snatched down hammocks and nets.

Nina heard nothing. 'How do you know?' She tore her hammock from its posts.

'They hear on radio that planes are coming. The Russians listen for us.'

Nina heard feet running in the darkness.

'This way!' someone said.

She followed, through whipping branches, bare feet placed unthinking. The night was eerily silent. Filled only with the sound of panting. Her own, and that of others in darkness. And their running feet. She bumped into other running bodies. Hit something metal. Then she heard a faint 'Whump, whump, whump,' growing closer and closer. Rocks falling from the heavens but this time on her.

The ground began to shake. Spasms of earthquake. Harder and harder. Nina thought she was falling behind the others. Another group knocked past her in the darkness. She couldn't see who or what they were.

'Whump! Whump!' The bombs nosed into the jungle, looking for the road where she had walked that day. Looking for the people who had used the road. 'Whump! Whump!' Louder and louder.

Suddenly, the sky roared. Nina couldn't see. Couldn't hear. She ran blindly, gasping for breath, across dark quivering earth.

Then, the roaring eased. The earth still jumped, but the earthquakes were moving away. Nina collided with something warm and alive. A man or woman. Hard metal tore at her shoulder. She had a sense of voices screaming around her but could hear nothing. She shouted a question but no one heard. Someone took her by the shoulders, mouthed an instruction. She shook her head. Hands pushed her forward along an invisible trail. She was walking now, instead of running, among other warm bodies, still sobbing with effort of her lungs to get oxygen back into her tissues. For one moment, she thought that the earthquakes had caught her again, then she realized that the child in her belly had thrust first one foot, then the other up toward her heart.

She didn't know how long she had walked before they stopped again. People milled in the darkness. Then someone slung a hammock and others followed suit wherever they found suitable trees. Nina tied hers to the nearest uprights and draped the mosquito net above her. The child was still churning inside her.

It's all right, she tried to assure it. We're all right now! She lay

104

shaking in the darkness until she fell asleep, as suddenly and brutally as if she had been coshed.

The next morning, they followed a guide through the jungle back to the main track, looking curiously at the daylight face of the quaking darkness through which they had fled. They had run a long way. When they finally reached the trail and retraced their steps of the day before, they saw that the air strike had knocked out the nearly-repaired bridge. They moved west along the brink of the gorge, descended, waded, rock-hopped, and climbed back up the far side. Then they moved east again along the opposite brink to rejoin the original trail back to the first camp.

A truck headlamp glinted high in the branches of a surviving tree near the trail. Fires smouldered among raw heavings of red earth. The earth on which the camp had stood was no longer there.

'Back we go,' said Auntie Eel cheerfully. 'No rice bags!' After a few steps, she added, 'No rice for us either. Oh well!'

Nina didn't hear. Her hearing did not completely return until mid-morning. She was just grateful not to carry rice. The new weight of her belly had begun to frighten her.

It was too late for them to reach the second camp before nightfall. They camped in the jungle. No fires were allowed by the route liaison officer. Iron Man caught five frogs. Nina declined a raw leg and ate a Dragon's Eye she had found on the way back to the main track that morning.

'Have you had children, Auntie Eel?' she asked suddenly.

The old woman gave a dry bark. 'Five.' She bit at her frog leg without further comment.

Nina hesitated, then decided not to ask how many had survived. For her own sake.

In the morning, the corporal led a group, including Nina and Auntie Eel, onward to the south to catch up with the earlier part of the convoy. Iron Man and six others of the men were ordered back to join the bridge repair gang at a new bridge site. That day, the monsoons started.

At noon, the sky turned black and split. A sheet of water slammed against the earth like an iron roof thrown by a hurricane. Like a hammer, it struck off leaves and branches and bruised Nina's shoulders.

In an hour it had passed. The sun was hot in the sky again, innocent as a child's eye, and the earth and jungle gently steamed. In the hot, damp jungle, tiny black leeches, like fragments of leaf, began to stir and smell blood.

Late in the afternoon, the corporal handed his group over to a sergeant and a new guide. They left the main track and turned eastward, back toward Vietnam. The new track was narrow and rocky, impassable for trucks. A monsoon-born stream had claimed it as a right of way.

The unladen porters climbed single file, up through deep ravines, following the flanks of the corderilla ranges. They crossed occasional single stranded spider's webs of swing bridges, under artificially thickened jungle. Once, when they passed a work party repairing one of the bridges, Nina half-noticed two spider men, busily weaving their web in the treetops above her. But her energy was turned inward. Her stomach had begun to tighten from time to time and she didn't know what it meant.

Don't come yet! she begged the child, as she waded through mud up to her knees. Not into this filth!

It would die if it was born here in this temporary river bed, among the leeches and mosquitoes, and bombs.

Please stay where you are!

Each time she slipped on a wet, mossy stone, Nina imagined her baby's head crashing against her pelvic bone. Each time she twisted to grab at a branch to keep from falling, she was sure that the cord had just been jerked tight around her child's neck.

Near evening, planes passed over them, flying west, invisible through the jungle canopy, with the high-pitched screaming of fighter jets, not the B52 roar of the night. The line of porters froze like rabbits among the rocks, until the planes were gone. Tiny explosions arrived on the hot air.

'The bridge,' murmured a voice. 'They're attacking the building teams.'

Auntie Eel hugged herself and rocked silently, staring at the ground, her thin dry lips tightly pinched. Iron Man had been sent back to help rebuild the bridge. Nina did not notice Auntie Eel's distress. Her child had not moved since sunset.

Someone lit a piece of vine. The porters passed the smouldering stump from hand to hand, to burn off the leeches. Nina tried to wipe the mud from her shins and thighs with pieces of leaf.

The route liaison officer passed down the line. 'We walk all night,' he said. 'This is a vulnerable area. We must move supplies south before the rains stop traffic. You sleep tomorrow when we reach the depot.'

106

Awkward with exhaustion, as they slipped and clawed their way through rocks slippery with mud and wet moss. Nina now moved with the delicacy of a spider. A still-vague discomfort had begun to grow at the bottom of her belly.

It began like a rat gnawing at the base of her stomach, just above the pubic bone. The rat bit, then stopped. Then she felt it again. Nina ignored the rat for two miles. She watched her baskets bouncing at the end of her yoke and counted strides.

They were two days south of the depot, where they had rested and eaten. A doctor in the field hospital there had examined Nina and told her that she was healthy but her time was close. She had been given a shoulder yoke, Thai-style, with a hanging basket balanced at either end, to make her carrying easier. Auntie Eel stayed close to her.

One. Two. Three. Four. Five. Six. . . .

Her brain was waiting for the rat again.

The column of porters came to a mountain river and began to cross a woven swing bridge. Nina trotted across the open slats, eyes averted from the grey boiling far below her feet, as if she were walking in the treetops. Then the sky slid abruptly sideways, and she fell against the narrow ropes that formed the side of the bridge. As she dropped to her knees, she felt the lowest rope cut into her stomach. Someone grabbed the back of her tunic. The basket on the forward end of her yoke slid gently off the hook, turned over once, twice, and looped into space. Nina's eyes tried to follow it. The sky slid round again and she had to clutch the slats of the bridge to keep from following the basket down into the river. The rat was back again, but now it felt like a tiger.

'It's coming,' she whispered. 'The baby's coming.'

Slowly, the hands on the back of her tunic hauled her upright again. 'Get her to the other side,' said someone behind her. 'Come on.'

The gaps between the slats of the bridge were chasms. She edged one foot forward.

'A little farther, that's all. Another step. Good girl.'

Nina launched herself across another chasm, clutching at the tiny spider's web of the hand-rail. The tiger tore at the flesh of her belly. She wanted to curl around the pain, to close out the tiger.

'Another step!' begged the voice. 'Just another step!'

The pain coiled Nina up, but the hands on her arms and tunic tried to hold her upright. They all stumbled and set the bridge into juddering motion. When it settled, Nina tried another step. Strands of dark hair stuck to her damp, cold forehead.

Please, she begged the hands, let me lie down. Everything will be all right if only I can lie down. She couldn't tell, over the roar of the river below them, whether she had spoken aloud or not.

'What's wrong?' asked another voice behind her. 'Are you sick? You mustn't get sick.'

'The baby,' Nina said. She could see the iron eyes in the rocks on the far bank, to which the ropes of the bridge were tied. Below the gaps in the bridge were now rocks, not roiling waters. Nina took another shaking step and doubled over. The hands tried to pull her up.

'No!' she screamed. 'Leave me for a minute!' The hands stopped pulling. Nina panted, waiting for the tiger to open its jaws. As the pain eased, she straightened and walked fast, across as many gaps as possible before the next pain.

The iron eyes on the rock grew larger. Nina now saw the frayed ends of the guy ropes, and the scramble of rocks at the far end of the slatted bridge. Miraculously, the pain hesitated, and she gained solid ground. Climbed the giant staircase of rocks at the end of the bridge. Then another contraction hit her, doubled in force.

Auntie Eel and another porter hauled her between them into the cover of the jungle. Nina squatted, panting as the contraction eased, trying to get her bearings during the lull in her body. Other porters scrambled up from the bridge.

'Is she hurt?' asked one urgently. 'We have to move off the trail, now! There was no warning from the Russian Round Eyes this time!'

Nina and her two flanking guardians lifted their heads and heard what the others already had heard – the sound of airplane engines, faint as flies on a sunny day, but growing louder.

Auntie Eel grabbed Nina by the armpits and heaved her to her feet again.

'No,' said Nina. 'I can't!' Her dark eyes stared blindly into her own pain.

The seat and inner thighs of her trousers were suddenly drenched as if she had fallen into a stream.

'Go away!' screamed Auntie Eel to the other porters. 'Get out of here! This is women only now! Shoo!' She flapped her arms as if at a flock of marauding chickens in her rice store. The approaching planes had become as loud as gasoline-driven lawnmovers in a neighbouring compound. The other porters crashed away through the scrub. Two of the women had begun to scream.

Auntie Eel thrust her wrinkled face into Nina's. 'Can you walk at all?' she demanded. 'Never mind,' she said, as she saw the look in Nina's eyes. 'One place is as good, or bad, as another.' She unbuttoned Nina's jacket, then began to pull the pins from her hair, refusing to look up as the planes flashed into sight above the jungle on the other side of the swinging bridge.

The noise was suddenly all around them, shaking the ground, and making the trunks of scrub saplings tremble. Then the scrub, the ground, the bridge and Nina's entire being were convulsed. She and Auntie Eel seized each other and curled together, hiding in each other. The ground jumped six times in quick succession.

'Holy Mother Mary!' screamed Auntie Eel in Nina's ear.

Nina didn't hear anything else the old woman said, or the last five explosions because her ears were numbed by the first one. Then came a lull, like the pause between her pains, filled only by the swelling roar of other planes. The ground began to jump again. Nina felt like a thin membrane between the forces outside her and those within. Any minute she would split wide open. A branch crashed to earth beside them, followed by twigs, then leaves. Nina lifted her head in the lull to find herself watching a small leaf twisting and turning slowly to earth.

The old woman had her head cocked, listening. 'Farther up the trail,' whispered Auntie Eel. 'The bastard Round Eyes hit farther up the trail.' She looked around. 'And behind us. So much for the sergeant and his "pregnant woman are bad luck." ' She paused and untangled one arm from around Nina. 'I'm as wet as you are,' she said sheepishly. 'With less reason.' She started to stand, settled back again, sat down, then returned to her knees. She hummed a few bars of music to herself then stopped abruptly, staring up along the trail. Her apparent calm was really shock.

Nina gasped for breath. The air was filled with dust and smoke, and floating fragments of ash and leaves.

'Iron Man. . .!' cried Auntie Eel. She half-rose, then sank back beside Nina. 'He's back at the other bridge. I'm losing my mind. . . .'

Nina didn't hear her. Her ears were still deafened. In any case, she had forgotten the planes. She had forgotten the bombs. She didn't notice the smoke or the fog of drifting débris. She didn't notice the ants and beetles which had resumed crawling in the dust beside her, nor the leech on her left ankle. She was working harder than she had ever worked, with absolute, burning concentration. The pain had changed.

Auntie Eel stood up, tested the various parts of herself. 'Back in a minute,' she assured Nina over her shoulder. She hesitated once more, took two steps back toward Nina, then crashed away into the undergrowth after the other porters.

Nina grunted. Then she gave an astonished little cry, half in pain, half like making love. Her body sagged, at peace, into relaxation warm as a summer lake. She wanted to slip further and further into the lake and drift, just drift.

Something moved slightly between her thighs. With terror, she remembered what she had just been doing. Frantically, she opened the top of her wet *panung* and reached down. There was no movement. No cries. Her hands found a soft slippery piece of pipe. Then she gripped a tiny arm and pulled her daughter up into the daylight.

The baby was breathing. The cord, still attached, was pink and pulsing. Nina laid her against the bare skin of her breasts and prayed to be told what to do next. The child stirred, as if dreaming.

'Wake up!' Nina begged her. 'Please, wake the hell up!' She hugged the baby tighter, willing her to join the world. 'Live!' she begged it. 'Oh God, what must I do to make you live?'

The tiny mouth opened and Nina heard a faint gargling sound.

'Give her to me!' said Auntie Eel, reappearing like a conjuring trick. 'I'll find the others in a minute . . . Give her to me! I thought you probably didn't know. . . ! And no family here!'

She hooked a gnarled finger into the baby's mouth. 'Such a simple thing!' she said. 'There!'

The baby gave a yowl of disproportionate force and opened her eyes. They were dark and startled. Nina watched them swivel out of control, then focus fuzzily and somehow appear both to register the world and to demand 'Where the hell am I?'

Nina held this fragile new life gently, as if it might still change its mind and leave again, afraid to give in to relief.

The child's eyes met Nina's. Aha! they said. There you are!

I thought all babies were blind at birth, thought Nina, as startled as her daughter looked. The child searched Nina's eyes, as if confirming her identity. With a passion that she had forgotten possible, Nina fell in love. More intensely than that distant three-year-old in the photograph had once loved Doi the gardener, and Simpoh Flower, and her gibbon Minou, and her parents. More even than the fifteen-year-old had loved her father's distant cousin, Thu. Far more passionately than the twenty-year-old would ever have risked. In spite of reason, which told her that such love was dangerous . . . that everyone could be lost, as everyone of importance in her life had been lost. Nina was shocked out of caution by her daughter's peremptory acknowledgement of her own self. For the first time in her life, she was the other half of an equation.

As she watched, the awareness faded and the tiny lids fluttered in

110

weariness. Auntie Eel reached to pull Nina's jacket open again. Without opening her eyes, the baby felt a nipple against her cheek, turned her head and clamped on.

A line of quicksilver spread from Nina's breast, through her chest and stomach into her toes. She bent and kissed the wet, black feathers on the baby's scalp.

'Little eyes see pretty things,' crooned Auntie Eel. 'Little nose smells what is sweet. Little ears hear pleasant sounds. Mouth likes luscious things to eat.' She gave a short, hard laugh.

Nina rocked gently as her daughter suckled and started to laugh. Everything was wonderful. And funny. She had never seriously considered the possibility of a daughter. She had let fear, and Thu's obsession with a son cloud her own imaginings. She gazed curiously at the enormous, bright red pudendum, out of scale with the rest of the tiny body. A girl, no doubt about it! With black hair and dark eyes. Her own father's genes had won. Those of her blond French mother and of Will John had not met after all. Thu would have accepted this child as his own, even if he had not forgiven it for being a daughter instead of a son. She stroked the wrinkled satin of her daughter's tiny legs.

'Lie back,' ordered Auntie Eel. She pressed on Nina's belly. Nina hardly noticed.

A girl. A daughter. Herself. She wondered if she had imagined that look of recognition, but still found something familiar in the fierceness of the tugging at her breast. She hardly noticed the milder pain of the after birth or Auntie Eel's manipulations of the cord.

She's so beautiful! thought Nina with surprise. Thick dark hair. . . . She bent to kiss it again. Skin as frail as the petal of a poppy. Long fingers with nails like the scales of a tiny fish.

Will John Haines, your daughter is beautiful!

She wiped the damp hair carefully with the corner of her jacket.

'What will you call her?' asked Auntie Eel. The calling name, not the private one. The name to divert the attention of jealous spirits. The servants in the big house had once called Nina 'Little Rat' to keep her from being carried off to the spirit world prematurely.

My little tigress, thought Nina. For safety's sake, let's call you Mouse. To disguise and protect the power I feel in you already. The strength in those kicks.

'Mouse,' she said aloud.

As if in acknowledgement, Mouse unhooked herself from Nina's nipple, looked searchingly at her mother for the second time and fell asleep. Nina watched her, fascinated by the lavender shells of her eyelids, by the long black lashes, by a raspberry mouth too small to imagine, by every quiver and twitch. When she finally looked up, she was surprised to find the rest of the world still there, a broken branch lying a few feet away, débris littering the trail. The bridge was gone. A large chunk of the far bank of the river had been blown down into the gorge. Auntie Eel had finally vanished.

Nina wondered if she and Mouse had been abandoned. But a full rice basket lay on the trail. And other parcels and bundles. Too much to leave, she thought. The troops need feeding. They'll come back.

Carefully, so as not to disturb Mouse, she pushed herself across the dirt and leaned against the pliable wicker side of the rice basket. In a short time, she too was asleep, drifting on the warm lake.

'It's no good!' bellowed the voice of the NVA sergeant now in charge of her unit of porters. 'No good! Do you hear?'

Nina coiled like smoke from a genie's lamp and rose into the sky, blossoming like a cloud from a bomb. Then she became a tree, spreading her canopy above the second layer of the rainforest. Her branches were filled with hundreds of tiny monkeys who chattered and played.

The sergeant stood on the ground far below, calling up in a voice made faint by Nina's attitude, 'It's no good.'

He began to chop at the base of her trunk with his machete. Her branches shivered with each blow and the monkeys clung tightly to keep from being shaken off like ripe nuts.

'One dead and three wounded,' said the sergeant's voice. 'How can we carry another one? And what about her load?'

Nina opened her eyes.

'Why don't you ask her opinion?' said Auntie Eel's voice. 'There. She's awake.'

Nina checked the reality of the small weight in her arms, bending her face to sniff lightly at the top of her daughter's head. She had been asleep for some time. The light was that of early evening. She felt sore and a little bruised but still wrapped in the same luxurious ease as after Mouse's birth. She looked up and smiled at the faces above her.

The sergeant glared down at Nina and Mouse. 'One of my strongest men is dead,' he said, 'and three others too injured to carry their loads. And now you! We'll have to leave all of you here and hope someone can come take you back north by muleback. I don't know what to do about all your loads!'

Nina climbed carefully to her feet, using her free hand for balance.

112

Once up, she felt surprisingly well. And lighter. Thin. Like a stalk of rice instead of a boulder.

'I can carry my load,' she said. 'Why shouldn't I?'

The sergeant spat on the ground without answering.

Nina surfaced into the chill of reality. 'It was a good birth,' she said. 'A good omen for the future.' She waited. Thu might have accepted Mouse as his own once, but not now that Nina had fled. She was barely out of his range now as it was. They could not be sent back north.

'How can you carry your full load while also carrying that?' The sergeant pointed at Mouse. 'And what if it cries if we run into a Royal Lao or American terrorist patrol?'

'She won't cry,' promised Nina. 'I'll suffocate her first.'

He snorted. 'It's not a risk I'll take. You stay . . . with the three wounded till transport arrives to take you back.' He turned away and began to tug at a fallen bundle, refusing to look at her again.

Nina took a step toward him. Her sense of physical wellbeing wavered. She was weaker than she thought. She tried to imagine balancing her yoke with one hand and Mouse with the other.

'Here,' said Auntie Eel. 'You don't know anything.' She had torn one end off a piece of ragged packing cloth draped over a broken branch and now knotted it around Mouse and Nina into a sling which left both of Nina's hands free. From her chauffeur-driven car, in a former life, Nina had seen women working in the *paddi* fields with their babies tied on in the same way.

The sergeant kept his head down as he began to transfer pineapple grenades from the bundle into an empty shoulder basket.

'Now,' said Auntie Eel to Nina, 'we must find some wood for a fire. You need cooked rice tonight. And we could all use some comfort.'

'Why find wood here?' asked the sergeant. 'You'll only have to carry it. We have dead men's rice and ammunition to carry.'

'It's nearly night,' said Auntie Eel. 'And why move on to a new target when they've finished here? If you ask me. . . .'

The sergeant glared back toward the ruins of the bridge.

'. . .not that it's my place to advise,' she added hastily. When the sergeant said nothing, Auntie Eel risked a further argument. 'We can cook rice. Our smoke will fit right in!'

The sergeant pulled on the end of his short nose, still contemplating the bridge. 'There's some point in what you say,' he conceded. 'Move up a hundred metres. The cover's thicker there.'

'Thank you,' whispered Nina to Auntie Eel. 'I only need a night's sleep.'

'Hmmh!' snorted the old lady. 'It's nothing. Such things should be obvious to our glorious leaders.'

The next morning, while Mouse still slept in the nest of a torn jacket, Nina found a yoke and one of her own baskets. She filled the basket with scattered grenades from a broken box. Then she tied a broken, half-empty sack of rice to the other end of the yoke. She tried it across her shoulder. It balanced. She fed Mouse, tied her on, lifted her yoke and joined the line of porters which had already begun to move off to the south after the guide. All her energy had focussed down to one small bright point – to leave this place safely with Mouse.

The sergeant was loading a crate onto another porter's pack frame. His eyes met hers. He frowned and opened his mouth to speak.

Nina's eyes told him that nothing would stop her while she was alive. And that even if he shot her, her body would keep walking.

'If it cries,' he said, '*I* suffocate it!'

And if he tried, Nina knew she would tear the flesh from his skull and his heart out through his ribs. But she dropped her eyes to hide her triumph. She moved past him into a green tunnel.

Nina fell into the soft bouncing step that kept her load in balance, Mouse tied securely against her chest like a part of herself. By mid-morning rumour had told her that the three wounded porters had died mysteriously during the night.

'Of course, their throats were cut while they slept,' whispered one woman porter. 'How could they be left there alive?'

Of course, thought Nina. How indeed? And, miraculously, she had been given a chance to carry Mouse out of reach of such darkness and ugliness.

For a while, Nina walked in a fog of exhaustion, contentment and terror. She was amazed how little Mouse interfered with the yoke and baskets. In spite of the tiredness from carrying rice, she was also amazed how well she felt after the birth. Her mother and her friends in Saigon had led Nina to expect what they always called 'an ordeal men would never put up with, if *they* had to go through it.' Her own mother had handed her over to a wet nurse immediately after birth, and then to an *ayah*. She had said nothing to make Nina expect the sensuality of motherhood, the intensity of the sharp tugging at her nipples while small hands brushed and stroked her skin. Nina had not expected the pure pleasure of new feet which had never touched the ground or of hands like sea creatures in a rock pool, or the delight of ears like pale unfolding flowers. She had not expected the inarguable peace of falling asleep, even along a jungle trail, with her sleeping child propped against her, sheltered in the crook of her arm. She had not expected the connection, the recognition which was a voluptuous confirmation of herself.

She forgot the tiger's jaws within hours; her dizziness lasted only two days. She remembered Mouse's birth as a fall through space across a clear boundary in time – before Mouse and after. Even life with her parents in the big house before it burned down, and her life in the streets afterwards had not been separated so distinctly in her emotions. She would look down and be amazed that time and space had existed before that small face with the intense dark eyes had been there to perceive them. She tried, unsuccessfully, to remember her own body when it had walked, eaten and made love alone, before it became the centre of the universe for the strong little mouth and searching hands. She was no longer alone. She no longer cared where life washed her up, as long as she and Mouse could be safe together. She wanted Will John to share this amazing transformation of the world.

Keeping Mouse quiet enough to satisfy the sergeant was another matter. In her first week, the baby hardly cried. She slept and sucked, then slept again. Then she began to wake for longer and longer. She stared intently up at her mother's face or at the moving pattern of leaves above their heads, as if decoding messages. As soon as the tiny mouth opened, Nina offered it a full brown nipple. Mouse would suck, then sleep again. Constantly alert, Nina brushed away insects which might annoy Mouse. She cleaned and dried rags she used as Mouse's diapers to keep the soft, fresh skin from chafing.

But once, when the convoy moved briefly out across an exposed ridge and Nina had sunk back into her own thoughts, the sunlight struck Mouse's eyes. She gave a peremptory cry of irritation – an oath and an order to her mother to put things right.

'Hush!' Nina quickly adjusted the cloth of the sling to shade Mouse's eyes. 'Oh, hush, my darling!' She raised her head like an alarmed doe. But the sergeant did not come crashing along the trail. For the next hour, Nina mused on the force of will shown by so small a body.

After three weeks, Nina's milk began to dry up. She begged camp cooks for extra rice, and shamelessly accepted what Auntie Eel and some of the other women gave her from their own portions. On Auntie Eel's advice, she drank water pooled in leaves and soaked rags in streams, to suck as she walked. She dripped water from the leaves into the baby's mouth. Even so, Mouse began to fret after feeding instead of falling asleep.

'Good baby, good baby!' crooned Auntie Eel, jiggling and stroking. 'Sleep baby. Grow to marry well. Grow to bury your parents well. Sleep now. Sleep now.'

But Mouse whimpered, cried, subsided and whimpered again.

Every night, Nina would slide among the sleeping porters to get as far as possible from the sergeant. Her sleep was broken. Even when Mouse was quiet, Nina feared she would wake, and tried to wake herself first, to offer the baby what little milk she had.

'What am I going to do?' Nina begged Auntie Eel. 'What can I do?'

Their route had turned eastward, toward South Vietnam. The escorting soldiers had become noticeably more alert. And every night, Nina heard distant rocks falling from the sky, ahead and behind them.

One morning, Mouse decided she had starved long enough. She opened her translucent lips and howled with rage.

'Oh God!' cried Nina. Mouse howled again, a piercing shriek of frustration far too loud to come from something so small.

Heads lifted around the campsite. The sergeant rose from a squat and crossed toward Nina and Mouse. Auntie Eel half-stood and froze.

Mouse howled again. The sergeant had nearly reached them. The other porters waited in silence.

'So,' said the sergeant.

Nina closed her hand over the baby's mouth. The tiny body wriggled like a beached fish but no sound emerged. 'See!' Nina cried. 'I won't let her cry!' She felt the tiny body convulse in her arms. She lifted her hand for the length of one gasp and clamped it tight again. 'I swear! I swear it!' She crouched with Mouse clutched against her chest, miniature feet drumming on her belly.

I must let her breathe! she thought wildly. She has to breathe!

The sergeant looked down at Nina. 'Yesterday,' he said, 'our regular forces met a terrorist guerrilla group one hour's walk from here.' He hesitated. His hands began to reach for Mouse.

Nina's lips curled from her teeth in a snarl. Her eyes burned the sergeant to ashes. Mouse had stopped fighting her.

The sergeant dropped his hands. 'If I hear it again,' he said. 'I kill it. No more warnings.' He turned and stalked away through the silent, frozen porters.

She's dead! thought Nina. I've killed her. She looked down in terror at the quiet body and met small dark eyes, still filled with life. And rage.

'Please!' Nina whispered. 'Please, please, please understand that you

116

must be silent!' She lifted her hand a fraction. Mouse inhaled. Nina replaced her hand, more gently. Then lifted it again. When Mouse had breathed once more, Nina crushed the little mouth against her breast. 'Forgive me!' she begged. 'I must!'

Mouse snuffled and glared, but did not scream. She still did not scream when Nina cautiously pulled her away and gave her a little water.

'He's right, you know,' said the man nearest to Nina. 'She could get all of us killed. Don't worry so much, it's only a girl!'

Nina gave him the look that had twisted the marrow in the bones of the *fumeur* owner, and stopped the sergeant's hands as they had reached for Mouse. Then, after a moment of thought, she gave the baby some of her own rice.

Mouse promptly vomited. Frantically, Nina pressed her to her breast to muffle the cry of discomfort.

Auntie Eel had sidled close. 'Chew it first! Don't you know anything?' She looked at Nina's desperate face. 'I didn't think before . . . try now. Here.' She offered part of her morning rice. 'Until it's like soup.'

Nina took a little rice and chewed. Like a mother bird, she dipped her mouth to her child's and fed it from her own lips. Mouse swallowed greedily and was not sick. Nina gave her a little more. Then a little more. After eight sups, Mouse closed her lavender, bright-fringed eyelids, and went limp. When Nina saw that her daughter was deeply asleep for the first time in days, she began to weep with relief.

117

6

Nina's pursuers were not what she had imagined as she walked the trail from the Tiger's Head or clung to Major Lucky's mule.

After his men found her tracks in the dust of the trail leading north, Thu had shrugged. 'Let her go,' he said. 'She's worthless.'

Nevertheless, the Meo women in the house knew better than to whisper or look at him sideways. His aunt, who was in reality the sister of one of Thu's father's wives, waited all night without sleeping until she saw him climb safely down from the lookout platform where he had spent the first night after Nina left, smoking his Chinese cigarettes and gazing along the northern ridge. When one of the youngest women dared to hold up the yellow silk *ao dai* Nina had worn on her first day, and then to giggle, his aunt had boxed her ears and sent her away from the villa to relatives in a distant village. A week later, the old woman presented Thu with a concubine chosen by herself from a village across the ridge.

The man who rang the doorbell of the big house in Saigon was a tall American in civilian clothes, slightly plump, with a baby's mouth, a boy's freckles, and the eyes of an aging Times Square hustler. While he waited, the eyes took in the gutted sandbags rotting in the drive and their replacements on the barricade around the verandah. They noted the grenade mesh over the windows and the new lock on the door. He leaned on the bell again.

A young blonde American woman finally answered the door. 'I'm sorry,' she said. 'I don't know where all the staff have gone. Can I help you?'

'I'm looking for Mme. Nina Martell,' said the man. 'Is this her house?'

The young woman looked nonplussed. 'I don't know. I'm new here. Let me go find out.' She hesitated, then decided to leave the door open. 'Come on in,' she said. 'I guess you don't look like a Viet Cong.' Neither of them was clear whether or not she was flirting with him.

Standing in the entrance hall, the man heard typewriters rattling behind the panelled door on his left. The door on his right bore a discreet wooden sign saying 'USAID. Please knock.'

The young woman didn't come back. Instead, a tired, middle-aged American man trotted down the formal staircase that rose like the half-spread wings of a gull to a landing on the floor above.

'How do you do?' he inquired politely without giving his name. 'I understand that you want to know whether a Nina Martell owns this house. May I ask if you're a friend of hers?'

'A friend of a friend,' said the man with the baby's mouth. 'He asked me to say hello when I came to town.'

'May I say who it is?'

'Is she here?'

'No. Not any more.'

'Do you know where she could be?' The tall man was polite.

'Off-hand, I couldn't say,' said the middle-aged American. 'Who's the friend?'

'That's OK,' said the tall man. 'I guess she's gone then.'

'You could say that.'

'Thank you for your help,' said the tall man.

Back on the street, he re-read the note of the directions he had written on the back of a business card. He looked up at the trees that foamed above the top of the compound wall. He studied a patch where the stucco had fallen from the wall, leaving the shape of a short-trunked elephant. Then he wrote in the margin of the card, 'Note 2. for WJH. @ 6/13/66. NM no longer in residence. Pres. loc. unknwn to occ. USAID?'

As he walked back toward the corner of the street, he eyed the chauffeur asleep in a parked car, the man pushing a broom without conviction along the sidewalk, and the legs of the *pousse-pousse* driver who appeared to be repairing the axle of his pedal cab.

Maybe, he thought. But only maybe.

When the middle-aged American man who had come down the gull-wing stairs left that evening to go home, he too eyed the chauffeur, the *pousse-pousse* driver, now asleep in his vehicle, and a begger stretched out along the wall. He was quite sure that someone had put a watcher on the house . . . there had definitely been one ever since he had moved into his office there, two months ago. He couldn't imagine what they were trying to learn.

Jimmy Putnam did not enjoy his eleven days in Saigon before

119

reassignment. He pretended to get drunk and watch Doris Day movies. He visited the National Museum, Souvenir Temple and Zoo. He had his hair cut and had a massage which went farther than he thought he had intended. He bought an *ao dai* for his sister and a necklace for his mother of shell casings carefully worked into flowers. He went to the library to double-check the word paranoia: 'a mental disorder characterized by systematic delusions, as of grandeur, or, especially, persecution.' He lay on his bed in the grilled and sandbagged military dormitory and stared at the ceiling.

He was more frightened moving around the crowded Saigon streets than out in the country looking for the enemy. In the city, there were always people you couldn't see, behind you, jostling you unexpectedly, roaring at you out of side streets on motor scooters. And some of them were enemies, except that he couldn't tell which. Any of them could have a knife. One of them had singled him out.

He watched Vung, the young maid who washed his shirts, and the eleven-year-old boy who swept the floors, and the venerable go-fer, a grandfather of seventy, who bought beer, cigarettes, condoms, knucklebones of the Buddha in lockets, girls, potato chips, VC ammunition belts, shirts made in three hours, and anything else the men might want. Not one of them met Jimmy's eye that little bit too directly.

He was afraid to fall asleep. He lay drained by the heat, eyes closed, fighting unconsciousness that would leave him as exposed as a sacrifice on an altar. He waited for whoever had written the note to make his or her next move. One night, he imagined telling his father about the problem and asking his advice.

John Putnam's deep, smooth voice said clearly, 'You've handed over the initiative, Jimmy! Since when did you ever solve anything with your back to it, running away? You were clear about your reasons for going over there. Get clear about what you think now. Then you'll be able to see what to do next. And do it!'

Jimmy rolled over, fumbled in his locker for a pencil and paper, lay for twenty minutes in the dark, then went into the toilets to write his own letter.

'Dear Brothers and Sisters in Freedom,' he wrote. 'Read a little more American history before you lecture me about white slave owners. I wouldn't be here putting my life on the line if I didn't *know* that freedom is worth dying for! Your own Ho Chi Minh turned to the American example for the Vietnamese Declaration of Independence against the French. "All men are created equal." But some men use words like "freedom" and "equality" to create a new slavery. I still believe

I'm fighting such slavery over here. Yours sincerely, James Putnam.'

He left the note on top of his locker. Having taken action, he was less afraid.

The reply was waiting for him two evenings later.

'Dear Brother, Go to the South Vietnamese refugee camps. Ask who bombed their villages, burned their rice, shot their fathers and brothers, raped their sisters. Ask which side – their enslavers or their liberators? Do not destroy us for our own good. Respectfully yours, One who would be your true brother.'

The correspondence was interrupted by Putnam's reposting to Ban Me Thuot where he was forced to focus on the enemy in uniform.

The unimaginable noise suddenly filled the sky. It came from behind the mountain range to the west rather than from the east as the night bombings did. First it wasn't there at all, then it was on them.

'No,' whispered Nina, running toward the basket where Mouse lay asleep. 'No more! I can't bear it!'

The jungle exploded around her. The ground heaved. Nina rocked with the shock wave and screamed, caught her balance, and threw herself toward the basket.

'No,' she screamed. 'Not me! Not Mouse! You don't want us! Please stop! Stop! Stop! Stop! Stop!'

The explosions swallowed her screams. A tree crashed to the ground. Air and earth had exchanged places. She inhaled floating particles of earth and tried to stand on what felt like nothing. Embracing Mouse's basket, she clambered to her feet and tried to run, out of the floating earth and the shock waves. She stepped on a leg which lay across her path like a fallen tree branch, and fell again. The earth shuddered and bucked her through the air. She had the insane sensation of having left the earth entirely before she hit the tree and lost consciousness.

'Here she comes,' said the voice. 'She's back.'

Nina struggled up through the black veil which pinned her to the ground, immobile and blind. She was in Thu's villa again, regaining consciousness. She had never escaped. She had to stand. To run, to save her child.

'Not too fast,' said the voice. A woman's voice. 'Take it slowly.'

She had to escape before Mouse was born. She rolled to her side, tried to raise herself and retched.

'You watch her,' said the woman's voice. 'I must go see to the others.'

The others. Nina managed to open her eyes. A green wall was revolving around her, like a fairground ride. She curled tightly into herself and waited for the giddiness to pass.

Suddenly, she went absolutely still. Something was terribly wrong. Her elbows were digging into the hollow of her flat belly. Her arms were tightly closed around emptiness. She waited two disbelieving seconds, for the apparent reality to correct itself. But a cold horror had already begun to grow up from the soles of her feet, spreading like icy flood waters through her limbs, her chest, standing her hair on end.

'Where's Mouse?' she whispered.

No one replied.

Nina heaved herself up onto both hands. 'WHERE IS MOUSE?'

She stared at the blank face of the woman porter beside her. 'Where is my baby? Where is she?'

The woman shook her head helplessly.

Nina clambered to her feet. 'Auntie Eel!' she screamed. 'Auntie Eel!' The old woman had her. Had taken her while Nina was unconscious. 'Auntie Eel!'

The woman laid a restraining hand on Nina's arm. 'A woman near you was hit. She's dead. Many are dead.'

'No!' said Nina between clenched teeth. She couldn't hear properly but could read the woman's face. 'No! Not Mouse!' She took two steps and fell to her knees. 'Help me find her!' she ordered the woman. 'For God's sake, she's here somewhere. I was carrying her. She can't be far!'

She climbed to her feet again and staggered toward a stand of broken bamboo. 'She's in here,' she said. 'Somewhere in here.' The bamboo canes came away in her hands as she pulled at them.

'You go look,' she ordered the woman porter. 'Go see if someone has already found her. A little girl, seven weeks old.'

Doubtful, the woman trotted away.

Nina heaved at the tangle of a broken treetop, then fought her way into the leafy mass. She found a severed hand trailing a length of limp grey string and a bloody hammock but not Mouse.

'She's here,' she said. 'Somewhere. Right here. Not far. Here.'

She found herself seated on the ground, with the green wall revolving again. She couldn't stand, so she began to crawl through the debris, reaching under branches, pushing aside ruptured bundles. She crawled to a mound of fresh earth, dug with her hands until she reached rock, moved to her right and began to dig again. She paid no attention to the rivulet of blood which ran down her arm. She was still digging when the woman porter returned with one of the soldiers.

'You must come to the First Aid station,' the soldier ordered Nina. 'You have a head wound and require treatment.'

Nina kept digging.

'You must come with us,' said the soldier.

'I don't think she hears you,' said the woman porter.

The soldier moved closer to Nina, who had begun to roll a broken boulder away from a gap unplugged by the roots of a fallen tree. Nina looked up.

'You must help search,' she ordered. 'I am lost.' Her braid was matted with blood from her scalp and her hands caked with blood and dust, but her voice rang with all the authority of the former head of a family empire. 'Help me!'

'Her head is bad,' said the soldier.

'You start over there!' Nina pointed back down the trail toward a ridge of dirt ploughed up by a shelf. 'I'll finish here . . . She's here somewhere!' She pushed herself to her feet by leaning against the broken boulder.

'What are you going to do?' the woman asked the soldier.

Before he could answer, Nina slid back down the boulder, spun back into blackness by the revolving green wall of jungle.

She came to on a litter, in darkness. It took her several minutes to decide that it was night, and that she was not blind. She watched shapes moving. She did not examine them, or question. Her brain held back from full consciousness. It refused all knowing, except that there was something too enormous to tolerate. She drifted, aware of movement at some point but not of its nature or direction. She thought she may have been given an injection but was not certain. Finally she sank back into sleep without fully reaching the surface.

She knew the second she woke up. Mouse was gone. A part of herself was gone. She was going to wake up like this every morning of the rest of her life, with the cold metallic heaviness in her stomach and the sense of emptiness. She tried to dig herself back into sleep, as if she could burrow through a wall in time into another reality and wake up with the small fragrant warmth in her arms.

After a few minutes, she opened her eyes and swung herself upright on the edge of the hammock where someone had placed her. Her head throbbed. The world was beyond a fogged sheet of glass. She reached up and touched a bandage she had not noticed before. Then her nostrils caught the fetid smell of dried blood and she saw the dark stiffening of a jacket sleeve, too far away to seem her own. There was dried blood in the cracked skin of her distant hands and under her broken nails.

She was in a thatched shelter without walls. A man lay beside her, eyes closed and face grey, on a pallet raised off the dirt floor on a rope sling. One of his legs was splinted and the other missing below mid-thigh. He was humming faintly, the way cats purr with pain. Other bodies slept in hammocks slung from the posts of the shelter. The dirt floor was criss-crossed by trails of blood. Flies buzzed in lines along the trails and on the eyes of the sleepers. Nina noted these things absently but only one thought churned in the sea of her dizziness. Mouse wasn't gone, only left behind. She must go find her.

Nina stood, experimentally. She tried walking two steps. The ground stayed where it should have been, more or less. On the far side of the shelter, a woman in a khaki bush shirt and olive uniform trousers was administering an injection to one of the bodies in the hammocks. Nina managed to cross the necessary fifteen feet.

'How far was I brought?' Nina asked the woman.

'A night's travel,' said the woman. 'How is your head this morning?' A stethoscope hung around her neck. Her uniform was streaked with blood and mud.

'Did we move north or south?'

'North.' The woman looked at Nina. 'Please sit down for a while. Don't do too much too fast.'

'Where is the trail?' Nina began to walk unsteadily out of the shelter.

'Please sit down, as I suggested,' said the doctor politely.

'I must go back and find my daughter,' explained Nina, equally polite. She reached for a pole holding up the edge of the shelter roof as dizziness hit. She felt the doctor take her arm.

'In a minute or two,' said the doctor. 'You can go back in a little while. Just sit here. . . .' She eased Nina down into a sitting position, her back against the roof pole.

Each beat of Nina's heart was a blow to the inside of her skull. She was going to be sick. But she had to go back to the site of the air raid. Mouse had been well-fed on Nina's rice. The night had not been too hot or too cold. There had been no monsoon deluge since the bombing. If tigers, or wild dogs had not found her. . . .

Nina climbed to her feet again.

'Where are you going?' asked the doctor.

'To find Mouse . . . my daughter.'

124

'Oh yes,' said the woman. 'That's right. Let me give you something first, for the pain in your head.'

Nina hardly noticed the prick of the injection. Then she felt darkness swooping in on her again. In a rage of frustration, she screamed, 'No!', just before the doctor eased her down to lie unconscious again on the ground.

When she woke up this time, a man in his fifties stood beside her. He was slight and grey-haired, in civilian clothes, and spoke softly, with the educated tones of a mandarin.

'I hear that you have lost your baby,' he said gently. 'You must be very, very grieved.'

Nina pushed away the metallic heaviness of her first waking. 'Yes,' she said firmly. 'And I must go back and search properly, now that I'm better. I was crazed with terror before, and probably dizzy from the blow to my head.'

'Please,' said the man. 'I understand your pain. I have lost two of my three sons. I ask you to believe me that there is no one left alive back there. The soldiers searched thoroughly. They did not find your daughter.'

Nina turned her head away. The world continued to spin around her.

'I know you feel angry with me for telling you this,' he said. 'But you must believe me. You will not find her. And we need you here.'

He did not understand. Nina became crafty. 'Where is "here"?'

'A Group 559 Base Camp. In Laos. For the time being, you are safe. The camp is in neutral territory . . . too many American allies for bombing, so far. You can rest, and recover. Then you can help us further.'

'Group 559?'

'Of the People's Army of Vietnam,' he said. 'In charge of moving men and supplies south into southern Vietnam, to support the struggle against the new American invader and its puppet government in Saigon.'

'But you're a southerner,' said Nina with apparent lucidity. 'I recognize it in your voice. How are you moving south?'

He shook his head. 'I went north in 1954, after Dien Bien Phu. To flee Diem's reprisals against the patriots who supported the National Liberation Front. Now I'm coming home again. Many of us are.'

'Where in Laos?' asked Nina, leaping at her gaol. 'Where exactly was I when I was hit?'

He shook his head again. 'Better for you not to know too precisely.'

Nina reared up. 'You *must* tell me!' she said. 'I have to know where my daughter was lost!'

Irritation began to colour his compassion. 'You would be vulnerable if you were captured,' he said. 'Please don't press me further. Concentrate on recovering your strength. Ease your grief by considering the part you can still play in our struggle. Our country's grief is greater than any of our individual sorrows. I will come see you again tomorrow.'

Nina watched him disappear along a narrow track into the jungle. Craftily, she sat on her hammock without further protest until after the late afternoon rice. After rice, the doctor disappeared into a nearby hut with other officers and cadres who appeared from the jungle. The amputee on the nearby pallet still hummed with pain and the other patients seemed to be dozing, flies notwithstanding. Nina rose and walked quickly away along the largest track she could see.

'Which way to the road?' she asked a man in black who sat smoking by the track.

He gestured in the direction she was already headed. Nina passed through a small clearing, unchallenged by a group of soldiers playing the four-colour card game, past the sand-bagged openings of bunkers and tunnels, along the tiny thread of trail, to the sudden widening of the main track. There, she stopped, bewildered. The jungle wavered as if seen through heat waves.

They had brought her north, the doctor had said. Then she must now go south. But she had no idea which way was south. She squinted up at the tiny flakes of sky visible through the leaves and the throbbing in her head. The setting sun was invisible through the jungle canopy, but the sky seemed brighter behind her. She tried for several moments to decide what that meant. Then she turned right and began to walk.

An hour and a half later, the scream of a small animal returned her at least partially to her senses. She stopped, knowing clearly for the first time where she was – alone at night in the jungle, without a weapon, compass, water, mosquito net, hammock, or food. Crippled by a serious head wound which was making her right eye blind with its drumming inside her skull. All she had was a stubborn, irrational hope. She might not even have the energy to return safely to the base camp. It was a miracle that she had not stumbled off the track. A firefly drifted brightly across her path. On. Off. On. Off.

She squatted in the middle of the dark trail, folded her arms across her knees and lowered her aching head. The darkness shifted and creaked around her.

But I'm looking for Mouse, she reminded herself. Must find Mouse! A shadow skittered across the track, four feet away.

You're not trying to save Mouse, Nina answered herself with icy clarity. You're trying to die too!

That possibility stopped her breath and the blood in her veins. If that were true, then she must, in truth, think Mouse was dead.

'No!' she moaned between clenched teeth. 'No, no, no!' 'Mouse!' she cried. '*Mouse!*' Her voice roused a sleeping gibbon who began to hoot the news of her presence. She called again and again, as she had after the bombing. Except that now she felt she was calling across a distance too vast to bridge with a human voice. She began, at last, to weep the tears for which she had so far denied the need. The gibbon faded into silence.

Finally, Nina eased out a last shuddering breath and stood. Her legs had cramped from squatting so long. She rubbed the backs of her thighs as she looked into the shifting, creaking darkness around her, suddenly afraid. She had revised her purpose.

If Mouse still lived, Nina would not save her by getting lost in the jungle, or stepping on a *krait* in the darkness. If Mouse had a chance to survive, Nina must survive. Limping, she started back north along the trail toward the hospital camp.

I must have proof before I give up, she thought. I won't accept it without proof! Until then, I stay alive and keep looking.

She marched unsteadily through rustling leaves, through clicks and screams and grunts and whistles, past moving shadows, watching eyes, and anti-personnel detection devices. She fell back into her hammock in the infirmary some time after 2 a.m.

7

Dan left early for the top fields on the morning after the bombing. Hue Hue followed him out of the tunnel where they had spent the night, but instead of lighting the brazier in their camp to heat water for tea as a wife should, she walked away from the tunnel into the scrub as she had done for the past ten days. Unhappily, Dan watched his young wife disappear from sight without looking at him or speaking. He knew where she was going. He had followed her for the first week after it had happened.

Hue Hue was kneeling at the edge of the fields, in front of the flatness, which had once been filled with wooden walls and a thatched roof. She stared straight ahead, hands lying loosely on her lap, at the corner of their former home where they had found the body of their three-month-old baby girl. She sat like that every day, not moving. Dan had watched her. She didn't cry, just sat. When it rained, she continued to sit, with water running down her face and hair and making small pools in her open hands. When the sun came out, she let it dry her as if she were a stone.

Dan had tried to make her eat or drink but she acted as if he weren't there. Then, in the late afternoon she would suddenly stand and return to their new home. She would collect firewood, cook his meal, throw the scraps to their pregnant sow, lie down to sleep, a little more silently than before the baby died but otherwise like herself. Then, the next morning she would go back to the ruins and take up her vigil again.

Dan's sister-in-law brought bits of meat and fish for Hue Hue to cook in the evening, and was tending their vegetable patch in place of Hue Hue, but everyone would be needed in two weeks for the rice transplanting. Dan's older brother had advised him to beat Hue Hue. Dan had followed her one day to the ruined house, intending to assert proper marital authority. But at the sight of her kneeling silent and still beside the stump of a broken banana tree, he had lost his resolve.

Dan ate two finger bananas instead of a bowl of rice and took his bird net with him to the fields. He thought for a moment, then picked up a large empty basket and a six-foot length of bamboo as well.

It was time to send to a larger village for a *tay phap*, he decided, as he climbed the gradually rising trail to the small field above their settlement where he grew corn. Hue Hue's spirit was disturbed. She seemed not to hear as well as before that bombing strike. Perhaps the baby's spirit had not been properly settled by the funeral and Hue Hue was listening to its cries. The *tay phap* would judge when he arrived.

He stopped at the top of the ridge and stared. The night's air strike had been even closer than he had thought, deep in his burrow in the ground. The jungle beyond his field had been cut down with a giant, fiery scythe. Jagged blackened spires of tree trunks clung to their fallen tops by shreds of fibre. Smaller trees at the edges of the main damage leaned against each other like a crowd of drunks, their shrivelled leaves dangling like lank hair.

They look like people, thought Dan. Their bark is pocked and shredded just like arms and legs hit by shrapnel fragments and cluster bombs.

Most of his field had been trampled by monstrous feet but it had been spared the scythe of fire. Dan let out his breath very slowly. Nearly half of his corn was spoiled, even if the field had not been burned. It was hard not to feel singled out for punishment.

He turned and looked back down toward their original settlement. His field was a half kilometre from the village. He could see the family graves clearly from here, on a high, open point where the land began to fall away downhill into the next valley. The nearest track from the North which the People's Army used was another 20 minutes fast walking, over two small ridges. Unless the men in the iron crows were very stupid, they would have known that the graves meant a village. They would have known that no village would lie on top of Uncle Ho's Trail. Or if it did, it would hide itself. It was easier to imagine malice than such stupidity. Glumly, he climbed the dirt terraces to inspect the damage to his corn more closely.

Suddenly, he saw the dull gleam of metal on the ground, under some fallen cornstalks. He tried to change the direction of his next stride and hopped sideways to avoid stepping on whatever it was. He bent and carefully lifted the corn aside. The object was a pineapple grenade. His body began an instinctive bolt backwards, but he stopped himself and reapproached the grenade cautiously. Even more cautiously, without breathing, he eased aside the grass which draped the top of the grenade. The pin was still in place.

Dan relaxed and picked it up. With his eyes now focussed to see them, he found six more grenades scattered through the ruined corn.

A strange crop, he said to himself. But it will help pay for the losses. He put all the grenades into the empty basket. Then he moved on into the tangled wreckage above his field. As he walked, he prodded delicately with the bamboo pole, lifting aside small branches with the tip. The pole hit something hard, hidden in a broken clumb of *lalang* grass. He slid the end of the pole gently back and forth across the surface of the hardness. The surface caught at the splinters in the bamboo.

Too rough, thought Dan. A rock, not an unexploded shell. He moved on, still prodding.

Though he himself had never been so lucky, other farmers in the area had found a dozen or more unexploded shells after air strikes, which they had sold to the local unit of Pathet Lao. A little extra money would help pay for the *tay phap*. Spiritual guidance didn't come cheap. Nor would a second wife to help him out if Hue Hue never got better.

By the time he had climbed the next ridge, skirting the worst of the nearest bomb damage, he had found only two more rocks. Then he nearly stepped on another grenade as he made a detour around the mass of a fallen treetop. No shells, but at least, he now had eight grenades. He laid the last carefully onto the clutch of lumpy eggs already in his basket, feeling a little puzzled. He had never heard of airplanes dropping grenades.

Then his pole hit something soft. Dan didn't want to look, but he did. It was only a gibbon, speared by the end of a broken branch. Then he saw a rubber sandal.

He refocussed his eyes yet again to look for what they did not expect to see. The grenades could mean that a travel party from the north had been hit. Such groups carried weapons of all kinds, to the soldiers fighting in the south. He looked back at the sandal. Perhaps they had cut a new trail through the jungle, closer to his village.

Reluctantly, he looked beyond the sandal for its owner, or parts of him, or her. To his relief, the litter on the ground was all vegetable matter. Then he looked up. A man lay draped across a tangled nest of branches, arms and legs dangling at strange angles from his joints. He wore boots and what looked like a uniform. Dan couldn't see the man's face, which stared up at the sky.

'Hey!' he called up. 'Brother!' The man must be astonished to be able to see so much of the sky from here, thought Dan inconsequentially.

The man didn't move. Dan wondered what to do next. Feeling silly, he asked, 'Are you alive?'

Still no answer. And not likely to be one, Dan told himself firmly. He started to try to climb up and realized that he would need help to get the body down. He wondered why the man's friends had left him behind. The villagers would bury him the best they could, but it was all most unsatisfactory. It was doubtless Dan's field that the spirit would haunt.

He shook the nearest branch but stopped immediately; the motion made the man look as if he were trying to wave to Dan, or to free himself. Dan stood staring up at the body, feeling as helpless as he did when watching Hue Hue kneeling before the ruined house. The patterns of his life were becoming harder and harder to understand. It was getting harder and harder to know how to behave. Feeling exhausted, he turned to go back to the village to fetch his brother and his brothers-in-law.

He found a second sandal hanging on a broken branch and tossed both into his basket with the grenades. He cheered up slightly when he next stumbled across an unbroken bundle of rice. The area would be worth a second search when he came back with the other men. He prodded with hope at a basket lodged in the base of a fractured stand of bamboo. The basket fell free and rolled heavily. The cloth around its contents seemed to heave and twitch. Dan felt himself go cold. The spirits had already begun to make mischief in this ill-fated place. He ran all the way back to the village.

When the four men returned, led by Dan, the bundle of cloth had rolled completely out of the basket. As Dan pointed it out, it acquired a lopsided peak, like a miniature mountain, then flattened again into its original grub-like shape. It rolled in a quarter turn toward them.

'There it is!' said Dan, with a dry tongue. 'That's what I saw!'

'Give me your pole,' said his older brother, Tai. Tai approached the bundle and prodded it lightly. It heaved and made an undefineable noise. Tai lifted the ends of the cloth aside with the tip of the pole. Then he dropped the pole altogether and bent to untangle the last wrappings.

'It's a baby,' he said. He lifted the cloth which served as a diaper and peered beneath. 'A girl.' He left the baby on the ground, stood up, turned to his younger brother, and grinned. 'Lucky you brought reinforcements!'

The baby cried faintly, once, then subsided.

Dan squatted beside the basket. 'What shall we do with her?'

'I don't need another mouth to feed,' said his brother. 'Where's this dead soldier of yours? Or is it a spirit . . . I'm confused now.' He grinned again and the two brothers-in-law joined him.

131

Dan ignored all of them. 'She's nearly dead. Look, she can hardly be bothered to cry.'

'We'll bury her then,' said his brother. 'What a lot of funerals! Let's see what else we can find to help pay for them.'

Dan searched the baby's basket for clues to its parents. She had been lying on an indigo cotton quilted jacket. The bottom of the basket had been torn away but the jacket was undamaged. Dan shook his head, thinking of the porcelain fish jar he had given Hue Hue for their wedding, which had survived, miraculously entire, unchipped, a few feet from where their daughter had been crushed to death.

He pulled off the sodden diaper and wrapped the baby in the quilted jacket. 'The dead soldier is up there,' he told the other men, pointing. Then he picked up the baby and ran back down the trail as fast as he had before. He passed through the new settlement to the ruins of the old one.

His wife was kneeling in her chosen place, back straight, her hands holding each other in her lap.

'Hue Hue,' he said urgently.

She ignored him, calm but distant.

'Hue Hue, look!'

She continued to contemplate the ruins of their house.

'Wife!' he ordered. 'Look what I have brought you!' He squatted in front of her, blocking her view of the ruins and held out the baby. 'She fell into our jungle with the bombs!'

The line of Hue Hue's gaze passed through her husband's face which had happened to interpose itself. Dan tried to lay his bundle on her lap but it rolled off. He pushed the baby back onto his wife's thighs and held it there with one hand. Up in the jungle, he had been certain he was doing the right thing, but now he wasn't so sure.

'Look!' he begged. 'Just look! The Heavens have sent us another child!' He lifted one of Hue Hue's limp hands with his own free hand and placed it on the child's bare body. She still did not look down.

Her fingertips moved slightly. Paused. Moved again. Hue Hue stiffened. Her eyes filled with terror. Dan felt her begin to shake. Gently at first. Then her body shook as if she were riding a runaway cart on a rutted track. She shook so hard that Dan could hear her teeth clattering together. He felt despair; he had only made her worse. The baby gave a faint cry of protest.

'She's hungry,' Dan whispered. 'Please . . . please, give her something to eat. You still have some left.' He pushed the baby up against his wife's body and pulled her other arm around to hold it. 'Try!' He waited.

Hue Hue continued to shake, staring straight ahead.

'Please, Wife. Hue Hue . . . please feed her.' He relaxed his hold on the baby tentatively. It did not fall. Though still trembling, Hue Hue was holding it. He lifted her hands so that the baby's head was near her breasts. He took his hands away and sat without breathing.

The baby knew where she was again. She turned her face toward Hue Hue and rooted in the fabric of the woman's blouse with her tiny nose and mouth. Weak with hunger, she knew what she needed.

Hue Hue looked down at last. 'It's not ours,' she said quietly to Dan, very gently, as if he might have been deceived and she was telling him disappointing news.

Dan's mouth was dry again. 'No,' he said. 'I know. But I think she must have fallen from the Heavens for me to find. There were many other things up there. . . .' He hesitated. 'But nothing else lived.'

The baby mewed with frustration at finding only a mouthful of blouse and kicked feebly. Her eyes fluttered open and glared up at Hue Hue.

'Feed her!' whispered Dan. 'Please feed her!'

Hue Hue looked down. 'She's angry,' said Hue Hue, as if observing from very far away. 'She's very, very angry.' She nodded. Her chest heaved. She drew a deep, rasping breath, then squeezed her eyes tightly closed against the tears which began to run down her face. Dan listened to the silence before her first sob. It came at last, then another, and another.

'She's so angry!' Hue Hue said between gasps. 'So angry! . . . Angry. Angry. Angry!' She rocked on her knees, repeating the word, clutching the baby to her.

Dan was afraid she would crush the child without realizing. The baby managed a scream at nearly full power. Hue Hue loosened her grip and looked down.

'Please, Hue Hue,' Dan whispered. 'Please!' Awkwardly, he un-buttoned the top of Hue Hue's blouse and pulled it away from her breast. 'Please!'

'Yes,' said Hue Hue to the baby. 'You're angry. I know . . . Oh, I know!' She shuddered as the child clamped onto her nipple. 'I know!'

As the baby nursed, Hue Hue continued to rock on her knees and cry, but more gently than before.

The doctor in the field hospital released Nina for work after four days.

'You're well now.'

Nina smiled and nodded obediently. If Mouse was dead, she would

133

never heal. But it served her purpose to carry rice again rather than to sit in a hammock in the infirmary slapping mosquitoes and flies, burning off the tiny black leeches and ticks, listening to rain on the thatch, and trying not to think. Her own need was as urgent as that of the People's Army.

Supplies were badly needed in the Parrot's Beak where the concentration of Viet Cong and North Vietnamese were gathering for a major assault on the south. Armies might stop fighting during the heaviest of the monsoon rains but they still had to eat.

As she carried her yoke and baskets in the following weeks, through mud often over her knees, Nina was obsessed. Her eyes constantly probed the thickets beside the trail. Whenever the porters rested, she searched. At night, she slipped away to retrace part of the day's route and hardly missed the sleep. In the occasional montagnard villages they passed, she leaned close to all babies to study their faces. She had nightmares that she stumbled across Mouse but did not recognize her. One evening, she sat for an hour watching another woman porter nurse her baby. The child was too old and large to be Mouse, but Nina kept her vigil until absolutely sure of its wide cheeks, low forehead and sad, sleepy eyes. She filled her time with searching to deny grief entry room.

She suspected she might be a little mad. Sometimes, as she hauled one foot after the other from the sucking mud and wiped the rainwater from her face, she imagined Mouse lying alive in her basket like a female Moses waiting for the Pharoah's daughter to find her among stalks of bamboo. She wrote and rewrote this story in her head. She tried to think how she could tell Will John about flying through the air and losing their child. Then tears and rain would run together down her face, while the earth pulled at her feet and an ulcer under her yoke ate at her collarbone. But she kept searching.

Looking back later, she could not put together a coherent picture of this time. She remembered a maze of trails. Blazes of hope, and disappointments. Faces of different guides. A kaleidoscope of officers. Certain porters, like Auntie Eel. Who died. The cold glow of fireflies smeared on the back ahead to keep her from wandering off the trail in the darkness. Small kindnesses. The sudden terror that the mud had no bottom and she would sink to the centre of the earth. Repeating Will John's telephone number again and again, even though he himself no longer seemed real. Exhaustion. Hunger. Maggots in her sores. Bombings. The emptiness as cold as metal. And searching.

She thought she remembered looking down one night on a river of headlamps as dense as the Saigon rush hour, flowing through the deserted jungle. Troop transports and tanks. Jeeps and gun carriages. But it seemed unlikely in this wilderness of muddy tracks and spider's silk bridges. She did remember riding at some point in the back of an open truck, with other porters. She could remember clearly the cascade of water trailing from its canvas roof, but its destination escaped her memory.

When did I form a rational purpose? she asked herself, later. Why didn't I do the easy thing and simply lie down beside the track to be shot?

This purpose had somehow arranged a second ride in a truck. And after a night bombing, when she allowed herself to become lost in the confusion, there had been yet another ride. Then a helicopter. These rides cost the rest of her rings, the pearl necklace, and one of the gold chains.

The rides were followed by six days of walking alone across the flatland, limping along dike walls toward the setting sun. On the second day, she hid from an armed patrol, until she saw that they carried guns with straight magazines and wore the uniforms of the Royal Lao Forces. She stole fruit from gardens and eggs from nests in the scrub. Four times, she was given rice and boiled vegetables by villagers. Once she was threatened away by an old man with a French carbine. She met others like herself, looking for a place to stop. Many times, she altered her direction because she thought she heard a baby crying in the scrub.

On the evening of the fifth day, she stumbled from the road and splashed across a *paddi* field to shelter in a bird watcher's hut. A man already lay just inside the door on a pile of rice straw.

'Do you mind if I share your house?' she asked politely.

He kept his face rudely averted. 'Buzz,' he said.

Nina leaned closer and retched. Flies were speaking for him. His lips were rimmed with their green, metallic sheen. The side of his skull wore a buzzing, shifting cap.

Nina retched again, her eyes on the improbable redness of the straw beneath him. Brighter than her rubies. Hot as chillis in a market. Too bright and hot!

She turned like a frightened deer and, motionless, felt through the space of the rice fields for the location of the gun which had so recently fired. Her eyes searched banana clumps, the rims of the dikes, another distant hut.

He's there! she thought. I am in his sights, now! I have stumbled into a brief pause in the killing.

She felt a cold terror, as if facing a demon of childhood fantasy. This moment is not my own. I don't belong here. It must not trap me!

Slowly, as if backing away from a tiger, she began to walk away along the dike-top path. This is not my correct death, she whispered to herself. Not correct. Not correct. She felt the heat of the gunman's eyes burning her across the openness of the *paddi* fields.

Another fresh body lay face down in the shallow pink water below her feet.

I do not see you, she told it. I am not here in your fate. Not here. Not here. The incantation shielded her back to the road. Many months later, she remembered that as the day she had decided to live.

That night, she lay against a crumbling wall under the fringe of burnt roof and watched the terrifying beauty of phosphorus flares light the earth and sky with unnatural clarity. She locked her scarred hands across her head to try to block out the sounds which followed, but the earth vibrated under her.

On the seventh day, she stood on a bluff looking across the smooth beige waters of the Mekong. On the far shore, about a kilometre and a half away, lay north-eastern Thailand. Across that endless water, another self – in which she no longer quite believed – had once arranged for a future.

In Bangkok, from his window in the Brighton Beach Guest House, which he preferred to the newer hotels, the man with the baby's mouth watched a dark blue American Chevrolet inch through the narrow, crowded street as slowly and painfully as an elephant down a snake's gullet. An old woman pushing a vendor's cart of brass and glass filled with coffee beans and watermelon slices on chipped ice, had blocked the way. Now, she stood staring over the car, waiting with infinite patience for the inconvenient object to evaporate.

The Thai driver swore and shouted. The white-skinned passenger in the back seat leaned forward, then rolled down his window and added his own shouts. The car rolled forward until its front bumper was nearly touching the brass and glass cart. But the old woman continued to stand, patiently. She seemed to be deaf, blind, and possessed of all the time in the world.

Heads appeared in windows, children danced in doorways. Someone shouted encouragement to the old woman and another voice yelled to the driver not to take any nonsense from anyone.

By now, the car's passenger was swearing at the driver for failing to remove the obstacle. The driver, caught between the two opposing forces, had begun to shake with rage and shame. The man in the window watched him now trying to persuade his passenger and superior of some other course than running the old woman down.

Then the car began to reverse. The children shrieked and the crowd cheered. The old woman waited until it had backed out of sight around the corner of the street. Then she began to push her cart again, slowly, without acknowledging the shouts from around her. She doesn't think the affair warrants a fuss, thought the man at the window. It had always been her street.

Both amused and thoughtful, he went back into the little room to continue writing the note interrupted by the first blatting of the car horn.

'Dear Will John,' he wrote. 'I checked with IDC here yet again. Nothing yet. Sorry. Who the hell *is* she?'

'No, no.' The boatman averted his eyes from Nina's gold bracelet and busied himself with lacing the tarpaulin roof of his launch. 'Too dangerous.' He laughed as if he had made a joke. 'Nobody takes boats across now. You stay here. Laos is very hospitable.' He smiled at no one in particular and began to whistle through his teeth. 'Not like Thai soldiers on the other side. They think everybody is Pathet Lao, coming over to blow up top secret American bases.'

'What about people who have to go across?' asked Nina desperately.

'The strong ones swim,' said the boatman. He threaded the rope through a grommet and bent double to pull it tight. 'Under the water,' he added. 'To avoid bullets.'

Nina looked out across the muddy, sliding beast of a river, a flat serpent twining between the sharp, protruding bones of the earth. It would eat her.

'Can you take your boat as far down as Vientiane?' she asked.

The boatman shot her a look. 'They have border checkpoints in Vientiane. You need papers. . . .' His trailing tone made clear just how likely he thought her possession of such things to be.

'But your boat can get down?' she repeated. 'No rapids?'

'The river is OK to Vientiane,' he agreed reluctantly.

'You're right,' she lied. 'I'd better stay on this side. Thank you for the good advice.'

She followed the riverside track downstream away from the village until it began to rise up onto the nose of a mountain range. She picked her way down from the track to a muddy limestone shelf above the grey water and considered the river's impossible breadth and speed. As the sun rose, she moved back into the shade of some tamarinds, where she sat, hardly moving for ten hours, staring at the river. She returned to the village, in the late afternoon, for food and a drink of water, then went back to the rock shelf to wait for darkness.

I'm not leaving you, Mouse, she assured her daughter from time to time. I swear I'll be back to find you. But a crazed rice porter, half-dead of exhaustion, will never find you. I must become myself again – whoever that may be – with my proper resources. And perhaps with the help of your father.

The reservoir of mobilizing power within her was shrinking hour by hour, the mud cracking around the edges. As she waited for the day to end, she could clearly imagine the moment when her courage would run dry, when all action would stop and she would suddenly freeze for eternity, with one foot suspended in the air, unable to replace it on the ground in the next step forward.

Not yet! she begged any listening deities. Please, not yet! Let me cross first! She hugged her knees and rocked slightly under the tamarinds to try to comfort herself. Mosquitoes bit her unnoticed.

The mountains of northeastern Thailand bit a first piece out of the setting sun, then swallowed the rest with surprising speed. Dusk tarnished the bright metallic glints of the river's surface. Then darkness erased the far shore. Nina sat rocking.

It must be done.

She rocked a little longer. Then, with decision, she stood up, tucked her *panung* up between her long, slim legs, and strode to the muddy edge. She stopped again for several minutes, feeling the warm water pull gently at her ankles.

This is nothing, she told herself. Compared to the last months, it is nothing.

The width of the river spread away from her. She felt as dizzy as when, as a child, she had lain looking up into the sky, trying to focus her eyes on infinity. She touched the small roll of possessions tied around her waist and began to wade slowly out through the sucking mud which had been dry land before the rains, and would become dry land again when the dry season returned.

She looked back at the lights of the village on the shore behind her, already small and distant on her right. The silhouette of a headland cut into the curve of river to her right. Ahead, lay nothing except a dull flat shimmer that blended gradually into the dark shadows of the Thai mountains.

The mud grew deeper. It sucked at her feet, then at her ankles and finally at her calves, while the warm muddy water climbed her legs. Small flies swarmed around her eyes and dived into her throat as her breathing deepened with effort.

138

Something alive wriggled from under her foot with horrid fluidity. A water snake? She staggered, splashed, then clutched for balance at the branch of a submerged, fallen tree. Filled with new terror, she froze to listen. The wet night air pressed down upon the surface of the river, filled with squawking night birds, humming insects, the syncopated plops of feeding fish, and a full chorus of frogs from treble to double bass. The only sound from the village was the faint thumping of a cleaver on a wooden block and the cadence of news on a transistor radio. Nina's splashes had not alerted a late night fisherman or patrolling village dog.

When the water reached the top of her thighs, she forced herself to tilt forward and began to swim into the darkness.

One stroke at a time, she told herself. It's possible.

The flies and mosquitoes followed her. She trod water to shake her head like a mountain pony, swallowed water, then plunged forward again, trying to stifle her choking and coughs. She could still hear the sounds from the village, across the water, distant but distinct.

The water was warm. An unseen shape brushed her legs. Her heart jolted and her breathing raced.

Just a fish. Only a fish!

The river grew faster; the village slid quickly out of sight behind the promontory which had been downstream from her lookout. Then she realized that she had turned into the current. The beast had taken her in its jaws. She fought to turn so that it pushed against her right side.

The moon began to flirt sullenly from behind dirty shreds of cloud, lighting the occasional flick of a bat or swift across the surface of the water. It was not strong enough to illuminate the far shore. Ahead, Nina could see only darkness. The dark beast beneath her pulled at her, inviting her downward, into depths as vast and dizzying as the sky.

Her arms began to ache and her legs felt heavy as logs. She swam and drifted while she gasped at the hot, damp air. Then she swam and drifted again. The moon suddenly sprang from behind its cover and lit the river like a phosphorous flare. Nina imagined eyes on the far shore picking out the dark spot of her head. Taking aim. She raised her head and allowed herself to look to see what distance she had left to cover.

She saw nothing, even in the sudden moonlight. There was no shore beyond the bright circle of river around her. Only the far distant bumps and peaks of the faint boundary between mountains and night sky. And though these had shifted upstream, they looked no closer than when she had set off.

You are swimming into nothing, she thought. You will swim forever, until the bottom reaches up and pulls you down. Terror suddenly caught up with her. The warm, tugging water had washed away the protecting numbness of the past weeks and months. The reservoir of her strength dried up. She stopped swimming, paralyzed. The beast would have her after all.

Then something hard on the surface grazed her shoulder and surged away downstream. She gasped in shock. Water burned into her lungs. Her body began to swim again. She struggled. Kicked. Splashed. She heard rapids downstream, though her brain tried to tell her that was impossible – all the rapids were upstream. There were none below her before Vientiane, fifty kilometres downstream. She heaved herself through the water to escape the dark beast that was pulling her down. Down stream over the rapids. Down to the bottom.

Her heart was trying to break her ribs from the inside. She rolled onto her back to try to rest. Then back onto her stomach. She counted strokes. One. Two. Three. Four. She floated again, than swam four more strokes. She floated and swam again.

Please! she begged. A village on the shore, a hut, a bicycle! Anything to make it real again. A sound. . . !

As if in answer, somewhere in the night sky with the now-exuberant moon, jet engines whined faintly and faded. A large fish jumped. The circles of his fall spread across her path. She saw herself framed by his rings, very small, very distant, splashing and gasping, breaking the moon's reflection, inching farther and farther out into endless darkness.

You're already dead, she thought. Look! There you are, a scrap of dead leaf on the water, among other dark scraps. The threads holding together your body and soul have finally broken. You are drifting apart.

The scrap of leaf kept swimming. Stubbornly, blindly, forever. Other dark scraps continued to float past.

Then she saw the light.

It was a hut, on a point in the shore which she had somehow reached without knowing it! Exultation flared in her. She put all her remaining strength into the next six strokes. Then she saw that the light was on the water, like herself, upstream and a little ahead of her. She drifted toward it, too exhausted for either wonder or despair.

As it drew closer, she saw a dark shape, like the one which had struck her shoulder, floating on the water and carrying a small flame. She lost momentum, sank, coughed, found the strength to strike out again. The flame was a candle protected by a wet glass chimney, sailing on a small woven bamboo raft about a metre square. She kicked twice more. Her fingers touched the bamboo of the *kratong*, a ceremonial raft large enough to carry only a candle and its glass armour.

She clutched the *kratong* with both hands, holding on against the pull of the bottom while her lungs battled for air. Her forehead dropped against the rough woven edge and her eyes squeezed tight with the effort to breathe. A little later, her brain began to make sense of what she had found. She remembered the rice straw in the bird watcher's hut. It was autumn. Time for the harvest festival.

Have I been lost for so long? she wondered. Has it been so long since I lost Mouse? Are the rains nearly over? Her grip slid on the wet bamboo. She clutched and splashed before she was safe again.

She opened her eyes and looked up at the sky. The moon was full. The scraps of cloud had gone. A full moon. She looked back in disbelief at the candle on the little raft. Somewhere there was still a world where festivals took place. Men and women still gave thanks to the River Goddess for her liquid bounty which let rice grow. Villagers along the river had launched flotillas of such lights, for the festival of *loy kratong*. One of their offerings to the River Goddess had come to meet her.

Nina gazed upriver. The surface was lit only by the moon. She remembered the hard shape which had grazed her earlier. Her *kratong* was the only survivor still en route for the sea. If it had survived the rapids below Chiang Khan, then the goddess's hand must be steering it personally.

You could do worse, she told herself. Her exhaustion was flooded with clarity and renewal of purpose. Though too small to carry her, the raft was large enough to trail her in its wake. Holding tight to the tiny lightship, she set off again for the faint line between the Thai mountains and the sky.

Suddenly, she found her arms tangled in water spinach, and her feet fumbling in mud. She lifted her eyes. Beyond the candle flame in its water-spotted glass chimney lay the solid darkness of real shadows. She swam a little farther, then tried to stand. There was no bottom, just soft, yielding mud like her nightmare on the trails. Then her foot touched rock. She swam three more strokes and stood on both feet, up to her breasts in water but on the other side, in Thailand.

She began to plunge toward the shore, which she now trusted to be there. She stopped. Lines on the water swirled out from the curve of the bank ahead. She turned downstream and guided the *kratong* back into the main current. It caught once on a submerged branch. She waded after it and set it free again, then watched it drift slowly away down stream. As distance dimmed its spark, she felt a pang of loss. Then she flung herself through the mud toward dry land where she fell into instant, dripping sleep without thought of snakes or any other danger.

141

8

Washington D.C. and Bangkok – 1967

Will John Haines had the cheerful but implacable curiosity of a four-year-old in the body of an elegant elkhound. He gave the world good reasons for why he did what he did, reasons like duty, patriotism or professional necessity, but the truth was that he had never lost the child's need to take apart, push open, question and dig, on the off chance that he might find The Answer, in whose existence he still believed at the age of forty-two.

He was intelligent enough to realize that for some people it might be better to leave well enough alone, keep their heads down and try to stay out of trouble. But he never felt that these limiting clichés applied to him. He understood that he was privileged. He was grateful that some good fairy who specialized in upper-middle-class families on the American East Coast had touched his pink forehead at birth and decreed not only long bones, red-gold hair, regular features, considerable brain power, and a natural ability to ride, sail and play basket ball, but had also granted him generally an easy ride in life. He never had to waste much energy on struggle. Such privilege left him free both to notice and to pursue his curiosity. It also gave him the unshaken self-confidence which only the unchallenged enjoy. As a result of this confidence – and a physical size which discouraged bullies – he was peaceable, kind, considerate and humorous.

Privilege did have some disadvantages. Particularly in his late teens and early twenties, he often felt guilty at his good luck in being dropped into that particular body in that particular family. He was aware that he had neither chosen nor fought for his good qualities and sometimes wondered what he would have been like if it had been left entirely to him, without help from the good fairy.

Also, being intelligent, he observed the state of the rest of the world and lived with a constant sense of being left out. He was happy enough to be spared the tragedies and life-altering accidents that he saw shaking and breaking other men, but nevertheless knew he was an outsider to the community of human suffering. He had a job which gave unbridled freedom to his desire to question and learn. Both of his parents were still happily alive in the big wooden shingled house on Narragansett Bay. His brother and sister were alive and reasonably content. The breakdown of his marriage had been his own fault and caused him more guilt over how he might have tried harder to connect with his wife than heart-break over the loss of the relationship.

Then he fell in love with Nina Martell, née Luoc.

A good friend, who was a poet forced by the economics of publishing to lecture on Victorian literature, told him that his obsession with her was nothing to do with love.

'She challenged your ego,' said the friend. 'She's the unattainable fulcrum on which you want to shift the world.'

Will John had laughed. He never felt threatened by criticism but always examined it for nuggets of possible truth. His friend was partly right. But he didn't want Nina only because, for once, life had tantalized him with something he couldn't have.

Their relationship reminded him of a visit he had made at the age of twenty-nine to the north island of New Zealand. During a tour of Maori country, as he was standing beside a steaming natural hot pond, the guide had told his group that the ground beneath their feet was only eighteen inches thick. Beneath that thin crust was the boiling centre of the earth. Will John had been torn between a craven desire to tiptoe away as fast as possible and the almost irresistible urge to stamp his foot. In the end, he had walked away casually, pretending that neither urge existed. Safely back in the Volkswagon mini-bus, he had been unaccountably ashamed and sworn never to let himself make that middle non-choice again. But of course, he had, again and again. Until Nina, when with exhilarating irresponsibility he finally stamped his foot.

And now you know, he would tell himself again and again, why everyone else keeps his head down, etcetera. Living creatures prefer to avoid pain.

His pain was complex. Sometimes he thought he hated her because he felt he had failed her. He sometimes hated her because she had lied to him and he had believed her, against his own better judgement, and therefore been a fool. He missed her so much sexually, all the time, that his over-educated sensibility could not find an unhackneyed, un-embarrassing way of expressing his agony. He missed the bizarre sense of kinship they had shared. Worst of all, he missed the amazing, open emotional self that he had been when he was with her.

Though finally shaken, the basic Will John had nevertheless

survived. Once he had delivered his written evidence and testified to the committee in Washington, he felt free, after a brief pause in neutral, to try to find her again. He did not know exactly what would happen then. But, after thinking it through, over and over for months, he knew that he would never resolve his pain without her help, one way or another. Whatever they might be in, they were in it together.

At the time that Nina was making her way from San Khom to Bangkok, across the flat dry lands of north-eastern Thailand, on foot, by brightly-painted local bus, and in the back of farm trucks, Will John was becoming frightened.

'I should have heard from her by now,' he told his poet friend. 'Something has happened to her.'

'Or she's changed her mind,' said the friend, who wanted to be left alone to develop an image which had come to him during coffee.

'Stick with it,' Will John wrote to the man with the baby's mouth, who was then in Vientiane. 'I'm grateful for all your efforts so far. I'll be out early next year, if my grant comes through. I'd be happy even for hints of where I might start looking.'

Being Will John, he was certain he would find her, or at worst learn what had happened to her.

The proprietor of the gold shop on the Yaowaraj Road had the slightly detached air of someone minding the shop temporarily as a favour to a friend. He leaned on his case of pagoda-shaped rings and turned Nina's last gold bracelet between his fingers. Then he looked pointedly at her black jacket, mended *panung*, scarred arms and dirty, broken nails. He laid the bracelet down on the glass counter top and seemed to dust off his fingertips without actually doing so. There were too many people like her in Bangkok these days.

'I don't handle this kind of thing,' he said in English.

Nina glanced down into the case at the harlequin rings set with a riot of zircons, ruby chips, amethysts and opals. 'Too expensive?' she asked, with understanding. 'What a shame! I have others I would like to sell too.'

Her English was better than his own. The proprietor reassessed the woman inside the beggar's garments. She had surprising authority for someone who looked like a street whore from the provinces. And she had once had earrings worth selling in those neat pierced earlobes of hers. 'Do you have a receipt of purchase?' he asked, his tone a touch less brutal.

'I am afraid, *monsieur*,' said Nina, with carefully gauged indignation, 'that in my rush, I forgot to bring any receipts from Vietnam.' She was too weary and unsure for this charade.

When Nina had first climbed down from the truck full of squealing, screaming pigs trussed in woven bamboo corsets, the westernized streets of Bangkok felt unreal after so many months in the jungle. The city's centre was the setting for the science fiction films of her childhood – a fantasy city of glass and steel built for an imaginary future. Except for a gigantic red Garuda bird spread-eagled in the sunlight high up on the concrete flank of one of the monster buildings, she would not have thought she was still in Asia.

Ground level was a little more recognizable but stunned her with noise and numbers. Cars and taxis, bonnets radiating heat waves, assaulted each other from assorted angles, horns blaring and drivers screaming obscenities as they wedged each other to a standstill. Motor bikes and bicycles caulked all gaps in the jams. The three-wheeled *tuk-tuk* cabs drove up onto the sidewalks, ploughing aside solid blocks of pedestrians.

I can't deal with this! Nina thought in panic, poised to flee. She inhaled gasoline fumes and steeled herself not to run from the sound of roaring engines. How can I walk through all that? And where do I walk? Her bank account might as well have been on Mars.

She searched dizzily for glimpses of the familiar among the shouldering crowds of office workers and the flashing signs that shrieked 'Pepsi', 'Kodak' and 'Mitsubishi'. With relief, her eyes found a crop-haired old woman balancing a yoke like the one she had carried, with live hens bound in feathery bouquets on either end.

Then she noticed an elderly *sam law* driver lounging in the passenger seat of his pedal cab, chewing betel. He was regarding with a disdain and disbelief which she recognized the mayhem in the street where he should have been plying his trade.

'Excuse me, Old Uncle,' she said to him, 'would you be kind enough to tell me where I might find a cheap place to lay my head and buy a little rice?'

The tired old eyes swivelled to her. 'Klong Tooey is best for cheap. Near the docks. Lots of ladies like you there.' He seemed to find her, unlike the street, all too believable.

Following his instructions, she asked along the plank walkways elevated above the river mud until she found the house perched like the rest on pillars above the water. It was shared by a group of women willing to let her sleep in an unoccupied corner of the small floor.

★

Nina slept for most of her first week in Bangkok. She would half-wake in a blissful fog, then remember. The cold, metallic emptiness would hollow her out to a chilled shell pretending to be alive. She would accept a little of the rice the women offered her, then fall asleep again, to fill the emptiness with dreams.

After a week, Nina's body had healed enough to refuse her easy refuge in sleep. She looked for ways to fill her time while her mind tried to heal as well.

The women were mainly from struggling farming families in the north or northeast, sent to the city to send money home. Four were prostitutes. They all 'washed plastic' – salvaged bright blue and orange plastic bags and opaque commercial wrappings from dumps and alleyways and washed them for resale.

Nina went to 'wash plastic' with two of the women, to earn enough *baht* to buy rice from a street vendor. She slept, wept a little, stared at nothing and waited to be reinhabited by the former self who could deal with Bangkok, a self who had lived in a large house in Saigon with servants, been driven everywhere she went, wore French and Italian clothes, opened bank accounts, loved both an American spy and a Vietnamese war lord, and run an opium empire. A self who might know what to do with a half-mad rice carrier who had borne and lost a daughter named Mouse.

On the jungle trails, pulling her legs through the mud and hallucinating from exhaustion, she had begun to fear that she was imagining the Nina who had transferred money from a bank in Saigon to a bank in Bangkok. She had wondered if need were inventing a Will John who had given her a telephone number in America to ring, who might or might not have already unravelled her future.

After two weeks in the slum of Klong Tooey, she knew that her former self would never come there. The rice-carrier had to visit the business woman's world if she wished to find her. So, Nina washed her hair in a canal and let it dry in the hot sun. She borrowed a black cotton jacket less torn than her own. She borrowed a needle and thread to mend the jagged rips in her *panung*. She took her last bracelet from its hiding place beside Will John's pale green jade monkey in the faded red-and-white checked cloth wrapped around her waist.

'Ah,' said the proprietor of the gold shop. 'I see. A refugee.' He picked up her bracelet again. It was twenty-four carat, and more finely wrought than the single bracelet displayed in his window as a come-on for his ruby chips and zircons.

146

'It's easy to find less reputable dealers.' Nina closed her eyes briefly and took a steadying breath. 'If one needs that kind.' She held out her hand to take back the bracelet.

'Two hundred *baht*,' he offered.

'I like your sense of humour,' she replied. Whose voice said that? she wondered.

He remained silent, awaiting her counter-offer.

She studied several price tickets through the glass counter top. Help me! she begged her other self. 'What's your mark-up?' she asked. 'That bracelet is worth at least a thousand five hundred.'

'Eight hundred,' he said glumly.

'Nine.'

'Eight twenty-five.'

'Seventy-five.' The man was a thief, but that seemed unimportant. In relation to her other losses, the money was nothing.

'Eight hundred and fifty.'

A small loss in a good cause. And she lacked the energy or will to battle further. 'Beggars can't choose,' she said tiredly.

In Pahurat market, she bought a straight black cotton skirt made in India, a sunny yellow silk blouse embroidered in Hong Kong, and a pair of low-heeled pumps from Korea. She changed clothes in an alleyway, then found a chipped full-length mirror beside a stall selling studded Levi-style jackets made in Pakistan and locally-made brown and green tiger-stripe camouflage uniforms.

She peered curiously at the shadow behind the hazy glass. She had not seen her own image for months, except the occasional fractured muddy ghost in a *paddi* or fish pond.

Who is that? she thought with shock. She leaned close to the glass to examine the alarming hollows, the new lines branded onto her face, the scars of infected leech and insect bites, of hunger and exhaustion. She looked into her own eyes and away again. Their expression frightened her.

She combed and pinned up her hair, which felt dry and rough. The clothes were already changing her, as she had hoped. Her body had begun to remember such pressures of waistband and shoe back, and these memories opened the way to others.

Who might she be now? Nina wondered, looking at the gaunt young woman who no longer looked like a rice-carrier. A typist? A salesgirl? Except for those enormous, bewildered eyes. She looked at the still infected sores on her thin arms. A refugee.

147

She remembered painting on the flawless face of a successful young business woman, the morning she left Saigon. She dropped her arms and continued to study the mirror. *After all that has happened, do you know where you're going any more than before?* she asked the stranger.

'Are you going to be all day?' The stall's proprietor, a youth in tight bell-bottomed jeans and platform shoes, swung the blank surfaces of his dark sunglasses in her direction like radar receivers. 'Or do you want to rent the mirror?'

The old woman's head, with hair dry and spikey as white grass, peered at Nina across a rack of striped jellabahs with tasselled hoods. One side of her face was grotesquely young, the skin drawn shiny tight. The other side was puckered into ridges like overtight satin. Her lashless eyes, behind sharp-edged rims of scar tissue, were grey and blankly friendly.

'Have you seen her?' she asked Nina across the rack in English.

Nina shook her head, smiling and distancing herself uneasily at the same time.

The old woman turned to a nearby stall holder. In her aging, sun-wrinkled hand, was a baby's feeding bottle, half-filled with milk.

Nina felt a premonitory chill. The stall holder shook her head in answer to the old woman's question. Nina and the stall holder watched the woman wander on with her question to another stall, and then another.

'Crazy,' the stall holder informed Nina cheerfully. 'English *farang*. Her baby was killed in last war, same time as she got burned. Walks around all the time, looking for baby. Always carries bottle, just in case she finds baby. How many years now? Crazy!' The woman shook her head reflectively and turned to a customer.

A coldness as deep and absolute as the nevermelting hoarfrost of the Arctic froze Nina in place, in the full mid-morning flame of the equatorial sun. She stood unmoving, watching the woman with the white grass hair as she asked and searched through Pahurat Market, carrying the bottle carefully filled with milk, just in case. Only when the woman had disappeared completely, could Nina remember what she had been about to do next.

The *Banque de l'Indochine et de Suez* was on the Wireless Road, not far from the American Embassy. Before she filled it out, Nina considered the oddity of the printed form she was given. She waited for a creature called an assistant manager. She answered three identifying questions, pre-set by that supposed self who had supposedly transferred funds there from the Saigon branch eight months earlier. She walked out of the bank with 2,000 *baht* – enough for a few days of food and a little rent for the corner of the house in Klong Tooey – and the beginnings of relief. The past Nina had been real after all, with a real life which had real consequences in the present. And she seemed able to come to the rice-carrier's aid.

On the street, Nina counted the money again, surreptitiously, alert for quick-fingered children.

Should I go back for more? she wondered. Then she walked on. She had rejoined this world enough to know that only fools carried large sums along the walkways of Klong Tooey. She could withdraw more when she had had time to think how best to use it. However unlikely it still seemed, she was edging back into a life where bank accounts, like baths and regular meals, were normal practice.

Now, she thought. Now comes the most frightening step. But she did not take it that day. She could not yet stretch so far. And there might be no ground onto which to step.

The next day, she walked past the public telephone in the Siam Center five times before she made herself pick up the receiver and dial 100. She gave the operator the number that Will John had burned into her memory the night before he disappeared from Saigon. With fatalistic calm, she listened to the dolphin clicks and whistles of the miles between them. The distance was too great; the call could not go through. He had given a false number. The tree she had flown into during the bombing strike had knocked the correct number from her head. He had never intended to speak to her again and the number was that of some drugs enforcement office.

'Hello?' The friendly American male voice spoke without identifying itself. 'Can I help you?'

'Could I please speak to Mr Will John Haines?' She waited to be told that she had the wrong number. That she had called a cinema in Hong Kong or a masseuse in Singapore.

'I'm afraid he's not here right now,' said the voice pleasantly. It paused. 'Who's calling, please?'

The receiver became slippery in her hand. He had given her the right number. She had remembered it accurately. The call had gone through, though to whom she did not know. Why did she think he still wanted her? Or would help her? What had he said to his committee in Washington?

She started to hang up in panic. Then told herself that the speaker was thousands of miles away. What harm could come of telling the friendly-sounding voice who she was?

'It's Nina Martell.' It felt strange to use that name again.

'Miss or Mrs?'

'Miss.'

The voice said nothing. After a moment, it asked, 'Do you want to leave a message for him, Miss Martell?'

'A message should reach me sooner or later,' Will John had said.

'Yes,' she said. 'I think so. . . .' *What have you done with my life . . . with our lives? You had a daughter, but she is gone. Help me!*

She no longer knew how to speak to him.

'What is your message please?' asked the voice, without a trace of impatience.

'Tell him I got out.' *He did make me promise to let him know, no matter what else,* she reminded herself. She imagined a reach for a pencil, or a whispered consultation. '. . . And that it took a little longer than I expected.'

'Where can he reach you?'

The question triggered panic again. Then she pulled herself together and said, 'I'm in Bangkok. He can't telephone me. I'll have to ring back.'

Again she imagined a pause for consultation. 'Give us a couple of days,' the voice said, more businesslike than before.

And just who is 'us'? wondered Nina. *Oh God, Will, why didn't we have more time at the end to tell each other the important things?*

'Why don't you ring back on . . . let's look at the time change . . . How about Thursday? About this same time?'

She nodded numbly, without speaking.

'Are you still there?' asked the voice.

She must have missed something it had said. 'Oh, yes,' she said quickly. 'Sorry. Thursday will be fine. I'll call. Goodbye.' She hung up and wiped her palms on her skirt. She walked as far as a teak bench outside a boutique selling northern hilltribe handicrafts before her knees gave way, weakened by the sudden renewal of hope.

Don't expect anything, she warned herself. *Wait, but don't hope.*

For the next two days, waiting for Thursday, she found it impossible to follow her own advice. She stayed away from Klong Tooey except to sleep. The rice-carrier was too strong there. She walked the streets of the old city, sat in the courtyards of the temple *wats*, and imagined those voices in America tracing Will John. Then she imagined them checking

150

her own file. Then she remembered her sense of absolute safety while lying in Will John's arms. She should never have let herself fall in love with a good man.

She had had the wit to be frightened of him from their very first meeting in Saigon eighteen months before. The tall, Yankee professor with the long straight nose, bright blue eyes and red-gold hair, on a research grant from some foundation whose name was never clear to her, had popped up with his notebook and camera everywhere she hadn't wanted him. She had seen him watching her at parties, in cafes, at the *Cercle Sportif*. She had felt his focus like the muzzle of a gun and his will power like the pull of gravity on a climber at a cliff edge.

'What do you want from me?' she had finally cried, over the din of voices at a reception for some new government minister or other. 'What do you *want*?'

He had merely smiled that confident smile which had so infuriated her. 'To talk,' he had said. 'Take it easy. I just want to talk to you.'

He was too tall, too good-looking, too assured, a man who had only to raise an eyebrow to get what he wanted. Well, he wasn't going to get her! Nina had glared up at him, speechless with anger at even his height, which forced her to crane her neck in order to meet his eyes.

'Take it easy?' she had repeated coldly.

How dare this American, who seemed to think he knew her, presume to tell her what she should do? How dare he say 'Take it easy' when yet another war – his country's war this time – was disrupting supply lines from the northern poppy fields? When Thu was openly cheating her and thereby advertising her vulnerability to her enemies? When that cousin, so-called partner, and lover had decided, even so, to carry her off to the mountains of northern Laos where they could grow opium poppies in cozy togetherness? When her family's main business, once franchised by the French government, was now illegal *and* attracting the attention of the American Mafia? When she no longer had the stomach for that business? When she felt exhausted, drained of power, drowned in a new sense of helplessness, terrified that she had lost both purpose and the will to fight?

'Do you know anything about "hard"?' she had demanded.

'No,' he had replied seriously, 'and it makes me nervous.' Then he had laughed into her eyes again. 'Why don't you let me practise on you? Come have dinner with me.'

'You make it sound like penance.'

' "I serve here voluntary." '

151

To her amazement, she had accepted. Even more to her amazement, she had let him reach for her and comfort her. He made her laugh. He listened carefully to what she said and heard her desires before she spoke them. He washed her, fed her and made love to her whenever they could snatch an opportunity. For the first time since she was six, Nina had begun to let another person take care of her. She had burrowed into her first sense of safety since her family's house had been bombed in 1955, after Dien Bien Phu. Seduced by the illusion that life could be easeful, she had too easily found herself lying, concealing the truth about herself and her business in order not to drive him away in horror.

Just one more day . . . one more week of respite, she would say to herself. I know it can't last, but, please God, give me just a little longer!

Once, when they were lying naked together in her big bed during the afternoon siesta, a random grenade had exploded in the street at the back of her compound. It was a relatively small explosion, but Nina sat up, rigid and wide-eyed.

The next one would be closer. Then would come the earthquake. The smell of burning. The fragments of wood and flesh.

They heard a faint popping shot, and another. Then a siren.

'No!' Nina cried. 'No! No! No!' She began to shake.

Will John wrapped himself around her like a child's blanket. They listened.

'I think that's it,' he said. 'All over, whatever it was. Everything's OK. It's over.' He stroked her arms, her neck, her back as if soothing a frightened cat. 'Saigon's secure. Nothing's going to harm us.'

'Not you,' Nina said. 'You don't deserve it!'

The siren sounded again and receded.

Nina snatched up her blue silk kimono and ran out onto the balcony of her bedroom.

The street beyond her compound wall was quiet again. No fire. No black columns of smoke above the lime trees that quivered in a faint, hot breeze. In her garden, a gold carp sucked a dimple in the surface of the lily pool. She went back to the bed, needing to explain to him. Wanting to explain what she knew was going to happen, each time she heard an explosion.

'Our . . . my father's . . . big house burned down . . . bombed while I was asleep.' Her eyes looked darkly back at the thing she was trying, so inadequately, to describe. 'To the ground . . .' She gave a disparaging, apologetic, mirthless little laugh at the gap between the words and

152

the memory. 'I always thought that was a figure of speech until I saw it the next day. There was nothing . . . part of the staircase . . . a piece of the piano on two legs, like the haunches of a water buffalo trying to get up with its head blown off.'

Will John pulled her gently down beside him. With his long, healthily-nailed forefinger, he traced the pale blue and cream petals of an embroidered chrysanthemum which lay across her thigh.

'The staircase,' she said into his shoulder, 'had led up to my room. . . .'

'Come with me to America,' he said. 'I want to take you out of this mess.'

Nina went very still. She suddenly wanted to cry.

Life without sandbags. Without explosions, and wire mesh across windows. Life in a white-painted wooden house on green grass, across the street from a white-painted wooden church. Life where children played with dogs, rode ponies and built sandcastles on unmined beaches. She couldn't imagine it. Her earliest memories included the sound of the Allies bombing Japanese planes at Saigon Airport. And Will John could not possibly know how great her 'mess' was.

She shook her head fiercely. 'This "mess" is my country!' She stood up and moved to the balcony door again. 'Anyway, you're married.'

'My marriage is finished,' Will John said. 'I spend too much time abroad. Divorce wouldn't be your fault, just mine . . . and hers. You don't have to worry about that. Please come with me!' He sounded slightly astonished at his own words.

'Life isn't so simple,' said Nina. 'You may be smarter, but I know more.'

'I know enough. Trust me.'

She turned and tried to read from his blue eyes whether he could really know and mean 'enough'.

'I trust you more than anyone I've known,' she said. But not enough to tell you the whole truth.

'Will you come?'

'No.'

'Don't you want to?'

'Oh, yes!'

'Then why not?'

She shook her head again, angry at herself for even imagining it might be possible.

He had asked again the following day.

153

She looked at his long limbs spread naked across her bed under the cloud of pink mosquito netting and leaned over him to press her bare breasts and belly against his warmth. Then she pulled away and sat on the edge of the bed.

'Why the hell did you ever come to Saigon? Why didn't you leave me alone? I was fine before! I knew where I was.'

'I'm not sure what you're talking about,' he said. 'But no one has that much power to change another person.' He stretched out a long arm and stroked the soft inside of her elbow. 'You only noticed me because I was already relevant.'

She turned startled eyes back to his face. I think he's right! she thought.

Then Will John had disappeared on one of his field trips to a village north-west of Saigon. While he was away, Nina had stood back from her life. With undefined purpose, she sold her two legitimate hotels, and four go-downs along the Arroyo Chinois, which had been rented to Chinese rice merchants. She put the money in an account in Bangkok. She invited tenders for the transport company she had built up herself. She moved money from Saigon to family accounts in Hong Kong. She told herself that she was merely occupying herself with her usual business. Then she began to suspect that Will John had made her pregnant.

'About America. . . ,' she began one night four weeks later, when Will John had returned to Saigon. Her voice revealed more than she had intended. He had raised his head abruptly from the notes he was making from a stack of tapes.

She was terrified by the joy on his face, and by the joy it made her feel. 'We'll see . . . it's complicated. . . .' She shook her head and fled onto the verandah.

But three days later, she agreed to meet an Italian-American from Tampa, Florida, who was interested in the sampan fleet that ferried her opium, and in the confectionery factory where the crude opium was transformed to opium base.

On the second of July, 1965, twenty-four hours after her pregnancy had been confirmed, and four hours before Nina planned to tell him he was to be a father, Will John had tagged along with the man from Tampa, Florida who had agreed to buy Nina's family's place in the Saigon opium trade. Will John had lied to her as much as she had lied to him.

154

Two terrible days later, on the Fourth of July, they had been invited to the same American barbecue. Nina had gone because any distraction seemed better than raging alone in the bedroom of her big house with the door locked against her curious servants.

The first firework had shattered the dust with a three-stage flare – red, white and blue. The crowd in the compound of the big house in the American quarter of Saigon cried, 'Ooooh, oooh, oooh!' as their faces changed from red to white to blue like the sky. Nina saw Will John's face changing colour across the lawn at the same time that he saw her.

The enemy! Just as her cousin Thu had once warned her.

She fled through the smoke of barbecuing chickens and the clinking of glasses to her car, which was parked in the street outside the attaché's compound.

'Take me home!' she told her driver, Tiny Albert. She braced herself for the next explosion. Only fireworks! she tried to assure herself. It's only fireworks! She clasped her hands together to steady them.

'Go now! You're too slow!' she cried.

Tiny Albert carefully folded his racing news and turned the key in the ignition.

The sudden bang shook the evening sky like a piece of rag. Nina quivered; a child behind the wall began to scream with terror. Will John pulled open the car door and dropped into the shadows of the back seat beside her. The smell of black powder and burnt paper followed him.

'Go away!' she cried. 'Please,' she added more quietly, for the benefit of Tiny Albert.

Will John slammed the door, enclosing them in the small private world. 'Sorry to chase you out here, but we have to try to talk! They want me back in Washington.' He spoke English; like many Vietnamese, Tiny Albert spoke fluent French.

An elephant stepped onto Nina's chest.

'I fly home tomorrow,' said Will John. His mouth was dry.

'Tomorrow?' When she managed to speak under the weight of the elephant, her voice was brittle. They had no time to put things right! Even in the awfulness of the last two days, she had secretly believed they would eventually put things right.

'Shall I go, Madame?' asked Tiny Albert.

'Not yet,' Nina said. 'Mr Haines is staying here.'

Tiny Albert turned off the ignition and reopened his racing news.

The car filled with silence. Nina and Will John both stared at their laps. Then, to be done with it, she flung at Will John the question which had kept her awake for the last two nights.

'Have you decided yet what you are going to say about me . . . when you report back to your special committee who want you back in Washington so suddenly?'

Will John crossed his long elegant legs away from her, and Nina's terror seized on this small move as proof of intended betrayal. The sudden shivering light of a Golden Spider silhouetted his large, long head. As it died, he faded in the dusk to a half-developed photograph. Nina watched, helplessly.

She knew every inch of him like a catechism – by sight, by touch, by taste and by smell. She looked away, out of her window into the street, and swallowed. Only two and a half feet away, he was as unreachable now as an object behind glass. A bright white flash in the evening sky suddenly lit up the car. Nina turned her eyes back to him, pleading.

'Will, what are you going to say about me, when you get back?'

The bang which followed the flash was damp and muffled.

He raised his hands as if warding off her question. 'I don't know.'

'Will. . . !'

He looked at the top of Tiny Albert's head bent studiously over the paper in the front seat. 'I really don't know! The whole American involvement has turned out to be so much bigger than anyone expected. I don't know how hard the Bureau is going to push for prosecutions. Or how many.' He exhaled a shaky breath.

She couldn't think of anything to say.

'Why the hell didn't you tell me sooner?'

She was shocked by the ferocity of his tone. 'You know why,' she said softly.

'I wasn't investigating you,' he said. 'I swear! If only you had told me, and told me that you were pulling out, I might have been able to protect you!'

'And risk losing you?' she shot back. 'Forget about your professional problems . . . speak personally. Would your all-embracing tolerance have stretched so far?'

He shook his head in despair. 'I know they'll ask me for a list of the contacts of that quartermaster, Clinton Clay. They may ask me pointblank whom Falacci was meeting the other night when I tagged along!'

'Won't it count for anything that I'm pulling out?'

He looked at her with what she thought was pity while a series of small explosions crackled beyond the wall of the attaché's compound. 'I

156

wish I could explain to you the American need for black and white,' he said. 'My countrymen have a low tolerance for ambiguity. They'll know what to do with Clay. And I'm terrified they'll cram you into the same pigeonhole.'

'I don't understand.' Her gold bracelets tinkled incongruously as she leaned toward him, both fists braced against the grey leather upholstery. 'What's so complicated about a change of heart? I thought that you Americans were a deeply moral people. I've made a moral choice!'

'Oh, Nina!' he said despairingly. 'Nina . . . Nina! Moral people are terrified by real moral sacrifice – I've observed three generations of them in my own family.' He leaned closer in his turn. 'They're scared witless of people who sacrifice real things, like money or power . . . on principle. It puts them on the spot, you see. So they find it easier to cry "scoundrel and hypocrite" than to believe.' They tried to read each other's eyes in the dusk.

Nina leaned back abruptly. 'Why didn't you tell *me* who you really are?' she demanded.

'I suppose I thought it was obvious,' he replied. 'The way I talked about the foundation . . . the amount of time I spent among the hill tribes even in the midst of hostilities . . . my scrutiny of their economy. Surely you guessed that I was as interested in their opium as their oral tradition!'

A low light now flickered silently behind the wall, throwing him into silhouette again.

'I didn't guess,' she said bitterly. 'I wanted to blind myself as much as you did. And to be fair, you did warn me not to make up a false Will John. Too good, too moral, too straight to be trusted with reality . . . a wonderful, if temporary, refuge.'

Irrationally, she prayed for him to contradict her, but he didn't. The light behind the wall died; the car was nearly dark. In the front seat, Tiny Albert still pretended to read his paper.

'How ironic,' said Nina, 'that I might have told my truth if I had known yours!'

'Do you hate me for deceiving you?' Will John asked.

'Why on earth should I? It makes you more like me.'

He made a noise in his throat which wasn't quite a laugh.

Nina watched his long fingers rub themselves back and forth along the shadows of his crossed shin.

'I'm afraid . . .' Will John said finally, '. . . desperately afraid for one of the few times in my life. I'm afraid of you, because you know

157

things I don't, and don't want to know, and wish you didn't know them either. Afraid for you, because. . . .' His voice thickened. 'Afraid for us.' He fell silent.

'Please fight!' she begged. 'Please fight when we both know it's over and you're leaving me alone forever, tomorrow! Don't keep pretending to be nice. Most men I know would pick a fight to make it easier to leave!'

'I don't want it to be easier,' he said. 'A terrible thing is happening to us. I want to feel it as the catastrophe it is.'

They looked at each other.

'Can't you lie?' she whispered. 'For me?'

'It's too late,' he said despairingly. 'Oh God, I wish I could! I would, but I can't. I'm afraid to lie. I don't think I'm clever enough to get away with it . . . not under oath. Not even when I want to! It's like being a virgin. I don't know if I have the expertise.' He turned his head away and looked out into the darkened street. 'I'd lie myself blue in the face if I thought I could undo the damage that's already been done. And that's quite an admission for a Calvinist Yankee to make.'

There was another silence.

'It seems clear enough to me,' she said at last. 'You cowboy, me Indian, as your American soldiers would say.'

'It's not like that!'

'Dress it up as you like, but it *is* like that!'

'Nina, have mercy!' he said. 'I'm out of my depth. I'm not a trained agent. Just one of thousands of tame information collectors chewing away at the world like termites . . . nibble, nibble, nibble, for whoever's interested at any particular time. Note it, file it, send it in. I have no power! I'm nobody! And the way intelligence collection is going, I'm nearly obsolete as well!'

'Information is power!' she said. 'You're pretending to be naive!'

'All right!' he said. 'But my life and my information have never conflicted before. Not like this!'

'Do you mean you keep separate consciences the way you keep a wife in America and a mistress in Vietnam?' If he wouldn't fight, she would have to. Without the clean-slicing knife edge of rage, she would not survive the rending. 'Tell me your secret!' she demanded. 'I never managed to keep my life separate from what I knew! That's why I am changing my life! With or without your help!'

If I tell him about the child, she thought desperately, he might try harder. . . . He might risk. . . . She stared out of her window and blinked. She would not let herself use tears against him either.

158

'Nina, please. . . !'

'Just please take your fear and your love, and any other emotion you've been trying out over here like funny clothes and . . . *va t'en foutre!*'

In the front seat, Tiny Albert's ears seemed to flare with interest when she dropped into French. He turned the page of his paper in near darkness.

Will John drew a deep steadying breath, exhaled and wiped his palms along his shins. 'My darling, this is crazy,' he said quietly. 'This isn't a real fight, it's panic. We've run out of time and can't handle it. Wasting the little time we do have. I haven't even said what I followed you to say.'

'I have the impression you've just said several things,' said Nina.

'I want you to listen for a minute.'

'I think you should get out of my car.'

'Listen to me!'

'Please!'

'Listen to me!' he ordered, leaning close across the grey leather upholstery. He captured her right fist in his hand.

She looked away. If she had to carry on without him, she needed to clutch to herself his former golden confidence, the belief that all can be made well. Not this pleading. Not this uncertainty and fear.

I've unravelled my world here, she thought. What have I done?

'Listen!' he repeated. 'We will be together, I swear! I'll make it happen! With luck, the drug issue will die down in time. New problems always shove out the old. I'll make it work! Now, please memorize this number.' He repeated it twice. 'It's my own emergency contact number. Call when you're clear on this end. And be patient. A message will reach me sooner or later. Now repeat it back to me!'

'What's the point?' Nina asked, 'Why know how to call your name if you won't throw me a rope?'

'This is the only rope I have right now,' he said sharply. 'Memorize it!' He repeated the number a third time.

She kept her lips closed, but the digits were nevertheless printed on her memory.

'We must salvage our trust,' he said. 'It's our only hope.' His other hand made a *kamikaze* dive for hers. 'I've always had trouble with flowery speeches. . . .' He hesitated. 'Even *in extremis* . . . particularly then. . . .'

'Try,' she said. 'If a speech is all I'm going to get.'

His hands tightened. 'You feel like another self . . . I can't explain. . . .'

159

She nodded, unable to speak. Unlikely as it seemed, particularly in the circumstances, she felt it too. 'I don't really want you to lie under oath,' she said. 'Not really. I'm sorry to have put you. . . .'

'Don't,' he said.

They sat silently for a few minutes. Nina swallowed against a sharp rock in her throat.

'I should go,' Will John said, shaking his head in unconscious denial of his own words. 'You shouldn't be seen with me.'

'Or vice versa, as you so sweetly didn't say.'

'I fly in the morning . . . did I tell you?'

'Please have a safe flight.'

They exchanged quick shadowy smiles at this absurd turn in the conversation. Their faces were close together.

Oh God!' he said. He opened her hand and buried his mouth in her palm as if he were trying to hide there. Without looking at her again, he placed her hand back in her lap, and reached for the door handle. 'Call me!' he said. 'Please!'

The car shifted on its springs, the door slammed, and he was gone. She had sold the rest of her life. She had nothing left except his child.

'We must salvage our trust,' he had said that night in Saigon. Now she had called his name and was about to learn whether or not he had been able to throw her a rope.

When Thursday finally came, she called the number again from the Liberty Hotel. She chose it for its name, and the tourist-filled anonymity of its shopping arcade.

'Oh yes,' said a different but equally friendly male voice. 'We got your message for Mr Haines. Unfortunately, he's out of the country right now.'

'I see,' said Nina. No rope. Hang up now!

'What did you say?'

She swallowed. 'I said, I see.' Her voice was hoarse. 'Do you know where he is?'

'I can't tell you that. But there is a message for you. . . .'

Her ears filled with the rushing of blood.

'Can you hear me?' asked the voice.

'Yes, yes,' she assured it. Had the voice said the message was from Will John?

'You're in Bangkok, right?'

'Yes.'

'Can you please go to the American Embassy on the Wireless Road and ask for the IDC representative?'

'IDC?'

'Interagency Defector Committee.'

After a beat of silence, she said, 'I'm not a defector.'

'Of course not,' said the voice. 'But it's a convenient contact.'

When Nina remained silent again, the voice continued, 'Ask for a man called Paul Karelian. He'll sort you out.'

'All right,' she said slowly. 'I'll do that then.' Perhaps.

She hung up. No mention of Will John.

'I don't know what this means,' she said aloud without realizing. 'I don't know the risks.'

A pair of elderly Englishmen strolling past, in matching taupe bush jackets and cotton caps, glanced at her in alarm.

She looked back, without seeing them.

Life was so unclear. She stared into a shop window full of the dark blank eyes of sunglasses, filled with nostalgia at twenty-seven for the clear purpose of nineteen.

Why would I go to the IDC?

After a long time by the window, she had two answers for herself: to try still to contact Will John, and to finish what she had started in Saigon when she sold out.

And what might the IDC do to me?

This was harder. They might help her. They might arrest her. She had no way of knowing which.

I'll go, she decided. The rice-carrier had nothing to lose. The young, former business woman might, just possibly might, gain everything.

But before she entered that world, she needed time to reassemble a little more of her former self, the one who was at home in shopping arcades and art galleries. Who wasn't cowed by eighteen-year-old corporals, didn't automatically shake every item of clothing free of vermin before putting it on, or start to fling herself to the ground when a car engine backfired. The one who didn't search the faces of children in the streets and turn to ice at the sight of a crazy *farang* with grassy white hair and a baby's bottle, carried just in case. The one who hadn't needed anyone.

I'll give myself a day or two, she decided, before I contact this Paul Karelian who is going to sort me out.

9

Vietnam and Laos – 1967

Bill McNeill believed that you could talk your way out of trouble, or you could fight your way out. It had never occurred to him that you might ever not be in trouble. His own choice had always seemed clear. In the streets of East Chicago, if you were six feet, two inches tall and worked out four times a week in the YMCA gym, you didn't waste energy talking.

When America got into trouble in Southeast Asia, Bill McNeill, two years out of high school, had gone out there to show the US Army how to cut the crap and win. He also wanted off the East Chicago car-assembly lines.

'That wasn't living! I might as well of shot myself right there,' he said shortly after his arrival in Danang to another fucking new guy who couldn't believe McNeill had volunteered. 'But I'm too lazy. I'll let some little dink do it for me.' He had grinned and swaggered away.

Instead, over the next three months, the uncooperative little dink shot his friend Tony. Then Tony Two, Bob, and Guru George. Four months later, after the helicopter just ahead of his was brought down by small arms fire, killing the pilot, co-pilot, navigator, their rear-door gunner, and four more friends, McNeill promoted the little dink to the status of serious enemy. He also eased up on making friends, as they tended to get wasted.

After becoming squad leader, due to sudden vacancy of the post, and playing hide and seek with a unit of VC for two weeks during which fifty per cent of the men were picked off by snipers or maimed by mines, McNeill was very angry at the VC and a little less certain about showing the US Army how to win.

After being sent out yet again, against his objections, to chase the same VC unit, and losing two men to the friendly air cover sent in to bail them out, McNeill also became angry at the US Army. One of the few maxims he had accepted from his devoutly Catholic father was that if a thing was worth doing, it was worth doing well. He began a list of officers he'd like to make write that out a thousand times then eat the paper, after wiping their asses with it.

The Army, on the other hand, liked Bill McNeill. He did what he was told, and did it well. Said little. Was reliable. Had initiative, but not too much. His application for transfer from the Infantry to Special Forces was approved. He didn't tell them that he just wanted to try to learn what the hell was really going on in Vietnam and had decided that the Infantry would be the last to know.

The grey-green sponge of the treetops suddenly melted into swaying, bowing wands. A mini-tornado made them do-si-do as the unmarked helicopter lowered itself toward the hilltop.

'Move it! Move it! Move it!' McNeill bellowed into the storm of swirling grass and flying dust and twigs.

Injured on. Waste of time. Poor bastard would never make it. Fire from the left. A carbine . . . a fucking carbine! McNeill swivelled his gun and let off a volley. Take it up! For fuck's sake, take it UP!

'Where have all the flowers gone?' bellowed McNeill, inaudible in the clatter of the rotors. 'Loooooong tiiiiime passsssing!' He waved to the white men in black pyjamas on the ground, then fired a long blast at the position of the carbine.

TAKE IT UP! I still got a job to do. I'm not going to die on the wrong side of the border rescuing a dead man!

Bangkok – 1967

At first, two days later at the American Embassy on the Wireless Road, Paul Karelian made Nina feel like Cinderella turned up unexpectedly to try on the glass slipper.

'I don't know Haines myself,' he said cheerfully, after signing her in and waiting while she was briefly searched. 'But he's in Bangkok now and again. A good friend of mine is a friend of his.' He gave her a clip-on pass and led her down a grey-walled, vinyl-tiled corridor.

I used to find places like this familiar, thought Nina in wonder. They turned a corner.

'Would you like Green Spot or a Coke?' Karelian paused by the huge cooler in the corridor, head tilted in question, hand poised by the frosted door. He was an inch shorter than Nina, dark, quick and jerky in movement like a bantam cockerel. His eyes assessed the black cotton skirt, yellow silk blouse and her face.

What was the right answer in this world? Not the native orangeade, she decided. 'A Coke, please.' Choose American.

Without missing a beat, Karelian opened the glass door, extracted

163

two green glass bottles, and prised off their tops in the set-in opener. Then he tacked across the corridor, shouldered open a door and held it open with his elbow to usher her in.

She felt his eyes on her as she looked around his office, remembering with sudden vividness her own office on Don Due Street in Saigon. But when she turned, he smiled and trotted to the desk. He put down both bottles of Coke, gestured toward a chair, and adjusted the slats of the wooden venetian blind behind the desk so the afternoon sun wouldn't glare into her face.

Nina sat carefully on the chair. She had not sat on one for more than a year.

'Well now,' Karelian said expansively. 'Let's just establish who you are.' He opened a file on his desk with shiny, new covers.

Nina could not read the various lines of print on the front cover. An invisible band was tight around her chest. The artificially chilled air hurt her lungs. 'Nina Martell,' she said for the second time. 'When can you put me in touch with Mr Haines?'

In the fairy tale, there were two doors, she thought. Behind one was the princess, behind the other a tiger.

'Any supporting documents? Passport? Letters addressed to you?'

She shook her head. 'In the circumstances. . . .' She had no idea where to begin. 'All lost,' she said. No passport, no visa for Thailand, no legal existence.

'That's too bad.' The bantam cock had its head on one side, deciding just what kind of insect was lying there in the dust.

'But you know who I am,' she said.

'I know who you say you are.'

'I'm afraid that's the best I can offer,' she said tightly. It had taken her two days to locate a self strong enough to risk being 'sorted out' by someone at the IDC. 'If it's any help, I was née Luoc and my Vietnamese given names are Le Thuyet. And when I was a baby, my *ayah* also gave me the nickname Little Rat to protect me from abduction by covetous spirits. . . .'

The way I called my daughter Mouse, to disguise the power of that tiny lioness. . . .

'Take it easy!' he said. 'Just tell me your last address in Saigon.'

She told him.

'Can you describe the house?'

She looked at him for a moment, then drew in a deep breath and began to describe the home she would never see again. She would prefer to discuss the opium trade. That had to be why she had been told to come here.

'Can you describe your bed?'

'My bed!' She leaned forward, incredulous. She felt heat rising up from her collar bone, anger and embarrassment together.

Karelian waited, ballpoint poised.

Nina saw a warm, private tangle of naked limbs – her own and Will John's – beneath the sheltering tent of mosquito netting. She remembered feeling safe, for the first time in years, inside the little world of that carved and gilded relic of a long-closed *Binh Xuyen* brothel. Now Karelian's sharp little bantam rooster eyes seemed to peer into that private safety.

'The one in your bedroom,' prompted Karelian. 'The one you slept in.'

'What do you want?' she demanded.

'Right this minute, to establish who you are.' His voice was patient.

Oh Will, she begged him. I hope you thought this would avoid other questions! Or were you enough in control even to think?

'A four-poster,' she said, looking directly at Karelian. 'Wood and gilt. Supported by carved caryatids, bare-breasted and holding garlands of flowers. The caryatids were once gilded but the gold-leaf had been worn off their breasts. It came from one to the *Binh Xuyen* brothels that Diem closed in the late 50's. Canopy, *eau de nil* green, and the mosquito netting. . . .'

'OK, OK!' said Karelian. 'That's fine!' He scribbled in the file. Then looked up and grinned. 'A brothel bed, hey? How well did you know Haines?'

The heat rose from her collar bone again, more rage than embarrassment this time. 'Just socially,' she offered through stiff lips.

Karelian nodded agreeably. 'He gives the impression it was a little more than that.'

'How much more?'

Karelian glanced down at the file, not long enough to read but long enough to let her know that there were things to be read. 'He thought a lot of you, Nina . . . had a lot to say in your defence.'

So, now she knew – Paul Karelian's IDC door hid the tiger, not the prince. Nina stared at him, trying to remember how to deal with the tigers in this world. 'Why was I asked to come here?'

'Haines seemed to think us meeting you could be helpful.'

'Helpful to you or to me?' asked Nina. Had Will John merely lacked the expertise after all, or was he final proof that she could trust no one in this world?

'Both!' said Karelian triumphantly, as if a prize pupil had just asked the right question. 'Helpful all around.'

'I want to speak to Mr Haines,' said Nina. I have to know what he intended for me!

'He's not in the country,' said Karelian. 'In fact, he's nothing to do with us anymore.'

Or with me, thought Nina dully. Is that the truth I have to accept? 'Who is he to do with?' she asked. Of course, she thought bitterly, he wouldn't have anything more to do with someone he had betrayed!

'Who knows?' said Karelian. 'Could be anybody these days. Anyway, I'm afraid you're stuck with me. I hope you don't mind.'

'And if I do?' She had to get out!

'You're free to walk out any time you like.' He was smiling but Nina couldn't connect his smile with his words.

'And if I walk out?' she asked, knowing the answer.

Karelian shrugged. 'Then nothing, I guess. Either way.'

'You mean, you won't help me if I'm not helpful back?'

'Seems only fair.' Karelian beamed and crushed a paper cup on his desk into a ball, then lobbed it over her shoulder into a wastebasket behind her.

'Just how do you see me helping you?' asked Nina carefully. She tried to remember the turns in the grey-walled corridor. One left and two right? But the guard at the door would stop her. Or would he?

'In a lot of ways,' said Karelian. 'Everything's grist for the mill, these days . . . particularly in Laos and Vietnam.'

She unclenched her hands and her feet. 'I'm a civilian, Mr Karelian. I don't know the kind of things I think you're talking about.'

'You never know what somebody's going to find useful.' He held a 6-inch ruler between his thumb and forefinger and whistled it back and forth through the air.

'Do you work for American Intelligence?' Once out of the Embassy, she could lose herself quickly in the insanity of the streets. She'd be safe from Karelian and the IDC in the maze of Klong Tooey.

'Of course.' He sounded surprised at the question. 'The different services only talk to each other here in the IDC office, when they're fighting over the goodies.' He laughed at his own joke, then suddenly pointed the ruler at Nina. 'But before you get all worked up, let me make something clear. I bet you think Intelligence is all spies shooting each other with poison darts, microdots, hidden radio sets and dead letter drops – like on the TV! I bet you don't know how much so-called classified information comes from open sources, available to anybody. Routine stuff.' He tilted his small dark head to cue her. 'About eighty percent,' he continued, when she refused to respond. The ruler had begun to whistle back and forth again. 'From newspapers, radio broadcasts, public speeches, gossip. Nothing sinister. And none of it means a hot damn until somebody in an office somewhere knits it all together into patterns. *I'm* one of those office men.' He pointed the ruler again. 'I'm real good at deciding what somebody else might want to know. I'll pass you on to just the right people. You leave that to me.'

She began to understand what they wanted from her. She saw no help for herself in this dark-eyed, sharp-featured little man. They weren't going to give her Will John. They weren't going to give her anything.

'And if I walk out . . . without your help, or vice versa,' she asked, 'will everything really be just as it was before I made that first call?'

'That's not what I said.'

'Would you mind repeating what you did say?' asked Nina. She felt the same agonizing slowness of mind as when the two men had stopped her in Tan Son Nhut Airport in Saigon. 'I must have missed something the first time.'

Karelian patted the open file. 'Some of the stuff in here could get embarrassing for you. To be blunt, ma'am, in some people's books you're a crook.'

'I understood that possibility when I came here,' she said. 'But I still came, in good faith, to put that file right.'

Karelian's hands fanned out a ghostly deck of cards. 'All right, Nina . . . everything on the table, then.' His tone was patient, almost pedantic. 'On one hand, you could be seen as a young woman fleeing from the terror of life under the constant threat of Communism and willing to do everything she can to help the people who want to help her.' He picked up his ruler and began to whistle it back and forth again. 'On the other hand, you could look a lot like an uncooperative, illegal alien. With a history of unlawful trading activity and professional associates who have criminal records . . . not a particularly desirable immigrant anywhere in the world.'

The rope Will John had thrown her that night in Saigon would not pull her to safety. Unless she was very, very careful, it would hang her. Nina stared at Karelian, trying to think rationally, then she stood and walked toward the door.

'I wouldn't,' he said. 'I'd come sit down again, if I was in your shoes.'

She had almost reached the door. Nothing he could say mattered. One right and two left? She would give up hope and effort . . . end up like the crazy *farang* with the white grass hair and the baby's bottle, searching the streets of Bangkok for a small dark-eyed girl and a tall, golden American.

'It won't take a lot,' said Karelian, 'to give you a personal police record.' His voice went tight and rose in pitch. 'You're clean so far in this country. The file's still classified. But it wouldn't take much! Do you know anything about Thai jails? Do you know what some of the guys in this building would like to do to a dink drug pusher?'

She put her hand against the door.

'Sit down, lady, and grow up!' His voice was thick with pure hate.

The reality of Thai jails finally reached her rational mind. Her hand fell. When she turned, he was standing, with his hand on an internal telephone.

She walked back to her chair. They sat down slowly, in unison.

'A dink drug pusher'. Part of her brain was still listening, still assessing. Will John had been right. She was in a pigeonhole with Clinton Clay, no matter what private choice she might have made.

'OK,' Karelian said. 'That's better.' His temper had vanished like monsoon clouds. 'Would you like another cold drink before we go on?'

Nina wondered if she had imagined the man of a few seconds before with eyes like an attacking Doberman. She shook her head.

'Now, then,' he said. 'Let's look at how you got into the country with no passport and no visa, and think about how you'll be allowed to stay.'

Forty-five minutes later, he leaned back. 'Great! There's some great stuff there! I think we're going to get along just fine. We don't get many coming in here and claiming to be hot off the Ho Chi Minh Trail! The boys will really be fighting over these goodies!' He stood up, stretched. 'Like a coffee?'

Without waiting for her answer, he lifted his phone and ordered three cups. Then he dialled again and asked for someone called Sloop.

'She showed up,' he said to Sloop. 'How about that!'

Sloop was a small sandy-haired man with a broken nose and a white scar through his left eyebrow, who wasted no time on spurious joviality. He said he was from Air Force Intelligence, and shook hands with a firm, calloussed grip while his eyes made a frank, non-sexual survey.

'When can I speak to Will John Haines?' she asked him in one last attempt.

He glanced at Karelian. 'That's up to Paul,' he said. 'I'm here to ask you to look at some pictures for us, as a trial flight.'

On cue, Karelian handed her a black cardboard photograph album.

'A trial flight for what?' Nina asked. She suddenly imagined that the picture would be Thu. Her breathing tightened. She opened the cover.

168

Sloop turned away to pick up his cup of coffee. 'Do you recognize him?' He made a quick pacing circuit of Karelian's office.

The first plastic-covered page held a single grainy, black and white blow-up of a detail from another photo. Not Thu. A Caucasian male, lean, forty-odd years old, wearing what looked like an olive drab uniform with short sleeves, but without identifying patches or insignia. His trouser bottoms were tied with string. A strange ghostly blur stood by his left shoulder where someone else had been painted out.

'No,' Nina said truthfully. 'I've never seen him.' They hadn't got her yet.

Sloop leaned over her shoulder and turned the page. 'What about this one?'

Two photos of a Vietnamese – a passport portrait and a candid shot at a restaurant table, of the kind taken by wandering photographers who make fortunes by selling back the rolls of film to men caught out with the wrong women. She knew this man. A Saigon black marketeer who specialized in military POL . . . petrol, oil, and lubricant . . . which he bought from the Americans and sold to anyone.

'Why do you want to know?' she asked.

Sloop said nothing. He had stopped pacing and was standing just behind her left shoulder again.

Karelian smiled encouragingly. 'Just say we have an interest in the gentleman.'

'Do you want to shoot him or make him Prime Minister?' asked Nina.

Sloop remained silent behind her.

The attacking Doberman re-inhabited Karelian's eyes. 'Don't blow it, Nina! You've been doing fine. Tell my friend here if you know this man. I think you do.'

Nina shook her head stubbornly. If she took this first step, she was theirs.

'We can try again tomorrow,' said Sloop.

'I came here prepared to tell you about the opium business,' said Nina. 'Not to spy on my own people for Air Force Intelligence.'

There was a beat of silence in the office.

'OK,' said Sloop. 'We understand. No hard feelings. Paul, do you know how to contact her?'

Karelian snapped Nina's file closed and put it back into the locked filing cabinet. 'Yeah,' he said shortly. 'Come on,' he ordered Nina. 'Let's call it a day and go get some mug shots for the file.'

★

169

She jostled her way through the hot bodies on the sidewalk toward the *Banque de l'Indochine et de Suez*.

Walk, don't run! Try to look like everyone else.

This time, she would withdraw nearly everything in the account, leaving just enough to avoid questions about whether she wanted to close the account. Fake passports were expensive but like almost everything else could be bought somewhere in Bangkok. And though she could live cheaply, she would need sweeteners for patrols, checkpoints, area crossing masters, and other realities of her unrealistic choice.

She asked the clerk for an ink pad.

I may just have time to buy a passport and leave before Karelian thinks of a reason to lock me up.

She pressed the ivory seal her father had given her onto the ink pad and then into the space marked 'signature'. The clerk looked at the amount and disappeared for authorization from a higher power. Instead of returning to his window, he unlocked the gate between the public and backstage.

'The manager would like a word with you.'

'It's been *what?*' Nina leaned forward, rigid with disbelief.

'Frozen.' After a beat, the Thai manager added in French, '*Gelée.*' His assessing glance was part curiosity, part prurience. 'It's noted here in the file: no further withdrawals to be authorized.'

'Whose authority?' she asked fiercely.

'It depends on the reason,' he said. 'Sometimes I make the decision. In your case, it was a higher authority.'

'Which one?'

'I'm not authorized to tell you.' He looked down at his desk top and moved his Shaeffer pen a fraction of an inch to the right.

'Why was it frozen?' Nina demanded.

'Sometimes it's a police matter,' he said primly. 'Sometimes government. No reason is given here.' He touched her file.

'Who does know?'

'You could try the regional director,' he said. 'Or perhaps the Chairman, in Saigon.'

Or perhaps Karelian, she thought with rage and despair.

'That's right,' said Karelian, unperturbed by her cold rage. 'Every account we could trace through your companies and your father's companies. As soon as your first call went through. Bangkok, Hong Kong. And Los Angeles, of course . . . Why don't you sit down?'

Nina ignored his suggestion and paced his office, with a caged leopard's fury. 'Do you mean, that if I hadn't called, it wouldn't have happened?' Oh Will, would this irony amuse you? It makes me want to scream. She pressed the shaking fingers of both hands against her lips, which had set such damage in motion.

'Your call made it a priority.' Karelian cocked his head, but severely rather than cheerfully. 'Anyway, who's to say these countries didn't just decide they don't like the way you made your money?'

Nina's outrage burst past her wisely silencing fingers. 'Even with a limited knowledge of local economies, I find that hard to believe!'

Karelian shrugged.

She glared at him. 'I didn't need to be blackmailed! I came to you prepared to tell you everything I could about the Saigon opium trade. But you started by assuming the worst. Will John warned me! . . . He must have told you that I was pulling out of the business!'

'He mentioned that you had told him of this intention.'

'And I've done it.'

'I'm sure you made a tidy profit,' said Karelian.

Nina felt dizzy. She had been right, there in the shopping arcade of the Liberty Hotel. She was not yet ready for this world.

'I'd be richer if I had stayed, believe me!' She was breathing hard. The creamy skin of her neck was flushed now with pure rage. 'Do you have any idea what's happening to the South Vietnamese economy since American dollars began to flood in? With all those new customers? . . .' She looked at his puckered little smile. 'What's the use!' she cried. 'You're not listening . . . you think you already know!' She turned to leave, then remembered that she had nowhere to go except the house in Klong Tooey and no money except the few *baht* she might earn washing plastic.

'Mr Karelian,' she said. 'I worked hard for seven years. I owned earth moving machinery and transport lorries, and warehouses. The money I made from selling those is mine by right and without shame!'

'Not yet, Nina.' He shook his head abruptly as if surfacing from a swimming pool. 'Not yet.'

'When?'

'Show us who and what you really are. We're honourable men. You show us and we'll look after you.'

She started to laugh, then realized that he believed what he had just said. He perched on his chair with a questioning look on his beaked little face, waiting.

'Exactly who is "us"?' she asked. 'In this case?'

171

'Everybody,' said Karelian. 'Army Intelligence, Air Force Intelligence, CIA, Navy . . . America!'

'Take your pick,' the Meo from Lucky's caravan had said. 'Vietnamese that way. Pathet Lao that way. Royal Army that way. . . .'

'And are all of you moral as well as honourable?' she asked.

'Are they different?'

She fought the persisting, hysterical urge to laugh. 'What about "good"?' she asked. 'In your land of opportunity, is one allowed to try to become good?'

'That's exactly what I'm giving you a chance to do here, by helping us!'

'No,' she said. 'You're giving me a chance to show I'm on your side. All of your sides. That's not necessarily the same as "good".'

' "If you're not for us, you're against us",' said Karelian. 'That's a practical fact. The bottom line in a condition of hostilities is: practical fact is truth. Honour and morality don't win wars! You give us practical help . . . we can debate all that other stuff over a drink sometime.'

She rubbed her temples with her fingertips.

'Are you going to take the chance we're offering?' asked Karelian.

Nina walked to the sealed window and looked out at a world sliced by the slats of the blinds. She would not stay in Bangkok. She could not return to Laos the way she had left. 'Will you give me a valid passport?'

'If we're satisfied.'

'What's my other choice?' Will John can't know what's happening to me, she thought. Lies or no lies, I knew him too well to believe he wanted this for me!

'Good girl,' said Karelian.

Karelian began to look after her as he had promised, by arranging immediate lodging with an American professor and his wife in a new, red-tiled, white-painted one-story stucco bungalow on a hot, bleak street which had no trees. As far as Nina ever learned, Peter Baker was simply a visiting lecturer at Chulalongkorn University. His wife Barbara seemed to be a good woman with far too much energy for the limited role allowed to her as an accompanying dependent in a country whose language she did not speak and whose normal functions had been taken over by a staff of cook, Number One Boy, maid, wash *ayah*, and gardener doubling as her personal driver.

When Nina arrived, escorted by Karelian, Barbara was listening to a tape of Thai phrases.

'*Sawat di kah!*' she cried. She placed her hands together and bowed slightly. 'I'm Barbara. Welcome to our home! Paul has told me a little bit about the terrible things you've been through.' She took Nina's hand in her own. 'You let us look after you for a while. It will be our pleasure! And when you're ready to talk about your experiences, I'll be happy to help you work them through.'

Nina found this greeting both warming and alarming.

Her room was a small, concrete box at the back of the house, with a Swedish modern chair with wooden arms and a single bed covered with an Indian print spread. A poster of Hong Kong hung on one wall and, on the bedside table, Barbara had arranged a box of Kleenex, a water carafe, a posy of freesias, a box of Nedick's mints and two orange paperback novels.

Barbara Baker pushed open the shutters of the small window in the far wall. It opened onto the servants' quarters where two small girls were bouncing up and down on their toes, nose to nose, chanting an unintelligible rhyme. Nina paused as she was putting her tiny bundle down on the bed, and listened to the high clear voices with panic.

How old would Mouse have been before her voice sounded like those? The cold emptiness weakened her, as if it had replaced her bones with iced water.

'Everything OK?' asked Barbara.

Nina nodded.

'You look a little funny. Why don't you have a lie-down for a while?'

'I'll do that,' said Nina. As soon as Barbara left her alone, she closed the shutters again, but the voices came through, only slightly muted. Nina wasn't sure she could bear to live here within constant range of those voices. She could also hear the cheerful clattering and shouting in the cookhouse – the cookhouse had been the noisy, joyful, indulgent centre of her early childhood. She listened to the wet slaps coming from the wash house and remembered the young wash *ayah*, Simpoh Flower who had been her big sister until Maman had decided Nina should no longer be familiar with the servants. She sniffed the smell of burning charcoal which had drifted up to her bedroom in the big family house. She nearly came unstrung.

Someone knocked on her door.

'Happy time in ten minutes,' called Barbara through the door. 'With luck, Peter might even get back before we finish the gin!'

Nina suddenly hated that cheerful, friendly voice. Rage felt better than emptiness. Her rage at Karelian had made her temporarily strong and purposeful. But she was too weary to keep on hating Barbara who only wanted to help. Hysteria finally nudged at her. Nina shook her head in bewilderment and disbelief. Her shoulders shook. Her throat ached. Her eyes ran with what were not quite tears. She sat down on the edge of the Indian bedspread to try to pull herself together before joining Barbara Baker for happy time.

The next day, a car collected Nina and deposited her at an acronymic office in one of the science fiction buildings of glass and steel, where Karelian introduced her to a man called Pat. Just Pat.

Pat had tight eyes above an orthodontic smile in a wide flat face. He said he was from the US State Department and asked her to identify more photographs and discuss names on a list, most of them Vietnamese.

'I still won't spy on my own people,' Nina said. 'Paul Karelian should have told you. I agreed to help if I could, but I have no right to do what you want.'

Pat's tight eyes pinched tighter. His upper lip lifted like a tapir's snout. 'You could be helping some of those people,' he said. 'Some of them just need confirmation of identity to get passports. You're hurting their chances.'

And the rest? she said silently. What do you want with the rest?

'You're not doing too well, Nina,' said Karelian.

'I'll tell you everything I know about the drug trade,' she said. 'There, I understand what I am doing.'

When they released her, she waved down the nearest *tuk-tuk*. 'Water taxi to Thonburi, please,' she said. She needed to think, away from the jostling bodies on hot concrete and the blaring horns. She clutched one of the metal posts supporting the fringed plastic canopy of the three-wheeled motor cab and let her thoughts find their way through the roar of the *tuk-tuk*'s engine and the clamour of traffic. I must leave Thailand, she thought. They won't accept my choice. They don't believe it. To them, I'm still a 'dink drug pusher'.

At a rickety landing stage, she climbed into a water taxi to Wat Arun, The Temple of the Dawn, whose towers rose above the water on the far side of the river. The low wooden boat had a long, egg-beater engine stretched behind like a mosquito's sting, with the same high-pitched whine. The openness of the wide, muddy water cleared her mind a little. She inhaled the rich smells of rotting weed, mud, jasmine in the hair of the girl in front of her, and the pungent dried fish in the basket of another passenger. As they passed through a mist of exhaust from a passing ferry and rocked across the wake of a tugboat, she felt a rush of pain for Saigon, with its own wide, muddy river, boat traffic and very similar smells.

At the temple, she climbed part way up one of the steep staircases of the central, towering *prang* which was set with millions of pieces of broken Chinese porcelain. There, above ground-level confusions, she perched on the steps, breathed in the damp air, and gazed out over the nearly-familiar river. An eight-man racing shell slid by, bizarre among the launches and high-tailed pirogues.

For a few moments, Nina studied the oily, swirling surface and its small cargoes of tangled weed, broken wood, and plastic bottles. A few feet beneath the surface, the occasional plastic bag turned and drifted in the shadows like a dying manta ray. She thought about throwing herself into the water and bobbing like the weed, sinking slowly until she slid into darkness.

Almost immediately, she knew she never would. If she had not given herself to the dark beast at the bottom of the Mekong, no water would have her. She had missed, or refused, her chance.

With that out of the way, she found it a little easier to think. So, she asked herself, where can I go? Not America . . . not without Will John! Even if I fool myself that he did not deliberately betray me, Paul Karelian does not seem likely to arrange a reunion. I myself closed the door on Saigon. Left too many enemies behind. And the war. She swallowed hard, searching the oily river for the reminder that it was not for her.

A baby cried just below her, near one of the pavilions, a mewling milk cry. Heart pounding, Nina waited until the mother appeared with the child tied against her, a tiny new-born. Nina wrapped her arms tightly around her body as if holding it together. Mouse would be bigger than that by now. Mouse would be sitting up. But probably not standing. Or perhaps she might. Nina knew so little about babies, only the brief wonderful lesson of her own. She looked away from the soft, rounded bare legs of the boy toddler who clung to the mother's *panung*.

I could go back to Laos, she thought . . . into the war. But I could look for Mouse. When not half-crazed with hunger and exhaustion. I could 'help' the Americans until they give me a passport, and until I can find some money. I could go back then and search properly! I will not become that crazy *farang* with her bottle. I will search properly, with all the resources I can find!

The idea felt both reasonable and possible. It allowed her to see a next step. It did not require magic or dislocation of reality. But it did need faith.

Now, thought Nina. Decide for once and for all whether Mouse is dead or alive, or you will never think straight about anything else!

She waited.

A pile driver thonked distantly. Transistor radios, car horns, boat horns, an electric saw.

I don't feel death, Nina thought. Just loss. It's unreasonable, but I do not feel as if Mouse is dead! I should know better, but I don't believe it. She stood up, leaning one hand on the sharp edges of broken china set in concrete. So! I choose hope. Laos and hope.

Two days later, the same car took her to a different office, where a man called Bill was waiting for her. He was medium everything – medium tall, medium fair, medium good-looking, medium nice.

The criminal no one can describe after the crime, thought Nina. She wondered where he would try to lead her.

'I'm a narcotics specialist,' he said. 'On loan to the Bangkok Police from the American Drug Enforcement Administration. Pleased to meet you. Please do sit down.'

She sat, feeling cautious relief. Paul and Pat may have accepted her limits after all.

'In fact,' Bill told her, 'I'm trying to finish my doctoral thesis while I'm out here. It's a bitch . . . Been working on it for eight years at Georgetown, but the pressure of work keeps getting in the way.'

'I wouldn't have thought this was the place to come for free time, in your field,' she said. I just made a joke, she thought in wonder.

He laughed. 'Too true! Too true! But the research possibilities are terrific!' He punched a button on his Sony tape recorder. 'Speaking of which, we should get started.'

At last, she shared a purpose with one of her new alien masters. She had nearly forgotten it. She had knocked her own house down when she had decided to sell her father's business. Now she swung the hammer recklessly at the remaining walls.

'Him,' she said a little later, touching a photograph. 'That's Farrentino.' She looked at the lumpy face with the uncertain eyes and soft, cruel mouth. One of the reasons I got out, she thought. And the others like him.

'AKA Farrentino,' interrupted Bill, speaking to the tape recorder.

'Unless there have been changes I don't know about,' said Nina, 'he's refining morphine base to a reasonable approximation of Number Four in a sound-insulated concrete shed behind the Heron Confectionery . . . Here, let me show you exactly where on the map of Saigon . . . there, just off the Arroyo Chinois.'

Bill interrupted to read the map coordinates into the tape recorder.

'Warehouses,' said Nina. 'Used as drops for pick-up of the base . . . Here, just north of the Navy docks. It's brought upriver by fishing sampans which follow the opposite bank. . . .'

She didn't see that she needed such a purpose as intensely as she needed a passport and money.

Four days after Nina's first meeting with Bill from the DEA, she had a second with Sloop.

'I'd like you to sign a statement,' he said, 'confirming that you will not discuss anything we talk about here in this room. Under any circumstances.'

'Why don't we just not talk?' asked Nina. She meant it as a joke, which he ignored. She signed the secrecy oath.

'Now,' said Sloop, 'Let's you and me make a fresh start. I'd like to talk about what you saw while you were carrying rice along the Ho Chi Minh Trail.'

'Did you see PAVN troops?' asked Sloop. 'How big were the travel units?'

Nina tried again to see the shadows squatting under the man-made roof of vines. They were as veiled as the world had been after she had hit her head on the tree. 'About a hundred, I think. . . .'

'Did you see any other third country nationals?'

She looked confused.

'Chinese or Russians,' he explained. 'Not Laotians.'

'Perhaps a Chinese officer,' she said. 'I really don't know.'

'What colour was his uniform?'

She closed her eyes with the effort. 'Olive drab.'

'Did he wear glasses?'

'Yes . . . I think so. . . .'

Sloop asked about fuelling stations for the mechanized transport, about the size of maintenance staff at the stations, about the nationality of the maintenance and other support staff.

Nina tried her best to remember, to please him, to earn her passport, but Mouse and mud and air strikes and leeches and flies and the ache of hunger and exhaustions blurred the details he wanted so badly.

'I'm sorry,' she said. 'We were like pack animals. Too tired to take much notice of what we did see.'

Sloop persisted, moving on to weapons. 'What did the Vietnamese regular troops carry? The irregular troops?' he asked. 'Grenades . . .

with handles or not? Smooth or ridged? . . . try to remember!' He barked the order as if willpower ruled such things.

She shook her head helplessly. Then a detail came into focus and she told him about the trellises and spiders' webs above the trail.

'OK, now what about tanks? You'd remember if you saw tanks!'

'Once,' she said. 'I think. Most of the trails I was on were too steep. But once, I think I saw a road. . . .'

She told him of her dream of a river of lights.

'I think you're a plant,' said Sloop.

'I'm sorry?' Nina was genuinely confused. For a second, the word meant a jumble of lianas, bamboo and fishtail palms.

'. . . A Communist agent, telling us a pack of lies . . . What the hell is so funny?'

'That's what he said to me,' said Nina. A sudden hysteria threatened her self control.

'Who?'

'The PAVN interrogator!' She shook her head. 'I'm sorry, Sloop! It's all so. . . .' She struggled for the word. 'So silly!'

'I'm sorry you feel like that.'

'*I'm* sorry,' she said quickly. 'I wasn't laughing at you, I swear . . . It's just that. . . .' She gulped. 'I've been under strain,' she said. 'The last few months have been . . . stressful.' She drew a deep breath. 'What other lies can I tell you today?' She burst into tears.

'Let's leave it for today,' said Sloop. 'No problem.'

When Nina returned to the Bakers that afternoon, Barbara asked her if she wanted to see the USOM doctor to get a tranquillizer.

'Did someone tell you I need one?' asked Nina. She wondered who had called.

Barbara blushed slightly. 'No, I just know that the kind of thing you're doing now can be a little stressful.'

'Barbara,' said Nina, 'are you watching me for them?'

'Don't be silly!'

Sloop resumed his questioning the following day with the same dogged politeness he had shown before his accusation. 'What kind of defences did you see along the trails? Any anti-aircraft installations? Would you recognize a SAM missile? Did you see *any* missiles deployed? Can you describe the anti-aircraft guns you did see? Air landing strips? Aircraft on the ground? What did you carry personally? Was it always the same? Did you ever carry weapons of any kind, or components?'

Nina answered flatly. She would spend no more personal coinage. Give no more hostages to rejection.

He returned doggedly to earlier topics, his voice and manner quietly depressed by her repeated failure to remember. 'Did you see PAVN troops?'

'My first day with the convoy.'

'How many troops travelled as a unit?'

'I said, I think perhaps a hundred.'

'Are you sure you didn't see any Chinese or Russian troops?'

'Reasonably sure. Except for that one officer I mentioned.'

'You're lying. We know that Chinese troops are using the trail.'

'Perhaps, but I didn't see them or if I did, I didn't recognize them.'

'What about Russians? Any Europeans of any kind?'

Nina stopped with her glass of iced water half way to her mouth. She looked at the glass as if unsure what it was and replaced it carefully on the little teak coffee table in the corner of his office where they were sitting that day. Absently, she rubbed her cold fingertips with her other hand. He had jarred loose a personal memory.

'I saw an American,' she said. She looked at Sloop as if for help. 'I think I did. I had forgotten until now.'

'A prisoner of war?' asked Sloop. His voice rose. The eyebrow not pinned down by the scar arched nearly to his hairline.

'No,' Nina said. 'A soldier. Along the trail one night. In camouflage uniform.'

'Impossible,' said Sloop, looking her straight in the eye.

She had been on one of her half-crazed searches for Mouse, by moonlight, along a stretch of trail where she had thought she might have seen movement in the scrub when the porters had passed. The tiger had stood just off the track. The black stripes of its face came into focus among the stripes of shadow.

The hair lifted on Nina's neck and scalp and along her arms. She and the tiger stared at each other. Then she saw that it had human eyes. The stripes were painted on. She saw the shadowy outline of one human shoulder; the rest of him was hidden in the scrub. She could not move.

If she opened her mouth to scream, she was dead. If she turned to walk away, the man tiger would silently overtake her from behind, and she would still be dead. She forced the muscles of one hand into a thumbs-up sign.

'It's OK,' she whispered in English through stiffened lips. She breathed in and out again. 'I'm a friend of Haines.' It was nonsense, but it might give him pause.

The eyes had not moved or blinked.

'Take a good look,' Nina said, 'so there's no mistake another time . . . you would make some people in America very angry . . . and tell your friends.' She raised her hand a little higher in farewell. 'I'm going to turn now and walk away. Won't tell a soul!' She groped for the most American words she could think of. 'See you later, alligator!'

She hadn't known, until she reached the first listening post outside the camp whether he would let her go or not.

'Impossible,' said Sloop. '*When* did you say this was?' He paced one of his caged bear circles. 'Just why did you assume he was American?'

Nina shrugged tiredly. 'I just knew.'

'He couldn't have been American!' said Sloop. 'Get that through your head. American troops weren't in Laos in 1966. It was a neutral country!'

At the end of their first week, he showed her a map. 'Where did you leave the convoy?' he asked.

'They don't tell either troops or porters where they are.' She smiled slightly. 'As protection against moments like this one.'

She studied the map. 'I know I never reached Tchepone,' she said finally. 'And that could be the first river I followed, but it's hard to be sure.'

'You're positive you weren't below Tchepone?' he pressed. 'You saw no roads south of Tchepone?'

'That's right.' She could see he was disappointed.

'Did you ever learn where the trucks terminated?'

'Tchepone,' she replied. 'When I escaped, the porters were still speaking of it as a destination.'

'Did you ever cross the border out of Laos into Vietnam?'

She stared at him incredulously. 'I may well have done. I assure you, I would never have known, one way or the other!'

'Why not?'

'Have you ever been in those mountains?' she asked.

'As a matter of fact, I have,' he said. 'And you're quite right. It's impossible to tell.'

It brought her up short and made her wonder how many other traps she had missed.

★

One evening, Karelian dropped by the Bakers' house. He perched like a watchful starling on the Danish modern sofa, which seemed to be US overseas standard issue to government employees, and waited for Barbara to leave them alone.

'Everybody's really pleased,' he assured her. 'Would you reconsider talking to Pat?'

'No,' she said. 'Are you any clearer yet about who and what I am? How soon do you think I might be given a passport?'

'Getting there,' he said. 'Getting there. Once our old friend Sloop has finished. . . .'

The following Friday, Bill, from the FDEA, took her to dinner at a restaurant cum nightclub on the road to Don Muang airport. Over Chinese honey-glazed duck, served with French-style shoestring potatoes, she confirmed that his new photographs were of Farrentino from Tampa and four men she had seen with him around Saigon. She identified the plump cheerful face of the quartermaster who had become her best customer for the new-style *ma thuy*. She put names to pictures of hamlets, dock areas and the concrete garage behind the Heron Confectionery near the Arroyo Chinois.

'May I?' she asked. She then removed from Bill's pictures those of Heron employees who had, in truth and innocence, been making only coconut chews and cinnamon hearts. 'Good guys!' she said. 'Look after them.'

Back in Bill's car after dinner, she listened to a tape recording of a conversation and identified the man who was discussing with Farrentino, in heavily accented Corsican French, through an interpreter, the most peaceable means of defining spheres of influence in the South Vietnamese drug market.

The following Monday, Sloop said, 'Congratulations! You've been given low level security clearance. Now we can get down to the nitty-gritty!'

'Does that mean I can have a passport as well?' she asked.

Sloop smiled, something he rarely did. 'You can't skip the country yet,' he said. His dark beige eyes watched hers try not to flicker. 'Sorry about that.' He ran a hand across his thinning, sand-coloured hair. 'Honey, with your record, where the hell could you go? And anyway, maybe we'll make you an offer you can't refuse.'

Another man was in the debriefing room, thin, gentle and smiling, with the arrogant shyness of the boy who has always been top in maths and physics. From Defence Science, explained Sloop.

Nina shook hands and went to lean by the window, looking down through the tinted glass into another world on the street below.

'We'd like you to give us a careful assessment of various factors in those air strikes,' said Sloop. 'Starting with accuracy of target acquisition. Did you have access to the body count after the attacks?'

Nina turned and leaned on the back of the nearest chair. She shook her head. She felt doors closing in her mind.

'Can you give me a personal estimate of the casualty levels?'

The last door slammed shut somewhere in her being. The sensation jarred her physically, though she knew that it was only her mind going on strike.

She shook her head again.

'Try!' urged Sloop.

'A woman I often walked with was killed one night,' she began. Auntie Eel. 'There were others. . . .' Mouse. She reeled internally, then veered back into semi-solid ground. She had decided about Mouse, half-way up the central tower of Wat Arun. 'One man lost both legs . . . There were flies crawling on his eyelids, but I think *he* was still alive. . . .' She closed her own eyes. 'There were pieces . . . I can't say how many people. . . .'

He glanced at her face and spread an aerial photograph on his desk.

The road was as visible as the wake of a boat on still water. Nina was shocked by the clarity of the detail. The tyreless hub of the overturned truck. The jackstraw tumble of broken pilings in the river gorge.

'That could be it,' she said. 'I don't know.' She turned her head away before any of the grey lumps could resolve themselves into bodies. She sat down on the chair and put both hands together between her knees, to keep them still. 'It's hard to tell.'

'Did you ever see one of these?'

She looked away, at the window.

'Nina?'

She looked blankly at the object in his hand. He offered it to her but she kept her hands between her knees.

'Did you ever see anything like this?' he asked again.

It was a fishing float nearly the size of a walking stick. The end of the shaft was sharp like a bayonet. The top was an olive drab cylinder about seven and a half inches long and one and a half inches in diameter. Nina shook her head.

'Are you sure?' he persisted.

She continued to shake her head while memory began to rise like hideous gas from the bottom of a swamp.

'No!' she said faintly. 'No, I. . . .' She had pulled one just like it from the ground and thrown it away. Then she had torn at the burnt stand of bamboo in which Mouse could have been lying. She shook her head again, but this time like a mare with a particularly vicious gadfly. 'No. . . .' She raised her eyes to Sloop's. 'What is it?'

'An infra-red anti-personnel device,' he said. 'It tells the planes where there's something alive on the ground. . . .'

She knocked over her chair as she stood and backed away to escape from the object in Sloop's hands. That thing had called in the Iron Crows! It had seen her running with Mouse and told the men in the sky how to acquire them as a target.

She screamed. 'NO!'

That relentless eye in the night had seen Mouse and pointed her out to be taken by envious gods.

Nina dropped onto the corner sofa and locked both hands over her head. With her head between her arms, she rocked and wept. 'No,' she said. 'Please, no!'

'Hey!' said Sloop. He touched her shoulder. Nina flailed a fist at him. He watched her weeping on his corner sofa for a minute, then called Barbara Baker to come take her home.

'Appears willing to cooperate,' he wrote on a memo form after the two women had left. 'No visible political bias. Possibly unstable emotionally. Recommend standard first level staff psychological testing before enhancing utilization.'

Jimmy Putnam sat on his heels beside the dying man. 'Here!' he said. 'God, I'm sorry! I'm sorry!' He held his canteen to the young man's lips. 'Maybe this'll help a little.'

You stupid asshole, he swore at himself. Nothing's going to help a man die. What a mess!

He gazed unbelieving at the red mud under the man's body. The guy was too small to hold so much . . . and he was still alive. I did that to him. I think I did.

'Come on, Putty!' yelled the RTO. 'You gonna get left behind!'

'I'm sorry,' Putnam said again to the man he had shot, who was dying. Water spilled down the man's chin. Putnam wiped it away. He had tried to hit the man. He had wanted to hit his target. He had known what that meant. He was no cherry. What was wrong with him now?

The dying man turned his half-open eyes toward Putnam. His right

183

hand twitched. 'Black soldier,' he whispered. 'Why you killing me? I am a man of colour too!'

Putnam's insides heaved. Part of him wanted to smash that mouth with his fist, part wanted to apologize again.

'You in love with that gook or something?' yelled the RTO again.

Helplessly, Putnam held the eyes of the man on the ground. The red lake kept spreading and spreading under the small body, not much bigger than his own younger brother. Maybe not much older.

'Finish him and get the hell out of it!' someone shouted.

'You want me to finish the job?' whispered Putnam at last. 'I think you're probably screwed up anyway.'

The man stared blankly, the disbelief now his.

'Tell me!' urged Putnam hoarsely. 'I'll do what you want!' He didn't know which would be worse – to leave him draining dry or to have to shoot him this close, this real.

The young man on the ground suddenly smiled and shook his head.

Putnam stood up, relieved in spite of himself.

The man on the ground started to laugh. Small noisy spasms shook his chest, like a child with croup. But he was laughing. He turned his head away and kept laughing, while the red lake spread past the tips of Putnam's boots.

For the next three and a half weeks, Nina lived in limbo. Sloop and Bill vanished. Instead, Embassy personnel officers gave her a battery of tests, both oral and written. Karelian told her that she was to receive a modest *per diem* for living expenses, to be collected from the IDC office. He invited her out to dinner. On learning that his reasons were purely social, she declined politely. She went to his office to read and sign copies of the transcripts of her last sessions with Sloop. She tied her expense money from the IDC into her faded sash and hid it beneath her bed.

The Bakers had an American-style shower, not just a tap set into the wall or a water jar and dipper, and a bath tub. In those three and a half weeks, Nina showered twice a day, and bathed nearly as often. She washed the lice from her hair and scraped the jungle mud from under her skin. She scrubbed her nails, her teeth, the breasts which had refused to feed her child, and the damp fork of her body but still felt the mud in her pores.

She slept, but her sleep did not wipe out the world as it had in Klong Tooey. In the Bakers' house, she slept nervously. She would stroke the Egyptian cotton of her pillow case, unable to believe its cool softness.

184

Then she would wake in hot, small hours and turn her sweaty head restlessly, sure that she was lying in a hammock again, beneath a sheet of plastic to catch falling bugs.

She had nightmares.

One night, Thu followed her from the Tiger's Head and recaptured her. She tried to hide the emerging golden head of her baby beneath her *panung*, and woke up shaking and wet with sweat, in her little concrete box above the Bakers' servant's quarters.

She read both novels on her bedside table but could not remember them. She began to read newspapers and magazines, to try to make sense of what had happened to the world while she had been absent. In her black cotton skirt and yellow blouse, with her hair scraped back into an elastic band, she accompanied Barbara obediently to her *ram wong* folk dance classes at the Thai Women's Culture Club, and to the Sports Club where she politely declined Barbara's offer to teach her squash. She also ignored Barbara's repeated hints that she was available any time Nina was ready to talk out her traumas.

Nina visited the Temple of the Dawn again, at sunset, and looked for a long time down into the beige, greasy waters of the Menam Chao Phrya flowing past its foundations. She walked through the Bangkok streets, studying the children's faces, trying to decide how old they were and how large Mouse would be now. She ate without appetite at the Bakers' table and from street stalls and vendors. She washed herself. She washed her clothes. She tried to sleep.

One night, she was lost on a dark plain, alone. Mouse was somewhere near, but invisible. Nina tried to hear her, to smell her, to feel for her warmth. In the darkness, she stepped on something cold and slippery. She screamed.

Her light went on. Peter Baker stood in her doorway holding a revolver, with Barbara close behind him.

'We thought you were being murdered,' he said.

'Do you want one of my pills?' asked Barbara.

'You're looking so much better!' said Barbara the next morning, as the two women drank coffee in the bright white plaster-walled dining room. 'You'd be really lovely if you looked after yourself a little better. With those enormous dark eyes and wonderful cheekbones, you could look like a French model! Let me take you shopping for some new clothes. I've nothing else to do. It would be fun!'

Nina looked down at her coffee cup. 'Fun?'

Barbara gave an apologetic but determined little laugh. 'You really have to break out of all that introspection! It isn't healthy.' She sipped her coffee. 'Most women think buying clothes is fun . . . *I* do, when I'm not trying to get something at the last minute. Didn't you ever . . . before you got lost in the jungle and . . . everything?'

I wore armour, thought Nina. Paris-labelled testimonies to status and power. Spells against my enemies. 'I bought clothes,' she conceded.

'*I* think it would help you get back to normal,' said Barbara, still apologetic but still determined.

Nina shrugged. Your normal, or mine? she wondered.

Barbara swallowed two mouthfuls quickly, to hide her sense of rebuff. How stubborn you are! said the clatter of her cup on her saucer. How wilfully determined to be wounded.

Nina looked at her nails, which had grown again, and the skin of her hands and arms which had healed and begun to smooth over from Barbara's creams and oils. She looked down at her lap. She had slipped into her mended *panung* for breakfast and shoved her bare feet into thong sandals.

'You're right,' she said to Barbara stiffly. 'It would be normal.' Barbara had reminded her how much she still fell short in the role she was trying to play for the Americans.

'Terrific!' cried Barbara, instantly reanimated. Nina saw a cloud shadow of relief pass over the woman's broad, fair, slightly freckled face. 'I'll get Mei Wat to call the driver for . . . what? . . . about 9:30, before it gets so stinking hot? You'll love my dressmaker! You two can talk French together . . . she's part French, like you.'

In the dressmaker's mirror, Nina could see that the frightening new hollows which had appeared between her bones during her time on the Trail had already begun to fill again. In the bare top of the emerald-green sundress she was trying, her shoulders and arms were again slim rather than gaunt. Her skin had healed to nearly its former creamy smoothness. Her eyes, as they observed this risen ghost of a past self, glinted with a faint spark of her former ironic humour.

'You *must* get the jacket, too,' said Barbara. 'You never know when you might need something a little more covered-up and tailored.'

Nina turned slowly, letting the feel of the tight waist and short full skirt awake still more memories of her re-emerging self.

'It's really not fair!' cried Barbara in slightly dramatic admiration. 'You have the figure of a young girl. Some of us never had figures to start with! And have you seen Dorrie Schultz since she had her baby? She's gross! Makes you wonder if it's worth it.'

186

Nina froze. She doesn't know! she tried to remind herself. You never told them! But anger began to rise, like a freak wave, first a small swelling on the surface. 'It's not fair!' Barbara had said. Then an ocean of rage rose up to blot out the sky. The rage crashed over her, ran from every pore of her skin, flowed from her hair and eyes. She kept her lips locked tight so it would not sweep Barbara away. She unzipped the dress, stepped out of it, left it lying on the floor, put on her old black skirt and yellow blouse and left without speaking one word to either Barbara or the dressmaker.

'Where *were* you?' cried Barbara when Nina finally returned to the house at 10:00 that night. 'I've been frantic! Peter even called the police. We didn't know what might have happened to you! A single woman like you shouldn't be out after dark in Bangkok! We were getting ready to drag the river! Why didn't you let us know you were all right?'

Nina turned dry, drained eyes on Barbara. There were violet circles under them again. 'I know,' she said coldly. 'It wasn't fair of me, was it?'

She went to her room and closed the heavy shutters against the cheerful sounds of the servants' quarters.

The next morning, Barbara was understanding, even forgiving. 'I went ahead and ordered that sundress for you,' she said. 'I thought it looked so lovely on you, and you'll need it. I hope you don't mind.' She concentrated on stirring her Sweet'n Low into her coffee. 'I hope I didn't upset you yesterday in some way. . . .' Under her light sunburn and freckles, she went pinker.

You're such a small part of my anger, thought Nina. But she couldn't say it. 'That's very kind about the dress,' she said.

Their eyes met. Barbara looked away first, deciding to smile.

Nina stayed angry, however. Her anger brewed like a tropical fever, always there, even on good days. She tried to be polite to Barbara, but every offer of more coffee, a swim at the Sports Club, or a new novel drew a rake along her spine and stiffened her lips around the correct words of gratitude. She didn't want any of these thousands of things of no importance! Barbara seemed to think that a new Thai silk dress, or ice in Nina's drink should somehow be enough to make her forget her loss. Though of course, Barbara didn't really know about Nina's loss in the first place, as she had never mentioned Mouse to Paul, Pat, Sloop or Bill. Barbara's slight wariness, even at her most relentlessly cheerful, made Nina feel guilty, and even angrier. She finally lost control the

187

evening that the Bakers insisted she join them and some friends for a barbecue in their small rear compound of concrete blocks and wilting flower boxes.

Their friends, the Thompsons, had two children, a sulky girl of eleven who kept her neatly permed head buried in a book through cocktails, and a blond boy of five who spent happy time throwing peanuts at the Bakers' caged mynah bird.

'Daniel! Stop that!' cried his mother from a sunbed. The adults carried on talking. Daniel carried on throwing peanuts.

'Daniel, I'm warning you!' said Mrs Thompson.

'He likes peanuts,' said Daniel reasonably.

'But not in his eye!'

'I'm not throwing them at his eye,' said the boy. He threw another which caught the bird on the back of its head.

'Please do be careful, Daniel,' said Peter Baker nervously.

'Do something about him!' Mr Thompson ordered his wife.

Mrs Thompson rose from the sunlounger, put down her gin and tonic, and closed in on her son.

Nina heard a flurry of ferocious *sotto voce* threats and higher pitched protest. Then the sound of a slap. The delicate, still baby-like curve of the boy's cheek reddened. His eyes filled with tears of pain, humiliation and shock.

The wave of rage swelled in Nina. She stood up and stumbled over tanned and slack-clad legs to get to the mother and child. She opened her mouth to scream at Mrs Thompson that if she didn't know how to treat a child, she didn't deserve to have one, when others wanted one so very, very much. Her hands clawed out to shake the wretched woman who did not recognize the joy and good fortune the heavens had wasted on her.

Startled eyes turned from Daniel and his mother to Nina. Her hands fell to her sides. She closed her teeth hard on her fury, but her rigid body and hot eyes spoke for her.

Mrs Thompson stepped back in alarm.

'I think I should go to my room for a while,' Nina finally allowed herself to say. 'Excuse me!'

As she left, she felt the embarrassment, the glances, and the what's-eating-her and you-know-how-it-is shrugs. Daniel began to cry quietly, slumped onto a sack of briquettes.

'Well,' said Mrs Thompson's voice brightly, when Nina was just out of sight but still within earshot, 'I don't know what she'd have done! Sorry, everybody, if I caused a little contretemps.' And Barbara's voice murmured soothingly.

In her room, Nina fell onto her bed and stifled her cries against her pillow. 'It's not fair!' she screamed into the musty feathers. 'It's not fair! Oh God, it's not fair! Not fair, not fair, not fair!' She wrung the pillow and thrust her fist deep into it again and again as if into some unidentified pink stomach. 'It's not fair!'

Oddly enough, when the storm had subsided, Nina felt clear-headed as if she had slept well and was now awake.

Karelian interrupted limbo with a telephone call at lunch time four days later. 'I'm sending a car to bring you to the Embassy at 4:30 tomorrow afternoon,' he said. 'The guy who could be your new boss is in town.'

'I'll ring the dressmaker to hurry up,' said Barbara when Nina told her. 'I just knew you'd be needing that dress and the jacket!'

Ethan Perry was sixty-four years old and nearly six and a half feet tall. In spite of his height, he was well-proportioned and noble as an ancient banyan tree. His wide, high forehead rolled upward like a mountain ridge. A peninsula of silver-grey hair bisected the great dome of his skull and dark blue eyes lurked in the shadows of his grey-fringed cliff-edge brows, looking too sharp to need the gold-wire rimmed spectacles on the end of his beaked nose.

'How do you do,' he said noncommittally and extended Nina a long-fingered, dry, manicured, liver-spotted hand.

Nina shook hands with equal reserve.

'Thank you, Paul,' said Perry. His voice was light for his height, a tenor just beginning to crack with age.

Karelian recognized dismissal and left them alone in his office without ceremony.

'Please sit down,' said Perry when Karelian was gone. He gestured graciously toward the chrome and brown leather sectional seating in the far corner of the room and stood back to let her go first. As he folded himself down onto a seat facing her, he adjusted his angles slowly, like a stork settling on a nest. The air conditioner below the window rattled like a man with phlegm in his throat. When Perry tucked in his firm chin and focussed on Nina over the top of his spectacles, she felt like a small animal caught in the headlamps of a car.

'Now then, Miss . . . ahh . . . Martell. . . .' The pause over her name was somehow diffident rather than arrogant. 'Has anyone actually asked you whether you want to work for us or not?'

'I wasn't aware that an offer had been made.' Are you what all the rest has been for? she wondered. And what do *you* want from me?

'I feared as much. . . .' The light tenor was touched with dryness. 'Can you remind me which languages you speak?'

'French, English, Vietnamese, scraps of Saigon Chiu Chao and a smattering of Meo,' she said. 'Who is "us"?'

'I'll get to that,' Perry said. 'First things first. Your father was a North Vietnamese by birth. So is this cousin who apparently carried you off in what sounds like a most romantic fashion but I dare say was nothing of the sort. Are you sure that your own sympathies don't lie with the North in the present "conflict" as I believe we are allowed to call it?'

'I've already answered that question, many times!'

'But not when I could watch your face as you did so.' He did not smile.

He was a different animal from Paul, Pat, Sloop and Bill. But that is not enough reason to trust him, she told herself.

'So tell me – where does your heart lie?' The dark blue eyes in the shadows of the cliff edges invited directness.

'My father once asked me the same question,' she replied.

'And you said. . . ?'

' "I don't know enough yet to choose." '

'And now?'

She still didn't know. 'Is this a practical or a philosophical question?'

Perry threw back his large head and gave a quick, surprising bray of laughter. 'Imagine living in a time,' he said, 'when the two can be separated so completely!' He settled more deeply in his chair and stroked the under side of his chin with the back of his long fingers while the intelligent eyes studied her. 'Our practical friends in the IDC have decided, after some debate, to recommend you for limited security clearance, as you may already know.'

'They did tell me that.' To her surprise, she was enjoying this conversation.

'You bring a rather special perspective to bear on Southeast Asia,' he said. 'Half French, with a Southern upbringing and Northern connections.' He peered over his glasses again. 'And thoroughly confused loyalties.'

He shifted sideways like a giant tree about to topple but merely took something from his jacket pocket before righting himself again. He put a French passport on the low glass-topped table between them.

Nina just looked at it for a few seconds. She reached slowly, expecting it to disappear, like a conjuror's trick. She picked it up. It was solid in her hand. She opened it, still not trusting. The face inside was

190

hers, one of Karelian's mugshots of the first day, a strange, strained, gaunt woman with eyes out of proportion to the rest of her face. The name was Nina Desanges. Nina of the Angels.

'As in "on the side of"?' she asked, unable to keep sudden elation out of her voice.

Perry's gurgling chortle took a long time to bubble to the surface; it had a long way to travel. 'Oh Lord!' he said, as if to himself and for no clear reason. Then he added, 'Poor Paul!'

She had escaped them. They had finally given her the means to escape! She smiled back at Ethan Perry. In spite of herself, and in spite of what he was trying to do, Nina liked him. She collected her wits. Tried to think what he would expect her to say next, if her soul and intent were blameless. 'Is this free of charge?'

'The question should be whether the price is too onerous.'

'How bad is it?' He would expect her to ask, but it didn't matter. She would pay their price for so short a time!

He grimaced in mock pain. 'A steady job, with use of company cars, pension plan, health insurance, permission to shop at the PX . . . and a priority seat on evacuation aircraft in the event of political or military emergency.'

'Doing what?' Money was now her chief concern. She forced herself to listen to his answer. It was, after all, the point of her last several weeks.

'Officially,' Perry said, 'you would be employed by the Southeast Asia Media Bureau, monitoring printed Vietnamese language sources, like newspapers, journals, government pamphlets, and so on. Translation and analysis . . . Very easy, very boring.'

She waited, while he sketched the emerging shape of the life he offered with such misleading diffidence.

'Once the powers that be are satisfied with how you've settled in, various other bodies might call on your services . . . as a translator, for example, or for your perspective on some particular issue. I might want you to interview someone, for instance, to confirm something that person had already told someone else.' He stopped.

Say something! she thought. You're supposed to be interested in your future! 'What are some of those bodies?'

'The Military and Civilian Coordinated Research Group is one that springs to mind.'

'That sounds like civilians doing research for the American military,' she said. 'Are you sure it's not like being a spy?'

The great tree swayed forward. Perry peered under his brows in self-mocking caricature of a stern schoolmaster. 'I'm afraid you may be a romantic, Miss Martell. Forget all those English and American movies you saw as a girl in Saigon. We don't have spies anymore. We have HUMINT resources, as I believe they're now called. And SIGINT, ELINT and several other INTS. We plug men into machines. Some people would prefer to eliminate men altogether and just play with machines. I think they think that machines are much less messy to mend.'

Nina smiled slightly. 'You're more of a romantic than I am, Mr Perry.'

'I'm a dinosaur,' he said firmly. 'Without illusions. But let's return to you . . . Karelian said you were definitely not "a clear-cut case". Which way are you going to jump?' He sat back with what appeared to be genuinely open interest.

He terrified her suddenly. He was too certain of his power. Like Will John. He knows! she thought. He can't be fooled.

'Is your own thumb up or down?' she asked him. 'Considering what you know of me.'

'*Moritura te salutam?* You're romanticizing again. In fact, I hope that you'll join us. I assure you I have a far greater tolerance of ambiguity than Paul, Sloop, Pat and Bill.'

She looked down at the passport in her hands.

'Would it be so painful to help us?' asked Perry. 'Given that you don't appear to be a member of the NLF or an undercover agent of Hanoi, is there something inherently wicked in being helpful?'

His style of blackmail was far more elegant than Karelian's. And more persuasive. Being helpful was almost like doing good.

'I don't know yet.' She looked back fiercely. She did not like him anymore. 'Duress can make these things hard to judge.'

He blew two brief snorts down his long nose. 'But don't let it sway your judgement, either. The choice made under duress *could* still be the right one. And consider your alternatives very carefully!'

He does know what I intend to do, she thought. She couldn't tell whether he was amused or angry. 'And if I say no?'

'Then nothing, I'm afraid,' he said. 'Just as Karelian told you. You continue to be an illegal immigrant. Your bank accounts remain frozen. Everything stays just as it is. Even if I did have influence in the appropriate quarters, you know too much to risk as a possible loose cannon. I'm afraid Karelian just might blow the whistle on you to the Thai police.' He suddenly produced a large white cotton handkerchief from his jacket pocket and blew his nose with an explosive honk. 'The pension scheme is really rather good,' he said.

'Karelian thinks he's one of a band of honourable men,' said Nina at last.

'Do you want time to think about it . . . really think?' Perry prodded the handkerchief back into place and watched her under his brows. 'Paul Karelian thinks that honour lies in being right.'

'And for you. . . ?'

'. . . It lies in *trying* to be right . . . and as fair as life will allow.'

The extraordinary thing was that she believed him.

'I would rather be a volunteer,' she said.

Perry shrugged. 'No one's counting those points.'

She held up the passport. She would tell this terrifying old man the truth, whether he heard it or not. 'For the time being, then . . . or is that too ambiguous even for you?'

Perry chortled again. He unfolded himself and stood up to his full, third-level jungle canopy height. 'I'll tell personnel to sort out payment and paperwork.' He held out his dry tough hand again. 'I've enjoyed meeting you,' he said sincerely. 'And though my nineteen-year-old, politically-committed niece would lecture me for a week for using the male-chauvinist-pig phrase, may I suggest that you try to lie back and enjoy it?'

He walked her down to the main door and signed her out. He put his hand on her elbow. 'On the subject of "for the time being",' he said gently. 'Though that passport gives you legal identity and a Thai visa, I really should warn you that you wouldn't get past customs with it. We had to use one already on the list.'

He smiled down at her.

The car was waiting for her on the Wireless Road outside the Embassy. Perry waved farewell from the top of the steps as if he were a relative sending her off on a journey. Nina looked back. She ought to hate him. And she should be weeping with despair. But she felt in that old man a force that might work for her, though she did not yet see how. He was on the other side but not an enemy. So she waved back.

That night, a thick, black, gelatinous membrane wound itself around her, hobbled her legs and bound her arms to her sides like a mummy's. Soft dampness filled her mouth and nose and burned deep into her lungs. She struggled. Finally forced one hand free, out through the dark membrane. Her hand vanished, cut off in mid-arm. Currents of cool air blew on her fingers. Something lay out there, unseen, just beyond her reach. She could move her hand freely, but she could neither reach that elusive something nor pull her hand back.

She sat up and turned on the light. She sipped some of the ice water made from boiled water which Barbara Baker had her number one boy put beside every bed each night. The next morning, she rang Karelian and asked to see Perry again.

'You just caught me,' he said. 'I fly back this evening.'

'I'm not going to pretend to be on your side if I'm not,' she said abruptly.

He had asked her to meet him after lunch on the terrace of his hotel, an old-style Singapore-sling and steamer-trunk stucco building with a modern turquoise-lined swimming pool, thatched cabanas and open-air dais for entertainers grafted onto the back. He sat now in a white wrought-iron chair far too small for his height, his majesty unimpaired by either the long, bony old man's shanks which protruded from his faded khaki bush shorts or by the rubber-thong sandals on his long, slim, horny-nailed feet. A puce bougainvillaea billowed from a Chinese dragon pot against the wall behind him. The moist air smelled of chlorine from the pool, and of coconut suntan oil.

'Pretend?' he asked. 'All of us are always pretending something.' He shook his large head soothingly. 'You go ahead and say what you like . . . I'll decide whether to believe you. Drink up, I want another gin.' He sat with his hands firmly on either arm of his chair, foresquare and solid as an ancient tortoise. 'Just be careful who you tell about your treachery.'

Nina looked away, at the glittering turquoise swimming pool. All the swimmers were Americans. She nodded. She felt better, lighter, as when she had begun to tell Thu the truth.

'I really am very pleased to have you "join the team",' Perry said. He put implied quotation marks around the last phrase as if to disinfect the sincerity of the first. 'For the time being,' he added.

Nina held her breath while a small tanned boy floated limply face down in the pool.

'What else. . . ?' demanded Perry.

The boy raised his head. Nina looked back at the sharp old eyes. Perry was making two impossible requests as easy as they could ever be. She drew a deep breath and dived. 'Do you know a man called Will John Haines?'

'Not personally,' said Perry. He didn't blink.

'I need to get in touch with him directly . . . not through the

Embassy.' Without the interference of Paul, Pat, Sloop and Bill. I need to know from him personally how far he betrayed me, she thought. I have to be sure of something in my life!

Perry nodded. 'I'll give it a whirl. Next?'

Nina looked back at the pool and swallowed. She sipped her almost untouched gin and tonic. 'I withheld a major fact from Karelian and the others. . . .' The ice in her glass tinkled with the faint shaking of her hand.

'More than one, I'm sure!' said Perry. 'For God's sake, young woman, finish your drink!'

Nina fixed her eyes blindly on the bougainvillaea behind him and tried to say the words she had not yet spoken to anyone since that night in the field hospital in Laos. She could hear Perry breathing in and out quietly as he waited.

'I. . . .' What tense? Have? Had? 'I have a daughter. . . .' She steadied her breathing. It was possible to say. Her heart still beat, although heavily. Her blood still flowed, unfrozen. 'Somewhere in Laos. I believe she's still alive.' She had exhausted herself and fell silent.

Perry dropped the hand he had raised to summon a waiter. His eyes closed briefly, as if in an old man's cat nap. 'Your only child?' he asked without opening his eyes. There was a hollow splash as someone dived heavily into the pool.

'Yes,' said Nina. A drop of water landed on her foot.

'How old?' He opened his eyes and took a small leather-bound notebook from a pocket of the baggy shorts.

'Seven weeks,' said Nina. 'At the time.' She began to smooth the skirt of the green sundress across her knee with fierce repetitive little strokes.

Perry sighed. 'As young as that.' He wrote in the tiny book, which fitted into the palm of his hand. 'I'm sure you know what you're asking.' He looked at her suddenly. 'That is what you're asking, isn't it . . . for help trying to find her?'

Nina nodded, unable to speak. The same clumsy diver battered the water again and splashed the hot concrete paving. A dark spot spread on the green skirt of her dress. She rubbed at it with her thumb.

'How did you . . . lose her?'

'During an air attack.' She tried to answer flatly, as she had answered Sloop's questions, as if someone else were answering.

Perry sighed again, looking like a weary old man. 'Well, let's eliminate the obvious. Start with the Red Cross Refugee Reclamation crowd . . . Are you sure you'll be able to handle their questions?'

'I'm used to questions.'

'Yes . . . well.' Perry studied her with the objective concern of a family doctor.

Nina's rage reawoke at his concern. Life was complex enough without kindly blackmailers, even ones she had decided to trust enough to ask for help. But she pushed the rage firmly back down into the cave where it lurked.

'I'll give them a ring before I fly out,' said Perry. He flagged down a waiter and ordered two more gins without consulting her.

Perry's concern about questions was justified.

'You do realize, don't you, that this isn't a refugee problem?' The fifty-year-old American woman sitting across the small wooden table from Nina had dark wine-coloured moons beneath her eyes. Her salt-and-pepper hair needed washing and her nails were bitten to the quick. 'We're really talking about a missing person . . . in what are virtually wartime conditions. You know yourself how disrupted Laos is . . . the fragmentation of services.'

She had taken Nina around the orphanage. She had shown her albums of photographs. Together, they had gone through lists of named and unnamed infants. She had put a baby into Nina's arms.

Nina stiffened. It was all wrong. The eyes were wrong. The weight was wrong. It smelled wrong. Its rubbery little legs lay awkwardly in her hands like a cheap toy. It reminded her of her nightmare of finding Mouse but not recognizing her.

It had already tainted her body's memories of Mouse. She thrust the changeling back at the woman who now sat across the table from her, before it could destroy Mouse altogether.

Besides weariness, Nina saw pity in the woman's eyes. She also saw the disciplined distance of someone who must regularly say unbearable things to people who do not want to hear them.

'It's possible. . . .' Nina began. She remembered the total rearrangement of the world after the bombing strike. She suddenly didn't know what she had thought was possible.

'You might as well give me a formal description,' said the woman. She dug into a drawer for a form.

Nina recognized the act of charity. 'She was wearing a torn-up blouse . . .' she said. 'Blue . . .' She drew a breath. 'I had put my quilted jacket under her in the basket. . . .' She stopped.

196

Instead of writing, the woman took both of Nina's hands in her own. The touch was both comforting and a portent of unbearable evil.

'You really do know, don't you,' she said, 'that there is very little chance your little girl will be found? Miracles can happen, but we can't count on them.'

Nina tried to withdraw her hands; the woman's grip tightened.

'I've seen many, many similar cases,' said the woman, 'and I know the odds against us. I have also seen many, many people held prisoner by false hope. They can't make a future for themselves because they won't let go of the past. You're young, still able to have children. . . .'

Nina jerked her hands free.

'Oh, I know you won't want another child until you have grieved properly for this daughter. But you won't be able to mourn her until you accept that mourning is called for . . . that you have suffered a real loss.'

'She is still alive,' said Nina. 'That's why I'm here.'

'She might be,' said the woman. 'But you must face the terrible truth that you will probably never know one way or the other. If it's any easier to accept, the truth is that she probably is not alive.'

Nina stood up. She refused to listen any more.

'She was very tiny,' said the woman. 'Too small to survive unless someone found and kept her, even if she did survive the air raid. I'll see what I can do, but I urge you to be realistic. Take time if you need it, but release your daughter. Mourn for her, and let her go.'

'We never found her body,' Nina insisted. 'We searched the area but never found her body!'

'Were any others killed?'

'Yes.'

'And did you find them?'

'I would know if she were dead,' said Nina steadily. 'I'm sure I would know!' She wanted to tear that head with the pitying eyes from the woman's body, beat those warm hands with her fists until they were pulp. The reality of the search was blurring the reality of her conviction.

'Ethan Perry called from Washington,' said Barbara Baker when Nina returned to the house. 'He wanted to know how you got on this afternoon.'

Nina felt a pang of loss at having missed his call.

'How *did* it go?' asked Barbara.

Look at her! Standing by for action at last! thought Nina. With PX

197

Kleenex at the ready! 'Buckets of compassion,' she said tightly. 'No joy.'

'I'm sorry,' said Barbara Baker. 'I really am sorry. . . .'

'It was an American plane,' said Nina.

'Pardon?' Barbara looked puzzled, then alarmed.

'Never mind,' said Nina. 'It's not your problem. Did Perry say when he would be back in Bangkok?' She had forgotten to ask him.

She would have liked to point out to him, beyond anyone's evasion, that it was an American plane which had taken her daughter, whom she was beginning to admit she would probably never see again. She would have hidden in a chair beside the pool of his hotel, while Perry quietly downed gin and considered what to say to her, as aware as herself of the ambiguities.

'Would you like a drink?' asked Barbara. 'To hell with Peter and his advisory meetings! You could use a drink and I could do with the company! Keep me company! Please!'

Nina recognized charity again, relentless charity like the Red Cross officer's useless questions about Mouse. But then perhaps the woman really was lonely. 'Thank you,' she said. What could a little return charity cost her at this point? She wouldn't be here any longer than it took to earn or acquire a real passport that would get her across borders. Ethan Perry notwithstanding.

10

Thu's son was born in a tunnel made by enlarging a small cave in the mountain side below the villa. The men in the planes were too far away to hear the young concubine's first screams. From an altitude of two thousand feet, the men stamped a box on the ground with their explosives, a square of coordinate numbers, on signals relayed from a distant command hootch. But the baby was only half way along his journey when the last reverberation shook the timber supports of the tunnel roof.

Thu, his aunt, and the midwife, crouched beside the mother-to-be, their faces a patchwork of shadow and orange glints reflected from the single, shaded lantern. In the silence after the last explosion, men might be moving across the mountain side, listening and watching for movement against the rocks or for a trap door to open. These men would throw grenades into the tunnels and caves and wait for the survivors to struggle out of the ground. But the elderly Meo woman, watching the midwife by the girl's feet, was more disturbed than frightened. She turned her head awkwardly to look at the face of her nephew, Thu, who crouched beside her near the young mother's head in the cramped, wormhole which was serving as a birthplace. His breath was short and his eyes were intense as he looked down at the girl lying on the uneven, rocky floor.

This is an important child, thought his aunt. Even more than most people know. A propitious entry into the world is more important than it has ever been. She looked down at the girl who had begun to pant again, like a dying animal. Apart from what it means to my nephew, the old woman thought, a child born now has so many dangers to face. And everything is wrong!

Her nephew's presence was explicitly forbidden by custom. Herbs and incense should have been burning by the mother's head to ease her labour, but Thu, the father who shouldn't be there, had forbidden it because the perfume might seep out into the noses of the men who might be walking outside the crack where they were hiding. In the villa, the doors and windows would have been thrown wide open to allow the free movement of good energy, just as the child should move freely from his mother's womb into this life.

The old woman tucked back behind her ear a strand of her own hair which she had unplaited to flow loose on her back. She had unpinned the girl's hair when her labour first started, but these were puny gestures. Nothing good could come of the close-pressing walls and three-foot ceiling of their burrow, or the packed bodies in the dark tunnel a few feet away. Neither she nor Thu nor the midwife could stand upright. The poor girl could not even release her pain with cries.

The girl panted faster. Then her eyes opened wide in fright. 'Oh!' she gasped. 'Oh!' Her voice began to rise.

Thu leaned closer. 'Be quiet!' he whispered. 'Be brave!'

She stared uncomprehending, as her final spasms began. 'Aiee . . .' she gasped again. 'Aieeee. . . !'

He covered her mouth with his hand. 'Be quiet!' he whispered again fiercely. 'The barbarian soldiers will hear you!'

She shook her head against his hand. Her eyes bulged, staring through him into pain she had never imagined. She clawed at his hand.

'Be quiet, or I will kill you!' he whispered. 'I will not let this one be taken from me!'

She looked at him wildly, half-hearing at last. Then another contraction arched her stomach into a lump hard as rock. A strangled grunting sound escaped through her nose. Thu loosened his hand a fraction so she could draw in a breath deep as a river, then tightened it again against her scream. There was a flurry of slipping movement like a landed fish between her thighs, and her body relaxed. A mewing sound came from the flurry of tiny limbs.

The midwife breathed out a tiny sound of satisfaction. Her busy hands seemed to chop at the shadows. The Meo woman leaned to inspect the baby.

'Colonel, it's a son.' Her eyes gleamed in the faint reddish light.

He exhaled a breath as intense as a war cry. 'A son!' In his excitement, his shoulder knocked against the stone wall of the tunnel. Then he settled back on his heels and held out his arms across the girl's body to the midwife.

'Give him to me!' he whispered.

'In a moment, in a moment.' The old woman was used to fathers. Even her nephew had to bow to the authority of women at a time like this. 'First the midwife must put him to her breast, so he does not cry.'

'Give him to me! I want to see him.' Even whispered, this was an order.

The old woman hesitated.

'He won't cry.'

No one dared push the Colonel too far, not even his aunt. She nodded to the midwife to hand the baby over, naked and still slippery with blood.

Thu felt the child come into his hands as naturally as the handle of his sword. The small moist head shaped itself to the hollow of his right palm. He hefted the 5 or 6 pounds along his arm and bent his lips to the damp blood on the child's head. Two dark serious eyes caught the light of the single lantern. The man and infant regarded each other. Thu was filled with exaltation; the Heavens had finally returned what they had once stolen from him. He would let no one have this one.

The mother, reviving, stretched out her arms for her baby, to see him.

'In a moment,' murmured Thu. To his aunt, he added, 'I said that the little general would not cry!'

Cradling the child against him on one arm, he reached with his free hand into his jacket and took from its sheath a small, triple-bladed weapon, like a starfish with razor-sharp tentacles. Mother, midwife and old woman made movements of anxious protest. Thu touched the tip of his finger against the end of a blade. A single drop of blood welled, black in the dim, orange light.

The baby, growing used to the sensation of air rather than amniotic fluid in his lungs, now began to notice the first hunger in his untried stomach. His mouth pursed and searched. Thu put his fingertip to the infant's lips. The tiny mouth closed on the finger and the drop of blood. The old woman made an involuntary hiss of dismay and disapproval but pressed the mother gently back onto the ground.

Thu was shocked by the strength of his son's jaws, soft gums, and mouth which was hardly larger than the circumference of his finger. For a few seconds, he lost himself in the connection between himself and that small, damp body. For those few seconds, they were one creature. Then he gently withdrew his finger.

'And now, *mon petit général*, you may have your mother's milk.' He passed his son back to the women, for the moment.

The old woman kept her head down as she busied herself with mother and child, to hide the disapproval in her eyes. As soon as daylight came and they were out of this worms' nest, she would make the proper, peaceful offerings in thanks for this arrival of a perfect new life.

201

She caught herself with alarm. Not perfect! she hastily assured any listening spirits. Not perfect at all . . . very ordinary . . . nothing to interest any of you! Nothing at all!

Thu squatted in the dark tunnel, forearms on his knees and watched his second child suckling. The reality of that tiny body, with its astonishing strength, stirred a deep sense of loss as well as joy. There was another one in the world as wonderful as this one. Somewhere in the world was the woman who had robbed him of that child, and the man, a Round Eye spy, who had tricked her into deserting her proper place in the world.

The English actor at the Bakers' dinner table, being entertained by Barbara during a British Drama League tour of *All's Well That Ends Well*, described a nightmare he often had: he walked onstage and realized that he was in the wrong play, one for which he did not know the lines and where he couldn't find the exit door. He explained, with humorous examples, how he would improvise dialogue while he frantically tried one door after another, sweating with terror. The worst thing was, he said, that the other actors didn't seem to notice anything wrong. They just kept on giving him cues to which they seemed to expect the correct response.

Everyone at the table had laughed. The man was entertaining, verbally quick and sensitive to his audience. Nina had smiled, but their eyes had touched once. Then met again. She knew exactly how he felt in those nightmares.

She had a new name, a bed to sleep in, friends to drink with at happy time, and a desk in an office of the Southeast Asia Media Bureau. She had the appearance of a social life; Barbara introduced her relentlessly to the large number of single men in town, with or without wives at home in the States. She had a salary (which she deposited under a false name in a small Chinese private bank, to grow into the price of a good quality false passport). She had a mended, rested body and a soul which had begun to wake up. She had everything except her daughter and a sense of being in the right play.

Her job for the Bureau was simple. The work was routine. Her sessions with Bill and Sloop had given her a clear line on what the Americans might like to know. She sat at her desk reading Vietnamese language newspapers and magazines from both the north and the south. She selected and translated all items which seemed relevant to a list of headings she had been given by her supervisor, an American woman named Muriel Wicks who looked like an aging Sandra Dee, with sharp eyes hiding behind the red plastic butterflies on the corners of her clear plastic spectacles.

'Anything that seems important,' Muriel had said to Nina on her first day. 'The break-down's on that list. Economically, politically, militarily . . . you know the kind of thing.'

She bent suddenly and scraped at the underedge of Nina's grey-painted steel desk. 'The guy before you was a real slob,' she said, peeling off a used Bandaid. 'Summaries are due on Monday and Friday. Try to break tradition and get them in on time. Have fun.'

Dear Will John, wrote Nina in an imaginary letter. Guess what? Now I'm a termite too.

For a few weeks, Nina threw herself into being a termite. While she had been in Thu's eagle's nest, carrying rice through mud, bearing and losing a child, and beginning to heal, the world had churned on without her. She had to catch up with it, to try to find a place in it for herself. Her job gave her access to the information she needed.

In her own country, she had just missed Air Marshall Ky's election to prime minister in June 1965, in place of Dr Phan Huy Quat, who had replaced General Khanh who had replaced Minh who replace Diem, the murdered Premier, whom the Americans had put first into power in 1955 and then renounced in 1963 as a dangerous failure. Elsewhere, she had missed the beginning of Chairman Mao's Great Proletarian Cultural Revolution in China in September 1965, which was to leave her country as the bone between two large and nervous dogs.

She had missed the first big conventional clash of the Vietnam non-war – the battle for the bone – in the Ia Drang Valley, in October. She learned that the number of US troops in Vietnam had grown from the 200,000 present when she had left to more than 400,000. She read the names of battles, then a few weeks later, with bewilderment, read the same names again. A formless sea of war seemed to be flooding her country, without logic or progress.

She learned that the United States was now regularly bombing North Vietnam, though it seemed that the bombing had not actually stopped since the beginning of Rolling Thunder in February 1965. One day, as she was reading names of bombed villages, she recognized several in the Red River Valley.

My father's village! she thought, with a twist of terror. Grandmother! She buried her face in her hands and remembered the old, old woman, frail and transparent as a dried leaf, who had clung to Nina and wept with joy at this unexpected granddaughter, come to bury the beloved son. Nina imagined the village as it might now look after being rearranged by tons of high explosives dropped or fired by both sides. The dried leaf of the old woman blowing in flakes of ash on the wind. Her father's coffin thrown from the ground and his bones scattered for animals to gnaw.

She became dizzy with information but could not stop devouring it, far beyond the brief of her job. She began to read the English and French language papers as well as the Vietnamese. In all these, she studied the claims and counterclaims of aggression, violence, outrage and atrocity. She read in North Vietnamese and Pathet Lao papers about the regular bombing inside Laos by Lao Air Force, South Vietnamese Air Force and American Air Force planes, and then searched English-language papers in vain for any mention of the same.

She tormented herself with pictures of old women squatting in vacant disbelief on the ruins of what had been the family home and the centre of its universe for more generations than anyone could remember, and with pictures in the Vietnamese papers of children who had lost their mothers. She wept over pictures of women who had lost husbands or children, searching their eyes and nodding in recognition.

She also cried at the pictures in American papers of US peace demonstrators, of rows of flag-draped coffins holding nineteen-year-old American bodies, and of American soldiers, weeping, carrying dead Vietnamese children. She looked at pictures of the confident faces of the men, on both sides, who were sure they were right.

Sometimes, she searched herself for a response and found that she had no emotions left to spend. Knowing that the act was a little mad, she would search photographs from refugee camps, studying the blurred faces with a magnifying glass. She never saw Mouse. So she translated the cold details of warfare from one of her two native languages into English, ate the Bakers' food and allowed their wash *ayah* to launder her newly-bought clothes. She smiled and improvised dialogue in response to cues from actors who were in the right play for them. Meanwhile, she searched desperately for the door offstage.

In all of her reading, Nina never saw mentioned news of the capture of a twenty-three and a half year old black university graduate, named James Michael Putnam, who had volunteered to help his country fight for the freedom of the oppressed.

★

'Him!' said Rocco. 'In the dark green seersucker jacket and red tie. Go fetch.'

It was Nina's first sortie with Ernest Rocco, one of the Information Liaison Officers of the body called the Military and Civilian Co-ordinated Research Group which Perry had mentioned. She followed the green seersucker jacket into the Chase Asia Bank and walked past the man after he joined a line at a window. His eyes flicked over the people around him as he inserted one hand into the manila envelope clutched to his chest.

Nina stepped back as if avoiding a blow. She knew that pitted face and narrow jaw. The opium smoke still reached out for her, even here among the noise and traffic and glass-fronted buildings. From Saigon to Bangkok, across a wilderness of mountains and the grey coiling serpent of the Mekong. Through the wall of all that had happened to her.

Both the cats and rats are leaving the ship now! thought Nina.

Rocco was waiting just outside the door.

'A Chiu Chao rice merchant from Cholon,' said Nina. 'But also an agent selling Yunnanese opium to the Alliance Corse. And he knows me by sight . . . I must go!'

'What was he doing?' asked Rocco, unmoved by her urgency.

'Making a deposit, I think.' She glanced back. The rice merchant was still in the bank. He had acted for Thu . . . she had seen them together.

'Did he see you?'

'I don't know. For God's sake, M. Rocco, I can't let him identify me!'

'You should have confirmed what he was doing,' said Rocco. 'It's important. Which window?'

She closed her eyes and tried to remember what she had seen before that jolt of recognition. 'Third from the left.'

'Why do you think he was making a deposit?'

'He had a full envelope of something that was making him nervous . . . Please, let's go!'

'Just hang on while I make a phone call,' said Rocco. 'If he comes, wave to that Buick over there.'

Perhaps he didn't recognize me, Nina thought. Perhaps I halluci-nated him.

'Right,' said Rocco, reappearing. 'They've got the son of a bitch in their sights. Let's you and me go get name, rank and number down on paper.'

Nina knew that the man's hard, opaque eyes had rested briefly on her face. His eyes had peeled away the protection of time and distance. She had forgotten to watch out for old enemies.

After that day, she stayed close to her office and the Bakers' house. She avoided the main business district and the narrow streets of the old city where black-market statues of the Buddha, carved jade and Imperial Chinese rosewood furniture were exchanged over cups of tea and bottles of Green Spot orangeade. She avoided all Americans with Italian names, who might be friends of the man from Tampa, Florida, who had bought her family's opium business.

Nevertheless, Nina had no qualms about re-writing the future of the rice and opium dealer, as a HUMINT resource or applicant for US citizenship or whatever the issue might be. Exposing him was consistent with her choice to leave Saigon. But her second excursion with Rocco began to make clear the price she was expected to pay for a passport, the appearance of a normal life, and legal permission to occupy (although shackled) a place in the world.

Rocco took her to a private house in a *cul-de-sac* off the Prasarn Mitr Road. Nina shook hands American-style with a nervous, crew-cut, forty-five or fifty year old Vietnamese. The man's eyes were frightened and his hands were soft and damp.

'Hello,' he said. 'Good day! I'm very pleased to meet you. I like Americans very much.'

'Mr Van wants to give us some information,' said Rocco, 'but his English leaves a lot to be desired. Maybe you could help us out.'

Van spewed out an eager flow of facts without prompting. He had been born in the Saigon delta, he said, and now lived in Luang Prabang in Laos. A cousin of his, from a village to the east had seen a big road being built by the PAVN, right through Laos, to transport their guns into Cambodia and South Vietnam. Van himself had seen a well-known North Vietnamese general in Luang Prabang. There were Pathet Lao troops camped in the area. He personally knew two Pathet Lao supporters in his neighbourhood.

'What's he saying?' asked Rocco.

'I'll let you know when he stops for breath,' said Nina. Now she was the bone between two dogs, both hungry in different ways. To Van, she said, 'What's your business in Luang Prabang?'

His eyes flickered briefly. 'I have a shop.'

'What do you sell?'

Again he blinked rapidly. 'Many things. I have a comprehensive stock.' He paused. 'Radios. Watches . . . such things.'

'What is the address of your shop?'

Van smiled broadly. 'It's very hard to find. If you wish to come, I must meet you and show you the way.'

206

'How long have you lived in Luang Prabang?'

'My family moved there from Vietnam in 1955.'

'Did you have to leave much behind?' asked Nina.

Van looked at her helplessly. 'No,' he said instinctively. 'Yes,' he corrected himself. He looked past her. 'Yes, we left much behind.' He continued to avoid her eyes. 'Is what I have told you worth anything? Will they pay me to tell them more?'

Nina looked at Rocco, wondering what to do.

'Come in the next room a minute,' the American said.

I won't pretend, she reminded herself. Either way.

I can't prove it, she thought, but I suspect he's in an office somewhere, or behind the desk of a library . . . somewhere with access to the media. He said nothing I haven't seen in print. Maybe even writes for a paper. He wants a reward. Wants onto the famous American payroll. Needs to be. . . .

She imagined Rocco's reaction to this opinion. Then she remembered the helpless expression in Van's eyes. And she did pretend after all.

'I'm not certain how much access to top quality sources he really has,' she told Rocco. 'Why not thank him for his time . . . give him something . . . and tell him that you already have this information but should he ever learn any *new* facts, you would be most pleased to show your gratitude? You never know.'

She returned to her newspaper cuttings in relief.

'Watch,' said the man. He drew his knife point down Jimmy Putnam's right bicep. The skin split neatly as a peach and bright clear blood drew a line down the brown skin to Jimmy's elbow, where it dripped less neatly to the ground.

Jimmy inhaled sharply but made no sound. He was tied to a post in the centre of the village, wearing a sign which said, 'Invincible American aggressor'.

The assembled recruits murmured. The encircling ring of village children squeaked and laughed. A naked toddler pushed forward to touch the bright red wetness.

'See! An American bleeds just as we do,' said the man. 'They have no magic powers . . . You!' He pointed to one of the seventeen year olds who had gathered for this lesson. 'If you take my gun and shoot him, he will die, like a buffalo. Here. Take it!' He offered his Mauser to the youth.

207

'Come forward. Don't be shy or fearful. Just do as I tell you. No more, no less.'

The young man shuffled out from the comforting shoulders of his comrades and took the strange metal weight in his hand.

'Where should you aim?' asked the instructor.

Jimmy Putnam met the pupil's eyes and held them. The young man's hand lifted, wavered and fell again.

'Where?' demanded the instructor.

'His heart,' muttered the youth.

'His balls!' shouted one of the others.

The instructor grinned but shook his head. 'At this range, with this weapon, choose the head for sure death. Raise the gun . . . that's right.'

Jimmy still held the pupil's eyes. The young man once again faltered. The gun shook in his hand. His eyes slid away from Jimmy's.

'A little higher,' urged the instructor. 'Hold it steady.'

His pupil put his other hand on the gun.

'Good. Can you imagine yourself now killing an American?'

The youth nodded uncertainly.

'Good! Now give the gun to a friend. When you are quite sure you will succeed, I shall let you pull the trigger. Maybe next time, eh?'

The next man Rocco took Nina to see threatened her.

'How much do you want?' he asked. 'How much would it cost to tell them I'm a good man?'

'I'm only the translator,' said Nina stubbornly. 'I don't have the power you imagine.'

'We'll mark you,' he said, smiling for Rocco's benefit. 'Round Eye mongrel bitch! I'll have your face marked so the Americans won't want you to whore for them no more!'

'And I've marked you,' said Nina coldly, calling on past experience. 'I don't make trouble for small men unless they start it first!' But in the past, she had had lieutenants and bodyguards, mongrel or not.

'What was all that about?' demanded Rocco.

'Nothing relevant,' said Nina shakily. She tried to tell herself that the man's 'we' had nothing to do with the Chiu Chao rice dealer. That this was not evil following her from her old life.

Nina found newspapers and journals safer than field work, even though they told her that the Communists had begun major actions in South Vietnam and American troop strength in her country had risen to nearly 500,000.

She had a brief and unsatisfactory meeting with Ethan Perry when he touched down en route to Saigon in September, just after Thieu had been elected the president of South Vietnam. Perry was distracted by concerns she knew nothing of, and they failed to make the direct contact which had originally helped reconcile her to duress. He did not mention Will John Haines.

The MCCRG used Nina to speak to many refugees like Van, the man with the anxious eyes. Some had real facts to tell. All of them, genuine and fake, hoped for something in exchange for their information, either money or refuge. Except one.

The rains had just started and the refugee camp was a plain of mud crossed by a network of planks. The woman was a Vietnamese peasant about Nina's age, who had been living in northern Laos.

'Yes, it's true, I saw five prisoners. All Round Eyes,' she said. 'Soldiers from the sky. From Beefeety two. The *kla* kept them in cages. Tiny cages they couldn't lie down in.'

American prisoners of war. Airmen from a downed bomber. Nina translated and explained, '*Kla* is local dialect for savages . . . montagnards. There's no love lost between them and the Vietnamese . . . north or south.'

Water was dripping insistently from the corrugated metal roof of the office hut. Splash, splash, broadening the muddy moat over which Nina had picked her way when they arrived.

'Where did she see these prisoners?' Sloop's beige eyes were unusually bright.

The woman's eyes swivelled and settled on the floor. 'In the mountains, a long, long way from here.'

'Which mountains?' asked Nina. 'Near a village?'

The woman shook her head helplessly. 'The Pathet Lao shelled our village. Thought Royal Lao soldiers were there. My baby was killed. How can I remember the names of places when I was running with the body of my child?'

Splash. Splash. Splash. Splash.

Blankness swallowed up Nina's thoughts. Explosions nosed closer and closer through the darkness. She flew through the air and woke up in a terrible new world. She closed her eyes. Grief did not recede slowly like a departing train, carrying pain away. It ebbed and flowed like the tide. One moment, she thought she was standing clear, above high water mark. The next moment . . . now . . . it snatched and tumbled her deep along sloping sands toward a dark, bottomless rift.

'What did she say?' demanded Sloop.

Nina opened her eyes.

Sloop was straining at his leash. 'Where did she see them?'

'She can't be specific,' said Nina. 'Sloop, I need to stop.' She wiped her cold, damp palms on her skirt.

He looked at her sharply. 'OK, but first try to pin down her route of flight. This is the best break we've had in months!'

Nina pulled herself together. To the woman she said, 'Where exactly is your home village?'

'Nowhere!' cried the woman. 'It's gone. Boom! Lots of dust and smoke and a big hole! I have no village!' The woman began to cry with open eyes. Tears ran down her face and from her nose. Her hands lay open and empty on her lap. 'I want to die. Why didn't the bomb take me too?'

Nina looked at Sloop.

Splash. Splash.

'Try again!' he said.

'Can you tell me where your village used to be?' asked Nina very gently.

'No more . . . no more. . . .' The woman rocked on her knees, her eyes open and unfocussed, spilling salt water down the brown crevices of her face. Her words slid into Nina's mind like snakes.

'It's no use,' said Nina. Her voice shook. 'I think we should stop.' No more. No more.

Sloop ran a hand across his lean face. 'Another fucking write-off!'

'I trust you mean as a HUMINT source?' asked Nina tightly. 'A "write-off" for intelligence purposes?' She knelt down and took the woman's hands. The hands gripped hers but the woman continued to stare into space with open, overflowing eyes. 'Can we try to get her antibiotic powder for these septic sores on her arms?' asked Nina. 'And at least one good meal?'

No one could give the woman back her village or her child. And now, ironically, she was in the wrong place for someone to give her the death she desired.

In the Landrover, on the way to Udon, where she would get a military flight back to Bangkok, Nina thought about the woman and her desire to die. Suddenly, she realized that Mouse would have been born sometime in the next few weeks.

She would have been one year old soon! Nina tried to imagine her larger than seven weeks but could not bring the image into focus.

'Do you have children?' she asked Sloop neutrally.

'Yeah, two,' he said. 'A boy and a girl. Trouble all the way, but worth it, I guess.' He turned the broken nose toward her slightly. The unscarred eyebrow rose. 'It gets to you, doesn't it? After a while . . . that stuff back there. I shouldn't let it, but it does.' He looked out the window for a while. Then, as if remembering his manners, he asked, 'You have kids?'

'No,' said Nina. 'No,' she repeated.

Sloop turned back to her to check her tone.

'When did your children walk?' asked Nina quickly.

'Well now. . . ,' he said, successfully distracted. 'I missed the girl . . . in Korea at the time. She must have been about 18 months, I think the wife said. But Gary now, he was on his feet by ten months. And tried to kick a ball to me before he was one!'

His wirey frame relaxed into the pleasure of memory for a few minutes. But Nina didn't notice.

Mouse would have been walking! she thought. I'm sure that she would have been, by one year. Nina's image of Mouse focussed at last.

She would have been one of those with a round little belly like a jellybean, jointed like a doll. With feet like plump little pillows, not sure that the ground would still be there for the next step, careening gleefully across the chasm between the arms of mother and friend, small face alight with triumph.

Nina squeezed her eyes closed, but tears leaked down her face. She turned to the window and licked the salt water from her upper lip.

The following evening, back in Bangkok, Nina went to one of the impromptu flower markets which had sprung up along the streets in preparation for the birthday of the Buddha in three days' time. She bought a garland of tiny pale pink orchids and a clutch of incense sticks. Without plan or deliberate thought, she wandered slowly toward the river.

What is best? she wondered. She forgot to watch doorways and the shadows of cross-alleys for the Chiu Chao merchant or his friends. Her feet felt the way, along the Siphya Road, past huge modern hotels, down a river lane onto a small wooden pier. Just downstream, a launch was unloading sunburnt tourists onto the Oriental pier after a tour of the *klongs*.

Nina looked down into the littered water, opaque in the dusk, much closer to her feet than it was at Wat Arun. She could smell the dampness and the rotting weed and petrol fumes from boats. She raised her head. Houseboats moored along the banks were already showing the warm

211

eyes of lanterns. Another launch slid by, agile on the current, outlined in coloured lights.

The river here was not as wide as the Mekong where she had crossed, but just as strong. The River Goddess could coil as easily along its back when she visited the sea.

You saved me, Nina told the Goddess. Look after my daughter. Please.

She lit an incense stick and stuck the end into a crack in the grey wood of the pier. Then she threw the garland gently onto the dark, roiling water.

For you, she told the Goddess. And for Mouse. Happy Birthday.

She watched until the pale pink flowers turned ghostly with distance, then faded into the moving, metallic shimmer of the river at night. Then she lingered, imagining that she could still see the garland, until a water taxi cut across its path and sent little waves slapping against the pilings of the pier.

The instructor prodded Jimmy Putnam out of the tiny bamboo cage. Jimmy tried to stand but his legs were weak. He scrabbled on all fours, then rose at last, unsteadily but upright.

'Eat!' ordered the instructor in Vietnamese. He pointed to a basket of rice and boiled vegetables on the ground inside the circle of recruits.

Jimmy reached down carefully, suspecting a trick, expecting a blow from behind, but none came. He ate a handful of rice.

Oh God, it tasted good! He ate and ate, licking his fingers, then the basket, for the last grains. He forgot his audience.

'Drink!' The instructor handed him a coconut shell full of water. Jimmy drank. Whatever the trick was, it was important to keep up his strength, to be ready for the chance to escape, when it came.

'Observe,' said the instructor. 'He eats like a starving peasant. And if you wait long enough, you will see him piss like any other man.' He mimed the act, to get through to his prisoner. The recruits laughed.

'Now,' said the instructor, 'you, you, and you. . . .' He pointed at three young men. 'Beat him!'

Jimmy didn't understand the words but saw them coming for him. The fight was short but vicious, on both sides. A kick to Jimmy's head, followed by a foot in his solar plexus ended it. He lay sucking painfully for breath with the sun beating onto his bruised face and listened to a lecture, with gestures, which was clearly pointing out his own techniques of self-defence.

From one squinting eye, he estimated the damage he had done. Not bad, given the odds. But he didn't think he would survive long when those bastards began to practise with real weapons. He remembered his apologies to the young man he had shot. None of this bunch seemed to share his weakness.

I'm going to die soon, he thought. I hope I can handle it!

Nina and Ethan Perry sat beside his hotel pool again. He was on his way home from Saigon.

'I'm sorry we didn't get much time together before, on my way out,' said Perry. 'How are you getting on?' This time he wore slacks, loafers without socks, and a short-sleeved shirt which exposed loose freckled skin over the wiry muscles of his aged arms.

'I'm trying,' Nina said. She wore a blue cotton shift and stretched long tanned legs out to the sun. 'I'm not sure why, but I'm trying.'

'Everyone seems very pleased with your work,' said Perry. 'In case you care.'

'I suppose I do,' she said, after a moment of thought. 'I'd like you to be pleased.'

'Good,' he said absently. 'Good.'

I don't know what I hoped for from this old man, thought Nina, but disappointment bit at her gently, nevertheless.

'No luck with your daughter, I gather,' Perry said.

She shook her head. She wasn't ready to tell even him that she couldn't shake off the words 'no more!' She certainly could not tell him about the garland she had given to the river.

'By the way, have you heard anything from Will John Haines?' he asked without warning.

'Will John Haines?' Nina repeated stupidly, thrown off balance. She felt the same panic as before making that call.

Perry raised his noble head and peered at her along his nose. 'The one you asked me to try to track down,' he said. 'He vanished for a while. Then I heard that he was back and asking around the Foggy Bottom to see if anyone had heard from you in the last year. I passed on your desire to make contact.'

'Thank you for warning me,' Nina said after a moment. A bubble of joy began to form under her breast bone. If he wants to see me, his conscience must be clear after all! He must have tried! The rest was the fault of Paul and Pat and Sloop and Bill. 'Asking for me?'

Perry nodded.

'Where was he asking?' she asked after another moment.

'Lord knows who's talking to whom these days . . . How do you feel about him now?' Perry's tone was casual.

Nina shook her head helplessly. 'How do I know? He delivered me over to you. But I'm surviving in spite of it . . . perhaps because of it.' She hadn't considered until now that this last might be true.

'Did you love him?'

'That's really none of your business!'

'You're quite right.' Perry still held her in his sights. 'Quite right.'

'I want to take you out of this mess,' Will John had said. 'But this mess is my country,' she had replied.

But *this* mess isn't my country! Nina thought suddenly. She gazed around the hot deserted concrete and empty sun loungers. Not now! The idea of being rescued began like a gentle effervescence in her veins. She was so weary, so confused. If Will John still wanted her, he could put things right. She had never asked, or let, anyone put things right for her before, except that one time before. Now she needed it. He could help her finish what he had helped her to start. Lift her away from the war and confusion and the Chiu Chao rice merchant's friends. As in her dream, he would fly with her high into the simplicity of the sky . . . to the edge of his bay, to the cabin on the lake in Maine. To peace among green trees, above fresh water filled with trout. She was suddenly drunk with the possibility that her own effort could cease.

'Are you sure he understood that I want to talk to him?' she demanded of Perry in panic that Will John might not have been sufficiently reassured.

'He understood.'

Will John did say that it would take time for things to settle down, she reminded herself. Be patient! I must try to be patient!

A week later, Nina saw the Chiu Chao rice and opium dealer drinking with Bill in the bar of the Oriental Hotel.

'Do you mind if we go somewhere else?' she asked her partner, one of Barbara Baker's unattached males in town for a while, who didn't like eating alone.

'Something wrong with your drink?' he asked jovially. 'Anything I said?' He looked around. 'Or do you just like classier joints?'

Nina smiled into his eyes and brushed a dark strand of hair back from her face. He was a geologist. On a research grant, he said. From an academic foundation, he said. Just like Will John. She would take no chances. 'Old boyfriend behind us.'

'There must be a few of those around,' said her date. 'A woman like you!'

And just what do you imagine that is? she wondered, as he escorted her tactfully through the door farthest from Bill from the Drug Enforcement Agency and the Chiu Chao merchant.

Nina was less frightened than she would have been before Perry's visit. Will John had learned too late what kind of woman she was, but now he knew and would come for her anyway. Take her out of a world where heroin dealers drank with drug enforcement officers.

I can't do this job anymore, she imagined saying to Ethan Perry. I don't see the point. I'm coming apart again, the way I did in Saigon, into French pieces, Vietnamese pieces, American pieces. I can't put it all together.

Hurry, Will John! Please hurry! I'm not sure how long my strength will last.

Then something happened that made her ring Karelian and demand Perry's number in Washington.

'You do realize what time it is here?' Ethan Perry asked.

'I need your help,' said Nina.

'Then wait a mo, until I put in my teeth . . . I don't hear well without them.' The receiver rattled onto a bedside table or desk.

She waited shaking, until she heard him lift the receiver again.

'Is it bad or merely urgent?' he asked.

'Both.'

Nina had returned to the Bakers' house from the Bureau and climbed their hot, bleak concrete steps with the evening sun still fierce on her neck.

'Oh, hi!' said Barbara. 'Guess what! A little package came for you this afternoon. I don't know where Mei Wat put it. Hold on . . . and would you like some lemonade? Mei Wat just squeezed some. I made sure she washed the lemons this time!' She disappeared down the white-painted corridor toward the servants' quarters at the back of the house.

'Mei Wat!' Nina heard her call. 'Mei Wat! Please come here!'

Nina sat down on the orange and brown Scandinavian settee. She couldn't think of anyone who might have sent her a little package.

'Here it is!' said Barbara triumphantly. 'She put it in your room, but she found it again. Lemonade's on its way.'

She handed Nina an official manila envelope, addressed to Nina Desanges, care of the Bakers. Inside the manila envelope was a small flat parcel wrapped in dirty cream rice paper. It had no name or address on it, no stamps or franking.

'Aren't you going to open it?' asked Barbara, leaning over her curiously.

215

There was a small note to Paul Karelian on a comp slip from the office of the US Consul. 'Is this one of yours?' it said. 'Item left at front security desk by messenger.' Paul Karelian had added, 'To N. *Are* you one of mine? Anyway, I think it's yours!'

Nina sniffed the parcel and hefted it in her hand. 'I don't suppose it will explode,' she said and watched Barbara back away. Reluctantly, she unwrapped the dirty cream-coloured paper.

It was a French passport. She opened it. Her passport, her real passport in her real name, which Thu had taken from her carryall. Now it was here, with her real name, but no face. Her picture – taken with pompous formality by a Saigon portrait photographer – had been cut out. Nina laid the passport on her knees so Barbara wouldn't see the sudden unsteadiness of her hands.

'What on earth. . . ?' asked Barbara, leaning close again.

'It's mine,' said Nina. You don't exist anymore, the passport told her. There is no longer a woman called Nina Martell, née Luoc.

'Is it from the Embassy?' asked Barbara, bending her neck to read the comp slip.

Nina shivered. She touched the second page of the passport through the hole where her face had been. 'I suppose so,' she said distractedly. The passport was telling her that she wasn't going anywhere, ever again!

She told her legs not to leap toward the window, that there were no watchers in the street outside the Bakers' small compound.

Why did I feel safe from Thu, here among the futuristic office blocks and traffic jams of Bangkok, if I knew that the Chiu Chao merchant was here?

She leafed through the passport, suddenly afraid that he had written a message. But the neatly sliced hole replacing her face was enough.

Bangkok and Saigon were both large cities. Her mistake was to think of Thu only in his eyrie on the Tiger's Head. She had ignored how much the fighting was jumbling together the different worlds.

Barbara shrugged her incomprehension of bureaucratic processes and moved on to her own preoccupations. 'By the way, Steve McDonough's had a heart attack . . . He's the poli-sci man you met at the Ivys' pool party. A mild one, thank God! It was a warning. These men of ours work too hard. I keep trying to tell Peter. They're not used to the heat . . . and to dealing with people with such different values . . . Where's that lemonade?' She headed for the door. 'Frankly, they all drink too much . . . no wonder they keel over. Steve's lucky – he'll get sent home now.'

Nina didn't hear her voice receding down the corridor calling 'Mei Wat! Mei Wat!' She saw Thu's scarred hand holding the knife that sliced her face from the page.

'How did he know where to find me?' she demanded of Perry on the telephone.

'I doubt if he did,' said the cracked tenor reasonably. 'You said it was forwarded from the Embassy?'

'Yes.'

'Then he's fishing . . . knows you're in Bangkok . . . or may be there. After all, that's where you were headed in the first place. Have you interviewed anyone in the last few months who might be suspect?'

Of course. 'I could have . . . how does one know? And I've visited the refugee camps. . . .' And there was the Chiu Chao rice dealer in the Chase Asia Bank.

'How badly does this cousin frighten you?' asked Perry. 'Enough to leave Bangkok?'

'Oh God. . . ,' said Nina. 'I don't know!' She tried to gauge her terror. 'I'm not sure I have the energy to keep running,' she said. '. . . or enough places to run to.' She had always planned to flee to Laos, but now. . . .

'Paris?' suggested Perry. 'Here?'

'Would I be allowed in? A "reformed dink drug pusher", as Karelian once called me? Am I *persona grata* enough yet?'

'Official memory is pragmatic,' said Perry. 'After all, they used the Mafia in Sicily during World War II. You've done good work for us. And I might be able to help.'

'Thank you,' she said. 'Thank you very much. But I don't have the energy to move my life again. I think I have to survive until the fighting's over, then try to go back to Saigon.' Unless. . . , she added silently. Unless! She would wait for Will John. Hurry! she urged him. Hurry! Before the 'mess' grows beyond my control.

'Good!' said Perry. 'To be frank, I hoped you'd stay out there. You're becoming more useful rather than less, the way things are going out there!'

'I'll keep my head down,' said Nina. 'As Rocco would say. He should understand.'

'If he doesn't, call me,' ordered Perry. 'And, Nina . . . if you're ever frightened again, please let me know. Take this brigand of yours seriously!'

★

217

With an excellent sense of timing, Peter Baker came to the end of his contract and returned to the United States with Barbara. Under a false name, Nina rented a small, old-style wooden bungalow near the Chulalongkorn University. She told no one except her employers the address. She hired a Cambodian cook and a number one boy, who were husband and wife, along with their teenage daughter as wash *ayah*.

Then, as her initial panic eased, she reminded herself that Thu had not come after her when she fled from the Tiger's Head, when her direction must have been plain to see. He must have let her go. Perry had been right – Thu had merely heard rumours that she was in Bangkok – perhaps confirmed by the Chiu Chao rice dealer – and tossed her passport into the sea of the city on the chance that it might wash up at her feet.

But why? she asked herself. Why bother now, if he let me go?

Please, Will, come now!

At work, while she waited for rescue, Nina became reluctantly caught up in following the plot of a hideous serial. She confirmed through an increasing number of interviews with the growing number of refugees that North Vietnam was now regularly moving heavy tanks and war matériel to the south, along the maze of trails and roads which continued to stretch and spread in spite of constant bombing. She read the contradictory figures for the numbers of dead and wounded, both the North Vietnamese figures and the American ones, for both their own dead and that of the enemy.

Please Will, take me out of this.

The war did not improve, but, as time passed like a broad river without landmarks on its shores, Nina's reawakened sense of Thu softened to a dark, elusive shape like those which had occasionally brushed her legs as she swam toward the Thai shore.

'It's for you,' said the Embassy secretary. 'Long distance from The World. Do you want to take it in the cubicle?'

Nina was too frightened to put the receiver to her ear. It was happening!

'Hello?' said a tiny man's voice in English from the receiver in her hand. She continued to look at it. 'Nina? Are you there?'

She put the receiver to her ear. 'Will?' She wasn't sure whether she had actually said it or whether her thoughts were as audible as a scream.

'Yes,' he said. 'It is. Hello . . . this seems very strange. . . .'

Nina sat down on the little wedge of stool screwed to the cubicle walls. Her knees were banging together. 'Will,' she said. '*Je ne suis pas sûre* . . . I'm not sure I can. . . .'

'I know,' he said, switching to French with instinctive grace. 'Long time, no see and all that. Still no see, in fact.' He sounded nearly as nervous as she felt.

'A long time,' she repeated. 'And a long way away.'

'Yes,' he said. 'As a matter of fact, geography is why I'm phoning you. It looks at last as if I might be coming out. . . .'

She watched her shivering knees from a vast distance, every molecule of her being willing him to say the right words.

'I wondered if we shouldn't at least meet . . . to talk a little . . . settle our gyroscopes, so to speak.'

She could hardly hear him through the pounding in her ears.

'What would you find easiest?' he asked.

'Nothing is going to be easy.'

'You're right,' he said. 'I'm sorry. . . .'

As always, his quick, sincere capitulation caught at her defences. There was a moment of silence.

She realized that she had written this conversation wrong. To begin with his original offer. After so much time. And he would have been a little changed. Her fault, to expect too much, too soon. Her fault for stampeding. She tried to sit back mentally.

'How are you?' he asked. 'Really?'

'Fine,' she said. 'Busy, as you may know. Accompanied by a few ghosts.'

'Am I a ghost?'

She didn't answer. Only if you want to be. She lacked the courage to say it.

'*Mea culpa*, again,' he said, misunderstanding her silence. 'Anyway, I'll be there in a few weeks, forcing myself upon you . . . in the nicest possible way. No pressure. No cheating. Just meet and talk. *D'accord*?'

'I don't know. . . .' she began struggling for balance.

'Commit yourself now, on oath,' he said. 'So you won't reason yourself out of it, the way I almost reasoned myself out of calling you today.'

'All right,' she said.

'Swear it!'

'I said all right!'

'It's too fragile for "all right". We both know that.'

'What do you want me to do?' she asked desperately. 'Swear on the head of my grandmother? On the tombs of all my ancestors? Prick my finger and draw an "x" in blood on the wall of the telephone booth?'

'I want you to feel dishonourable if you're tempted to back out.'

'You trust my honour at this point?'

This time, he was temporarily silent. 'I always have,' he said. 'It's your opinion of mine that worries me. I'll call again when I know my flight date. Agreed?'

'Will, do you know what you're doing?'

'Oh yes!' he said 'Though my record may be against me, I do know what I'm doing!'

There it was at last!

'All right,' she said, with sudden unreasoning joy. 'Call me.'

Within hours of Will John's call, Nina's animal awoke after more than a year of dormancy. She began to wear flowers in her dark hair so their sweet scent could go with her everywhere. Suddenly, she noticed what she ate. She savoured the sharp tang of lemongrass, the crisp oiliness of fried dumplings, the smoothness of noodles, the mustiness of mushrooms, the heat of the red and green chillis. In the few weeks before Will John was to arrive, at polite dinners in the many western-style restaurants, with the men whose wives were at home in America, she again enjoyed the character of good wine in polished glasses, and the pleasure of crisp linen and glinting cutlery, remembering past evenings with Will John and imagining those that lay ahead. One night, when she returned home, she dug out the little jade monkey and put it on the table beside her bed.

She bought new clothes at last, for fun, wondering how she would look to Will John's eyes in this sea-green silk dress, or that Madonna-blue blouse. She bought gold bracelets to adorn her long slim wrists and a red bikini. She bought shoes with high heels to show off her ankles again.

I'm sorry, Barbara, she laughed at her mirror. It's not fair, it really isn't. And you did try so hard. I realized it, even then. And may even have appreciated it in a twisted way.

Then she would examine her naked body critically. Would he still like her breasts now that their top curves were more convex? Would he mind the small scars on her long legs, from infected insect and leech bites, which had never faded? At least, the 'most beautiful and mysterious navel in Asia' had become its former, neat-edged, shadowy pool of a self.

But I would trade it with such joy for that ugly, protruding button, thought Nina, if I could still have Mouse!

Nevertheless, once, whirling in the energetic incongruity of a Scottish reel danced on a teak floor while bats swooped past the chandeliers and gecko lizards croaked in competition with the pipes, Nina had an astonishing thought.

I feel happy! she thought, as her dark hair swung out behind her like a fan and her hazel-flecked eyes laughed up at her admiring partner. I didn't think it possible ever again, but I am! Filled with a sense of well-being. For a moment at least.

The men who took her out felt how alive her animal had become. They sensed its untried newness, which was nearly raw, and it appealed to them. She was wary enough to make an interesting chase, and oh, how satisfying, how almost virginal. How necessary, to show her what was possible! And how responsive that dark-haired, creamy-skinned female energy would be to the right man!

She didn't mind when they tried to take her to bed. Her rage seemed to have vanished into the bottom of its cave. Patiently, she explained that she was involved elsewhere. Over and over, she politely answered questions about how she found Americans (or French, or English), whether she would like to live in the States, (or France of England), and whether or not the Vietnamese really liked the Americans. She listened to the English and French explain what the Americans were doing wrong, and to the Americans justifying the American role in the war in Southeast Asia, and to how much these men missed American television, autumn in New England, their children, or a really good pizza. She could be charitable. She was leaving them all, any moment now.

She felt protected even when she went with Ernest Rocco to the refugee camps. She still scanned the faces of the children, trying to gauge how large Mouse might have grown by this time. Every so often her heart would still crash against her ribs and her mouth would go dry when she saw a child with a particular set to its ears and a certain breadth of forehead or wideness of eye. But these torments were short-term. She would be leaving soon. She would be able to tell Will John everything about his daughter, even about her own madness and guilt. About the searching. About the garland on the river. He would know what to say. He would cry the same tears, and they would heal each other.

Five weeks later, Will John finally telephoned again. 'The gods are against us,' he said. 'I've been given a different assignment. Not in Thailand.'

221

He didn't even try to pretend that it was academic research, and she wouldn't have believed him, not with what she now read and heard about the plight of the Meos who were being left unrescued and without re-supply as the Americans withdrew from the highlands of Laos and Vietnam. 'I will come to Bangkok when this other thing's over. Be patient, my darling. I will ring. I swear!'

'Fine,' she said. 'I would like that.' She hung up. He's not going to come! He may be smarter, but *I* know! She couldn't cry. She felt cold, and muzzy, as if she were getting influenza. Disoriented.

She returned to her desk and sat staring at the cluttered top. After an hour, she went home, without explanation, and lay awake on her bed from sunset to the following dawn. She picked up the little jade monkey again and again, to throw it away. Each time, however, she replaced it on the bedside table.

She did her job mechanically. She refused all further invitations to dinner from visiting *farang*. She danced no more Scottish reels or square dances. She ate just enough to spare the feelings of her Cambodian cook, who took unemptied plates as a personal insult. She lay awake at night, trying to find sense and purpose in the continuation of the mind and body that were herself. She tried to tell herself that Will John would call again, but she knew that she had done it again – made up a man who was too good to be true. With the same man.

How stupid, how gullible you are! she raged. How did you survive in the opium business for seven years when you think like a lovesick adolescent?

No longer minding whether or not old enemies found her, she began to take refuge from herself at night in the Bangkok streets. The noise and electric energy which had first stunned and frightened her now distracted her. She remembered similar nights in Saigon when the world revived from the torpor of the day and people tried to cram a whole life into the few cool hours of darkness.

Dressed again in a *panung* and sandals, she would stroll and eat noodles from vendors with portable brass mini-kitchens hanging from their yokes. She bought grey chipped ice with syrup poured over it from a woman in a stall made of bomb crates. She drank tiny cups of coffee in Vietnamese cafes and chewed coffee beans from glass cases pushed like wheel barrows, which also sold toffees in waxed paper twists and watermelon slices on shaved ice.

She avoided the bars, which were crowded with soldiers, sailors and airmen who had come to Bangkok for Rest and Recuperation. She watched them roam the streets and plunge into bars with their arms around mini-skirted whores in white lipstick.

Will John with me, she would think wrily. What was the difference?

A great deal! said another self. And he has still promised to come!

But she shook away such wishful fiction like a gadfly.

Most of the men among whom she moved on the streets were American, but there were also Australians, Thai Rangers and Air Force fliers and mechanics. There were Filipinos, and sailors from the British Navy. There were merchant seamen of all nationalities. There were also men who were merely tourists – Japanese men, American men, English men, Dutch men, German men, and Canadian men. There were very few women on the Bangkok streets at night except the whores.

I lived in a man's world in Saigon, thought Nina. I should feel right at home now. Perhaps that world is pulling me back.

In the streets were buyers for all of the thousands of jostling sellers whom Nina watched elbow and shove each other away from their prey. There were buyers for the women, for the girls, for the boys, for the transvestites and transexuals. Buyers for whisky, for cold tea masquerading as whisky, for beer, for tee-shirts, for suits made in one night, for gemstones and knuckles of the Buddha in cheap lockets. There were sellers and buyers for Marlboros soaked in hash oil, for Thai-sticks, for uppers, downers, and for horse.

Do I still fit in here after all? Nina would wonder. After giving up everything to escape? Was I fooling myself that I could buy innocence again by sacrifice? My mother's God could arrange such a transaction . . . Is Bangkok out of His jurisdiction?

One evening she settled against a wall to watch a trio of quick-eyed ten-year-old boys tug at uniform sleeves and offer small plastic bags of white powder. Only one man pulled angrily away. They made fourteen successful sales in half an hour. Then, chattering and laughing, they squatted near her feet and shook some white powder onto a piece of tin foil for themselves. Nina shivered. She couldn't watch any more. She had once been implicated in that white powder.

That world will never pull me back! Never, never! As she turned to walk away, she met the eyes of a man who was standing nearby. It was the man who had pulled away. She hadn't felt him approach again. She pushed past and began to walk fast.

'What do you think?' asked an American voice. The man had followed her. He caught up with her.

'That evil is often stronger than good,' said Nina. She walked faster.

223

'I *know* it is.' The man walked beside her. 'I've seen the proof.' It was an educated voice.

Nina walked a little faster.

'Anybody with his eyes open has seen it,' said the man.

She glanced sideways. He was in uniform. She shook her head. She didn't want this conversation. She didn't want to share this knowledge with a stranger in a worn American uniform. She didn't want to be followed at night by a strange man.

He put his hand on her arm, lightly.

'I'm not a hooker,' she said.

'I know.' He was tall and thin. Shorter than Will John or Perry but taller than Nina.

His thin face turned green then pink and green again under the blinking neon sign above their heads. His eyes were invisible in the shadows of his brows.

'And I'm not a rapist or murderer,' he said. Dark green and dark pink shadows alternated below his cheekbones. 'I'm off duty.' He smiled slightly.

Nina considered the tight dryness of his voice and the tension being transmitted by the hand on her arm. She wasn't certain about his disclaimer.

'May I hold your hand?' Without waiting for her answer, his hand slid down her arm and took hers. He held her hand out in the multi-coloured light and examined it, turning it over, feeling along her fingers with his own, which were calloussed and long. Then he grasped it palm to palm, experimentally. She heard him sigh.

'Is it all right?' His hand was hard, rough, and very warm. 'I really need to hold someone's hand.'

She half-laughed, still alarmed. 'I think so . . . I'm not sure.'

They began to walk.

Why am I doing this? wondered Nina. But he was right, there was something very comforting about another warm human hand.

He strolled slowly without talking. Now she could see his eyes as they caught the light. They darted from face to face in the crowd, inspected wares on stalls, glanced behind him. He seemed content not to talk, but the muscles of his arm were tense against hers.

I'm not in physical danger, Nina decided. That's not what feels wrong. 'What's your name?' she finally asked.

'John Doe,' he said. After a few more strides, he said, 'Sorry, that was rude. It's Gabriel.' Instead of asking her name, he asked, 'Will you have dinner with me?'

224

'I've eaten.'

'Eat again.' His face was lifted, looking over her shoulder, scanning the street. His hair was long, for a soldier.

'Gabriel,' she said. 'I'm not Thai, I'm Vietnamese.'

'Are you a VC?'

'No.'

'Then have dinner with me. Please!' He sounded calm, in command, but she felt an urgency in him, which was not purely sexual.

'I must go back. . . .' she began to say.

'So must I,' he said. 'Tomorrow. I'm not sure I can. Go back. There.'

His voice was flat and factual but a certain note in it sent a slither of chill through Nina's gut. She recognized this moment of his. Her own had come when she squatted on the eastern shore of the Mekong regarding an impossible journey. She looked down at their linked hands and nodded.

'I don't want to talk about evil,' she warned him. 'I can't. . . .'

'Nor can I,' he said. They stared at each other in the bright light which poured out of the open front of a restaurant and bar. With his grip still firm on her hand, he reached up with his other hand and smoothed her forehead with his thumb. For some reason, that small gesture erased her last alarm.

'I've already eaten dinner too,' he said. He began to walk again. Nina went too. Her knees had begun to shake.

He was staying in a small, inexpensive hotel in a small back street not far from the river. The Thai concierge accepted a few *baht* from Gabriel and vanished back into her private quarters without looking at Nina. His room had no air conditioning. Pale chinchook lizards skittered out of sight under the bed when they opened the door. He opened the wooden shutters across the windows and let in the light of a street lamp. He did not turn on the light in the room. He put something under the pillow on the bed and returned to stand in front of her.

Nina smelled teak, and mould, and frangipani, and the foxy smell of his body waiting quietly three feet away from hers.

'We don't have to do anything,' he said. 'But I'd like to hold you.'

She held out her arms. 'Let's see what happens.'

His body reminded her of Thu's. It was wiry and alert, even when pressed against her. His arms held her tightly, like Thu's, as if she might disappear. It felt strange to be hugged. It had been so long.

'Come lie down,' he said into her neck. He went to the bed and took off his boots.

Self-consciously, she followed him and lay down against him, her neck on the opened arm he offered. She listened to him breathe in and out four times while he stared up at the dark ceiling.

What am I doing here, she asked herself.

'Oh God!' he said. 'Oh God! Oh God!'

'Shhh,' she whispered, turning to him. 'Please. Don't!'

They reached at the same time, each as desperate as the other. Nina helped him pull up her skirt and tugged urgently at the tails of his shirt. She felt his hands in her hair and his mouth on her throat and breasts, through the fabric of her blouse, even while she struggled with the fly of his uniform trousers. She felt warm, damp skin beneath her lips, and then his weight. She opened her legs and pulled him against her with all her strength. She felt him enter her and lock her into his arms. They held each other as if trying to hold onto everything that ever had been, or could be, taken away. He came almost immediately and broke free. 'I'm sorry,' he said.

Her lips opened and pressed against the muscle of his arm which was braced beside her head. The hot night air between them felt cold on her skin. She was trembling. 'Please,' she whispered. 'Please come back! I need to hold on, too!'

He dropped his head against hers and nodded. Then he sat up. Carefully, he undressed her, button by button, layer by layer. Then she undressed him. His body was brown, lean and tightly muscled with a band of paler skin around his hips. She felt the hidden eyes watch her as she carefully laid his shirt, with airborne wings and other patches she didn't recognize, and then his trousers across the foot of the bed. She lay back and stretched out, her arms above her head. He put a hand on either side of her head. Then he lowered himself onto her, slowly laying each inch of his skin against hers, a little at a time, until she felt the blanket of his warmth covering her from head to foot.

They sighed in unison.

'Just like this,' she whispered, 'forever.' Her hands shaped themselves to his shoulder blades.

His weight lay so still on her for so long that she thought he had fallen asleep. Then he began to run his dry mouth along her eyebrows and across her lids, along the edges of her ears, across her collar bones on a long slow meander toward her breasts. By the time he entered her again, they held each other with their first intensity, but their rhythm had softened and slowed. They moved smoothly, locked together in the cold light of the streetlamp outside his window, for a long, long time until they slid together into release. He gave a long low cry as if in pain. Nina found herself in tears.

226

'I'm sorry.' This time she said it. 'I don't know why. . . .'

'No, no,' he said. 'I know. I know!' He stroked her forehead, her cheeks, her lips. 'I know.'

He woke her early the next morning. 'I have to make a flight from Don Muang to Tan Son Nhut. You stay here till you're ready.'

Her first awareness was the warmth of his hand lying in the arc between her shoulder and neck. His eyes were bright blue, like Will John's. His hair was light brown. He was as attractive by daylight as by streetlight. Then she noticed how thin his face was, and the dark circles under his eyes. She reached up and pulled his face down to hers before more thoughts could appear in either of their eyes.

'Thank you for a good night's sleep,' he said against her hair. 'That may sound crass but you can't even begin to imagine what a compliment it is!'

Nina kissed him again, reluctant to let him go. He returned the kiss hard, then pulled free and stepped back from the bed.

'Well,' he said brightly. 'I guess I'm going! Back!' He gave a wry nod of his head. 'To Vee-et-nam! Take care of yourself.' He turned and vanished through the peeling door of the room.

Nina wanted to scream for him to come back. She wanted to run after him and pull him by the arm back to safety. Instead, she curled on her side among the tangled, grey cotton sheets, embraced his damp pillow and began to weep.

An hour and a half later, she was back at her desk reading a North Vietnamese description of a battle in the Parrot's Beak. But though her days continued as mechanically as before, Gabriel with the bright blue eyes had unlocked Nina sexually. After their night together, she lay in her new bed, in her new bedroom, in her new house, awake now with a fury of appetite and sense of loss.

Dear Miss X . . . Mrs X? wrote Gabriel Simpson in his head. Dear Angel of Mercy. I wish to God I was lying with you in that Bangkok fleapit instead of here (also lying, but less comfortably) in a hole on a mountain-top in a place I'm not allowed to tell you, with NVA artillery teasing us from across the valley. Letting us know, with the occasional shell, that any time it pleases them . . . Whammy! They've read the right psychology books – the suspense is killing us, literally. Celeski charged out last night, got tangled in the wire and walked straight back into one of our own directional mines. There may or may not have been someone out there. Are they friends of yours? Enemies? Do you know

227

that even while I was inside you, I wondered whose side you were on. But it didn't matter. That night, you wanted to hide as much as I did. And if you are my enemy, at least I've seen your face!

Do you know something else? You may have been my last fuck. Ever. Now there's a thought! . . . Oh shit! . . . INCOMING!

Nina heard it on the radio. Muriel Wicks came to get her from her office.

'I think you'd better hear this,' she said.

On the 31st of January, 1968, Tet Mau Than, the Tet of the Year of the Monkey, the North Vietnamese and Viet Cong had launched a coordinated attack on all major cities, towns and military bases in South Vietnam. A handful of VC in South Vietnamese uniforms had taken the US Embassy in Saigon and held it for 6 hours. President Thieu had declared martial law.

Like Diem in 1955.

It's never going to stop, thought Nina.

'At least it's going to force the Vietnamese to make up their minds which side they're on,' said Muriel. 'Now that it's not just the military taking the brunt of it all!'

Nina wondered about her friends in Saigon. Chinchook and Simpoh Flower who had once been her maid and her best friend. She wondered about Gabriel with the dark circles under his bright blue eyes who had gone back to 'Vee-et-nam' to gaze again upon the proof of evil he said he had seen. Though she was certain she would never know, one way or the other, she needed him to survive. She closed her eyes. If she could conjure up the sensation of his body's warmth, it might not leave the world.

Suddenly, like a vicious pike from the bottom of a lake, an image swam to the surface of her mind. She saw the hand she had found while looking for Mouse's body. She had picked it up without thinking. She felt its coldness and the damp strings of its trailing veins and tendons. Her teeth began to chatter. Her hand pushed it away.

'Are you all right?' asked Muriel.

Nina gritted her teeth.

'What's the matter?' asked Muriel.

Nina shook her head. 'It's never going to stop!'

'Of course it will,' said Muriel. 'They'll all be at the negotiating table before the end of the year, you wait and see. The Communists have shaken everybody up. You wait and see!'

'Who did you say has been taking the brunt of it?' asked Nina between clenched teeth.

228

'Pull yourself together,' said Muriel. 'You're out of it. You have nothing to worry about.'

Gabriel Simpson sat hunkered down by the LZ. He looked as if he had been there forever, an oddly shaped boulder, dirt-coloured, mottled with stains, nearly mossy. For six hours, he had been waiting to be lifted out to a base in the rear. For all six hours, he had been waiting for the bullet from nowhere to keep him from getting back. He was too close. This was when cosmic irony always came into play.

He flicked his eyes around the perimeter and the treeline beyond, and took refuge with the woman inside his head. His eyes tried to close.

Dear maybe-the-last-woman-in-my-life, I'm still alive, if you call it living. Not sure what I've done to deserve to get this far. There's a push coming, but supposedly not until after the native New Year . . . the Tet. Received wisdom of senior command tells us that the gooks always drop everything . . . even throw down their guns in the middle of a firefight . . . to see the New Year in. They felt in more of a hurry than that, up at the camp.

. . . Come on! he begged the silent sky. Come on!

I dreamed about you last night . . . not sure when I slept long enough to dream, but you got in there somehow. You're stubborn like that . . . keep popping up. Like my friend Jimmy who's somewhere out there too but I don't know where. I'd like to talk to you again, and all the rest. Maybe the rest first, then the talking. I'm too tired to be sure. Anyway, there you were, walking towards me, arms spread in welcome, smiling. It made me feel good. Safe. Sexy. No violins in the background, but they would have been appropriate.

You lucky son of a bitch! I said to myself. Then I saw the man behind you with the knife. He gathered up your hair in one hand and sliced it off. The skin of your nape looked very pale and fresh, as if light had never hit it before. Like a camellia petal. I tried to yell at him, but somehow had turned the volume off. Then he cut off your right arm. Then your left arm. I couldn't move to stop him. He was very precise, very neat. Arranged the pieces on the ground in the right order, as if you were going to be reassembled. When he began to slice the nape of your neck, I felt I was going to explode, but your head kept smiling at me, even after he laid it on the ground.

'Why, Gabriel?' it asked, still smiling, but sadly, as if you realized how hard I was trying to get to you.

Simpson surfaced and listened again for engines in the sky. He scanned the treeline and closed his eyes.

Are you still alive? In one piece? I don't need a degree in psychology to figure out that dream. They told us on the radio they were sending in a second bird for the 'yard team. I didn't see it. Haven't seen any of those boys yet. And the camp wasn't far off being overrun. Jesus, I hope they're OK! I'd have stayed if . . . Those guys have been keeping us alive for weeks. We should have made them go first. The PAVN will treat them as traitors. Oh God, why didn't I insist that the Meos flew out first? I wanted out, that's why. Scared. I should have refused to go first!

Get me out! he begged the silent sky. Get me out!

Ironically, the increase in patriotic fervour in the North Vietnamese media, and its urging of the people to be steadfast, to hold faith, etc., suggested to Nina that the North Vietnamese leaders thought the Tet Offensive was a failure. If she read between the lines of official speeches and press releases, they seemed surprised by the US decision to halt the bombing and negotiate. Then the President's decision began to change her own life.

'We'd like you to go back into business,' said Bill. He sprinkled a teaspoon of tiny beige dried fish onto his rice and reached for the grated coconut.

They were eating at Pat's house. Nina had not seen the man from the State Department since her first refusal to identify photographs of her countrymen. His wife had been sent home to the States in the general anxiety after the Tet Offensive, and there were only the three of them at the table. Pat's Number One Boy, an attractive woman of thirty-five or so, in a *panung* and bare feet, was serving them a Thai-style chicken curry.

'Thanks, honey,' said Pat. 'We'll help ourselves now.' He watched the woman leave the room with appraising, possessive eyes, then turned back to Nina.

'We'll set you up with a generous bankroll,' he said. 'Move you up to Chiang Mai. Most of the tri-border dealing goes on up there.'

Nina took a careful sip of the, no doubt boiled, iced water with boiled water ice cubes. The faces of both men were serious. 'Business?' she asked. 'Dealing?'

Bill avoided her eyes.

'Come off it,' said Pat. 'You're over twenty-one. We need a window into the area now that the US presence in Vietnam and Laos is being stepped down. We Americans all got to put our hands on the table to show how clean they are. You have a history in the trade. Nobody'll

230

wonder if you happen to turn up again with a new name to pursue old interests.'

But they might feel they had a few scores to settle with a traitor, thought Nina. She shook her head.

'What do you mean?' demanded Pat. He glanced at Bill.

'I mean, no.' Nina shivered. That world would never have her again!

Bill picked up one of the little dried fish from his plate and broke it in half with apparent fascination.

'It would help us,' said Pat. 'The end of Turkish opium has everybody jumping around like rain on a griddle. With our own men out of the mountains, we have to keep the hill tribes happy. We need people with their ears to the ground. Without the 'yards, we've got no security in the north!'

'No!' said Nina fiercely. 'I pulled out of the business three years ago. I've told you everything I know about it. You have no right to ask me to go back in!'

'I'd have thought you'd enjoy it,' said Pat. 'A taste of the old times . . . Bill has agreed – we'll let you keep any profit you make.'

Nina threw her iced water in his face.

This time, she calculated the time change before she called Washington.

'What kind of line are you on?' asked his cracked tenor, when she had started to explain.

'Open,' she said.

'Stop right there,' he instructed her. 'Can you hold the fort until I come out in two weeks?'

'I don't know.'

'Let me know if not.'

'Thank you,' she said. 'I will.'

'You're being naive and you know it,' said Perry, his tone gentler than his words.

They were beside the turquoise pool of his usual hotel again, under a large blue and white umbrella advertising Campari. It was nearly midday. The sun was frying the concrete and the sun loungers were deserted.

'Why shouldn't they ask?' he continued. 'You might have said yes. They're pragmatic men trying to deal with chaos in a pragmatic way. You must try to forgive them.'

Now she could hear definite irony in his voice.

231

'Forgive them for sending me back among men who would first cut off my breasts then kill me for treachery?'

'I'm sure that Karelian and Co. have great faith in the security of their investigations,' said Perry. 'They'd be highly insulted at the idea that you were in danger from a leak.'

'And, worse, they used my history in the trade to blackmail me. . . !'

'Their request doesn't mean they now *approve* of opium trading,' said Perry.

'Stop playing devil's advocate!' She slammed her glass down on the table so hard that an ice cube leapt out. She threw the cube hard onto the hot concrete, where it shattered. The sharp-edged fragments melted instantly. 'You know that approval or disapproval are irrelevant to pragmatic men.'

He smiled into his gin. 'In any case, I never approved of the recent fad for Intelligence being involved in operations. It blurs perceptions and judgement . . . Why don't you have a swim to give credibility to that rather attractive red bikini?'

'The natives know better than to swim in this sun,' she said tartly. 'This suit is to keep me cool . . . Ethan, if I'm certain of anything, it's that I can't go back! I would undo everything . . . more than you can imagine. I would have nothing left.'

I shouldn't have worn this bikini, she thought. It was meant for Will John.

Perry regarded her, his large domed head tilted slightly to one side.

'Does that sound too melodramatic?' Nina asked. 'Does it embarrass you?'

'Makes me a little uncomfortable,' he said. 'Only because I've never "been there", as my niece at Cornell would say.' He pushed out his lower lip. 'Come to the States.'

'To do what?'

'I expect we could find something.'

She inhaled and exhaled the mixture of chlorine and ylang-ylang. Was this the form that rescue would take then? Not flying, but skulking? Not carried, but alone?

Perry put down his empty glass and looked over his shoulder for a waiter. 'I'm a desk man,' he said to the swimming pool. 'There's always space in analysis for someone with your background. And right now, a new department, section or committee is being born every minute, to check up on some other department, section or committee. Demand is outracing the supply of informed, intelligent . . . Aha!' He raised one long, immaculately manicured, liver-spotted hand. 'Think about it . . .

232

Two more of the same,' he said to the waiter. 'Think about the alternatives.'

He sat comfortably silent, his eyes half-closed like a lizard on a rock, until the new drinks arrived.

'It would get you out of the clutches of the boys with operational yearnings,' he resumed, as if they had never paused. 'My side of things is relatively restful – as long as you don't mind that the policy-makers never read anything you produce, and ignore what they do read. Apart from that, it's a pleasant life.'

I can't go to America alone, Nina thought. Without Will John. It's too far in every way! 'Thank you for the thought,' she said. 'But, no. Just please try to get Bill and Pat "off my back".'

'I feel old when those two just look at me,' Perry said, nodding his large head in understanding, '. . . with their stainless steel eyes. Thank God for seniority! Right, I'll see what I can do.'

Perry collected her from the Bureau the following evening in an Embassy car and drove her home.

'It's squared,' he said. 'And not much hard feeling. They'll find someone else . . . were most eager to let me know how easily, in fact.'

He came in without being invited. 'How the hell did you get one of the old wooden houses?' he demanded.

'Luck.'

'You've just made me nervous for the first time,' he said severely. 'We like to be the only distributors of "grace and favour".'

'That's ego, not politics,' she said.

'Touché!' he said cheerfully. 'In fact, I now want to ask you a favour.' Having invited himself in, he now waited to be asked to sit.

'I'm sorry, I've no more gin,' Nina said as he arranged his long arms and legs in, across, and around a rattan armchair.

He waved his hand. 'Don't worry, this is business . . . you wouldn't know, but I've been out here advising on the establishment of yet another new body. A new section at the Embassy, answerable directly to the Ambassador, for the screening of refugees. To serve as a filter for information . . . direct it to the appropriate service agency. I put your name forward and hope you won't embarrass me by refusing, should they offer you a job.'

'Refugees?' she asked faintly.

'Third country nationals,' he amended. 'But primarily refugees.' He lifted the cliff-edge brows slightly in question. 'Yes? No? You already do very much the same kind of thing for the MCCRG now and again. It could be painful at times, but then, you may find the chance to do some good on a personal level.'

Nina said nothing. She smelled charity again in this 'favour'. 'I would report directly to the Ambassador?'

'To his office.'

Not to Karelian. Not to Sloop or Bill. Not to Pat. Nina shrugged.

'Right,' Perry said. 'That's done.' He placed his hands on the wide rattan arms of the chair and levered himself to his feet. He looked at her with sudden alarm. 'You did agree, didn't you?'

'Of course, Ethan,' she said, half-laughing, half-enraged. 'Of course. What did you expect?'

Jimmy Putnam did not know about the Tet offensive. He knew only that all the men and boys over fifteen had vanished from this new village. His present guard was a fierce young woman of twenty-five or so, constantly armed with a semi-automatic rifle, who must have been one of the first females in Jimmy's life to remain unmoved by the sweetness of his smile. At this point in his capture, he did smile from time to time. He felt lucky.

He had been removed without explanation from the custody of the military instructor before any of the increasingly bold recruits had decided to show off and pull the trigger. Now he had to find fire wood and carry water for the villagers, to dig, to split bamboo, to dig up tree roots – to be out of that cage felt nearly as good as being free. He had dysentery badly, but the villagers gave him strong tea to bind his gut, water to replace what he lost and as much food as they had themselves. For Jimmy's bulk, it wasn't enough. But he could steal fruit while he was working, and was free to move around, under guard, during the days while he worked. He occupied his mind by learning Vietnamese, mostly from the children and the two widows for whom he did the most work. He began to think that he might survive after all, and be either liberated by his fellow Americans or returned as a POW when the whole mess was over.

Then, one afternoon, without warning, he was bound, blindfolded, and marched away by four North Vietnamese in uniform. As they left the village, he heard one of the widows shouting in protest.

The darkness frightened him. Not knowing what was going on around him frightened him.

If they want to shoot me, he reassured himself, they could have done it in the village.

234

After several hours of marching, he was manhandled into the back of a jeep. Then they marched again. Then waited. Then a short march, down a steep track.

When his blindfold was finally removed, Jimmy had a quick glimpse of a heavy grate swinging shut and a lantern beyond it which quickly retreated, leaving him in the cold dankness of an underground cave. He felt his face. The blindfold was really gone. He knew he had seen a lantern for those few seconds. But he felt blind. He could see only darkness thick as velvet. He felt a flash of panic.

I can't stay here! I can't bear it!

Carefully, he sat himself down on the damp stone floor. Pull yourself together! Your eyes will adjust in a minute. He leaned back onto his hands, then jerked them off the floor. With growing irrational terror, he felt again for the stick, or whatever it was. It was a bone. Attached to other bones. A pelvis. Ribs. Skull. Shreds of cloth.

Jimmy scrabbled across the floor away from the dead man until he hit a stone wall. He wrapped his arms around his shaking knees and buried his face to blot out the cave.

Mother! Oh God, Mother! Help me! Help me out of here!

11

Unlike Thu, Major Lucky had had no son to replace the one he had lost. He did, however, still have his hamlet intact. The Avenues Marie Antoinette, de la Chapelle, Maréchal Foch, Deux Magots, Bonaparte, Prudhon, and St Cyr still lay in a faint and dusty but unbroken *patte d'oie* below the surveying lenses in the sky above, still punctuated by the comma and exclamation point of the pagoda and Cenotaph. The statue of Major Lucky, now finished, still adorned the Place in front of the Palace, surrounded by octagonal beds of red-orange cannas.

However, Mihailo Rogov now refused to come to the villa, no matter what bait the Major dangled. The Russian knew the risks of chancing to be in the wrong place at the wrong time, under a falling shell unable to make fine distinctions of race, nationality or political belief.

'It's a bombshell,' Major Lucky assured Rogov. 'The piece of good luck that life sends to each man no more than once!'

Rogov's launch waited at anchor below the knobbly-kneed pier on the Ou River. The Russian eyed it wistfully. 'Another new buffalo?' he asked Lucky, slapping two mosquitoes at once. His record was five.

'I'm saying no more.' Lucky's eyes gleamed with the sly satisfaction that always made Rogov want to slap him instead of mosquitoes.

What an earthquake of flesh a slap would set off! thought the Russian. 'What do you want from me, precisely?' he asked.

'Check the name,' said Lucky. 'Just check the name!'

Major Lucky had checked the name already. It had taken Grégoire Ince three months to get back to him, and cost Lucky the opium harvest from a good-sized village, but the results had been worth it. His newest American prisoner, a mere footsoldier purchased from some ignorant Tai farmers, was worth nothing in himself, beyond a certain propaganda value in the place of his capture. The bombshell was the prisoner's father.

'*Bon voyage!*' called Lucky cheerfully from the pier.

The eggbeater engine of the Russian's launch pulled it backwards in a frenzy of churning muddy water. As the boat turned downstream, Rogov ignored Lucky's mocking salute.

Oh, my superior friend, reflected Lucky. I'm going to relish our next meeting so much more than you!

It made no difference to Jimmy Putnam that in his final days in office in early 1969, President Lyndon B. Johnson ordered the end of all special ground operations against the North Vietnamese. What did matter was that the man who now held him, a Major Lucky, had finally taken him from the cave after a period of undefined blackness that nearly broke his mind. Jimmy was now locked into a chicken run in the open-roofed inner courtyard of a walled prison building, where he could tell day from night and hear other human voices to remind him that the world, in some form, was still real.

Nina was grateful for her new work for the Ambassador's special committee, even though it was sometimes painful as Perry had warned. She could see the point of it. She was able to facilitate a visa here, or help locate a relative there, as well as to assess the information which refugees from Laos and Vietnam brought with them. She shared problems and made friends, both among the staff of the refugee camps and relief organizations, and among the refugees themselves.

Her closest Vietnamese friends were a married couple who ran a restaurant on the beach in Pattya, a resort south of Bangkok on the coast of the Gulf. She met the Ngos by chance when trying to find a temporary foster home for a ten-year-old Vietnamese boy whose parents were missing but not confirmed dead. She would spend days- off sitting on their terrace, looking past neon signs at the sea and chatting of holidays in Dalat, the mountain resort north of Saigon, or comparing Thai beaches to those at Cap St Jacques, now known as Vung Tau. But Mr Ngo had been a civil servant in Saigon; he didn't know who she had been but he knew that she now worked for the Americans. A slight uneasiness would always quiver in the air between them.

Major Lucky, meanwhile, still waited for a response from the Russians to the message he had given Rogov. It didn't come. Lucky became first impatient, then angry.

This silence is a snub by that jumped-up bureaucrat, he fumed. A deliberate insult! He probably never even passed my message on!

Lucky began to investigate alternative ways to exploit his 'bomb-shell'.

In late 1969, Nina was asked to travel north to Chiang Mai to talk with Vietnamese-speaking Meos being resettled in Northern Thailand. She asked for twenty-four hours to think.

'I must go directly to the meeting and return to Bangkok the same day,' she said, after a sleepless night visited by the angry spirits of her father's former colleagues.

As she trudged down the track to the resettlement village from the main road where her jeep and driver had parked, she wondered what she would do if she recognized any of these Meos, from Thu's eyrie or Lucky's caravan.

But the tribesmen waiting in the huts at the bottom of the rocky track were strangers. They had been driven from their villages in the northern mountains by the advancing North Vietnamese.

'They mean to wipe us out,' said the former headman of one abandoned village. 'They are slaughtering whole villages, even the children. They must kill us because they can't control us. We are too powerful. We are too good as soldiers. We can make our own guns.'

And you have money from opium, thought Nina.

He told her, and others confirmed, that the use of many of the US special forces and CIA camps in the mountains between Laos and Vietnam was becoming impossible. There were, they said, growing rumours and reports of American POWs in Communist-controlled areas of northern Laos. They also told Nina that US helicopters were now flying most of their opium out of the mountains of Laos in place of the old mountain pony and mule trains. To them it seemed a fair trade for Meo guns, loyalty and men.

When Nina returned to Bangkok, she found a message on her desk. 'A Will John rang. Please call him back.'

Under tight control, she waited until 2 a.m., to allow for the time change. With cold fingers, she dialled the number on the message sheet. A woman answered.

'Could I speak to Will John Haines?' Nina asked, startled by the apparent calm of her voice.

'I'm sorry, he's not here yet,' said the woman. 'He doesn't usually get home till six-thirty or seven. Would you like to leave a message?' Her

238

voice was soft but matter-of-fact. She sounded used to taking messages for an absent husband.

Nina was in a nightmare loop in time. And she recognized absolute finality.

'No thank you,' she said with extreme politeness. 'I'll try his office.' She hung up.

I was right! I did know! She had a sense of manic self-control.

He hadn't been able either to lie for her or to get a divorce!

'Well, Will,' she said aloud to the teak panelling on her bedroom wall, still deceptively calm. 'I think that's it! Really it. The end. No more making up anything! You were just too nice for me altogether!'

Then a hideous thought wrenched at her gut. What if he had divorced, and that woman was a second wife?

Nina picked up the little jade monkey from the table by her bed and threw it with all her strength against the wall. It bounced and clattered unharmed onto the teak floor. She threw it again, harder. It still remained unbroken. She snatched it from the floor and marched out of her bedroom, through the entry porch and down into the concrete drive. In a fury of frustration, she searched the dark garden for a large enough stone. With a wedge of granite hauled from the edging of a flower bed, she smashed the little monkey first into sharp-edged fragments, then into chips, then into milky dust. She scrubbed the dust with her feet until it was erased by darkness. From 2:45 until dawn, she rolled and twisted among the damp sheets. There were no princes in this world, only tigers. No genies. No rescue. Unless she rescued herself.

Strangely enough, Nina found finality, even awful finality, easier to live with than dying hope had been. She simply closed down part of herself and shifted that energy outward. The lives of others had more meaning to her than her own. America was now closed to her, and she no longer recognized what she heard of her own country. She accepted her present place and present role. The force of her now-restored energy which she put into this role was considerable. She worked every day and as many nights as possible. She volunteered for extra assignments. She drove the Ambassador's office nearly mad with follow-up queries. She did not recognize the multi-layered rage which fuelled her as she tried to sweep up and reassemble pieces, whether of information or of other people's lives.

Except once, on a street near the University, when she and a large American headed for the same gap in the crowd. They collided and he swore at her. Nina had started to reply when she read the legend on his tee-shirt: 'Kill them all and let God sort them out!'

239

Nina looked from his printed chest to his pink face and back to his chest. A blind, murderous fury rose in her at this callous hopelessness, like that of a child walking away from a ravaged playroom. Like Will John, they thought they could solve everything, for everyone. Then when the problems turned out to be harder than they had thought. . . !

She tried to organize her thoughts into punishing words. She would spit in the man's face. Then kill him. Then she was paralyzed by the inadequacy of all these urges. She raised her hand as if to brush him away. To the surprise of both, he stepped aside and let her pass.

Behind her, he said, 'Crazy dink bitch!'

She whirled, ready now to attack, but he lowered his head and walked away. She stood in the street, breathing hard, cheated of release. Finally, she walked on, to continue her own sorting out, with or without God's help.

Major Lucky and Grégoire Ince met in Vientiane.

'How's business?' asked Lucky.

'Never better.' Ince smiled and polished his glasses with the tail of his sports shirt. 'And what trick have you got in the bottom of your bag?'

Lucky told him.

Ince hissed between his teeth and rocked his round head from side to side doubtfully. 'Very delicate!' he said. 'Whew! Well, that's my boy! I'll have a go.'

In 1970, the Meo headman's predictions to Nina came true; the Special Forces bases in Laos were abandoned. In early 1971, dissension raged in Bangkok – where the venture was leaked sooner than in America – about an American raid on a prison at Son Tay in Laos, to rescue reported American prisoners of war. The raid was launched from the Thai bases of Udorn and Ta Khli. It was a dry hole. There were no POWs there when the rescue force arrived.

One body of Bangkok opinion considered the raid on Son Tay as yet more proof of US incompetence – in particular a failure of Military Intelligence – through over-reliance on electronic intelligence collection and lack of communication in the command structure. Opposing opinion held that the raid on Son Tay was a master stroke of Machiavellian tactics, never intended to rescue prisoners but aimed from conception at the 200 Chinese troops and Russian advisers said to have been 'accidentally' killed in the attack.

In the spring of 1971, the South Vietnamese invaded Laos and disrupted the steady southward flow of arms, men and supplies for the North Vietnamese. The number of refugees increased. More and more Vietnamese and Laos applied for US citizenship. Nina was regularly offered bribes in exchange for help in furthering these applications. She received two more threats from men who couldn't believe that she was both incapable and unwilling.

The most painful case was that of her friends, the Ngos, who ran the restaurant in Pattya, and were not refugees, strictly speaking. For reasons Nina never quite understood, Mr Ngo fell foul of local police and turned out not to have proper papers.

'They knew that!' he cried. 'The police always knew that! It didn't matter before. But now they want too much!'

'Please,' begged his wife, pushing an iced coffee across the table towards Nina. 'Please talk to your American friends. You can get us proper papers. Please!'

Nina talked to everyone she knew, including Perry. There was a brief interlude of hope while strings were tugged. Then she had to go face the Ngos in Pattya.

'I'm sorry,' she said. 'More than I can say. It seems that you . . .' She looked at Mr Ngo. '. . . joined a revolutionary youth movement, while in Saigon University. You're considered a bad security risk.'

'What can I give you?'

'I don't want anything! I just can't!'

'You could!' cried Mrs Ngo. 'You could if you wanted to!'

Will John must have felt helpless in this way when she asked him to lie for her.

Nina kept trying. She even made a personal visit to the chief of Bangkok Police. The Ngos were sent back to Vietnam the following month, just after the North Vietnamese Army shifted from guerrilla tactics to all-out conventional war.

In 1972, Bangkok gossip made Nina aware that a US fighter bomber squadron along with nearly 2,000 pilots had been relocated from Danang in South Vietnam to a base in Thailand. More Meos were evacuated from the Plain of Jars, in Laos. Then in December, it was announced that MACV Headquarters was to be moved from Saigon to Nakom Phanom in Thailand. The Americans were leaving the ravaged playground. Nina watched it all from the safety of Bangkok with a chilly helplessness. She felt deep in her bones that her life would be changed yet again. That she would never be relieved of effort.

In the few hours of non-working solitude she allowed herself, she became aware that she was lonely. She missed the Ngos and their neon-lit beach. Missed Will John. Missed Ethan Perry. Missed Gabriel Simpson. Missed Mouse.

As the Peace Accords began to settle into shape in 1973, Nina considered beginning a low-key affair with a doctor she had met at one of the refugee camps. His compulsion to work and emotional weariness both matched her own. She saw him only when he came to Bangkok on his days off. He wanted to eat, drink, make love and not to talk, all of which would have suited her perfectly. His love was drained by the hundreds of men, women and children whom he was unable to help enough. Then they had their first and only fight.

'I don't understand how one country produces you all,' Nina had said one evening. 'The destroyers and the healers – and both equally dedicated to their jobs.'

Ben Jalelian responded with such a rage of fury and frustration that they made up immediately, before they destroyed whatever slight comfort they gave each other. However, Nina pulled back. Ben was as precariously balanced as herself.

Soon after her fight with Ben Jalelian, a letter from America was delivered to Nina at her office. She looked at the postmark, then at the handwriting. She threw it unopened into her wastebasket.

It lay all afternoon among the crumped letterheads, coffee-stained newspaper clippings, broken elastic bands and crushed, sticky paper-cups. At the end of the afternoon, Nina locked her desk and filing cabinet. She looked at the letter and straightened her desk lamp unnecessarily. Then she bent suddenly and transferred the letter from wastebasket to handbag as furtively as if shoplifting.

When she arrived at her old wooden house, she changed with slow deliberation from her western work clothes into a *panung* and thong sandals. She poured herself a whisky, told the cook when she would want dinner, and sat down in one of the rattan chairs on the open wooden deck surrounded on three sides by rooms of the house. She stared up at the blue evening sky, watched a swift hi-jack a mosquito four feet above the deck, counted the first evening croaks of the gecko behind the shuttered doors of the dinng room, sighed, and opened the letter.

'. . . I admit defeat,' Will John wrote. 'King Kong bows his head in surrender to the fates. I tried several times to ring you but we missed – I would rather have told you . . . no, correction, I'm more comfortable writing . . . the coward's way out. My wife became pregnant. With my cooperation, obviously, but not my collusion or desire. Estranged husbands and wives seem to have this strange compulsion to copulate – perhaps in the illusion that the act is now shorn of the complexities of married life. That is not an excuse that a gentleman should make, but I am desperate that you do not think I was deceiving you when we spoke. I did know what I was doing!

'Now, obviously, she and I must look closely once more at our relationship, or lack of it. I don't know what I am doing any more, or at this moment, at least. I loved you. I probably still do. Something in me changed when we were together, and I think it may be permanent. I wish I liked and admired myself in all this as much as I do you. I'm grateful. . . .'

The sheets of thin airmail paper rattled in Nina's hands.

So am I, she thought. You should have left me alone, but I'm still grateful!

'She's an obsession now,' said Will John's poet friend. 'Be reasonable. You're about to become a middle-aged, first-time father.'

Will John tried to laugh. 'I'm usually the one telling other people to be reasonable. I'm a little frightened that one major setback can unhinge me so completely.'

'It hasn't,' said his friend. 'You just like to think so. You've been bitten by the romanticism of encroaching middle age . . . nostalgia for all that unmade hay, all those unburnt candles, uncrossed bridges, unsown oats. . . .' His focus became distant as he groped for more clichés for his list. '. . . stones unturned, songs unsung, rosebuds ungathered, frogs unkissed. . . .'

'Shut up!' said Will John violently. 'Please,' he added, lest his friend feel offended.

When Ince reported that the French considered the matter too hot to get involved with, at that moment, Lucky began to regret the money he had paid for his brown American prisoner. He began to mind the inordinate amount of food that seemed necessary to keep the young man in trade condition. He would stare reflectively through the wire at his acquisition and wonder whether to still maintain him as a long-term investment, or write him off as a short-term loss.

In late 1972, as US troop numbers fell from 159,000 to about 24,000, and the most intense American bombing operation of the entire war was mounted, Nina was called more and more often to Chiang Mai in northern Thailand. The former capital had become a focus for refugees, deserters of all races and politics, and cross-border opium traders. As Americans were pulled out of Laos and Vietnam, all other eyes into those countries became more and more valuable, her own included.

In January, 1973, a peace agreement was signed in Paris by North Vietnam, South Vietnam, the United States and the Vietcong. However, South Vietnam refused to recognize the Communist provisional government in the south, and continued to receive US aid. Real peace remained elusive. Fighting resumed in March at the end of the first 60-day ceasefire.

Nina did what was asked of her. Each year, a few days before the Buddha's birthday, she threw a garland of pale pink orchids onto the oily surface of the Menam Chao Phyra.

While Nina was busy in Thailand, Bill McNeill from East Chicago, who had long given up on winning the war, was crossing between Vietnam and Laos with a small Studies and Observation Group, checking whether American prisoners of war were being returned according to the agreements between the US and North Vietnam. He gave cameras to Man and his other Meos, who came up with the pictures: Americans in secret hospital camps, Americans in special prisons, men mutilated by torture or injuries sustained during capture. McNeill collated eye-witness reports from montagnard agents from both North Vietnam and Laos. He passed on these reports, backed up by the photographs, and waited for further orders.

'Did you know your countrymen are being set free?' Major Lucky asked Jimmy Putnam. Fortunately the young man spoke French. It relieved Lucky's impatience to be able to torment him. Sometimes he imagined actually torturing him, telling him first about the young son, murdered by American terrorists.

'Sent home?' asked Putnam. 'Is the war over then?' Joy took a minute to swell to the surface through numbness and disbelief.

'So it appears,' replied the major. 'And prisoners are being exchanged.'

'When will I go?' asked Jimmy. He had begun to tremble uncontrollably. 'Oh God, I can't believe it's finally happened.'

'Happened for some,' said Lucky. 'Your joy must be unselfish. Be happy for your fellow countrymen! I am going to keep you forever!'

On the television in the bar in Bangkok in 1973, McNeill watched the freed American prisoners file off the plane. Every man was walking unaided.

'Where're the others?' he muttered to himself. 'Where're the ones in wheelchairs? Or stretchers?' He waved away the hostess, who was smiling a five hundred *baht* smile, in a bikini bottom and nothing else, except a peace sign drawn in lipstick between her naked breasts.

The American president raised his arms exultantly above his head. 'All our boys are home!'

McNeill stood abruptly; the hovering waitress darted away in alarm. It's a fucking lie!

Eyes raised and heads became suddenly attentive. For a minute he thought he had shouted the words out loud. He was going to kick over the table. Throw his glass at the moon-faced jerk from Reuters and the Thai smoothy who were slumming it over a shared bottle of Scotch. IT'S A FUCKING LIE! His hands wanted to throw his chair at the used-car salesman on the TV screen selling the United States another piece of crap.

The bar owner, a fifty-five year old Saigonese woman in a pink cardigan and Levis stood up slowly behind her leatherette-covered cash desk, her eyes on McNeill.

His hand trembled as he replaced his glass carefully on his table. He drew in a deep breath and made himself walk out of the bar between undisturbed tables, unbroken glasses and unthrown chairs, into Patpong Lane 2. Behind him, the television was playing band music and the bar owner waved to the hostess to let him go.

'There is now reason to think that you were mistaken . . . that many of the reports are unsubstantiated.' McNeill's CO looked him straight in the eye.

'You and I know they goddam well weren't!'

'*I* don't know any such thing.'

'The photos. . . !'

'Undated and unsubstantiated as to source and location.'

'I know the men who took those!' exclaimed McNeill. 'My best Meos. If they say they took those pictures some place at a certain time, they did!'

The officer nodded. 'I'll make sure your assessment is noted. Thank you. We appreciate your help.'

McNeill tried going over the CO's head. He tried talking to two journalists in Bangkok. He did not think of himself as an emotional man, but he began to become aware of the anger. It felt like a parasite gnawing its way into his liver, making him nauseated, like an amoeba or fluke.

As Major Lucky had said, the war only appeared to be over. Violations of the cease-fire agreements continued. Nineteen seventy-four ended with expectations from Bangkok and Washington of a North Vietnamese build-up toward a massive effort against South Vietnamese forces in 1976. Nina continued her work, and to wait for the change in the order of her world.

Bill McNeill took a duplicate set of the Meos' photographs and explained the situation to an old friend, now attached to the Assistant Chief of Staff for Intelligence of the Air Force, Bangkok.

'Sorry,' said the friend after two weeks. 'I hit a stone wall too. Everybody wants this goddam war to be over. America's out and wants to stay out. I think you'd better face reality.'

'Reality is guys still out there,' said McNeill.

Reality is betrayal.

Bill McNeill understood expediency, and the moral imperatives of survival. He did not understand betrayal.

I re-upped to see this thing out, he thought. To hang in there with the guys doing the dirty work, no matter what I thought of the work itself.

Night after night, he lay awake. I did what they asked me and now they tell me it has no meaning. 'Unsubstantiated'. Those men I saw, and Man saw, and the others saw, and photographed . . . did what they were asked. And now their lives are 'unsubstantiated'. Worthless. They think we're all worthless.

The liver fluke of rage sat under his ribs night and day, month after month, even when he went home at last, in 1974, to find out what else he could do besides be a good soldier.

'No one has asked for you,' said Major Lucky to Jimmy Putnam in the thick wire chicken run. He snapped his fingers for a cigarette and the young Meo girl who had replaced wife Number Two in his affections, handed him a cigarette and lit it with the gold lighter. 'Do you think anyone cares?' asked Lucky.

Jimmy didn't answer.

'I doubt it myself,' continued Lucky cheerfully. 'No one seems interested. No one at all. I didn't tell you before, but I *have* sent word that you're here. In your position, I would definitely wonder whether anyone cares. Do you ever wonder?'

He's lying to torture me, Jimmy told himself. It's not true. The fat little asshole is trying to torture me!

But Lucky's words came back at night, and during the endless hours of the day. Jimmy didn't know exactly how long he had been here in this wire cage but it was a long time. He had made marks for the days, then forgotten whether he had already counted a day or not. He was unsure of the months, of how many days to count before starting another. But he could tell just by looking at the sticks of his arms and legs that he had been a prisoner for a very, very long time. Long enough for someone to do something to get him out if they were ever going to.

In January 1975, the Vietnamese provincial capital of Phuoc Long fell to Communists. This caused mild alarm, but no panic among Vietnam watchers in Bangkok and Washington.

Nina was therefore shocked by Perry's telephone call in February, on a secure line.

'I'm coming out to collect you,' he said. 'Have second thoughts about it later, once you're safely here. It's now or never.' His tenor cracked with unusual emotion. 'You see, I can be melodramatic too! It's now or never!'

'Ethan, what the hell is going on?' This is it! Nina thought. The next crumbling away of my life . . . I've been waiting for it ever since MACV moved out of Vietnam!

'Can't say, I'm afraid. But you're smart enough to read between the lines. I'm going to need you over here, and if you don't come soon, even I won't be able to get you into the country.'

The implications of what he had just said made Nina cold. 'I can't come to America. I have to stay here!'

'Humour a dinosaur today,' Perry said. 'I need you! How fast can you pack?'

'It's as bad as that?' she asked, knowing it must be.

'I'm afraid so. By the time you can get organized, you'll need me to walk you through . . . and don't tell anyone you're leaving.'

'*Mon Dieu!*' she said.

'Quite!'

'Why will you need me?' Need is a seductive word. 'People need me here.'

'There's no one for them here. We need Vietnamese speakers, badly! . . . People with cultural sensitivity. And a sense of mission.' Even now, a slight irony disinfected his underlying intensity. 'You don't have to stay forever.' He hesitated. 'Make another moral choice. Come do good.'

Life pivots on such small points, Nina thought, like an old man

247

knowing the right words. 'All right,' she said helplessly. It made as much sense as anything else. 'Come and get me.'

'No one wants you enough even to try to bargain for your life. No one cares. Why should I?'

That evening, Major Lucky tramped angrily up and down along Putnam's cage. 'Why waste food on you? Why waste men to guard you? You're useless! Worth nothing. I think I'll kill you.' Lucky paused.

Putnam lay curled up on the ground. Pretending not to hear.

'Why don't you save me the trouble,' asked Lucky, 'and kill yourself? You Americans think you can do everything. So, figure out how to end your worthless life and save me the trouble!'

He was quite sure that such a thing was impossible for Putnam. Lucky was not going to kill his prisoner. He had had a better idea.

Ethan Perry snored gently beside Nina for most of the numbing hours in the airplane, a protector whose long legs had relaxed into her seat space. Nina drank the free Business Class champagne and watched meals appear from the steward's trolley like a conjurer's trick, multiplied by mirrors. She wanted to hide inside herself and try to feel what was happening to her. To dream out her dreamlike state in order to wake. But she was constantly distracted and overwhelmed by objects being announced or offered, like the infinitely multiplying dinners: hot towels, sleep masks, padded socks, complimentary decks of cards, funpacks for the children, duty-free alcohol, perfumes and watches, life jackets under the seats, oxygen masks which would materialize in case of need.

They were following the sun and slowly catching up with it. Nina watched the protracted dawn. Its pink brightness glowed around the edges of clouds, in contrast with the stale greyness of dozing, cotton-mouth passengers behind the pulled-down window shades. As the brightness grew outside the plane, Nina drifted in and out of restless half-dreams.

She was roused by the announcement that they would shortly be landing at New York John F. Kennedy Airport, followed by the instruction to fasten her seatbelt and place her chair back in the fully upright position.

She had a sudden, shocking, exhilarating view from her window of Manhattan in the early light, implausibly clear in outline, impossibly high, rising from the sea as abruptly as the rocks of the bay of A Long. There was not even a Garuda on those alien towers. She had seen them in photographs, an abstract composition, a half-noted bar chart of irrelevant figures. Now, she felt sick with terror and excitement at their beauty, strangeness and reality. Is that what I have chosen? What on earth is it?

12

Laos – 1977

Will John Haines sat balanced on his buttocks, forearms on kneecaps, strong long-fingered hands loose between his shins, on the wide weathered steps of the verandah of an abandoned French hotel in the jungle of northern Laos. As a boy, he had sat in much the same way on the steps of his grandparents' porch, looking dreamily out at the rumpled waters of Narragansett Bay designing the future. Now, he was a tall man with red-gold hair, wearing a borrowed white cotton sailor's sun hat which was too small for his large head. The pale skin on his long straight nose and jutting brow bones was flaking after two days back in the tropical sun. On first look, he seemed potentially comic – too fair, too large, too contented, too peaceful for jungle where the gibbons were occasionally shocked into silence by artillery and automatic weapon fire.

Any latent comedy faded on a closer look. Under the borrowed hat and red-gold hair, the blue eyes were windows onto constant thought. His clean, regular features were underpinned by emphatic bones in nose, brow and chin. His long wrists were strong and glinted with gold in the afternoon sun. His height, when unfolded, would be imposing. Alone on the sagging steps, under the sinking tropical sun, he looked immensely calm, self-assured, and reassuring, in the way other men respect and women find sexy. As always, he seemed unaware of either possible opinion.

He was an hour and a half by foot from the Thai-Laos border, waiting with considerable interest to see what was going to happen next.

I should probably be afraid, he thought, then he continued to enjoy his waiting, among the ghosts of the former French Union of Indochina.

The hotel sign had fallen from the roof and now leaned askew against the gap-toothed verandah railing. Each letter in the words 'Hotel Bellevue' had been outlined with bulletholes, so neatly that the centres of the 'o's and 'e's had fallen out. Will John imagined the focussed anger of a gunman willing to take the time for such precision.

★

Life fascinated him. As a youth, he had believed that its amazing, seductive secrets could be stripped bare by books. He had been an academic for six years before he decided, on the contrary, that books were a tease – a waving of veils – and had begun to look elsewhere for his answers. He had then pursued direct personal research with the same gusto as, aged eleven, he had consumed *The Count of Monte Cristo* under the bedclothes by flashlight. Luckily, this switch in personal focus came during work on his Master's degree, at the same time as an academic's usual switch to original research. It also came at the time when a growing number of government foundations in America were beginning to finance such research for their own reasons. Luck was on Will John's side yet again; he ended up with a Ph.D in Folklore and Anthropology, and in the right job for the wrong reasons.

He had no romantic image of himself as a spy or intelligence agent, nor any illusion about the vital importance of the titbits he collected so happily and analyzed along with his scholarly research. He understood, quite correctly, that he was making minute contributions to a vast pattern. He did not mind his insignificance; it seemed to balance his unfair share of life's advantages in other realms. It was enough to enjoy waiting in deserted hotels for unknown stool pigeons who wanted to trade titbits of possibly useful fact for American favours. From time to time, real joy bloomed for him, in the rare moments of stumbling over an absolutely new idea, or when the pattern of known facts suddenly enlarged itself in his understanding. He was a glutton for knowledge and his work, with its first-hand fact-chasing and occasional revelations, suited his temperament and intellect perfectly.

Will John watched pale little chinchook lizards dare themselves closer and closer to his unmoving feet, bellies as translucent and fragile as a child's eyelids. A cloud of tiny flies wavered and swooped around his head, blending with the waves of late afternoon heat rising from the ground. Through this miasma, beyond the wide flagged approach to the steps, he could see young trees growing from the moss and lichen at the bottom of a crumbling swimming pool. Beside the pool, a Chinese-style pavilion threw its exuberant curves toward the sky as if trying to grab hold and arrest the slow sideways slip of its peaked roof. Beneath the roof, an ice-cream vendor's case was rusting under its chipped enamel.

He wished he could show Nina this place. The ruined grandeur would have moved and amused her, as it did him. She would have understood the ambiguities.

251

His contentment acknowledged its true source and flickered into cautious joy.

Nina. Nina. Nina.

Even the sound of her name warmed him. He said it silently, twice more, as an incantation for the future. It was going to happen, in spite of everything. He would find her and then find somewhere wonderful for them to hide, to begin the long mending. This time, he knew what he wanted and knew he could make it happen. He would make his world embrace her as totally as he had done.

He had tried sincerely, but failed, to reconcile with his wife. They had reached an amicable agreement about Louise's future. She had been a genuine accident, not a deliberate act by his wife. He was fond of the child but did not see himself in her, or a soul which he recognized.

He had recognized Nina when he had first seen her. Not just as a beautiful, self-contained, confident-seeming woman. As kin, in some strange way. How strange, he thought, that my own genes seem more alien than someone from a different race and culture. He would take Nina to his grandparents' home on Narragansett Bay, which was now his own. To the cabin on the lake in Maine. He would show her the blazing beauty of a New England autumn, when the mountains glowed as if planted with bougainvillaea in full bloom. But even more beautiful. And less hot. Less dangerous. He expected to do full penance before earning those joys, but was a willing penitent.

He looked up at the verandah surrounding the hotel and suddenly saw the line of Nina's back and hips as she had leaned on the railing of her own balcony, wearing only a thin silk kimono. An embroidered chrysanthemum had lain across one shadowed curve just where he had planned to place his hand.

He shifted his buttocks on the stairs; physical memories must not distract him from the afternoon's project, one of a few final tasks before he would muster his courage and call her in Washington.

He refocussed his eyes on the secondary jungle around the hotel and cocked his large fair head to listen. A stand of tall grasses grated drily on his left. In the trees behind the hotel, a flock of gibbons were still hooting their outrage at his intrusion to anyone who would listen. He heard nothing out of the ordinary. He could decipher old palm leaf manuscripts but not the irregular green humps on the far side of the dried-up swimming pool. His many acquaintances who had fought in the jungle would doubtless be able to see and hear more than he could.

On the other hand, he thought, they might also have learned to be properly afraid, not merely interested. He listened to his own, regular breathing and observed the steady tick of his pulse against the wing of his open collar. His ability to keep his feet firmly on the rational path made him attractive to the funding foundations, but sometimes he wondered whether he was missing the highs, both of terror and joy, that seemed to fuel other men.

Except with Nina, a recalcitrant part of his brain reminded him. You didn't miss the highs or the lows with her. And you'll have them again, he reassured himself. Right now, keep your mind on business.

He looked back at the jungle without urgency. He would see or hear the would-be informer who had asked for this meeting when he or she was ready.

He heard them behind him on the verandah. He rose and turned, noting for negotiating purposes that the man above him had chosen to establish superior status, with a higher position, leaving Will John as suppliant, halfway up the stairs. The man was gazing down with an intense satisfaction which Will John found off-key in a prospective informer. And though the man was unarmed, the four men with him, standing behind him at a respectful distance, carried AK.47s. All five wore black uniforms like those worn by the PAVN and many guerrilla groups. The leader, with the oddly satisfied expression, wore a Colonel's 3-star collar patches.

Will John felt a shadow of uneasiness stir in his chest.

'You stole my son,' said the man gently in French.

Will John Haines usually understood most things most people said to him. Understanding was part of his job. Now, he stared up with unaccustomed incomprehension at the man standing above him on the verandah of the abandoned French hotel.

'I'm sorry . . .' he said, 'I don't think I understand.' His mind scrabbled to make sense of what the man had just said. There was a rational explanation, if only he could think of it. There was always a reason if man's mind could only find it.

'You . . . stole . . . my son,' the man on the verandah repeated slowly, as if Will John might be a little slow-witted.

Lao or Vietnamese, noted Will John's brain automatically. Probably French educated. Or employed by the French.

Why is he looking at me like that? demanded another part of his brain. Why the triumph in his eyes? Why does he seem to know me? Will John's body felt fear seeping in like the first shadows of dampness on the wall of a cracking dam.

Like most rational men, he was frightened by things he could not explain.

The man sighed. The intense, inexplicable satisfaction in that sigh sent a small cold current of fear to the tops of Will John's knees.

He's insane, thought Will John.

In other circumstances, Will John, himself an attractive man, would have dispassionately described the face above him as handsome, even beautiful in a ravaged way, like a stone sculpture left to weather for centuries in the jungle. The face had the same cheekbones, cat-like eyes and clean-edged curve to the lip that Will John had seen in the ruined temples of Cambodia, before all the shooting had started.

In other circumstances, Will John would have been amused by the absurdity of the scene: a blond giant of a man, a peaceable American professor of folklore and anthropology with extra-curricular interests, being accused of kidnap by a madman two thirds his size, in the uniform of a guerrilla warlord, surrounded by his troops on the verandah of a derelict former French colonial hotel, complete with ice-cream freezer, in the mountains of northern Laos.

He might, perhaps, have also been amused to remember that he himself had insisted on leaving behind at the Thai-Lao border the squad of Royal Lao soldiers assigned as his bodyguard for the trip to the hotel.

But the careless angle of the four guns on the verandah, unmistakeable in intent, was too much for Will John's usual sense of ironic detachment. He had faced guns before, but in explainable, and therefore manageable circumstances.

In the silence left for his answer, Will John could hear the bats behind the shutters squeaking and rustling, in preparation for evening flight. He swallowed and heard the dry sound of his own mouth.

'I have no sons, my own or anyone else's,' he said. 'Would you please be kind enough to explain?'

The man smiled. In other circumstances, it might have been an attractive smile. 'You're not in a position to demand explanations.'

Will John could hear the pulse in his neck beating against the side of his collar. He had been an arrogant idiot to leave the Royal Lao soldiers five miles back along the overgrown grassy track once known as an *autoroute nationale*. Briefly, he let himself hope that they might have become anxious about him, and were even now about to burst from the scrubby jungle around the hotel.

'No soldiers,' he had said. 'No guns. Nothing provocative.'

Not in the troubled border area between Laos and Thailand. Not with a new informant who might prove useful in the future. Not to a potential new human intelligence resource.

He had been pleasantly aware that he was more or less accepted among the hilltribes of northern Thailand and Laos who crossed back and forth over the battle-lines of national boundaries as casually as the wild mountain cats. He had been pleased by the image he had gleaned, of himself as a crazy but peace-loving *farang* with a voice-capturing machine and notebook, who was always asking questions, spoke Thai, made a stab at several montagnard dialects, ate anything he was given and could match a Meo drink for drink. He had thought it quite natural that an anonymous would-be informant might ask for him by name. Always honest with himself, he had privately admitted that he was flattered to be known and trusted, not just another ghetto-American from Bangkok locked into the tiny world of PX, Sports Club, and English-speaking servants. He had walked alone into this insanity from pure hubris. He had no one but himself to blame.

'I realize,' he tried again, still hoping to refocus insanity into clarity, like a blurry film in a cheap cinema, 'that many sons of all nations have been lost. . . .'

'No,' said the man quietly. 'I accuse you alone. Not your war-mongering country. You alone.' He moved to the front edge of the verandah. His eyes were intense but without any shadow of madness. 'You deprived me of my first son – my support in this life and my caretaker in afterlife. What penalty do you think is fitting for such a crime?'

Will John shook his head helplessly. The world was suddenly beyond his control.

The man on the verandah gave an order in Vietnamese. Two of his four men moved forward toward the verandah steps. Will John saw the black cloth hood in the hands of one of them, swung his arm to fend it off and fell backward down five steps to the ground. The rifle butt that he just managed to see coming hit him in the chest. While he was still gasping with pain and shaking sense back into his head, the black hood slid over his face and was drawn tight around his neck. He thrashed out with his long arms, felt one fist connect solidly, then found himself on his knees, clutching his solar plexus, retching and struggling for breath after a second blow from the rifle butt.

'Please,' said the man's voice, still gentle. 'That was not polite of you. Stand up now.'

Will John tried to inhale and managed a painful wheeze.

'Stand up!'

He tried to raise himself on one leg, but the knee buckled.

'I do not repeat orders.' A light exploded on the right side of his head and he wanted to be sick again.

Oh God, not inside the hood! . . . Think! he ordered himself. Solve this. Find the way out! There is always a way . . . as long as you can think!

A blow on his back sent him staggering against the bottom step. He broke his fall blindly with his hands. A splintered stair edge gouged his chin. Hands shoved him up the steps. His brain was too busy trying to keep him upright to be able to think.

Washington D.C. – 1977

With her beige raincoat pulled tight around her, Nina stood under the dark rim of trees around the Mall and surveyed the sea of fog in its centre. Ahead of her, the giant stone needle of the Washington Monument was quilting together layers of mist. Beyond it, she saw nothing but fallen cloud stretched out on the grass. The air was metallic with exhaust fumes.

I'll never find him, she thought. We could pass within ten feet of each other! Thank God! I can go home . . . say I lost him in the fog.

'Start at the Monument and walk toward the Lincoln Memorial,' Perry had said. 'You'll meet in the middle. No waiting around in public for either of you that way.'

As if that somehow makes the job easier, she thought.

After two years working for Ethan Perry in Washington, Nina had become muted. To Perry, who remembered her from the hot, tormented, sunny war years in Bangkok, she now suggested an object floating just under the surface of a lake, inviting inspection just as it slipped a little deeper into shadow. He felt obscurely responsible, and helpless to do anything about it. She is drawn, he often thought, palely fragile like a sun-loving flower forced to grow in damp shade. At that moment, he was fretting in his office, wondering whether he had been too drastic in his attempted cure.

The wall of fog on the Mall diffused and redirected all sounds. A steam hammer tut-tutted somewhere in Washington's permanently dug-up streets. Above the soft, damp sluicing of traffic, an airplane rumbled and whined, feeling its way, sounding much too low and close, along an electronic beam into Dulles International. As it passed overhead, Nina fought the need to throw herself flat onto the wet green grass.

How many years will it take? she wondered. Before that stops?

Closer than steam hammer, cars, or plane, a pigeon cried rape and murder.

Nina shivered inside the layers of gaberdine and wool, of facings, interfacings, linings and interlinings intended to fortify her against the damp chill. The spring, her second in America, was as tight-lipped as Perry had been when they had talked, just as unwilling to relax into ease and warmth. For a moment, in her mind, a violent equatorial sun burnt away the fog, and glinted off the puddles, the lenses of spectacles, and the teaspoons on the tables of the sidewalk cafes in Saigon.

Stop that! she told herself yet again. That's over. Gone. Learn to be resigned, even if resignation is not in your nature. She jumped off the edge of the world toward the stone needle.

After ten strides, the wet grass had soaked her high Italian boots. She paused and bent to peel a damp magnolia petal from the water-blackened leather on her left foot. The petal was cool, smooth as dead flesh, and as purple as a bruise at the end she held between her finger and thumb. She stared at it.

Like many things in America, where she had too much time in which to remember, it shimmered with half-remembered alien import. Christmas trees, for example, drowned her with longing for her early childhood, when their resinous smell persuaded her for a few heart-breaking seconds that she was back among the pines of Dalat, safe with her parents and *ayah* in the villa above the lake. And there had been that odd moment during the past winter, by a freshly-frozen pond. Before coming to America, she had seen ice only in cubes and blocks.

One cold bright winter afternoon chilled by alien winds, a boy had sent a stone sliding across the brittle surface. The ice sang out a high, clear note, like a crystal wine glass when you run your finger around its rim. The boy's friend cried, 'Listen!' in a tone of childish wonder. Nina and the two boys listened to the ice sing again and again, under more stones, and Nina began to weep tears beyond her control.

Now, she dropped the flesh-like magnolia petal abruptly with undefined horror, and hauled herself firmly back into the present. She turned ninety degrees at the plinth of the Monument and nearly stepped on a body lying face down on the grass. She stopped, thinking of booby-trapped bodies that destroyed those who bent to help.

But this was Washington D.C., in 1977, and the body was a young man in jeans and an olive drab rainjacket. He rubbed his hidden face back and forth along his folded arms.

Nina let out her breath and leaned forward. 'Are you all right?' she asked softly.

257

'Fuck off!' he said to the grass. 'Just fuck off!'

She walked around him. After a few yards, she wondered whether he had thrown her off course. She looked at her watch again.

'John Putnam?' she called quietly, so quietly that he might not hear.

The steam hammer still rattled. Another airplane searched along the electronic beam for Dulles International.

He's not coming, she decided, once more bracing herself upright against the engine in the sky. I can go home with a clear conscience.

Then she saw a dark mushroom in the greyness, its cap a black umbrella, the stem a beige raincoat and dark trouser legs.

Oh hell, she thought. Please turn away. Be someone else!

But the mushroom grew rapidly until she was looking into the face in John Putnam's campaign photo, now under a red plaid wool cap. John Putnum was the first black mayor of a small, once-racist southern California town.

'B.Sci., *magna cum laude*, from Yale,' Perry had told her. 'Then structural engineering at MIT. Defeated when he ran for the state legislature but pulled enough of the hispanic vote and middle-of-the-road Silicon valley working man to be elected mayor by a hair,' Perry had said. 'Not to be underestimated. Try to locate his motives.'

They looked at each other.

'I'm John Putnam,' he said.

'Nina Desanges.'

His eyes searched her face as they shook cold, damp hands.

I can't do this! thought Nina. How can I find the arrogance to judge this man's veracity and his motives for 'making trouble'? The quotation marks were Perry's, quoting whoever his source had been.

'Why do people insist on hoping?' Perry had asked.

'Because it's easiest,' she had replied, from considerable experience.

'Thank you for coming.' Putnam's voice was deep and clear, with the unrushed enunciation of a man used to speaking in public. Like the formal handshake, the polite phrase carried more than usual intensity.

Just be professional, Nina exhorted herself. Stick to professional tactics and phrases. You'll get through somehow. Begin now. Assess. Him. Mayor John Putnam. Middle-of-the-road. No sign of revolutionary tendencies. Nothing extreme. Successful middle America, as Perry would say.

His laced-up shoes looked English. The Shetland jumper under his

258

open raincoat had an embroidered lion on the breast. The raincoat had enough buckles and tabs to be a genuine Burberry. He was not what she, a foreigner, would have expected of southern California. And certainly not what Perry and his colleagues might expect of a possible subversive troublemaker.

Putnam turned and began to walk beside her back toward the Lincoln Memorial from which he had just come. He held his black umbrella between them against the fog which was turning to half-rain. They walked ten feet in silence.

Nina's feet were cold in her wet boots. Her scarf was damp. 'You have something to show me,' she prompted, to speed the inescapable.

'Is there any point?' Putnam asked the underside of the black umbrella. 'It costs me . . . don't ask unless you're really going to listen.'

She admired the way he had put her on trial instead of himself. 'Please go ahead.'

He stopped walking and fished a paper from an inner pocket of his raincoat. 'The letter no one wants to admit has been written.' He handed it to her. A photocopy. 'From my eldest son, James,' he added, as if she did not already know. He held the umbrella carefully over her and the letter as she unfolded it.

'*Mon Dieu!*' she whispered after the first glance. She had been right, and Perry, with his endless confidence in her, had been wrong. She wasn't going to be able to handle this.

'Look at the date!' Putnam said hoarsely.

Nina had already seen it and registered its meaning. She reminded herself to breathe again. She tried to form a professional phrase but her English was slipping. Even after six years of frequent, and two years of constant use, it still deserted her at times of great stress. She only half-heard yet another plane passing overhead.

'Well?' begged Putnam. 'What do you think?'

She shook her head numbly. What would Perry say now? Or Bill or Sloop or Pat? She formed her question word by word in French and translated it into English. 'When did it arrive?'

'Last month,' he said. 'Just before I telephoned Senator Quincy. For one whole month, I've been pounding on doors. I used to think I knew a lot of people in Washington. . . .'

The letter's date said it had been written three months before it had arrived. It was dated December 16, 1976. Four months before this day.

'Dear Mom, Dad, Princess and Pipsqueak. . . .' it began.

The mayor's son was more or less all right, everything considered, he said. Though he had the runs again – all the time – and several ulcers that wouldn't heal. . . .

259

Nina skimmed over the conventionally permitted health news and stopped a second time at the next sentence.

'They've moved me again,' it said. 'Just as I was getting used to Son La. The mountain behind this camp is so steep it's called the Cloud-Stirrer. . . .'

She glanced up at Putnam. 'The Vietnamese never permit such specific geographical references.'

'What are you trying to say?'

She shook her head and kept reading. The letter became less coherent but the sense was clear.

'Have you really given up? They say you have! Dad, you always said faith could move mountains . . . with the help of a little hard work. I have faith in you. Please get me out of here! Don't stop working on it! Don't give up! I know they've abandoned me! Don't let them! I'm going to die out here and it scares me. Sometimes you don't seem real anymore . . . Right now, I'm not sure whether I'm writing to anybody or not. Maybe I'm making you up because I need to, ha, ha. Does that sound crazy? Please . . . if you're really there . . . get me out! I don't know how much longer I can hang on!'

Your loving son,
Jimmy

Nina made herself read the postscript:

'If Junor and Falacci got back in one piece – give or take a little – and you ever hear from them (if they're real too, ha, ha again) tell them I'm glad they made it out, and to keep a six-pack of Bud cold for me or I'll skin their asses if I do get back.'

She folded the letter carefully but kept it in her hand. Jimmy Putnam's father was as real as Mouse's had been, once.

'My son was killed in action in Vietnam in 1969,' said Putnam. 'Nearly eight years ago! The army shipped his body home and we buried him. Miss Desanges, what is he doing writing to us now from Laos?'

And that's the question no one wants to answer, thought Nina. And that everyone hopes I can make go away. 'Are you quite sure that he did write it?'

'Oh yes!' said Putnam thickly. 'Jimmy wrote it all right! I know my son's voice! My wife agrees. We searched our hearts, believe me, before we decided to reopen things!'

260

Nina nodded. 'Did you consider that he might have written it seven years ago and that the date has been changed?'

'That's what the Senator suggested, though he hasn't actually seen the letter.' Putnam pinched his lips together. 'He never explained to me either,' he said, 'why, in that case the Army treated Jimmy as dead. Didn't just say he was missing?'

'It's not always that clear cut in war,' said Nina softly. 'It wasn't necessarily a deliberate lie.'

The fog enclosed them in silence.

They've closed the airport, Nina thought with relief. Because of the fog. At least I don't have to deal with the planes!

'Then why won't the Committee agree to evaluate this letter?' demanded Putnam. 'Why does the Army keep assuring me that Jimmy is definitely dead? What about the letter from his commanding officer saying that he signed the KIA certificate in clear conscience and that he still stands by his signature? Why refuse even to have someone look at the letter, until I leaned on every contact I have in Washington and threatened to go to every liberal paper in the country?'

'Retreat can be painful,' said Nina reasonably, professionally, 'if you have much invested in holding a position. Nixon said in 1973 that all American "boys" were home. Did he lie? The Vietnamese said that all POWs had been freed. Were they lying? The two governments are in negotiation right now. The US would rather not be forced to call the Vietnamese liars.'

The broad squat bulk of the Lincoln Memorial began to take shape ahead of them. The fog had turned into feeble rain.

'There's still a state of *de facto* war in Southeast Asia,' said Nina, resolutely professional. 'It would take a major, unarguable piece of evidence to change anyone's position.'

'With respect, Miss Desanges, that's politics not justice. And it's their problem, not mine!'

Nina shook her head. 'Unfortunately, your problem is finding the unarguable evidence.'

Putnam pointed to the letter which Nina still carried.

She shook her head again. 'If I had a strong reason to do so, I could make a good case against that letter. . . .'

Ethan, I hope you're proud of me, because I'm not proud of myself!

'. . . For a start,' she continued, 'it's atypical, unlike any other letters I've seen from known POWs. The paper is unorthodox – unlined, without the usual printed instructions that prisoners are to write only on the lines, and only about health and family matters. . . .'

'You mean the NVA pass out personalized stationery?' said Putnam.
'. . . And those geographical references are impossible.'

'Are you trying to say you think the letter's a fake?' Grit roughened the smooth, deep politician's voice.

'Only that it's unusual,' Nina answered steadily. 'And that arguments can be found to discredit it. But I think you already know that.'

He looked away from her as they walked toward the Memorial.

Nina tried to remember what she should do next, officially. But every time she looked at John Putnam, she forgot again.

'What are you going to do now?' he asked between clenched teeth. 'Miss Desanges. . . ?'

'I'm sorry?' she said distractedly.

'What are you going to do now that you've seen this letter?'

'Pass it to the Committee via my superior,' Nina said. 'With a report. I know it's a lousy answer but it's the truth.'

'What will you say?'

'I don't know.'

Putnam stopped. He drew in a long shaky breath. And exploded, all smoothness in his voice roughed by the harsh edge of pain. 'And *they* won't know what to say either! Oh, they'll talk about it for a while, then move on to the next item on the agenda while my wife and I sit out there in our house in California wondering who or what is buried in Jimmy's coffin, and what to tell our other children, and how to live the rest of our lives not knowing whether our son is alive or dead. Jimmy's letter will disappear in the system while we go crazy trying to live with uncertainty, after we thought we had come to terms with grief!' He closed the umbrella distractedly, then opened it again. 'Do you have any idea what it's like to lose a child?'

Nina opened her mouth to reply. Her breath caught. I told Perry he should send someone else, she thought. I *told* him! Her breath caught again in the first sob. No! she thought. Oh, no!

Putnam watched her, at first shocked, then with growing concern. 'Miss Desanges. . . ?'

Nina shook her head. She hugged herself with damp arms and shook her head from side to side. She turned away to hide from him, but her back shuddered with the force of her weeping.

'I'm sorry,' said Putnam. 'I had no idea. . . .' He dropped the umbrella on the wet grass and put his arms around her. 'My God, I'm so sorry!' He released her and bent to pick up the umbrella again. He opened it and held it above their heads with one hand while he put the other arm around her again.

They stood with water dripping from the edges of the umbrella while Nina tried not to soak the front of his Burberry.

'Can you tell me?' he asked.

She shook her head against his chest. I'd like to so much! she thought. But I can't, not yet. She began to feel in her pockets for a handkerchief.

He released her and fished among his layers of gaberdine and tweed for a fresh red and white checked cotton square. Nina wiped her eyes and blew her nose, while he placed a comforting arm loosely around her shoulders.

'I'd like to . . .' she began. She gave her eyes a final wipe and carefully folded the checked square. She gave him a pleading glance to beg his forgiveness for what she was about to say. 'But I'm afraid we still have official business. I can't hope to help you if I go to pieces now. I'm sorry, but I must keep that copy of the letter and warn you that it is classifiable. . . .'

He dropped his arm and stepped away from her. The light, cold near-rain blew in her face again.

'. . . containing specific references to the security of foreign relations and foreign activities of the United States.'

'On what authority?' His voice was suddenly dangerous.

'Statutorily,' she said. 'I'm really sorry, Mayor Putnam. Executive Order something or other . . . I can look up the precise reference if you wish.'

Putnam stared at her now with hatred.

'They will want the original.'

'I don't have it,' said Putnam. 'It was destroyed.'

'Are you prepared to swear to that?' she asked.

'This is my only copy,' he said between clenched teeth. 'Send your goons to search my house if you like.'

Nina lowered her head and kept going, now that she had begun. 'I must then warn you that it is an offence to keep and/or disclose information which has been classified.'

He said nothing.

Nina put the letter carefully into her coat pocket and began to walk at random into the drizzle. She had to get away or she would drown in his rage and pain.

'For a time there, I thought you were listening,' said his voice behind her.

Nina kept walking.

A sudden grip on her arm pulled her off balance. 'You can't walk away just like that with the proof of my son's life! I want to know something about the woman who's going to type up the report that could bring my son to life again or leave him to die in truth!'

'It doesn't matter who I am,' said Nina.

'Like hell!' said Putnam. 'You're the most important person in my life right now!'

Nina pulled her arm free. 'I'm a translator, interviewer and analyst,' she said, tiredly. 'Someone must have thought that I could be impartial in this case . . . I'm outside any particular service. Not quite official . . . to avoid embarrassment. But with enough background to form a reasonable judgement.' She headed away again, toward the squat, rain-furred monument.

Putnam followed. 'What background?'

'I interview refugees,' she said, 'from Laos and Vietnam.' She trudged grimly across the wet grass toward the growing bulk of the Lincoln Memorial. At least, she could escape the rain which was sticking her hair to her head and creeping down between the neck of her raincoat and her scarf. She glanced at Putnam. He had forgotten his umbrella and was nearly as wet as she.

'I hear many things,' she continued, 'including rumours of Round Eye prisoners still in Southeast Asia. Much is true, but some, I believe, is the invention of frightened, homeless people who hope it will buy them special attention and favours from Americans.'

'Are you suggesting that Jimmy's letter has been concocted in order to buy something from the Americans?'

She heard a new intensity in his voice and flicked another glance at his face. He seemed to be deep in troubled thought.

'It's possible,' she said. 'The truth is, I've never heard a rumour about a black POW in that area of Laos . . . not that there might not be rumours, just that I've never heard them.'

As they passed beneath some dripping trees, whose wet black branches were hazy with pale spring growth, a sick pigeon scrabbled in panic between the roots of one tree, too weak or damaged to fly away.

Putnam seemed to gather himself. 'Miss Desanges, I have put the truth into your hands. Are you brave enough to see it and fight for it?'

She was on trial again. 'Mayor Putnam,' she said carefully. 'Life has forced me to believe that men can create their own truths, which last as long as those men hold power. . . .'

'They also create their own lies! Like the lie that my son is dead . . . that he died in 1969. And they do it only as long as we're cowards enough to let them!'

She marched up the wide stone steps of the Lincoln Memorial toward the shelter of the pavilion over the giant statue. Putnam followed.

'I'm asking how brave you are,' he said. 'I know what I'm doing and what I'm asking of anyone who helps me . . . particularly an impartial analyst, who seems to like being outside the main system. I'm not naive, in spite of any impression I may have given you. I know I may send my business down the tubes. I may lose the mayorship. But I don't care. Not any more. My wife and I have been through too much. When we learned our son was dead, we tried to understand why. We buried him under the American flag. We tried to understand when some of our more radical friends didn't come to the funeral . . . We did our best to try to live the rest of our lives. To keep our other two children from feeling guilty they're still alive. And now. . . !' He swallowed audibly and was silent for a few seconds. Then he said quickly, 'In an awful way, it was easier than now.'

They climbed in silence up into the cathedral-like space around the huge statue of Lincoln, out of the rain. Together, they turned to look back down the Mall toward the Monument, just becoming visible through rising cloud.

'I know,' said Nina at last. 'I really do know.'

'Then tell me honestly, do you think *I* created my own truth . . . that the letter's a forgery and I just can't accept the truth that my son is really dead?'

'I think you believe he's alive,' said Nina. 'I don't know what I believe.'

'How will you decide?' He furled his umbrella and turned it round and round in his hand. 'As you seem to be the only help on offer.'

She lifted her head to watch a tiny sparrow beat its way high above them across the ceiling of the stone pavilion. The sound of its wings echoed, improbably loud. 'Will you answer one more hateful question?' she asked. 'Before we go any farther.'

He nodded. 'I can't imagine what's left, but ask.'

'As a father . . . it's clear that you want your son back. Are you absolutely sure, as a politician, that you understand and want the international politicial repercussions of an official inquiry?'

'Yes,' he said with conviction. 'Absolutely. My son went over there to fight for freedom. He believed it, whether it turned out to be true or not. I have to fight for his freedom now. I accepted the cost of my son's death for his country . . . with difficulty and with pain. But I did. Now I believe that his country has a moral duty to accept the cost of his life!' His eyes challenged her to disagree.

Nina did not disagree. A reckless sense of purpose was lifting the hair on the back of her neck. Ethan Perry would have been alarmed by the life that came into her eyes and the flush that climbed from her neck to her rain-spotted cheeks. She touched the pocket which held the letter. 'Who are Junor and Falacci?' Her previously controlled voice was slightly breathless.

'Just men Jimmy mentioned in letters from time to time,' Putnam said, his own mouth suddenly dry. He had sensed her gear change.

'Do you know if they made it back?'

Putnam shook his head. 'I've no idea. He mentioned lots of names in his nine months. Why?'

I couldn't find my daughter, Nina thought, but I will help find your son! I can try to do the good that Perry promised me. I probably can't do much, but even a little is better than nothing!

'What are you going to do?' he repeated. 'What are you able to do?'

'Junor and Falacci aren't referred to in Jimmy's file,' she said. 'I can try to talk to them. They might have something to add to the picture of his alleged death.'

Putnam reached for her hand.

'I may not be allowed to talk to them,' she added hastily. 'Junor and Falacci may have nothing to add. And in the meantime, please don't discount the official channels. You're not the only family applying pressure, as you know.'

'Thank you!' said Putnam.

'Don't count on too much,' she begged. 'Not after all this time. With the power balance in Southeast Asia as perilous as it is. Please don't count on too much!'

'I have a good feeling,' Putnam said. He held her hand in both of his and shook it in farewell. 'I have a sense of movement. I was right – you are a courageous person.'

'No,' said Nina faintly. 'I specialize in flight.' But he was already headed back down the steps into the rain. She watched him go, feeling both excited and guilty but unsure why or to whom.

She rang Perry from his former brother-in-law William's Georgetown *pied-à-terre*.

'So, what did you make of the letter?' Perry's high tenor asked amiably, his earlier anxiety under control.

'On this telephone?' Nina asked.

'Why on earth not?'

'Because it's not good news,' she said.

266

There was a long silence. Nina could see herself in the gilded wood, eagle-topped hall mirror. Her eyes were puffy from crying and her wet hair was plastered to her head like a seal's fur. Still holding the receiver, she bent to unzip one sodden boot. When she pulled it off, her stockinged foot left a damp, narrow print on the polished maple floor.

Perry had arranged for Nina to rent his brother-in-law's house soon after she arrived from Bangkok. William's marriage to Perry's sister had broken up and he had moved to Oregon. His town house was a modest, two-story, brick and white-painted wood dwelling tucked between larger, clapboard monuments to Federal neo-classical grandeur. Through the silk damask draped windows of her elegant neighbours, Nina could see Louis XV chairs, English Chinese Chippendale mirrors, and faultlessly coordinated silks and chintzes being brushed and vacuumed by black, uniformed maids.

By contrast, Perry's brother-in-law's house was shabby, its furniture early American rather than European – a Duncan Phyfe neo-classical settee and sideboard, and waxed, wooden Shaker chairs, candlestand and chest. Worn braided wool rugs lay on bare polished wood in its bedrooms. Faded cotton chintz draped the maple four-poster bed (for Nina, a diminished and distorted reminder of her own ex-bordello extravaganza, with bare-breasted caryatids and pink mosquito netting in her house in Saigon). But this house and its furnishings were shabby in the right way, as Perry managed to convey without actually saying so, like an English country house owned for generations by the same family. Like the house of Will John's grandparents on Narragansett Bay undoubtedly would have been. Nina gathered from occasional visitors, mainly casual acquaintances from work, that shabby was 'OK' if your own great-grandfather had left the burned ring in the wax on the chest and your own grandfather, as a boy, had chipped the leg of the dining table.

The house was a revelation to Nina in a country that she had expected to feel as raw and brash as Paul, Pat, Sloop and Bill. Its continuity with a past comforted her in some way. Nevertheless, that past was not her past. Each time she walked through the iron gate and between the two standard balls of bay in white Versailles tubs to enter the gentle arrogance of the worn, antique-filled interior, she felt like a trespasser. After nearly two years, America still felt like an inventory of objects, both pleasant and unpleasant, which she could not collect together inside herself with a sense of rightness or possession.

Georgetown itself, she hated. It reminded her of the smug self-containment of the Saigon French quarter, an island of privilege in a sea of slightly threatening 'others' whose chief purpose, for the islanders, was to act as servants, caretakers and labourers. The way she herself was eyed on the streets was coloured entirely by how she was dressed.

Saigon had fallen two months after Ethan Perry collected her, and the American Embassy in Bangkok had been swamped with applications for US residency or citizenship. On its televisions, the world had watched terrified Vietnamese clawing at the Saigon embassy gates and being beaten away from American helicopters. America was closed.

Perry had arrived unannounced at his brother-in-law's house to sit with Nina as she watched the helicopters lift off with living bodies clinging to the skids. He stared at his feet while she sat upright with her hands pressed against her mouth in horror.

'You knew!' she cried, spilling incredulous rage and guilt onto the nearest available object. 'You knew this was going to happen! Why did you make me slink away? You made me a coward and a traitor! How can I live in this country now?'

When he didn't answer, she tore her eyes from the television. His right hand lay across the cliff-edges of his brows, hiding his eyes. His left hand, on the chair arm, shook uncontrollably.

'How can any of us live here?' his voice asked huskily. 'All of us really knew, even you. And I wanted you here for my own selfish reasons. Would you please turn that thing off?'

Their relationship had changed subtly once Nina arrived in Washington. Seen on his own ground, Perry was both stronger and weaker than he had seemed to Nina on his visits to Bangkok. It had taken Nina several months to detect the hidden American aristocracy to which he belonged: the descendants of exiled rogues and younger sons of English younger sons who, in the early 17th century, had claimed to make a nation out of a wolf-and-Indian-infested sea of trees. In spite of the democratic face that America offered to newcomers, Perry and his ilk were still a major force in the worlds of finance and politics (even though their children had gone to India to seek inner worlds). Their voices still carried into the places that mattered even while they appeared to defer to more recently arrived Americans, and to the morally superior position of the men who had, in fact, claimed use of the land long before they arrived.

Ethan Perry usually seemed so at ease on his own ground that, without intending it, he made Nina feel intensely foreign. His Yankee vowels made her own voice sound, in her own ears, affectedly throaty and Frenchified. His height, though less startling in this nation of giants than in Asia, made her feel shrunken and unimpressive.

On the other hand, on his home ground, he lost the omnipotence of a transient genie and gained human weaknesses. Nina learned, though only after six months, that he was a widower with a married daughter in Utah. His only sister (divorced from William, the owner of the *pied à terre*) had remarried and now lived on St Lucia. Away from an official role in his work, he was a lonely, slightly shy man.

Now he and Nina met outside of work in an easy, friendly way, once a week or so when Perry was in town, then would not see each other for months, when one or the other was busy or out of the country. She found that she needed him. He was her only witness to an earlier life. He had known not the real Nina, whoever she might have been, but a Nina at least more real than the present one. For his part, he seemed to enjoy her company as well as find her a useful escort, from time to time, to receptions, dinners or balls. And at first, she worked to earn her place in his universe, trying, as it were, to make it fit.

'I didn't know you had it in you, Ethan!' cried their hostess, in a pleated silk, imitation Fortuny. 'She's adorable! Darling. . . .' Catherine Addams kissed first Perry, then Nina. She gave Nina a knowing and approving look. 'Good wine comes in old bottles, darling. Smart lady! . . . May I call you Nina? Now, let me introduce you to some really fascinating people who know all about your part of the world! They're absolutely dying to meet you!'

With a helpless look over her shoulder at Perry, Nina let herself be dragged away by the hand.

'Isn't she lovely!' cried one woman she met. 'She makes me feel so fat and pink!'

'Did you ever meet Madame Nhu?' asked another. 'Do you think she really said that about monks barbecuing themselves? I met her in Paris and she seemed absolutely charming.'

At one reception, a journalist shook her hand warmly as he asked, 'And just how did *you* manage to get on board one of the flights? Whose popsie are you?'

At an early cocktail party, a man talked eagerly to her through bourbon fumes about his favourite restaurants and sights in Saigon, asking if she had tried, had known, knew what had happened to them. A friend of his had cut in with an anecdote about 'this amazing woman in Danang' and asked Nina to go to bed. Another man at another cocktail party said politely, 'Sorry ma'am, I can't shake hands with a dink, however pretty,' and turned his back.

There were, of course, men and women who met her eyes with the same guilty knowledge she knew her own must hold, and that she had seen in Ethan Perry's the night that Saigon fell. But both Nina and the people to whom she had the most to say avoided saying anything of any importance. It wouldn't have entertained. It would not have amused. It would probably have embarrassed the others.

So Nina smiled away insults and related charming anecdotes across starched white linens and Irish crystal. She laughed when others laughed, at other people's jokes. She rationed her words so as not to bore. Her work was made easier by the social effect of her dark beauty and her potential, if properly handled, for political chic.

Fortunately, Ethan Perry disliked large parties; he preferred quiet dinners *à deux* or Sunday afternoon strolls. Sometimes, when they had eaten well and finished a bottle of wine between them, she would see a contented warmth in his face as he watched her across a restaurant table or the pale, grey-blue carpet of his brother-in-law's drawing room while she served him coffee and port.

'Young animals don't know how lovely they are to the old,' he said once, and ducked his large head to the tiny china demi-tasse cup, in immediate, embarrassed retreat.

'I've heard the mayor is quite a persuasive character,' Perry's voice now said at last.

'Yes,' said Nina tightly. 'He persuaded me that he sincerely believes the letter to be genuine, in every way.'

'What do you think? You've seen other POW letters.'

'I don't know,' she said. 'I really don't.'

There was another silence during which she pulled off her other boot. Then he said, 'Hell and damnation! How did you leave it?'

'That I would pass the letter on to IPWIC with a report on the meeting.'

'And he said, "Thank you very much, now I'll go home and wait quietly to hear from you"?'

'I also said. . . .' She tried to keep her voice flat. '. . . that I would try to talk to two men whom Jimmy Putnam mentioned in the postscript to his letter. In case they might remember something about the day he was supposed to have been killed.'

Perry's tone sharpened like a reproving schoolmaster. 'The mayor must have been persuasive. You had no authority to make that offer.'

Nina scowled at the woman in the mirror, who wavered behind the

270

old, handmade glass, as elusive as she had been in the Pahurat market in Bangkok. 'I know, Ethan,' she said. 'But I did. Tell me not to talk to them.'

Perry remained silent.

'Sooner or later,' Nina added, 'Putnam will think of the same thing. He's no fool and he won't give up now. Don't you want someone else to get there first . . . even if it could make you the most hated man in Washington?'

'Why don't you bring the letter round here to my office?' suggested Perry's voice. 'I'd like to take a look at it myself. I haven't had lunch yet. We can grab a sandwich while I have someone run those two names through the computer. There's just time to get all the forms signed before everybody goes home.'

Nina was still too shaken by her meeting with Putnam to feel triumph.

'Take a taxi if you don't feel like swimming,' added Perry.

'I only swim when I have to,' said Nina. She hung up, found a pair of dry shoes and put her wet raincoat back on.

'You look like a drowned rat,' he said, when she arrived. 'Why didn't you take a taxi as I suggested?'

'Because the taxis didn't realize you had decreed it and were all full.' She smiled as she handed him her raincoat. His office decoration was tasteful-official, leavened by personal accumulation. Nina settled down on a leather-upholstered sectional seat beneath an original Edward Hopper gouache and beside a lumpy clay rabbit in a nest made by Perry's niece at the age of six. The hair still prickled on the nape of her neck.

'One easy – if that's the appropriate word – and one dry hole,' said Perry a little later, reading the computer print outs. 'Victor Falacci was wounded. Receives 30% compensation for loss of right leg below the knee. Cheques go to this address in Queens.' He handed Nina the print outs at the end of a long arm.

She took them eagerly.

'Harold Junor, Junior, on the other hand. . . .' Perry began to unwrap the polythene straitjacket around a plate of sandwiches which his secretary, Midge, had brought in and left on his leather-topped desk. 'Junor returned alive,' he said. 'With a Purple Heart, but has never claimed compensation. No address. No known employer. No telephone. Has never been in touch since he was discharged. All

271

correspondence goes to his widowed mother at the address given there . . . Here's that pastrami on rye for which you've acquired the unfortunate taste.'

He gave it to her and folded himself down into the Eames chair behind his desk and bit into a chicken sandwich. He watched her set the sandwich aside without noticing it and return to the print outs. 'Go carefully, Nina. Don't make this Putnam boy into a cause.'

Nina looked back defiantly over the flimsy papers. 'I understand very well what's at stake,' she said. 'On both sides.'

He made an impatient noise. 'Oh, my dear, you're ripe for a cause. I know the symptoms.' He chewed carefully, as people do when keeping false teeth in place.

'What's wrong with a cause?' demanded Nina. 'If it's a good one?'

Perry chewed as if he hadn't heard her.

'*You* sent me to meet Putnam,' said Nina.

'Are you claiming the right to define "good"?'

'No more than you,' she replied.

Perry chewed a little longer. Then he said, 'What the hell, take a departmental car if you like . . . charge for gas. Care for some coffee?'

13

As part of her early attempt to fit in to America, Nina had bought a car and, after six months of lessons, finally learned to drive it. She had observed that only one small tribe, living on the island of Manhattan, seemed able to ignore the national rule of wheels. Elsewhere, shops were strung out around vast parking lots like maintenance sheds along airport runways. Banks, photo developers and post offices dispensed overdrafts, negatives and stamps to customers through car windows. Restaurants shoved chicken-in-the-basket and burgers through windows into cars still in gear. Nina had tried at first to walk, as she had in Saigon and Bangkok. After a few months of feeling like a very small rabbit pursued by baying mechanical hounds, she began to understand the absurd rumour that in Los Angeles, one could be stopped by the police for the suspicious activity of walking.

In fact, once she had her license, she found physical power and freedom behind the wheel. She prowled the outskirts of Washington and rural Virginia, exploring new territory and taking possession of it. She speeded on the freeways, letting the sound of wind empty her mind. She would imagine turning the key and driving west to the edge of the Pacific, to sit and gaze at the curve of horizon which hid her real home.

That night, after her meeting with Perry, Nina drove up to New York as soon as she could throw her toothbrush and a change of clothing into a bag. She was suddenly desperate to escape the greyness and drizzle and permanently excavated streets of Washington. She arrived in Manhattan in the early morning and stayed for what was left of the night in a small hotel on the west side, which Midge had booked for her.

In addition to the television, coffee-maker and mini-bar she had come to expect in American hotels, her single bed had a small sign announcing that it had Magic Fingers. Nina put fifty cents in the slot on the side of the frame. The magic turned out to be a noisy mechanical jiggling of the mattress. No detectable fingers.

She went to her window and looked down. The street lay far below;

opposite her window, a slice of space between buildings was crossed by a constant stream of moving lights. Like Saigon, New York never stopped. For the rest of the night, too excited to sleep, she listened to the surge of abruptly raised voices, the swish of traffic, the rattle of trucks hitting potholes, sirens, airplanes, sudden creaks from the heating pipes, and a game show on the television in the next room, at five o'clock in the morning. The sounds were as dense as in Saigon or Bangkok.

She rose at eight and went back to her window. In the slice of space between the two buildings opposite her hotel, above honking traffic and the tops of a valiant line of trees in a riverside park, she could just glimpse the grey water of the Hudson River. On the street, two old men were walking small dogs, a young woman was jogging in the company of a Great Dane, and two people of undefineable sex were still sleeping in nests of blankets in doorways, like the refugees in Saigon after the 1955 Partition, or like those in Bangkok when the war had begun to spread in the rice fields of Laos and Vietnam. A woman in a fur coat was examining something in a garbage can, and dozens of other people were walking very fast with their heads down.

Ethan Perry hated New York. Nina found it exhilarating and disturbing. She had loved it on her first visit (to attend the opening of an exhibition of Vietnamese refugee painting in a small SoHo gallery). It was a circus, a denial of everyday life. In disbelieving joy from her seat at a sidewalk cafe, she had allowed a middle-aged man on roller skates, dressed in blonde wig and tinselled ballet dress, to wave his benedictions onto her head with a sparkling fairy wand. She had rejoiced in the polyglot energy of the voices in the street, in the food stalls, in the late-night activity, in the sudden appearance of clowns, musicians, tap dancers and fire eaters, in the sheer weight of life. On later visits, she noticed the homeless sleeping under lumps of blankets, the beggars, pimps, hustlers and lunatics. And the anger.

New York's noise and dirt, like its traffic jams and shouting, honking drivers reminded her of Bangkok. And like Saigon, it was trapped in the bubble of its own being, responsible for being *the* place. New Yorkers, like the Saigonese, seemed to think of everywhere else as 'oh, there. . . .' Sometimes such reminders were comforting, sometimes harsh as the broken bottles under her feet. Nevertheless Nina preferred New York, with all its arrogance, impatience, intolerance, dirt, and uncomfortable familiarities, to the defensive chilliness of Washington, an artificial city struggling to preserve its heart.

She made coffee in her room, retrieved her car from the hotel parking lot three blocks away, and drove out to Queens across the Triboro Bridge, like a salmon swimming upstream against a torrent of cars and bodies already pouring onto Manhattan. In spite of the confusion of four-lane roads on the mainland, Falacci was easier to find than to talk to.

'Sure, I was on that operation. So what?' Falacci had sounded angry and suspicious as soon as she showed her identification and explained, more or less, why she had come. 'Why the hell are you asking about all that now? The poor bastard's been dead for eight years, or near enough!'

The muscles of his face had clamped themselves tight to the bones. He glanced at the closed door of the kitchen where his wife had retreated after pouring Nina and Falacci each a glass of beer.

Nina sat on the tweed-covered sofabed, next to a well-polished, three-foot rubber plant in the box-like living room of his second-floor apartment and tried to decide whether he was going to lie or not.

Falacci had probably once been a high school athlete, short but strong, now fattening slightly with middle age and inactivity. He had a pleasant, rounded face and black hair still thick enough to suggest greying temples rather than eventual baldness. His eyes were like fragments of smouldering charcoal, opaque grey on the surface and red-hot underneath.

'His father wants it re-checked,' said Nina, evasively.

'I think it stinks.' Falacci didn't seem angry at her personally, though the two hot, opaque coals never stopped assessing her. 'Nobody wanted to know back then, at the right time. Why didn't someone check up on loose ends back in '69? Why ask now? Why is it less embarrassing now? You didn't care how he died in '69. What's different now?'

And why you? his eyes asked.

He launched himself up out of his tweed-covered armchair with a heave of his arms and crossed the oriental-pattern carpet to top up her beer, just to show no personal ill feeling. He had a good prosthesis and moved well in spite of his weight.

'Jimmy's father has received a letter,' said Nina carefully, 'which suggests that Jimmy might still be alive.'

'A POW?' asked Falacci. 'After all this time?' He spilled the beer he was pouring for himself. Patiently, and without speaking, he put down the bottle, re-crossed the room to get a Man-sized Kleenex from a box on the sideboard, wiped up the spill from the glass-topped sidetable and threw the tissue away.

'Not that it matters,' he said finally. He did not return to his chair but stood by the window looking down into the street where children's voices were screaming in mock blood lust and terror. 'I understand what you're asking but I still can't remember what happened that day. Just that we got hit. I woke up in hospital. Most of me woke up . . . some of me decided to stay behind.' He made the little joke as if he had offered it many times before, to soften the ugly fact he felt he presented to spectators.

'Don't you even have an image of where Jimmy was relative to yourself during the attack?' Nina persisted. 'Just a sense. . . ?' This is for his father as well as me, she reminded herself.

'It's too late for me to start to remember.' Falacci moved to the door and stood waiting for her to take the hint. 'Sorry, I really can't help you.'

She felt him watching her cross the wide, scarred concrete sidewalk, through the skateboards in the street, to her car. That was supposed to be the easy one, she thought. Now for the dry hole. It was still mid-morning.

After leaving Falacci, Nina drove around Queens for 25 minutes looking for a public telephone which had not been vandalized. When she finally found one, Harry Junor's widowed mother was curt.

'When he wants to see me, he comes here. That's all I know.' She hung up, without even a ritual goodbye.

That's it, then, thought Nina.

Sorry, Mayor John Putnam. Information about your son is inconveniently unavailable. Nina couldn't imagine being able to say such words to him. She sat in her car and considered what to do next.

Ethan would think I was being stubborn, she thought. Unreasonable. Hooked on my cause.

On the other hand, it was a sunny Saturday morning. She was alone, miles from what she temporarily called home, with an empty spring day ahead of her. She needn't return to Washington to buy or clean anything. When you lived alone, you could starve and live in squalor if you liked. And besides, the sun was shining. You made the most of what was on offer.

What can I lose by trying?

She lost herself for nearly forty-five minutes until she found La Guardia Airport, left the car in a long-stay carpark and took the shuttle to Boston. At Logan Airport, she rented another car, bought maps and headed north on the Interstate 95, toward Mrs Junor's farm,

276

an in-holding in the midst of Forest Service land in northern New Hampshire.

Boston was new territory to her. As Nina slid around the edge of the city on a current of traffic, her eyes moved with interest from the waters of the harbour across dereliction to a Florentine tower, from plate glass skyscrapers down to two-story 18th century red brick.

This place is different, she thought. Safely unfamiliar. Exotic. I must come back.

In the northern fringes of the suburb of Melrose, three-story wooden houses with wooden shutters peered down at the road over the edge of the cutting. Sheathed in either clapboards or shingles, they were painted apple green, ochre, brown, smoky blue, white, pale pink, rose pink, oxblood, and grey.

As if, thought Nina frivolously, there's a rule you can't paint your house the same colour as any other in the block.

She stepped a little harder on the gas pedal. Traffic was light. The weekend-home-on-the-Cape crowd had already swarmed out of the city the day before, on Friday afternoon. The rest of the population seemed to have parked on the vast shopping malls strung out at intervals just off the highway.

The houses along the embankment gave way to miles of young pines which bristled with fresh green growth at the end of each dark branch like girls who had just had their hair tipped at the beauty parlour. Nina was still amazed to find so much unoccupied space so close to the cities of America. At home, and in Bangkok, every inch would have been claimed and used, often by several people at once.

That's why Americans can be so open in character, she thought suddenly. They can retreat into private space; they don't have to live in a state of perpetual negotiation.

She rolled down her window, put her foot down hard on the accelerator and waited for the rush of wind to blank out the dangerously poised thoughts of home. Instead, the problem of Falacci and Junor tilted her into thoughts of Gabriel from Bangkok.

I should have asked his last name! Why didn't I ask him? She shook her head once again at her own stupidity. Then, I could have had someone check him on the computer . . . to see whether he's alive. My last lover.

She looked at her speedometer and lifted her foot slightly. He doesn't feel dead, she decided. Just gone. Like Mouse.

The metallic chill began just under the sudden knot in her throat and spread downward through her chest.

Oh God, will it never leave me? She listened to the fluttering of her scarf and the wind roaring against her open side window, but the chill reached her gut. She tried to change the subject to the problem of locating Harry Junor.

What will I say to his mother. . . ? Can I tell her that I have been a mother too? She tried to imagine Mrs Junor. And then Junor's childhood. Perhaps he had a dog, like Will John. Did he grow up hunting squirrels with a .22? Was he already a good shot before he went to Vietnam?

Then a brief fantasy intruded of Mouse growing up in America – on a tricycle like the little boy who lived three doors away from Nina in Georgetown . . . in a treehouse, like Will John's, with American friends like the freckled children in films . . . playing with a puppy on an improbably green lawn. Then she realized that she was driving too fast again and began a catalogue of the physical world to distract herself from inner pain.

Look at the sunlight! she told herself. Let it lift you.

She noted the swelling hills on either side of the road. Measured the distance between emergency telephones. Carefully read the names of vanished mayors and state governors which now identified bridges. She sniffed the resinous air and was suddenly ambushed by the memory of summer evenings in Dalat.

She had played doctor under the pines around the villa above the lake, with her gibbon Minou as long-suffering patient. She had hidden behind the hammock on the verandah, to eavesdrop on her parents. One night, she had heard a new voice talking with her father in the dusk. Its vibrations had tickled her stomach and held her prisoner in the dark, immobilized by a passion only half understood.

It had been Thu's voice. When introduced to this new, distant cousin the next morning, the adolescent Nina had felt sick to her stomach with nerves. She had lowered her own eyes because his eyes had weakened the muscles above her kneecaps, and because she had wanted more than anything to touch the dark, curving lock of hair on his forehead with her shaking, twelve-year-old fingers.

If he had inhabited a different world, she now thought, I wonder how our story would have ended.

A broad curve in the road brought the sun full onto her face and shoulders, and she took a fresh grip on the present, like a resolute terrier.

She stopped once to stretch in the sun beside a waterfall dashing down into a culvert beneath the highway, then drove on when she realized that the place threatened to free a memory. She told herself to enjoy the sudden openings of lakes, with alien names like Winnepisaukee, Squam and Pemigewasset Pond, that punctuated the valleys and held the hills apart. After two hours, she took a long curving exit off the highway and stopped for a mug of coffee in a plastic-laminated hamburger factory.

The aging waitress conspired to cheer her on as she skated on the fragile surface of the present. The woman, in a paper housemaid's hat and gingham apron, brought Nina endless refills of American coffee, offered three flavours of doughnuts and Danish, made little friendly jokes, and did not ask where she came from.

Only the tumble of rubbish from an overflowing trashcan in the parking lot made Nina's determined lightness waver for a moment. Her eye selected two pieces of plastic suitable for washing and resale, and an uneaten sandwich still in its plastic wrapping.

Someone could use those, she thought, before she stopped herself and turned away to her rented car to resume her sunlit odyssey.

Dusk seemed to come early, as the hills swelled into mountains. The air grew crisp, as it had in Dalat. Nina stopped for the night near a dot labelled Twin Mountain on her map, in a small inn which was a ski lodge in the winter time. Inside the automatically closing screen door, she paused with relief. Almost nothing was familiar.

The air smelled of beeswax and bayberry. Heavy beams as broad as her shoulders braced a massive wooden ceiling dotted with the dark eyes of pine knots. Log fires – one in the entry hall and two others beyond open doors – sparked and dropped red-hot coals from giant andirons onto stone hearths. The pine-panelled walls were crowded with muskets, moose antlers and crossed snow shoes. Outside the dining room door stood a stuffed black bear; inside, petrified trout and pike in glass cases gazed down at the tables in wall-eyed alarm. Through the dining room windows, Nina could see mountains, receding into dusky space, touched by fingertips of final light.

A man greeted her guardedly from behind three racks of postcards on the reception desk. While she registered, she felt him watching her with open curiosity.

Don't spoil my mood by asking where I was born, she begged him silently. Or demand my response to stories about your son, or the son of a friend who was 'over there'. Not today. Please!

In spite of his scrutiny as he showed her to her room which had the same soul-scouring view into space as the platform on the Tiger's Head – and the equally open curiosity of her waitress at dinner, Nina clung to her fragile sense of sunlit adventure. Her sleep was filled with people and places which escaped her when she woke.

The next morning, her stomach was too tight with nerves to consider sausages, cereal, pancakes, cornbread, waffles, Danish pastries or bacon. She upset the waitress by choosing only black coffee and a homemade roll, which she finished quickly, impatient to set out in search of Harry Junor's mother. After three hours of winding roads and places scattered among rock and pines, with names like Goback Mountain and Dixville Notch, she found Mrs Junor's mailbox.

The miniature quonset hut of galvanized metal leaned on a rotting post at the top of a long rutted driveway. It had a hinged front that dropped down and a red metal flag to be propped up to alert the postman to outgoing mail. The hand-painted letters were barely legible. 'Harold P. Junor.' Senior, now deceased, according to the military computer. A wooden frame house, its paint scoured away by weather, was just visible through a screen of large oaks. Nina guided the car around the potholes in the driveway and climbed the half-flight of wooden steps onto the porch.

Mrs Junor stayed behind the closed screen doors. Through the wire mesh, Nina could see that she was thin, sun-cured, and had probably never worn make-up in her life. An apron covered her blue man's workshirt and a pair of denim dungarees.

'I telephoned. . . ,' Nina began, suddenly wishing she had left it at that.

'I guess you didn't listen very good,' said Mrs Junor.

Nina swallowed. 'I'm really sorry to bother you,' she said. 'But I do need to talk to you about your son Harry. I thought perhaps. . . .'

'Where are you from?' Mrs Junor interrupted.

'Washington,' Nina began to explain. 'I work. . . .'

'I mean, where are you *really* from? You ain't American!'

'I am now,' said Nina firmly. Yesterday's lightness and faith in her purpose had evaporated. She tried to smile an American smile, open and friendly, without hidden embarrassments or disguises. 'I need to talk to your son about a friend of his. I'm doing it for the friend's father. The friend is James Putnam – Harry may have. . . .'

Mrs Junor pushed the screen door hard and stepped out, forcing Nina to retreat to the top of the verandah steps.

'Young woman, you just git!' She waved her arms as if shooing a flock of chickens, or herd of cattle. 'You and your kind have done enough to mess up my son. Now, git, before I go fetch my husband's .22 and shift you myself.' She advanced fiercely to the top of the steps; Nina descended five steps to the overgrown yard.

'I may not know much anymore,' continued Mrs Junor, 'but I know a slit-eyed dink when I see one, and I know one of those slimy fuckers from Washington Dee Cee, and when I see both kinds mixed together it makes me want to puke!' She drew a deep breath. 'My husband and me paid our taxes and raised our two boys to be good Americans and look where it got them! One dead and one good as. Because of people like you.' Her voice had begun to shake. 'If I was you, I'd shift!'

Nina fled back to the rented car and bumped back out across and around the potholes, almost as deep in places as mine craters. In the rear-view mirror, she saw Mrs Junor attacking last year's dead ragweed beside the verandah steps, with a scythe. When she reached the main road again, Nina pulled over and leaned her hands and forehead on the top of the steering wheel.

I should have left it alone! Oh, Mayor John Putnam, what made you think I am brave enough, or strong enough to help you?

'People like you. . . .' Mrs Junor had said. She hadn't meant race alone.

What makes you like you are? Nina asked a tangle of year-old bittersweet that was strangling a bleached wooden fencepost beside the car. What you think or what you do? I've already changed what I do so many times! She reached through the open window and picked a bittersweet berry, a shrivelled yellow-orange globe in a split, red-orange cap, and held it in her palm.

Will John could have understood this world in which she was now stumbling. He could have assured her that life bent to one's will and that man's desires are considered when the gods are making up their minds. Man had merely to decide what he wanted.

Will, I'm not sure I can live in your world without your assurance to protect me, she thought. Sunny Sunday or not, I should have stayed in Washington – chilly, defensive, and without its heart – just where I belong. She tossed the bittersweet berry back into the tangle of its bush and started her car.

She drove slowly back to the nearest hamlet, called Paris, and stopped at a restaurant on its outskirts for a chance to think as much as for lunch. The wood-shingled building had red-checked gingham curtains at the window and no-nonsense Formica-topped tables in the dining room. Three young waitresses in jeans and short gingham aprons all smiled and stared as she came in. Nina ordered a Mixed

Seafood Special and coffee. Her waitress paused to whisper something to her friends.

I'll go back to Boston for the night, Nina decided. This is insane.

'This place mat is made from one hundred percent recycled paper,' she read from the paper rectangle on the table in front of her.

I'll go back as soon as I eat, she told herself.

The teenage waitress brought her a basket of rolls, a saucer piled high with acorns of butter and a little bowl of raw vegetables with a pool of dressing, pink as cheap face cream, in the middle. There was already more on her table, before her meal arrived, than she had sometimes eaten in five days in Saigon, years ago, while she was changing from a spoiled, fifteen-year-old French mademoiselle into . . . who knows what. The largesse of this country still overwhelmed her most when a modest restaurant like this one could take it for granted.

The girl hovered curiously.

'You have good weather up here,' said Nina politely.

'Mostly,' replied the girl. She rearranged the sachets of coffee-creamer, Sweet-n-Low, white sugar, raw sugar, and coffee crystals in their stainless steel nest while she studied Nina's New York designer sweater and amber earrings. 'You come far?'

How far do you want to know? thought Nina. 'Washington,' she said. 'The weather stinks down there.'

The girl smiled. Then there was a pause while she went to bring a pot of coffee to fill Nina's cup; four pots were brewing on the multiple hotplate, all full, though there were only three other diners in the room.

'Were you born in Washington?'

Though the question was politely indirect, Mrs Junor on the subject of slit-eyed dinks had made Nina cautious. 'My mother was French,' she said.

'Oh,' breathed the girl, as if her question had been answered, not evaded. 'French! What on earth are you doing up here?' Here in the pits, her tone said. In the boonies. She left to replace the coffee pot on the hotplate.

This is it, thought Nina. Decision time. Go back to Boston and play tourist, or catch a late shuttle to Washington. Quit while you can, with reasonable honour. Be warned by Mrs Junor.

The girl returned to Nina's table.

But then, thought Nina, it does no harm just to answer the girl's question. She knew she was fooling herself.

'A friend of my brother lives up here,' she improvised. 'He left a sweater at my brother's place in New York. I had come up from Boston

282

anyway and offered to drop it off. But the friend's mother didn't seem to know where he was . . .'

This is a terrible story, she thought. Full of holes. Paul Karelian, Bill, Pat and Sloop would have hooted in derision, but the girl seemed to be accepting it. 'In fact,' said Nina, 'she didn't even let me get as far as the sweater. Told me to clear off.'

'Who is it?'

'Harry Junor. Junior.'

The girl nodded seriously. 'I'll bet she didn't like you asking about him. Won't talk to anybody about anything hardly, anymore. My mom says she'll never get over it. Mrs Junor won't . . .'

Get out now, Nina told herself. You're not going to like this! 'You can't blame her,' she prompted.

The girl nodded. '. . . what with Dicky getting himself shot down in his helicopter,' she agreed. 'It's terrible. . . .' She was interrupted by a buzzer from the back of the restaurant announcing the arrival of Nina's Mixed Seafood Special, with salad and hold-the-fries.

Mrs Junor had lost a child. Perhaps in the same place as Nina. Or near. Perhaps helping to kill children like Mouse. Nina clasped her hands tightly in her lap. She didn't notice the other young waitresses eyeing her uneasily. And Harry, 'as good as' . . . She looked up as her own waitress came back from the kitchen. What good does it do to trade dead child for dead child? It leaves women like me and Mrs Junor. . . .

The girl squeezed an oval platter onto the crowded table top, and refilled Nina's coffee cup. She met Nina's eyes, laughing, but slightly flushed. 'If your mother was French, can you say "I love you" in French?'

Nina smiled, unaccountably cheered. *'Je t'aime.'*

The girl repeated it twice. Then Nina wrote it for her on a paper napkin, from the hundreds in a holder next to the four kinds of sweetener. The girl repeated it twice more before she folded the napkin and tucked it into the back pocket of her jeans.

'Why is Mrs Junor so upset about Harry?' asked Nina as she casually speared a fried clam.

'I thought you knew,' said the girl. 'He must have left that sweater a long time ago.' Now she studied Nina's face, suddenly uneasy.

'You know how men don't like to tell us things,' said Nina. 'And I gather that Harry is a little hard to pin down.'

The girl hesitated and looked around as if for guidance from her friends. They were busy. She sighed, leaned forward, and lowered her voice. 'He's crazy. A trip wire man. You know what that is?'

283

'No,' said Nina. 'You'd better tell me.' She stared at her fork and put it down. The clam had tasted like an elastic band.

The girl leaned closer and dropped her voice lower. 'He's still fighting the war, my dad says. Can't get over it. He's hiding out somewhere in the woods, like he's still one of those gorillas.'

Nina's heart accelerated and the back of her neck tightened. 'Does he ever come into town?' She wrestled a chicken lobster tail out of its pink, hinged cradle, then put it down on the plate. She couldn't eat. 'What does he do for food and supplies?'

'Well, my friend Donna, works at the Shop 'N Save's never seen him. Nor Ben at the liquor store . . . Excuse me.' The girl went to answer an upraised finger at a nearby table.

Leave it alone! Nina ordered herself. She pushed her knife and fork to the side of her plate. Protect yourself a little!

The girl returned, bringing a red plastic tomato full of catsup she had forgotten earlier.

Nina asked, 'Does anyone know where he is?'

The girl shook her head meaningfully. 'Not for certain. Somewhere up on the family land – they got an in-holding – hundreds of acres of rough woods you can't farm. It's all Forest Service land around them. Just trees. My cousin saw him out there right after he got back.' The girl tucked her denim-covered bottom onto the edge of the unoccupied neighbouring table, between the sugar and the napkin dispenser. 'A lot of the guys used to go up there to hunt deer and squirrels, before it was fenced off. Now all the land is posted. Forest Service and the Junors'. My cousin said that Harry put up his own signs too. Crazy signs.'

Nina fingered a packet of raw sugar; its contents shifted under her fingers like a half-filled sandbag. She was unable to believe what she had just decided to do.

Perry would be appalled. Even Putnam wouldn't expect it of her. But Junor had disappeared right after he returned from Vietnam. Unlike Falacci, he might not have already said everything he had to say.

She looked around the civilization of Formica tables, a choice of sugars and multiple coffee pots. She remembered waiting by Cassidy's airplane, and the feel of Thu's knife exploring her ribs. She remembered walking through the night to throw herself on the mercy of an opium-dealing war lord. She remembered stumbling, blind and deafened, through the darkness, trying to escape the explosions which nosed closer and closer in the jungle. She remembered, with reason-threatening intensity, the impossible, unbearable loss of Mouse. In that context, Junor held little terror. He was the most interesting thing to happen in two years. She stared down at the wreckage on her plate.

Steady! she told herself. Anyway, local gossip always exaggerates. And I'll be careful. She was suddenly in a hurry to get on with it. She asked for her bill.

'Isn't it OK?' the girl asked anxiously, looking at the clams, shrimps and half lobster remaining on Nina's plate.

'I'm a small eater,' Nina reassured her.

The girl scribbled on a pad attached to her belt and gave Nina the bill. 'How do you say a lot? In French.'

'*Beaucoup*,' said Nina, as she paid. '*Je t'aime beaucoup*. Whoever he is, he's a lucky man.'

'You bet he is!' the girl grinned happily as she scooped the money into the pocket of her gingham apron. 'You have a good day,' she ordered, as Nina rose to leave. 'Come back soon.'

Nina knew it was a ritual phrase, but it still made her feel better, after Mrs Junor. She shouldn't need to be made to feel better, but she did. Then she began to wonder once again how Mrs Junor's son, who still thought he was 'one of those gorillas', felt about slit-eyed dinks from Washington Dee Cee.

Nina drove past the Junors' leaning mailbox and turned right every time she met another road. From time to time, she saw the same fluorescent red 'No Trespassing' signs nailed to trees on her right. She didn't know exactly what she was looking for, just something, a clue, a sniff. Her excitement and nerves of the day before had steadied into concentrated energy.

After 50 minutes, she reached the mailbox again. She had gone in a circle and seen only two farm houses, an abandoned school bus, painted olive drab over its orange-popsicle orange, and a lucky white horse grazing in a green field like an advertisement for something very expensive and manmade. All the logging roads and drives on the Junors' side of the road had had chains across them.

She sat and thought for a minute, then began to circle the Junors' land again. The first farmhouse, on the side of the road across from the Junors' land with its red signs, was unoccupied, temporarily. A wheelless car was propped up on concrete blocks in the driveway amidst a scattering of tools. A large Scottish collie with movie star eyelashes tried to tear the door off Nina's car. When no one came to investigate the uproar, Nina reversed back down the gravel onto the main road.

The second house, on the Junors' side of the road, looked vacant as if

285

it might be for sale. She parked her car and walked past the chain across the driveway, up the dirt track past the house to an empty hay shelter, two storeys high, with a corrugated iron roof, concrete floor and no sides. It held only a worn tractor tyre and an old icebox, minus its door. No track or trails led onward into the wooded hills beyond. She saw no well or pump. She peered through dirty windows into the dead, empty rooms of the house and went back to the car. The sun had reddened and begun to relax down into the dark bristles of the pines. She might drive all night and never find Junor.

I'll give it until dusk, she told herself. But I won't find Harry Junor because he doesn't want to be found. It's as simple as that. Then I can tell both Mayor Putnam and myself that I tried.

She stopped suddenly on a small bridge and looked down into the stony water of the mountain stream. Then she moved forward to let a large yellow-orange, operational school bus squeeze past. She looked back at the little stream under the bridge and considered the matter of Junor's water supply.

A stop sign flipped up on the side of the bus. Two girls and a boy, carrying square metal lunch boxes, began to walk up a dirt track which was not blocked off by a chain. As the bus pulled away, Nina touched her horn lightly. The children looked back and clumped like cells on a slide, united against a stranger. The younger girl was probably the age Mouse would have been.

I'm afraid I'm lost,' said Nina. 'Do you think you could help me?'

'Stay here,' the eldest girl hissed to her siblings; they followed her toward Nina's car.

'It's a slope!' said the boy. 'Don't get too close.' He dropped into a crouch and pointed a finger at Nina. 'Bang.' He blew on the end of his finger and tucked it into the pocket of his jeans.

Nina nearly drove away. Then the oldest girl asked, 'Yeah?'

If anyone had located a dangerous, forbidden kingdom, it would be children, anywhere and of any race. The graver the warnings, the more likely they would have tried.

'I'm looking for someone,' said Nina, trying to smile, feeling like a 'slope'. 'But I'm not having much luck.'

'Who's that?' The girl spread protective wings around her younger siblings.

'Harry Junor.' Nina held her breath. The three children's eyes slid and swivelled in silent conference.

'Is he a friend of *yours*?' The girl sounded incredulous. The wings dropped.

'Not really,' admitted Nina. 'More of my younger brother.' Brothers could be useful; she would have liked to have one who had not been killed before she knew him.

'Well,' said the girl. Again, the children traded silent coded messages, then looked at Nina. 'Maybe we know, but you better not try to go there. He's dangerous. Specially for you!'

'Really!' said Nina, sounding fascinated but feeling sick. 'Why is that?' She didn't want to hear why Harry Junor was especially dangerous for her, but that information came with the rest.

The girl hesitated tactfully, trying to decide just what kind of 'slope' Nina was. . . . 'Well . . . you know . . . He was over in Nam. And all that.' Her fear of offending Nina had taken the edge off her suspicion. 'Anyway, my dad says he's dangerous for anybody. And my brother here has seen the signs he put up in the woods.'

That's it, thought Nina, suddenly eased by decision. Fate has arranged it.

She took five dollars from her purse. 'If I swear not to tell your parents, or any one, would you show me where those signs are? Just the signs.'

Again, they held a silent, visual conference.

'We don't all need to go,' said the girl. 'Orville can take you.' She held out her hand for the money.

Nina cursed her Italian shoes and narrow skirt; she had dressed for respectability, not cross-country hikes. But it's nothing compared to the supply trails in monsoon season! she thought. In spite of her unsuitable clothes, she moved like a hunting cat, alert, graceful, focussed and alive.

Orville politely heaved up the lowest strand of the barbed wire fence so Nina could roll under it. Then he led her through a head-high belt of five-year-old Forestry Commission pines, to the edge of a field dotted with scrubby seedling oaks and birch. On the far side of the field, about two hundred feet away, a mixed woodland rose in slow undulations toward a high rocky ridge. Nina noted that the stream which ran under the road bridge seemed to flow down from those hills.

'He's in there, somewhere,' said Orville *sotto voce*, pointing into the woods. 'That's what my dad says anyway.'

'Where are the signs?'

He put his finger to his mouth for silence, crept forward, paused to listen, then crept forward again, pointing his toes inward like an Indian. Then he motioned her forward silently, just the way it was done in the movies. He pointed into the shadows of the trees.

Nina saw the first sign just inside the woods, hand-lettered in black on white-painted board, unlike the fluorescent red, printed No Trespassing signs. 'KEEP OUT, DANGER.' There was another sign to the right and yet another to the left, nailed to trees inside the perimeter of barbed wire fence which separated the edge of the field from the woods. 'KEEP OUT, DANGER.' All the same. And not any crazier than many other signs she had seen.

'Can you find your way back OK?' whispered Orville, his skinny young body already inclined in the direction of retreat, his tanned, bony face both uneasy and envious.

Nina looked at her watch. Four o'clock. Two and a half hours of light left, more or less. 'Yes, thanks. Thank you very much, scout.'

He saluted and dashed back across the expanse of oak and birch saplings.

It's odd how much more alone one feels in woods than on a mountain top or a beach, thought Nina. Then she thought, this feels real again.

She crossed the first line of signs. Now she moved clumsily, making as much noise as possible. The last thing she wanted was to sneak up on Junor unexpectedly. The woods were a little like secondary jungle, mostly scrappy regrowth with a tangle on the floor which hadn't yet been shaded out by long-term giants. Nina followed what could have been a deer trail. Then she stopped dead. Another black-and-white, hand-lettered sign was nailed to a large sugar maple ahead of her.

'DANGER. MINES.'

Junor was serious about his privacy.

She didn't quite believe the sign, but she dared not ignore it either. She slid carefully along the groove of the trail, feeling with the toes of her Italian shoes, studying the bumps in the dirt, scanning the underbrush for an oddly-angled branch which might, conceivably, trigger a booby trap. After nine feet, she stiffened with one foot in front of the other, arms slightly open for balance, like a tightrope walker on a breaking rope.

The trail stopped at a hole in the ground, three feet across, four feet wide, and four feet deep. From the bottom of the hole, the pointed ends of sharpened sticks stared up at Nina like missiles ranged in a silo.

A *punji* pit! she thought. Nina swallowed. Then she realized that it was open, uncovered, undisguised. She was supposed to see it . . . it was no more than another sign. But the sign language was becoming more vehement. For the benefit of anyone who dared pass the first perimeter of barbed wire and signs. It was probably no more than that.

She looked closely at the brush beside the track, started to walk around the pit, and stopped.

'Harry Junor!' she called. 'Are you there?'

Nothing moved among the trees.

'Are you there? My name is Nina Desanges. I need to talk to you. Please!'

She listened. The woods were silent. No breeze. A few insects. A quick volley from a distant woodpecker. Her nose received stronger messages than her ears – last year's mouldering leaves, oak tannin, the recent, gamey passage of a fox, and, faintly, woodsmoke. Sharper and fresher than jungle smells.

Something touched her back, firmly. Exactly on her spine, just above her waist. Her breathing stopped. Her blood beat at the inside of her skull. The hair rose on her neck like a warring tomcat's ruff. She imagined the dark unwavering spot of the gun barrel. The image sucked up her thoughts like a black hole in the universe. She saw herself lying on the brown leaves in two bleeding halves, severed at the spine, like the man in the bird-watcher's hut who had stained the rice straw bright red. She sucked in a jerky breath and smelled a man among the other smells, not unpleasant, but distinct, like the fox and the damp leafy earth under her feet.

'Turn around,' said his voice. 'Very, very slowly.'

She turned, slowly as an American sunset, slowly as the moon, hands open and a little away from her sides.

He was thin, just under six feet tall, long-haired, mid-blond and bearded. A dirty headband of torn cloth held his hair out of his eyes, which were bright green and clear as emeralds. A towel hung around his neck, his rifle across his back. He wore torn jeans, a plaid flannel shirt, an Army-issue knife in a sheath on his belt, and no shoes. He was still holding out the forefinger he had pressed against her spine. It had not been a gun after all, but he was no less frightening for that.

'Mr Junor?' Her voice quivered slightly, even though his rifle was across his back. She was much farther from Formica tables and coffee percolators than she had expected to be.

'You're out of your head to come in here!' he said.

Nina nodded sincere agreement, not trusting her voice.

'A real live gook!' he said, in wonder. 'Do you know what I used to do to people like you . . . what I still do in my dreams?'

'You're awake now,' she managed to say with a dry tongue. 'Wide awake.'

'Can't you read?'

She nodded again. Then she said, 'But I have to talk to you about James Putnam!'

Junor stepped back and breathed hard a few times. 'Get out of here. Please.'

The 'please' reassured her slightly.

'If you know what's good for you,' he said. The green eyes looked her up and down. 'Holy shit!' he said. 'A real live one!'

She drew a sudden, necessary breath. 'I'll go in a minute . . . I do know what's good for me – it's just that I get other ideas that seem more important . . . like finding your friend James Putnam.'

He stared at her then made a noise that tried to be a laugh but didn't make it.

'Jimmy's dead,' he said. 'Did they forget to tell anyone? Now why don't you fuck off?'

'May I take something from my purse?' She kept her eyes on him while she fished out a copy of Putnam's letter. She held it out toward Junor. He let her keep on holding it.

'You've got nothing of interest to me,' he said. '*Nada*. None of you out there. You don't exist anymore.'

'It's from Jimmy to his parents,' said Nina. 'Look at the date.'

In spite of himself, Junor's eyes moved to the letter in her hand. 'Nineteen seventy-seven,' he said. 'He died in '69!'

'He mentions you,' said Nina. 'Hopes you got back safely.'

Junor's hand took the letter. She watched him read it. He wiped his free hand over his face, as if cleaning it, then read the letter again. He stared past her into the trees for a long time, then read the letter one more time. His eyes returned yet again to the postscript.

'Oh shit!' he said. 'Shit! Shit! SHIT!' He closed his eyes and threw back his head.

He stood for a long time, head back, breathing fast and shallowly as if he had been winded, sucking his breath between gritted teeth, his eyes screwed tightly shut. Then he threw his head forward and exhaled like a swimmer emptying his lungs. He was still for another moment.

Nina touched his arm.

'I'm OK! I'm OK!' he shouted. She stepped back and waited.

He sobbed and gasped like a drowning man, reached out blindly and struck at a tree. Hit it again and again, with both fists. He turned and slammed his back against it, still gasping and sucking at the air. Then he began, frantically, to try to smooth out the letter, which he had crushed in his fist, against the tree.

'It's only a copy,' said Nina. Not a physical part of the man who had written it.

Junor had forgotten she was there. Nina took an involuntary step backward at the rage in his eyes.

'Do you like to see a man make a jackass of himself?'

Nina didn't answer. 'No' was as bad as 'yes'.

He wiped his free hand over his face, roughly, as if clearing his sight after surfacing from deep water. When he looked back at her, the green eyes were still glinting, but the rage was under control.

'I want you to help me,' Nina said. 'Help me find out whether he really is alive or not. If you want to. I took a chance that you would.'

'*Want to*? I'd do goddam well anything!'

'That was the chance I took,' said Nina.

'Yeah,' he said, after a moment. 'I guess you did.'

He stood, thinking silently, undecided, glancing at her sideways in appraisal.

'Mr Junor,' she said firmly. 'I am not scared of you.' That was not entirely true.

He laughed abruptly and the rage left his eyes. 'You should be,' he said. 'Didn't they tell you all about me in town? Can't you read?'

'I don't believe everything I read . . . or hear.'

'Well, well,' he said. 'Makes a change.' He looked down at the letter which he was still smoothing against his thigh. 'You really are dumb!' he said. 'I'm not good news.' Again, he gave her a sideways glance. 'That's all.'

'I took a chance on your feelings for Jimmy,' She waited again, afraid she might have gone too far.

He turned and began to walk into the centre of the woods, still carrying the letter. Nina followed the rifle slung over his shoulder. Neither spoke; she supposed he might be a little out of practice. They stopped in a clearing about two hundred feet further on. It held the litter of a temporary campsite – an orange crate, coffee pot, a small fire built between two logs, over which he was drying some strips of meat. There was no tent or shelter.

'Coffee?' he asked. His tone was ironically hospitable. He wasn't that much out of practice talking.

She nodded. Now she had to keep him going. She looked around. 'Where do you sleep?'

'That's my business.' His suspicion sharpened again. He covered it by smiling as he handed her a plastic cup of black, unsweetened coffee. It seemed to be his only cup. 'I like to move around.' He squatted down beside the fire, not drinking.

'OK,' he said. 'Talk to me! If you want to so bad.'

Nina crumpled onto the dried leaves and moss as gracefully as possible in a straight skirt. She felt like a collapsing water buffalo. Though she had practised several approaches in her mind, the words fell out unadorned. 'Jimmy's father thinks he's still alive . . . that the letter is genuine, and written when it says it was. Do you think it's possible?'

Harry Junor looked at her for a long time, shaking his head slightly in discomfort or protest. Then he held up a fist with the fingers tucked tight together above the thumb. 'We were like that, Jimmy and me,' he said finally. 'Like that.' He disappeared for a moment into his private thoughts. 'What I'm trying to say is that I'm not sure I trust myself to remember right. I *want* him to be alive too much. I don't trust my memory. Do you understand me?'

The hunting cat went very still, crouched over its forepaws, even the tail motionless. 'Chance it,' said Nina. 'Could it be true? From what you think you remember.'

Junor's mock hospitality had gone. He glared at her, teeth together, lips apart in a near snarl. 'I dunno. I dunno.'

'Tell me about that firefight,' she suggested gently. 'From the beginning.'

'Sure,' Junor said, exhaling hard. 'Sure. No sweat. Got no problems about it. Not much to tell. We walked into an ambush. That's all.' He offered each word neatly, with precision and without emotion of any kind. 'I took a hit in the head. Probably why I'm screwy now. And that's it.'

Nina sipped her coffee. The dark brown surface shivered in concentric rings when she lowered the cup to her lap. 'Where was Jimmy relative to you?'

'Bug off, lady!'

'Try!'

He studied some oaks and maples as if they were a screen where he saw the fight replaying itself. 'Just beyond Falacci,' he said at last. His words came slowly, like water seeping from a blocked pipe. 'Billings was walking point. He just kind of disappeared. You know . . . vaporized like on television in space shows for kids.' He tried to make it sound like a joke. 'Then Falacci got hit.' He paused. 'I could hear him. . . .'

Nina suddenly heard the screams in the silence after the last bomb had fallen, screams that cut through the settling dust and scraping of tardy falling branches. She shook her head to drive the sounds away. Junor was now staring straight down, into the centre of the earth.

'Did you see Jimmy get hit?'

He looked up sharply. 'No,' he said at last. 'But I had blood in my eyes. I must have looked like a complete wipeout . . . that's why they left me behind . . . didn't bother to finish me off even. . . .' He studied the oaks and maples again.

Nina finished her coffee and handed him the cup. 'Your turn.'

He filled it for himself without comment and drank, huddled down into himself. She could feel his distance from the oaks and sugar maples.

'Did you see the VC take any prisoners?'

'Jesus, I just told you I had blood in my eyes.' His voice was flat and steady. 'And a detached retina it turns out – they told me in hospital . . . but I heard them shoot three survivors before they took off.'

'How many did that leave unaccounted for?'

'Count out Billings and Falacci and me and the guy that carried me out . . . and the three they shot . . . that leaves two. I guess they could have taken two with them. I thought maybe I saw them take two. But Jimmy P. was counted KIA so I wasn't sure.'

Nina had to steady her breathing. She didn't know if he realized what he was saying to her.

'Harry,' she said aloud, unable to stop. 'Are you sure you didn't see Jimmy taken prisoner? How many black guys were in the unit?'

'Fuck off!' he said violently, the rage back in his eyes. 'Just fuck off and leave me alone.' He stood up and threw the dregs of his coffee into the scrubby undergrowth.

'How many black guys were in the unit?'

The plug in the pipe finally blew. He wheeled back toward the fire and stood over her. 'OK,' he shouted. 'OK! I thought I saw them take Jimmy! Are you happy? Does that help anybody? Is it any better for his folks than thinking he got killed . . . for him to be rotting over there? How do you think it makes *me* feel? I'm OK. They didn't take *me*! How do you think I feel?' He was panting as if he had run up a mountain.

It didn't make Nina happy either. And it might not help anyone at all. But it felt like the beginning of truth. She pulled up her knees and grabbed them for support. 'I suppose that's what I came out here for you to tell me,' she said quietly. She looked up at him. He was still fighting for balance, trying to slow his breathing. 'Isn't it funny how hard we try to make a success of something we didn't want to do in the first place?'

'Like being a soldier?'

Nina was startled into laughter. 'Yes, I suppose so. Didn't you want

293

to be one?' She needed time to take in what he had just told her about Putnam.

'Me?' Junor nudged the end of one of the fireplace logs carefully with his bare toe, and blew out a breath, like a horse. 'I meant other men, mainly. I wanted to be a soldier, or thought I did. Meanest squirrel hunter in the county.'

His relief at the change of subject was so clear that Nina hoped she would be able to reel him back to Jimmy Putnam.

He poured himself more coffee. 'Went off to be the best gook-getter in Vietnam. Just like John Wayne.' He sat down cross-legged on the far side of the little fire. 'Yee . . . how!' he added drily. 'Didn't last long.' He looked at her levelly. Can you handle that? the green eyes asked. As a gook?

'I had a talent,' he said. 'I guess it's a talent . . . kept me alive, anyway. If you call it living. It got me some shinies, besides my Purple Heart for the detached retina. My Mom's got them . . . she needs something.'

'Why did you come out here?' asked Nina. 'Instead of staying at home?'

'You wouldn't be interested,' he said flatly.

'I asked.'

'Well,' he said. 'Imagine that!' He sipped at his coffee, the other arm wrapped tightly around his knees. 'She's interested,' he informed the trees above his head. But the plug had blown earlier. The water had started to flow again.

'Well,' he said, watching Nina carefully for signs of boredom, disinterest, too much of the wrong interest. 'I got no guilt. I know I was in active combat. One day I was in the bush with friends, killing gooks. . . .' The clear green eyes checked with her again.

She looked steadily back.

'. . . And the next day . . . two days later, really,' he continued, 'I was on a plane headed Stateside, still wearing my dirty uniform. I really stank!' Again, he offered the small touch of humour. 'Didn't know anybody on the flight. Nobody else from my unit was going home. There were some other guys, all strangers – headed home like me. First we all sat kind of hunched down in our seats, waiting for something to keep it from happening. Then after we took off, we all went a little crazy . . . yelled, shouted, got brained until we fell asleep . . . then there we were. Home. Just like that! We all went our own ways. No debriefing. No brass to shake our hands. Just my Mom standing there by herself, blubbing her eyes out, not knowing what to say. Me neither.

294

' "Hi, Mom. Neat to see you again. How're things? Too bad about Dickie. I expect you're wondering if I brought home any gook ears." '
He was still watching carefully.

Nina kept her face neutral.

'Clean jeans and *pyjamas* for God's sake!' he said reflectively. 'I couldn't get used to any of it. People didn't want to talk about where I'd been and made it clear I should stick to saying how great it was to be back. Except a few of the guys who wanted to hear all about yellow pussy and how many babies I shot.' The green eyes were angry but clear.

Nina tried to hold his eyes but this time could not. Now she turned her head away to study the oaks and sugar maples. She took a long time before speaking again. 'You didn't come out here just because you couldn't make small talk with fools any more.'

'Too right!' he said. 'You see, I wasn't a normal person any more. Not crazy . . . that's different. I just wasn't normal for *here* any more.' He stopped and his face began to close up.

'Why?' she asked. 'You seem fairly normal to me . . . as these things go.'

'You're lying or you got no perception.' He smiled a little. 'No perception at all.' He lapsed into a silent, private conversation for a few minutes.

Suddenly he raised his head and stared back into the trees. 'One week after I got back, Mom came in like she used to, to wake me up. My feet must have been sticking out of the covers. Anyway she took hold of my big toe to wake me up, as a kind of joke.' His hand began to try to cover his mouth. 'When I came to, I had my hands crossed on her throat. In about four more seconds she would have been dead. It was pure reflex . . . I was just doing what I had been taught. That's what I meant when I said I had talent.' He looked directly at Nina for the first time in several minutes. 'I can't ask anybody to live with that. When I'm out here, they're safe, so I'm safe.'

He grinned suddenly, without humour. 'I tell myself if anybody's still dumb enough to come out here, in spite of the signs, then it's their funeral.'

'I won't make any sudden moves,' Nina promised. 'But I don't see anything crazy in wanting to protect other people. And are you sure about the reflexes? Are they still there after eight years?'

'I can't take the chance,' he said. 'I can't stop knowing what I know. Anyway. . . .' He leaned forward conspiratorially, half-mocking his own seriousness. 'I'll tell you the real truth. I like it out here now. It's quiet. I can hunt and fish. It's a good life. People leave me alone . . .

mostly.' He shot her another glance.

'I know, I'm sorry,' she said. 'I'm going; it's nearly dark.' She stood up and began to brush leaf fragments from her damp skirt.

'Sorry I can't offer you supper,' he said, rising politely. 'There's not a lot in the icebox.'

'Thanks for the thought,' she said. 'Maybe next time.' She looked at him inquiringly. 'I might need to come back, to talk again. Would you mind?'

He shrugged. 'It's your funeral.' Then she realized he had made a real joke.

She took a card from her purse and offered it to him. 'That's who I am.'

He accepted it and looked at it briefly before slipping it into his shirt pocket.

'One last question,' she said, 'and then I really will leave you alone.'

'You gonna do something about Jimmy?'

'If I can. Where were you that day? Can you remember?'

He rubbed the back of his head. 'That's two questions.'

'Can you?'

'Hell, I had to sign all sorts of papers saying I wouldn't tell anybody that.' He bared his teeth again. 'I guess it doesn't make too much difference where I'm locked up.'

'Some of it has already come out, in the last few years,' said Nina. 'Anyway, you put yourself out here.'

'Don't kid yourself.' He stared into the past again, leaving her in the present. 'We were over the border into Laos,' he said. 'On H. and I. Harrassment and interdiction. Our last three. . . .'

'You were in Laos in 1969? It was a neutral country!' As soon as she had spoken, she remembered the indignation in Sloop's voice in Bangkok, saying exactly those words. 'It was a neutral country!'

'Maybe *they* were,' said Junor, 'but the VC hiding over there sure as hell weren't. Believe me, we weren't the only ones going in! Everyone sterile. Unmarked choppers. No US ID markings anywhere on us. We wore black pyjamas, Chinese tennis shoes and carried commie AK.47s, in case we got picked up.'

They stared at each other across the little fire, thinking the same thought. He began to look angry.

'I guess I never wanted to think about that,' he said slowly, as if each word had a nasty taste. 'I suppose because Falacci and I were medevaced out like normal, I didn't think about how we were on the wrong side of the border. I mean, it happened all the time. I suppose Jimmy could have got listed KIA because you can't bargain for the release of a POW who officially wasn't there.'

296

14

Laos and Washington D.C. – 1977

The scent of perfume woke Will John. It was Nina's. He tried to reach for her but could not move. It was dark. He was pinioned to a wooden surface. His eyes could just make out broken beams and patches of night sky through a collapsing roof above his head. The air was cool. They had flown in a small aircraft and then climbed to bring him here. Into the mountains, he assumed. He heard a scratching sound and turned his head, but he saw only rubble in the shadows of the large, half-wrecked room where he was a prisoner.

He inhaled again and still smelled Nina's perfume. The scent gave him a feeling of dislocation, as if he were back in her big four-poster bed in Saigon, inside the mosquito netting which had seemed to shield them from the world.

A sudden thought jolted him. Perhaps he hadn't dreamed it. Perhaps she was here! Or had been here! The thought was insane. But, with his heart thudding, he prodded at a pattern of ideas which refused to come into focus. He felt a conviction which had nothing to do with rationality.

He replayed the scene at the hotel in his mind. The missing son was another insanity which seemed unreal and real at the same time. This conflict between feeling and knowledge was rare for Will John.

It's the effect of darkness, he told himself. Of sensory deprivation. Of a real dislocation in place.

He began to rehearse everything he had read about the effects of captivity on the human mind.

As the sky lightened above the gaps in the ceiling and behind the lines of the closed shutters that made up one wall of the room, he reassembled himself, fact by fact. Detail by detail, he caulked the cracks in the solid structure of self split open by surprise, terror and physical pain. He was nearly complete again, he thought, when someone began to fold back the wooden shutters. He saw the silhouettes of a woman who was opening the shuttered wall and of a man who crossed to stand above the platform bed where Will John was tied. In the early daylight, Will John recognized the man on the verandah of the abandoned hotel.

'I'm going to kill you,' said Thu. 'In time.' He looked into Will John's eyes. 'Perhaps.' He turned and left.

Will John recited the litany of interrogation techniques which he had once learned with vicarious curiosity. Create uncertainty. Reduce confidence through physical humiliation. Cut subject off from familiar environment. Induce fear. So far, so good . . . classic . . . recognizable. He was back in a known pattern.

He strained against the bonds on his ankles to relieve the rawness of his wrists for a moment. What had he read that other men had done in these circumstances? Recited Shakespeare, imagined themselves stripping a car engine or building a house, step by step. . . .

Why am I here? his brain interrupted its own attempts to maintain calm. Terror quivered in his chest and drove the late Sonnets from his memory. Why me, Will John Haines?

He drew a deep breath and began to conjugate Latin verbs. '*Amo, amas, amat.* . . .'

Will I live to let Nina know how I still feel about her?

'. . . *amamus, amatis, amant. Amabo, amabas, amabat.* . . .'

He had nearly finished the irregular forms of the fifth conjugation when an old woman in a black jacket and turban appeared with a bowl of rice gruel which she placed beside his head. As she turned to go, she glanced down at him for the first time since entering the room.

'Devil!' she muttered. 'Demon!' He could hear the whisper of her bare feet on the wooden floor as she left again.

He stared helplessly at the rice gruel, wondering if this were to be his first torture. Then one of the soldiers who had been at the hotel came into the room and untied his hands so he could eat.

Nothing else happened for the rest of the day. Tied flat again on the platform bed, Will John tried to construct the activity outside his room from fragments of sound. He heard women and children talking and calling. None of the voices was Nina's. A mule brayed. Two roosters – a tenor and a counter-tenor – competed in endless antiphony. Will John heard the harsh shouts of military drill and, later, the same repeated in the shrill voices of children. He heard the thudding of a cleaver on a block and the faint cries of birds from the sky above the ruined ceiling. He identified fourteen different insect noises and the rustling of two sizes of lizards. He thought he could hear bats creaking and scraping somewhere in the ceiling crevices.

As the sky outside his room grew white with sunlight, he recited Verlaine's poem written from prison. 'In the sky which I see above my roof, a tree is blowing. In the tree which I see, a bird sings his woes. . . .'

Then he reviewed mentally the last set of notes he had made for the Area Field Study and decided what changes he would make when he returned. He slept for a few hours during the afternoon, though his wrists and ankles now alternated between numbness and excruciating pain. After he slept, he revised his notes once again and then began to compose a mock-serious lecture for graduate students on the perils and pitfalls of field research.

When his evening bowl of rice was brought, by the same old woman, Will John decided that he had survived his first day of capture reasonably well.

The next morning, his first sensation was that he was going to lose his hands and feet if he were not untied. Then he saw the picture of Nina propped beside his head. He twisted his neck to try to see it better. It was her passport photograph. The embossing of the official stamp had raised a blister on her cheek. Suddenly the pattern in which he was trapped whirled like a roulette wheel. The ball was still bouncing but he felt the wheel slowing. Any minute now, it would stop. Emotion flooded him like the sea rushing into a cavern. It was half terror, half helpless rage.

Then he realized that the man was back, still as a stalking cat, watching Will John's awkward twisting and straining in the effort to see.

'Where is she?' demanded Will John. 'What have you done with her?'

'Aaah,' said Thu. Satisfaction showed in his eyes. 'Wrong question. What did you do with her? What did you do with my son?'

'I swear,' said Will John, 'that I do not know what you're talking about!'

'The child!' said Thu. 'My child, which she was carrying!'

'Your child?' Will John repeated. 'She was pregnant with your child?' He closed his eyes to think. He felt sick again.

'My son,' said Thu. 'Unless you know differently.'

Will John opened his eyes again. He heard the danger in that casual remark. He understood the implication precisely. The danger was no doubt Nina's as well as his own. He fought the confusion of shock and pain. 'No,' he said. 'I swear I knew nothing of any child!' He needed time to think. His confusion was dangerous.

'I loved her,' he could say. 'But she wouldn't have me. She said she loved someone else – one of her own countrymen. . . .'

299

He imagined the ironic amusement in the intelligent, knowing eyes above him.

'I was interviewing her for a book I was researching . . . I was investigating American involvement in the opium trade. . . .'

No. Say nothing, he told himself. On the principle of name, rank and number. Give him nothing. Learn what you can yourself. 'I know nothing about a child,' he repeated.

'You're a liar,' said Thu gently. He left the room.

Alone again, Will John surfed on repeated waves of panic and despair. Again and again, he found himself tumbling helpless and out of control. If Nina had really been pregnant by Thu, then she had been sleeping with them both at the same time. This was at the time when, with amazed exhilaration, he had felt like the other half of that small, slim, dark-haired woman who was part woman warrior, part terrified child. He now felt rage that she had made a fool of him. Then he felt desolation. Then he reminded himself that it only *might* have been so. Then he knew that his natural stance of emotional self-protection had been justified after all. Then another wave of despair rolled him onto the rocks and left him gasping.

At some point in the afternoon, he remembered the techniques of interrogation. He had forgotten the most important: convince the prisoner of your superior knowledge; separate him from other prisoners so they cannot reinforce each other's morale; make them mutually distrustful; imply to a prisoner that another has already betrayed him.

Remember the classic patterns, he reminded himself. Hang onto the patterns.

'Tell him to untie me,' said Will John to the old woman when she brought his evening rice. 'Untie me,' he said in Meo. His voice was firm and carried authority.

In the late afternoon, three armed men untied him and escorted him from the room, down a flight of wooden steps, across a packed dirt parade ground, down some rock steps to a bamboo cage which had been built in a fresh raw scar in the rock. It was just long enough for him to lie down in and four feet high, made of bamboo as thick as his wrist, lashed together with steel wire. He blinked in the light of the evening which was brighter than the shadows of the room. The little cage had no cover and the rock floor beneath it was hot from the now-setting sun.

His wrists and ankles oozed blood but at least he could move his arms and legs. He spent an hour stretching and bending all his joints and rubbing his deadened muscles. His spirit lifted at having something new to look at, however limited. The cage was set between a ten-foot cliff and the sharp-edged rubble which had been sheared from the little cliff by an exploding shell or bomb. He could see a narrow slice of the terrace above him, between two rocks, a large boulder, and a vast expanse of sky. A spider was constructing a murky tunnel in a crack at the bottom of the cliff. Ants traced purposeful arabesques across the loose rubble. Once in a while, someone crossed the slice of view of the terrace. He would have enough to occupy him for a little longer.

As it grew dark and bats began to swoop from cracks in the peak above the cage, Will John stretched out gratefully on the still-warm rock. His feet stuck out but he could straighten his knees. He thought about Nina, and his conviction that he had smelled her perfume on the first morning. He probed for the pattern in the strange new shape reality had assumed. He decided that Thu was lying about the child to torment him. Then, to distract himself from the weakness of that argument, he began to recite the multiplication tables, starting with one times one.

'Let's salvage what we can of the situation,' said Perry on the telephone when Nina arrived back in Washington and rang him. 'Have dinner with me. Tell me then.'

He took her to a small house on the edge of Georgetown, recently turned into a restaurant in spite of the neighbours' objections. It held only a dozen tables and was all pale peach linen, *ficus benjamina* in baskets, and signed Artist's Proofs on the walls. Perry normally favoured English-style carveries with oak beams and patterned carpets or else what he called 'splendidly awful' cafes and coffee shops from the Bakelite era. She wondered if he were trying to please her, and if so, why.

'Falacci has put the war away,' she said, when they had been settled at an isolated table in a small conservatory at the back of the house. She looked down into the exquisite, crab-centred flower of mango slices on her plate.

She was sitting in the sun in the garden of her parents' big house in Saigon, mango juice running down her face and wrists, sweet fibres caught in her teeth, and sticky strands of hair glued to her cheeks. Simpoh Flower, her best friend, her older sister, chewing on her own mango stone, growled like a dog. Both little girls laughed and swung their bare legs from the garden bench. Nina's *ayah* laughed, too, and carefully slit the skin of another smooth, orange fruit with her little knife, for Minou, Nina's gibbon and imaginary sister, who was complaining impatiently from the back of the bench.

I want to be there, Nina thought, not sure whether she meant the time, or the place. Oh God! I want to be there again!

She looked up to meet Perry's look of quizzical concern.

'Distracted by memory,' she explained.

' "What's memory but the ash that chokes our fires. . . ?" ' murmured Perry. He turned his fork in his angel-hair pasta. 'Tell me about Falacci.'

This mango had been picked too green; it needed time and sun to sweeten it. Nina sighed.

'He's coping with his own problems,' she said. 'Doesn't want ours or anyone else's. Wants nothing to choke his fires. I can't say I blame him.'

Perry ate two baled parcels of pasta without speaking. He had the gift of remaining silent when a lesser man would have spoken merely to fill the void.

As Nina ate the tiny mound of crabmeat, her mind again slid back, in spite of her will, to half-remembered picnics on the beach at Cap St Jacques. The three-year-old girl of the photograph which Thu now had, with her safe world still gathered around her – mother, Simpoh Flower, *ayah*, Doi their chauffeur and her first love. Minou, chained to the handle of the huge wicker food basket. Nina could still remember the oblique, eight-cornered shadow cast on the hot sand by the parasol which had seemed vast as a pavilion, and the sun on water too bright to look at. She could still feel her *ayah*'s hands brushing fragments of white crab shell out of her hair.

'And Junor?' Perry's voice interrupted the past.

'You aren't going to like Junor,' she said.

'What was the problem?' Perry was watching her again under the cliff-edge brows.

'He's a prisoner of war,' she said.

'Is that a figure of speech?'

'As real as Jimmy Putnam,' she said. 'Behind barbed wire and perimeter defences. With the difference that he's his own jailer and in upstate New Hampshire.'

Perry silently rolled another bale of angel hair.

'He can't decide which is more dangerous – himself or the world,' said Nina. 'But he believes the two have to be kept apart.'

'Why doesn't he see a psychiatrist?' suggested Perry. 'Or get in touch with one of those groups that are supposed to "talk it out".'

'How?' she demanded. 'No one sees him. No one talks to him. He doesn't talk to anyone. He's in solitary confinement!

Perry looked down at his plate and drew lines with his fork in the cream on the bottom. 'Perhaps,' he said quietly, 'he feels he deserves it.'

Nina felt unexpected rage burn up her neck. 'Perhaps he does,' she said. 'And no one's doing anything to make him feel differently!'

Perry gave her a strange smile. 'You're an unexpected advocate for the defence, aren't you?'

She put down her knife and fork. 'You have the wrong defendant in the box! Jimmy Putnam survived that firefight. Junor saw him taken prisoner. And they were on the wrong side of the Laos border at the time! Try putting those pieces together and then tell me who the villains are!'

He drank some Perrier and wiped his mouth with the pale peach linen napkin.

Displacement activity, Nina noted. Like a disturbed cat grooming itself.

'How sure is he?' asked Perry.

'Putnam was the only black soldier out that day.'

Perry nodded. 'I see. Yes, I can see.'

'What are you going to do now?' asked Nina.

'You haven't told his father yet, have you?'

'No,' said Nina. 'What are you going to do?'

Perry drank more mineral water, staring past her at the carved wooden garland of fruits and flowers on the wall behind.

'Pass the information on to IPWIC, I suppose. I'll have to sleep on it. Maybe the group at Fort Belvoir . . . you talked to one of their majors about that application from Macao, remember?'

Nina recognized the subtle diversion. But this was not a matter of refugee vetting. Her major had not belonged to the group he meant now. 'No, Ethan!' she said sharply. 'I meant longer term, to get Jimmy out, not pass the buck!'

'What else would you like me to do?' asked Perry, with an equal edge to his voice. 'File quintuplicate requests for another lunatic rescue attempt? Insist that someone stands up in Paris or Geneva and makes a denunciation . . . without hard evidence to support such an action?'

He stopped himself and leaned toward her, propped on his elbows, his large head suspended from his boney shoulder ridge. His voice regained its usual level tone. 'Dear Nina, the basic picture is still the same. The only difference is that you have clarified an historical detail – James Putnam wasn't killed when he was thought to have been. We still don't know that the letter is genuine. It's not like you to jump to conclusions like this.'

'You jumped too,' she said. 'When I first told you. Then I felt you change gear. You believe the letter could be genuine too.'

She felt the watertight doors shutting. The pupils of Perry's grey-blue eyes shuttered down to pinpoints under the brows. He leaned back in his chair and closed his long arms across his large body. However, he said reasonably, 'I suppose I might have done, at that. "Such tricks hath strong imagination." ' He opened his arms again and let them lie along the quilted curve of his club chair. 'For a minute there I think I must have imagined myself as the man who wrecked the US-Vietnam Peace Accords by calling the Vietnamese liars.'

Nina was impressed; few men would so readily sacrifice face in order to win the real point. But she also felt lonely.

'What about Mayor Putnam?' she asked. 'He's expecting to hear from me, or someone.'

'I'll get in touch,' said Perry. 'His weekly call to me is overdue, in fact . . . Ahh . . . At last,' he said, as the waiter arrived with the main course.

For the rest of dinner, they discussed the controversial incumbent mayor of New York, whether or not fish feel pain, and Perry's eighty-nine-year-old aunt, who wore a fox stole and kid gloves even in the summer and spent every Tuesday afternoon with a niece in the vaults of the family bank making a definitive inventory of the family's valuables. Not for the first time, Nina admired Perry's particularly American gift of appearing to make fun of himself and his family while being impressive at the same time. Will John had had it too.

Just as Perry dropped her off at his brother-in-law's house, however, Nina allowed herself to ask, 'What do *I* do now?'

'Write your report and go on to the next job, my dear,' he said quietly. 'I did warn you. You've done a regrettably good job. Jimmy Putnam is some other poor department's problem now.'

Two endless weeks later, during which Nina had done nothing much except read newspapers in a tiny office with flickering fluorescent lights, make eight fruitless calls about Harry Junor, stare out of her window, and translate an encounter between a Washington welfare worker and a forty-seven-year-old Vietnamese woman who needed surgery for cancer, she called Perry.

'Have you heard anything yet about Jimmy Putnam?' she asked.

'I pushed the message out in a bottle but nothing has washed back. I have to confess, I didn't expect much. They're not going to mount any commando raids at this juncture.' He paused. 'I'm sorry. I wish I could give you more positive news.'

304

She wished she weren't so angry with Ethan. She picked up another newspaper, and put it down. She decided to ring IPWIC herself.

'The matter cannot be discussed on the telephone,' said the man's voice. 'If you care to make a formal inquiry in writing, someone will get back to you.'

Another two weeks passed. Perry had still had no news. Then Mayor John Putnam called Nina at her Washington *pied-à-terre*. Perry had said that Putnam knew everybody – including, it seemed, someone willing to hand out William's unlisted telephone number.

'What's going on?' Putnam demanded, his voice tightly wound. 'You didn't get in touch about Junor and Falacci.'

'Where are you calling from?' Nina asked. Perry hadn't told him, then.

'I'm back in Washington,' Putnam said.

I should check with Ethan, thought Nina. She wavered for only five seconds. 'How about a stroll?'

'Same place?'

'Fine.'

They agreed on a time.

I'll call Ethan after I meet Putnam, Nina decided. She didn't want to have to disobey a direct order. I did warn Ethan that I wouldn't pretend, she reassured herself.

The early summer was less grudging than the spring. The sun was bright. Nina wore a short-sleeved red cotton dress, a little prematurely, for the pleasure of feeling the sun's warmth on her bare skin. There was no mist in the void between the two monuments, only green, green grass, striped by a mower and littered with tramps, picnickers, early tourists, office escapees, dogs, pigeons, and a group of Vietnamese playing soccer. Nina walked past gum wrappers, silver paper, polystyrene hamburger boxes, empty film canisters, and one young man, unshaven, lying flat on his back staring up into the sun. She realized with shock that the ball-playing Vietnamese looked small; she had been adrift among giants for a long time. As she passed the game, she glanced quickly, to see if any of the players' faces were familiar from interviews or photographs stapled to printed forms.

Putnam wore beige slacks and a navy blue blazer over a knitted cotton shirt. Nina's original impression of him still held – a responsible, solid citizen, sincere, intelligent, dignified, and middle-of-the-road. If he had strayed from the middle, he had been pushed.

He interrupted their ritual greeting abruptly. 'What did you find out?'

'Has no one been in touch?' she asked casually.

He shook his head.

'Let's walk,' she said, for time to reconsider her professional impropriety.

'I don't care if you have bad news,' said Putnam. 'I just need to know. To know *something*! I am only half-alive, not knowing!'

When Nina still didn't answer, he caught her arm. 'What's wrong? Please look at me,' he begged.

She stopped and turned to face him.

'Jimmy really *is* dead. Is that what you have to tell me?'

'He survived that fight,' said Nina.

Putnam didn't move. Nina stared away angrily through threatening tears down the Mall, across the pigeons and picnickers and the young man who was still staring up at the sun. Then Putnam flung his arms around her and hugged her so hard that she exclaimed in pain. When he released her, he was crying. 'God bless you,' he said. 'Thank you!'

'I've only made it worse,' protested Nina. 'I didn't say that I learned he's *still* alive. Rationally, the odds are against it. It has been a long time. Americans aren't used to the living conditions out there. Apart from his captors, you must consider disease, parasites, attacks by western forces on sites where POWs may have been held . . . I've been there, and I know what he would face.'

'How did you learn?' asked Putnam. He wiped his eyes with a blue spotted cotton handkerchief.

'I'm sure I shouldn't be telling you, but Harry Junor saw him taken prisoner.' Even in her refusal to pretend, she did not think it advisable or necessary to tell Putnam that it had been a black exercise into a neutral country as defined by the Geneva Accords of 1955.

'Thank you, God!' said Putnam, mainly to himself. 'I don't believe it! It gives me faith! It makes everything clearer.'

Nina looked at him. They started to walk again, along a paved path.

'So what's happening?' asked Putnam. 'Why wasn't I told?'

'The information is churning through the system,' said Nina. 'You should have been told, but bureaucracy takes its own sweet time.' She looked at Putnam again. 'It isn't clearer at all,' she said. 'There's no proof of any kind that Jimmy survived after capture. There's no proof he didn't write that letter seven years ago.'

'Then why send it now?'

Nina shook her head.

'I'll tell you,' said Putnam excitedly. 'Jimmy is alive and they want something for him. The letter is an opening move. They want to trade him.'

Nina felt a seismic irregularity in his voice. 'For what?' Her senses had gone inexplicably on the alert.

Putnam's glance reproved her for pretending ignorance. 'He's a bargaining chip . . . we've been hearing about bargaining chips. . . .'

Something had slipped subtly in their relationship. His face, however, showed nothing but intense thought, and the aftermath of his earlier emotion. They walked in silence toward the Lincoln Memorial. Nina lifted her face, inviting the sun, and found herself trying to remember something Putnam had said in their first meeting which she had let pass at the time.

Nina wondered how much of the Washington gossip Putnam had heard. How many had he read of the reports of POW sightings since 1966, which still slipped through into the press in spite of the official reluctance to discuss such disruptive subjects in public. She wondered whether, in his optical glass business in Silicon Valley, he had heard the conflicting stories of the high-tech crowd. But if he had, he would also know that those possible live POWs, who existed in the gossip, in the newspaper articles, in the classified high-resolution photographs, and in the diplomatic innuendo, were not allowed to write letters listing places they had been held. They had not been allowed to write letters at all, not since 1973.

'I do trust you, you know,' said Putnam.

Why did he say that? Nina asked herself. 'I'd rather you didn't,' she said.

'Is that a wish or a warning?' They looked sideways at each other.

'Just a wish,' said Nina. 'At the moment.'

'Thank God,' said Putnam. He stopped and looked up the stone stairs into the high, shadowed vault of the Memorial. The great blind stone eyes of Lincoln gazed down at them.

'When this was built in 1902,' said Putnam, for no apparent reason, 'everyone knew what it meant to be a good American: brave, free, patriotic, industrious, independent, God-fearing. Tolerant. Look at that monument . . . you can tell how they felt then. It's square. Solid. Confident right angles. Now it's all a lot more complex.'

He appeared to be talking to the statue seated high above him. 'For example,' he asked it, 'who's more patriotic – the man who fights to defend his country . . . or the one who fights to keep his country out of a war he thinks is wrong?' He turned to Nina. 'This is a monument to freedom. But when we talk about freedom, whose do we mean? My kind, or that of a headman of a Vietnamese village?'

'Do you know whose freedom you mean?' she asked, looking upwards, like Putnam. She had remembered the snatch of conversation from their first meeting. 'I could send my business down the tubes,' he had said.

'Well,' he said now, 'I do know for a start that you just have to pick your own way of being American and stick to it. Otherwise you'll get confused. That's clear enough. It's choosing the way that I find so hard.'

'I'm the wrong person to ask,' said Nina. 'I'm still working on the basics of how to be human.'

The seismic disturbance in Putnam had increased. Nina could feel it, as she had the explosions of distant shells through the soles of her feet. There was more for her to do on this job after all.

They climbed halfway up the steps and turned to look back toward the Washington Monument whose long straight sides were just beginning to waver in a foretaste of summer heat to come. The young man still lay flat on the grass, now face down, very small and far away.

'You asked me earlier what was going to happen next,' she said to Putnam. 'I think the real question is what are you going to do? That's what you've just been talking about, isn't it?'

'What would you do in my place?' He rubbed his mouth with his fingertips, then thrust his hands deep into the pockets of his beige slacks.

'I don't know all your options,' she said.

Putnam shot her a sharp questioning glance. Then he smiled gently. 'Just call me a good old-fashioned kind of American who believes in life and liberty for all, even if happiness is sometimes in short supply.'

As soon as they had parted, Nina telephoned Perry from a public phone booth.

'Exactly what did you say John Putnam does for a living when he isn't being mayor?'

'He started and now runs a small high-tech optical glass company, in California, in the town where he's mayor. Microscope lenses and mirrors, that kind of thing. High quality, low turnover. He'll never be rich but he filled a very special niche.'

308

'Does he have a contract with the Department of Defence?'

Perry paused so long that she thought he was not going to reply.

'I believe he does,' he said at last. 'I'd have to check to be sure . . . Nina, I think you're going to have to tell me why you want to know.'

'Of course,' Nina said. 'But remember about jumping to conclusions. I'll get back to you if I may.' Perry's information had made her stomach queasy.

'By the way,' she asked, counterattacking to divert his curiosity, 'have you told him yet that he buried the wrong body?'

She would have missed the tiny pause if she hadn't been listening for it.

'I haven't heard back from the powers that be,' said Perry. 'It's still under discussion. Be a little careful with him in the meantime, please.'

Focused again, Nina then spent seven hours in the library at Georgetown University ploughing through publication summaries and indices. She left the library thoroughly depressed by her success in finding what she had been looking for.

Why am I doing this, Nina asked her wavering reflection in the eagle-topped mirror as she dialled the number Putnam had given her of the friends' house in Washington where he was staying.

The image of a burnt and shattered stand of bamboo invaded her mind. Her own bloody hand pulled frantically at the canes. . . .

'Hello?' asked a stranger's voice.

This time Nina and Putnam met in the airy, high-tech shop of the Space Museum set on one side of the hall.

'Who approached you?' She spoke softly but without warning. 'Was it before or after Jimmy's letter came?' She watched for the effect of her grenade. At first nothing happened.

Putnam fingered a foil packet of dehydrated strawberry ice cream, as eaten by American astronauts in space. 'I think I'll get some of this for my youngest boy,' he said. 'He wants to be a space scientist the way I wanted to be a cowboy.' He looked up, heavy-eyed. 'There were a lot of black cowboys, you know.'

'Will your youngest boy take over your business?'

Putnam's hand moved slowly to a pack of freeze-dried baked beans and rested there. 'He's only eight; it's a little soon to know.'

'Mayor Putnam . . .'

'John. For God's sake, John. Please. All this mayor and mister business makes you sound like you're interrogating me!'

'Who was it? What do they want?'

'May I use your Christian name?'

'Nina. Please answer me. Was it before or after the letter?'

'I think you've gone mad,' he said, still studying the range of space foods.

It's almost an impressive performance, thought Nina, but he hasn't objected to quite the right things. His focus is askew. Oh God, I was right! 'It was after the letter,' she said. 'The letter was to soften you up. You would never have considered it otherwise.'

Putnam finally looked up from the freeze-dried baked beans. 'What you're suggesting is outrageous. Do you really expect a serious answer?' He had finally got it right.

'You want to trust me to tell you the truth,' Nina said passionately. 'Why can't I want the same? It's not hard to imagine that you would be under pressure anyway, given your business, and a Department of Defence contract . . . It's almost routine for them to try. You want to enlist me on your side! I swear I'm not your enemy! Tell me who's doing the asking.'

Putnam flushed the colour of raw liver. He dropped the packet of freeze-dried ice cream, bent to retrieve it, and had to steady himself on the counter edge as he straightened up again.

'I think you hoped your government would take up your cause and spare you a terrible choice,' said Nina. 'You brought them Jimmy's letter to give your country a chance to save your soul.'

Putnam stood braced against the counter edge.

'John,' she said gently. 'Do you have any idea what would happen if I reported this conversation? Though it's only an unfounded accusation and a denial. But that's all it would take.'

Putnam stared at the floor.

'They'd check everything – your tax returns, your books, your holiday plans, your wife's friends, your golfing companions, your telephone bills and every call, what you eat for breakfast, and the dust in your trouser cuffs. You would be refused further export licences. Or, alternatively, you would get them and then every shipment would be secretly monitored.'

'Haven't you already reported what you suspect?'

'Of course not! You would have noticed, I assure you! I told you I was not your enemy.'

Putnam didn't seem to hear her reassurance. His face had set into the blankness Nina had seen on the faces of peasants in photos, caught between the VC and US troops, powerless in their dilemma except to wait for fate to make its next appalling move.

310

What would I do in his place? thought Nina. If it were Mouse?

'John,' she said gently. 'I have experience in living uncomfortable lives. I think you're a patriotic man by nature. I don't think you would like swimming in those waters. Treason is like a flat beach – long, long shallows and then, when you're not expecting it – the deep!'

'I gave my son to fight for the survival of truth. Now I believe more and more that he has been abandoned for the sake of some other "truth".' He glared at her. 'That's the real treason! You were right when you said I'm a patriot. We've all heard the arguments that world peace depends on an equal balance of power . . . why isn't it my patriotic duty to do what I can to maintain that balance?'

'Do you really believe that?'

Putnam rubbed his mouth with his fingers again. 'If it's true for one side, why is it treason when applied to the other?'

Perhaps he didn't care how much he was confessing. Or perhaps it was a relief.

'Now I think you may be creating your own truth,' Nina said, 'as other men do . . . as long as we let them.'

'Leave me alone,' he said. 'Please leave me alone!'

'No,' she said. 'I think you wanted me to ask! Now, where do you want it to take us?'

'Dear God, how do you think I can choose?' His voice began to rise. 'I try to examine my conscience . . . to be rational. I pray for guidance. My God, I pray! But there're no instructions from Up There! Not about this. Not yet. I'm a man and a father and a public servant . . . I'm losing my balance . . . coming apart!'

His raised voice was attracting attention. Nina was afraid that his white-knuckled hands would tear the glass front off the display shelf he was clutching.

'Pay for the ice cream if you're taking it,' she said quietly. 'Then come outside.'

Putnam pocketed his change with shaking hands and followed her back out into the bright sunlight, carrying the freeze-dried ice cream as if he weren't sure what it was or why he had it.

'I'm going crazy,' he said. 'How can you choose between two impossibilities and stay sane?'

'One choice is more impossible than the other,' said Nina.

'What do you mean?' he raised his face to the bright blue sky and waited.

'Jimmy was captured on the wrong side of the Laos border,' she explained. 'He was there illegally, in defiance of international

311

agreements. Under orders, but still illegally. Party to what is officially a criminal act by the US Government. If he is alive he's doubly valuable. As pressure on you and as potential propaganda. Are you quite sure that his price isn't so great that it won't tilt the balance of power the wrong way?'

Putnam stood in the white sunlight reflecting up from the terrace outside the museum, shaking his head numbly. 'I don't care! I don't care! I have what they want. And they have my son!'

'When were you first approached?'

'Five years ago . . . with money.'

'And you refused?'

Putnam nodded.

'Because your DOD contract was too valuable to risk?'

'Because I knew who they really were, in spite of the Belgian passports!' His indignation was genuine. He looked at her for the first time since his outburst in the museum. 'I didn't consider it because I didn't think it was right.' His face crumpled. 'I still don't. That's what's so awful. I still know it's not right!'

'But five years later,' said Nina gently, 'they have learned your price.'

There was a long silence.

'I almost wish he had died,' said Putnam. 'I could never say that to my wife. But it would be cleaner.'

'Have you agreed to deal yet?'

'No,' he said. 'Not really. I just haven't said "no" this time.'

'Let me go back to my superiors,' begged Nina. 'This changes everything! Let me say that you volunteered to me that you were approached. Tell me it's all right with you.' She touched his arm lightly. 'I think you want that or you would never have raised the subject of choices with me.'

'What will anyone do differently?' Putnam asked tiredly.

'How can I know what they'll decide?' she said. 'But I can tell you what I see. You'll destroy yourself if you give away military technology in exchange for your son. You said I was a person who liked truth. Well, you're a man of honour, whether you like it or not. You haven't the stomach for treason any more than I did for lies. *Tant mieux, tant pis,* that's the way you are. Accept it.'

She drew a deep breath. 'I also know that it's impossible to sacrifice your son a second time.' She closed her eyes briefly against the glare of the white concrete. 'No one can ask that of you. But what you've just told me takes Jimmy's case out of the political arena of US-Vietnamese diplomatic negotiations. It's now the province of old, experienced, cold-war players . . . on both sides . . . who aren't as careful of each other's feelings as diplomats are.'

'Why should I believe anyone, even you?' Putnam asked. 'And what can you do that I couldn't?'

Nina stared at him in despair. 'I didn't want to talk to you in the first place,' she said fiercely. 'I knew I was going to get involved in something I couldn't bear. But I did and I am. And if I say I will try to make something happen, I will! I can't answer for anyone else. You'll have to be happy with that.'

'I don't know,' said Putnam. 'I don't know!'

'Try to think straight,' she said. 'You have two choices now: you try to go ahead alone and end up in prison, or you let us try to save your soul.'

He looked at her for a long, long time. She recognized the agonizing slowness of mind that accompanies terror.

'John,' she said shakily. 'I left a child somewhere in Laos. I don't know whether she's alive or dead, but, like you, I believe that she's alive. I want you to have Jimmy back almost as much as I want my daughter. For God's sake, let me see what I can do, before you start to destroy yourself!'

He continued to look at her, almost as if she hadn't spoken. Then he half-smiled in weary resignation. 'If that's your best offer,' he said. 'I'll stall them. Tell your superiors not to make my son wait too long.' Then he turned and walked quickly away, into the line of trees that held at bay the noise and fumes of Constitution Avenue.

'They have to do something now!' Nina took two quick steps to keep up with Ethan Perry's long legs and cursed her high-heeled sandals. 'Don't they?'

'It's a lovely afternoon,' Perry had said when she telephoned. 'Why don't you help me return my library books? I feel like playing hooky. I'll meet you outside, in the sunshine.'

In other circumstances, Nina would have been amused by his flat cap and tweed jacket on this sunny, early summer day.

'Aah, "the girls in their summer dresses",' he said approvingly when he saw her. 'Red suits you.' It was part compliment and part delaying tactic. He straightened his back and sniffed the air. 'We lived outside all summer when I was a boy, even slept out in the boathouse. I don't suppose I changed clothes for three months at a time if my mother and grandmother could be evaded. Thank goodness we all went swimming every day!' He peered at her along the ridge of his nose and held out a full octave stretch of books in one long-fingered hand.

313

'One country-house murder with no loose ends,' he enumerated. '*Mansfield Park*, revisited yet again. One temporarily unfashionable German philosopher. One collection of English gardening essays which resolves the knotty problem of choosing the best snowdrop. . . .'

I've never heard Ethan chatter like this! thought Nina. He's seriously worried. 'Somebody has to take some kind of action now!' she insisted.

'Putnam should have come forward five years ago when they first contacted him,' said Perry severely.

'Would you have called that kind of attention down on your own head?' asked Nina. 'Particularly if you had said no?'

Perry pursed his lips and tucked his books under his arm. Nina had to skip again to keep up; he was walking very fast.

'Did he say what they were asking for?'

'No,' she said.

'He's no fool,' said Perry. 'He must know that it's not the Vietnamese. They can't even afford to feed their own people. They're asking for farm machinery and power stations, not material for defence research . . . not yet. They don't have the capability, certainly not at this level.'

'Exactly what level would you say it was?' asked Nina.

'Way above both of our heads!' He gave a snort of dry amusement. 'Did he mention agent nationality?'

'Belgian.'

He gave another snort. 'I should have guessed. *Le plus ça change*, eh?'

'I wouldn't know,' said Nina. 'Does John Putnam make laser mirrors for research in designing "smart" missiles?'

Perry turned his large head, suddenly resembling the American eagle focusing on a rabbit. 'Did he tell you that?'

'No,' said Nina. 'But I read the papers and popular paperbacks. The US loses hundreds of thousands of dollars worth of computer technology to Russian scientists each year. Via West German conduits among others. Much of it simply purchased, through more or less legitimate agents, then transferred east by a form of international sleight-of-hand. And you told me that Putnam probably had a DOD contract.'

The eagle still had the rabbit in its sights. 'You have an active imagination,' he said severely.

'Not imagination, just a visit to the University library,' she said. 'I spent seven hours looking through Soviet bloc open source publication summaries – just the kind of thing I used to do in Bangkok. It was obvious that six major Soviet scientists doing x-ray laser research a few years ago have stopped publishing in technical journals. I then asked myself what they could be doing now that can't be published . . . particularly in view of the rumoured work we're doing on guidance systems.'

'I won't insult your intelligence by denying it,' Perry said. 'But leave it alone. It's not your territory, or mine! It's mainstream and we're both way out on the fringe! You'll get yourself into trouble I might not be able to undo.'

'I just want to know that something will be done to get Jimmy Putnam back, if he's still alive!'

Perry straightened to his full six feet, six inches. 'Of course something will happen now,' he said, 'but I have no idea what. You're too old to expect anyone to promise a happy ending!'

Nina shook her head in frustration.

'Unhook your heartstrings,' said Perry. 'There's nothing more you can do for your black mayor. And Jimmy Putnam is not your daughter!'

Nina turned her head away. There was a dead pigeon in the gutter, half-covered by a crumpled paper napkin and a broken green glass 7-UP bottle. 'Well then,' she said after a moment, in a very small voice, 'is there any chance of setting Harry Junor free?'

Perry lifted his cap and rubbed the mark of its leather band on his high forehead. Then he took the cap off. 'I'm very sorry, my dear. I don't mean to sound like the enemy. Let me get rid of these damn books, then walk me home . . . I won't be a minute. There's something I wanted to tell you.'

'I'll stay out here in the sun,' said Nina, feeling a premonitory chill. She watched him disappear under the dirty brick Gothic arch of the local lending library, past a bulletin board advertising lectures on local history, meditation groups and women's self-defence classes. She had known there was something other than Putnam bothering him when they first met that afternoon and, whatever it was, it concerned her.

'Come have a sherry,' he ordered when he re-emerged under the brick arch. He tucked her hand under his arm. 'Old man's prerogative,' he said and patted her hand which was caught in the tweedy crook of his elbow.

Nina's alarm increased. He usually avoided physical contact except in the ritualized gestures of courtesy.

'Ethan,' she said. 'What's going on? Is immigration going to take away my resident alien status? Am I going to be thrown out? Have the Florida Mafia finally realized who I am?'

315

'Don't be silly,' he said. 'Nothing like that.' He said nothing for a few more steps.

'Your old friend Haines. . . ,' he began.

Nina poised between elation and terror.

'It seems,' said Perry, 'that he was over the Thai-Laos border doing an update on that Area Field Study he was involved with . . . waving his tape recorder at singing grannies and centenarians with total recall . . . Anyway, he hasn't come back out. I only heard by chance. After allowing two weeks for all the usual snafus in transport and so on, the Study Centre has finally raised the alarm.' His voice was unnaturally jaunty.

'How long has it been since he was due out?' Her own voice was quiet.

'Nearly four weeks now.'

I shouldn't care, she told herself. He's dead for me. I want to keep him that way. 'Has there been any word of any kind?' she asked. 'Were there disturbances in the area?'

'No more than usual,' said Perry. 'And so far no ransom notes from dissident Shan guerrillas or disgruntled Meos we left behind to face the PAVN.'

Nina was falling through space. Everything in her once familiar world was being taken away. Everything was disappearing. From the age of fifteen, great chunks of her life had broken away beneath her in avalanches of falling rubble, like a crumbling chalk cliff. Her parents. Her home. Her husband. Her city. Her country. Her child. And now Will John. Even if he had not been destined to be her lover again, or her husband, he had been a guide, a beacon which had illuminated paths she had not seen. She had loved him totally, with feelings made more intense by knowing that he would leave her.

'Thank you for telling me,' she said. 'I think I would like to go home. I should have worn a warmer dress.'

'Why not come in for a quick sherry. We're nearly there.'

She felt Perry's concern, and also his ambivalence.

He's afraid I'll fall apart on him, she thought. Terrified that he'll have to mop up female tears.

'Really, I'm sure,' she said. She smiled up at the sharp grey eyes under the craggy cliff edges. 'The Will John chapter of my life was several volumes ago.'

I thought I had replaced love with anger, she thought, but it didn't work. I still owe him too much.

316

Perry nodded and released her hand from his bent elbow. 'Shall I let you know of developments?'

'*Bien sûr!*' she said. French still broke through when the surface cracked.

Safely back past the bay trees in the Versailles tubs, among William's Federal antiques and dried flower arrangements, Nina sat on the striped silk of the Duncan Phyfe settee and rocked with her arms wrapped tightly around her, holding herself together.

I'm not sure I can bear it, she thought. I'm not sure I can lose him again. I don't know how much more I can lose!

To her own surprise, she found herself going to the little kitchen and putting some cold rice from an unwashed pot onto a saucer. Beside the rice, she placed eight grapes. She took the saucer out into the walled terrace behind the house and placed it in the centre of a raised flowerbed, beneath a white camellia. She had last made such an offering in Bangkok, and before that, as a child in the company of the servants and Simpoh Flower.

It you're over there, she said silently to the spirits of the plants and animals, you must be here in this country as well. I know there's nothing you can do to bring back Will John, or Mouse, or Jimmy Putnam. But keep me company, at least! I feel so alone!

She sat on the terrace until after dark, her face turned upward like a second offering. Somewhere, above the orange-tinged feverish glow of the city, was the same sky that had burned with heat above the garden in Saigon and the Tiger's Head.

15

For a long time after Nina drove away from his apartment in Queens, Victor Falacci stood by the window, listening to the children in the street below, trying to stop being so angry. From the side of his eye he saw Becky pop out of the kitchen and stand waiting for him to speak. He wished she wouldn't always do that, as if she were frightened of him.

'Who was she?' Becky asked at last.

'A stupid, snooping bitch,' he said. After another pause, he added reluctantly, 'From Washington.'

Becky sniffed at the faint traces of Nina's perfume and raised her eyebrows. She didn't smell very official, she wanted to say, but didn't. It was another one of those times. Batten down the hatches, everybody – Daddy's in one of his moods.

'What about?' She waited. 'What was she snooping about?'

Her husband glared at her. 'Nothing important,' he said. 'Nothing for you to worry about.'

He crossed from the window toward the door of their apartment without looking at his wife. 'I'm going out to get some new batteries for Lucy's bear.'

Becky Falacci watched her husband's hips and legs as he walked. He still looked good from behind – better than most men of his age.

'OK,' she said finally. When the door closed behind him, the tips of her shoulders dropped fractionally. She didn't know why he still couldn't trust her enough to talk about the things that sometimes hung over both of them like a summer storm in the making. He goddam well ought to trust her.

She had waited for him the whole awful year he was in Vietnam, even though they were only engaged. She had hung in there when he had broken their engagement after his discharge. She had seen that he had been through something and might need a little time to sort himself out. She had waited, in spite of all the advice from her friends and family, until he had come to his senses and decided that marriage was a good idea after all. She had told him, and meant it, that she couldn't care less whether he had lost a foot and part of his leg . . . It wasn't his foot she had fallen in love with. And she had stayed around through the last four years. What the hell else did he need from her to prove she could be trusted?

As he walked to the electrical store next to the pizza place under the elevated stop, Falacci's rage transferred itself onto Becky's silent questioning. It made him feel he was failing her. He wanted only to protect her. The shadows that sometimes slid around the walls of his skull weren't things he ever wanted her or Lucy to know about. He wished *he* didn't know them! He loved her, he loved Lucy, he loved the daily details of marriage and family life. He just couldn't seem to make her believe how much he loved it all.

Unlike his year on the borders of Vietnam, spent mainly in scrub jungle above his head or mud up to his waist, waiting for an innocent-seeming tree, or patch of track, or even a child, to kill him, his life now was controllable. More or less.

He liked its predictability and even its pettiness. He *enjoyed* putting out the trash cans. He *enjoyed* trying to get the charcoal going for a barbecue. He *enjoyed* solving the small problems of his family or his staff at the supermarket where he was manager; their very smallness meant that they could be solved. He enjoyed things that he knew drove some other men mad. He knew he was lucky.

His year in Vietnam had given him a gift. In exchange for eleven inches of bone and flesh, he had been given the awareness that his life was happening to him. He could feel its texture and temperature as he slipped through its current. He would never arrive at his last moment, like so many other people, crying in shock, 'Hold on a minute! How did I get here?' He was in extra time and meant to make the most of every minute of it. He hated to waste any time being angry. He wasn't really angry at Becky anyway, he decided, but with himself, for not making her see how safe he now felt with her, and how much he treasured this safety.

By the time he reached the drug store under the elevated train track at the end of his block, he was angry only with that slope-eyed bitch from Washington. It was like he was a tightrope walker and she had shaken his wire. Just seeing her had stirred up the shadows in his skull. Then her information had made him feel helpless again – the way he had felt helpless for most of his year in the army. What the hell did she want him to do with the knowledge that Jimmy Putnam might be still alive, over there? Slit his throat?

He bought the batteries and walked home again, thinking: Jimmy

319

can't see those kids hitching roller-skate rides on the backs of cars. Jimmy can't buy a slice of sausage and green pepper in the Pizza Palace. Jimmy can't hear the elevated trains or the traffic, or the new re-release of Purple People Eater blasting out of the Record Rack on the corner. Jimmy can't walk out to the store, like I can, and then go home to his family. I can and Jimmy can't. Why me and not him? What did I ever do to earn it?

He was glad that Becky was back in the kitchen. He went into Lucy's room and watched his hands reload the talking bear he had given her for her third Christmas.

'Hello, Lucy,' it grated. 'I love you.'

As he placed the lavender-furred creature on his daughter's pillow, he suddenly thought of Gabriel Simpson.

He had met Simpson in hospital after being wounded. In civilian life, they might never have done more than nod. But in neighbouring beds, in the grey, uneasy hours of early morning, kept awake by the moaning, swearing and nightmares of other casualties and by sudden grenades of their own pain, he and Simpson had talked. Still raw from their direct look at death, they had wandered in and out of their own thoughts and each other's, sometimes aloud and sometimes silently. By the end of their six weeks together, without ever meaning to, they had learned and exposed so much that it had embarrassed them afterwards, whenever Simpson stayed at Falacci's house on his rare visits to New York. They had never been so close again. Nevertheless, in spite of the embarrassment, each of them took comfort from the presence of the other.

Falacci felt like calling Simpson now, except that Gabe wouldn't have a telephone in that cabin of his up on his mountain top. To Falacci's surprise, he found himself sitting on the sofa writing Simpson a letter. He went immediately to mail it. When he came back, Becky saw more clearly than Falacci himself how much weight he had dropped into the mailbox on the corner.

'What've you got?'

'Christ knows.' A piece of flesh, white ends of bones, strings, collapsed tubing.

'Call it one VC body.'

Onto a pile of hands, half-heads, a thigh still attached to part of a pelvis though dislocated at the joint.

'Call it forty-seven.'

'It was only one unit. . . .'

'Forty-seven. Get on the fucking radio . . . forty-seven. We got us forty-seven!'

320

Sunrise reflected off monsoon puddles, the water a delicate pink, more water than blood. A bulldozer rooted out a pit and began to shove the fragments into it.

Gabriel Simpson rolled off his bed and came to his feet by the cabin door. He could no longer remember where those puddles had been, but they were so clear in his dream that he was certain they had been real. He hesitated for a moment then pulled the door open and stepped, naked and sweating, out into the bright night on his hilltop.

The air was skin temperature. The world around him was silver and blue. The ring of trees, the pelt of grass in front of his cabin, the sky thick with cold fires, were all cool blues. The blades of the grass were edged in mercury. There were no warm colours in this night – no reds like the blowing highland dust or pinks like the bloody pools. Just a few lavender highlights. The orange squash and pumpkins in his garden patch, a red flannel shirt left lying across his bench, had become black. Even his own body, already brown from working without clothes during the first hot summer days, was almost black in the silver light. His slim, bare foot was a dark backdrop for the ice-green beacon of a firefly tangled in the grass.

For another minute or two, he tried to remember where those puddles had been, and what he had done there.

He sighed, then squatted to part the grass gently. He observed his hands shaking. The firefly righted itself and began to climb an arch of stem.

Gabriel Simpson had found Falacci's letter in his box at the local post office in the small town where he bought his milk and coffee and cigarette papers. He had looked at the unopened envelope, while he checked out the messages from his head, his stomach and his breathing. They told him he was having a so-so day – not a bad one but not a good one either. He put the letter into his pocket for later, when he had his woods around him and the wall of his cabin behind his back. He was pleased at the contact but it also made him a little nervous. Contact with Falacci took him back. He had to prepare himself for the journey.

He sometimes thought of himself and Falacci as mariners once wrecked in a black and churning sea. They had fought their way to shore together and were now bound by an experience they would both rather forget. He liked that image. It was a good way to handle the whole thing.

Watching the firefly crawl painfully up the stem of grass, flying wings protruding like wisps of petticoat from the thicker protective wings, he knew the letter was the reason for the dream, his first in a long time. What Falacci had written was a bad dream in itself – to be over there still! He couldn't imagine how Jimmy P. could still be sane enough to write a letter . . . if what Falacci wrote was true. He had to decide about that likelihood first. The firefly suddenly seemed to decide that it had worked hard enough and flew away. Its cold, blinking light faded like an aircraft disappearing into the night sky.

Simpson went back into the cabin, rolled himself a smoke and returned to sit on his bench, bare back against the unpeeled logs, long, slim toes nosed down into the silver-eged grass. Then he got up again to get his rifle. He laid it across the bench. He knew he didn't need it. He had been making himself leave it on its hooks on the wall more and more. He was totally and ironically aware that getting it down tonight was self-indulgence. But he still needed it.

He had made an agreement with himself, during the long process of getting steady again after the war, to take it slowly, not ask too much at a time. He could step outside himself and look at himself as a rather slow and uncooperative patient. He thought the prognosis was good however, as long as the objective doctor side of himself stayed in charge. He knew that he was really in New Hampshire. He knew that no one was going to shoot at him from the dark treeline. However, the rifle lying on the bench would harm no one.

He listed aloud the jobs to do before the autumn – a mantra to steady himself. Cut and split more wood for the stove. Buy beer and wine to see him through a hot July and August when the world was best avoided. Ditto tobacco, salt, matches, etcetera. Finish door on the new root cellar. Plant potatoes for same, next week. He almost managed to burrow back down into internal peace.

Then the stillness in his mind was filled again with the blowing red dust and the whomp-whomp-whomp of helicopter rotors which had arrived on the mountain top with Falacci's letter.

Remember the good parts, he adjured himself. Remember the good! Like those children in that village whose name he had forgotten. Like standing on a mountain top, looking out over the green coral of the valleys, feeling your insides hollow and filled with lightness. Like the woman in Bangkok whom he had recognized, as she had recognized him, though they had never met before. He shut his eyes tightly and tried to recapture the brief peace he had felt while she had been holding him tightly against her. But the whomp-whomp of the rotors was too strong.

To drown them, he said, 'The deer are eating all my sprouting corn.'

He often spoke aloud to himself, deliberately; it amused him to confirm, even for his own private enjoyment, the opinion of his parents' friends that he was definitely strange, if not actually psychotic.

'If you would only get your hair cut, darling,' his mother would say, in a weak defensive move. 'Hippies are out of fashion now. Didn't you know?'

His father's tactics were more offensive, as suited a former lieutenant decorated in World War II and successfully returned to the normal civilian responsibilities of man. 'How long are you going to waste yourself up there impersonating Thoreau?'

'These days it's called "being into self-sufficiency," ' Gabriel corrected him drily.

'Ahh,' his father would murmur reflectively. 'So that's what the younger generation call wasting a degree *magna cum laude* and four years of tuition, board and room.'

Decisive moments seldom appear as such until later. Simpson had no sense of decision as he sat naked on his bench with crumbs of bark from the log walls printing themselves on his tanned skin. He felt discomfort, like the uneasiness that precedes nausea. When the work mantra failed to soothe him, he tried analysis.

There was fear in there somewhere. Remembered fear. Fear of being captured . . . as Jimmy had been. Lying on his side in water, digging his back into the mud of the dyke wall while the voices passed by above his head, along the dyke top path. He could pin down that slippery feeling . . . that taste in his mouth like the electricity between a scrap of aluminium foil and a filling in his tooth. Fear was logical. He lifted his hand from his rifle where he hadn't realized he had put it.

Guilt. He took a deep breath. That was a big one! Guilt because he felt so goddam happy that he wasn't writing a letter like Jimmy . . . perhaps . . . from God knows what place, in who knows what state. No decent human should feel happy that someone else was suffering and he was not. Particularly a friend! And if I had stayed up in the camp as I should have done, and sent the Meos out first, he thought, the POW might have been me!

This was harder to deal with. He took another deep breath. Come on, Gabe, he told himself. You're not happy because Jimmy's there. You're just happy it's not you. That's logical, not wicked. But the foretaste of retching remained.

He couldn't let himself near the real source of his discomfort. He had become a man of peace. Embraced a life of hard work, and the search for a tranquil spirit. He had rejected the Machine, whether green or pin-striped.

He heard rustling from the spring garden. The goddam deer again! He didn't need the meat so he left his gun where it was and yelled. He listened to the animals crash away into the woods. He had become a man of peace – how could he admit to himself that the largest part of his discomfort was excitement? Part of the thrumming in his centre was excitement. Vietnam had excited him even when he hated it most. He still had trouble accepting that fact. How could man ever do away with war if part of him secretly thought it was fun?

William McNeill felt Simpson's excitement when he appeared the next day at McNeill's truck depot.

'Hi, Gabe,' said McNeill. 'What's up?' Simpson didn't often come down off that hill of his – usually when he didn't like his own company. McNeill didn't mind being the alternative to being alone. He didn't mind very much at all these days. It was a pleasant way to live.

Simpson gave him Falacci's letter without preamble, then helped himself to a beer from the cooler while McNeill read.

The two men were so different that they might have been written as contrasting characters in a play. Simpson was thin and nervy, long-haired, and graceful as a greyhound under his heavy work clothes. He had long since trained himself not to make casual references to Veblen, Locke, Descartes or Nietzsche. He avoided betraying knowledge of the existence of Avigadro, the number of words for snow used by the Eskimos, the name of Monet's garden or those of past Nobel Prize winners who included one or two of his father's friends. This careful paring back of himself to basic man, however, could not always hide either his true identity as a university faculty brat or his relatively late introduction to basic man at the age of twenty-one when he volunteered to escape from academic privilege via Vietnam.

William McNeill was tall, bullet-headed and tanned. He was well-muscled now from hard work rather than work-outs in the gym. He was still heavy-jawed and crew-cut. He was quieter, however. He thought before he spoke, said nothing unnecessary and never said anything poetic, fanciful or frivolous. He was almost exactly what Simpson, aged seventeen, had thought of as basic man.

When McNeill finished reading Falacci's letter, he put the letter on his desk and placed his hands precisely on his knees, as he did each time

324

he sat down. His movements were cautious, as if he were so large that he had to keep checking that all the bits of himself were in the right places.

He felt, though he never said it, that he had life pretty well under control. He had come through Vietnam better than a lot of men he had seen – better than Gabe for example. His only problem, that he could see, was a low tolerance for bull-shit.

He had had nine jobs in the first 13 months after his discharge from the Army in 1973 but left them because some kid who didn't even know where Vietnam was had started giving him guff about the 'way things are done in this office' or about his attitude to the company. With his recent experience, he couldn't take that kind of thing any more. He had seen too many men killed through six-month officers who didn't know their arses from their elbows – there had been good officers, but they were just as scarce as good office managers. He had survived Vietnam by trusting only the man fighting beside him, whose ass was just as much on the line as his own. When you depended on each other for survival, it made for trust.

After the ninth job, McNeill had borrowed money from an army acquaintance who was now a lawyer, rented land from the state, and begun farming Christmas trees. Then he started his own garden maintenance business, contracted to big local firms who liked to fancy up their acres of macadam parking with ground cover shrubs and sapling trees. His first planting of Christmas trees would be croppable in three years. He had nearly paid back the loan from the maintenance business, which though still small, was growing. McNeill was doing very well, though he would not have said it out loud even under torture.

'What do you think?' Simpson seemed to be studying the four pick-up trucks parked outside the office window, neat between white lines. He was amused to note that McNeill's own truck was parked away from the others, in direct eyeline from Bill's desk. No one could go near it without being seen.

McNeill wiped the sweat from his palms on his blue denim kneecaps. As often happened, Simpson, to his own annoyance, was unable to wait for McNeill's voice to engage gears.

'You were out there, Bill. Checking the numbers. You always said it was bullshit that "all our boys" came home. You said the delivery was short, by a lot!'

McNeill continued to wipe his palms with a circular movement as if polishing his knees. He had told Gabe a little. But not about the photographs of the men who never showed up. Or about his visits down to see the Inter-Agency Prisoner of War Intelligence Committee. Or about the aerial photographs he had handed over before leaving Cam Ranh Bay, and never been able to trace afterwards. Or about the men he and Man, his Meo guide and partner, had personally seen behind barbed wire and bars, and still there as far as he knew. Unless they were dead.

'That's right,' he said. 'I was checking that we got them all back.'

This time, Simpson made himself wait. He had stopped being fooled by McNeill's apparent slowness after they had gone out together the first time.

McNeill reached out and touched Falacci's letter. 'Jimmy's done well if he survived this long,' he said reflectively. He looked carefully at Simpson, who had refused to sit down. 'Why did you bring it to me?'

Simpson's nervous walking stopped. For a count of two, he was absolutely still. 'I couldn't ignore it . . . go on cultivating my garden as if I didn't know! Who the hell else could I bring it to?'

McNeill read Falacci's letter again. 'It doesn't sound like that woman actually showed him Jimmy's letter. If he wasn't going to tell her anything, it's the first thing I'd have showed him, in her place. With his name in it, to get through to the personal. Shake some memories loose in his head.' He crossed his legs and carefully arranged the hem of his jeans around the ankle of his workboot. 'I'd like to see Jimmy's letter myself.'

'Do you think it could be a fake?' Simpson sounded oddly hopeful.

'Would be nice,' said McNeill. 'A few people down in Washington would like to think it's a fake, too.' His large head made a slow scan round to Simpson. 'I'd hate to find myself agreeing with some of those characters I met down there. Did you want me to check it out a little more? With Putnam's dad? Maybe talk to the woman, whoever she is?'

'Yes,' said Simpson. 'That would be good.'

'Are you sure?'

Simpson looked startled. 'Yes.'

McNeill brushed dust off the corner of his desk and straightened the corner of a pile of papers. 'If Falacci's letter got you this churned up, how will you feel if I get positive confirmation on Jimmy?'

'How will it make *you* feel, Bill?' asked Simpson.

'Same as this letter from Falacci . . . like I ought to do something. That's why I'm about to take two days off work at peak time.' He looked directly at Simpson. 'Are you willing to take the risk?'

In spite of the time he had known him, Simpson was still caught unawares by finding that the slow-moving McNeill had suddenly shot

326

ahead and left him way behind, open-mouthed. 'Risk?' he repeated, though he knew exactly what McNeill had meant.

'Can you handle it?' asked McNeill.

Simpson felt nauseated and slightly giddy. He wished he were sitting on his mountain with his back against the rough bark of his cabin wall, with nothing to worry about but deer in his garden. 'I'll just have to find out, won't I?' he replied. 'It's too late for anything else. If I back off, I'll have to live knowing that I did . . . I have too much garbage like that in my head as it is. What the hell, go ahead. Prove what you like.'

'OK, Gabe,' said McNeill soothingly. 'OK. Let's not make a federal case out of it, yet. Check in again on Thursday.'

His telephone rang. He picked it up. 'McNeill. Yup. No problem, Mr Sweeting. I'll send Ronnie Blake around. I got to go out of town for a couple of days. . . .' He waved a large hand at Simpson who let himself out to flee back to his mountain top where nothing happened, as far as he could possibly control happening and not happening.

As he manoeuvred his cross-country motorbike around the sliding gravelled curves of his road, Gabriel Simpson swore aloud, again and again. He was not entirely clear what he was swearing about.

He left the bike in the lock-up shed he had built at the end of the logging-road that cut around his land and walked the last quarter mile along his track. Some days he could make this final climb without watching for movement among the trees, without straining his ears for a sound that shouldn't be there. This afternoon, he was jumpy again, all the old reflexes working on autopilot; he couldn't help himself. He felt naked without his gun. It frightened him to feel so afraid.

At last he reached his cabin and pressed his shoulders against the logs of his refuge. He gazed along the V of interlocking ridges which carried his eye to a distant pair of peaks, two old, worn East-Coast-of-America mountains, soft and rounded as a woman's breasts. Hers had been soft and round in the same way, in the light from the streetlamp outside his hotel room in Bangkok. Exciting and comforting at the same time.

His breathing finally steadied. He pulled his mind back from Bangkok, before it could sneak off toward Laos and Vietnam. He imagined his way through constructing a smokehouse on his mountain top. He thought about Jimmy Putnam. He discussed with himself whether he was ready to get a dog, which would need looking after when he had just begun to look after himself properly. Then he found himself thinking about Vic Falacci, who was alive, and Boucher, and Joey Billings and several others who were not.

He rose suddenly, walked down to his vegetable patch and squatted to examine the frail pointed blue-green tubes of emerging onions. An early whippoorwill beyond his cabin anticipated dusk with its plaintive instruction. Something rustled among the sapling oaks beyond the checkerboard of corn hills. Simpson froze, still holding a seedling onion delicately between finger and thumb. His mouth went dry and his pulse began to thunder in his ears. Very, very slowly, he turned his head toward the rustling. It was not repeated. He waited, the early evening sounds suddenly as loud in his ears as if someone had turned the volume to maximum. He saw movement, then heard the rustling again and saw a shape against the undergrowth. A doe had come like himself, to check the progress of his garden.

Simpson unclenched, muscle by muscle, limb by limb. 'You can have some too,' he said quietly to the deer. 'But not yet. You have to be patient.'

The doe froze in her turn, spotted him and crashed away in panic into the dusk.

'How generous I am,' he said drily, aloud. 'A real softy now!' He returned to his bench with a can of beer cool from the new root cellar. After one swallow, he got up again and brought his rifle outside for the second night running. He had let it get into bad shape. After another swallow of beer, he began to strip and clean the gun. His hands carried out a precise sequence of orderly actions while his thought swarmed like an overturned ant hill. He kept trying to meditate on the clean outline of the doe's head and the twitch of her ears adjusting like a radar receiver, but his thoughts zigzagged from Jimmy, to McNeill's question about risk, to red mud made redder with the blood of friends, and to his own, peculiar excitement which had the electric taste of fear.

16

'What does defeat taste like?'

Will John sat up in the cage and shielded his eyes against the sun. His captor was a dark silhouette. 'I don't know yet,' replied Will John. 'I'll tell you when I do.'

'I'm asking you as an American,' said Thu. 'Your personal situation is of little relevance one way or the other.' They spoke French again. 'How does defeat taste?'

Will John squared his back against the bars of the cage and did not answer.

'It tastes like conceit,' said Thu. 'Like arrogance.'

'Not cowardice?' asked Will John drily. 'Why don't you say cowardice or stupidity, like others I've heard?'

'Because the people who say that are wrong,' said Thu. 'Your soldiers were often brave and generous with their lives. But you Americans were too conceited to think it worth understanding the patterns in which you found yourselves.'

'Do you understand me?' asked Will John.

Thu blinked. 'I understand that you're a clever man who knows how to argue better than how to fight. Don't try to fight with me. You'll lose.'

'I would not fight you in any case.'

'How sensible.'

'I think you are more comfortable at war than at peace.' Will John tried to see the man's eyes. He had to establish a relationship with him, make himself a real person in the man's mind, rather than an abstract enemy. 'I'm the opposite.'

'You would fight if you had to, to stay alive,' said Thu.

'No I would not,' said Will John. 'Although I admit to a terrible curiosity about what it would be like.'

'Do you prefer learning to living?' asked Thu in disbelief.

'Learning *is* living. When I stop learning, I'll start to die.'

'I learn only what I need to stay alive,' said Thu. 'What you're talking about has no place in my world.'

Will John leaned forward slightly. 'But your people have always revered learning far more than my people . . . you call us barbarians . . . learning for you is an organizing principle of the universe.'

Thu raised his chin and looked down. He took a small step back from their involvement. 'You refer to the mandarins. Their world is as dead as yours. Do you think I write poems to the peach blossoms each spring, or pause to recite an ode before I cut off a man's head? I make my order for myself. I don't worry about being in harmony with a bunch of layabouts in the Heavens. Every man who survives now makes his own order. And please don't generalize about "your people" – that's another form of conceit.'

'You're right,' said Will John. 'I would like to learn not to generalize.'

Thu weighed the apparent concession. 'Is there nothing you would rather not know?'

Will John hesitated. He had often pondered that question in the past. 'No. I don't think so. If it exists, I want to know it.' He considered. 'I don't necessarily enjoy knowing it.' Then he began to wonder if he had exposed too much about himself while trying to open up his opponent.

Thu shook his head in mock disbelief. 'Perhaps I'll become your teacher,' he said. 'I could make you curse me for opening your eyes.'

'No doubt,' said Will John, now certain that he had said too much but refusing to show weakness by backing down. 'But I would curse and observe at the same time.'

'We shall see,' said Thu reflectively.

'Please don't think I'm issuing a challenge,' said Will John. 'Under the circumstances.'

'I trust you wouldn't presume to,' replied Thu. 'As you say, under the circumstances.'

Nevertheless, the unmade challenge was taken up two days later.

Two soldiers pulled Will John from the cage. Then, insofar as differences in height allowed, they frogmarched him up onto the parade ground. They dumped him in the centre and withdrew to the perimeter, where they had left their rifles.

Will John stood upright for the first time in four days, unfettered and unconfined. It was almost enough to make him feel happy. But the way that the slowly gathering crowd pointed at and discussed him, made him feel like a Christian slave awaiting the lions.

Children sat whispering and giggling along the edge of the verandah, women peered from behind the splintered wooden pillars, four *Binh*

Xuyen lounged in the dust at the side of the parade ground. Two more armed men leaned on the edge of a cistern. Even a hen had perched on a corner of a nearby roof, as if to watch whatever was about to happen.

Will John stretched and gazed back at his audience with curiosity. They seemed to be a mix of Vietnamese and Meos, the men mainly soldiers and the women and children, presumably, their families. Suddenly, one small boy dashed forward, touched Will John's arm which glinted in the sun with small golden hairs, and ran back to his place, screaming with laughter. Then Will John was deluged. The children darted at him from all sides, still laughing and giggling. They stroked his bare arms and, when he squatted on his haunches, his red-gold hair. One little girl pulled at his blond eyebrows which had been bleached white by the sun. Over their heads Will John saw one boy still on the edge of the verandah, his eyes serious, swinging his bony legs. The child's eyes reminded him of Nina.

Will John turned his mind to the damage to the villa. The main pavilion, where he had been tied for his first two days, had been hit by rocks torn loose from the peak behind it by a shell or bomb. One twenty foot section of the bamboo palisade was newer than the rest. The charred stumps of a small clump of trees still stood beside what was no doubt a rebuilt hut.

'The Colonel!' he heard someone say, under his breath. 'Colonel Thu!'

The children scampered off the parade ground. The soldiers straightened. The women stopped whispering. Thu descended the steps from the look-out platform, crossed the verandah and paused for a moment beside the boy with the serious eyes which reminded Will John of Nina. Thu touched the child's shoulder, almost unconsciously, as if for good luck, then went down the verandah steps and stood before Will John.

'Today is my first lesson for you. We will fight.' Thu laid a long-bladed knife with a wooden handle in the dust of the little parade ground. He stepped back and kicked off his sandals.

'No,' said Will John. He felt a quiver run through their audience. The boy perched on the edge of the pavilion verandah stopped swinging his legs.

Thu removed his jacket. 'Are you afraid?'

'Of course,' said Will John. 'I'm not an idiot.' He sat down on the ground.

Thu handed his jacket to the boy. 'You're right to be frightened, but I'm afraid you have no choice.' One of his men gave him a second knife, like the one he had placed in front of Will John, shaped like a long-bladed breadknife with a razor-edge instead of saw-teeth.

331

'You're wrong,' said Will John. 'I do have a choice.'

'*You* are wrong!' shouted Thu suddenly. 'You fight or you die! Pick up your knife!'

'That *is* my choice.' Will John continued to sit in the dust. 'I made it many years ago. I will not fight.' He was as terrified as he had been at the abandoned hotel. He was in unmapped territory. About to find out what he was when it *was* left up to him, without help from the good fairy. Luck was about to become irrelevant. He was afraid of dying, but he was just as afraid of learning that he had coasted through life on nothing but luck, without real convictions or real courage.

Thu stepped over the knife in the dust. He bent and placed his knife tip against Will John's throat. 'But now you are tasting the reality of that choice.' He pressed just hard enough for Will John to feel the point draw blood as delicately as a mosquito. With a sense of disbelief, Will John braced himself for the full thrust.

Thu stepped back. 'Pick up the knife.'

Will John's eyes swung around the huddled women and children, the seven *Binh Xuyen*, watching, utterly still. Adrenaline was flooding his body now, telling it to fight. He could choose to fight. His size and length of arm gave him some advantage over Thu's undoubted expertise. He might be able at least to damage the man who had humiliated and terrified him. He might even win. He looked at the soldiers. They would respect a winner . . . they might shoot him, but they might not. Then he looked at the watching, breathless children and remembered that he had once, in the safety of a university campus, believed that he had principles.

Even through the shortness of his breath and the cold knowledge in his gut, he was ironically aware how much that ring of witnesses made a resolution inevitable, one way or the other. Neither man would give way in front of all those watching eyes. He was glad of them. They reduced ambiguity.

'I do not believe in fighting,' he said in Meo. He repeated it in Vietnamese. 'I do not believe in fighting.'

'Pick up your knife!' Thu's voice was hard and angry.

Will John leaned forward, stretched out a long arm and picked it up. The surrounding people exhaled audibly. He tossed the knife toward Thu's feet and leaned back again.

The two men stared at each other, balanced as delicately as if the combat were physical. After a moment, Thu also dropped his knife. He reached out his hand; one of the *Binh Xuyen* placed a pistol in it. Thu crossed to Will John and placed the muzzle against his head.

Will John could not stop the reflex jerk of his head away from the cold point of pressure. His entire being contracted into small, hard kernel. Will I hear it? Will I hear it? He clutched at the question to prevent thought in the second before all thought would end. Will I hear it? The question lost all meaning, became just another noise in his head amidst the thundering of his blood.

After ten seconds, when nothing had happened, Will John rediscovered a dry, thick muscle in his mouth that was his tongue. He drew a breath that he had not expected to take.

'The Americans lost the war,' he said unsteadily, 'because they did not understand their own purpose while your people were sure and firm in theirs. Now the situation is reversed. I will not fight!' His voice cracked but became clearer as he spoke. 'I look forward to learning what comes after this. I thank you for teaching me. Carry on.' He closed his eyes.

No one on the parade ground breathed as this silence grew longer than the first.

'I refuse your request,' said Thu. 'I will not add to your knowledge.'

Will John felt the small, hard pressure lift from his temple. He opened his eyes again.

'Besides,' said Thu with disdain, 'I am a soldier, not a butcher. And you are not a man, but a buffalo. I see something better to do with you.' He slammed the pistol back into the hand of his soldier and stalked up the steps onto the verandah. The boy still sat, swinging his legs again, staring at the golden-haired giant trying to get to his feet alone in the middle of the parade ground.

For seven hours, Will John sat in his bamboo pen and clutched his knees, jaw rattling, thighs jerking, cheek muscles jumping, trying to tell himself that it was a natural reaction to imminent death. What he could not forgive himself was the dark wet patch on his trousers.

'Coward,' said the boy from the verandah in French. '*Poltron.*' Squatting outside Will John's pen, he offered the word almost experimentally.

'Consistent,' said Will John to himself. 'Thank God! Just consistent!' He closed his eyes again and drew a deep breath of relief. The trembling was beginning to pass.

'*Chien battu,*' said the boy. Whipped dog.

Will John opened his eyes. 'I'm not so sure, I'm happy to say . . . Not so sure at all.' He closed his teeth to stop their rattling. He had faced the moment of decision . . . would never have to face it again. He had done it. Himself. Chosen. He was committed. It would be easier the next time, and the next. He was quite sure that Thu would provide a next time. He only had to carry on as he had now begun. He was lifted briefly on wings of euphoria.

'I like to fight,' said the boy proudly. 'I'm a good fighter.'

'I'm sure you are,' said Will John. 'I suppose you'll need to be.' He wished the boy didn't remind him of Nina. 'How old are you?'

The child pulled back. 'I don't talk to cowards,' he said. He stood up, kicked a bamboo bar of the cage angrily with his bare foot and disappeared down the stone steps toward the small gate of the fortress.

Euphoria lowered Will John back onto the rock floor of his cage and flew elsewhere. As the downward swing of his emotions continued, Will John began to search the storehouse of his brain for distraction from that inevitable next time.

'Then Odysseus stood staring at what was his own land. . . .' he recited aloud. 'Crying mournfully aloud . . . da dum, da dum dum . . . What do I do here. . . ?' I should have majored in classics, he thought. Instead of Southeast Asian folklore and anthropology.

For what he reckoned to be two weeks, no one else spoke to him. The old woman who had called him a devil brought his rice gruel, with occasional pieces of vegetable. One of the soldiers collected his slop can and returned it empty. Lizards scuttled through the bamboo bars of his cage and birds landed on its top. One of the soldiers laid a piece of matting across part of the top to give him a little shade.

Will John made up as many different names as he could think of for the small segment of eroded limestone mountain range that he could see between the rocky buttresses surrounding his cage: a lower jaw with missing teeth, a comb, an arthritic hand, the handles of forks sticking out of a jar, the spinal column of a turtle, a lumpish aurora borealis. He did press-ups and stretches through the bars of the cage. He polished his teeth with the corner of his filthy shirt hem and cleaned his nails with a sliver of bamboo from the cage. He picked the lice from his clothes and any skin he could reach.

He exhausted his memory of the *Odyssey* and began on fragments of the *Mahabharata*. He tried to trace a continuous line through the crazing of the surface of the split rock face nearest his cage, following each line from fork to fork, retracing when he reached a break. His aim was to get from one corner to the other. He never did this for more than a few minutes at a time, lest he succeed too quickly.

Meanwhile, he continued to try to determine the routine of the villa by sound – the women's voices, shouts from the parade ground, slamming of cooking pots, anticipatory grunting of excited pigs about to be fed. And by the occasional flash of movement across the visible fragment of mountain range.

Occasionally he looked up to see the boy, with or without one of his companions, standing on a rock above his crevice, staring down. At first, he spoke to them but each time they vanished. After that, he remained silent, enjoying even the silent presence of another human being.

When he thought he was unobserved, he tested the wire bindings of the cage, and the toughness of the wrist-thick bamboo bars. He studied the movements of the sun during each day and made minute scratches in one of the bars, as had been suggested in case of capture during his brief training so long ago, to help keep yourself anchored in reality. He wrote letters to Nina in his head.

. . . You are a deceitful bitch. A Lilith. Kali, the destroyer of men. . . .

. . . my darling, I feel that I betrayed you. It was never meant. I tried to undo damage already done and was not strong enough. I failed you. . . .

. . . forgiveness is a patronizing word, but. . . .

. . . perhaps we might still find it useful to meet, as we had planned, to discuss the alternatives . . . With best wishes . . . very best wishes . . . Sincerely . . . With love . . . Yours. . . .

Thu suddenly appeared in the gap between the rocks one evening as the sun dropped beyond the Tiger's Head.

'You do not matter.' Thu leaned against the rock face, across which the consecutive line was nearly traced. His voice sounded oddly clear to Will John, so close. 'You do not exist. I will keep you forever. You have no reality except that lump of dust your soul inhabits there in the cage.' He folded his arms and observed the effect of his words. 'This is all you will ever see – these rocks and this sky, and that small piece of the mountains. Your learning is finished.' He regarded the big American with triumph.

Will John fought the sucking of despair. 'In that case I must now pursue wisdom.' He tried to smile. 'You have driven me from chasing knowledge to inviting wisdom. I'm sorry that we are enemies.'

He heart Thu's intake of breath.

'Don't presume!' said Thu. 'Don't condescend. You are not enough to be even an enemy to me. You are a tick. A mite in the coat of a mangy three-legged dog in the gutters of Saigon. The egg of a louse on a whore's twat. Don't dignify yourself!' He stalked away.

Wisdom did not visit. It did not even acknowledge Will John's invitation. On the second night after Thu's visit, Will John picked up the flake of stone to scratch off the passing of another twenty-four hours as the egg of a louse but dropped it again without making the mark. He imagined the cross-hatchings of 'forever' covering the bars of the cage, from top to bottom of each bamboo pole. Even the wire lashings were scarred. If those tiny marks were the only effect on the world of his continued existence, he saw no point in either the existence or its record. He was a closed circle. An endless loop. He looked with fresh eyes at his cage. For the first time, he sought a means of possible self-destruction.

He worked with his thumb nails along a ridge of bamboo bar. After half an hour, he was able to pull away a six-inch splinter. For a few minutes, he felt the satisfaction of success. Then he looked at the splinter directly. How could he use it best? Though the edges were sharp, he would have to saw doggedly to cut his wrists. The point was too dull to reach his heart, unless he could fall on it and guarantee that it would miss all ribs and cartilege. Rationally, the best solution was to insert it through one eye into his brain. The best rational solution made him want to vomit.

'*Poltron*!' The word was whispered. For a moment, he thought the voice was from inside himself. Inner and outer were blurring more and more as his isolation stretched itself forward into time. '*Lâche*!' said another whisper.

He raised his eyes and saw the boy's face, chin propped on forearms, at the top of the overhanging rock. Will John wondered which way the boy intended him to take the insult. The boy swung one arm out, opened his fist and dropped a hard beet-red mangosteen into Will John's cage. The fruit hit his knee sharply and rolled into the dust. He picked it up then gazed thoughtfully at its source.

'*Lâche*!' The boy seemed to be waiting for a response.

'Clarity, if not charity,' Will John said shakily. 'This time, you're right! Thank you. *Merci bien*!'

The boy vanished like a startled lizard.

Will John prised at the tough husk of the fruit with his thumbnail. He had been wrong. His courage on the parade ground, with Thu's pistol cold and hard against his head, had not been for once and for all. It was not just a matter of carrying on as he had begun. He was going to have to commit himself again and again. The battleground would keep shifting. And Thu had almost won this time.

Will John finally bit through the bitter husk and stripped it away from the soft, white, sectioned flesh inside. The juice was sharp and sweet at the same time, counteracting the bitterness of the husk. He rolled the central seed of the largest section around his mouth. The fruit tasted of peach and lemon, though its perfume suggested something thicker and more cloying. He remembered eating mangosteens inside the tent of mosquito netting over Nina's big, four-poster bed in Saigon. Laughing and being silly. Long ago in another universe. When he had still felt guiltily untested by life.

' "What a piece of work is a man!" ' he said around the mongosteen pit to the lengthening purple shadows and swooping cliff swallows. ' "How noble in reason! How infinite in faculties!" ' He spat the seed into his palm, examined it and put it into his pocket. 'You better believe that, you egg of a louse!' he told himself. 'It's your only weapon against the clever Colonel!'

He picked up the bamboo splinter and snapped it carefully in half, then broke each half into half yet again. He lay back onto his ragged mat, bending his knees up to keep his feet from sticking out of the cage, and began to recite to the darkening sky, ' "Then came Grendel out of the mist clouds, over the moorland, bearing the wroth of God. . . ." '

Two nights later, he was bundled through the darkness, down a steep track into a cave somewhere below the villa. Crouched against a dripping rock, with a rifle barrel grating against his rib, he listened to the explosions shake the mountain. For an almost unendurable and incalculable time, he thought that his mind would slip its moorings in panic and helplessness. He was surprised, when they emerged from the cave in the early morning light, to find that he was, nevertheless, still sane. It seemed as if it must be so only by chance, as he had been unable to exert his will during the long night. He spent the day tied loosely to a tree near the mouth of the cave, while another cage was build; the first had burned during the night, along with the rest of the villa. He could hear the keening and weeping of women. A child had been killed.

You can stop now, he said to the Heavens. I know enough now. Please stop!

Even so, and in spite of new pains in his arms and legs, he felt steadier than he had since being captured.

17

'Just where do you fit in, Mr McNeill?' Mayor John Putnam carefully shook sugar into his coffee from the dispenser on the coffee shop table.

McNeill had called the town hall in Arcangelica, California, left his name and number with a message for Putnam. Putnam had rung back the next day to say that he was in Washington, D.C.

'I'd like to talk to you about Jimmy,' said McNeill. 'Can we meet?'

He had listened to the long silence on the line. Then the Mayor's voice had agreed.

'How about tomorrow afternoon?' asked McNeill. 'You say where.'

After a little hesitation, the mayor's voice suggested a coffee shop near the railroad station.

'I'll be there,' said McNeill.

They had settled in a booth where McNeill could get his back to the wall and keep an eye on the entrance to the coffee shop. They ordered coffee and Putnam had a Danish pastry.

'A friend of mine served with Jimmy,' McNeill said. 'He heard a rumour that Jimmy might still be out there.'

Putnam cut an edge off the sugary snail of his Danish. 'How strong a rumour?'

'Like a letter you got from him, dated this year.'

Putnam didn't look up from his surgery on the pastry. 'Are you official, Mr McNeill?'

'Do I look official?' McNeill smiled. He was wearing his blue jeans, work boots and denim jacket.

'It can be hard to tell,' said Putnam. 'The clothes, no.' He studied McNeill closely now. 'The rest . . . could be. But you haven't answered my question.'

'I'm not official.'

'Then we shouldn't be talking.' Putnam sipped his coffee as if it were laced with arsenic. 'Who *do* you work for?'

'Myself,' said McNeill. He placed his large hands slowly on either side of his paper doily place mat and leaned slightly forward. 'I grow

Christmas trees, and run my own garden maintenance business. I'm the only boss I can work for any more.'

Putnam pushed away the plate with his uneaten Danish. 'You're wasting my time, Mr McNeill. I thought you were someone else.'

'Someone official?'

'Yes . . . Please excuse me, I don't have time to waste with nuts.' Putnam began to rise.

'I'm not a nut, Mr Putnam, any more than your son is dead.' McNeill spoke with more force than he usually allowed himself.

Putnam looked directly at McNeill for the first time since they had met. He settled heavily back into his seat.

'The men who made it back care about the ones who didn't,' continued McNeill. 'We were responsible for each other out there . . . and if a friend got killed, you felt you maybe didn't look after him enough. Maybe he looked after you better, because here you are, safe and sound.' He looked away, at the glass-fronted case full of blueberry, cranberry and bran muffins. 'It's not always easy to live with . . . and it's worse if you don't know exactly what happened to them.'

Putnam had not taken his eyes from McNeill's face. 'If you're not a nut and you're not a spook, why did you take all that trouble to get in touch with me?'

'I'd like to see a copy of Jimmy's letter.'

Putnam shook his head. 'Sorry. It's been classified.'

They looked at each other.

'But you got a letter?'

Putnam nodded. Then he said angrily. 'I don't know why I'm supposed to hide the fact! But they tell me that something is finally being done officially and I'm not to mess things up for them.'

'That's encouraging news,' said McNeill mildly. 'I'm glad to hear you found some fucker down here you can trust.'

'There are several "fuckers" here in Washington that I trust,' said Putnam almost primly. 'Just in case you're reporting back, Christmas trees notwithstanding. I'm putting my trust in the US of A one last time. Tell them that too. Including Miss Nina Desanges! One last time.'

'They won't hear it from me,' said McNeill. 'Would you mind just telling me what Jimmy said? So I can try to put his friend's mind at rest.'

'You really don't work for any government agency?'

'On the level. I grow Christmas trees and shovel shit onto bushes.'

Putnam picked up his fork again and toyed with the glazed apricot which was the yoke in the fried egg of his pastry. He sighed. 'Do you have a pencil? I know it by heart. . . .' Slowly, he dictated from memory.

McNeill looked down at the napkin on which he had written. 'It says too much,' he said. 'The PRVN doesn't let that much information rattle around loose.'

'That's what she said.'

'Who said?'

Putnam smiled. 'Just one of the "fuckers" I'm trying to trust.'

McNeill deliberated. 'Well,' he said. 'If they don't live up to what you want, let me know.'

Putnam's eyes filled with alarm. 'What do you mean?'

'Don't panic,' said McNeill. 'It's just that I volunteered for three tours and spent the last one mainly tying up loose ends. If nothing happens officially, it makes Jimmy one hell of a loose end.'

'What are you trying to say?'

'Just that I'm interested in your problem,' said McNeill. 'Can I stay in touch?'

Putnam looked away. 'Of course. But, Mr. McNeill, don't get mixed up in it.'

'I won't jam your spokes,' said McNeill. 'I won't do anything to make things worse for Jimmy than they already are!' He put a business card on the table. 'If you ever want to get in touch with me, that's where I am most of the time.'

Putnam picked it up and looked at it absently. He put it into his jacket pocket, so deep in thought that he only half noticed McNeill calling for the bill and laying out five dollars on the table.

'No, no, let me,' he protested politely.

'It's the least I can do,' said McNeill.

Just for the hell of it, and to indulge old habits, McNeill followed Putnam back to the house of friends where he was staying. He enjoyed the tracking, and it gave him time to think about Putnam. He was surprised, even though the sidewalks were reasonably crowded, that the man didn't seem to notice. On the other hand, the mayor obviously had a lot on his mind.

Before heading home, McNeill went to the public library and looked in the Washington telephone directory. Nina Desanges was not listed. Just for fun, he also checked New York, Boston, Philadelphia, and Baltimore, with no more success.

★

340

'He warned me off,' McNeill said to Gabriel Simpson. They were in McNeill's office. 'Maybe I can't blame him.' He looked at Simpson interrogatively.

'Except that he started the hare in the first place,' said Simpson. 'By showing Jimmy's letter to that woman who visited Vic.'

'That's right,' said McNeill. Simpson often felt that McNeill used him to check conclusions, like adding up a column of figures twice.

'Her name is Nina Desanges, by the way,' said McNeill. 'Pretty fancy.' He studied the napkin on which he had copied Jimmy Putnam's letter. 'Phong Saly . . . Jimmy was being moved around Laos. "There are no American POWs in Vietnam," the man said. It's no lie – they're in Laos.'

'You've decided he's still there, haven't you?' Simpson felt sick again.

McNeill moved his telephone three-quarters of an inch closer to the edge of his desk and aligned it parallel to the edge. 'I don't know . . . yet. Do you want to come help find Harry Junor, the other guy who survived with Vic Falacci? And maybe track down Miss Desanges, who went to see both of them.'

Simpson suddenly saw McNeill as a piece of his own machinery – tipped over the edge of a ridge, brakes off, just gathering momentum as it began to roll downhill. He himself had pushed it over the edge and now had to wait until it reached the bottom, one way or another.

McNeill seldom repeated questions. He simply waited until his answer came back. The habit unnerved people who didn't listen well.

'I'm sorry?' said Simpson, catching up. 'Come with you, you mean?' The possibility threw him into confusion. 'No,' he said. 'Thanks. I have to go back. There's too much to do this time of year . . . to get the garden in.'

'OK,' said McNeill.

One reason Gabriel Simpson liked McNeill, apart from respect and shared experience, was that McNeill simply accepted. Simpson felt free in his company. Nobody else he knew made him feel that free.

'Can I come up to you when I get back?' asked McNeill. 'I don't know how long this is going to take.'

'Sure,' said Simpson. 'That will be fine.' But he was lying. His fragile peace would not survive the act of waiting. His mountain top was feeling more and more vulnerable, closer and closer to the rest of the world.

Harry Junor stood on the deer trail with his rifle pointed at McNeill.

341

McNeill had enjoyed finding him, even more than following Putnam along the Washington sidewalks. After sniffing around, and noting, as Nina had done, the announcement-like quality of the *punji* pit, he fired a single shot from his Colt.45 then sat down on a log to wait.

Junor was slipping. McNeill heard him several seconds before he saw him, and had turned to face the space into which Harry Junor stepped.

'Just fuck off,' said Junor. 'I don't care who you are, get the hell out of here.'

McNeill looked at the green eyes, and the tension of the muscles in the young man's right arm. He looked at the ridged tendons on the back of his right hand, which was on the trigger of the rifle.

'OK,' McNeill said. He stood up slowly, hands away from his sides, and the gun inside his denim jacket. 'We're on the same side.'

Junor didn't move. The tension stayed in his trigger hand.

'Jimmy,' offered McNeill. 'Jimmy Putnam.'

'Get out!' said Junor.

'I want to talk . . .' said McNeill.

'I *don't*!' interrupted Junor.

'. . . about Jimmy,' continued McNeill.

'Jimmy's dead. He's dead!' said Junor. 'Do you hear me, he's dead!'

'That's not what you told that woman from Washington.'

'I don't care what I told that dink! She tricked it out of me. He's dead. And you can fuck off with your questions, same as she can!'

'OK,' said McNeill reasonably. He stepped backward over his log. 'I'm going.' He took a step backward. 'I was over the border too,' he said, watching Junor carefully. 'About the same time as you and Putnam.'

A tremor ran through Junor's body.

McNeill took another backward step. 'I'm going to drop a business card on the ground,' he said. 'Then I'm going to turn around and walk out of here. If you ever want to talk, you have my business telephone number on the card.'

When Junor didn't reply, McNeill dropped his card and turned to walk out of the woods. After six strides, he paused. 'Harry, you still there?' He turned slowly back to face the younger man, hands away from his sides. 'Is it OK with you if I try to talk to that woman who came up here?'

'I don't care what you do,' said Junor. 'Just get out of here!'

'Sure, I'm going,' said McNeill. 'She didn't happen to leave you her name and telephone number, did she?'

Junor looked away.

'I won't bug you again,' McNeill promised. 'I'll go bug her instead
. . . if I can find out where she is.'

'Take the goddam thing!' said Junor. He yanked a small piece of
white card from his pocket and sliced it through the air toward McNeill.
'I just want to get shut of the lot of you!'

'Gabe! Gabe!' yelled McNeill as he approached Simpson's cabin.
Sometimes Simpson was nearly as jumpy as Junor had been.

Simpson didn't answer. He wasn't in his cabin. McNeill called again,
but heard nothing except the distant rumble, faint as the humming of
blood in his own ears, of the plane which was pulling a length of thin
white wool yarn across the top of the blue sky.

'Gabe, it's McNeill.'

He went behind the cabin and saw Simpson, standing still, waist-
deep in the ground. Simpson raised a hand in what could have been
either greeting or warding-off.

Simpson didn't bother to lie about having heard him. He climbed out
of the hole. 'Let me go clean up a little.' He looked back into the
ground. 'Another water tank. I get more run-off from the cabin than I
can store. The garden nearly dried up last summer. Let's go sit down.'

'It's coming on,' said McNeill, as his large head and quick eyes
covered the arc visible from the bench against the front of the cabin.
'Sometimes I think you work about as hard as I do.'

Simpson smiled. 'Let me get you a beer,' he said. 'My new root cellar
keeps it nice and cool.'

'Sure,' agreed McNeill.

Simpson disappeared into a mound which projected like a stubby
nose from the falling contour of the mountain top. He reappeared with a
can of Budweiser, then asked, 'Do you mind if I get stoned? I think I
need it.'

McNeill shrugged. 'Sure. There's nothing up here to watch out for.'
He sat down on the bench and placed his hands carefully on his knees.

'Except us.' Simpson wished he could control the twanging sensation
in his centre. 'Except us. Watch out for us.' He disappeared into the
cabin for his pouch and returned to sit beside McNeill on the bench.

McNeill watched Simpson's quick brown fingers rolling the joint. 'I
have one or two favours I can still call in, but we're getting to the point
where we're going to need money. If we take it any farther.'

Simpson licked the cigarette paper very carefully. He sealed the little
tube and twisted one end. He kept twisting and twisting the little point
of tissue-fine paper.

'Are you beginning to know?' he asked.

'Nothing's proved,' said McNeill, 'but it's shaking down. You know how we sometimes used to know, before we went out, whether it was going to be OK . . . or whether we were walking into a bummer?'

Simpson nodded. McNeill knew, proof or not.

'Jimmy didn't die in 1969,' said McNeill. 'He was captured. Junor denied it yesterday, but you should have seen the poor bastard when he was saying it. I'm going to go with what he told that woman who talked to Vic Falacci. And I'd like to know who she is and who she's working for. She's a slope, by the way – I find that kind of interesting. The way I find Jimmy's old man interesting. There's too much going on.' McNeill looked at Simpson, who was holding his breath.

After a count of three, Simpson exhaled slowly and leaned his head back against the bark of the logs. 'I wish I'd never brought you Falacci's letter.'

McNeill began to polish his denim kneecaps with the palms of his hands. 'We'd all do a lot of things differently if we knew how they would turn out,' he said, 'but it probably wouldn't change much.' He picked the beer can up from the bench and took a swallow. 'Jimmy would still be wherever he is whether you brought that letter or not. Even if Vic never wrote to you. Even if that woman never talked to Vic. Nothing would be different for Jimmy.'

'How much do you think the Interagency Committee knows?' asked Simpson, almost hopeful.

'More than we do.' McNeill thought briefly again about his photographs. He had his rage pretty well under control by now but could feel a brushfire still smouldering in there somewhere.

Simpson's eyes were closed. He looked asleep, except for his bare right foot which seemed to be keeping time to a very fast piece of music.

'Gabe,' said McNeill. 'You're not responsible for what I do. Have you got that? You're not responsible.'

Simpson nodded without opening his eyes. 'Like you don't feel responsible for Jimmy?'

McNeill didn't answer. Then he said, 'That's different. He's . . . family . . . in a weird way. He's in trouble.'

' "Do your duty and leave the rest to the gods," ' murmured Simpson. 'I envy you your single-minded sense of purpose.' When he received no reply, Simpson opened his eyes to see if McNeill were angry.

'You screwy vets are all the same,' said McNeill. His voice was friendly, but Simpson knew that blows had been exchanged, however lightly.

He started to laugh quietly. Everything was screwy. Him. McNeill the runaway truck. Jimmy Putnam, probably alive and not-so-well in Laos. His own father, Professor *emeritus* Simpson, worried about reviews of his latest book in the academic press which nobody read. And whatever it was that had happened to the twenty-one-year-old Gabriel Simpson, B.A., *magna cum laude* in History and Literature of the Renaissance and Reformation, with a grant for graduate school. Everything was screwy except the doe with the radar ears who just wanted to beat him to his corn. The realization had a comforting simplicity.

'I'm going to try to get positive confirmation,' said McNeill. '. . . Are you OK?'

'Fine,' said Simpson. 'Fine. And getting better.' He looked out at the two breast-mountains, away from McNeill's concern. 'Won't you join me . . . put it all away for a change?'

'I'll just sit a while, if you don't mind,' said McNeill. 'Then I got to get back to tidy up at the office, if I'm going to take any more time off.'

'You do just as you like,' said Simpson. 'Be my guest. Go. Stay. Have another beer. Do as you like. Please.'

'I will,' said McNeill. 'Thanks.'

After leaving the Army, McNeill had gone to three newspapers; only one small inside-page paragraph appeared in print, about 'allegations' which threatened the peace negotiations between the United States and Vietnam. He stayed in touch with friends still in the military. He knew that some of them knew the truth – like his friend with Airforce Intelligence – but no one seemed able to break through official determination that the war should be finished. He was out of step with the country's mood. Nobody wanted information which would almost surely lead to more fighting or, at best, disrupt the so-called peace negotiations.

In this time, he held and left his nine jobs, and slept with and left three different women. McNeill then quit his ninth job, said goodbye to a fourth woman, and started to think about the future he was lucky enough to have, even if other men didn't have one. He suddenly decided he was wasting something he maybe didn't deserve but should try to hang onto since he had it. He borrowed the money and began raising Christmas trees. But though he did well, part of him stayed angry.

The anger still lurked in him like a parasite. He wished he could belch it out. He didn't like to think about it and dealt with unwanted thoughts the way he piled a thick layer of bark chippings on sprouting weeds. He had accepted that neither he nor anybody else was going to get any more orders. He had no further role in the unfinished job. He scanned all the newspapers and kept clippings about anything to do with POWs and Vietnam. He read books to try to put the whole experience into a wider, defusing context. He had lived with his parasite more or less under control until Jimmy Putnam's letter made him ashamed of being relatively content. Sitting against the rough log wall, beside Gabriel Simpson, he suddenly said, 'I was right all along and I let those turds shut me up!'

When he returned to his office, he closed the door and unlocked the filing drawer in which he kept the clippings. It was so full, he was going to have to move files out of another drawer to make room for expansion. After ten minutes, he found the two inch by two inch advertisement he was looking for. He wrote to the PO Box number in Pheonix, Arizona. Then he called Miss Nina Desanges at the number in Washington that Junor had given him.

The tall, heavy-jawed man in a denim jacket and the small, dark-eyed woman in a New York suit and amber earrings, eyed each other across the soy sauce, napkin holder, and toothpicks on the Formica table top in a booth in a Vietnamese restaurant in Washington.
    'Why did you choose this place, Mr McNeill?' asked Nina, smiling. 'To make me feel at home?'
    'I like the food,' said McNeill. With a large hand, he brushed imaginary crumbs from the Formica, which had been scrubbed so often that patches of the printed woodgrain had been rubbed away. 'And I'm not comfortable in those fancy offices of yours.'

Nina had refused the strange man's request to meet her away from the office. Then he had mentioned Harry Junor. Nina had left Perry the name and address of the restaurant and the time she expected to return. As soon as she met McNeill, she knew what he had been. His eyes, his movements and the position he chose in the restaurant gave him away. She never asked American men whether they had been soldiers in Vietnam but often found that she knew, one way or another.

'I like the food too, as it happens,' she replied. 'Was it a lucky guess?' She smoothed a strand of dark hair back into her chignon with a gesture which was half-seductive, half-gauging.

McNeill smiled for the first time, slightly, acknowledging the female across the table but intent on his business and not to be softened or distracted. 'It made sense,' he said. 'Since I heard you were Asian. . . .' The grey-blue eyes double-checked. '. . . part Asian . . . and involved with Jimmy Putnam.'

'Jimmy Putnam?' Nina repeated. Her eyes widened and her back stiffened. 'I thought you wanted to talk about Harry Junor. I had hoped you could help me. . . .'

'You've been asking around about Putnam,' said McNeill. 'Spreading the story that he might still be alive.'

'That's right.' Nina readjusted both thoughts and defences. Guilty excitement began once more to clench her scalp around the roots of her hair.

McNeill left a silence for her to continue to fill. But she declined.

Finally, she gave in. 'Mr McNeill, one of us is going to have to talk. And as you asked for this meeting, I'm afraid *c'est toi le chat*!'

He nodded agreeably. '*D'ac*. Fair enough. . . .'

Nina put a mental tick beside French, basic at least.

'Please?' The waiter arrived at their booth with pad and pencil. 'You wish something to drink first?'

'You order,' said Nina, and sat back.

McNeill did, in reasonable kitchen-Vietnamese.

Over there a long time . . . enough to bother learning the language, Nina thought. Front-edge.

'I'm a friend of a friend of Putnam's,' said McNeill, when the waiter had left. 'We'd like to know if something is being done to get the poor bastard out.'

Nina's chin lifted. 'So would I.'

'You mean, nothing is?'

'I don't know.'

McNeill looked down at his lap and smoothed his palms along the tops of his thighs. 'Well now,' he said reflectively. His rough palms rasped against the fabric of his jeans. He pulled the front of his jacket straight and looked up. 'Do you mind telling me how you come into it?'

She told him the American part. The grey-blue eyes assessed her as she spoke.

'And where do you go from here?' he asked.

'Nowhere,' she said. 'I'm off the case.' She tried to keep her anger and frustration out of her voice.

McNeill processed her words and tone. Then he nodded. 'Who is on it? Who does know what's happening?' he asked.

347

'I don't know that either.' And I couldn't tell you if I did.

The flat surface of his eyes sparked with rage, as fleeting as lightning. He blew out a quick, impatient breath. 'Nothing's happening,' he said. 'You know that as well as I do.'

Do I? was the properly evasive reply. But Nina did not give it.

Instead, she weighed up the knowledge in McNeill's eyes under that flat, grey-blue surface. She watched the internal stillness that made every action count, except for the occasional, almost furtive gestures of keeping order. Why had he come all this way just to have her confirm something he already knew? She made an improper decision.

'You're wrong,' she said. 'I'm sure something *is* happening. But I suspect Jimmy Putnam will be dead before the due process of whatever it is finally unravels itself.'

The intensity of McNeill's focus was undisturbed by the arrival of their Black Cat beer, salad and noodles.

He's hearing what I'm saying! thought Nina. I think it's what he wanted to learn. A suspicion grew in her mind. She looked at him directly across her glass. 'You have nothing to fear from me, Mr McNeill. I'll help in any way I can. But I'm afraid I've nothing more to tell you.'

She watched him rock back. He folded his arms and planted his spine firmly against the back of the booth. Her suspicion set into belief, unconfirmed by evidence but solid as granite. He too was involved.

'That's real nice of you,' McNeill said, smiling again, with the slightest twist of irony. He engulfed the spoon handle in his fist and bent his large head to his noodles.

The restaurant owner, having heard that they spoke Vietnamese, edged up to their table. He had come from Phan Thiet, a coastal town north of Saigon and Vung Tao. The rest of lunch was spent in cautious, general chat among the three of them, in which a friendly link was formed and huge chunks of information were carefully avoided.

As Nina and McNeill shook hands outside the restaurant after lunch, he said, 'Thank you for being so helpful.'

Nina ignored the possible irony. 'Please stay in touch,' she begged, and waited for him to ask what about.

He didn't ask.

Back in her office Nina avoided Perry until he was likely to have forgotten to ask about her lunch with the stranger.

Hang on, Jimmy! she thought. Someone more effective than myself just may be working on getting you out.

★

348

McNeill thought about having someone check up on Nina Desanges. Then he decided it was better not to let anybody official know that he was talking to a Vietnamese *métisse* who worked for Intelligence.

Ten days after his meeting with Nina, McNeill had a reply from the box number in Phoenix, Arizona. The day after that he drove down to Newark Airport in his blue pickup truck and had a call put out for a former Air Force pilot who was now flying domestic airlines routes to the West Coast.

18

Will John heard the high, clear voices of children on the parade ground above his cage.

'I fight with all my heart,' cried a single treble.

It sounded to Will John like the boy who looked like Nina, whom Thu had touched lightly in passing like a good-luck charm.

'I fight with all my heart,' echoed a ferocious, high-pitched chorus.

'I fight with all my strength,' shouted the leader.

'I fight with all my strength,' replied the chorus.

'My heart and strength are for my country!' The young voice was fierce and passionate.

'My heart and strength are for my country!' came the shouted response.

'Bayonets!' shrieked the leader. '*On guard*! Up! Smash! Slash! On guard!'

Will John tried to imagine the scene on the parade ground, which sounded only slightly like the war games he and his brother and friends had played in the summers on Narragansett Bay.

Thu stood very still on the wide verandah of the ruined pavilion, sandalled feet slightly apart, hands clasped behind his back. The rolled sleeves of his black uniform shirt uncovered the webbing of scars on his hands and arms. Apart from these scars, he seemed unmarked by having been a soldier from the age of fifteen – for nearly two-thirds of his life.

He watched intently as his seven-year-old son drilled the other children. They carried wooden guns, but a real knife blade had been lashed in place of a bayonet to the end of Hien's toy-sized mock-up of a semi-automatic rifle. Hien's face had the fierce intensity of a child who knows that he is acting like an adult.

One by one, the young soldiers launched themselves at a dummy set up in the dust on Thu's right, a scarecrow in an olive drab uniform, with a white head made of a rice sack and roughly painted western features. One by one, the four boys and two girls screamed an ululating war cry, sprinted across the dust and stabbed at the scarecrow with the muzzles of their toy guns. Thu's son, Hien, watched his troops, his mouth moving with their cries.

Hien ran at the dummy last. He stabbed his knife blade upward into the chest below the red Russian star on the pocket. Then he thrust his blade lower, into the belly. He grunted, twisted and levered his gun upward. The fabric split and rice straw stuffing exploded from the dummy's belly. Flushed with the expectation of approval and unaware of the straw from the dummy lodged in his hair, Hien called his squad to order and marched them into position facing his father.

'Well-drilled,' said Thu, still not smiling. He spoke to each child in turn with suggestions or praise.

Then Hien paired off his soldiers for exercises in unarmed hand-to-hand combat. His father noted with interest that he matched himself with the largest boy, who was a head taller than himself.

Brave, thought Thu, but perhaps a little arrogant. He would have to keep an eye on that potential weakness. With only mild interest, he watched the first two pairs fight. They were the sons of his soldiers and of the local farmers. Except perhaps for one ten-year-old Meo and his nine-year-old sister, none of the children showed the same promise as Hien.

Then it was his son's turn. Both boys removed their jackets. They circled each other warily for several seconds. The larger boy made a lunge and Hien stepped back.

Good, thought Thu. Don't rush. Study your opponent. Knowledge is better than brute strength.

The larger boy, Doi, suddenly let out a fearsome yell and lunged again at Hien. Thu held his breath. But Hien seemed unperturbed. He slipped under Doi's arm, turned and hooked one of Doi's legs with his own.

Unconsciously, Thu let out a small sound of relief. Doi stumbled onto his knees. Hien leaped like a jungle cat onto his back and knocked him face down in the dust. Hien then grabbed one of Doi's arms, set his knee on the straightened elbow. It was over.

Thu prepared to say 'Not badly done.' Then, to his surprise, Hien produced a small knife from his clothing and mimed a *coup de grâce* across Doi's neck. He stood and looked up at his father.

Thu nodded to the flushed, upturned face. That hidden knife interested him. It also occurred to him that his son had chosen Doi because the older boy had recently grown and become slightly awkward. Perhaps Hien was wily rather than arrogant. Thu almost smiled. 'Dismiss your men,' he said.

Hien turned and prodded the fallen Doi lightly with his toe. 'Up, you pregnant buffalo,' he ordered under his breath.

All approval vanished from Thu's face. 'Hien! Do as I said and come here!'

Hien felt as if a sudden, black monsoon cloud had swallowed the sun. He dismissed his squad quietly and climbed the steps to the verandah.

When the boy stood beside him, Thu said fiercely but quietly, so no one else could hear his anger, 'Never insult someone you have vanquished! You may kill a man you overcome but never insult him! If he is an enemy and survives, he will pursue you even more bitterly. If he is friend beaten in playful combat, he will become a secret enemy.' Thu glared down at his son. 'Doi's pride was wounded enough by his own failure. I am teaching you to be a leader, not a bully. One leads because others choose to follow an inspiring and instructive example. What kind of example was that, just now, to gloat?'

Hien looked sideways, down at the polished silver-grey wood of the verandah floor. He tried to concentrate on a beetle which had landed on its back, in order not to cry. As always, his father was right. He had been feeling pleased with himself about beating Doi, who was nearly twelve and much heavier than himself. He had let himself become arrogant.

'Apart from that,' said his father, 'I am happy with your work today.'

Hien nodded but could not look up; tears still threatened. He wanted to please his father in every way. Sometimes he thought he would never get it right, even if he lived to be thirty or more.

Thu touched his son lightly on the hard bony point of his small shoulder. The arm below the shoulder was thin but already firmly-muscled. Thu resisted the impulse to put his own arms around the small spare torso, and rub his face against the sun-warmed black hair. For the boy's own sake, he could not indulge his own rush of softness. Instead, he removed a rice straw from Hien's cowlick.

'Let's go eat now,' he said. 'Then we will go together to take an offering to your mother's spirit.' Though Thu privately thought that rituals were for peasants and women with nothing better to do, he knew Hien would recognize the plan as a gesture of affection. He turned to climb the steps up to the lower observation platform where the two of them often ate in the evening.

Hien didn't move.

'Come,' said Thu sharply. 'Don't sulk.' His voice softened again. 'Come eat, *mon petit général*.'

★

352

Thu adored this boy beyond his own belief or even desire. He had not wanted to live with the constant terror that something might happen to the child. Thu hated this vulnerability even while he loved its cause. His own life was nothing to him, often risked and as many times preserved.

Thu had been fond of the mother but had not loved her. Since her death, a few months after childbirth, he had missed her body. He thought that Hien perhaps missed something in having no mother, but the young concubine left no emptiness for himself. She had begun to complain of discomfort and tiredness, as woman do, and he had been almost relieved by the cessation of anxiety which her death brought him. He had missed his old aunt far more, when she had died of feverish dysentery and a sad heart after the villa was bombed, but the grief had passed. The thought of losing Hien, on the other hand, opened a void as giddy as a cliff edge.

He had to make the boy invincible. He could not tolerate the idea that his son might carry scars like his own, the gift of the managers of the colonial French copper mines in Tonkin. Thu was making Hien a soldier, trained as he himself had not been when taken captive by the French at the age of thirteen. His son would know early in life how to move through the country like water and, like water, slip through the fingers of anyone who tried to contain him. Hien would know how to defend himself, how to return the attack, how to humble his enemies so they would never attack him again.

Thu watched the child push a fragment of chicken casually from the edge of the low carved table onto the stone platform where they sat cross-legged to eat. A kitten from one of the many litters in the compound was curled into the crook of his son's dirty knee. Though Thu did not smile, the child would have seen warmth in his father's eyes if he had dared raise his own from his rice basket.

They spoke seldom. Thu was comfortable in speech only when he was instructing or giving orders. But their silence was comfortable. The boy began to forget his earlier humiliation as he planned an afternoon excursion with his friends to a cave in the cliffs below their compound, on the way down to the river. After he and his father had gone together to visit his mother.

As Thu chewed delicately at the double comb of a small fish's spine, he watched his son and reflected on the hidden knife. That knife interested him a great deal. The father who was terrified of that cliff edge of possible loss found the knife reassuring. Hien appeared to have realized already that rules may be broken at any time, and that it is better to do the breaking than to let someone else do it first and take you by surprise. Hien might yet survive on the field of war that life had shown itself to be. Thu put the fishbone on the table. If only he could have taught the other one in the same way.

He pushed his rice bowl away. He had no appetite. The evening was too hot. And the thought which he held away from him with all his strength had managed to slip into his head again. Somewhere in the world was another one as wonderful as Hien. Somewhere, probably in an America he could not imagine, was another son. His eldest son. He had never seen him or even been told of his birth, but he knew that he existed. He had felt him under the tight skin of his mother's belly, like a small animal slipping from underfoot in the dark.

Thu glanced again at the half-healed scab on Hien's left kneecap, at the neat lobes of his close-set ears, the long curve of dark lashes over the downcast eyes, the smooth skin over the small firm muscles of his bare arms, the shadows of his ribs and faint fluttering of heartbeats under the skin just above one small brown nipple. Thu knew every part of this son; he had often made inventory while the boy was asleep and open to his gaze. The other son was no more than a startled, fractious movement against his palm.

He had loved that mother. Abruptly, he unfolded his legs and rose from the table.

'Are we going to mother?' asked Hien anxiously.

'Later,' said his father. 'Later. I must see to something.'

He walked back down onto the verandah and stood staring across the parade ground, past the eroded limestone pinnacles on the interlocking shoulders of mountains beyond. The thatch of the stables needs renewing, he told himself. And the rising billows of magenta and scarlet bougainvillaea must be cut back before they blocked the gate to the river.

Emotional pain has no purpose, he reminded himself. It is also dangerous, because it distracts a man from survival, and sometimes even makes him question the worth of survival.

But, in pain or not, he had been beside himself with rage when Nina had run away for the second time, taking his child with her. Even without the child she carried, she had been worth more than most men. A woman warrior – brave and wily, like himself. With the rare ability for a woman not to ask foolish questions but, instead, to watch and then to act. He had felt at ease in bed with her after passion had drained itself, which was a rare comfort. He should have killed her when his men first brought her to the villa but the unborn child had stopped him.

354

That, and the fact that she was the only mortal, man or woman, to whom he had ever spoken of his bad times or trusted with even a hint of the anxiety and weaknesses which sometimes terrified him.

He tried to turn his mind to the problem of a leaking reservoir but without success. He should have killed her, child or no child. He had lost both of them anyway. To a man he had underestimated as a rival. To the American in the cage which he could not quite see from here, a pirate from yet another country in the long list of those who had pillaged his country.

He heard a sound behind him, delicate as a lizard in the grass. It was Hien, waiting. Thu looked at the boy who pretended to be looking at the distant mountains too, instead of importuning his father to keep his promise.

'Go fetch some joss,' said Thu. 'We'll go to the graves now.'

As the boy vanished toward a hut on the terrace below, Thu saw clearly how much he had failed that shadowy eldest son, Hien's half-brother. It was the first and only time in his life when he had not either put right or avenged a wrong which caused him pain. The pain would stay with him, blurring his vision, clouding present pleasure, until he found a way to remedy it. Killing the man was not enough, but he could not think of another remedy extreme enough for the ill.

'When did it arrive?' asked Perry.

The trans-Pacific cable crackled.

'What?' demanded Perry.

'This morning, on my desk,' said Paul Karelian faintly. 'The memo, that is. The note itself showed up in the Udorn Red Cross Office yesterday sometime . . . it's being looked at in the lab. Nobody knows when it was actually left on the bunk in the refugee camp. You know how hard it is to pin the slopes down on anything when they're not sure how you're going to like it.'

'Do I?' asked Perry.

'I don't know why *I* got it,' said Karelian. 'Haines is nothing to do with our department . . . wrong colour eyes! She's nothing to do with me either, anymore, you lucky old bastard.' He laughed a distant crackling laugh.

'Please wire me the exact wording immediately,' said Perry. 'Let me know about the source of the paper and so on, and send a copy. Thanks.' He hung up. He didn't particularly wish to be abrupt with Karelian. He was fond of Chesterfield's injunction to his son that a gentleman was never rude by accident. But he admitted that he might have eased interdepartmental relations slightly more if he hadn't been preoccupied with whether or not to tell Nina of this new twist. He was anxious enough about her at the moment, as it was. This new information filled him with an irrational terror.

After her meeting with McNeill, Nina became restless. She walked for hours after work, along the Potomac, through the streets, in the countryside on Sundays with Ethan Perry wryly begging mercy for his aging bones and trying to keep pace where his long legs had once outdistanced her. She drove aimlessly, then was shocked to see the number of miles on the clock.

One evening, she found herself cleaning out the cupboard in the front hall. She surveyed the resulting pile of newspapers, old work files, a broken umbrella, a single shoe whose mate had been lost and a tartan wool scarf left by a forgotten guest. On impulse, she pulled from its hanger a beige nylon fold-up raincoat with matching tie-on hood, which she had always hated, and threw it onto the rubbish pile as well. I'll give it to someone, she reassured the guilty self who remembered a world where nothing must be wasted. She looked back into the shadows of the cedar-lined closet where her heavy winter coat, her mackintosh, and her windbreaker were hanging with far too much space around them.

It's as if I'm moving house. Her next thought was that she could no longer bear to stay in this house with its two drumstick bay trees, moth-proofed closets, electric kitchen and antiques from someone else's past.

There's too much peace here. Too much nothing!

She sat thoughtfully on the Duncan Phyfe settee. She rearranged the needlepoint cushions, stitched by someone else's wife or grandmother, into the precise positions in which she had found them waiting for her. I miss my own ghosts, she thought.

I want to go back!

She waited for the silent, empty house around to claim her, hold her, offer her the sense of being *there*.

Oh God! I want to go back! The idea shook her like a possessing spirit. Terrified her. She began to laugh and cry at the same time. She picked up a needlepoint cushion and threw it against the book case. She threw the other two after it and watched them bounce off *The Golden Bough* and the complete works of Jane Austen in the Modern Library edition. She went into the hall, where she kicked the pile of rubbish against the front door like a child kicking fallen leaves.

Why not? she asked herself in the eagle-topped mirror. There's nothing of mine in that closet. I can even leave my winter coat here. She imagined grabbing the windbreaker and her handbag and walking out past the bay trees for the last time. She would walk with huge strides, like a goddess mounting a whirlwind, right across this country, step from island to island across the Pacific Ocean, to her home.

If I'm right about Bill McNeill, he will need local help to find Jimmy Putnam. Even a former Special Forces Round Eye won't get far without it. Nina dismounted from the whirlwind for the moment and went to the little kitchen for a plastic trash bag. She began to clear the floor of the hallway. Carefully, she folded and set aside the scarf and the raincoat for re-cycling.

She closed her eyes and stood again on the eastern bank of the Mekong, unable to imagine the next day, swearing to her daughter's spirit that she would return. Twenty minutes later, she telephoned Bill McNeill's work number, which she had verified before meeting him.

McNeill had to wait for the noon flight in from Los Angeles the following day to find his pilot friend. The pilot wangled McNeill a free airline employee's ticket and walked him onto the afternoon flight to Phoenix, Arizona.

In Phoenix, McNeill hired a Chevrolet sedan and drove forty miles into the desert, following directions in the telephoned reply to his letter to the PO Box in Phoenix. By half-past five, he was following a high wire fence on steel posts, which seemed to enclose the entire American south-west. Finally, he arrived at the electronically-controlled, white-painted metal gates of the Flying F Ranch. He called the house, barely visible on the horizon, on the telephone hanging from one metal gatepost.

'My name's William McNeill. Mr Fields is expecting me.' He hung up before the voice on the other end could reply, got back in the car and waited. The telephone on the post began to ring. McNeill ignored it. It rang twelve times, then stopped. Then McNeill heard the electrical whine that set the heavy gates into motion. He had pretty high hopes for Fields. The rancher used his money the way McNeill was using his time. You spent what you had.

Fields didn't waste his own or anyone else's time. McNeill was in the poolhouse with his host for exactly twenty-three minutes. He explained his intended course of action. Fields listened without comment. When McNeill finished, Fields asked one question: 'Who was your last commanding officer?'

When McNeill told him, he nodded curtly. 'I know him,' he said.

'So check me out,' said McNeill. 'He'll say all the right wrong things.'

'Don't try to teach your grandmother,' said Fields. He wrote McNeill a cheque for $15,000. 'And don't waste my money!'

'This is only enough to start checking,' warned McNeill.

'I said, don't waste it!'

McNeill stared down a German Shepherd as he backed slowly into his rented car. Fields would listen again. And there were others like him, all around the country, some financing official operations, and some favouring the freelancers. Men like himself, who weren't quite satisfied with the way things had turned out.

When he returned to Newark that evening, he checked into a motel near the airport and called his friend the pilot.

'Intercontinental is a pain in the ass,' said his friend. 'And why Bangkok? You returning something you picked up on R and R?'

'Did you get me a seat?'

'Of course I did! What did you think? I just want to hear some gratitude coming down the line.'

'I'm grateful,' said McNeill.

'But not for four days. There's a standby list of airline employees two miles long . . . mainly the stewards.'

'OK,' said McNeill. 'No problem.' He needed time anyway to get Fields' cheque cleared. He also needed time to figure out how to find a human needle in the haystack of Southeast Asia without calling the wrong kind of attention to himself. All of his own contacts were military – exactly the wrong people.

He didn't need a visa for Thailand. If he weren't back home before his fifteen free days were up, he's just leave Thailand and go back in again. He decided, however, to go home for his suit. The last thing he needed was for Customs to take him apart as a hippy pusher and find the large denomination bills that would be in his wallet. There might be a difference of opinion about how much was enough for personal use and how much required a signed currency declaration.

He drove back up and spent a day and an evening in his office, making contingency plans for his absence. There was no message from Gabe Simpson. He was staring out of the window toward his truck, parked in isolation on the tarmac lot when Nina telephoned.

★

'I thought you were a type who works late,' she said. 'I'd like to come with you to Laos.' She listened to the silence on the line and wondered if he had hung up. She had stampeded like a buffalo calf. Then she heard the faint sound of a throat being cleared.

'Who said I'm going to Laos?'

'Are you worried about your telephone?' she asked. 'My line is OK.' Her earlier conviction about McNeill suddenly ebbed away.

'Listen, Miss Desanges,' said his voice flatly, after a few more seconds, 'I don't know where you get your information but your source is a little mixed up. I'm going out to Thailand to look up an old friend . . . in Chiang Mai.'

'My mistake,' she said, a little reassured by Chiang Mai. 'It's just that I may be going out there too. And I'm still happy to help you out, as a more-or-less local.'

There was another long pause. 'Funnily enough,' he said with reluctance, 'I could use a little help picking up my friend's trail.' He hesitated again. 'My friend's a Meo.'

A Meo! Nina had once made business decisions on less information than this. She imagined how hard it was for McNeill to tell her even this much. 'I know a few people in Chiang Mai,' she said. She knew one or two men in Chiang Mai who would still know the Meos well, through the opium trade, but they were old contacts, former colleagues of her father's. They would ask McNeill who had given him their names. Except for Thu, her father's world thought she was dead, or as good as. By her own choice, she wanted to stay that way.

And if she were right about McNeill, official American contacts would be too dangerous for him. 'The Area Field Studies people might be able to help,' she suggested wickedly.

'Maybe,' said McNeill without enthusiasm. 'But maybe not.'

Nina grinned to herself. Suspicion pretty well confirmed. 'Maybe not,' she agreed.

Then she remembered an Englishman called Howard whom she had met once briefly with Perry. An old friend of Ethan's from the OSS days. Now 'gone native' and known in Chiang Mai as a local eccentric.

'There is a man called Howard,' she said to McNeill. 'Fairly straight. Deals in tribal handicrafts. He went out from England in the '30s to work in the teak industry and stayed. May have been involved in intelligence during World War Two but now retired, as far as anyone retires. Speaks Thai and a little Meo and Karen. I'm told he knows the tribes.'

'Would he talk to me?' asked McNeill.

'Mention Ethan Perry. My superior.' Forgive me, Ethan, she thought. 'But please remember, this is not an official contact.'

'No problem,' said McNeill's voice pleasantly. 'As I said, it's just a friendly visit.'

Since he wasn't in the mood for Christmas trees, McNeill decided to use the rest of his waiting time to drive into Boston, where he reopened contact with an ENT surgeon who had been a CIDG medical specialist and later a medic with McNeill's unit for four months in 1969. They had met again in 1973, in Saigon, and since 1975, had met once for a drink and dinner before returning to their now very different lives.

The surgeon listened to what McNeill had to say.

'I don't suppose you're up for something active yourself?' asked McNeill.

'God no!' said the surgeon. 'But thanks for thinking I could hack it. I'm about to give up squash for golf!' He had thought when McNeill first asked to meet that the man needed another job again. 'You just want some names, right?'

'Right.'

'Let me get back to you. I haven't thought about this kind of thing for a long time.'

'Lucky you,' said McNeill, smiling.

'I don't know anything . . . just that you're interested in talking to a certain kind of guy with a certain kind of experience, right?'

'Right,' said McNeill again. The doctor walked him out of his office.

'Congratulations,' said McNeill, looking around the consulting room, which was lined with chairs bearing the Harvard emblem on their backs, in gold. '*Veritas*,' they said. Truth. 'You've done real well,' said McNeill.

He also called a man named Henry Spiegel, once Captain Spiegel. A medic in Vietnam and now a doctor, Spiegel, along with his regular practice, was joined in uneasy alliance with the Veterans Administration in Boston as a medical consultant for war-injured Vietnam veterans applying for compensation. McNeill had referred acquaintances to Spiegel in 1974 and 1976.

'Sure I remember you,' said Spiegel. 'Are you kidding? How are you?'

'I'm OK,' said McNeill. 'I'd appreciate a little help though. Can I come talk it over with you some time?'

'Is this for you personally?' asked Spiegel, with only the faintest of gear changes in his voice. 'This is an office phone,' he added.

'I'd like to talk about some people you might know, professionally.'
Spiegel was silent for a minute. 'I can't break confidentiality.'
'Can I come down?'

There was an even longer pause. 'Sure,' said Spiegel, 'I'd like to see you again. But I don't think there's much I can do for you except take you out for a beer.'

'That'd be fine,' said McNeill.

After calling McNeill, Nina could not concentrate on anything. Work lost the hypnotic insistence which had saved her in Bangkok. The wide-ranging books in brother-in-law William's shelves were so much blurred paper. Newspapers contained only horrors to be thrust aside. She ate abstractedly from open packets which fell under her hands, from trays of canapés shoved under her nose at receptions, and from plates urged on her in restaurants by Ethan Perry. She found herself prowling the house, making coffee, and staring out at the drumstick bays at 4:00 in the morning.

Three days before the Buddha's birthday, she went to the Washington Cathedral, slipped into a side chapel and lit a candle for Mouse. She raised her eyes from the tiny flickering flame to the smiling plaster face of the mother with her child.

Holy Mother Mary, we haven't spoken for some time. Do you mind?

Into her mind squeezed a long-faded image of herself in a ruffled dress, with curled hair, clinging to her mother's hand in Saigon's red brick Cathedral, overwhelmed at six years by all these other, Round Eye, spirits to be appeased.

I haven't got the balance right yet, she thought.

She crossed herself, left the Cathedral and looked for a florist. When she found one, she bought a vase and a spray of tiny shell pink orchids, which she took back to the Cathedral and tucked in among the lights of the candles.

On the third day of waiting for a flight, McNeill drove back down to Newark, feeling uncomfortable in his lightweight, drip-dry suit and carrying only the money, a flight bag with basics, the two hundred permitted, duty-free American cigarettes, a camera with a telephoto lens and the full legal limit of five rolls of film. Taking off for Asia as a civilian was a new experience. He thought about it most of the way to Honolulu.

When the flight put down at Kai Tak Airport in Hong Kong, McNeill persuaded a representative of the airline to rewrite his ticket.

Instead of arriving in Thailand through Don Muang Airport at Bangkok, he took the alternative route to the northern Thai city of Chiang Mai. Thirty hours after leaving Newark, McNeill, in jeans and a tee-shirt, was hiring a motorbike from a tout near the eastern moat gate of the old city, and breathing in the heat.

McNeill sniffed the air and suddenly felt happy. He had not been aware of that sensation for longer than he could remember, not that he ever thought about it. The rich mix of spice, rotting vegetation, dank water of the old moat below the former city wall, excreta, jasmine and petrol fumes touched some irrational source of pleasure buried too deep for reason to find and analyse. The smell of balsam fir in the mountains at home made him happy in the same way.

That's why I grow Christmas trees, he thought suddenly, in a rare moment of self-analysis. I like the way they smell! The realization pleased him too.

He bought a bowl of noodles from a vendor with a portable brass stove on one end of his yoke and a portable brass cupboard for bowls and spoons on the other. He ate the noodles with an enormous spoon, astride the saddle of the motorbike. As his bones warmed, his sense of contentment increased. He allowed himself just to sit on the bike, to watch and listen, drinking occasionally from a lukewarm bottle of Singha beer.

On the far side of the moat, white-skinned tourists in sunhats were aggregating slowly around a small brown man holding aloft a sign which said 'Umbrella and Silk Villages'. A young woman in a navy blue skirt and white blouse advertised 'Lamphun and Leprosarium' from a much smaller clumping of sunhats.

McNeill hadn't been back to Chiang Mai since 1967. He was pleased how little it had changed. He had heard that the city fathers had politely refused the opportunity to turn the quiet northern town into a second R&R haven for US servicemen, thereby passing up the profitable disco bars, amusement arcades, and massage parlours which enriched Bangkok.

He watched the women with a slight sense of surprise at his own sudden interest. He had organized sex into his life as neatly as his pick-up trucks ranged between their parallel white lines in the macadam parking lot. Usually, it stayed where it belonged. He watched the secretaries and shop girls, and the worn-out breeders and the hill-tribe women in what looked like fancy dress when it was walking along a concrete sidewalk. Lazily he observed and enjoyed their slightness, and the way their hands opened more when they gestured than the hands of American women, turned back at the joint between fingers and palms like daylilies. He watched the clean, cool flat faces, trying to pick the sinitic tribal faces from the more Malaysian Thais. He found himself imagining that he could really hear the brushing of all those cream and tanned thighs, walking in all directions around him. Attractive as she was, Nina Desanges in her fancy suit hadn't reached him like this.

It must be the heat, he thought, and stretched comfortably. Maybe, he told himself. Maybe later. He enjoyed the thought.

He tossed the empty beer bottle back to the vendor, an eleven-year-old boy, who immediately began to open another.

'*Proong nee*,' called McNeill. 'Tomorrow.'

He wheeled the bike along Tapae Road past open-fronted shops selling a smorgasbord of local handicrafts to tourists who didn't have time or want to bother to visit the specialized villages around the outskirts of Chiang Mai. Lacquerware, hammered silver bowls, lengths of silk and cotton cloth. He walked slowly, his usual deliberate movements relaxed to an even lazier rhythm. He stopped beside a four-foot high carving of an elephant and sniffed again. Teak. Warm, pungent like sandalwood but slightly sour.

The elephant guarded the open front of a shop which displayed a range of teak elephants from two inches high up to the size of the guardian at the door. However, McNeill wasn't interested in the elephants; his eyes were on a pile of embroidered cloths, unlike the silks and cottons in the previous shops. These were crusted with red, gold and yellow threads, embroidered by hill-tribe women. Some also had patterns of ivory beads shaped like rice grains. On the back wall of the shop hung a display of heavy silver Meo collars, hollow rings open at the back and fat as New York bagels.

Before going into the shop, McNeill checked out its occupants. The proprietor was alone. He wore a sarong and leather sandals but his accent was pure Oxbridge. Local gossip reported that Howard avoided talking to Americans to keep it that way. At first glance, he could have been an elderly Thai – thin, tanned, with cropped grey hair and the universal webbing of age across his face.

'Mr Howard?' McNeill asked. He received a guarded nod. 'I'm a friend of a friend of Ethan Perry. . . .' He didn't like coming out of cover even this much.

Howard carried on straightening a pile of woven bags but gave a grunt which could have been encouragement to continue.

363

'I'm looking for an old friend of mine who used to live near Chiang Mai. A Meo. Used to operate up near Chiang Saen. . . .'

McNeill let the reference hang in the air. Chiang Saen was on the border with Burma and Laos. At the apex of the Golden Triangle. He knew that Howard knew that a principle product of the hill tribes had always been opium, even more than silver and embroidered clothes. Howard specialized in the hill-tribe handicrafts.

Howard turned from his bags and let McNeill wait while he scrutinized him.

'He'd be in his late forties now,' said McNeill.

'I'm not as much in touch as I used to be,' said Howard. 'Why don't you go out to the Old Chiang Mai Culture Centre south of the city? One or two of the old head boys hang out there, building up their pension funds by letting tourists take their pictures. But they're still all there, in every sense of the word.'

I know your type, his old eyes said. And I have no reason to let you know whether I'm the same or not.

'They do quite a good typical Thai banquet out there,' said Howard. 'The tourists like it. Might be worth trying. The man who introduces the hill tribe dances afterwards is a helpful sort.'

McNeill thanked him and pointed the bike out of Chiang Mai. He checked to see if anyone followed him. Nobody did. And Howard didn't seem like he worried much about anything any more. If this Old Chiang Mai Culture Club came to anything, the risk of using an official contact might have been worth it. McNeill's earlier lazy contentment gave way to his more usual pleasure in purpose. Either way, he was having a good time.

He enjoyed the banquet too. Seated cross-legged at one end of the long, low table beside a Spanish honeymoon couple, he didn't have to make chitchat with strangers, which would have spoiled his mood. He smiled at the beautiful girl with the off-centre topknot who served him, savoured the chillis and tang of lemon grass and listened to the *gamelan* musicians chasing each other in an accelerating game of musical tag.

The best part of it was that he was not armed. He did not have to remain alert. The musicians weren't, possibly, about to pull weapons from under their *panungs*. The serving girl hadn't, possibly, already reported his off-duty presence to someone offstage. He examined each part of the exotic-familiar experience in this new context of peace. The pleasure of that first deep sniff of Chiang Mai air was still with him. The realization continued to flood in – he had been waiting for the first really good excuse to come back out to Southeast Asia in peacetime.

When the floor show started, he sharpened his attention. The master-of-ceremonies whom Howard had mentioned as a 'helpful sort' did not appear. Instead, his role was taken by a self-possessed young woman in a silk jacket and long silk skirt. The first two hill-tribe folk dances were performed by Karen and Lisu couples. However, the third group were Meos. The girls were wearing the turbans that McNeill remembered so well, but the performers were far too young for him to have known them except as children – probably all students at Chiang Mai University or one of the church colleges, earning a few extra *baht* to pay for books and trips to London or New York.

As two young men, who looked no older than twelve or fourteen, finished a sequence of carefully contrived gyrations with enormous swords and began beating at each other's blades like bad Hollywood extras, McNeill caught the eye of his waitress.

A mixture of Thai, English and three five *baht* notes, brought the missing MC to McNeill's end of the table before the applause for the sword fight had died.

'Very impressive, don't you think?' he asked McNeill. 'We are making excellent progress in assimilating the diverse tribal groups into the mainstream of Thai culture and economy.' Though wearing the old-style Thai court dress, he talked like the government-employed professor he was.

'Sounds better than revolution,' said McNeill gravely. 'Good luck taming the Meos.'

The MC shot him a quick look. 'Quite,' he said. 'I consider it a priority, as do many of my colleagues at the Thai Hill-Crafts Foundation, to find a real economic alternative for them. You may have noticed an increase in Meo silver and the number of woven bags in Chiang Mai shops. We are hoping to open a new, specialized outlet in Bangkok this year.'

'Admirable,' agreed McNeill. 'In fact, I'm looking for one of your old cowboys. Just for old times' sake. Used to work up in the Chiang Saen region. Across the border. I expect you're keeping an eye on people like him these days.'

The MC gazed toward the orchestra's dais where two of the players were chatting, another was examining the sole of his bare foot, another was intent on her little fingernail and yet another was poised, impatiently alert, glaring at the empty ring of the xylophone-like *gamelan* of an absent colleague.

'Excuse me, please, for one moment.' The MC rose, vanished, and reappeared again at exactly the same time as the missing player.

'Interestingly enough,' he said to McNeill, as if their conversation had never been interrupted, 'I was speaking just a few minutes ago to a member of the Border Patrol Police who dropped by this evening . . . that is why I did not play my usual part in the evening's entertainment, by the way . . . The Border Patrol are very helpful in the project of finding both domestic and foreign markets for Meo handicrafts. Of course, they are aware of where the different sources are located. Perhaps you would like to meet this man.'

McNeill would.

McNeill left the old city early the next morning through the White Elephant Gate on its north side, turned left and took the road north-west through rice-paddis, toward Doi Suthep, a mini mountain of 1,000 metres topped by a temple which overlooked the city from a distance of twelve kilometres. He was tempted to open out the bike on the long, straight ribbon of road across the plain. Then, already travelling at considerable speed himself, he was overtaken by a blaring, careening bus draped with passengers and cargo which included several screaming pigs tied on top in woven bamboo swaddling clothes. He nearly hit two chickens and a dog before he steadied the bike and decided to test the engine another time.

But then, ten minutes later, just past the Chiang Mai Zoo, the road began to climb away from the plain. He had left the buses behind in the parking area from which tourists and pilgrims climbed on foot 290 steps up to the gilded sanctuary on the summit of Doi Suthep. The temptation of a clear road was too much. McNeill emptied his mind and leaned happily into the hairpin curves. For the next five kilometres of still-climbing road, he let himself open the throttle and burn round the bends, making love to danger as he had not allowed himself to do for a very long time.

On the peak beyond Doi Suthep, he reached the summer palace of the Thai king, turned the bike around and retraced his route downhill for 400 metres to a dirt track, which he took. When this track crossed another, he parked the bike, as he had been instructed the night before, tucked a carton of cigarettes under his arm and began to walk to the left down the new track.

Five minutes into the steep descent, a small girl in a black and red embroidered costume and with a shop-full of silver around her reed-like neck, slid from the rock where she had been sitting and scrambled down the track beside him.

366

'You take my photograph, mister? Five *baht*.'

'Not today,' said McNeill in English. 'I got business with the head honcho.'

Cheerfully unperturbed, she followed him chanting, 'Photo. Photo.'

The track ended at a scattering of huts across the mountainside. The huts were set on the ground, not on stilts like those in Thai villages. A half dozen more children came on the run.

'Take photo?' they asked. 'You American?' 'Come see typical Meo house? Specially for you.'

'I want to see Mr Man,' said McNeill.

'OK. OK.' The horde veered away toward the far end of the village. The little girl from the rock took his hand. Her small wrist clattered as a dozen silver bracelets fell toward her elbow.

A man wearing black folk costume, with short-cut hair and a slightly balding pate was sitting comfortably on the ground in front of one of the huts. As McNeill approached, he concentrated on the two and a half foot long water pipe, through which he was smoking an American cigarette.

McNeill tossed the carton of the cigarettes onto the ground beside the water pipe. 'If you want to get cancer that bad,' said McNeill, 'I can help you out.'

The man's head jerked up. 'Holy shit!' he yelled in English. 'Cowboy!' He leapt to his feet, dropping the pipe in the dust and flung himself at McNeill. He slammed McNeill on the back with both hands in what was half war dance, half embrace. McNeill returned the hug, lifting the smaller Meo two feet off the ground.

'You old bastard! You come to take my photo after all these years?'

'I can't afford it, you son of a bitch,' said McNeill.

'I don't believe it!' said the Meo. 'I don't goddam well believe it! Hey, put me down!' They stood and grinned at each other.

Women and more children came out of the huts to investigate the uproar. Most of the women wore the black Meo turbans but two wore curlers and hairnets.

The Meo said something in his own language which McNeill couldn't quite follow though he once could have done.

'This man nearly killed me, twenty times,' the Meo translated for McNeill.

'And this man saved my life, the stupid fucker!' said McNeill.

The two men exchanged one quick, furtive, serious glance, then veered away from the past back to the present.

'Let's have a drink,' urged the Meo. 'I bet you miss the lousy beer!'

367

'I miss a lot of things,' McNeill heard himself saying, though he had never thought about it before, not so clearly.

'Beer, women . . . bombs . . . The good old days!' The Meo shook his head in mock nostalgia. 'Wow!' He slung a small, scarred hand up over McNeill's towering shoulder like a grappling iron. 'Come on, you old buffalo, let's make whoopee!'

'You'll miss the first bus-full of tourists,' said McNeill as he stooped and let himself be led into the hut.

What both had first said was true. What they hadn't gone on to tell their audience was that McNeill had fought like a demon to get the Meo, his Number One Wife (one of the women in curlers) and his son, now grown and working in Udorn, onto an Air America flight out of Laos in 1973. McNeill had successfully argued that the Meo was compromised as an agent for the Americans and needed a resident visa and new home in Thailand. Most of their montagnard colleagues in the same unit had been left behind and executed by the North Vietnamese.

'What the hell you want, coming back here? After you take my photo?' The Meo had taken McNeill for a stroll up a track to a clearing above the village which had once been a field burned out of the jungle but now lay fallow. The blackened trunks of former trees stood out like three-day stubble against the dry channels of early erosion. In the village below them, they could see the pink, khaki and pastel blue clothing of a party of tourists who had arrived half an hour after McNeill.

'How much do you hear from across the Laos border?' asked McNeill.

The Meo made a face. 'Enough. A few army checkpoints and Border Police patrols don't mean much to the mountain cats.'

'Do you ever get back?'

'Are you crazy? I got family over there . . . what's left of it. Meo territory is Meo territory. Those are our mountains, man! Laos, Thailand, Burma, Vietnam, makes no difference. Sure I get back! You homesick or something?'

'I heard somebody is . . . if he's still alive. I'd love to know if it's just horseshit or if it could be true.' McNeill lifted the camera strap over his large head and offered it to the Meo. 'I got five rolls of film and a good telephoto lens. On a long shot that anybody gets close enough to use it, it would be useful. Otherwise a word or two is good enough to start with.'

'Any somebody?' asked the Meo.

'Uh-huh. James Michael Putnam. He's one of the brothers.'

'Where do I start looking?'

'I got four names for you.' He told him the place names in Putnam's letter.

The Meo swung the camera on the end of its strap and watched it as if trying to hypnotize himself. 'You motherfucking turtle,' he said. 'I'm retired. Got a great gig smoking home-grown *bhang* for the tourists . . . instead of stewing in a refugee camp somewhere. Planning to get fat and have a coronary just like an American.'

'I've got start-up funding,' said McNeill. 'With pictures and map coordinates, I'll get a lot more.'

'I don't mean that,' said the Meo. 'I'd do it for nothing. For fun.'

They both stared down toward the village and the pastel patches that appeared and disappeared behind the upper huts.

'For the good old days, hey?' The Meo looked at McNeill.

'They were OK,' said McNeill. 'In places.'

They started to climb back down toward the village.

'Thanks,' said McNeill.

'How long've you got?'

'How long will it take?'

'Tell you afterward?'

'Fair enough.'

The Meo walked McNeill back to the bike. 'Get your ass back here a little sooner next time. Then maybe we can relax and have some real fun.'

While McNeill was in Thailand, Gabriel Simpson began to dream again. For two nights in a row, he lay sweating, muttering 'Cease firing! Cease firing!' between clenched teeth.

He was surrounded by a circle of dancing, headless bodies. The bodies were kept upright and in motion by a barrage of gunfire. They jigged and danced closer and closer, the white knobs of their neckbones glistening in the moonlight, swimming toward him on the hot metal wave of bullets.

'Cease firing!' he screamed. Then the bodies would fall and stop reaching for him. But they jerked and flicked closer and closer. They reached for him with the stumps of their wrists.

'CEASE FIRING!' screamed Simpson.

While McNeill was still away, Nina's telephone rang one night at 10:30. It was Mayor John Putnam.

His voice was thin with distance and very shaky. 'I've had another letter from Jimmy! It says. . . .'

'John, I'm not sure about this line,' interrupted Nina.

'Good!' said Putnam. 'I want everybody to know . . . Hello, anybody else listening . . . please pay attention. I have just had my last letter from my son, who wasn't dead after all, last time but will be now!'

'What does it say?' asked Nina.

'They're going to shoot him in exactly one month unless I stop stalling and contact the agent in Brussels. "I'm not worth feeding," my boy says. "Not worth a bowl of weevilly rice!" ' Putnam's voice caught. 'They won't let him write again.'

Nina leaned against the wall of the front hallway for support. What can I say to him? What should I say?

'So much for your good advice, Miss Desanges! Write another report telling your committee how grateful I am!'

'Call Brussels tonight,' said Nina. 'Do you have a number?'

There was a pause. 'Yes. But it's the middle of the night there.'

'Then they'll believe how frightened you are!'

'Are you telling me to agree?'

Nina slid down the wall into a crouch. She breathed in deeply. 'What else can you do?' She switched the receiver to her left hand and wiped her cold, wet palm on the nightdress over her thigh. I think I'm thinking straight. 'Save Jimmy!'

There was another pause. 'At any price?'

'That's your decision,' said Nina. 'I gave you my opinion.'

'You mean, that advice just now was not official?'

'Have any of our chats been official? I told you what would happen if the authorities learned about the Belgian contact . . . you haven't forgotten, or done anything stupid that I don't know about?' She prayed for Putnam to understand. 'I just hope they aren't listening, no matter what you said earlier!'

The pause this time was very long.

'Right,' said Putnam finally. He sounded very tired. He might have figured out who else could be listening, to his telephone, not hers. 'I'd better get the news of my capitulation started along the wires. It took three months for Jimmy's first letter to reach me.'

Nina waited until the next day to tell Ethan Perry in person.

'You did the right thing,' he said. 'He'll have to take it a step further. We can hold up the export licence to buy time . . . assuming the approach is still through European channels.' He looked at her sharply. 'I'll do what I can! I can't do more!'

'I feel I'm on the wrong side of a one-way mirror,' said Nina.

'Of course. We all do.'

When he returned to America, McNeill's mind wouldn't stay on work. He had to bite his tongue to keep from telling superintendents with nothing better to worry about where they could put their poison ivy. He sent Ronnie in his place on as many jobs as he could. He tallied up deliveries of baled peat and granular fertilizer with only half his brain. The other half was making lists of strategic considerations . . . buying arms in-country, fall-back positions, and local guides. He doodled endless combinations and recombinations of manpower. All lists and doodles went into the locked filing cabinet with his clippings. He lay awake at night chewing over and over the problem of undetected insertion. When he drove out to look over his three-year-old trees, he mentally moved an eight man team on their bellies through the low bristling cover. He imagined Military Intelligence knocking on his door, alerted by Miss Nina Desanges who had called four times in his absence. He did not return her calls.

Four days after his return, McNeill's phone rang.

'Dammit!' said Nina's voice, indignantly and small with distance. 'At least you could tell me how your friendly little trip went! I had hoped we could meet – I have some rather urgent. . . .'

'I'll give you news when I got it,' said McNeill. 'Mr Howard was very helpful. Thanks.' He hung up. That woman bothered him. Personally, he could have liked her. She seemed to care about Jimmy Putnam. But how far could he trust a Vietnamese who worked for US Intelligence, for God's sake? Even if it was just a desk job like she said. And where did she get those eyes, like the eyes he had seen on a lot of soldiers – like the world they saw now was such a small part of what they knew? Whatever she knew and however she had learned it, he didn't expect her to feel she owed him, for one, many favours. And now that he had Man, he didn't need anything else from her. He'd be an idiot to trust her.

When the telephone rang again, McNeill took the receiver off the hook and put it into his desk drawer.

When Simpson didn't come back down to find out what had happened in Thailand, McNeill drove up to the mountain. Simpson offered McNeill lunch but didn't ask about Chiang Mai.

'Do you have a picture of Jimmy Putnam?' asked McNeill.

'I might,' said Simpson after a long pause. 'You want me to dig it out?' His tone suggested that 'no' would be welcome.

'Thanks,' said McNeill.

Simpson knelt and hauled a cardboard box from under his bed. 'I'm going to throw all this stuff away someday,' he said. He tossed a wood-toggled, canvas and leather North Vietnamese ammunition belt onto the floor, along with a boonie hat, an olive drab shirt, a pile of letters girdled by a rubber band, a small bamboo crab trap, a Vietnamese copy of a US tiger-stripe camouflage uniform and a pair of half-rotted jungle boots. He shook some photos out of an envelope and riffled quickly through them.

'Here he is . . . third on the right . . . with the arrow.' He tossed a picture to McNeill. 'All the guys with arrows pointing at them are dead. Here's another . . . closer up.' He stuffed the rest of the pictures quickly back in the envelope, put the envelope in the bottom of the box, piled the contents on top and shoved the box back under the bed. Then he went out of the cabin and sat down on the bench beside the door.

'Is it OK if I borrow these?' McNeill lowered himself carefully onto the split log bench beside Simpson.

'Sure!' said Simpson brightly. 'Have them!' He crossed his arms tightly across his bare chest and closed his eyes. 'You're getting serious about this.'

'Depends on what I get back from my friend in Thailand,' said McNeill.

'Going to Thailand in the first place is already serious.' Simpson scratched one bare foot without opening his eyes.

'Let's wait and see,' said McNeill.

'Waiting can seriously damage your health,' replied Simpson.

'Call me at once!' said the message from Nina Desanges waiting on McNeill's desk. He threw it in the waste basket.

19

When her son Harry opened the door one Sunday morning and walked in, Mrs Junor was careful, like someone watching a deer or a squirrel, who doesn't want to startle it into flight.

'Coffee?' she asked. She rose to make a fresh pot before he could refuse.

'Can I use the phone?' he asked.

She shook the coffee pot upside down over the garbage can, trying not to ask who he wanted to call or why it was important enough to bring him to the house after three months without contacting her. She wasn't the kind of woman to feel hurt that he hadn't come home just to see her. She was just happy to see that he wasn't sick and still had some meat on his bones. He needed a haircut and shave, but she had long ago given up on both subjects. That kind of thing had worried her years ago but seemed unimportant now.

The telephone was in the front room. Junor shut the door of the kitchen firmly behind him as he went. Mrs Junor put the coffee pot on the stove and stood by the door listening. For a while, she couldn't hear anything at all. Then she heard dialling but no talking. She crossed quickly back to the table and sat down with her coffee. He came back into the kitchen, tucking a card into the breast pocket of his shirt.

'Did you get through?' she asked, getting up again to pour his coffee before he forgot he wanted it.

'No. But it's not important,' he said. He sat down uneasily and looked around the kitchen. 'You got a new tea kettle.'

'A little while ago. Would you like a sweet roll?' If she had known he was coming she could have baked something. But she didn't bother cooking much any more, just for herself.

'Sure.' His sudden smile included the green eyes, and his mother thought she was going to burst into tears.

'They're just prefabricated garbage from the A&P,' she said gruffly.

'Taste great to me,' he said. He ate fast and finished his mug of coffee. He looked around again.

'Another cup?' she begged.

'I got to go fishing,' he said. 'There's a big old pike I'm after and I got a feeling he's hungry this morning. Thanks for the breakfast.'

'Any time,' she said. She followed him onto the porch. As he trotted down the steps into the yard, she couldn't stop herself from asking, 'When're you going to try again with that call?'

'I don't know,' he said. 'It's not important.' He waved and disappeared around the side of the house.

Mrs Junor ran from the porch through into the back bedroom. From the screened window, she just caught a glimpse of him across the woodpile as he vanished up the trail into the woods behind the garage. She dropped her eyes to her hands, which were resting on the flaking sill. Her nails were short and rough, the skin of the hands wrinkled. She thrust them into the deep pocket of her apron, then sighed.

'I should of took off my apron,' she said to the cat on the bed. 'But I didn't know in time.'

McNeill snatched up the telephone, thinking it might finally be Man.

'Please don't hang up,' said Nina Desanges quickly. 'A mutual friend has been given one month to live by his doctors. I thought you would want to know.'

Oh shit! thought McNeill. Now what do I do? 'The guy we talked about down in Boston?'

'Yes.'

He thought for a quick moment. 'I appreciate you telling me. Can he be visited?'

'He's still abroad.'

'What do foreign doctors know, anyway?'

'The diagnosis is pretty definite!' she said. 'Though there may be a little leeway.'

'Thanks for letting me know anyway.'

'And, Mr McNeill. . . .'

'Thanks,' he repeated and hung up. What did she think he was up to? And who else had she told? He leaned his large fists on the sill of his office window, noting absently that Ronnie Blake's truck was still out. She couldn't know. There was nothing to *know* yet. Unless Man had a hot line to Washington, and that was a crazy idea!

Nevertheless, McNeill considered it calmly for a moment. No way! he decided. Man's loyalties were personal. Miss Nina Desanges only suspected. In which case, this urgency about Jimmy could be to flush him, McNeill, into the open. Then she could go to her superiors with something concrete.

McNeill lifted a hand in greeting as Ronnie Blake pulled into the parking lot. But what if her information was true? McNeill watched Ronnie Blake leave his truck crooked between the white lines, as usual. The man'd be in the office in a minute, wanting McNeill's attention when McNeill needed to think.

Man can find out for me, he decided. Everything hangs on Man. Come on, Man, baby! Come on! It's been nearly two months!

'How's it hangin', Bill?' asked Ronnie Blake cheerfully as he hung his plaid wool cap on the hook labelled with his name.

Man called two days later. The voice on the telephone was muffled by distance or by fish chewing on the undersea cables.

'Cowboy?' 'I think I got something.' The Meo's voice was carefully flat but he couldn't quite hide his glee.

'No joke?' A small hard fist clenched in McNeill's stomach. 'Enough for me to come get?'

'Yeah,' said Man. 'We'll have some real fun this time . . . And listen, can you bring my wives some lipstick by Charlie? Don't matter what colour. Just something sexy.'

'Sure,' said McNeill. He looked at his desk calendar. Friday. He'd have to subcontract out some jobs if things took off. Even if Miss Nina Desanges was just stirring him up, the coming dry season was the time for any operation . . . essential for out-of-shape Americans.

I'm getting ahead of the evidence, he reminded himself. Like that *métisse* woman in Washington. 'Is next Thursday OK for you?' He began to scribble another list on a piece of paper.

'Terrific,' said Man. 'Listen, maybe I should meet you at the Bhubing Palace. I'll find you in the gardens. Morning sometime.'

'Eleven o'clock, next Thursday? Your time, not mine.'

'See you then,' said Man.

Local arms, wrote McNeill on one list. Uniforms. Cover. Supplies. Fallback. RTO. Guides. On another piece of paper he wrote, Marlboros – 2 cartons, Charlie lipstick – two.

This time, McNeill went to Chiang Mai via Don Muang, the Bangkok airport. Again, he felt the same expansion of spirit, the warmth and reawakening of appetite. This time, however, he was too intent on his purpose to linger in either city, even for the sake of the brushing brown thighs he had passed up the time before. In Chiang Mai, the tout near the eastern moat gate recognized him.

'Hi, Boss,' he said. 'You like same bike? Where you going this time? How about a nice girl to sit on the back?'

'I drive too fast – she'd fall off,' said McNeill. 'Maybe *proong nee*.'

Again, the road across the plain to the hump of Doi Suthep was crowded with early morning marketers, scratching chickens, bicycles, buses, and the occasional buffalo. This time, it was also a long string of lakes and puddles left by an early morning monsoon rain. Again, except for one whining, labouring tourist coach, he lost the traffic after Doi Suthep as he began the five kilometre climb up toward the King's Summer Palace. A Volkswagon minibus from Wild West Tours was parked at the top of the track down to the Meo village. McNeill carried on to the palace on the next peak where he had turned around the time before.

The Summer Palace was too new for McNeill's taste. He found a damp seat in the park, near a bed of magenta orchids, with his back to a large arbutus tree and a good field of vision. While he let his mind drift, his ears and eyes remained alert to the burring of cicadas, the small rustlings of lizards and birds, a distant aircraft, and a labouring engine which echoed thinly off a nearby mountain slope. For the moment, the sun bounced off a metallic sky and steam rose visibly from the paths. The heat loosened his bones. He sighed and spread his arms open along the back of his bench. He tensed as a flying squirrel suddenly swooped across his peripheral vision, then he relaxed again.

Man stepped into view a few yards away along one of the paths. Today he wore blue jeans and a beige Lacoste knitted shirt. McNeill's camera and telephoto lens hung from his neck and a flight bag was slung across his shoulder.

'Hi, Cowboy.' He sat beside McNeill and pulled two bottles of beer from his bag. He opened them and handed one to McNeill. Then, apparently as an afterthought, he reached again into the bag and handed McNeill a folded Thai newspaper. As McNeill's large fingers explored the paper, Man pulled on his beer and surveyed the gardens. 'Picturesque, hey?'

McNeill found the photographs. 'Holy shit!' he breathed.

The first picture was a grainy blow-up of a detail from a 35mm telephoto shot. In gaps between clumps of vegetation, McNeill saw two heads in profile and the back of a third head.

'Your guy's in the middle,' said Man. '. . . if it's him.'

The central profile was unquestionably darker than the one behind. The man's hair was a thick black halo around his head.

'Unless there's another black guy over there in the same place, that's him,' said McNeill. 'But who the fuck is behind him?'

'Look at the next one,' said Man.

The second photo was also a blow-up from a 35mm telephoto shot.

'Work party,' said Man. 'Two armed guards.'

Putnam, if it were he, was caught three-quarters full-face. McNeill took a hard, cynical look, allowing for the persuasive power of desire. It still looked like the Jimmy P. in Simpson's snapshots. McNeill laid the photos on his thigh and wiped the palms of his hands on his knees. Then he let himself look at the other two men – the other profile and the back of the head of the first photo.

'What do they look like to you?' he asked Man.

'Round Eyes,' said Man.

'Yeah,' said McNeill quietly. 'Did you get close enough to hear them talk?'

'Not this time,' said Man. 'But they all seemed to understand each other OK.'

'Three Americans!' said McNeill. 'We're going to start World War Three, no joke, Man, my man!' He rubbed his chin. 'I don't suppose you picked up any local chat about these guys getting wasted to save rice or something?'

Man shook his head. 'You got news?'

McNeill shrugged. 'Enough to make me want to speed things up.'

'I'll see what I can learn.'

Man had also taken four shots of a fortified village from nearby high ground, close-ups of two gates, and a series of shots panning past the village from a low angle showing the contours of the mountains behind it and covering approximately 120 degrees. There were four shots of a series of openings in the cliff face.

'That's the village where the guards took them back,' said Man. 'Funny place. Do you need it more formal?'

'No,' said McNeill. 'That's enough for me. Have you got the map coordinates? And any idea of the manpower in there?'

'You gonna get them out?' asked Man.

'You gonna help?'

There was a short silence as Man drank some more beer. 'Real help? Not just holiday snapshots?'

'As real as you can get.'

'Like the old days?' Man was studying the orchids.

'Better than that,' said McNeill, carefully. 'It'll be just us. To screw up or luck out. No REMFs. We'll be the generals.'

'We. . . ?'

'You and me,' said McNeill.

377

'Since you're in a hurry, finish your beer and gimme the bottle,' said Man. 'You and me are going to take a trip up to Fang.'

The Meo climbed on the back of McNeill's bike, with the flight bag strapped on the rack behind. They wound on up and over the mountains and then dropped back down past the Mae Sa Waterfall to join Road 107, the main route north from Chiang Mai to the junction of the Laos and Burmese borders at Chiang Saen. They stopped twice, once for lunch at a roadside stall and once for Man to make an offering at a spirit house shaped like a miniature Thai temple, set beside the road as it arched over a rocky ridge.

Fang, 152 kilometres from Chiang Mai, on the Burmese border, was like a California gold-rush town. For a short time, its gold had been crude oil. As they approached the town, McNeill saw an abandoned oil boring, the pump now lolling like a weary, heavy-headed bird. There were no visible signs of the real gold, which still flowed out of Fang – the crude opium from nearby Burma and Laos. But if you could read what signs there were, you knew that the boom was still on.

The streets were full of people who didn't belong there – bright-eyed Thai soldiers, Border Police, regular Thai Police, Kuo Mintang Soldiers, Laotians, Burmese, Americans, Swedes, French. There were also Shan, Meo, Yao, Lisu, Lamet, Karen and Akha tribesmen.

McNeill parked the bike by a banana clump just off the main market street. Man gave a small boy a few *baht* to guard its tyres, mirror, saddle and tank of gas. The two men strolled slowly into the town along an unpaved track, past thatched, stilted houses, bicycles, foraging chickens, naked children, and tribal women with babies on their backs, wearing silver jewellery stacked as high as that of Man's wives.

'They're Yao,' said Man. 'The Viets call them Man. . . .' He grinned. 'I guess that's how I got my name. My mother was a Yao.' He broke off to call a greeting to a man on the verandah of a very large thatched house set back just off the track. A gasoline-powered electrical generator sat hunched in a wire cage in the yard in front of the house.

'Let him get a look at your face,' Man instructed McNeill.

McNeill did so, then asked, 'Chinese?'

'Yeah,' said Man. 'Kuomintang. Got chased across the border by Chairman Mao. Smuggles opium. Married Meo girl. He's got good sense.' Man stopped in the street and clapped his hand to his head in a mock fit of inspiration. 'I got it!' he cried. 'I'll find *you* a Meo wife, when we're done. Then you can stick around a little bit. How about that?'

378

'Ask me again when we're done,' said McNeill.

Man turned abruptly down an alley and then again into the shadows of a corrugated iron-roofed shed which was the back side of a sword and gun shop on the main street. A thin man in a dirty singlet and cut-off jeans was filing a strip of metal clamped in a vise on a work bench littered with mysterious geometries of iron and steel.

'Hey, Loopy!' said Man in English. 'I brought somebody for you to meet.'

The man raised his eyes. McNeill recognized the look in them. They held the bitter humour which men sometimes choose as the alternative to madness. They had searched and not liked what they found. And were still active, not passive receivers of impression.

'Loopy La . . . Cowboy McNeill.' Then Man said something to La in Meo which was too fast for McNeill to follow.

'I told him you were a businessman,' Man explained. 'Old-fashioned business. Loopy here got his name 'cause of what he used to do with his planes.'

'Planes?' asked McNeill.

La spoke for the first time, in English. 'Rice drops.' He gave a final delicate touch with his file and laid it on the workbench. 'To hill-tribe refugees running from the Pathet Lao and the PAVN.'

'You were a pilot?' McNeill kept his excitement out of his voice. When Man moved, he moved fast.

La nodded and slid off his stool to insert his wide bare feet into a pair of rubber flipflops.

'Trained by US Air Commandos,' said Man. 'Number One in Laos in his day.'

'Dropping rice?' asked McNeill sceptically.

'And other things,' said La.

'Isn't Fang a little low altitude for you?' asked McNeill, looking around the workshop. 'Being an airman *and* a Meo?'

La smiled briefly. 'I still fly.'

'Freelance now,' added Man. 'Ain't we all!'

As La disappeared briefly into the room beyond the workshop shed, Man added *sotto voce*, 'He run out of mountains. All the Meo run out of mountains.'

La walked them back to the motorbike. Man asked about La's wife and the son who had crossed back into Laos. La asked Man how much the *farang* tourists were tipping these days for a photograph, and said he hoped that both of Man's wives were each cuckolding him at least twice daily. Both Man and Loopy La spoke to the Kuomintang soldier, still on his verandah. Nothing more was said about business, old-fashioned or otherwise.

Man and McNeill were back in Chiang Mai before midnight and went to a food stall with tables and benches by the east moat gate. The bike tout had vanished. In his place was a drinks vendor selling saffron, magenta and acid green syrups poured over chipped grey ice, and sugar cane juice from a hand-turned mill operated by his tiny son.

As soon as the two men settled on a bench with US Army surplus metal plates of sticky rice and curry, another small boy darted up and proffered an apparently unopened pack of Marlboro cigarettes.

'You like very special cigarettes?'

'What's so special about those?' asked McNeill.

The boy winked. 'Extra special ingredient,' he whispered. 'Hash oil. Only fifty *baht*.'

Man unleased a quiet stream of Thai invective which sent the boy trotting off, laughing, toward a noisy group of *farang* who were falling out of a Tavern-and-Grill across the moat.

Man and McNeill talked about McNeill's list until the last lantern was extinguished and the last vendors had wheeled away their carts and trotted home with their yokes. Man slept on the floor of McNeill's guest house, and four hours later, they continued to talk over bacon and eggs at another stall. McNeill drove Man to the parking lot at the base of Doi Suthep, where they made last minute notes among the parked coaches, cars, minibuses and three-wheeled motor *samlaws*.

'I guess that's far as we can take it,' said McNeill at last.

'I'll go shopping,' said Man. 'And try to get someone into that village. Call you in about five weeks, OK?'

McNeill would have liked to hear sooner. Even assuming that Nina Desanges's news was faked. Five weeks took them into September, early October. But he couldn't push Man faster then Man would now push himself. 'Five weeks,' he agreed reluctantly. 'And take it easy.'

'Look who's talking!' said Man.

McNeill handed over a large roll of dollar bills. They sketched ironic salutes. Man disappeared between the cars. McNeill waited for him to reappear on the road up to the Summer Palace, but the Meo seemed to have vanished. Then he saw him on a shelf of rock half-way up the shoulder of the peak, swinging his flight bag like a school boy on a picnic.

The baby was crying inside a hut. It was the only living thing in the hamlet. Even the chickens were gone.

380

'Leave it!' said Simpson to Boucher.

'Poor little bastard!' said Boucher, entering the hut.

'LEAVE IT!' screamed Simpson. He threw himself onto the ground just as the hut, Boucher and the baby exploded into flaming fragments.

'Oh God!' said Simpson, rocking back and forth on his bed. 'Oh God, oh God, oh God!'

For several months, Piotr Rogov had postponed passing on Major Lucky's 'bombshell' for reasons he did not examine with his usual private rigour. Irritation with Lucky's melodramatic secretiveness may have been one reason. Rogov chose to define his reservations in terms of 'inconclusive evidence'. In any case, he and his superiors in Bangkok had been far more concerned with the recent, furtive installation of US ground to air missiles in Thailand as supposed protection against Communist retaliation against airstrikes launched from Thai bases against Laos and North Vietnam.

Then Rogov had finally been allowed home to Leningrad on leave. He had found his young wife Sophia over-bright in manner and less lusty than when he had seen her last. His mother-in-law was critical of his table manners and his father-in-law patronized him, all of which made Rogov wonder what had been going on in his absence. He returned to Thailand physically sated but emotionally unsettled and, as a result, forgot entirely about the name of an American prisoner that Lucky had trailed like a matador's cape.

When Rogov finally remembered the name, the entire Soviet Trade Mission was preoccupied with a series of battles between the NVA and US Marines at Khesanh, a village propping up the western end of the Demilitarized Zone in Vietnam. The North Vietnamese newspaper, *Nhan Dan*, was claiming Khesanh as the American Dien Bien Phu. The likelihood and implications for Laos of this possibility kept Rogov too busy to follow up the report he had finally made. Lucky asked twice about the progress of his bombshell, then mercifully, seemed to forget about it just as much as the Russians had. Their relationship did not improve.

Suddenly, years later, with the war officially ended and new battlelines drawn between the USSR and China, someone tidying up loose ends wanted follow-up action.

The man, whoever he may be, is probably dead, thought Rogov. . . . Of a stroke while pulling Lucky's plough. After all this time, now they want me to buy him!

After he returned from Chiang Mai the second time, McNeill began to move fast. The ENT specialist gave him six names. Henry Spiegel gave him another twelve plus a few decoy names. McNeill and Simpson drew up a list of eight more. Twenty-six. It didn't leave much slack, but McNeill didn't want to go too public. For example, a former colleague now with the DIA in Washington could have helped, but McNeill didn't know where that man had gone in his head since 1973. After thinking about it, he didn't call him. It was bad enough having that woman on his back!

He did decide to take a chance on an East Chicago friendship even though it went back a long, long way.

Lance Sawyer was on duty when Bill McNeill called. He listened without saying much but his eyes were on the two privates from the typing pool who rattled on, unaware that the receiver had become slippery in Sawyer's palm.

'Let me call you back,' he said. He listened, then scribbled down a number. 'OK . . . Tonight or tomorrow when I've thought it over.' He hung up and wiped his hands on the seat of his uniform trousers though he would have chewed the nose off an enlisted man he saw do the same thing.

He sat down at his desk, unable to remember why he had stood up two seconds before the telephone had rung. To get something, probably.

McNeill was up to something. Sawyer was half-angry that Bill thought he would swallow that reunion bull and half-grateful that Bill hadn't come clean and made his own dilemma worse. Sawyer had a decision to make. The idea of Cowboy McNeill acting as reunion secretary for anything cracked him up. It wouldn't impress any of Sawyer's superiors either, if he got caught out.

The Army had been good to Sawyer. He could see it that way now that he was back home alive and in pretty much one piece. Vietnam had been good to some men like himself – the ones it hadn't wiped off the face of the earth.

At nineteen, black, and looking at a lifetime on an East Chicago car assembly line, he had volunteered for Vietnam to get away from home and become a hero. The worst part of that first year had been coming home to learn that his friends and family didn't think he was a hero. They thought he had been out there killing Third World brothers. But he had learned some good things about himself in that year and nobody was going to take those away. He had guts, and not just on the streets. And he could make decisions under pressure.

His officers had given him the credit he deserved. At 27, he was an E7 sergeant with higher to go and a job with security clearance which opened a world a hell of a lot bigger than East Chicago. He had friends who had shared his experiences. He knew that no matter what the Army asked of him in the future, he had already survived the worst.

The Army was his family now, and his social world. He didn't question it, though he did wonder sometimes about the civilians who gave the Army its orders. Bill McNeill had been a good soldier too. And now he was trying to make Sawyer consider just how he defined the Army – the system and its rules, or the men.

While he waited to hear from Sawyer, McNeill went to see Henry Spiegel again.

Spiegel, wearing shorts and no shirt, was eating a TV dinner in his back yard when McNeill arrived. McNeill noted the well-exercised muscles and flat stomach. Spiegel was serious about keeping fit.

'We're in go-mode,' he told the doctor. 'I need to put together two teams and get him out.'

'Have you got official backing now?' Spiegel's voice receded and surged as he threw the aluminium platter into a trash can beside the house.

'I don't want it,' said McNeill. 'I've been that route before.'

'My professional opinion is that you need a long rest.'

'Here's the photograph.' McNeill laid the copy of Man's first picture on Spiegel's Formica-topped side table.

Spiegel picked up the picture and studied it intently for a long time. 'You trust the source?'

McNeill nodded.

'Give me time,' said Spiegel. 'It's quite a thing to take on board!' He turned the photo over as if looking for a family album style note of names and dates. Then he handed it back to McNeill.

'I need more names,' said McNeill.

'I'll see who else I can ferret out. Go easy, McNeill. You're in deep waters.'

'How about you? Are you in there too?'

Spiegel turned away to search the pockets of his shirt which hung over his chair.

'Jimmy'll need a medic, after this long out there,' said McNeill.

'Ease off, McNeill! I know all the arguments!' Spiegel found a pack of cigarillos and lit one with shaking fingers. 'The men here need me, too . . . Sorry, Bill, do you smoke?'

McNeill shook his head. 'Take your time. We could get in really deep shit.'

'Story of my life,' said Spiegel. He stubbed his cigarillo out again. Then he said, as if answering McNeill's question, 'Bill, do you have any idea how many forms I fill out in a week?'

'McNeill? It's Sawyer.' The typists were at lunch and Sawyer was alone in the office this time. 'I slept on it and decided I can't refuse an old Army buddy a chance to get together with his other old Army buddies.'

'That's good news,' said McNeill. 'Got a pencil handy? Here come the names: Peter John Wilmington, Michael R. Bennett. Hugh Oyama, no middle name or initial. Robert Hoskins. Gaylord Smith. Jesus Burra. Sebastian Xavier Donoghue. George L. Cucic. . . .'

'That's going to be some party!' said Sawyer. 'Can I come?'

'Sure,' said McNeill. 'I'll let you know when I get it together.'

'Let me double-check,' said Sawyer. 'You want just their addresses and phone numbers. Nothing else. Is that right?'

'That's all.' He would have liked their specialities but wouldn't push Sawyer that far.

'I'll go run these through now,' said Sawyer. 'Maybe get back to you tonight.' And maybe run a search for common service units, he thought, to check just how much bull McNeill was shovelling his way.

'Thanks,' said McNeill. 'I couldn't do this without your help.'

McNeill called Mayor John Putnam in Archangelica, California.

Putnam was terse. 'The official word is now that Jimmy wrote the letter, but a long time ago. However, "the situation is in hand". Sorry I can't be more positive, Mr McNeill. And thank you for your concern.'

'Mayor Putnam, has there been more news from Jimmy?'

'No comment, Mr McNeill.' Putnam hung up.

McNeill began to make his telephone calls.

The first name on McNeill's list was Michael Bennett, from a suburb of Boston, who was out the first time McNeill called. The second name was George Cucic, also from Boston.

Like Sawyer, George Cucic had found his career in Vietnam, but it took him longer than Sawyer. For two years after his discharge, he drank too much, couldn't keep a job because he always picked fights with the bosses, and lost his girlfriend who, unlike many others, had

384

waited for him to come back. He drove too fast and was arrested twice. Once was for doing 127 mph on the Palisades Parkway out of New York on a friend's motorbike. The second time was for driving his Chevvy in circles on the Boston Common at 2 am, ploughing up the spring mud across the street from a Vietnamese supermarket. He had been so blasted he didn't know he was doing it. Nor did he know that he had attacked and nearly killed the arresting officer. The judge had put him on probation and referred him for psychiatric treatment; he considered killing the judge. However, it was a shrink or jail.

For the next three months, George tried to keep himself from killing the shrink who kept analyzing George's flashbacks and dreams in terms of childhood trauma and anal retention. Then, he got lucky. The shrink passed him on to another one, who had seen active combat too.

'What's the point of this shitty farce?' asked George at their first meeting.

'Don't know and don't care,' said the shrink. 'But whatever it is, it sure beats recycling guys to go back into combat as fast as possible because some fat-ass officer needs to keep up numbers. Do you want pills?'

'Nope.'

'Do you want to tell me anything?'

'Nope.'

'Great,' said the shrink. 'Then maybe I can have a turn sounding off . . . Do you mind?'

'Nope.' George began to feel interested for the first time.

The shrink lit a cigarette after offering one to George. He put his feet up on the desk.

Man-to-man, thought George warily.

'I get so teed-off,' said the shrink. 'By all the guys who come in here thinking they're Attila the Hun because they did something in Vietnam that their mommies wouldn't approve of. Or cracking up because they shit themselves in combat like most other poor bastards . . . me included . . .' He looked at George. 'You don't do that, do you? Think that you should have done something different and kept someone alive? Even think you were responsible for the whole goddam war! *And* for losing it!'

George looked at the floor.

'I bet *you* don't think for one minute that you're abnormal, secretly, deep down inside. Well, I want to tell you something: abnormal behaviour in an abnormal situation is normal. And I'm here to tell you, Vietnam was abnormal.' He put his feet down again. 'Tell me I'm wrong!'

George shook his head, smiling slightly and looking scared.

George began to accept things he remembered. He dug out other things he had put away, and became resigned to the fact that there was a lot he would never forget. But these memories were in the past. His problem – he even began to use the word – was to decide what to do with the present and all that time that came after it.

He stayed angry that the US had lost the war and that people seemed to blame him and the other soldiers for losing it, but he recognized and accepted this anger. He also accepted that there was no way he could go back and win it. Nor was there any point in going to war at home, against people who didn't even know he was fighting them. There was even less point in going to war with himself.

Then one night a drunk pulled a gun in a bar on Washington Street. George talked him down the way his counsellor had done with him. After he had disarmed the drunk, he paid the bar keeper $20 not to call the cops and took the man home with him.

The man was a vet. They talked all night, and killed a bottle of Jim Beam. The other man had never talked to anyone in the six years he had been back. He cried, which would have bothered George in the old days, before he had seen it happen in a group he had joined, and done it himself. He thought about that night for the next four days. Then he asked his shrink to tell him how he could learn to help too, officially and full time.

The call from the man called William McNeill frightened him. The solid base he had been shoving under his own feet started to shake a little. He didn't know if he had the strength to deal with it all again, for real, not just in somebody's head. And that was what McNeill was really talking about.

Go find out, he told himself. If it worries you, go with the worry. Face it. He's not asking for you to sign on the dotted line. Go to his goddam meeting!

The next man McNeill called, in Pittsfield, New York, slammed the telephone down without speaking. The next, in Augusta, Maine, listened, then very politely said he wasn't interested. The next, in Providence, Rhode Island, gave a guarded yes. The next said 'Fuck off, whoever you are!'

And I paid for a call to Los Angeles for that! thought McNeill.

A man called Donoghue, from Nashville, Indiana, said yes, he would come to a meeting. And so did a man called Hoskings, from Miami.

McNeill himself hung up on a man named Lambert, in St Louis, when he was asked if he minded having the conversation tape recorded. By the time he reached the end of the list (excluding Mick Bennett who continued to be out) in the middle of the following afternoon, he had twelve yeses, including Henry Spiegel. He was just about to try Mick Bennett again, when Nina Desanges walked into his office.

McNeill stood up automatically. 'What the hell. . . ?' he demanded, less politely.

Nina saw his eyes drop to his desk and his right hand pull back from the open file on the desk top. He looked past her.

'I'm alone,' she said. 'And unofficial. I just wanted to finish a conversation without having you hang up on me.' She saw him relax one degree, but only one.

'You stupid bitch,' said McNeill, in a level voice.

That's his first admission, thought Nina. She shook her head. 'Nobody followed me. If you have problems, they're not of my making.'

She looked around. His office was just as she had imagined it – plain and immaculately tidy, everything for a purpose. On the walls were a calendar for a seed company, a large work organizer and a map of the state. A row of labelled coat hooks. Named pigeonholes for employees' mail. A locked cabinet for keys. A rifle over the door. No pictures, or photographs of hostages to fortune, like wife or children.

'I appreciate your caution about the telephone,' she said. 'So I came to tell you in person . . . I'm not bugged, miked or otherwise contaminated. You can check if you like!' She tossed her handbag onto his desk and held her arms away from her sides.

For a minute, McNeill imagined what she would do if he ran his hands over her body. Then he said stiffly, 'That won't be necessary.'

'Thank you,' she said, with glacial irony. 'May I sit down?'

'Are you staying that long?'

Nina took a deep breath and sat on the hard bentwood chair by his desk. Now McNeill allowed himself to close the folder holding what looked to her, upside down, like a list of names.

'OK,' said McNeill. 'Like a drink then?'

'No thanks.' She dug herself into the chair, and watched him sit slowly down behind his desk, cross one shin over his knee, straighten the cuff of his jeans and consider how to tell her to get lost.

'Mayor Putnam has had a second letter from Jimmy,' she said without preamble. 'Saying that he has been given one month more to live.'

387

'That's terrible,' said McNeill. 'But you already told me.'

Nina's rage and frustration drove her to her feet. She leaned over the desk, trying to reach the stubborn pig of a man on the other side. 'For God's sake, McNeill, I'm trying to help . . . Jimmy and you!'

'Miss Desanges, what the hell are you talking about?'

'Is he in Laos or North Vietnam?' she demanded. 'I know parts of both. I want to come too! As a translator . . . a go-between with the local population . . . anything!'

They stared at each other across the perfectly square pile of incoming mail on his desk top.

'My friend I had the drink with knows the area,' said McNeill firmly. 'So do I, if it comes to that.' They continued to stare at each other. McNeill leaned forward suddenly and braced himself on his elbows. 'But it doesn't come to that. Run away home, back to Washington, Miss Desanges! Summer's a busy time in my business.'

'Please!' said Nina. 'I can't take any more lies. I know you're planning to go after Jimmy. I can't prove it, but I know it! And I want you to go, more than you can imagine. And I want to help! I have to help!' When she heard the passion thicken her own voice, she realized suddenly just how intensely she needed to be part of McNeill's search. She held his flat grey-blue eyes with her own dark ones, her pupils large with fervour.

'Oh Jesus!' said McNeill again. She had touched something. She felt him struggling.

She leaned forward too. 'Please!' she begged again.

Then he shook his head. 'No, Miss Desanges. Even *if* I was going to do what I think you think I'm going to do . . . you're the last person I'd let near me! A government spook, or near as dammit! I wish I hadn't looked you up.'

'Thank you for remembering who took the initiative,' she said tightly.

'I don't think you'd blow us,' he explained more gently. 'But it just isn't a necessary risk. You know all about limitation of access to information.'

She glared at him, fairly and squarely caught.

'Anyway,' he said. 'Laos and North Vietnam are no places for ladies in high heeled shoes.'

'Ah,' she breathed, with suppressed feeling. 'Don't jump to patronizing conclusions, Mr McNeill.'

'Aren't you a lady?' he asked blandly.

Nina gave him a mock-sweet smile. 'Straight from finishing school with Group 559.' There, you self-satisfied son of a bitch! she thought. She saw new assessment in his grey-blue eyes but no softening. Then she realized he had probably learned exactly what he wanted.

'No,' he said doggedly. 'The main issue is . . . would be security. Nothing personal. Sorry.'

She recognized a will as strong as her own and far more implacable. She stood up, fighting tears of frustration and humiliation. 'I won't take up more of your time, then,' she said. 'But just for the record, I'm reasonably familiar with parts of the mountains above the Ou River in northern Laos and I swam the Mekong 50 kilometres above Vientiane. I could even mark an airstrip or two for you on the right aerial photograph.'

She marched out of the office. She concentrated on finding the rented car and her car keys, on opening the door, sliding in smoothly and starting the engine without a hiccup; McNeill was watching her from his office window. As she turned out of the parking lot onto the highway, she tooted her horn in insolent farewell.

Idiot! Cochon! she swore at him as she headed back towards the Interstate Highway south. *Bête comme vos pieds!*

For the first ten miles, as she drove back toward Boston and the Washington shuttle, she killed Bill McNeill in as many different ways as possible. After ten miles, she admitted that much of her rage was frustration at not having persuaded him, and anger at herself for having bungled. Stampeded again.

After fifteen miles, she admitted that she was angry at McNeill only because he had refused to answer her own need. Reason told her that he did not need her . . . that his position was logically correct. After twenty miles, exhilaration began to seep into the rage. Rude as McNeill had been, he had also confirmed, as much as he ever would, that he was going after Jimmy Putnam. And however angry, Nina was convinced, after seeing him this second time, that he stood a good chance of success in whatever he set out to do.

Her anger slowly transformed itself to a different energy. She overflowed with the power that had kept her upright under rice sacks along muddy tracks, carried her through corpse-filled *paddis* and pulled her across the Mekong. It was the energy which had once confounded her father's enemies and kept Thu at bay. She didn't see how it could be contained in her office. It would blow out the genteel walls of brother-in-law William's Georgetown house.

What do I do now? she finally asked herself. Now that I have admitted to myself how strongly I feel?

After Nina left, McNeill finally reached Mick Bennett. Bennett became his thirteenth yes.

Mick Bennett was in good shape. He still had the body he had at twenty, just as big but no bigger, with a round innocent face. He played basket ball or football every weekend with friends. He had a reasonable job that paid well enough. Good marriage. Good life style. He and Julia had a car each. His wife had everything she needed to make life as easy as it was ever going to be. They had two cats and a pedigree boxer that Julia bred to sell the pups. No children, which didn't bother Mick as much as it did Julia. Apart from that, everything was great.

Bill McNeill's phone call gave him a stomach pain, as if he wanted to be sick but couldn't. He wasn't quite sure what McNeill wanted, but he got the gist and it threatened everything he had. Then, about an hour after McNeill's call, his phone rang again.

'For you, *again*!' said Julia. 'Aren't you a popular boy tonight?'

'Micky? It's Hugh . . . Hugh Oyama.'

'Blow me down!' said Bennett.

Oyama never rang first. Bennett had rung him from time to time since they were discharged together in 1968 and ended up together in the Boston area. Oyama brought various girlfriends to barbecues. He had bought one of the boxer puppies. He and Mick sometimes got together to watch football on television and bitch cheerfully as men do when there's nothing serious to complain about. They steered away from their feelings about being pulled out of Vietnam after the '68 Tet Offensive. There was a lot they didn't talk about.

Bennett liked Oyama. He knew that his family were *nisei*, interned by the American government somewhere out on the West Coast during World War Two. He had sometimes wondered how Hugh felt about that when he was fighting for America in Southeast Asia, but Bennett never asked. He liked Oyama but never felt close enough to ask embarrassing questions. Oyama was a reliable friend, one you could trust with your life, as Bennett had done, but not a talking friend, like Julia.

'What's up?' asked Bennett. 'Everything OK?'

'You'll never guess what just happened,' said Oyama. 'I think maybe I need to talk to somebody. . . .'

'Yeah. . . ?' asked Bennett carefully. 'Sure. Like to come over?'

'Is Julia around?' asked Oyama.

'Yes,' said Bennett. What a weird question for Oyama to ask! 'She'd love to see you,' he said. 'You know she thinks you're cute.'

'Can you get away?'

'Is it that bad?' asked Bennett. This was very unusual.

'I'd rather talk to you alone. What about a coffee at Ho Jo's on Route 128?'

'Sure,' said Bennett, 'but give me a clue. You raped your landlord? Found a million dollars of Mafia money in a suitcase in the back of your car and don't know what to do with it. . . .'

'Bill McNeill. . . ,' Oyama began.

'Oh shit!' said Bennett. 'How long will it take you to get to Ho Jo's?'

20

Ethan Perry left his office with dread. He had procrastinated, hoping to hear of official developments, before he told Nina about the letter left on the bunk in the refugee camp outside Udorn. When he could no longer justify waiting, he knew he had to tell her face to face. As he paced with long strides through the streets of Georgetown toward his brother-in-law's house, he distracted himself by observing all that he passed with the sharp, poignant interest of an old man who knew that all sensation would be switched off in the imaginable, if not imminent, future. Haines's predicament had made him reflective, as well as uneasy *vis à vis* Nina.

What have I really done with my life? he interrogated himself. How strange to be thinking in the past perfect tense, he then thought, as he observed the white lace trimming of geraniums on Federal facades as immaculate as expensive new lingerie. He sniffed the freshness of minute, newly cut lawns.

He did not know Will John Haines well – but then, he felt he knew few people what he would consider well. From what he did know, he had always thought of Haines as a younger version of himself: a reasonably intelligent nosy parker who used research of one kind or another to pursue the constantly elusive, salty centre of life. Haines still seemed to believe, as he himself had once done, that somewhere in life's tangle of appearances and complexities there lurked a concrete 'rightness', if only it could be found.

Perry had been intrigued by the crisis Haines had clearly suffered upon his return from Saigon in late 1966. After meeting Nina and reading her file, Perry had begun to surmise the nature and extent of that crisis. He envied Haines a turmoil of such genuine content.

His own crises had been those of missed opportunities or of not being listened to, crises of ego and self-image. Of politics rather than passion. His one personal tragedy – the death of his wife – had been blurred by occurring while he was involved professionally in the crises of 1954–1955, when the French were kicked out of Southeast Asia and the contenders to replace them had been jostling and eying each other. The

392

main residue left in his soul by that tragedy was guilt that political crisis had made him forget to grieve for hours, and even days, at a time.

Perry had been perfectly clear about his own motives in taking Nina on as an analyst, apart from her sterling qualifications. They were part envy, part complicity. Now Haines seemed to have been catapulted into the centre of a pure melodrama. And Perry, after a lifetime of seemliness and right behaviour, of measured patriotism and stern protestant morality, of intelligence, rationality and moderation, envied Haines the chance for his melodrama, even at the possible cost of life.

Of course, you have far less life left to lose, said Perry's inescapable, ironic, self-monitoring internal voice. It's easy for you to envy the risk . . . And here you are, where you don't want to be. He turned into the gate, between the paired bay trees in their white Versailles tubs. He did not smile as he usually did, at their stiff pomposity, padlocked to the wrought-iron railings like opera-goers in evening dress protesting wrongful arrest.

He let Nina take his jacket and old wool cap bought between the wars, across the street from the British Museum in London, which he still wore as a memorial to the fervent young graduate student he had once been. Today, she was looking more French than Vietnamese, in jeans and a loose blue cotton sweater with a bare neck, her hair tied back with a scarf – more suited to sailing out of Saunderstown and Newport than the beach at Vung Tao. For some reason, this reassured him, though the sharpness of her gaze did not.

'Sherry?' She walked to the butler's tray by the wall. 'More bad news for me, Ethan?' she asked over her shoulder.

'We've finally had word about Will John Haines,' Perry said.

Nina stared at the faceted stopper of the cranberry glass decanter, which found itself in her hand. Oh God! Nothing more, please!

'He's alive,' Perry added quickly. 'He's fine . . . we think.' He sounded self-conscious, like an over-parted actor, and very faint through the pounding of blood in her ears. 'It's good news that he's alive!'

Nina replaced the stopper carefully in the neck of the decanter, picked up his sherry and turned slowly. She carried the small brimming glass of straw-coloured fluid carefully across the pale blue-grey carpet. The sherry slopped across her fingers and made small dark spots on the carpet.

'Here you are,' she said, with great deliberation. 'Let me find you a coaster. Brother-in-law William wouldn't appreciate a white ring on

393

that candlestand.' She turned away to burrow into a drawer in a Duncan Phyfe mahogany-and-satinwood Greek Revival sideboard.

Perry cleared his throat and sipped the dry sherry.

Nina gave him a coaster, started to pour a second sherry for herself, then abandoned it on the tray. 'What do you mean, "He's fine . . . we think"?' she demanded. 'Don't go silent on me! Where is he! How long have you known?' She sat stiffly on the striped sofa, facing his chair.

'He's being held,' said Perry, 'somewhere in Laos . . . we think.'

'In Laos,' she repeated faintly. She remembered to breathe again and released a long shuddering breath. 'What was the message, Ethan? Let's have the rest of it!' She remembered her own drink and rose to get it, feeling unfocused and out of control. Will John in Laos. Nina in Washington. The world upside down.

' "The tiger has him." Unquote.' Perry finished his sherry, watching her down the ridge of his nose. 'Good melodramatic stuff.'

'The *tiger*. . . ?' Nonsense was becoming sense.

'Yes,' said Perry. ' "Has" . . . present tense. Not "had" or "got" or "ate" or "killed" . . . "has".'

She began to pace; her sudden nervous energy felt as if it would blow the walls from around the room's comfortable, retiring dignity. ' "The tiger . . ." ' she repeated. 'What tiger?'

He shook his head. 'Just "the tiger".'

'*Mon Dieu!* The tiger!' She shook her head, swinging the tail of thick hair back and forth across her shoulder blades. 'The tiger! How strange. . . .' She reached the window of hand-blown glass and pivoted round on the balls of her feet. She did not allow herself to think, yet, but waited for sense to fall into place without being pushed. 'What else? What else did it say? What do they want?'

'That's about it,' said Perry. ' "The tiger has your Will John Haines." ' He spoke the message quickly.

'What language?'

'Vietnamese.'

Of course. 'Any name? Ransom demand?'

'No signature, no demand,' said Perry, watching her closely.

'How strange,' she said again, though it was not strange at all. 'It makes it hard to know what to do next.'

Perry nodded agreement.

'How long have you known?'

'I waited a little while,' replied Perry evasively, 'to see. . . .'

Nina stopped in front of the white-painted bookcase and placed her hands very precisely on two large, leather-bound volumes, as if estimating the distance between them. She decided to give sense a little push. 'Ethan. . . ,' she said dangerously. 'Who is "you" in the message? Whose Will John Haines is he supposed to be?'

He looked down at the backs of his long hands, and at the gaps between the large-knuckled fingers. ' "No good for keeping money or secrets," grandmother always said.' He looked up and met Nina's fierce eyes.

'To whom was it addressed?' She braced her back against the book case. Her face was white and her voice ferocious. Life is about to lurch forward, she thought. 'ETHAN!'

'To you,' he said with resignation and despair.

Sense fell into place. Nina covered her mouth with her joined hands and stared at Perry for several seconds with eyes as wide and dark as the night sky. 'Then I know where he is!' she said, hoarse from the still-forming implications of her words.

'I was afraid you might,' he said.

'You need more sherry,' she observed distractedly.

'I'm fine,' he said, clearly lying.

'What's being done?' she asked.

Perry sighed. 'As much as can be.'

'And what exactly is that?' she demanded. 'Ethan, this is Nina speaking. Remember Jimmy Putnam? I want you to tell me precisely what is being done to rescue Will John Haines!'

Perry stopped pretending to drink his sherry and set it aside. 'A discreet representation has been made to the People's Democratic Republic of Laos,' he said. 'They claim to know nothing about him . . . claim that he isn't even in Laos.'

'They're lying!' said Nina. 'Or ignorant. He is in Laos. I think I know which tiger! And where. I just need clearance to see Big Bird photographs of northern Laos . . . above Vientiane.'

'I don't know. . . .' Perry began.

'Ethan, I have managed not to hate you over Jimmy Putnam . . . because you have helped me as much as you could without sticking your neck out too far. Don't make me lose my respect for you now!' I want to know how brave you are, John Putnam had said to her.

'Don't threaten me, Nina!' said Perry quietly. 'I've been making up my mind for myself for a long time.'

'I'm sorry!' she said immediately. 'I had no right to say that. But Ethan, I can't bear it! You know me well enough to understand what it means . . . I think I can find him!' She burst into tears. 'Oh God! I think I can finally find someone!'

'Don't . . . please,' said Perry uneasily. 'Nina!' He cleared his throat and leaned forward in his chair as if he were going to rise to comfort her. Then he leaned back again. 'I suppose I could ask to see Big Bird photographs of Laos myself. No reason why I shouldn't.'

Bill McNeill gave his knees a quick final polish with the palms of his large hands and cleared his throat. In his office, the self-conscious noisy profanity of the men who knew each other and the polite assessing chat of the strangers died instantly away. A last small explosion of a beer can being opened served as a full stop. In the silence, McNeill heard someone swallow.

'We're all here tonight for different reasons,' he said, 'but the bottom line is that we're all willing to go back.'

Now, no one even swallowed.

'Anybody who misunderstood me before should go now,' said McNeill. 'No hard feelings and thanks for coming.' He looked around the office at the fourteen men who were the result of forty-three phone calls. They sat on all three of his extra chairs, perched on the window sills, leaned against his filing cabinets and sat cross-legged on the floor along the wall. No one moved.

'Back out there? Who would be that stupid?' McNeill asked. He looked around again. The man called Cucic had his arms crossed tightly against his chest and was glaring at the floor.

'Almost anyone would,' McNeill answered for himself, 'With a good enough reason. And I've got that reason for you.' McNeill heard the tightness in his own voice. He wanted to make it work. He cared too much. He was out of practice at caring. Cool out, he instructed himself or you'll blow it.

'I'm not interested in why you agreed to come tonight,' he said. 'I don't care if you want to go back to do it right this time, or to see what the country looks like now, or to look up some whore you promised to marry. I don't care if you're just bored out of your skull and miss the excitement . . . or the mud.'

He heard a sound which was less a laugh than an acknowledgement of his awkward attempt to lighten things up just a little.

Gabe Simpson, Henry Spiegel, Mick Bennett and Hugh Oyama, he already knew. Stillwell, Lewis, Burra, Hoskings and Smith had been Spiegel's suggestions. Donoghue, Doucette, Friel and Lima had been put forward by the ENT specialist.

'What I don't want,' he said, 'is anybody who still needs to prove he's a hero.'

396

He saw Bennett and Oyama, who had arrived together, exchange a look. Stillwell, Burra and Cucic were studying their shirt fronts. The rest were watching him like they were trying to decide just how crazy he really was.

'I'm not crazy,' he said, and was startled by the genuine laugh he got.

Simpson nodded reassurance at him. 'You're reading minds, Bill,' he explained. 'It's OK.'

'I'll vouch for McNeill,' said Henry Spiegel to the group. 'He's no crazier than any other ex-Special Forces maniac. He's obsessive, highly self-motivated, eccentric, unable to adjust to civilian life, can't take orders from idiots and never takes no for an answer . . . absolutely normal.'

This laugh shattered the last of the early oppressive silence.

'OK,' said Mick Bennett. 'Give us this reason for going back.'

'Someone still out there.'

The silence returned, denser than before.

'A POW,' said McNeill. 'Who didn't come back in '73.'

'Sure,' said Scoot Lewis, after a second. 'We know there must be men still out there. It stands to reason. We know there are about 1,300 missing or unaccounted for. Even Graves Registration admits there are 1,300 they can't do anything about.'

'This one's already listed KIA,' said McNeill. 'I know where he is and have proof that he was alive five weeks ago.'

'Holy shit!' said Bennett softly.

The man called Peter Wilmington took his glasses from his thin face and began to rub them on the arm of his shirt.

'Where is he?' demanded Lewis.

'This is a backout briefing,' said McNeill. He smiled. 'That information's still classified.'

'KIA?' asked Oyama. 'Not MIA?'

'What difference does it make?' Lewis sounded angry.

Oyama faced him unhappily. 'It's hard enough to think about all that without opening up something that seemed to be closed . . . Okay?'

'Sorry,' said Lewis.

'How official is this meeting?' asked Burra suddenly.

'Not at all,' said McNeill.

'You mean, you're not an agency spook setting us up?' asked Doucette.

McNeill, Simpson and Spiegel all gave spontaneous barks of derisive laughter.

'I guess not,' said Doucette.

'What's the official position?' asked Burra.

'On what?'

'This POW.'

'He doesn't exist,' said McNeill. 'As far as anyone can find out, including his father. Officially, he's dead.'

'I think I misunderstood when we first talked,' said Burra. 'I thought maybe you had secret government funding, or something . . . that somebody gave you the nod. . . .' He stood up. 'I'd like to leave, if that's all right. I can't afford to get into trouble right now.'

'That's what this meeting's for,' said McNeill. 'Thanks for coming.'

'Good luck,' said Burra. 'I think you're going to need it. That doesn't mean I don't wish it for you . . . and that poor bastard over there. I'd like to help, but. . . .' He opened the door. 'Good luck, and stay out of jail!' He put his head back through the door. 'And don't get wasted now the war's over!'

'Anybody else?' McNeill scanned the room. One down, fourteen to go. He preferred a team of twelve but could go ahead with a minimum of eight. He felt the nervousness of desire creeping up on him again.

'I'll need to think it over,' said Wilmington.

Cross him off, McNeill said to himself. Too bad . . . the Doc said Wilmington was a crack shot, nearly as good as Simpson. And he had been cross-trained as a medic. Thirteen.

Cucic recrossed his arms and legs. 'What's the official military success rate for this kind of thing?'

'As far as I know,' said McNeill, who had made a careful investigation of that exact question, 'Special Forces carried out about a hundred operations between 1966 and 1973.'

Bennett whistled.

'They got one POW out,' said McNeill, 'And he died later from injuries. The rest were dry holes.'

'And those teams would have had massive logistical support,' said Cucic. 'All the resources of Defence Intelligence . . . satellite intelligence . . . Blackbird overflights. . . .' He left his meaning hanging clearly in the air.

'That was the problem,' said McNeill. 'As I see it. Too many people were involved. There were too many chances for things to go wrong. Too much time to get intelligence through the system. Too many chances for leaks – the Pentagon's a sieve, Langley's a sieve, Fort Bragg's a sieve. And there's not one Thai installation that doesn't leak worse than a number ten can used for target practice!'

Shut up, Bill! he ordered himself. Or you will definitely blow it.

398

'And,' he added in spite of himself, 'they depended on the wrong kind of intelligence – from machines instead of men.'

'We definitely know this man stands,' said Cucic at large.

'Give me another explanation for ninety-nine dry holes!' said McNeill, helpless to stop himself. 'And don't try to tell me the men on the ground fucked up every time – they were too good for that!'

Most of the faces in front of him were frowning. That's the last time you let yourself blow, McNeill raged. You may have wrecked it already! He wasn't sure what he would do with his life if this operation didn't come off. In the last few weeks, he had learned that he couldn't face forty more years of Christmas trees.

'Let me take you through the theoretical position,' he said quietly. 'If we go ahead. I think I can show you why our odds aren't as bad as you may think. But I want to read you something first.'

' "The greatest act of war is to subdue the enemy without exchanging blows." ' McNeill read from the little book. 'A Chinese general wrote that two and a half thousand years ago, and we haven't learned yet!' He turned to another page and read again. ' "All warfare is based on deception." ' He turned again. 'He will win who, prepared himself, waits to take the enemy unprepared . . . Let your plans be dark and impenetrable as the night, and when you move, fall like a thunderbolt . . . An army without spies is like a man without ears or eyes . . . Make use of local spies." ' He closed the book and laid it on his desk. 'The VC and PAVN took a few tips from that little book, believe me. And that's what we'll do.'

'As strategy,' said McNeill. 'I see small units – clandestine and combat-avoiding, with local intelligence and guides. Two groups inserted separately. Once in-country, reliable rear support from local population.'

'Gentlemen,' asked Bennett musingly. 'Does anybody else see a resemblance between this man and Mandrake the Magician?'

'Relative advantages,' continued McNeill ignoring the interruption, 'Logistically, we'd be about even. Surprise would give us the advantage if we can stay undetected.'

'If. . . ,' said Cucic.

'Weapons and matériel would be obtained in-country to avoid problems with customs, probably locally made or captured. The source is already indentified and confirmed in principle, but exact details of weapons and delivery are still unknown. Therefore, odds are impossible to calculate at this time and distance.'

They still seemed to be with him.

'The enemy are, and will be, far superior technologically, in both detection and targeting capabilities,' continued McNeill. 'We wouldn't be able to carry effective countermeasures and would have to depend on stealth, evasion, and human intelligence. Clear disadvantage, on paper, is to us.'

Oddly, this admission seemed to cheer Cucic. Friel, however, was frowning harder than ever.

'Not Mandrake,' said Lewis suddenly. 'Houdini.'

'We would also be at a disadvantage in numbers,' said McNeill. 'That's it then – Two counts against, one don't know, and one count in favour strong enough to swing it.'

'You'd have to be pretty sure of your local intelligence sources,' said Stillwell.

'Source,' said McNeill. 'I am.' He looked at Stillwell's sceptical expression. 'He watched my back for a year. And here I am.'

'Why will any of this small-unit clandestine stuff work now when it didn't help us in Vietnam before?' This time it was Lima.

McNeill drew a deep breath and tried once more to cool out. 'It *did* work last time!' he retorted. 'We trained Ho and his men as guerrillas in the 1940's to fight the Japanese . . . it worked then. And then, after we dumped Ho in the '50s to support some prick for Premier who couldn't even keep his own family under control, and pushed Ho into the arms of the commies, we used the same tactics ourselves.' Helplessly, he felt himself gathering momentum again.

'In 1965,' he said, 'we had the local montagnard militia all gung-ho, the villages secured, the peasants whose support we needed pretty much happy with their new roads and wells and anti-malaria shots. Then some prick over here in Washington decided that bombs can tell the difference between a good guy and a bad guy and turned us into the enemy!' He stopped abruptly. 'You know better than to believe what most people tell you about little men in black pyjamas. America didn't lose a guerrilla war. It lost a big battalions, high-tech war, against Russian and Chinese tanks with infinite rear support!'

Friel and Lima blew out air like spouting dolphins. Bennett scratched himself vigorously along the ribs, looking sideways at the others in the room.

'Is he a Meo?' asked Simpson suddenly.

McNeill knew who Simpson meant. 'Yes.'

'And he still wants to know us after we left them high and dry in '73?'

'I helped him down,' said McNeill. 'And his family.' He felt Cucic,

400

Lewis and Smith sharpen their focus. A friendly Meo in place was good news to anyone with the experience to know.

Friel and Lima stood up together, almost as if they had rehearsed it. 'I'd like to. . . ,' said Friel. 'I thought I could . . . wanted to, but. . . .'

'Me too,' said Lima. 'Come on, I'll give you a lift back to town!' He dived for the door with his head down.

'So long,' said Friel. 'Good luck.' He followed Lima to the door. 'It's weird,' he said, 'being all together in a group like this.' He hesitated as if he were going to say something more. 'Anyway, good luck.'

The men remaining in the room listened without speaking to the sound of two car doors opening and closing in the parking lot, and the sound of the engine starting, reversing, shifting up and fading away.

Bennett stood up. 'I'm going to make a speech now,' he said. 'McNeill has hogged the podium long enough. The rest of you keep your yaps buttoned till I say I'm finished.' He walked to the front so he could face them. 'Back in 1968. . . .'

He was cut off by a sardonic handclap started from Oyama and Lewis. '. . . I told you jokers to shut up,' he said with dignity. 'This is serious . . . Anyway, back in 1968, I didn't think there was a bullet with my name on it. I knew for sure that I was in line for the one that said "For whom it may concern." But here I am, with a beer belly and two cars. I've had nine years I didn't think I'd get . . . nine years with Julia that she didn't think she'd get.'

All barracking had died.

'I knew men who had died who deserved those nine years more than I did . . . I mean, I was a *creep* in high school.' He looked around as if for the laugh that was not going to come. 'Anyway, it used to worry me a lot when I got back. It seemed weird to be back when I didn't expect it and didn't deserve it.'

Someone murmured the beginning of either protest or recognition.

'You know what I mean!' said Bennett. 'Then I decided I must have been sent back for some reason, only I couldn't see what it was. When Bill called, I thought maybe this was it. I think this is it.' He folded his arms and exhaled shakily. 'I don't believe I'm fucking saying this!'

'I feel the same,' said Oyama.

'If I could tell Julia, I think she'd agree,' added Bennett.

'Like hell she would!' murmured either Smith or Lewis.

'She would,' insisted Bennett. 'She'd say it was the turn of that poor bastard who's been over there all this time.'

'You can all think about it,' said McNeill. 'There's no rush. I'll get in touch in the next few days.'

401

'No need,' said Simpson brightly. 'Nothing's changed for me. I'm always happy to try a little flooding therapy or. . . .'

'Stow it, Gabe!' said McNeill.

'Nothing's changed,' said Simpson, abruptly earnest. 'I'm in. There's no way out that isn't kidding myself.'

'You know my feelings, Bill,' said Spiegel.

Lewis shook his head.

Mentally, McNeill crossed him off the list. Damn! His other marksman! He felt his hunger like a pain. They were getting so close. He wanted twelve but would risk going ahead with eight. Eleven were still possible but only five were even fairly sure. One medic and one weapons specialist – Spiegel and Simpson. One engineer – Oyama. Bennett – radio man, cross-trained in weapons. And himself. A crucial three to find.

'No rush,' he reassured the rest. 'Take your time. I'll get in touch.'

Simpson stayed behind. 'You're kidding yourself, Bill.'

'What about?'

'About not exchanging blows with the enemy – the "greatest act of war" as your Chinese general said.'

'We can try.'

Simpson shook his head. 'These guys all came tonight because they want to go back to war.'

'They want to pull Putnam out!'

'No, Bill. No. They want to finish off their own unfinished business.'

McNeill stared at his desk top. 'I think you're overcomplicating things, Gabe. I mean, Jimmy *is* unfinished business. There's nothing wrong in finishing that!'

Doucette called the next day to say, no. Hoskings said, no. Smith said, no. Then came two calls from Stillwell and Cucic, both to say yes.

Seven! said McNeill. Come on, God, how about just one more?

Peter Wilmington wrote a letter explaining why he didn't feel he could contribute anything very positive to the project. Donoghue called to say he's like to go one step farther, if he could. McNeill said, yes, but put a question mark in his mind against the man's name.

Then Scoot Lewis, the marksman whom McNeill had crossed off in his mind, rang to say that after sleeping on it for a couple of nights, he would like to come along.

It's on! thought McNeill. With nine. He was almost scared at how good it felt to know what to do next.

'It's not here,' said Nina in despair. 'The sheet I need isn't here!' She stood in a gap in the paper patchwork laid out on the floor of the unused office in the Technical Documents Library. 'Why are so many missing? Didn't you request a full set?'

Perry had been dozing uncomfortably on a plastic chair during much of the four hours Nina had been going through the satellite photographs.

'Yes, I did,' said Perry. 'Are you sure?'

'See,' she said. 'I've matched edge coordinates. This fits here. . . .' She stretched down to a grey-shaded square of a close-up mountain range. '. . . along this edge of this. But there's nothing to go to the east. And the river is interrupted, there.'

It was the river in the painting above the bed in the villa, which had been a map after all. Here, in a cold office in a borrowed country, she had recognized the snake-like twistings around grey contours of mountains, like the face of a friend not seen for years.

'I'll try again,' said Perry. He stood up stiffly from the moulded plastic chair designed for people shorter and younger than himself.

He returned forty-five minutes later. 'It's absolutely ridiculous!' he said, huffing and puffing in exaggerated indignation which was only partially assumed for effect. 'This should be a complete set, but it's still low resolution . . . only fifteen feet. It seems that I need to apply in advance for close-look . . . even as a departmental head! The theatre operational groups seem to have grabbed all the goodies.'

'As long as it's a complete set.' Nina reached gratefully for the new photographs.

Perry rubbed the bottom of his spine and gazed balefully at the plastic chair before sitting again. 'Age may have its privileges,' he said. 'But modern seating isn't one of them.'

Nina riffled through the photos, reading the coordinates. She selected two photographs and picked her way from gap to gap to clip them to the illuminated board on the desk. She stepped back and stood looking, with her head on one side. Then she moved close again and pulled the magnifier over one of the pictures. She moved the magnifier to the other.

Check again, she told herself. Hold back against knowledge. Let it take you by force. She went back to the first photo again, then returned to the second. 'One, two, three, four, five, six, seven, eight . . . the peaks in the range,' she said. 'Ethan, don't go back to sleep!' Her throat had constricted around her voice. Knowledge was arriving like flood waters after a monsoon downpour. The grainy greys of the photographs were taking on colours in her head – light greens, acid greens, dark greens, greens which were almost black. And smells of mould and sweetness and the gamey traces of passing animals. Her ears were filled with buzzing, chittering, whooping, grating, whirring and the rustling of leaves like taffeta petticoats.

' "Fat chance" of sleep,' Perry murmured. 'As my niece would say.' His eyes were totally alert.

'Here's your tiger!'

Perry came to look over her shoulder.

'Here he is!' She could see the unnaturally hard geometry of what was probably Thu's villa. She ran her fingers over a lighter line, free of trees, south of what was probably the Tiger's Head. Then she touched the ridge running north from the peak. 'I do need a higher resolution for this one sheet!'

'You're not Imagery cleared,' Perry said. 'And I'd have to give a reason in writing.'

Nina stared at the photograph, tense as a clenched fist. 'What about enhancement?' She had not forced knowledge but it had arrived, nevertheless, to take her over. A wilderness had settled into a set of coordinates on an aerial photograph.

'What exactly do you want to determine?' he asked.

'Whether there's a trail here.' She drew her finger along the mountain ridge to the north of the bump she had called the Tiger's Head. She felt the ice water of terror in her gut, which in no way countered the force of her knowledge. Here – if there were a trail – was where she had waited for the shout from Thu's men as she had walked away toward Major Lucky. Here, she had walked, waiting for a bullet between the shoulders from Thu's gun.

'At this scale, it's too narrow to read as a line. If there is a trail. . . .' The face she turned toward Perry showed only her knowledge and excitement, not her terror. '. . . I can show you where Will John is being held.'

'Why do you think you know?'

'I have a cousin I have nicknamed The Tiger. . . .' She was stopped by the unhappiness in Perry's eyes.

'The same cousin who sent you the defaced passport?' he asked.

She nodded, reluctantly.

'And that peak is the villa where he took you,' he said.

She nodded again.

404

'Oh, my dear. . . ,' said Perry. 'I don't think I like this situation at all.'

She turned back to the photograph and waited. After a moment, he leaned over her shoulder. 'Show me this possible trail one more time. A former colleague of mine deserted to the nit-pickers. I am prepared to "lean on him".' He put inverted commas around the Hollywood gangster's phrase with ironic theatricality, as if that would somehow make this situation – which he didn't like – less serious.

'Nit-pickers?' asked Nina.

'NPIC . . . National Photographic Interpretation Centre. They're inter-agency . . . Olympian in their detachment . . . have no stake in territorial protection.'

'Please do "lean on him",' she said. 'I want you to be as sure as I am. It's like recognizing a person you haven't seen for a long time. You're afraid you'll make a mistake, but when you see them, you *know*! I know where Will John is!'

'One step at a time, all the same,' Perry said gently. He began to help her gather up the photographs.

She heard him clear his throat and braced herself.

'Nina. . . .' He tapped a handful of photographs on the desk to even out their edges. 'There's no confusion in your mind, is there?'

'I don't understand,' she said, knowing exactly what he meant.

'About who you're looking for?' He harumphed unhappily and inserted the photographs back into their envelope.

'Do ambiguities alter the main picture?' she answered finally.

He was back in two days with confirmation of the trail. Nina marked a copy of the photograph, and he went away again. Nina was reasonably patient for a week. Perry assured her that he had passed on the photograph and her information. After two weeks, she began to ring Perry daily. After three weeks without further news, when Perry dropped by to give her some minutes of a meeting he wanted translated from Vietnamese into English, Nina exploded.

Perry looked uncomfortable. 'I have no idea what's happening either.' He wandered along the white-painted lines of his brother-in-law's built-in bookcases as if studying the titles ranged on them.

'Ethan! Look at me!' Nina was poised in the middle of the pale blue carpet as if about to attack him. Her fists were clenched and her lips white around the edges.

'Is this another Jimmy Putnam?' she demanded. 'Is Will John too embarrassing, too?'

'Nina, I really don't know!' He ran a hand over his high, broad dome of a head. 'At least five different departments and committees in the various services and the State Department are working full time on problems like Will John and Jimmy Putnam. We don't know what's in their minds. They don't advertise their priorities to other departments unless they want our assistance.'

'And they haven't asked yet for your assistance in either case!'

He shook his head. 'Not yet.'

'Then nothing has happened and nothing is planned!' she said. 'You know it's not!'

Perry returned to the bookcase and raised his head as if reading the spines of a set of Victorian travel books. 'There's a slight feeling in certain sectors that Haines rather brought it on himself.' He thrust his hands deep into his trouser pockets and jingled nonexistent change.

'What on earth do you mean?'

'It seems,' said Perry to *Voyages in the Holy Land*, 'that he refused to take the military escort which the remnants of the Royal Lao Army provided. Left it at the border and went to the rendezvous naked. The Laotians are in a panic that the US will think they abandoned him . . . not without reason. Certain elements in the military do tend to think the worst about native troops, as you know. The Vientiane station is trying to reassure them but that leaves Will John looking either naive or irresponsible. "A Lone Ranger fixation" someone said he had. Anyway, he's a civilian, and only loosely attached to the company. . . .'

Nina left the room. She understood what he was doing but she couldn't bear it.

Perry followed her to the little kitchen at the back of the house.

She kept her head down, peeling a clove of garlic.

'This isn't what *I* think or want,' he said. 'It's the current state of reality.'

She began to chop the garlic, without answering, concentrating intently on the minuteness of her task. Her shoulders and arms were stiff with rage.

Perry stood in the door of the kitchen, his great dome of a head just missing the top of the frame. 'You've been living with that reality long enough now to understand it,' he said.

Fiercely, she sliced the stems from four tomatoes, squeezed them viciously over the sink and threw them into the blender belonging to Perry's brother-in-law.

'I know you were involved with Haines,' he ventured. 'But I always wondered just how much. . . .'

'Ethan, shut up and go away,' said Nina. She bent to remove a green pepper from the refrigerator.

'Harumph.' He cleared his throat uncomfortably. He watched her decapitate the pepper and remove the seeds. As she sliced it into rough chunks, her knife left deep grooves in the wooden cutting board.

'Aren't you taking this a little. . . .' he began.

She tossed the pepper into the blender and turned the machine on. In the small kitchen, it roared like an aircraft engine. She turned a stiffened back toward Perry and appeared fascinated by the smearing of red and green against the glass of the blender.

'I'll let myself out,' he said inaudibly under the mechanical din.

Just as he was about to shut the front door behind him, she switched off the blender.

'I could lead them right to him!' she called from the kitchen. 'Like picking an apple off the supermarket shelf!'

As soon as Perry had left, Nina went out to a nearby bookstore where she bought a large map of northern Laos prepared by the Defence Mapping Agency Aerospace Centre in St Louis, Missouri, with a scale of 1:500,000. She already knew what she was going to do, but not how she would do it.

21

'My place?' Simpson couldn't keep the panic out of his voice.

'It's the logical place,' said McNeill. 'Isolated and the right kind of terrain. There's enough room. And you sometimes hunt so a shot or two won't bring in the State Police.'

Simpson looked out the window of McNeill's office, at the trucks between their lines. McNeill knew how much he was asking and didn't care. Simpson tried not to feel enraged. And he was angry with himself for the panic that McNeill's perfectly logical request had caused.

'I suppose it makes sense,' he said. McNeill seemed to be somewhere else, and Simpson felt bereft in a way he couldn't define. 'All right,' he agreed. 'You can use my place.' The hair follicles on the back of his neck tightened and coldness rippled under his ribs.

'Good,' said McNeill. 'Here's a list of some stuff we'll need, and some cash. Can you get it?'

Simpson took the list. I've never invited anyone but you up there before, he said silently to McNeill. Not even my family. He wanted McNeill to acknowledge the enormity of what Simpson was conceding but McNeill seemed to take it for granted. He wouldn't have done, before the last Chiang Mai trip.

'Stay cool, Gabe,' said McNeill.

'What the hell are you talking about?' Simpson stalked to the door. 'I'd better head for the supermarket.'

McNeill watched Simpson's motorbike until it disappeared around a bend in the road.

In the next week, Simpson bought beer, whisky, wine, bacon, paper plates and cups, eggs, tuna fish, beans, condensed soup, cheese, candles, paraffin, rifle shells, rope, heavy string, baling wire, plastic sheeting, garbage bags, razor blades, a cord saw, and three metal-case cigarette lighters, endearing himself to the local shopkeepers as he never had before.

'A few friends are coming up to do some hunting. College friends,' he explained. A total of nine, in the end.

'He must be getting better,' the shopkeepers said to each other. 'Never much liked company. Getting sociable again. Good sign.'

'The amount of liquor he bought. . . ,' said the owner of the liquor store, '. . . keep your heads down when those boys start shooting!'

Bennett and Oyama were the first to arrive, at 4:17 on Thursday afternoon. Bennett parked his car in the turning circle and they crunched on foot up the track toward the cabin.

'Where the hell's Gabe?' asked Bennett. 'Oy, Simpson! . . . Fuck this backpack – weighs ten tons!'

'That's middle age,' said Oyama cheerfully.

'Nope. My Colt and two boxes of lead . . . Anybody home?'

The two men emerged from the trees and saw the cabin on the brow of the hill above them.

'Simpson! Your guests have arrived!' bellowed Bennett. 'Get out the cocktail snacks!'

The cabin was silent. Nothing moved. The two men hesitated slightly then followed the faint track leading upward through the grass. Bennett poked his head through the open door.

'Anybody home?' He turned back toward the hillside.

Oyama stood gazing at the distant peaks. 'Feels good up here. I can see why Gabe likes it.'

'Simpson!' yelled Bennett. 'I'm going to eat your fucking porridge! Then sit in your chair. And then I'm going to sleep in your goddam bed!'

'Maybe he went shopping,' suggested Oyama. He sat on the bench in front of the cabin and leaned against the log wall. 'This is really OK!'

McNeill arrived next, on foot, carrying a large, bulging pack. 'Where's Gabe?'

'AWOL, boss,' said Bennett. 'But I found some beer, so everything's cool.'

The second car, carrying Lewis, Cucic, and Stillwell rocked and grated up the track to the turning circle at 5:15. Lewis reversed the Pontiac and parked it pointing downhill, as if ready for a quick getaway. Stillwell put his head out the window and howled. 'Ak-Ke-La! Wolf pack, owowowouuuuuooooo!'

Donoghue arrived alone on a motorbike and climbed the track to the cabin quickly.

Spiegel arrived last. Simpson watched him from his cover behind some blow-down birch as he had watched all the others. The older man hauled his backpack from the back of his station wagon, fiddled with its straps and zippers, took off his windbreaker, folded it precisely and undid some of the straps on the pack to stow the jacket. He locked the car. Unlocked it again to get a map and a box of cigarillos from the glove compartment. He put the cigarillos into the breast pocket of his sweatshirt and patted it. Then he stood looking up the hill along the track to the cabin.

Displacement activity, thought Simpson. I know the feeling.

Spiegel took the cigarillos out of his pocket, lit one, and leaned against his station wagon.

Simpson watched Spiegel smoke and imagined walking up the track alone. He saw himself lurking, like the deer, in the edge of the woods, not quite able to step out into the once-silent space around the cabin. He stepped out from behind the blow-down.

'Godalmighty! Don't do that to me!' said Spiegel. 'You'll short-circuit my pacemaker!' He glanced at Simpson's rifle.

'Sorry.' Simpson stepped over a fallen log, lifted a branch of sassafras out of his way and joined Spiegel in the turning circle.

'I was remembering,' explained Spiegel. 'Being out on ambush and wanting to smoke. And the number of guys who did it. I used to die, I wanted to so much . . . but I never did. It was my superstition. Smoke, and you get taken out. I used to think somebody in my unit would frag me, just to get an officer who would let them smoke.' He offered the little box to Simpson. 'Like one?'

Simpson shook his head.

'No,' said Spiegel, 'I suppose you're right. Time to plunge into the thick of things.' He rubbed his cigarillo on the sole of his shoe and put the butt into his pocket. 'It's good of you to let us do this.'

'Yup!' said Simpson with feeling. 'Thanks.'

As they slowly climbed the track, Spiegel said, 'You know, I never got together with a group like this before . . . not in nine years.'

'Wow!' said Lewis. 'What a place! This is great! Really great, Gabe.' He bounced on the balls of his feet like Ali, then dropped into a defensive crouch. 'We're going to have fun! We're going to have us a *lot* of fun!'

'Where's Oyama?' asked McNeill.

'Gone for a walk,' said Bennett. 'He'll be back.'

'We've got four days,' said McNeill, 'to get rid of our beer bellies and remember what we used to know.'

'Who said we forgot?' demanded Cucic.

'That'll be great,' said Lewis. 'Man, I keep fit. I'm not as soft as all that yet. There's this great gym near where I work. Only the guy there doesn't give a back rub like the mamasan in Danang.' He winked and gave a nostalgic wag of his head.

'What's he on?' Cucic muttered to Bennett.

'Dunno, but I want some,' replied Bennett.

Simpson went into the cabin to make a pot of coffee. Out of the side window, he could see Oyama walking slowly around the patch of garden, hands jammed into his pockets, head down as if counting the pumpkins.

'Bill, may I say something?' asked Spiegel, when Simpson had poured them all paper cups of coffee. 'I'd like to clear up some details of procedure.'

McNeill nodded.

They had settled on the bench and ground around the front door of the cabin. As he handed round the coffee, Simpson decided that Oyama, Stillwell, Spiegel, and Donoghue were about as happy as he was. Bennett had elected himself jester to lighten the mood, Lewis was spinning in his own private orbit and Cucic was letting nerves make him aggressive.

'Bill and I agree that it would be helpful to decide formally to organize ourselves into a military unit. It's the pattern we all know. Our reflexes respond to that pattern. . . .'

'Yeah, but *how* do we respond?' Bennett was smiling but only just.

'I took that for granted,' said Lewis.

Donoghue nodded.

'I expect most of us did,' said Spiegel, 'But I just want it to go on record, so there's no misunderstanding sometime in the future. You've probably already figured out that we make up two A teams. And I think we should agree that Bill is our commanding officer for the duration of the exercise.'

'If it's OK with you, Captain Spiegel, it's OK with me,' said Bennett.

'Yo,' said Lewis. The rest nodded agreement.

'Right,' said Spiegel. 'Bill will assign roles in due course. Bill. . . .'

McNeill leaned forward and put two photographs on the ground in the centre of the irregular circle of men. 'These were taken last month. That's our target.'

There was a surge of movement to the centre, muttered conversation and passing of the photos and then the silence of deep preoccupation.

'Oh man!' said Bennett at last. 'Oh shit! The poor bastard's really real!'

'His name is Jimmy Putnam,' said McNeill. 'He was taken inside Cambodia in 1968.'

Oyama had closed his eyes as if he were asleep. Lewis was still holding one of the photos, staring at it.

'Simpson knows him,' said McNeill. 'He got the first word.' He looked around the circle. 'I'm not going to tell you any more . . . not till the end of the weekend, in case any of you changes his mind about coming along.'

'I won't drop out,' said Cucic, 'Unless you're a goddam liar and the whole thing's a fraud. Those photos are enough for me . . . assuming you know where they were taken!'

'The man with the camera is the one taking us in,' said McNeill. 'Now, drink up and let's go for a walk.'

'Come on, Bill! Ease off!' begged Bennett. His round face was red and lines of sweat ran down from his hairline. 'We got to take it slower at first. Some of us are really out of shape. I don't want a heart attack at thirty!'

McNeill's 'walk' was a four mile run, down Simpson's drive, across the highway and into Forestry Commission land. They thudded down logging roads, along endless avenues of dark pines and spruce, past clearings filled with stumps and abandoned machinery. McNeill's large, awkward-looking frame bounced along easily. Like Spiegel, he ran every day. He watched the others. Bennett and Donoghue had a long way to go. Gabe ran like a greyhound; he was used to sprinting up and down his mountain.

'I want to live . . .' panted Bennett, 'long enough to see how those women look now . . . when I'm not wondering if they've got . . . glass up their pussies or . . . are about to call in the local VC goon squad.'

Lewis looked angry when he ran, head down, brows clenched, fists pumping. Oyama was running in a trance and Cucic was tiring, though not as much as Bennett and Donoghue. As they began the ascent back up to Simpson's cabin, the last two and Stillwell slowed to a walk.

'That was instructive,' said Spiegel wryly, when they reached the cabin.

'But do I want to know what I learned?' retorted Bennett from the ground where he had flung himself flat on his back, limbs akimbo like a large bearskin rug.

'Give up?' asked Oyama.

'No way!' said Bennett. 'Gimme time. I'm gonna dig this gig! Right, Lewis?' He lifted his head from the ground to look at Lewis, who was seated nearby, stretching his hamstrings. Then Bennett let his head flop down again. 'Right,' he answered himself.

'Chow time,' said McNeill. And when it gets dark enough, we'll carry out a night exercise.'

'Can't we work on our bird-naming and knot-tying badges,' begged Bennett. 'Just for the first night? And what about dirty jokes and songs around the campfire? We could build up some espree duh core!'

Donoghue disappeared sometime during the preparation of food. Heads lifted and turned at the sound of his motorbike starting up in the turning circle.

'He's the only one with any sense,' said Bennett, to break the silence.

Back to eight, thought McNeill. No slack left.

By midnight, the Alpha Group friendlies, operating from a base in the turning circle had successfully captured a six-pack of beer from the target root cellar. However, the smaller number of Beta Group hostiles had made one kill and taken one prisoner. Simpson, reluctantly, had made the kill. Bennett had crawled up and practically begged him to do it. Both groups returned to supply base in the cabin to drink Alpha Group's liberated six-pack and two more from the cellar. The exercise had broken what ice had remained after the run.

'You stupid fuckers sounded like a goddam herd of elephants!' said Cucic. 'I could have taken you single-handed.'

'So why didn't you?' retorted Stillwell, a surviving attacker. He stood, leaning against the cabin wall. Bennett was sprawled on Simpson's bed. Spiegel, by tacit consent had been left the single chair. The others sat around the wall, or leaned against the still-warm wood stove, picking twigs and leaves from their hair and clothing.

'Because we could hear him grunting like a rutting hog,' said Lewis, the attacker who had actually extracted the six-pack. 'Every time he had to move.'

'They fell for it,' said Spiegel, the Alpha Group leader. 'Diversion . . . magic!'

'Bennett's quiet tonight,' observed Lewis.

'Cause I'm dead, you dumb bastard,' said Bennett cheerfully.

'Where's Gabe?' asked Oyama.

'What's up, Gabe?' McNeill followed Simpson through the dark to the root cellar on the side of the slope. Simpson sat against the little door, arms tight around his knees, staring at his bare feet. McNeill squatted beside him, a large dark blotch on the lighter background of drying grass. 'Does it bring back too much?'

'Everybody's having too much fun!' said Simpson. 'It's in their eyes. They're having a ball . . . except for a few minutes when you showed them Jimmy's picture. They miss it!'

McNeill said nothing.

'*I* was having fun there, for a while,' said Simpson. 'Got a body count of one, all by myself. It felt good, for a minute. A real buzz!'

'Nobody really misses it,' said McNeill.

'They miss something!' said Simpson. 'Listen . . . right now, to their voices!' They sat in the dark listening. A whoop of laughter came from the cabin, and the sound of two voices vying for the floor. 'You miss it, Bill. You haven't had so much fun in years. Admit it!'

McNeill sighed and settled his buttocks back onto the grass. 'I feel I know what I'm doing – and *that* feels good.'

'Well, it scares the shit out of me, if you want to know,' said Simpson. 'I was witness to evil and I still don't know what to do with it. I feel now like. . . .' He raised his face to the sky. 'Oh, to hell with it.'

'Like what?'

'. . . like snakes, twitching and stirring, like when they're just waking up in the spring, or if you pick up the rock they're under. When I start to have fun, like tonight, I feel we're about to wake those snakes up.' He lowered his head and pressed his kneecaps into the hollows of his eyesockets.

'Do you want to stay here?' McNeill's voice was light. 'It's OK.'

'Oh, it may scare me, but I have to go,' said Simpson, almost drily. 'I thought about it enough while you were over there! I've seen Jimmy's picture. I know he's there and can't get home. It's real. I can't walk away again, like I did at the end of my tour and leave the other poor bastards to carry on. I've got enough shit there already behind my shoulder that I'm not looking at.'

This time there was a very long silence. Finally McNeill said, 'I don't want anybody doing this trip as a kind of group therapy.'

Simpson laughed. 'Well, you've got quite a little problem there, Mr McNeill, because there's nobody who isn't doing just that!'

'I'm going to get Jimmy out,' said McNeill, a little stiffly.

'Sure, Bill. Sure. No sweat.'

'I'd like you to come,' said McNeill. 'You're the best shot in this group for sure, and one of the four best I've ever seen . . .'

'I'm the very best that I know,' said Simpson. 'Bar none. Have been since I was seven. That's terrific, except that I came back from war a

414

goddam pacifist! I don't believe in war as a way of solving anything any more, and I just happen to shoot better than I can write, or analyze a text, or play the piano, or grow pumpkins . . . probably better than I screw!'

'You've got a free choice,' said McNeill. 'That's why this time is different.'

'Bullshit,' said Simpson. 'The first choice may be free, but after that, circumstances take over. They've already taken you over. . . .'

But McNeill had turned away to head back up the hill to the cabin for a post-exercise de-briefing.

Forty minutes later, Oyama came down the hill to where Simpson was still sitting.

'Everybody's turning in,' he said. 'It's like Copley Square at rush hour. Is it OK if I sleep out here somewhere?'

'Sure,' said Simpson, 'Take your pick.' He waved his arm across the hillside. 'You have a free choice.'

'Do you want to be alone?' asked Oyama.

'Not really,' said Simpson. He watched Oyama arrange himself into a dark caterpiller in the silvery grass and wrap a ground sheet around himself. 'Maybe I'll go get my bag and come down here too.'

In the middle of the night, he thought he saw Bill McNeill walking across the hillside. He waited until he was certain he could identify the shape, then went back to sleep.

McNeill woke everyone at 6:00 on Friday morning. After breakfast, they began timed laps, wearing backpacks, around a course which Simpson had helped McNeill set on Wednesday. The course traced a sagging curve around the mountaintop, cross-country and through an area of heavy blow-down left by the last winter's storms. Spiegel and McNeill were the judges – Spiegel with stopwatch and McNeill with a time sheet. The others had been assigned to teams which took turns as referees along the course.

'Bennett!' shouted Simpson. 'Get the fuck under that tree, not around it!'

'I'm not doing the course!' panted Bennett. 'Come to the cabin on the double! Spiegel's gone berserk and is beating the shit out of McNeill!'

That weekend, after studying her map, Nina flew from Washington to Boston, rented a car again, and headed north to see Bill McNeill. She wished now that she had never made that first impulsive visit. All she had to do now was convince him that she wasn't a Defence Intelligence spy trying to infiltrate his mission.

His office was in disarray. A broken bag of chipped bark was leaking onto the floor just outside the half-open door. A plaid wool jacket had been slung over the bentwood chair. Two mugs stood on the desk top in a pattern of dried coffee rings. A teenage boy was muttering into the telephone while examining his dirty work boots, which were lodged on the desk edge. As Nina pushed the door further open, he swung his feet down and stood up in a panic which ebbed as soon as he saw who she was.

Or who I'm not, she thought, looking at the wadded paper balls which had missed the wastebasket and an open can of Coke on the window sill.

'I'm looking for William McNeill,' she said.

'Not here,' said the boy.

'I guessed,' said Nina. 'Where might he be instead?'

The boy wavered between flirtation, patronage and hostility. 'Why do you want him?' You, of all people, said his eyes, hostility winning.

Me of all people because I'm a gook? wondered Nina. Or because I'm female? Or because I look too flashy and citified?

'I'll tell him that,' she said politely but firmly. 'Are you in charge at the moment?'

Hostility moved over to let patronage enter his eyes, along with a tinge of pride. 'Right now, I am, yeah. Mr Blake's out on a job.'

'Do you know where Mr McNeill is?'

'Nope.'

'Is he out of the country?'

'Dunno. He's away till Monday.' He sat back down behind the desk.

'When is Mr Blake back?'

'Dunno.'

'Soon enough for me to wait for him?' asked Nina.

'Dunno,' said the boy. 'Sometime tonight.'

'I'd like to leave Mr NcNeill a message,' she said with resignation. 'Do you have some paper, and an envelope?'

He opened four drawers before he found them.

When she had finished writing, Nina sealed the envelope and placed it herself into Bill McNeill's carefully identified pigeonhole.

'Holy shit!' said Bennett.

Watched by most of the men, Spiegel hit McNeill again. 'Why are you here?' he demanded.

McNeill stood with his hands tied together behind him and looked at the floor. Oyama was behind him holding a rifle. Spiegel hit McNeill again, hard enough to throw him off balance.

Cucic stepped forward. He was still panting from his last run around the course. 'Ease off!' he said to Spiegel. 'This is only an exercise.'

Spiegel turned on Cucic 'Did you write the rules? Do you know what the rules of this exercise are?'

'While we were running our nuts off, you seem to have apprehended a hostile,' said Cucic. 'Sir!' he added sardonically.

'And would you care to tell me what my instructions are, in that eventuality?'

'To my knowledge this was not generally determined before beginning the exercise.'

'Well, let me remind you of something that seems to have slipped your mind,' said Spiegel. 'There are a lot of rules in combat that nobody's going to read out to you beforehand. And a lot more get changed, and somebody just might forget to write you a memo. It's easy to forget. Every one of you has been making assumptions ever since you arrived about how safe you are and what you think the circumstances are. Well, start changing that mind-set right now. Don't take anything for granted! Do that in the field and you're dead. When we get out there, it will be too late to change.'

He glared around the group, including Stillwell who had just arrived, breathing hard. Cucic balanced on his toes as if considering an attack on Spiegel.

'What's going on?' demanded Stillwell.

'Yeah,' said Lewis to Spiegel, 'but we know we're not really back in Nam. We're having a great weekend up here at Gabe's place. You can't ask us to really believe we're in danger. Not yet. It's not possible.'

Spiegel turned his back on him. 'Carry on questioning the prisoner,' he said to Oyama. 'Sit down, Cucic!'

'I thought Bill was in charge,' muttered Cucic.

'Sit the fuck down!' bellowed Spiegel. 'Your goddam leader has been captured! He's a fucking prisoner of war! Can't you get that through your head?'

'Heeeey. . . !' Cucic half-started to sit but rose back up again, fists closing.

'Prisoner!' barked Spiegel.

'Sit down, Cucic,' said McNeill. 'And listen up. I'm about to break down under interrogation.'

'What's going on?' demanded Cucic at large. 'Will somebody tell me!' As a compromise, he perched on the edge of Simpson's table.

'Join the dummies' club,' said Bennett.

'Now,' resumed Spiegel to McNeill. 'You're going to tell us what you are doing here. My personal opinion is that you're a Kuomintang opium smuggler, but the consensus of my colleagues is you're a Russki spy.'

'I'm a Pathet Lao sapper,' said McNeill. 'Last night, I laid mines in the woods around this cabin, and set non-explosive booby traps. The mines don't carry large charges – they're real but they probably won't blow your feet or balls off – just shock the hell out of you. The booby traps could smart a little. Protect your eyes.'

'Are you serious?' asked Simpson. He already knew McNeill was. That was why he had been crossing the field at 4:30 am.

'Yes.'

The fire which Simpson had made in the glass-fronted stove to cook breakfast spat two small explosions of sparks into the silence while the group stared at McNeill.

'Come on, man . . .' said Oyama, dropping out of his character as co-interrogator. 'Is this on the level?'

'Yes.'

'Spiegel,' implored Bennett, 'is he still playing a game?'

'No,' said McNeill, 'I'm not.'

'I don't know,' said Spiegel.

'Lunch!' said McNeill. 'Would somebody like to untie me?'

Oyama obliged.

When McNeill was free, Simpson asked again, 'OK, Bill. Now the game's over. Were you kidding?'

McNeill gave him a long cold stare. 'How many times do I have to tell you. The woods are mined.'

'I got it, I got it,' said Bennett. 'It's a good idea. Great. I like it. Just tell me, is it just the woods? What about the cabin? You're such a sneaky bastard. Can we eat lunch without getting indigestion, or have you mined the cabin too?'

'Make your own mind up,' said McNeill.

'Holy shit!' said Bennett once again.

Though lunch passed peacefully, McNeill could feel the change in their rhythm. The group's new alertness survived through the first part of the afternoon, during which Simpson led them down to a stream to fill their backpacks with rocks.

At 3 p.m., when McNeill set up a row of Number Ten tin cans, one for

418

each man in the group, no one had yet detonated one of the supposed mines. No one had yet seen a booby trap. Then again, no one had gone very far off routes covered that morning during the timed laps, the trail Simpson had taken to the stream or the area right around the cabin.

'You got us,' said Lewis admiringly. 'We bit. Hook, line and sinker.'

McNeill shrugged and drew a long line in the dirt parallel to the line of cans. 'Get your backpacks.' He reached into his own, took out a rock, and lobbed it through a lazy arc into one of the cans. 'Every rock, goes in a can doesn't go back in your pack.'

'Unfair!' complained Bennett cheerfully. 'I played football. "Bulldozer Bennett". Never touched the ball in four years of high school. The rest of you're probably baseball or basketball champs.'

'I was a runner,' said Simpson, hefting a rock. 'I did cross-country to avoid throwing balls.' He threw and missed the can. 'Balls bring out the worst in man.'

'For every one missed,' said McNeill, undeterred by the obscene barracking that followed Simpson's double-meaning, 'two go into your pack . . . which you're going to run up and down the hill with.'

They threw rocks for forty-five minutes. At first they were noisily obscene. Then they settled down to serious competition.

'I've filled my pack four times already,' said Spiegel. 'You sure you still want me to come to your party?'

'As long as you let Oyama throw your grenades for you,' said Bennett. 'Or Bloody Bill McNeill.'

After grenade throwing practice, they ran up and down Simpson's track for nearly an hour, past the turning circle almost to the main road, then back up the mountain again, carrying their loads of rocks. When they arrived back at the cabin, red-faced and panting, McNeill said, 'One more time.'

'Come on Bill, ease off a little,' begged Bennett. 'We're getting there. We're getting there!'

'I'm not convinced yet,' said McNeill. 'But there's hope. Come sit down and I'll show you what I hope we'll be carrying when we can get out there.'

'Tough son of a bitch, isn't he?' Bennett asked the rest of the group. 'But good with animals and children.'

They adjourned to the bench in front of the cabin and hauled Simpson's chair out of the cabin. Lewis sat on his pack.

McNeill brought out a Chinese sniper's rifle, an automatic pistol and a Chinese copy of an AK.37. 'Pass them round. This is what we're

419

likely to get out there. You'll all get a chance to practise before you go home.'

They took it in turns to dismantle and reassemble the weapons, and to squeeze off one or two shots at the cans. Dusk was thickening fast and the first fireflies were beginning to blink over the grass of the hilltop.

'It looks like an airfield out there,' observed Lewis.

Bennett opened a bottle of whisky he had brought with him and beer was passed round.

The mood of the group began to relax and mellow, helped along by exhaustion and alcohol. When the weapons were put away, serious drinking began, except for McNeill, who sipped a single beer. He felt high and didn't want to blunt the edge. He hadn't felt that edge for a long time – just a little, perhaps, in Fang, with Man.

Simpson began to dump cans of cream of tomato soup into a saucepan and Oyama piled cold cuts onto paper plates.

'There's more beer over in the root cellar,' said Simpson.

'Yo!' said Bennett. 'That sounds like my kind of errand.' He trotted away downhill.

The explosion came two minutes later. The echo seemed to circle the mountain twice.

Spiegel, Stillwell, and Lewis hit the ground while the echoes still rattled from mountain ridge to mountain ridge. Simpson knocked over the tomato soup and found himself crouched, staring at the sizzling red rivulets burning black on the sides of the iron stove. Oyama just froze, with his left hand full of sliced pastrami. Only McNeill was still standing, motionless, looking down the slope toward the root cellar.

'Bennett!' whispered Spiegel. 'Oh my God! Bennett!'

'He's OK,' said McNeill.

Nobody moved. The silence was just as shocking as the explosion.

'Oh my God!' murmured Spiegel.

Then they heard Bennett coming.

'You goddam fucking bastard!' he was saying. 'You motherfucking bastard, son of a bitch bastard, McNeill!' He was breathing hard, nearly in tears. 'I'll kill you! I'll fucking well kill you. I swear to God. . . !'

He stopped when he saw the others slowly raising themselves from the ground. 'I could've lost my hand!' he said. 'Do you know what this bastard did. . . ?'

'Exactly what he warned us he'd done,' said Spiegel. 'Exactly what he said.' His voice was shaky. He brushed dead grass from the side of his thigh. 'Alpha plus, Bill.'

'I got burned,' said Bennett. 'He nearly fucked me up! Bill, I swear I'll kill you!'

'Good,' said McNeill.

'Nothing seriously hurt but dignity,' said Spiegel. He picked some leaf from his track suit pants.

Nobody spoke. Bennett just stood, still breathing hard, staring at McNeill.

Simpson got up from behind the stove and looked for a cloth to wipe up the charring puddle of soup. Oyama began to place the pastrami onto the plates carefully, one slice at a time. He went round three times, then stopped and leaned on the table.

Lewis sat on the bench and dusted off the knees of his jeans. 'What a bunch of heroes we turn out to be!'

'We don't need heroes,' said McNeill.

'A moment of truth,' said Spiegel. 'Now we all know what assholes we really are! What a relief to get it into the open! Bennett, you were spared a pitiful sight.'

Bennett advanced a few more feet. He examined his right hand and shook it loosely in the air. 'Dammit, Bill!' Then he sat down on the bench beside Lewis and nursed his hand. 'Bastard,' he said under his breath but with diminishing force. 'Bastard.'

Then he suddenly looked up again. 'Shit! I forgot the beer!'

There was a collective intake of breath. Simpson stopped rubbing at the stove with his steaming cloth. He and Oyama looked at each other.

'Anybody going to volunteer to hold my hand?' Bennett stood up. 'OK, no volunteers. But so help me, Bill, if you've double-trapped it, I really will kill you this time!'

He marched away into the darkness, following exactly his earlier path. The group waited much longer this time for his return. After four minutes, there had been no second explosion. After seven minutes, Bennett reappeared, triumphant with four six-packs. He placed them at McNeill's feet.

'There you are, you son of a bitch. There's the goddam beer. And the last time I go anywhere tonight. And when I have to go for a slash, you're going to walk right in front of me!'

He poked his head through the cabin door. 'Where's the chow? We definitely need new caterers – good staff is so hard to get.'

'Ease off,' said Oyama. 'Just ease off, as you would say.'

Their noise level that evening never reached the heights of the night before.

True to his promise, Bennett took McNeill by the arm and marched him out the door with him when he needed a pee.

'Don't do anything we wouldn't do!' called Cucic.

'Belt up!' said Bennett, 'Or I'll use you for my sweeper.'

'He's done it!' crowed Lewis to the rest in the cabin. 'We're fucking there! He's got our heads turned round the right way, right here in the good old US of A!'

'Not yet!' came McNeill's voice, receding in the night toward the privy. 'You just had your last meal you're going to get up here!'

'But we have two days to go,' protested Oyama. 'And I'm hooked on cold cuts!'

Lewis gave a mock-fiendish laugh. 'A resourceful soldier is never at a loss. Remember what the teacher told you at jungle survival school. We can always eat each other. Too bad you haven't got a dog, Gabe old buddy!'

By 3 a.m. Saturday morning, Lewis, Stillwell, Cucic, Bennett and Oyama had raided the local general store. They reappeared on the mountain noisy with triumph.

'Get up, you bunch of pansies, and look what we brought you for breakfast!' bellowed Bennett. 'So stick this up your ass, McNeill!' He dropped onto the ground two filled brown paper bags which announced that they had been made from recycled paper.

Stillwell kicked the nearest sleeping bag, which turned out to be Spiegel.

'We left money for what we took,' explained Oyama.

'Yeah,' said Lewis. 'Adding it up was the hardest part. You'd think these Mike Foxtrots never got past first grade!'

'Good job,' said McNeill. 'I hate to miss my breakfast egg. How much trace did you leave?'

'Not a thing! Not one box of Cheerios out of line by even a hair!'

McNeill considered the situation briefly. 'Stillwell, set up a listening post in the turning circle.'

'Nobody saw us.'

'Come on, Stilly baby,' said Bennett. 'The man's right. And what about our cars?'

'There's a logging road a quarter of a mile east of the bottom of my drive,' said Simpson. 'You can drive around the chain. A couple can park in there. Spiegel, why don't you park your station wagon down the other way, near the fishing spot by the bridge.'

'Please, sir,' said Stillwell. 'Send me down my breakfast. I went to a lot of trouble to get it.'

★

Oyama replaced Stillwell at 7 a.m. At 10:00, he trotted back up the hill.

'Vehicle approaching,' he said. 'ETA, two minutes.'

'Get your packs and into the woods!' said McNeill. 'Scram!'

The sheriff was fatter and less fit than Oyama. He arrived eight minutes later, puffing and red in the face. McNeill and Simpson were sitting on the bench outside the cabin sipping mugs of coffee.

'Hi, Gabe,' he said. 'Sorry to bother you so early.' He nodded affably at McNeill, but his eyes were cool.

'Bill McNeill,' said Simpson. 'Sheriff Barker.' After a beat, he asked, 'Like some coffee?'

The sheriff had put his head through the cabin door. 'No thanks,' he said. He strolled away from the bench to look down the slope toward the root cellar.

'Had any trouble up here lately?' he asked.

'Quiet as a tomb,' said Simpson.

'What about those college friends of yours?'

'What's up?' asked Simpson. 'Did somebody drive off the road on the way home?'

'There was a break-in down at Dooley's, last night. I was wondering if maybe you guys got a little over-excited or something. . . .'

Simpson shook his head.

'How bad?' asked McNeill. 'Any damage?' His pulse was beginning to settle now that he had decided that Nina hadn't sent Barker.

The sheriff swung back around to study McNeill's bulk. 'As a matter of fact, no. A real professional job.'

'Doesn't sound like a bunch of drunks having a reunion,' said McNeill mildly.

'They left enough money to pay for what Dooley reckons they must of took.'

'Doesn't sound very serious,' said McNeill. 'Nothing much to lock anybody up for.'

'I guess not.' The sheriff maintained his pointed scrutiny. 'I just don't like wise-ass trouble makers.'

McNeill nodded his large head in agreement. 'Sounds like kids.'

'Have some coffee, sheriff,' said Simpson with dangerous glee.

Sheriff Barker switched his gaze. 'No thanks,' he said. 'I just feel I ought to say, Simpson. . . .' His eyes swung to the interior of the cabin again. 'A lot of people aren't too crazy about having somebody who might be a nut living up here . . . they worry about their kids and dogs.' He placed one foot over the threshold and peered at something. 'You could get a lot more trouble from the locals than you do, if I didn't keep things cooled down from time to time . . . How many guns you got up here?'

'My hunting rifle,' said Simpson, suddenly sobered. 'For which I have a licence.'

'You're sure that's all?'

'The others brought theirs but they took them home again.' Simpson didn't look at McNeill.

'Uh huh!' The sheriff gathered himself to leave. 'Just don't take advantage, you understand?'

'Of course,' said Simpson stiffly. He and McNeill watched the sheriff disappear onto the track down through the trees.

'Them and us,' said McNeill. 'Cowboys and Indians.' He was relieved it was nothing more than that.

'I've opted out of all that,' said Simpson.

'It's not up to you,' said McNeill. 'They've got to punish someone for losing the war.'

Sunday was spent in serious rehearsal of what to do if ambushed, if one of them was wounded, if they had to pull back under fire. They practised silent signalling. They trooped off in a convoy of cars to a cliff above the little fishing river where they practised basic rock climbing and rappelling down a vertical rock face.

'Put gloves on your lists,' said McNeill.

They went over equipment lists, necessary injections, blood groups and Thai immigration procedures.

'And get fit,' said McNeill again and again. 'We're none of us young as we were.'

As they gathered themselves to go home at dusk on Sunday, McNeill produced some patches, crudely machine-embroidered onto felt.

'We can wear these,' he said. 'Nobody'll know what to make of them if we're taken.' He handed one to each man. The patches showed a pair of joined hands and the motto, *Fratrem liberare*. To free a brother.

The men accepted their patches silently and seriously.

'I'm going back out there now,' said McNeill, 'To organize rear support and intelligence. I call you all when I get back and we'll meet to bring you up to date. We're going for this next dry season . . . between November and Easter. I'll have firm dates at our next meeting.'

'And now back to the real world,' said Bennett.

'Nope,' said Stillwell. '*This* is the real world, only they don't know that.'

'I hope to God you're wrong!' said Simpson.

'You mean,' said Spiegel to Simpson, 'that you hope they never have to learn what you know is real.'

After they had all left, Simpson felt lonely for the first time since he had moved up to his hilltop. He walked restlessly around his garden patch then back to the bench where even the long open view toward the twin-breasted peaks failed to soothe him.

22

Laos – 1977

'Bangkok don't believe you actually have this American Putnam in your possession,' said Rogov. 'We don't believe he's still alive. It's been too long since he was captured. If he had been in Hanoi, or somewhere with proper facilities. . . .'

'I have proper facilities,' said Lucky. 'How careless to wait so long to get back to me, if that is what worries them. I confess that I had given up on all of you.'

The two men stood once again on the knobbly-kneed pier above the Ou River. Rogov drew a deep breath and slapped a mosquito, hard. His own role in the delay was one he preferred to blur as much as possible. As for his superiors – for two years they had said they preferred to deal with Hanoi on such matters, where there were procedures to follow, rather than with local brigands. Unfortunately, this prisoner was not in Hanoi but here, in the armpit of Southeast Asia and they now wanted him, brigand or no brigand. Someone finally bothered to read my report, thought Rogov glumly.

'They're not certain enough of his worth to want to gamble,' said Rogov.

They had been certain about that pilot, thought Rogov. Certain enough to whisk him back to Moscow for interrogation before Rogov had been able to ask much more than his name. So much for dreams. Rogov was still here, slapping mosquitoes on the pier above the Ou River.

'Not certain of his worth?' Major Lucky's voice rose in dramatic indignation. 'I suppose I should be grateful that they ever got around even to considering it!'

There's more than a grain of truth in that, thought Rogov. He glanced down at the boatman waiting in his launch.

'Captain,' Lucky said, aquiver with reproach. 'Oh, Captain Rogov . . . Mihailo. Do you take me for a bumpkin?'

Yes, thought Rogov viciously. A bumpkin! A greedy *stuckach* . . . informer! A slave dealer! An Asiatic mini-Hitler. An ignorant, treacherous, francophile, opium-dealing bandit. With delusions of grandeur.

426

'Never that,' he answered smoothly, irony more or less under control.

'Don't let him know the value of what he's sitting on,' his senior officer in Bangkok had said. 'What ever you do, don't let him know!'

'But he *will* know,' Rogov had said despairingly. 'If we show sudden interest after all this time!'

'You underestimate me,' said Lucky. 'And you may be too late. I am not without my own connections, of one kind and another.'

It was going to look as if Rogov had handled the whole affair badly. 'They won't like that,' said Rogov severely. 'They won't like other fingers in their pie!' He waved an irritable hand into the cloud of gnats around his head. '*If* he were to turn out to be of value,' said Rogov, 'what are you looking for?'

'The father is willing to talk,' said Lucky, as if dealing a full house.

Rogov's hand paused in midair as if asking permission to speak. 'He's *what*?'

Lucky just smiled.

'How do you know?' asked Rogov.

'I contacted him.' Lucky raised the point of his chin, unpleating the folds beneath it slightly, and held the Russian's eyes defiantly.

Rogov was speechless. He was going to be in very serious trouble. He didn't care. He had had enough . . . of dragging on and on in this arranged marriage . . . of the heat and mosquitoes . . . of feeling like a pimp to a series of intelligence whores . . . of pretending to like it. 'You!' he exploded. '*You* contacted the father? You? A provincial bandit who likes to dress up in French clothes and pretend to be a cultured man. . . !'

Lucky's eyes had gone metallic, like pewter.

'How dare you presume?' demanded Rogov. 'How dare you think you could handle the father, or do anything with what he can offer? Do you realize what damage you may have done?'

'To what?' asked Lucky quietly. 'To whom? To you . . . perhaps. And with great pleasure.'

The two men eyed each other like gladiators searching for the gap between breastplate and shield.

'Go home!' said Lucky with sudden fury. 'Go home and tell your masters to send someone who doesn't make stupid jokes with long-time friends. Tell them I want to speak to someone with more authority . . . who has a wider perspective of world politics than you, my friend.'

For one dangerous moment, Rogov was tempted to take Lucky's advice. To get out of Southeast Asia. Never to have to sit in that damned launch among the mosquitoes. Never to have to be polite to this ass again. It had felt wonderful to tell him at least one home truth. Rogov was tempted to continue as he had begun. Then reason returned and he pulled himself together. There would be too many other 'nevers' accompanying such an act of professional suicide.

'I'm afraid you have to deal with me,' he said stiffly. 'Or not at all.'

Lucky marched several fierce paces before he deigned to reply. '*If* I deal with you people at all,' he said, mimicking Rogov's earlier emphasis. '*If* you have the sense to know that what I'm selling costs more than a few boxes of machine gun shells . . . a few military knickknacks for the silly, ignorant natives. . . .'

He stopped and faced Rogov with such intensity that the Russian thought he was squaring up for a bout of fisticuffs.

'Listen to me carefully, my friend,' said Lucky. 'You're not an American fobbing the Indians off with beads and gewgaws. I'm talking politics now. I'm talking about alliances, and military support. I want you to back me in trade against the Kuomintang bandits! I want the Russians to fly my opium to Bangkok!'

Rogov started to laugh. He didn't mean to. He didn't even want to. It was the kind of helpless, snorting, giggling fit that used to overcome him in school. He had managed to control it then, after two beatings by teachers. It had threatened again from time to time during his army training, then eased during his years in England as a mature student. It alarmed him because it never seemed proportionate to the apparent cause. Each trigger seemed to unplug a deep artesian well of hysteria. Now he stood snorting and shaking on the wobbly wooden pier, peeking through eyes half-closed by laughter, at the cold rage and indignation on Major Lucky's face. 'It's too much!' he wheezed between gasps for air. 'It's all too much. . . !'

I just want to go home, he thought with passion. I don't care if I'm stripped of my rank and end up as a clerk in a town hall somewhere! I don't care if I have to teach elementary arithmetic to idiots in Vladivostok or count turnips on a collective! I just want to go home!

'I'll. . . ,' he began. He gasped for breath. 'I'll p . . . p . . . pass your message on,' he managed to say before giving up and letting out a full-bellied whoop.

'I forbid it!' said Perry. He sat in the wing-back chair, his large hands set squarely on the ends of the arms, like a monarch issuing an edict. 'I don't understand what you hope to accomplish.'

428

'To persuade my cousin to set Will John free!'

'You are absolutely mad! You don't even know for certain that your cousin is holding him. Not for sure!'

'What do you mean by "know", Ethan? how do you achieve certainty?' Nina flung herself in a circle around the living room like a panther around its cage. 'I *know*! I can't produce rational arguments and documentary proof . . . but I know!' She turned on the old man sitting straight-backed in the wing chair. 'Don't you ever just know something, without all your paraphernalia of reason and proof?'

He looked at her silently. 'Often,' he said. 'But I seldom act on it.' He studied his legs, stretched across a yard of pale blue carpet. 'For example, I know that if you go wandering off into northern Laos in this insane mercy mission you want my help with, I will not see you again.' He sounded angry.

Nina stopped in mid-stride. Her dark hair was loose; she threw a strand back over her shoulder. 'Does that matter?'

Perry cleared his throat. 'It would be most inconvenient.' He cleared his throat again. 'I suppose I had hoped to have someone to annoy when I retire next year. "Adopt-a-grandpa" . . . that kind of thing.' He glared at her. 'But that is not why I am forbidding this adventure. It's both impractical and dangerous! The Communists may now control most of Laos, but they're still fighting off all the other factions. Territorial control still shifts like the tides. And between you and me, China is beginning to shuffle her feet in the wings. You'd find yourself in the middle of a battlefield!'

'It wouldn't be a new experience,' Nina said quietly. 'And I'm not sure I don't miss it.'

'Ah,' said Perry, as if he had been winded. After three seconds of silence, he returned to the attack. 'And how would you get there? You can't hike in to the Tiger's Head as if on one of our Sunday strolls. The Air Force can't fly you in through PAVN and Russian radar.'

Nina felt the warmth of power slipping through her veins, along with her blood. She recognized the sensation from many years before, when she had outfaced the Corsican Carbone and other business opponents. She had felt it when challenging Thu, in the early days of their relationship. She had felt it each time she had known that only she, alone, was responsible for making a certain thing happen in her father's world. Recognizing this revived sensation almost distracted her from her present purpose.

'You only have to fly me to Chiang Mai,' she said. By believing things, she had once made them happen. Even Bill McNeill would recognize the force of her decision.

429

'I won't authorize anything,' said Perry stubbornly.

'Not even a holiday? I have a lot of accumulated leave due.'

'And you want to take it in Chiang Mai?'

'Where else?' She held his eyes.

'Why?' exploded Perry. 'Why are you so determined? What do you owe this man, Haines? He left you pregnant in Saigon and basically shopped you to us, even if that wasn't his intention!'

Perry's brutality almost checked her momentum. The warmth hesitated in her veins. Then she said, 'Will John didn't know I was pregnant. Don't blame him for that.' She pulled up a hassock and sat squarely in front of Perry. 'Ethan, how do you think that a French-Vietnamese *métisse* found the courage to sell her father's opium business . . . considering the clout fathers carry out there?'

'Not to act out some fairy tale of marriage to Will John Haines and life happy ever after in American suburbia,' said Perry, stating a fact. 'You weren't that naive, not with your history.'

She smiled. 'When desperate, you use any available source of strength. Will John gave me a bearable image of myself. He was a beacon marking my escape route. My illumination.' Her smile faded. 'I hoped, of course . . . one is never completely pure in motive. And there was the baby. . . .' Now she couldn't look at Perry's angry face any more. 'And I may still love him.'

'Don't go,' said Perry.

'Help me.'

He looked away.

'If Will John is still alive, and Thu sent that message, then my cousin wants something more,' she said. 'I think he wants me. Logically, therefore, when he has me, he will let Will John go. Will John is Thu's "bargaining chip".' She leaned farther forward and tried to intercept Perry's eyes which were fixed on the candlestand. 'There's a rational argument for you.'

Perry continued to gaze at the candlestand. 'There's nothing rational in merely trading one life for another. Nothing is gained.'

'One may deserve more than the other.'

'You're not making some insane atonement for sins you imagine you committed in the past, I hope!'

Perhaps, thought Nina, in surprise. Perhaps that is part of why I feel I must go. But there's something else too that I don't yet see clearly. She shook her head mendaciously.

'Not to atone,' she said. 'To be consistent. Help me be consistent,' she begged. 'Help me act on the only reality by which I can still define myself – the choice I made at twenty-six, with Will John's help, whether he knew it or not. Help me to do what I believe is right.'

Perry shifted his gaze down his long legs to his feet in their Gucci loafers.

'All right, Ethan,' she said, 'I just want to go back. All the rest is true too, but at the bottom, I have to go back!'

After a very, very long time, he nodded.

'Don't look so miserable,' said Nina lightly, feeling sudden grief at losing him, even in her triumph.

'But I am,' he said, sounding surprised.

She slipped off the hassock and knelt beside his chair. *'Je t'aime beaucoup.'*

Perry nodded again, opening and closing his folded hands like a nursery game.

'I wish that didn't make you look just as miserable,' she said.

'It has such a valedictory ring.' Perry watched his hands continue to open and close. 'I think I'm just jealous,' he said with forced dryness. 'I wish your life here were enough to keep you.'

She leaned forward and stopped the restless movement of his hands with her own hand. His gaze, when he looked up was as direct and clear as a child's.

'I'd come with you,' he added suddenly, 'if I weren't so old.'

She settled back on her heels beside him and held the sharp gaze of this aging bird of prey. 'And I'd stay with you, if I were a little older,' she said.

He pointed his noble nose at the pale blue ceiling. 'I'm not sure the old ticker can take such a compliment. Too much emotion altogether. Why don't we adjourn for dinner and discuss your overdue holiday in Chiang Mai?'

She laid her hand again on one of his; it covered a little more than half. 'Ethan, *je t'aime, vraiment.* Truly.'

'Yes,' he said. 'And you understand me too. To hear it in bald English would cause a stroke on the spot. Where did you put my cap?'

Two days later, he arrived at her house with a plastic bag full of travel brochures for Thailand, including several for Chiang Mai.

'You're to write this holiday off to expenses,' he ordered jovially. 'I need someone to have a sniff around the tri-border sources.'

He followed her into the house and handed over his jacket and cap. 'There's a local Thai newspaper editor I'd like you to look up for me,' he said. 'An old friend from OSS days . . . used to be a damn good

431

photographer. I like to stay in touch with him personally.' With his drink, he took his usual seat in the wing-back chair by the fireplace. 'And there's Howard the professional Brit, of course,' he called after her, as she went into the kitchen for ice for her whisky. 'I'd like to know if he's still alive and kicking. The old guard keeps dying off. . . .' He raised one bristling eyebrow at her when she came back into the room. 'In fact, you'll be far too busy to go off looking for some *farang* who got himself into deeper water than he meant.'

She bent and kissed the top of his head, just where the peninsula of silver hair encroached on the high, wide dome. The reality of what she was going to do had just begun to stir the pit of her stomach.

'I still wish you weren't going,' he said. He caught her hand in his dry, long-fingered one. 'There will be nothing I can do to help you if you leave Thailand.'

'I know,' she said. 'Please tell me that I won't be on your conscience.'

'You're really frightening me now,' he said. 'Why does this cousin want you back so badly?'

'Family sentiment,' she said lightly. 'You know how we are about family.'

Nina and McNeill met in New York in a coffee shop in Pennsylvania Station.

'Lady, get off my back!' said McNeill as he reached the table where she was waiting. 'Do you know how much damage you could do showing up at my place, leaving me billy-doos where anybody could open them?'

'Not as much as you imagine,' said Nina tightly. 'And it's time for us to start talking frankly. If I were going to blow your mission, which you assure me is not taking place anyway – much as I wish it were – I would have done it by now! I want you to listen to me for a few minutes.'

'Let's go sit in a booth!' He walked away without looking to see if she had followed.

Nina ordered two cups of coffee at the counter to give herself time to calm down. 'I'm going into northern Laos,' she said after she had sat down opposite him. 'As soon as possible. I need help getting to a certain place, starting in Chiang Mai. If, by any chance, you and your old drinking friend over there had any suggestions, I would be grateful. If you knew anyone I could travel with, I would be even more grateful. And if you would stop insulting my intelligence by lying, I'd be most grateful of all.'

McNeill seemed engrossed in soaking up with a wad of paper napkins the coffee which had slopped into his saucer. 'I'm sorry, Miss Desanges,' he said finally. 'There's never been anything personal in all this. I think I'm a little jumpy. It makes me jumpy to have an employee of Defence Intelligence trying to horn in. I already used a contact you gave me. Apart from that, I worked hard to stay away from official channels. I'm sorry if I made you mad.' His apology sounded straightforward and sincere. 'But I still don't want to say where we're going, or when, or why. I hope you understand.'

It was as much of an admission as he was going to make.

'I'm going after someone too,' she said, focusing on him the full force of her will. 'Also without official backing. I need your help. So does the man I'm going after.'

McNeill studied his hands, then shook his head. 'Sorry.'

'Then I hope we don't fall over each other,' said Nina. 'I don't want Round Eye Boy Scouts clogging up the trails and making the Border Police and crossing masters jumpy! If we can't help each other, could we at least arrange to stay out of each other's way?'

Again McNeill shook his head. 'Nothing personal, as I said.'

Nina leaned heavily against the back of the booth. Neither the official or unofficial Americans would help her. In Bangkok, she had once thrown iced water in Pat's face for suggesting she approach the only allies now left to her. She wished she could talk to John Putnam about making choices.

Harry Junor watched from behind the old garage until his mother's old pick-up truck disappeared down the rutted driveway. When the sound of its engine disappeared in the direction of Winnepaka where she did most of her shopping, he let himself into the kitchen through the screen door.

She should lock up when she goes out, he thought. But she said she never had and she never would. It was unneighbourly, and if someone wanted to break in, they were welcome to anything they reckoned was valuable enough to take.

He looked around. There wasn't much to steal. She was right about that. But the world had changed. He'd have to talk to her sometime about the kinds of people there were these days. She couldn't imagine. Even old ladies weren't safe.

From old habit, he lifted the lid of the crockery cookie jar. It was empty except for a piece of crumpled cellophane and some dried-up raisins that looked like mouse turds. He replaced the lid quickly and went into the living room to telephone. He dialled fast, before he could change his mind. He'd let it ring ten times.

Someone answered on the seventh. 'White Mountain Property Maintenance.'

'Mr William McNeill, please,' said Junor.

'I'm sorry, Mr McNeill is away from the office at this time,' said the man on the other end.

Junor took a deep breath. 'When's he back?'

'I'm afraid I don't know,' said the man. 'But you just missed him. He's out of the country, in fact. Can I help you until he gets back?'

'No,' said Junor. 'That's OK.' The receiver was slippery in his hand. He hung up.

Out of the country and the man didn't know when he was coming back! That gave Junor all kinds of crazy ideas about what McNeill could be doing.

He prowled the living room for a few minutes, then went upstairs to look at his old room in the gable of the steeply pitched roof. The small, wooden-walled cubicle with the single bed was neater than it had ever been when he lived in it. The other difference was a big picture his mother had put on his chest of drawers, his high school graduation picture, with his medals pinned to the velvet picture frame, and his silver cup from swimming and some dumb ashtray he had made out of clay when he was about ten. There was also a bunch of plastic roses and lilac in a jar by his picture. Like in a cemetery, thought Junor.

He left his own room and stood for a long time outside the closed door to his brother's room. But in the end, he couldn't go in. He knew that his mother had put Dickie's picture up in there, like his own in his room. He went back downstairs and out into the open air of the front yard. He didn't feel like going back up into his woods yet.

Milkweed was growing up through the steps and poison ivy was sneaking out from under the porch itself. The milkweed pods had split and the little parachutes of silk were blowing all over.

The yard will be full of milkweed next year, thought Junor. His mother was letting things go. Tough as she was, she was getting too old to do it all. He went round to the back of the house to the woodpile. The axe was leaning up against the wooden saw-horse and a log lay on the sawed-off stump that was the chopping block, with the splitting wedge still stuck in it. Junor split it and a half dozen more logs, to burn off the effect of his crazy thoughts about McNeill and his trip out of the country. Then he went back into the kitchen, dug around for a pencil stub and a scrap of paper and left a note.

'Back in a week to phone again. Love, H.'

★

434

A few weeks later, when Mrs Junor returned from Winnepaka with the groceries, she knew somebody was in the house. She hesitated a minute at the door then marched in. If anybody wanted to bump off an old lady, she would give them a hard time first. She put down her brown paper bags and took the .22 off its hooks over the door where her husband had hung it. Then she went upstairs. She could hear whoever it was clearly now.

Probably a squirrel got in, she told herself. Or a bird. Animals always sound bigger than they are. Particularly when you live alone.

'Who's there?' Lord, I sound old and scared, she thought. 'Who's in there?' she demanded outside Harry's door.

'It's me.'

She pushed open the door. He was on the floor with his butt in the air, digging under his bed.

'Where's my stuff?' he asked. 'Where'd you put all my stuff?'

She leaned the rifle against the wall in the hallway, so he wouldn't see it and think she was getting nervous in her old age and start to worry. 'What "stuff"? What kind of word is that?'

'My uniform and stuff.'

'I put it back in the chifferobe, in case you needed it. What're you doing down there?'

He pulled out a cardboard box with papers and photographs held together with rubber bands. Then he took his uniform, washed and pressed, from the cupboard and put it into the box. 'I'm going to get rid of this junk,' he said. 'Give it to somebody else.'

'If you say so.' She leaned on the door frame. 'Who you got in mind?'

'I don't know,' he said. 'Just so it's not me.' He stood up and grinned at her, with the box under his arm. He carried it downstairs as far as the kitchen door. He put it down beside the door, suddenly undecided. He looked at the box for a minute. 'I'll find somebody.'

'How about some coffee?' She felt him watching her as she reached to put the rifle back up over the door.

'Sure.' He left the box, with relief. 'Here let me.' He put the gun on its hooks and sat down at the table. As she made two cups of instant coffee, she saw him looking back at the box again.

'I suppose you want to keep Dickie's. . . ?' he asked suddenly.

Mrs Junor picked a fruit fly off the top of the coffee in the second mug. She didn't use her china that much. 'Well, he's dead, isn't he. You just give yours away. That's fine with me.' And good riddance to it! She sat down and brushed away a crumb from her breakfast toast. 'That's just fine!' She brushed again at the clean oilcloth. 'Would you like to sleep down here tonight? Like you did before. I won't bother you or nothing.' She tried to keep any pleading note out of her voice.

He looked at the rifle she had brought upstairs with her to investigate a noise, then at his box beside the door. Then he looked at her. 'I might,' he said. 'Don't know for sure, but I might.'

23

Nina arrived in Chiang Mai two days after McNeill, Simpson, Cucic, and Lewis had already travelled north to Fang. She had changed planes in Bangkok, without stopping in the capital. Another self lived there, waiting like an unsettled spirit to repossess her; she had several exorcisms to perform before she could safely return. As the Thai Airways flight left the central plains and began to fly over the swelling of mountain foothills, covered in the grey-green sponge of secondary jungle, Nina became cold and sick with excitement. The silver scales of flooded rice fields on the flanks of the sleeping dragon mountains stirred shadows of the past lodged somewhere deep in her being. Of travelling to Dalat with her mother. Of looking down from the Tiger's Head, with Thu's hand resting on her nape, while the swifts brushed past in the dusk and bats squeaked on the edge of her hearing.

She had thought she had a plan, but the reality of the country beneath her, and the vastness of mountains that waited for her, stretching away to the east, unravelled her thoughts. Then the green mass of Doi Suthep rose from the Chiang Mai valley, topped by the golden spike of Wat Prathat, and the plane began to descend into Chiang Mai International Airport.

Outside the airport, Nina resisted the importuning taxi drivers and chose a three-wheeled motor *tuk-tuk* for the short journey into the city. Under the flapping blue plastic awning, she turned her face to the undeterred sun and sank into the clamour of the motorcycle engine and the driver's transistor radio, playing *gamelan* rock, which was strapped on top of the battery by his feet. A garland of plastic jasmine and tuberose on the awning frame whirred in the wind beside her ear.

In spite of old enemies who awaited, the heat unfolded in her bones and opened her spirit like a flower. The life in the streets – the barber, the vendors and tea sellers, the children, the buffalo asleep on the tarmac, the indignant chickens, the bicycles labouring under bundles of straw and wicker baskets of ducks and bunches of bananas as large as the driver, the honking taxis and the buses painted and garlanded like weddings, the mangey three-legged dogs nosing in the gutters, the smells of damp and freesias and sewage and rosewood and curry powder and dried fish, the school girls in white blouses and old women squatting beside flat bamboo trays of duck eggs and lemon grass calling cheerful obscenities to each other – all overwhelmed Nina's senses. This place was not home, but it was very like home.

Perhaps I can manage without my father's old friends, she thought. Maybe I don't have to look for friends of the Chiu Chao merchant. Perhaps I can find a way!

She checked in at her hotel, an anonymous modern refit of a 1930's guest house not far from the Eastern Moat Gate, changed from her American suit into a white silk blouse, green cotton skirt, and sandals, tucked money and her passport into a shoulder bag, ignored the hotel coffee shop and stepped back out into the noisy heat of the streets to buy sticky rice and vegetables from a stall.

Here I am! she thought. Just being here is too much. I need time that I don't have, to take it all in, before I tackle the problems of getting into Laos past military checkpoints, guerrilla patrols and the territorial boundaries of opium war lords. I need time to relearn things I have tried to forget. She looked eastward, toward the mountains which rolled away and up, secret, only half-mapped, toward the Tiger's Head, where the two men who were the two conflicting halves of her life were waiting for her.

And somewhere in all that, is also Mouse, she thought, with the twisting of grief that would never let her go.

My darling daughter, she said silently, we do what we can to put things right. But what man can, seems never enough. He is so much better at destruction.

She gave twenty *baht* to a passing, orange-robed priest, to make a little merit, according to Thai custom, before beginning to find out just how much she would be able to do to put things right and what it would cost her, including perhaps her life.

She went first to the shop of Perry's old friend from OSS days, Howard-the-Brit. She was the only customer in the aromatic clutter of carved teak animals, piles of bright red, blue, green and saffron cloth, baskets of rough silver bangles, thin beaten silver bowls and woven, tasselled handbags for the tourists. Howard raised his head from an abacus like an ancient turtle disturbed on a sunny rock.

'A desk-man, is he?' said Howard, after Nina had introduced herself as a colleague of Perry's and passed on his greetings and news. 'I told him he should stay out here!'

Nina had a fleeting image of a young Ethan Perry, fair, gangling and sunburned, his bush shorts still new and crisply creased, being tempted by the exotic East. 'His wife's death may have made him grab onto the familiar,' she said.

'All the more reason to cut loose,' said Howard.

Nina touched a carved teak tiger, then a small rosewood monkey. 'Are you still in personal contact with the Meos?' She smiled into Howard's old, tanned, webbed face, trying to reach the man behind it.

Howard's gaze sharpened. 'If you're interested in folk culture, I can recommend. . . .'

'That's not what I meant.'

'Is this still a message from Perry?' Howard was uncomfortably quick, seeming suddenly less like an ancient, sunbathing turtle than a watchful lizard.

Nina studied him. The 'OSS days' were a long, long time ago. Howard was a local, Ethan Perry a *farang*. It was time to become her father's daughter again, not Perry's protegée, as a favour to Perry if nothing else. She shrugged in answer to Howard's question. 'He hoped you would help me, but didn't know what I would ask.'

Howard suddenly slapped at a silverfish that darted from under a pile of woven bags.

'I need to contact someone in Laos, above the Ou River, nearest town Muong Sai.'

'Telephone,' said Howard. He snorted at his own joke. 'Why?' he demanded abruptly.

Nina hesitated, weighing the opposing threats. It was no use. She would have to raise the old ghosts. Otherwise, she was in danger as a suspected US agent. 'I used to trade in opium,' she said flatly. 'Before I knew Ethan. I would like to reopen some old contacts.'

Howard's eyes went as opaque as the pottery shards in the basket by his sarong-wrapped hip. 'I stay out of all that,' he said. 'Messy business. I suggest you stay out of it too, if you're rusty. It's a bun fight up here. No place for outsiders. Or nostalgic dabblers.'

'I see,' said Nina. 'How much is this monkey?' She paid his price without haggling. 'Did a man called McNeill ever show up here?' she asked, as she tucked the little monkey into her bag.

Howard slammed shut the drawer of his old-fashioned cash register with a crash. He looked at her again. 'Is he a friend of Ethan's too?'

'More a friend of mine,' said Nina.

'Just as well, then,' said Howard, 'as you'll no doubt be stumbling over him in a dark alley somewhere.'

439

Hell and damnation! thought Nina. I'd like to strangle McNeill! He could have helped me! We *are* going to get in each other's way! She thanked Howard and turned to leave the shop.

'If it's just transport you're after,' said Howard, 'there's a pilot called La up in Fang who runs the gunshop on the main street . . . flies across the border now and again. Just don't ask too many questions as a friend of Ethan Perry.'

'I understand. Thank you,' said Nina once more. She left Howard's shop and stopped to look in a window full of tiny bird and elephant opium weights. Who will Howard tell? she wondered. And how long will it take? She walked on, past two shops filled with antiques smuggled over the border from Burma, and took a *tuk-tuk* on Prapok Klao Road to the bus station, where she waited two hours for a bus to Fang.

Fang did not distract Nina from her fears, like Chiang Mai. She did not like Fang, or the men in its streets. There were too many soldiers and police of all kinds. Too many casually inquiring eyes that slid away when challenged by her own. As she looked and asked for La's gunshop, she watched for the man who had worn the Boston Marathon tee-shirt, or the Chiu Chao dealer whose cold eyes had touched her face in the Bangkok bank. Fang was their town now, more than Chiang Mai.

La shook his head. 'Not possible, I'm sorry,' he said in English. He was wearing an open white shirt over his singlet, shorts and flipflop sandals.

Nina fingered the banknotes in her purse. 'Perhaps I underestimate the fare.'

La looked down through the glass-topped case between them at a pair of Mauser pistols and an old flintlock rifle, lovingly polished. 'Not the fare,' he said softly. 'Just my lack of interest.'

Nina stood stubbornly among the gunmetal glints and polished wood of his stock. She could smell damp cardboard, black powder and throat-tickling chemicals. He was not disinterested at all. She had felt his interest palpably, as soon as she told him where she wanted to go. I can't do this anymore, she told herself. I'm out of my depth. She felt frustrated and afraid.

La said, 'I should stay in Thailand, if I were you.' He turned away to light a paraffin lantern hanging from an iron spike in the back wall of the gun shop.

At least I can leave this town!

440

Nina walked quickly back through the mud lakes in the street toward the bus station. If she had missed the last bus, she would have to sleep in Fang.

A man fell into step beside her. 'This way, please,' he said in English.

'Go away,' Nina said. Her voice resonated with authority, but her muscles began to jump. If he put his hand on her arm, she would scream and claw out his eyes. Before the darkness came, this time.

But he did not touch her as the man in Saigon airport had done. He moved his hand slightly so that Nina could see his pistol, a small one but lethal enough at this range.

'This way, please!' He edged her into an alley off the main street.

Not here! thought Nina. Not executed in an alleyway! It cannot happen now! All of her muscles seemed to be jumping. She looked over her shoulder. The man's eyes were nervous, not cold. They met hers before they turned away.

I'm still real, she thought. Not a thing. But why is he speaking English to me?

They reached the end of the alley and turned left. The man pointed to a brightly-lit house with a wide verandah, just ahead on Nina's right. A searchlight on the eaves pulsed in time with the throbbing of the gasoline-powered generator in its front yard. Nina walked helplessly past the generator, up the steps onto the verandah. A small man in an olive drab uniform and bare feet sat cross-legged on the bleached teak floor, smoking a cigarette and drinking Perrier water with sliced lime.

'Sit down,' he ordered her in English.

Nina drew a deep breath and tried to think herself back into her father's world, where invitations could be made at gunpoint for the sake of efficiency rather than carnage. She was glad he had asked her to sit. Her legs would have given way in any case. She dropped to the floor and tucked her feet under her.

'Why does an employee of US Intelligence want to contact opium dealers in Laos?' the man demanded. 'Which agency sent you? Who should be notified of any accident you might have?'

Therefore the English. Nina hadn't told La who she worked for. Just her name and that she wanted to enter Laos. So it had been Howard. By telephone, like his joke. He was a local, all right! Even if I survive, she thought, I'm not sure I will tell Ethan . . . he no longer needs to know such things. She stared back at the man in the uniform.

Compared to my cousin Thu, you are harmless, she tried to reassure

441

herself. Nevertheless, that humid, insect-filled night felt colder than the winter fog of Washington.

'I have friends in US Intelligence, like many people,' Nina said as steadily as she could. 'But whoever told you I work for them is a fool, with no more knowledge of our world than a child.'

'*Our* world?'

Please God, let Paul Karelian's security be as good as he thought it was! Let this man not know what I did in Bangkok! Let him not be a friend of Thu . . . or Carbone! 'My name is Luoc Nina,' she said.

In the silence which followed her words, a mosquito's whine surged and faded. A firefly blinked diagonally across the verandah, and a dog barked once, across the lane. The man flicked his cigarette butt in a red arc over the edge of the verandah into the yard. At the edge of Nina's vision, the shadow of another man bent to pick it up.

Nina looked back at the man on the verandah. Chinese, she thought. Not Thai. Possibly Meo. Whose side is he on? Which faction does he support? Is he Thu's ally or enemy?

'Prove it,' said the man.

Nina swallowed. 'Is Emile Carbone still alive?' she asked.

'Retired in Vientiane.'

'He knows me.' And owes me a favour, in the end, she thought. 'Tell him that Ninette sends her greetings.'

'Luoc's daughter died,' said the man. 'Or so the cousin says. Punished for her treachery.'

'The cousin is lying, on both counts.'

'Not for the first time,' said the man.

No friend of Thu's then, thought Nina with relief.

He lit another cigarette without offering her one. 'And what would Luoc's daughter want in Fang if she is alive?'

'To settle some old business with that same cousin. She would be in Fang looking for help from her father's old friends.'

The man re-crossed his legs. 'What kind of help?' He sounded interested in the conversation for the first time.

'Border crossings and safe passage in Laos.'

'Ah.' The interest faded. 'You need a mere go-between . . . a grease merchant . . . not a pilot like La or a soldier like myself. Try a Round Eye toenail paring in Chiang Mai called Ince. Grégoire Ince. Office in the New Asia Hotel. Now, please leave Fang to carry out your family feuds. Luoc's daughter or not, you are unwelcome here.'

And of no further interest to himself.

The man with the pistol escorted Nina to the bus station. The last bus had indeed gone. The man then ushered Nina into a bar where he found someone with a car and willing to drive her back to Chiang Mai that night, for a price, which Nina paid. The man seemed surprised that Luoc's daughter did not have her own car and driver.

Not knowing for whom the driver worked, Nina maintained a silent outward calm on the journey. But she felt sick for forty kilometres. I was right to leave Saigon! she thought. So right! I lost the stomach for the business long ago!

The following evening, as arranged by telephone, Nina waited for Grégoire Ince, the Round Eye toenail paring, to find her at the food stall nearest the Moat Gate. She watched bodies ebb and flow across the bridge. No sign, so far, of Bill McNeill in a dark alleyway or anywhere else. On the far side of the moat, a late tourist coach disgorged its passengers, hot and sated with a day at the Working Elephant Farm. Swarms of children and vendors descended on this new prey like gnats.

Nina's attention was caught by four men, three white and one Asian, eating and drinking beer at a nearby stall. They wore bright shirts and drip-dry chinos, blue jeans and Bermuda shorts. When the Asian, who looked Japanese, backed away with a camera, the other three threw their arms around each other's shoulders and called ritual male insults at the cameraman. Quintessential tourists. But their energy level was wrong. There was something muted and edgy in their laughter and obscenities.

Nina listened to their barracking. Americans. Perhaps former soldiers returning for a nostalgic wallow in old haunts. Then she realized that beneath all those bright shirts, drip-dry chinos, jeans and plaid Bermuda shorts, not one of the four was even slightly overweight. She studied them idly while she waited for Ince.

The oldest, a tall man with a balding head and weight lifter's arms, turned his head again and again to scan the crowds in the streets. They're waiting for someone, too, Nina thought. Then she noticed that, in spite of the heat, they were all wearing boots.

Nina stared at their booted feet. Ready for the jungle.

Beyond the men, a heavy man in rimless spectacles pointed himself toward Nina. She saw him coming and looked back at the four lean men in combat boots. What if they're with McNeill?

The heavy man was shoving between two food stalls, showering apologies and greetings around him in Thai.

Unless there's a third lunatic rescue mission underway in Chiang Mai, thought Nina, I'll wager anything, those men are with Bill

McNeill! He's in town. Why would Howard lie? The more she looked at the four lean men in boots, the more she was sure she was right.

What would McNeill do if I turned up now? she wondered. Would he at least tell me where he's going? Let me tag along across the Mekong? Or be even more certain that I'm an Intelligence plant? Who is the better risk – jumpy, hostile McNeill or the unknown toenail paring called Grégoire Ince?

A boy tugged on the oldest man's arm. The man bent his head to listen, nodded and spoke to the others. In an agony of indecision, Nina watched them pay their bill with counterfeit casualness and then lurch drunkenly, it would seem, into the shadows of a narrow street behind the boy.

I'll risk McNeill, thought Nina. As she stood up to follow the men, Grégoire Ince slid onto the bench beside her. Nina looked once more after the men.

Don't stampede! she told herself. They way you blundered into Fang. Not this time! Will John's life may depend on it . . . and your own. She sat down again. She needed to know what Ince might be able to tell her about Thu's world, before she re-entered it.

'I'm trying to pick up old threads,' said Nina to Ince. It felt better to be speaking French again, even to a toenail paring recommended by a Nationalist Chinese bandit, than to pretend an interest in the opium trade. 'The man in Fang said you were a wonderful source of gossip . . . knew everyone.'

But whose friend are you? she wondered. You don't look like a villain.

Ince had a friendly face, round and full cheeked, with a convincing smile. He was solid rather than fat, thick through the chest and shoulders like a Russian *basso*, but tapering to small, clean, pale feet in open sandals. His weight plumped out his wrinkles and made him look younger than the fifty-odd years he probably was. However, his cold, seen-it, know-it, don't-care eyes gave him away when she caught sight of them once through his lenses, like two small fish in murky water.

'I only gossip to friends,' he said. He held up one finger to the boy with the cooler of Singha beer.

'How do you choose your friends?' asked Nina sweetly.

'By how friendly they feel.'

Nina opened her purse. 'Does nationality matter?' Her voice and face remained innocent.

Ince had answered that question before. 'You refer to currency, of course,' he said. 'No, I'm not particular.'

Nina laid several ten dollar bills on the table. 'Is that friendly enough? For a start.' Perry's parting gift had been to have the Bangkok account unfrozen. Nina had been delighted to note that interest had been allowed to mount since 1966.

Ince smiled a cherubic smile and picked up the money. 'Another one,' he said to the boy with the beer. 'For my friend here. What can I tell you?' he asked Nina.

She skirted around her main question, while she got her bearings. 'How is my old friend, Major Lucky?'

'You do have funny friends,' said Ince.

'He did me a favour once,' said Nina. 'Of sorts.'

Ince drank some beer and studied her through his glasses. A lantern was now reflected off the lenses so that Nina could no longer see his eyes. 'I ask myself,' he said reflectively, 'just what threads you want to pick up.'

'There's only one thing up here,' said Nina.

'Not any more, dear lady. Not any more. As the Major will be the first to tell you. Look around you. Who do you see on the streets?'

'Tourists and soldiers.'

'Exactly,' said Ince.

Nina drank for a moment in silence. 'So the gallant Major has branched out. . . .' She glanced at the twin lanterns reflected in his glasses. 'Let me guess . . . He's opened a tourist hotel.'

'Hardly!' said Ince. 'He's hanging on, in the new People's Democratic Republic of Laos, but between you and me, he won't be able to keep up his balancing act forever. Sooner or later, he'll fall, to one side or the other, and the opposing side will pounce. Unless he's careful, he won't be forgiven.' He leaned his large, round head close to hers. 'I've heard that the Russians are giving him a hard time at this moment.'

'In his old or new business ventures?' asked Nina.

Ince shrugged. Then he said, 'We're merely friends, ma'mselle, not intimates.' In fact, he didn't know. Lucky had complained about the Russians but been irritatingly mysterious about the reasons.

'And what about his neighbour, Colonel Thu?' asked Nina. 'Have the two of them avoided killing each other all these years?'

Ince's interest shifted up a gear.

'With difficulty,' he said. 'They were forced into reluctant collaboration after the PAVN knocked the Meos off their magic mountain and out of Long Tien, into refugee camps and the American state of Montana.'

'How do they handle transport in and out of the country now?' asked Nina. Meaning their opium.

Ince understood her perfectly. 'Mercenary pilots,' he said. 'It's an expensive business for both of them. A little more, of course, for Lucky.'

Because Thu still controlled the only air strip in the area, thought Nina. 'The new government hasn't stopped the flights?'

Ince shook his head. 'Not as far as I know. The Communists have their hands full enough with the pockets of resisting Royal Lao and neutralist guerrillas. They're turning a blind eye, for the moment . . . and probably bolstering their ailing economy as well . . . so what's new?' He nodded knowingly at his beer. 'There are several old American-trained cowboys up in Fang and Chiang Saen who fly over the Lao border in old American planes.'

La, thought Nina.

'Some Americans too, I hear,' continued Ince. 'Who didn't want to go home when the party was over.' He waved at the boy for two more beers. 'Of course, they lose more than they used to . . . planes shot down . . . somebody asks for more grease than they will agree to, and makes trouble . . . the Royal Lao Army loses control of an area just as a plane tries to land there.' He chuckled. 'Sometimes, they just have lousy luck . . . *Santé!*' He raised his beer to her and she raised hers to him.

Nina had trouble imagining any circumstances bad enough to force Thu to deal with Lucky. 'The world is changing!' she said.

'Not for the better,' said Ince. 'Even if I say so myself! By the way, Thu had a spot of that lousy luck, I just mentioned. His eagle's nest was hit by American planes trying to stop military transport on the Chinese road into northern Laos. They missed the road, I'm told.'

Nina felt a thud of panic. 'What about Thu?' And Will John?

'Oh, he just shifted a few yards into the jungle and carried on, like everybody else does . . . except where the jungle has been poisoned with yellow rain. That's quite different, of course . . . That's why we have so goddamned many refugees!'

'When was this?' Nina tried to imagine the effect of a bomb on the villa beneath the Tiger's Head but could only conjure up the smoking ashes of her family's big house in Saigon. Then she wondered if Will John had been killed in the attack and she had come this far to rescue a dead man.

'Can't really remember,' said Ince. 'Anyway, Lucky insinuates that it wasn't completely accidental. He may know even more than he's telling about that one.' Ince tilted the twin lantern reflections at Nina in what may have been a knowing look. 'After all, as you undoubtedly know, your cousin Thu is thought to be pro-North and he controls a respectable mini-army, for those godforsaken parts. The Americans are very good at strategically useful mistakes . . . Look at that prison raid at Son Tay!'

'Tell me,' said Nina, hardly listening. Ince was telling her that Lucky, who had had her dropped in the middle of a battlefield in the Plain of Jars, seemed also to have called in an air strike on Thu's villa. A North Vietnamese calling in American planes against another North Vietnamese. It was worse than insane!

'The Americans didn't find one single POW,' said Ince. 'But they did, coincidentally, happen to kill at least 200 Chinese soldiers who shouldn't have been there either.'

Why did I imagine that changing worlds would help anything? Nina asked herself. What world did I imagine I would find elsewhere?

'Have I upset you in any way?' asked Ince.

She rearranged her face into neutral. 'In fact, it's Thu that I particularly wanted to contact.'

'Why?' asked Ince.

'I think he may want to kill me,' said Nina lightly. 'And I can't live with the suspense any longer.' The black joke rang true as soon as she spoke it aloud.

Ince was stopped in his tracks for a few seconds. 'Aren't you a helpful type!' he exclaimed after a moment. 'I wish *I* had more enemies like you!' He lined up the four empty bottles. 'Getting to him will be expensive.'

'How expensive?'

'Well,' reflected Ince, 'Thu's a long way from here. The border's tricky now that the Pathet Lao basically control the country. There are no roads except that superhighway the Chinese keep pushing south from their border . . . and of course the old American one the Meos used until they got bumped off their sacred mountain.'

'How expensive?' repeated Nina. 'Summarize for me.' She had a sense of terrible familiarity with the woman who was now speaking. However reluctantly, she remembered the old games.

'Do you want an armed escort?'

Nina shook her head.

'Two thousand.'

'*Baht?*'

Ince choked with fake laughter. 'Dollars. And if you try jokes like that, I'll make it pounds.'

447

'What does that joke buy?'

'Liaison,' said Ince. 'My valuable time and expertise at pointing out stepping stones in a quagmire.'

'But not the stones themselves?'

'Those are extra.'

'You're mad,' said Nina.

Ince leaned close again. 'Darling,' he said. 'Inflation has hit the boondocks. I could add up all the postage stamps for you, but it isn't worth either of our time. You're in a seller's market. A very large number of sellers. And the problem is that you must buy from every goddamned one of them!'

Nina waited.

'You don't know who they are and I do. I will, of course, give you a provisional list of taxes, tolls, fees for crossing masters and so on, as well as instructions.' When she still did not reply, he added, 'Seriously. Unless you want to try swimming the Mekong on an inner tube like that old monk and hiking in blind and naked, so to speak.'

Nina nodded in abrupt resignation. She had no desire to prolong this dreadfully familiar game, nor did she want to hike or swim, ever again.

She paid him half in advance.

Ince did not call her at her hotel for three weeks. Nina thought she would go mad. She wanted to act before terror hit. She was going to meet both Thu and Will John again, at the same time, and on Thu's territory. Will John might or might not have survived the air strike. Thu had once let her walk away, but who could know what time might or might not have done to his anger?

It's right! she told herself. What I'm doing is right!

She watched for McNeill or the men she had seen by the Moat Gate. She kept her ears open for rumours of a large group of Round Eye men, but asked no further questions. They seemed to have vanished from Chiang Mai.

While she waited to hear from Ince, she moved openly, recklessly, around Chiang Mai. All danger seemed now to lie ahead, not in the ghosts of the past. She went to Doi Suthep and climbed the 290 steps between the undulating giant *naga* snakes which formed the balustrades. On the top, she surprised herself by buying a sheaf of incense sticks and making an offering at the gilded *stupa* of the main shrine. She visited the silk and umbrella villages, and the daily work show at the elephant farm. She took a tourist coach to the Bhuping Palace and to the waterfall at Mae Sa.

I have missed it all! she thought one evening, as she strolled in a maze of narrow old streets. More than I would let myself admit. Again and again, she inhaled deeply the smells which had for so long been replaced by others. She bathed in the sense of familiarity – of the food, the flowers, the tree shapes, the smells, and the sounds – not exactly like those in Saigon and Dalat, but very close.

She made more offerings of food and flowers at the tiny *pi* house shrines. Raised a Catholic, she told herself that she did not really believe in the *pi*, but she felt their energy and presence through the belief of other people. The full population of the world was now restored by this second layer of spirits. Those miniature temples, on street corners and in gardens, at crossroads and on mountain passes, in holy places where a major spirit had once sat down for lunch or taken a bath, all defined one small, satisfying area of a world in which, otherwise, she saw no signs of immutable order of any kind.

At last, Ince called her.

'Be in Fang,' he said. 'In the morning, the day after next.'

Nina met him again, by the library in the temple, Wat Prasingh, to pay him his second $1,000.

'Take plenty of pocket money,' Ince said, after giving her precise instructions for her second trip to Fang. 'But keep it in your underpants.'

'Do me a favour,' she said. 'Let Fang know I'm coming at your invitation.'

'Don't worry darling! Everything's sorted out. You're old history now.'

Wearing a wrap-around Thai cotton *panung*, a loose blue cotton jacket, and a Burmese-style conical hat, with her belongings in a small, woven bamboo suitcase, Nina again took a bus to Fang. In Fang, she slept uneasily in a small guest house, with her suitcase against the door to warn her if it opened. The following morning, in spite of Ince's assurances, she avoided the lane where the Chinese soldier lived.

She presented herself to a Sergeant Wu, formerly of the Kuomintang and now an unofficial, auxiliary Border Patrol policeman. For a fee, Wu drove her in a jeep to a small airstrip north of Fang. For a second fee, he loaded her onto an unmarked helicopter otherwise full of beer, the parts for a mechanical pump, antibiotics, and four large wooden crates labelled 'Sewing machines. Made in USA'. There were two Thai pilots in Border Patrol uniforms and a door gunner. Liftoff was watched only by a half-dozen small boys dozing on the backs of grazing water buffalo.

Nina crouched on the floor of the juddering, racketing machine and watched green velvet and green coral-covered mountains roll away beyond the floor-mounted machine gun in the open door. The buffalo, apparently used to the noise, continued to graze as they shrank to dark dots. A little later, the great flat snake of the Mekong twisted into sight. The helicopter slid noisily down over the surface of the river and landed in a jungle clearing on the far side, in Laos.

Nina was off-loaded with the beer and antibiotics. The mechanical dragonfly strained upward, clattering, into the hot sky. Nina paid a landing tax to a Lao who shuffled out of the shed into which the beer and antibiotics had vanished. Then she began to walk north, parallel to the river, along a dirt road, carrying her bamboo suitcase. Sweat was already puddling behind the money tied in a cloth around her ribs.

A patrol of soldiers in black uniforms sent her on a detour into a rice field. She felt eyes watching her as she passed through a tiny hamlet perched on a long spit of land between the river and a series of fish ponds. She walked faster, in spite of the growing heat; she was trapped on the spit, with nowhere to run. Forty-five minutes later, she began to climb a bluff above the river. A half an hour after that, she looked up at the black-streaked, pocked and scrofulous stucco of an abandoned French watch tower from the ruined battlements of a former fort. A Lao carrying an American M.16 collected an area border tax and told her to wait.

Nina sat on the battlements until sunset, remembering her last wait on this same shore. The mountains still snatched at the falling sun and swallowed it with amazing speed. She looked down at her hands, unscarred now, with polished nails.

I can still go back, she told herself. Why? she replied at once. What is waiting for me back there? In a strange way, she was enjoying herself.

Just as the last bright paring shrank to nothing behind the purple ridges, a tiny girl of about eight years appeared among the weeds of the overgrown fort and summoned her with a peremptory nod for a ride in an ox-cart to a landing strip.

The flight in the dark, in the small, unmarked, single propeller plane terrified Nina even more than the prospect of meeting Thu. Their route seemed to zigzag across all of northern Laos. The pilot, who was not La, flew low, skimming shadowy treetops which, to Nina, looked only a few feet below the wings. Her heart tried to escape through her throat as they skimmed up over sudden swellings of mountain ridge and dropped again like a fairground ride. Once, she clutched at the strap beside her as the pilot abruptly banked into a 90 degree turn and lost altitude at the same time. Sometimes, she saw the thick darkness of mountains on both sides of the plane, as if they were flying through a tunnel. She decided that he had asked her to pay in advance because she would probably not live to pay him on arrival.

They landed twice on small airstrips. Each time, the pilot, a Meo, told her sharply to stay hidden in the plane. He did, however, allow her to pay the landing tax on both occasions.

Just before dawn, a double row of lights flared in the dark jungle ahead. They were expected. The pilot put her down on Thu's landing strip, turned the plane and took off again without stopping his engine. The lights were doused as the plane passed them, as if it had blown them out. They had been alight for less than eight minutes.

Nina stood in the shadowy pre-dawn light, inhaling the thick smoke of the extinguished flares. Shadowy figures were already manhandling the barrels into the jungle along the airstrip. Then she saw the two soldiers waiting for her in the mouth of the trail up to the villa. She began to walk toward them, past the place where Cassidy's body had lain and where she had waited for Thu's knife.

As Nina climbed the track, followed closely by her escort, she tried to decide what she felt but was numbed by conflicting terrors and expectations. The very familiarity of the track made her feel unreal, as if she were merely thinking or dreaming herself back into a former self.

Then she saw the small face observing her from the shadow of a banana clump. It had a broad forehead, large wide-set eyes and pointed chin. Neat ears were folded tightly against the small skull. The impossible had happened.

Nina's breath, her heart, the blood in her veins, her thoughts, all seemed to stop. Then she flung herself up the track, fell and cut her shin on a rock, unknowing. She scrambled back to her feet. Her heart would explode in her chest.

'*Mouse!*' she screamed.

The small face vanished.

'*Mouse!*' Nina flung herself up the next steep natural rock step.

The child darted off the track, across the abandoned field.

Nina was deaf to the shouts of the soldiers behind her. 'Wait!' she cried. She slipped, fell into an erosion channel, and climbed out again. 'Oh God, please wait!' Sobbing and swearing in frustration and terror that the child would vanish she yanked her jacket free from the claws of a bush. 'Wait!' She groped and clambered up across the field she had crossed so many times before, but when she came to the track again, the child had vanished.

In despair and exhaustion, Nina sank onto her heels. The soldiers slowed to a normal pace once they saw she was headed toward the villa.

Nina rocked on her feet. Life was not real. It was a dream after all. She was back on the jungle trail the night after Mouse disappeared, carried like a twig on flood waters around a malign circle of time and space.

Please! Are you there? she called again silently, as she had that night. Or am I mad? Have I slipped sideways out of reality into a world I don't understand?

She stopped rocking at the sudden thought that there may have been no child. That she had imagined it. Pursued a ghost of the child she had carried in her belly along this track. Perhaps reality was solid after all, but she was mad. Medically mad. The possibility was an anchor, of sorts.

The soldiers stood below her on the trail, whispering among themselves, a little frightened by her strange behaviour.

She began to rock again. Then let me examine how mad I am, she thought. I came here to try to persuade Thu to set Will John free. To accept me as a hostage if he still values me enough for that. To discharge my debt to Will John which I feel so strongly even if I don't entirely understand it. As she thought these things, she observed that her centre remained firm, without the cold slidings and seismic shiftings of madness.

Perhaps my strength has finally dried up. That would be logical. But it's not madness.

But I *saw* her! insisted another internal voice stubbornly, and set off the sideways slippage of reality once again.

A sound above her on the trail snapped Nina back into absolute clarity in the present moment. Her animal self tensed and waited, all senses turned up to full.

Thu stepped down from between two rocks, followed by the child. Nina stood up slowly.

The child was a little boy, barechested and wearing a knife. He had Mouse's broad forehead and wide-set eyes, her pointed chin and neatly-set ears. Like Nina herself. Like Nina's father. And like Thu who resembled Nina's father.

'There!' whispered the child urgently, his eyes wide and his small fists clenched with excitement. 'Is it mother's spirit? Is it?'

Thu touched the boy's shoulder to silence him.

Nina's pulse thundered in her ears. She looked at Thu wordlessly and he at her. She looked at the child; had it been Mouse, she knew she would have died on the spot, exploded with joy, her life traded for her daughter's. However, it was not Mouse, and Nina was still bereft. But she was also sane and a tenant in reality.

'Is it mother?' demanded the boy urgently, once more.

Thu pressed again on the boy's shoulder. 'So,' he said to Nina. 'There you are!'

When Nina spotted Spiegel, Oyama, Bennett and Lewis, they were on their way to their first rendezvous with McNeill, Simpson, Stillwell and Cucic, in a hut just outside Chiang Saen, a village north of Chiang Mai, on the Thai border with Laos and Burma. Each of the two teams had a medic, arms expert and marksman, engineer, and radio man. Each had a map, and before leaving Chiang Saen, McNeill made sure they were double-primed.

They were seated on the sagging bamboo floor of a small, stilted hut belonging to a local farmer and his wife.

'I don't plan on losing anybody,' McNeill said, 'but how many screw-ups do you all know about that happened just because a unit misplaced the one man with the necessary information?' As seven heads nodded, he spread the Tactical Pilotage Chart on the woven floor and clicked on a strong flashlight.

'Jimmy's here,' he said. 'And still alive.'

The men leaned together over the white oval of light on the map.

'Not much else is,' observed Bennett.

'Less people for us to run into,' McNeill agreed. Even with one ear cocked for MPs alerted by Nina or her superiors, he was feeling good. Everybody primed. No more back-out briefings. Go-mode, for real! He gave the men a chance to fix in their minds the map references and general topography of the target area. Then he slid across the creaking floor to the top of the ladder which led to the ground, and whistled. In a moment, two Meos climbed up into the hut.

'This is Gaur, our first guide and Loopy La, our pilot,' said McNeill. He watched his group assessing the newcomers in the dim, orange light of the lantern which hung from the roof beam.

'Gaur, here,' he explained, indicating the first man, 'lives over in Laos. He's going to take us across the river.' McNeill could feel the excitement in the little hut. The mission was getting real for everybody.

'Listen good,' said Gaur in firm English. 'You got to understand why we don't go the most direct route. Laos is all mixed up. Here and here. . . .' He indicated on the map. '. . . you got General Phoumi Novasan's people – right-wing, US backed. No problem. But then we got to go through here. . . .'

Once more, heads bent close to the map and the bright oval thrown by the flashlight.

'The pass is tied up by neutralist guerrillas,' said Gaur. 'Tight patrols against VC, PL and Phoumi's forces . . . maybe friendly to you, maybe not. Here, farther south. . . .' The light moved again. '. . . we got Khma Bou. He's neutralist too, but different. The Thais don't like him because he wants to take back some provinces from Thailand that used to be Lao. Here, you got lots of PL and PAVN Communist forces, and radar.' On the map, he pointed out two peaks guarding a mountain pass. 'And up north at target area,' he continued, 'you also got PAVN, but they're mostly watching Chinese border now. Once we get to here. . . .' He pointed to a spot north of the radar indicated earlier. '. . . we hit beginning of chain of safe villages, mostly Meo – or what's left of Meo – and some Free Lao.' His finger skipped along a series of mountain ridges.

'We have to stay out of sight,' said McNeill. 'Of all those guys, except the Meos.'

'I think I'll shut my eyes and hang onto somebody's shirt,' said Bennett.

'Why doesn't Mr La there just fly us in?' asked Stillwell.

'The radar sandwich on those two peaks,' said McNeill.

'So where does La come into it?' Cucic sounded both angry and nervous.

'On the way out,' said McNeill. 'When all hell is breaking loose behind us and we really got to move! With a man who may or may not be able to walk.'

'So what happened to that sandwich?' demanded Lewis.

'Two flights are cleared,' said La unexpectedly. Everyone looked at him, slightly startled. 'Opium runs following an agreed pattern, on agreed dates.'

'We have to get Jimmy to the airstrip in time for La's last run,' explained Spiegel, with a glance at McNeill.

La now gazed at the group silently.

'Where's the nearest strip?' asked Lewis.

'Six to eight hours fast walking along this ridge,' said McNeill. He showed them on the map.

'And what if Jimmy can't walk?' This time it was Cucic. 'He could be in shit shape.'

'The cameraman is up there now,' said McNeill, 'arranging a diversion with some local Free Lao. It seems like the guy holding Putnam is a North Vietnamese, and so are most of his men. My friend, Man, reckons the Free Lao – who are holding this river valley – would like any excuse for a good fight with their old enemies.'

'Do they by any chance believe it will win them American support and gratitude?' murmured Simpson.

'I don't know what Man is saying to anybody,' said McNeill equably. 'As long as it works!'

They climbed down from the hut into the compound. Those with light hair dyed it black in a basin provided by the farmer's wife. Then they stripped off their civilian clothing and changed into the black uniforms and assorted headgear which the farmer had delivered in wicker baskets.

In a Meo turban, Simpson, with his light eyes in a thin, tanned face, looked like Lawrence of Arabia, while Bennett suggested a New Year's Eve costume party, lacking only whistles and streamers. McNeill, Cucic and Spiegel chose battered forage caps. The rest wore baseball caps, Chinese officer's caps, or PAVN helmets with camouflage netting.

'Lewis and Oyama look great,' observed Bennett. 'But close up, the rest of you guys are a joke.'

'You're all too goddam tall,' said Gaur. 'You better walk on your knees.'

Joking stopped as they collected and inspected the weapons and the equipment which had also arrived in wicker baskets. There were two American M.16s. The rest of the guns were Chinese, including Chinese copies of a Verrey pistol and accompanying signal flares. Cucic and Spiegel drew the M.16s. Simpson field-stripped his Chinese sniper's rifle, then practised loading and unloading it several times. He tried to imagine pointing anything again at another human being, but his mind jammed.

'Noisiest goddam canteens I ever heard,' complained Stillwell. 'Must be World War One issue.'

'Be grateful for small favours,' said Spiegel. 'Ever drunk water that's been in a gourd?'

McNeill had wanted to cross the Mekong in two separate groups, but Gaur said that the Crossing Master refused to make two runs and it was better not to argue. McNeill paid the Crossing Master, and the Thai soldier who just happened to be there. They crossed after dark in two unlit sampans, one pulling the other.

Across the Mekong in Laos, they picked up a second guide and the two teams separated again. McNeill and Gaur left a half an hour before Spiegel and his guide. Separately, they left the narrow flat band of riverside *paddis*, fish ponds and water cress farms and began to climb. Still in two groups, they hid the next day and walked again the second night. They had 140 miles to travel, including several detours around military checkpoints.

'One thing they got right in Nam,' panted Bennett on their third night in Laos, as his group hauled itself up a narrow ravine, 'was airlifts.'

'Just keep remembering that Communist radar sandwich on those two mountains just ahead,' said Spiegel.

Getting up and over the pass between the two radar installations took them four more nights. On the eighth night, on the far side of the radar installations, they regrouped in an area still held by resisting Free Lao. The Meo guides went off to the nearest village for supplies while the Round Eyes laid up in a deserted, half-burned village.

That was the night Simpson began to have real trouble. The position of the huts felt familiar, even though he knew he had never been there before. A hut stood just where the hut with the baby had been. Lewis, looking for a soft bed, poked an exploratory head through the burnt half-wall.

'NO!' screamed Simpson.

The others hit the ground. Simpson stood, trembling, with his eyes closed, trying to get a grip on himself while the others began to get back to their feet, not looking at him.

They hid in the village for three days. Simpson pretended to sleep most of the time, to hide his shakes from the others. The fourth night in the village, when even McNeill's rhythms were becoming spikey with impatience, they heard a clattering in the sky; their guide led them along a narrow animal trail to a clearing where an ancient unmarked American helicopter was churning up clouds of sticks, leaves and dead grass.

'Where the hell did they get this bird from?' demanded Stillwell. 'It's an old gunship!'

'Hallelujah!' said Bennett. 'Who cares?'

McNeill and Gaur negotiated and paid the pilot and co-pilot, both Meos. Gaur stayed behind.

They drew red flashes of ground fire as they skimmed over a low, dark ridge. While the pilot hovered, they bailed out two ridges farther on, onto the landing pad of an old US Special Forces camp.

'Heads down!' ordered McNeill.

A squad of local Pathet Lao arrived a few minutes later. Watched by nine pairs of eyes in blackened faces among the rocks and scrub of nearby higher ground, their five indistinct shadows quartered the abandoned field below the deserted camp and prodded nervously at the grass with their rifles.

Finally, with evident relief, the Pathet Lao leader said, 'Nobody here.' He looked up at the ruined camp – at the collapsing sandbag walls, rusting corrugated iron, and random tangles of barbed wire – as if considering whether to disturb its ghosts.

'It didn't stop,' he said decisively. 'Just went over the top of the mountains.'

He left with his men.

No one in the deserted camp moved for an hour. After an hour, they began cautiously to stretch themselves, examine their feet and scratch at insect bites. An hour and a half after that, a voice from below one rotting sandbag wall whispered, 'Cowboy?'

McNeill showed himself. Their new Meo guide climbed up to join them, followed by two more men carrying coils of bright puce and fluorescent nylon rope.

The descent into the valley east of the ridgetop camp took two more days. Then the group, now travelling together, hit another mountain ridge and began to climb in earnest. They descended again. Then climbed again. And descended again. The Meo escorts seemed to dance up the slopes.

'I want to die,' puffed Bennett. 'Please God, give me a heart attack, right now!' He placed his left foot above his right one and heaved his weight upward. 'Just temporarily.'

On the twelfth afternoon, they hit the crest of a ridge between two higher peaks and looked down a vertiginous staircase of stacked cliff faces towards the glinting splinters of a river far below.

'The track goes down that way,' their guide said, pointing diagonally down along the highest cliff edge. 'But there's a PAVN checkpoint on the river crossing. Caravans have to go that way . . . no other way round for mules and ponies. We go down ropes tonight.'

'After *dark*?' asked Cucic. The others looked down toward the distant river.

'What about the crossing and the other side?' asked McNeill.

'No problem,' said the Meo. 'Me and my friends go this way all the time. Much cheaper. No tax.'

Their guide led them north-west along the ridge, away from the

PAVN checkpoint, to a minute track which sidled diagonally down the topmost cliff in the giant staircase. Then they stopped and pulled back into the shadow of an overhanging boulder to wait for dusk.

'I hate heights,' said Bennett mournfully. 'When all my friends were playing Tarzan off the garage roof, I was smoking in the basement.'

The Meos had marked a rock at the top of the descent. One of them went down the rope first, to locate the top of the next section. Then, one by one, the Americans rappelled down the first cliff face.

'Hey!' said Lewis, as he hit the lower ledge. 'What about that!'

'Beats climbing,' Bennett agreed, sounding surprised.

When all eight Americans and three Meos were strung out along the five-foot ledge, they edged twenty yards to the marker at the top of the second section of their descent. Again, they dropped, one at a time, with the Meos belaying, this time onto a semi-circular platform of rock. There was no break between the next two sections. The rest point between them was two feet deep and three feet wide. Two Meos went first, one to guide each American with urgent whispers and reaching hands, down onto the tiny ledge. The other threaded a rope through a permanently fixed pulley and continued downward. The sound of the river below grew steadily louder. They were still exposed on open rock as the sun began to rise.

'Quick now!' urged their guide. The Meos were watching the crevice of the gorge below. 'Patrol along the river soon!'

'At least we can see where we're going,' muttered Spiegel to Oyama who was just ahead of him in a traverse to the top of the last rope.

'I think I'd rather not, thanks all the same,' said Oyama, his eyes on the ledge which was only a little wider than his feet. 'How do you think I got this far?'

'I feel like a fucking fairground duck!' grunted Bennett.

On the last rope, they dropped suddenly through the roof of the jungle into renewed night. They counted heads, and set off along a narrow, dark tunnel through the thick waterside growth. When their guide told them to wait, they took off their packs and hunkered down along the trail. One of the Meos vanished toward the roaring of the mountain stream.

'I got foot rot!' announced Bennett indignantly.

I still don't believe I'm doing this, thought Simpson. Nothing they were doing seemed real. He had stopped shaking as soon as they left the burnt-out village. Now his body was running on autopilot, seemed to be doing all the right things. But he felt that it was someone else's body.

Bill, on the other hand, has never looked so happy since I've known him, he thought. That goes for Lewis too, though maybe he always spins like this. Even Bennett's OK, in spite of his bellyaching. Spiegel's reserving judgement. Cucic is working it through . . . he's into confrontations. And winning, I think. I'm out of touch with Stillwell . . . he's closed up in a private world. Oyama and I are avoiding each other . . . feeling the same. Neither of us has enough reserves to risk contamination with the problems of the other. And defining it doesn't make any of it feel more real. He dropped his head onto his knees and pretended to sleep. But then his brain racketed with questions about the Meos . . . why do they want to help? What do they owe us? *Are* they helping, or leading us into a trap?

When the dull flakes of sky visible through the top of the tunnel had turned to bright, sunlit sparks, the scout returned. 'Patrol gone back to checkpoint now,' he said.

They followed him out of the green tunnel, down to the noisy, foaming water's edge. While one of the Meos carefully pulled the branches of a tree and a mound of undergrowth back over the opening onto the trail, the other two fished in the shadow of a large rock and hauled a dripping arc of rope above the surface.

'We pull ourselves across on this,' the chief guide explained. 'Middle is up to chest.' He grinned. '*My* chest. You're OK.'

They picked up the main trail on the far side of the river, well past the checkpoint. With the Meos ahead and behind them, they followed the trail along the river gorge for three hours. In the late morning, they cut uphill again. They laid up at midday to sleep for a few hours and began to climb again at dusk.

An hour before dawn, two and a half weeks after leaving Chiang Mai, they emerged onto a long, narrow ridge which hung like an undulating bridge in the darkness. They turned north and followed a faint track for forty-five minutes.

'Cowboy?' a quiet voice asked suddenly. Man stepped onto the ridge-top track.

'We're on the home straight now,' said McNeill. 'Gentlemen, this is the guy who took the photographs.'

Accompanied now by Man and two of the other Meos, they walked until dawn. In the faint grey light, Man called a halt. 'OK,' Man said. 'Now take a good look where you are.'

They were midway along the ridge between a tall rounded peak to the south and a lower one to the north, barely visible in the early mist.

459

'That's where we're going.' Man pointed north, to the lower, mist-draped peak. Then he pointed south toward the higher one. 'Loopy La's air strip is just down the east side of that baby. If we get separated, rendezvous at the north-west corner of the strip. It's on the map as a light line, not named. Circle 90 degrees east from the end of the track and cut downhill, just by that bump like a baby's dick. . . .' He pointed. 'You should hit it . . . the strip . . . in about two thirds of a kilometre. If you get lost, find this trail again and start over.'

Spiegel shielded the flashlight beam and marked his map while Man continued.

'The guy that controls the airstrip lives just on the far side of the peak. He don't like you Americans much . . . bombed his house . . . but he really don't like Major Lucky.'

'Does he know we're coming?' asked McNeill.

'He knows somebody's coming. But not. Americans. Try to keep your heads down. He's been sweetened. Loopy La'll take his opium out just like always, and everything should be OK.'

'It should be fine,' said Spiegel reflectively.

'Should be,' said McNeill. An uneasiness was barely noticeable under his skin. And speaking of Loopy La reminded him of the time pressure. 'How many hours are we from the target area?' he asked Man.

'About four,' said Man.

'Can we risk daylight travel?'

McNeill watched Man thinking. La would make his first flight tomorrow. And they didn't know how long it would take them to snatch Jimmy P. Success depended on not having to rush. Eight Americans and three Meos weren't going to storm a fortified village . . . not if they wanted the prisoner alive. They had to take time to observe and to finesse Putnam out of wherever he was being kept.

Finally the Meo nodded. 'If you let us carry your guns.'

'Like hell we will!' said Cucic and Lewis together.

'Good idea,' said McNeill.

Now Stillwell protested. 'What if we meet some Indians?'

'That's exactly why you're going to give the man your gun,' said McNeill.

Bennett, Oyama and Simpson had already handed theirs to one of the Meo guides. Still protesting, the rest did likewise. Then the three Meos and eight Americans began to walk north through the early morning light, their eyes drawn east over the mountains to the climbing dish of the sun.

'I never forgot these sunrises!' said Bennett.

'Fucking beautiful!' agreed Lewis quietly.

Man stared ahead along their track. 'Quick! We tie you up now!'

'No way!' protested Stillwell.

'We tie you up!'

'Do it,' ordered McNeill. 'And get your turbans off!'

By the time the small patrol of Pathet Lao crested the next ridge, the three Meos had their Round Eye prisoners under control.

'For the Major,' explained Man in Lao, to the sergeant who was leading the patrol.

'So many?' asked the sergeant. He was plainly uneasy but unable to define his discomfort. 'You need help?'

Man shook his head. 'I said the Major is a very civilized man, educated in a Round Eye school in Switzerland. They think he will bargain for their release. Coming along like babies.'

The sergeant studied Man with open suspicion. 'Where did you get so many?'

Man shrugged. 'We're just paid escort . . . up from Ou valley.'

'What the hell is he saying about us?' demanded Stillwell.

'Shut up!' said Man tersely.

The sergeant studied McNeill and Cucic who were the closest to him. Then he looked thoughtfully at Stillwell. 'They're in good shape!' he observed. 'Where the hell they been kept?'

Man leaned close, confidentially. 'Would you like an M.16?' he asked the sergeant.

'Modified?' The sergeant's eyes moved on to Simpson and Spiegel.

Man laughed derisively. 'No! Original, no-jam version.'

'Where is it?' At last, the sergeant looked back at Man. Man held out Cucic's gun.

'That's mine, you mother-fucker!' said Cucic in genuine fury.

Man grinned. 'Too bad, Sunny Jim!' he said in English. 'I think it's maybe this man's now.'

'How much?' asked the sergeant.

Man considered. 'For you,' he said, 'it might even be a gift.'

The sergeant examined the gun.

Man lifted a belt of ammunition over his head. 'On the house.'

'You little shit!' bellowed Cucic.

One of the Meos hit him on the side of the neck with his rifle butt.

'Easy, George!' warned McNeill. The Meo now pointed his gun at Cucic. 'It's OK.'

'You could have fooled me!' said Cucic with fury.

461

Man put the ammunition belt over the sergeant's head. 'Looks good!'
He saluted, casually and nodded his men forward.

The Pathet Lao left just enough room for the other group to pass.

'Don't look back!' hissed McNeill.

'That's my fucking gun back there!' shouted Cucic.

The same Meo hit him again.

'Sorry, Cowboy,' said Man. 'He's trying to hit him light.'

'I think Cucic deserves an Oscar,' said Spiegel under his breath.

'I'm not fucking acting!' said Cucic. He rubbed the side of his neck
and glared at the Meo. 'Nor is that little bastard over there!'

Simpson saw a head among the rocks beside the track. It peered as if in
disbelief, ducked out of sight. Then the whole man appeared, bent low,
running north along the ridge.

'Man!' said McNeill. The Meo tossed Simpson his rifle. The open
track which exposed the Americans also left the Major's sentry
unprotected for several yards. If he left the track, the Americans could
run to a position above him before he would have time to reach the
treeline farther down the slope.

'Take him!' said McNeill to Simpson.

Simpson hesitated. Man tossed McNeill his rifle. Simpson took off
his safety catch.

I'm not doing this, he thought. It's not happening.

The sentry bounded toward the top of a small ridge and disappeared
over it.

'Gabe! Do it!' begged McNeill, already raising his own gun. 'You're a
better shot!'

The track to Lucky's hamlet crossed one more, slightly higher ridge
before it dropped away out of sight.

Simpson half-raised his gun.

'Goddammit, fire!' said McNeill.

Simpson raised and fired in what seemed like one single action, in the
few seconds that the sentry was scuttling over the second ridge. The
single crack echoed around the neighbouring ridges. The man fell on
his face as if he had been pushed and tried to keep on scrambling. But he
was already dead.

As silence returned, flies began to buzz again in the dust by the men's
feet. Simpson stood with his rifle still on his shoulder, looking ahead
with the rueful disbelief of a man watching an unharmed stag disappear
into the trees. Except that his stag was on the ground.

'I know where to take him,' said Man.

Following Man, Spiegel and Stillwell ran forward, siezed the arms and legs of the fallen sentry and began to carry him off the track. Smith, bent double beside them, held his shirt beneath the body to catch the blood. One of the Meos and Lewis, with his gun, dropped behind some rocks at the top of the ridge, to watch the track to the north. Bennett, Oyama, and Cucic began to scrape away the puddle of red mud where the man had fallen. The third Meo followed, carrying all the remaining guns.

McNeill looked at Simpson and decided not to say, 'Good shot!' Instead, he said, 'Watch our backs to the south, Gabe. I'll sweep.'

I pulled the trigger after all, thought Simpson numbly. Why did I need to prove it to myself again . . . that circumstances are stronger than convictions? What do I do with that fact now?

Only birds and lizards watched them covering their tracks down toward the jungle cover lower on the slopes.

They carried the body to a cave under a cliff where the mountain shoulder was suddenly sheared away, and left it deep inside the earth. From there, they clambered for a mile down a small, nearly dry water course for a mile to another series of small caves.

'We stay here until tomorrow,' said Man. 'I'll go later to find the best way back up to the village.'

'We can't afford to wait!' protested McNeill. 'La's flying now and the rains'll start any day!' But common sense told him that they needed to lie up till the first furore over the missing sentry died down.

The others were grateful for the stop. Dirty, bloodied and exhausted, they gnawed at the last of their jerky and examine their sores. Lewis caught a lizard and offered to share it, with no takers. They took turns slipping in pairs down to the trickle of water which, even at the end of the dry season, still moistened the stream bed they had followed to the cave. Man vanished.

He returned to the cave in the early evening. 'Boy, oh boy, they're all stirred up! About twenty armed men in the village and a few more from other villages.' He beamed. 'My cousin in the village says of course, they don't know who or what they're looking for. Maybe tomorrow, when nothing happens tonight, they'll calm down and we can move up closer.'

'What about La?' asked McNeill. 'Can we make one of his flights if we wait?'

'Maybe not the first one, now,' said Man. 'Second one, pretty sure.

And I sent messenger down to Free Lao to hold on till day after tomorrow.'

'Not tomorrow?' asked McNeill.

Man narrowed his eyes slightly. 'Better to have time to figure out what we're doing first. I think we still make La's last flight.'

McNeill rubbed his palms over his knees. 'You're right, Man, my man. Better not to go off half-cocked.' No point getting worried too soon, he told himself. But the whole thing was taking longer than he had thought, even without this new delay.

'You're sure Jimmy's still alive?' he asked Man.

'My cousin says so,' replied the Meo with the faintest coolness. 'Or I'd of said.'

While they waited, McNeill took the men through the plan again. With the help of the Meos, they would lie up tomorrow somewhere nearer the village. Man's contact inside the village would tell them where Putnam was. They would then assess the situation and make final detailed plans for the snatch. Then they would wait for the Free Leo diversion in the valley the night after next to draw off most of the Major's soldiers.

In general terms, Spiegel's team, plus Man, would deal with any guards on Putnam (non-fatally, if possible), snatch Putnam, and run south with him to the airstrip. McNeill's team would provide diversion in the village, pulling out on signal from the first team. Lewis and Simpson, both good marksmen and fast runners, would hang back on the trail to delay possible pursuit until the men with Putnam had a good start toward the airstrip.

If unseen, they should have a good start on any pursuers. And, if they were really lucky, the Major might blame the Free Laos in the valley for the loss of his prisoner.

'We're counting on you and this cousin of yours, Man, my man,' said McNeill in the darkness of the cave. 'As long as we got accurate information, we got no problems. Just like that old Chinese general said.'

He's having a wonderful time, thought Simpson, listening to the energy in McNeill's voice. A little nervous but having fun. I wish I were. He squatted with his Chinese sniper's rifle across his knees. He still felt numb. He had known that the body's drive to live blots out any moral considerations. He had known it when he and McNeill first talked about this crazy idea of trying to rescue Putnam. How many times do you have to prove it to yourself? he wondered. Circumstances take over, so you better choose them carefully!

464

And I'll tell you something else – he recognized the in-charge doctor's voice addressing the obdurate patient side of himself – there better be a point to it all this time. We better get Jimmy out, or a certain Gabriel Simpson is going to be one screwed-up little boy!

Early the next morning, they took a cautious look at the village from distant high ground.

'Weird,' whispered Smith to Lewis. 'Don't look like any hamlet I've ever seen!'

McNeill and Man went closer. Man left McNeill, and slithered away into the scrub to find his cousin in the village. McNeill raised his head cautiously to study the lay-out. Big main gate, big enough for trucks and jeeps. Even if they were locked up at night, Oyama and Cucic could take care of opening them.

Right now, the place was wide open. Cattle and three buffalo grazed outside the bamboo palisade, with small boys watching them. Two old women were sitting just outside the nearest gate chewing their cuds and brushing away flies. McNeill continued to observe and wait for Man. After an hour and a half, Man returned, beaming.

'You lucky son of a bitch, Putnam's in there OK,' he whispered, 'in the Major's jailhouse. It's easy to get into, my cousin says. Only one guard. The Major thinks the mountains are good enough prison.'

'What about the other two in the photos?'

Man shook his head.

Even so, it was better than McNeill had dared to hope. Until he could get everything slotted into place, he always felt like ants were crawling under his skin. Now he felt great. They knew where Jimmy was. They knew the nature of their problem and it didn't seem that big. He and Man exchanged looks of pleasure.

'OK,' McNeill said. 'Let's go back and tell Cucic and Oyama to start getting their toys ready for tomorrow night!' He began considering different ways of getting to the jail without raising the alarm.

Before they had gone fifteen feet, a farmer sprinted out of the jungle, from where the trail leading west met the treeline. He ran along the edge of the field past the quietly munching buffalo, and through the gate in the palisade. Man dropped into a pile of rocks. He peered in the direction of the sun, then uncased his binoculars. McNeill sank down behind a clump of *lalang*.

For about seven minutes, nothing more happened. Then something else moved by the treeline. Man focused his binoculars. By squinting, McNeill could see enough to shock him to his boot soles. Four white men, in camouflage uniforms, wearing saggy tropical field

465

hats and carrying AKS rifles, were headed for the main gate of the hamlet.

'Round Eyes!' whispered Man, without lowering his binoculars.

'I don't fucking believe it!' said McNeill. 'Who are they?'

Man peered through his binoculars a little longer. 'No patches or . . . Hold on, I got a little red star here . . . on the hat. Looks like the Major's got some *raydoviki* for company.'

'*Raydoviki?*'

'Russian for raiders,' said Man. 'Just like us, only I bet they got permission to be here.' He stiffened. 'Hold on! There's more!' He wriggled himself lower into the rocky ground like a bottom-dwelling fish disappearing into the sand.

They came from the treeline, one at a time, well strung-out. Silently, with growing despair, Man and McNeill counted twenty-four black uniforms and twenty-four weapons.

'PAVN,' murmured Man. 'Regular troops. Oh, brother!'

A squad of North Vietnamese and a *spetznatz* team! Ants started to crawl under McNeill's skin. He hadn't planned for this, anywhere among the contingencies. Insufficient intelligence. He thought he had considered everything, but he hadn't, and he couldn't see his way around this one. 'What the hell is going on up here?' he muttered.

He and Man began to wriggle backwards down through the rock and scrub to tell the others.

24

'I knew you would come back,' said Thu. He turned and began to climb the track toward the villa, taking it for granted that she would follow. The boy climbed after him, with wide-eyed backward looks at this woman who was not the spirit of his dead mother after all.

Nina climbed numbly after Thu and the boy. Her thoughts felt like an inconsequential jumble. Thu had begun to go silver at the temples. And he had been pleased to see her. She had seen it in his eyes before he could hide it. She had not found Mouse, but when the boy asked 'Is it mother?' she had nearly cried 'yes!' Then the trail suddenly looked unfamiliar. And then she realized why. It was taking a new route upward, around craters blown into the mountainside.

The main gate of the villa was not exactly where it had been. Thu opened one arm in ironic welcome and stood back to let Nina enter first. If Perry had been able to get her an updated, higher resolution aerial photograph, she might have been better prepared for what she now saw.

Rain had washed former mud walls into indistinct ridges. The reservoir where the fingerling fish had snatched at gnats had become a grass-covered hump. The parade ground and former terraces had been rearranged into a foreign terrain of broken rock and raw mud. A giant foot had stepped on the palisade beyond. With a sense of dread, Nina raised her eyes to the main pavilion. It was gone. The bare rock was blackened like the remains of a campfire.

Thu followed her eyes. 'The second airstrike,' he said. 'They only tapped it the first time.' His voice was bitter. 'We repaired it all, so they visited again. With a little more success. Now we live under cover, farther down. It makes no difference to us!'

Could it have been me and not Major Lucky? Nina asked herself in terror. Did I say something in Bangkok, to Paul or Sloop? Did I let slip something that brought the iron crows here? She joined her hands as if in prayer and turned slowly, hoping still to replace this strange disorder with the image she had carried in her head. When she looked back at Thu, her horror showed in her eyes.

'It makes no difference!' he said again. 'Come with me. I want to show you something.' He took her arm. For a moment, they were both distracted by his hand, closed around the bone and flesh of her elbow. Then he led her across the irregular ground which had been the parade ground toward an edge where the rock terrace had been sheared away. Hien followed close behind.

I'm not ready for this yet, thought Nina. Everything is happening too fast!

'There he is,' said Thu. He pushed her forward to look down on the man in the bamboo cage below. '. . . Your mighty American who redesigns our mountain tops and our governments!'

Will John was still alive.

'An object lesson for our children,' Thu said. 'Not to be awed by imagined omnipotence!' He was watching her face.

'He has changed while in your care!' said Nina faintly.

Will John sat in the cage with his knees drawn up and his eyes closed like a meditating monk. His skin was drawn tight around his bones. Its former smoothness was scarred by infected sores and dark leathery patches where it had been badly burnt by the sun. Both his red-gold hair and his coppery beard were shoulder length. He had pulled his hair back into a rough plait.

At the sound of their voices, he opened his eyes.

They are still bright blue, thought Nina. Something familiar at last! She was afraid that Thu would feel the thudding of her heart through the hand still holding her elbow.

For a moment, the blue eyes looked up blankly. Then they filled with terror. Will John tried to leap to his feet and hit his head against the roof of his cage. He dropped to his knees and stared up through the bamboo bars at Nina and Thu.

Please! Nina implored him silently. Please! Don't say the wrong thing! Don't say anything! The critical moment had come too soon and caught her unready.

'Well, M. Haines,' said Thu in French. 'Which do you say is more important now – living or learning?'

Nina looked at Thu in confusion, but Will John seemed to understand Thu's purpose. He glared up at Thu, his lips tight and white over his teeth.

'I know enough,' said Will John. 'Don't hurt her!'

'You don't want to curse but observe at the same time?' asked Thu softly.

Will John shook his head. 'No. I do not want to learn anything more!'

'Would you fight to save her?'

Nina saw a tremor run through Will John's gaunt frame. Please, she begged him silently. The trap is so obvious! Oh God, please say that I don't matter enough!

The two men stared at each other.

Say no! prayed Nina.

'Yes!' shouted Will John. 'Yes! I would fight!'

Thu gave a sigh of satisfaction.

Will and I are both dead now, thought Nina. Being a prisoner has altered Will John's judgement. She was afraid to look at Thu.

'Are you satisfied, Colonel?' demanded Will John more quietly.

'On one count at least,' replied Thu.

'Of course,' said Will John, 'it means nothing to you – the concession of the egg of a louse. . . .' He looked from Thu to Nina. His eyes held a darkness she had never seen before but also, to her surprise, the faintest flicker of his old humour. 'He's a clever son of a bitch,' he said to her suddenly in English. He shook his head at some private thought. 'How did he trick you into coming here?'

'Speak French!' ordered Thu sharply.

'I came of my own free will,' said Nina to Will John, in French. 'And for a good reason.' She willed him to hear the caution behind her words, and the possibility of hope, so that he would not make another *kamikaze* act of defiance before she could weigh the consequences of his first one. Then Thu pulled her back from the rock edge.

Thu turned to the boy. 'Go away now, Hien. I want to talk to this woman.'

The boy gave Nina a last, long searching look and scampered away over the rubble. Thu climbed onto the blackened rock where the main pavilion had once stood and up new wooden steps to the observation platform. Nina followed and looked out once again into the vast space between the Tiger's Head and the distant plateau.

Between the new bomb craters, the mountain slope below the villa, once covered in jungle and thick scrub, had been shaved by a monstrous razor. Here and there, black, branchless trunks of former jungle giants stood alone and bare like stone age monoliths. Below the devastation, farther down the slopes, minute women bent and straightened in grey-blue-green poppy fields.

'Where is he?' asked Thu abruptly.

Briefly, Nina felt reality spin again. 'Where is who?' She had caught up with him by the time she had finished speaking.

'Our son.'

That reality had been so long ago, and so much rewritten. Numbly, she shook her head.

'Why did you come back, if not to return him to his father?'

'I came because you sent for me.'

He started to speak, then stopped. Finally, he said flatly, 'You're nothing to me now. Why should I send for you?'

She contradicted him gently. 'I have very acute hearing. You sent and I came.'

He walked to the edge of the stone platform. In the silence, an insect whirred in a tuft of grass on the trail above her head.

He doesn't know what he feels either, Nina realized suddenly. Will John's defiance doesn't seem to matter. Thu doesn't know what he wants any more than I do! The balance is not yet tipped either way.

'What have you done with the child?' Thu asked again.

'The child', this time, not 'our son'. She could avoid the question no longer. 'It was a girl,' she answered quietly, 'and she . . . died.' The truth in a way. Mouse might live, but Nina was not going to find her.

Thu still looked out over the edge of the stone platform into space, as if he had not heard.

'She looked like Hien,' said Nina. 'Even as a newborn. I loved her more than I had thought possible . . . for the few weeks that I had her.' Her legs gave way unexpectedly and she sank to her knees on the rock. 'She was bright and fierce. I loved her more than myself. As I think you love Hien.'

He continued to stand looking out into space. 'How did she die?' he asked finally.

The truth could tip him two different ways.

'I lost her during an air strike against the PAVN supply trails,' she said at last. 'I was carrying rice. . . .'

'American planes?'

She tried to read his tone. 'Yes,' she said. 'I think so.'

'Do you hate them for that?' he asked. '. . . The Americans?' His voice was neutral; his eyes still looked into space.

Careful! Nina warned herself. 'No,' she said. 'Not any more.'

'What a pity,' said Thu. 'I would have given you the pleasure of executing the prisoner yourself.'

Nina's thanksgiving for having sensed the trap was short. He crossed back to stand over her.

'It's clear to me,' said Thu, 'that you came because of him!'

'I came because of your message about your prisoner,' said Nina. 'That is not exactly the same.'

'You are willing to trade your life for his!'

His instinct for the truth, or near-truth, had always terrified her. 'Cousin,' she said, half-laughing, 'I know you too well to think that would be possible! I know that if you truly believe that, yuu will kill both Haines and me anyway.'

'He would give his life for you.' His eyes were now appraising as he looked down.

'That's his business,' said Nina.

'Then what do you want?' asked Thu. 'Why did you come back?'

More important, thought Nina, is what you want. 'Why did you take Haines prisoner?' she rejoined. 'And keep him so long?'

'Because,' said Thu, 'I couldn't think of a death severe enough for his crime.'

'What was his crime, exactly?' she demanded. She suddenly saw the way out, for all of them. It was a question of simple logic.

Thu's mouth tightened. He looked away.

Nina held her breath. Admit the truth, she urged him silently. Admit the truth and save us all!

Then he looked back at her almost defiantly. 'He stole you and the child.'

Nina let out her breath. If she had not already been sitting, she would have had to sit now. 'Then, Cousin, you must let him go.'

The silence grew so long that the sun elongated itself perceptibly above the eastern mountains.

He already knows, thought Nina. 'I have not seen Will John Haines since I left Saigon,' she said. 'He did not take either me or the child. He is innocent of the crime you want to punish. As a man of honour, you must let him go!' How ironic, she thought, if Thu will not believe the truth!

'You're lying,' he said.

'Then you must choose to believe that I came here to die with him.'

Thu dropped onto his haunches beside her. 'Why did you come back?' he demanded savagely. 'Give me an answer I can believe!' He put his face close to hers, as if truth gave off a detectable radiation, like heat. 'Why did you run from me a second time, if you weren't going to him? Why did you run away again?'

She did not let herself pull back from his anger. He had admitted that he had cared. A large change. 'I was still afraid of you,' she said.

'We had begun to share truths.'

'That was also frightening.'

'So why have you now come back?'

'Because I wanted to!' she cried, giving the only answer of which she was now sure. 'I don't know more than that. You must teach me why I wished to return! You show me the reason! I only know that I wanted to come back! And I believed that you wanted me to come!' As she spoke them, her words felt right.

Their faces hung a few inches apart. They stared into each other's eyes. Then Thu pulled back and drew a deep breath. He settled on his heels, raised his face and gazed up at the sudden sheet of sunlight flung over the Tiger's Head.

'You're not afraid of me any more?'

'I've put you into context,' said Nina, with the faintest touch of dryness in her voice. She folded her hands to steady them.

Thu shot her a sideways look. 'And in context, I'm no longer frightening?'

'I can live with it.'

He considered her answer for a few moments. Then he stood up and walked to the stone edge again. 'If you had stayed, our daughter would still be alive.'

A shard of glass stirred in her chest. He had found the one truth she could not look in the eye: Thu would have accepted Mouse as his own. In running away the second time, Nina had made the wrong choice and lost Mouse. She pressed her kneecaps into her eye sockets and rocked in pain.

'Perhaps she would be alive,' he conceded. 'Perhaps not.' The warmth of his hand fell on her shoulder. 'Who knows?' His hand tightened. 'Who knows,' he said again.

Nina coiled tighter into her pain. Thu's hand moved to her neck beneath the knot of her hair and squeezed gently. He squatted beside her. His hand ran lightly down her spine, then up again, and came to rest again on her shoulder, alert as a bird prepared for flight.

'You're still young,' he said. 'You can have another child.'

Nina stopped rocking.

'Is that perhaps one reason you came back?'

She raised her head, shocked by the force of the idea. 'I don't know. . . .' she murmured in surprise. 'I never thought. . . .' Suddenly, she imagined the warm, fragile weight of Mouse in her arms and smelled the sweetness of her hair. She felt the strong, demanding little mouth on her nipple and the imperative signalling of small hands against her skin. 'Oh God. . . ,' she said, closing her eyes. 'Perhaps!' The sensation of Mouse was so strong she could not bear it. The possibility of having that sensation again was drowning her.

'But not here,' she heard herself say. 'Not here, in the middle of war. . . .'

Thu's hand pulled her around. Nina reached blindly and burrowed into the curve of his embrace. His grip was tight, as in his sleep, as if he were afraid she would disappear.

They sat without speaking until the full circle of the sun broke free of the snagging mountains to float at liberty in the hot sky. Finally, Thu said, 'I have business to do, alas. The harvest is underway.' He leaned his mouth against her hair. 'It has been a very long time. . . .' He was hard against her thigh. With one hand, he opened the buttons of her cotton jacket and pulled the fabric aside. 'As you're here. . . .'

She felt the warm air on her skin and his fingertips on her nipples.

'All is as it was,' he said lightly. 'As far as I can see at the moment. And if I look any farther, I won't be able to face my men.' He stood and looked down at her, his eyes still a little wary. 'Full inspection later. Please report!'

After Thu left, Nina remained on the platform, gazing out toward the limestone peaks, trying to catch up with a reality which had suddenly spun ahead, leaving her giddy and gasping like a fairground rider.

I didn't expect to feel happy, she thought. I'm not sure that I have reason to feel happy. Thu and I have some slippery stretches still to cross on our tightrope of truth. The question of Will John's survival is not yet resolved. I don't know what to do about that, or what to say to Will John, or even how to get a chance to speak to him. She gazed out at the familiar limestone seagull on its crooked post and the squashed limestone top hat. But I'm back in the right play. The script feels right even if the ending still frightens me.

The boy was watching her from a perch on the highest of the rebuilt steps with the predatory interest of a young cat.

'I thought you were my mother's spirit,' he explained shyly, embarrassed by his earlier mistake. 'You look like me.'

'And I thought you were my daughter,' said Nina. 'You look like her. And my father. That's nice but strange. Are you disappointed that I'm not your mother's spirit?'

He shrugged unconvincingly. 'I don't care.' He paused as a happier idea struck him. 'I'm a very fast runner. Shall I show you?'

'I know already,' said Nina. 'I learned when I was trying to catch you. You ran faster than a mountain buck!' She felt nervous. She wanted to touch him, to see if his small warm body and thick dark hair felt anything like Mouse who might have looked so similar.

Hien looked pleased but shrugged again in modest disclaimer. He and Nina smiled at each other shyly. 'I'm a good fighter too,' he added *sotto voce*. 'But Father says I'm not to brag.'

Carefully, Nina said, 'You can brag to me if you like. If I were your mother, you could brag all you liked and I wouldn't tell your father.'

Hien nodded seriously. 'One day,' he said, 'if you wish, I'll take you into the jungle and show you how well I can hunt.'

'Show me as much as you like, any time. Please.'

'I have a gibbon, who comes when I call him,' said Hien, gaining momentum as his offerings continued to meet with approval. 'Shall I show you now?' He studied her again with his original quizzical seriousness.

'Please!' said Nina. She rose, crossed to the steps, and followed him down. 'I had a pet gibbon once – her name was Minou – but she had to be kept on a chain.'

'How terrible!' said Hien. He signalled with his head that she was to follow him out through the ruins of the gate which led down towards the river. On the steep track, he reached up to offer a small dirty hand to help her down over a boulder.

Nina took his hand, smiling and weak with terror at the intimation of something valuable, which could again be lost.

After meeting Hien's gibbon, which swung down from a branch onto the boy's head just as Minou had once swung from the coronet of mosquito netting over Nina's bed, Nina and Hien climbed back up to the ruined villa.

'Do you ever speak to the Round Eye prisoner?' she asked the boy casually.

'Sometimes,' he said. He reached up to break a bamboo stalk, then abandoned it. 'He's a coward, you know. Father says so. He won't fight like a man. Even when Father said he would shoot him, he just sat there in the dirt.' He climbed a few more steps. 'Everyone laughs at him.'

'Who is "everyone"?' asked Nina, beginning to understand the exchange between Thu and Will John. Will John's judgement might be less damaged than she feared. Like Perry, he may have sacrificed face in order to win the main point.

'All the boys,' said Hien. 'We're already crack shots. And I always beat Doi who's bigger than me at. . . .' Hien fell silent as he remembered the entire episode of his first triumph over Doi.

'There are different kinds of courage,' said Nina.

Hien paused and balanced on one leg to pick at something from the sole of his dirty bare foot. 'That's what M. Will says.'

'What do you think?'

Hien shrugged once more. Then he said, 'My father is very brave!'

'Beyond any doubt,' Nina agreed. She looked at the small averted face. 'Do you think he would mind if you took me to talk to the prisoner again?' she asked. As she couldn't imagine ever being allowed to talk to Will John alone, Hien was her first choice for chaperone.

Hien put his foot back on the ground and surveyed Nina with level eyes. 'I don't think he would stop you,' he said. 'But I better stay there too.'

Will John had been waiting for her. He rose onto his knees as she and Hien climbed up from the gate to the shelf of rock where his cage stood. 'Oh God, Nina. . . ,' he began.

'I really did come of my own free will,' she assured him. 'I'm in no danger. Please don't worry. Are you all right?'

Will John nodded and settled back on his heels. *'Bonjour, Hien,'* he said to the boy. *'Comment ça va?'*

The boy ducked his head to hide a half smile but did not reply. He and Nina sat on some broken rocks outside the cage.

Being near Will John again seemed quite natural, now that she was here, and strange as the context might be. He seemed to feel the same. They smiled at each other in shared disbelief and pleasure.

'Long time, no see,' said Will John in English. 'If, in fact, you're really here . . . I sometimes get confused.'

'I am really here,' she said. 'I would touch you to prove it, but I'm afraid the boy will report to his father.' She noticed thousands of tiny scratches on the bars of the cage, in groups of five.

'What are you doing here . . . of your own free will?' he asked.

'In Washington, I thought it was a noble act to get you out. But now I suspect the reason is more selfish.'

'That's good news on both counts,' he said. 'What are the chances of the first?'

'Better than even.'

His skin pulled so tightly over his bones that it seemed about to split.

'You sound as if we were chatting over a cup of coffee,' she said. 'It's funny – we were both more nervous during that first telephone call you made to Bangkok.'

'I've learned to take what comes,' said Will John. 'And that reduces anxiety, quite a lot.'

475

They studied each other in silence, laying the new foreign image of the other over the remembered image, like film transparencies. He shook his large red-gold head in disbelief.

'I used to imagine how I could explain away the past to you,' he said. 'But all those arguments seem irrelevant now.'

'I know,' said Nina.

'Will he let both of us go?'

Nina glanced at Hien's fierce surveying stare and shook her head.

'Would you come, if he did?'

She took longer to answer this question. Finally, she asked, 'Can you really see me shopping every Friday at the supermarket in the shopping mall, in our station wagon?'

He closed his eyes. 'No,' he said. 'Though I've tried. Over and over, tried very hard.' He opened his eyes again. 'And I've tried to give up Narragansett Bay.'

'And you can't?'

His new quietness was shaken by a deep tremor. 'I want to die there, not here!'

Then they sighed in unison, realized what they had just agreed, and smiled in sad complicity.

Hien looked from one face to another, with bright assessing eyes.

It's still easy with Will John, thought Nina. So easy. It's the rest of life that would be the problem.

'I thought you had been driven mad by captivity,' said Nina. 'When you told Thu you would fight for me. I apologize for underestimating you.'

He shook his head. 'He and I understand each other. We've had a chance to get acquainted while he's been leading me through the Valley of Shadows.' His voice was dry. 'And you and he are surprisingly alike in some ways, even though he's a terrifying pirate and you are the woman I loved and still love more than any other.' He offered the protestation simply. 'Your minds both work in the same fast, direct way. You would both die before admitting weakness. You're loyal and tenacious in your different ways, though I question your choice of cause in trying to save *me*. . . .'

' "Only because you're relevant," ' she quoted back at him. 'That won't change.'

'No,' he agreed. 'It won't for me either.'

'Has he treated you well?'

'Well enough that you mustn't make it another cause.'

Hien shifted his thin backside on the rock to signal his discomfort with so much English, which he could not understand.

'Hien,' said Nina, in Vietnamese. 'This is a good man. He is a friend of mine, whom your father is going to set free. We are discussing old times, and not saying anything to harm anyone.'

'Father says he's a coward,' said Hien.

Nina looked at him helplessly.

'Save that boy,' said Will John with sudden passion. 'There's a cause for you! Save the child, if you can! He's being made into a killer. I've been sitting here for weeks and weeks listening to it happening.'

'I would have to change his world,' said Nina. 'Otherwise I might be killing him.'

'Stop talking now!' said Hien.

'We'll speak French,' said Nina. 'So you can hear what we are saying.'

'He suspects an alternative,' said Will John. 'Or my supposed cowardice would not make him so angry. He sits and studies me.'

'He wants us to speak so he can understand,' said Nina.

Will John smiled at Hien. 'He is my silent friend when I am lonely,' he said slowly, in French. 'Until I look at him or speak, then he's gone like a Spirit of the Yellow Leaves.'

Hien looked away but again nearly smiled.

'We may not have another chance to talk,' said Nina. 'Ethan Perry is a good man, and he knows almost everything we won't be able to say to each other. When you get back, please ask him to start pulling strings for Thai residency, for three. Lord knows how he can clean up the principle party for official consumption!'

Hien was frowning with concentration.

'Is all this really your free choice?' asked Will John. He searched her eyes.

'So far,' said Nina. 'Though I have no idea how I'll put Ethan's string-pulling to Thu.' Or if I'll survive long enough to put it to him, she thought.

'You'll no doubt manage,' Will John said ruefully. 'You really won't reconsider the supermarket?'

She shook her head. 'Please don't. The choice is clear but not easy.'

'I know,' he said. 'Ditto.'

'Anyway,' said Nina, 'you're not free yet.'

'*Que sera,*' said Will John. 'And, my darling, whatever happens, I'm grateful.'

'Ditto,' said Nina. She began to rise.

'One last thing. . . .' said Will John. He looked away from her for the first time. 'I'm not sure you can answer this . . . The child that I'm supposed to have stolen. . . ?'

477

Nina glanced at Hien. 'It was yours,' she said in rapid English. 'A beautiful little girl, and she was lost when she was seven weeks old.'

Will John sat back and his face twisted. 'That's a little hard to take as it comes . . .'

'I nearly told you on that awful Fourth of July. . . .'

'I'm so sorry!' said Will John.

She realized that he meant to comfort her as well as himself.

'I'm glad she was mine,' he said. 'It's ignoble, male ego, but I'm very, very glad!'

She felt him beginning to settle back into himself. 'What did your wife have?' she asked.

'A girl as well. Louise. Very like my wife. . . .'

'Don't waste her,' said Nina. 'I wouldn't forgive you for wasting a daughter!'

'I think we stop now,' interrupted Hien uneasily.

'I'll make him send you back,' said Nina quickly. 'I swear!'

Will John nodded and raised a thin hand in farewell as Nina followed Hien back down the broken terraces, across a flattened section of bamboo palisade and into the scrub.

Thu and his villagers had moved down the mountainside to the east of the villa, onto a wide shelf high on the side of the river gorge. From the scattering of huts in the shade of a few pines and wizened dipterocarps, Nina could hear the faint grumbling of water far below, muffled by the scrubby jungle.

'Father says we will build a new villa on another mountain top, not so close to China,' explained Hien, as if apologizing for the modesty of the settlement. 'Here, we're at least close to the caves, in case the iron crows come again.' He turned a suddenly cool eye on Nina. 'I don't know where Father wants you to sleep,' he said. 'But you can come have morning rice in our hut.'

Most of the women were already in the poppy fields. A girl with one arm and a badly scarred face scooped up a small basket of sticky rice for Nina. After eating, Nina climbed back up to the ruined villa, followed by Hien and two of his friends. One of the boys had also been badly burned; his eyelids were drawn down toward the outer corners of his mouth and one ear was half the size of the other. While they played and wrestled, Nina sat on the observation platform until the sun grew too hot. Then she accompanied Hien and his friends down to the river.

'Always stay on the track,' he warned her. 'Many shells are still in the jungle. Two of my friends were killed. . . .' He veered away into

478

the water. Nina sat on a rock and watched them swim and fish until sunset brought the coolness of a mountain evening.

Thu returned shortly after sunset. The women had come back from the poppy fields and taken their jars full of sticky brown sap away to a hidden kitchen in the jungle where a few women remained to boil and purify it. The rest began to cook the evening rice, feed the tethered ducks and pigs, and call to the children who darted between the huts. Thu stalked past the old women seated outside huts tending toddlers and past a circle of men sharing Chinese cigarettes to squat on the ground beneath the thatched porch of his hut.

His day had dissipated the wary closeness of their dawn. He did not greet Nina or deign to comment on the modesty of his new style of living. Both he and Nina were silent as they ate sticky rice and boiled vegetables served by a woman from one of the other huts. When she once looked up and caught him watching her, he looked away.

He called to the woman who had served them and handed her his half-empty rice basket. 'Go sleep with Cousin Tranh tonight,' he said to Hien.

The boy's eyes swung from his father to Nina and back again. He stood up and left without speaking, taking his rice basket with him.

Nina heard Thu's intake of breath at his son's bad manners, but he did not call the boy back. Instead, he rose and went into the hut, taking the lantern with him.

'As you still seem to be here. . . ,' he said from the doorway. It was an order, not an invitation.

'So,' he said. 'So. Finally.'

She could hear the dryness of his mouth and the tightness of his voice. Their years apart were snapping at him like angry dogs.

'So,' she agreed, carefully. She wondered if he could see her blouse front jumping over her heart, in the dim orange light of the lantern which he still held.

He turned away and hung the lantern on a peg. Then he blew it out.

Nina shivered. 'Must we find each other in darkness?' she asked.

'It seems appropriate.' His shadowy form crossed the hut to the back wall and sank down onto a low wooden platform bed.

I'm in the right play, thought Nina, but I don't like it.

'Come,' said Thu. 'Or are you going to run away again?' He threw the shadow of his jacket to the end of the bed.

She slipped off her sandals and sat down beside him. 'Cousin. . . ,' she began.

'It's safer not to speak,' he said harshly.

His hands undid the buttons of her blouse and tugged at the folds of her *panung*.

'Wait . . .' she protested. She wanted to be tender . . . to learn if they could reinvent their passion, testing each other slowly, making no mistakes. She wanted also to set her terms. She half-resisted, half-helped as he pulled the pieces of cloth from her body.

'You thought I would make love like I fight,' he had said after their first time together, delighted by his own perception. 'I don't always fight.'

She had laughed with surprise at having her mind read. He was right. She had not expected such private gentleness and delicacy from a man who led so violent a public life.

Now he was fighting. In the darkness, she couldn't see his face, but she felt the rage in his hands as he pushed her down onto the sleeping mat and held her there.

'No!' she protested. 'Please. Not like this!'

He entered her roughly, too soon, then punished her with his thrusts.

'No!' she cried. 'No!' She pushed at him with her hands and twisted under him but he was already finished. He slumped over her for a brief moment, then rolled off. She swallowed against a sharp stone of desolation which had lodged in her throat. I have made another terrible mistake, she thought. I thought I could put it all right again. I tried again to do what is beyond me.

The silence grew thicker, harder to break.

'Are you still so angry with me?' she asked at last.

He lay beside her looking up at the shadowy underside of the thatch.

'It seems so,' she answered herself, after a moment.

He said nothing, but his anger filled the hut.

She was paralyzed. There was no other play to move on to, and this one was intolerable. She felt herself being turned back into a disposable thing and thought of what it had cost her to arrive at this moment. Heat began to burn up from her neck, rage to drum in her ears. She forgot safety, forgot to guard Thu's dignity, forgot all the reasons why, in a former life, she had once hidden her own rage. She forgot even her mission to save Will John.

Between her teeth, she said, 'Well, Cousin, I am angry too! When I learned that you were cheating me after Father died, I wanted to kill you, not because of the money . . . because you taught the world that I was vulnerable . . . when you should have been protecting me! I have been angry with you for years! You were my family, my partner, my lover, and you exposed me in a field to wild dogs and tigers!'

He turned onto his side away from her.

'Don't hide!' she said fiercely. She hauled on his shoulder to make him face her. 'The truth is that we have done terrible things to each other!' She pulled again at his resisting shoulder. 'And we have to admit it . . . both of us!' Rage boiled higher at his stony silence. 'But the other truth is that for some reason, we still seem to wish to try to be together. You wanted me back, and I came. And here we are!'

His back lay like the barrier of a mountain range between them.

'Speak to me!' she cried.

He didn't move.

With every ounce of her strength, powered by rage at past betrayals, she hit him on the shoulder with her clenched fist. Along with pain, as that frail arrangement of small bones and cartilege connected with the continent of his blade bone, she felt a mixture of terror and deep satisfaction.

He spun and leaped like an attacking cat. His weight crushed her to the sleeping mat; his face hung a few inches above her own. He was breathing hard.

Terror and satisfaction still warred in her. 'Here . . . we . . . are!' she repeated. She could hardly breathe beneath his weight. 'Now . . . what?' She took two shallow breaths with the top of her chest. 'That was no way, just now . . . to make a child!'

He lay across her, pinning her arms to the mat with his hands. She sucked for air again. 'I can't breathe!'

He released her arms and took his weight on his own hands.

She took a grateful breath. 'I won't punish you, but I won't be punished either.'

He remained suspended in the dark.

She felt light, almost giddy. She had thrown overboard almost all her ballast. And she was still alive and he was still there. She raised one hand to touch the back of his neck. She ran her finger along the hard ridge of tendon to his shoulder.

'Cousin,' she whispered urgently. 'We have no other life but this one. I came here by free will. Where we go from here is your choice.'

He groaned and rolled onto his back, pulling her with him, on top of him, holding her tightly. She pressed her face against his cheek and felt his hands cup her head to press it even closer.

Then he released her and stood up.

'No!' she cried in despair. But he was lighting the lantern.

★

481

In the warm, orange flickering light, he was still beautiful. Though new silver touched his hair, the years had not softened the clean lines of his limbs and torso with even a hint of fat. When he lay down again, beside her, she ran her fingers in familiar wonder from his ear lobe, along the high cheek bone, through the valley above his collar bone, across his ribs and along the curved muscle from his hipbone to his groin. The webbing of scars was like decoration scratched onto an elegant clay vessel. His breathing was shallow and his shadowed eyes watched her intently.

Then he scooped her hand off his belly and pulled her to lie against him. 'Not yet,' he said.

She put her head on his shoulder, her arm across the scarred chest. Later, she thought she might have slept, arcing from sleep to thought and back again like a leaping dolphin. Sometime in these hours, the last of the jettisoned ballast drifted out of sight and she sank into a deep peace. She remembered feeling a similar peace with him in the past, which she had not allowed herself to trust.

I was right, then, not to trust, she thought during one of her arcs upward from sleep. Have we both changed enough to trust it now?

She raised her head to study his face in the lantern light. He seemed to sleep. The dark forelock had fallen back, leaving his brow wide and exposed, like Hien's.

He never valued his own life, she thought with new clarity. But now he has Hien. The boy is not a speck of dust to be blown away in the wind. To learn to value any life is a very big change for Thu.

He opened his eyes. For a moment, they held terror. Then he recognized her. The relief which followed the terror told her more than any words he could have spoken.

They reached at the same time. His mouth closed on her breast, then moved to the other. He fed like a hungry animal on her collarbone, the line of her chin, her eyelids, her lips, the soft insides of her elbows, her belly. His hands stroked, located, greeted and confirmed, leaving a trail of fire on her skin. She clung to thought and judgement, still afraid to let go.

'Is all as it was?' she whispered when he paused once for breath, meaning to echo his morning joke.

He raised his head. 'Is that a large or a small question?' he asked. His hand lay warm on her thigh.

She drew a sharp breath. This was the man she remembered. 'Can you answer the large one?'

He looked at her in the lantern light for a very long time. Then he

482

watched his hand trace a line from her navel to her dark triangle of pubic hair while he seemed to examine his own thoughts. 'The large answer is that I think not,' he said. 'Not at all as it was.'

'Is the change good?' she asked, to be sure that she understood him.

'Oh, yes!' he said. 'Except for the new fashion of beating husbands-to-be. That must stop immediately!' His hand tightened between her legs and he lowered his face toward the one she was raising toward him. '. . . and the amount of talking!'

His weight and warmth moved onto her. Welcome, welcome back! she thought, before she wrapped her arms and legs tightly around him, and all thought slid away beyond reach of caution.

'A general,' said Thu.

'What?' murmured Nina sleepily. She half-turned in the circle of Thu's arm and tucked her buttocks deeper into the curve of his hard, warm belly and thighs. First light was just reaching the ground through the thin jungle canopy.

'He will be a general,' said Thu to the back of her head.

She opened her eyes and saw that the odd scratching sound near the door of the hut was a foraging hen.

'. . . our son,' said Thu.

'There are other things to be,' said Nina softly. 'And places to live where it might not be as necessary to be a general. . . .'

She lay in the stillness of his thinking.

'All is most definitely not as it was,' he said finally. 'You have become much more contradictory.'

She turned to face him. 'I learned from you, do you remember? . . . That good energy comes from the coupling of the tiger and the dragon. My darling tiger, what would you do with a chinchook lizard?'

The old familiar mockery appeared in his eyes. 'I'm glad you remember at least that much! You seem to have forgotten all my other lessons in good manners.' But he was smiling, nonetheless.

' "All is not as it was",' she reminded him gently. She turned her head and kissed the arm which encircled her.

'In any case,' he continued, 'I had already decided that we must leave this place.'

She left the subject there for the moment. When she turned to face him, he pulled her on top of him again and stretched his arms above his head.

'So?' he said.

She grinned back down at him. 'So!' she replied. She slid down and bit gently at his left nipple. 'So!' She bit at the right. 'So! So! So!'

483

25

Man took one of his men and was gone for three and a half hours. For most of that time, McNeill sat opening and closing his fingers as if he were doing exercises. Simpson watched McNeill. Bennett had his head down on his knees as if pretending not to be there. Smith and Oyama were on guard a little way down the hill. Spiegel wrote in a tiny notebook with a pencil stub. Stillwell watched the direction Man had gone. Lewis sorted through his pack. Cucic seemed to be asleep with his head on his pack.

'Maybe he's blown,' said Stillwell. 'They got him.'

'Never,' said McNeill tersely.

'You trust him, don't you, Bill?' said Simpson.

'I sent him in there, didn't I?'

Simpson had never seen McNeill so close to the edge of his nerves. 'OK, OK,' said Simpson soothingly. 'That was my nerves talking.'

'Maybe we should change position,' suggested Stillwell. 'It shook me up a little to learn he knows Russian.'

McNeill glared, then shrugged. 'Fine. Let's move.' He picked a place where they could see both the track from the village and their former position.

Man finally appeared out of the scrub, alone. He hunkered down on the opposite side of the trail from the old lay-up and began to pick his teeth with a twig. After fifteen minutes, McNeill signalled to him and he slipped around the side of the hill to join them.

'Good news and bad news,' Man said. 'Good news – the PAVN got Lucky's men under guard in the jail and are picking the rest up one by one as they come into the village. So we only got the twenty-four of them and the four Russians to worry about at the start. More good news – my cousin says as soon as the Major heard that the *raydoviki* were coming, he moved Putnam out of the jail, probably into one of the caves farther down the mountain that he sometimes uses like high security lock-ups. The ones in the photos. . . .' He looked at McNeill. 'I went and had a look. There's somebody down there, OK, with one guard. My friend stayed to get a better look.'

'The other two in the photos not in the caves either?' asked McNeill.

Man shook his head. 'Gone a long time. And now the really bad news – the *raydoviki* want Putnam too. When the search of the village didn't turn him up, they took the Major into the Palace to talk to him, private. It's been two hours already. And the PAVN are talking to the Major's men. They say the Major's in deep shit for messing the Russians around and anybody who wants to stay healthy and get old should think about how to be helpful.' He looked at McNeill. 'I agreed with my cousin that the villagers are very smart to get the hell out of that place.'

McNeill felt the tension among his men.

'How secure is your source?' asked McNeill. 'Forget the cousin crap. Could they tempt her?'

Man looked at the ground. 'She used to live on that mountain where the chopper put you down. The PL shanghaied her husband. A Chinese patrol burned her village down . . . after the North Vietnamese shot all the men for suspected collaboration with the United States. . . .'

Simpson and McNeill exchanged glances. There was an uneasy pause.

'Listen!' said Man angrily. 'She don't like the Chinese, the PL, or the North Vietnamese Army. She don't like the Russian Round Eyes. You guys're the only ones she don't hate. . . .'

Yet. The word hung unspoken.

'What does she expect in return for helping us?' asked McNeill.

'Nothing,' said Man flatly. 'I didn't promise nothing. You can't give her what she wants – that's another husband . . . another mountain. She just wants to get back at the guys who took away what she had.' He stopped and looked at McNeill's face. He slapped the American on the biceps. 'Hey, Cowboy, I know you always did what you could. I got no complaints.'

'Lucky it's the right cousin,' said Simpson. 'The one who's mad at the Chinese, the PL and the PAVN.' He locked eyes with McNeill.

Spiegel rubbed his chin as if checking his heavy stubble. 'If the Russians want Jimmy P. badly enough to come out here and get him, they'll play rough with the Major if they have to,' he said. 'They don't want to hang around here and upset the PAVN and Chinese any more than we do.'

'I think we got to go tonight, without the Free Lao diversion.' McNeill looked at Simpson as if for confirmation. Simpson nodded unhappily.

'I agree,' said Spiegel. 'No diversion, but a better chance of catching our flight! How're we going to do it?'

The Russians had already stopped talking to Lucky. They were about to allow the PAVN to pull his arms out of their sockets, thereby transferring the wrath of any sympathetic bystanders from themselves onto the traditional enemy.

Lucky's terror had at first been outweighed by outrage. For a start, the *spetznatz* officer spoke in bad French to the PAVN captain who translated into Vietnamese for Major Lucky. Secondly, Lucky was willing to negotiate. But these brigands weren't listening. They wanted this American for free!

'I found him!' he had protested, though strictly speaking he had not. 'I fed and nursed him! I have been useful to you in the past. You still need me! You owe me something!'

The first of these two points carried no weight with his interrogators. They had been patient until after the midday rice because they hoped Lucky would decide to tell them without coercion. Lucky's second point about their debt to him was slightly coloured by hints Rogov had dropped in three recent consecutive reports, about Lucky's political promiscuity.

'Can you remember who you're talking to?' asked the Russian. 'Are you sure you haven't confused us with the Americans?'

'It can sometimes be difficult,' Lucky had said in his best Swiss boarding school French, 'to tell one thug from another.'

The officer laughed, as if he appreciated the joke. 'String him up,' he said to the PAVN captain. 'If you have any trouble, I'm sure he can tell you how it's done.' He left the room.

'Can I trouble you for some rope?' the captain asked Major Lucky politely.

McNeill asked Simpson to come with him back to the morning's look-out point. The gates of the hamlet were still open. The villagers were already slipping away into the jungle. The arrival of soldiers of any kind always boded ill. Women with babies and bundles pulled larger children along with them. One old lady, not two, sat by the open gate. The small boys had deserted their buffalo and oxen which were now scattered around the mountainside grazing, or settled slackly here and there on the ground like great grey and rust-coloured balloons half-filled with water.

'I wonder how the Major's holding out,' said McNeill. 'Once the Russians have Jimmy, we can kiss him goodbye.' He looked at Simpson, who nodded.

I should be flattered, thought Simpson, that he needs me to confirm. 'Without the Free Lao diversion,' he said, 'we may get Jimmy out of the cave and find twenty-eight armed men with nothing to do but chase us . . . plus any of Lucky's men they can recruit.' He turned to McNeill with a sudden awful thought. 'By the way, Bill, what happens if we engage the Russians?'

'We can't!' replied McNeill. 'Absolutely no way! I've been thinking about that since I saw them this morning. As if we didn't have enough problems, we can't shoot at a Russian! We just can't!'

'Maybe they won't want to engage us, either. Maybe they'll be just as scared of setting off another war.'

'Maybe,' said McNeill. 'I wish I knew how important Jimmy is to them.'

They stared down at the hamlet. As they watched, eight PAVN soldiers came out of the gate and stood arguing and pointing in different directions.

After watching them for a few seconds, McNeill said, 'I guess the Major hasn't broken yet – they don't know where to start looking.'

A few seconds after that, they heard a long, high-pitched scream from the Major's palace.

The first thing that Thu did next morning was to order Will John's release. Thu met him on the remains of the upper terrace.

'You go with the first shipment of cargo tonight. Until then you are my guest.'

Nina, Thu and Will John ate morning rice together on the observation platform, where Thu could keep an eye on the track down to the airstrip. The first bundles of raw opium were already being moved.

Will John walked shakily, unused to exercise. Nina also observed that he had to concentrate to keep his mind on their bizarrely polite conversation.

'We must move soon,' observed Thu as he peeled an orange. 'The soil is dead. Poppies won't grow here much longer. I must find my Meos another mountain.'

'A good soldier and brave man can always find an occupation in the tri-border area of northern Thailand,' said Will John casually.

Thu did not deign to lay claim to Nina in front of Will John by either gesture or act, but he was alert to every flicker of energy that passed between her and his former prisoner. Will John and Nina tried to avoid looking at each other either too much or too little; under

Thu's sharp gaze, the exact degree was surprisingly hard to gauge.

'You are at liberty until the evening,' Thu told Will John. 'Please feel free to walk about, but stay on the tracks . . . we have lost two farmers and two children to unexploded shells.'

In fact, an armed guard was never far away from Will John. Nina decided against trying to talk to him again. The guard would undoubtedly report the contact to Thu, and though she felt nearly safe with him now, the balance could still be easily tipped.

It will take time for us to trust again, she thought. Time and a shared child.

It was an odd day. She wanted only for it to be over, as if it were a comma in the flow of life. Several times, she saw Will John's red-gold head pass through her line of vision. She would think of urgent things to say to him then remind herself that he was flying only out of Laos that night, not off the edge of the earth. In a few days, he would be talking to Ethan Perry.

As she waited for the day to pass, she thought often about Ethan Perry and his sudden passionate desire to take part in her lunatic mission. She tried to imagine herself back among the antiques on the pale blue carpet. The result was pleasant, but unreal. Then she would look around the jungle clearing where an old woman was picking ticks from the head of a naked male toddler and three ducks protested indignantly from under their hemispherical basket prison. It all felt more real than the Duncan Phyfe candlestand and Victorian travel books, but it was not the final scene of her play.

I may not be an American mall-shopper, she thought, but I'm not a poppy farmer's wife either.

When she climbed to the observation platform during the afternoon, Will John was sitting in the blackened rubble of the pavilion, the guard leaning a few yards away. They smiled but did not speak. More than anything, the freedom Thu had given Will John to roam convinced Nina that he did indeed mean to leave this mountain top.

At dusk, just as Will John was about to be escorted from the main gate to the airstrip, he looked at Thu. 'May I. . . ?' He touched Nina's hand.

Though stiff and wary, Thu made no objection.

Will John picked up Nina's hand and kissed it gently. 'My first teacher,' he said. He turned to Thu and bowed slightly. 'And my second. Among other things, I have learned never to begrudge myself good fortune when it deigns to visit. May it visit you generously in the future, Colonel.'

'Thank you,' said Thu formally and noncommittally.

Hien, carrying a rifle whose length was two-thirds of his height, was part of the escort party. He stood near Will John, looking past him.

'*Au revoir, M. Hien*,' said Will John. He held out his hand. 'I will think of you when I am in America, and hope you might sometimes think of me.'

Hien looked at Will John, then at his father. Then back at Will John's hand.

Mouse would have decided for herself, thought Nina with absolute conviction.

Hien looked at Nina, shifted his rifle to his left side and took Will John's hand. Unsmiling, he shook it twice, hard, then dropped it, shouldered his rifle and stood smartly to attention, staring straight ahead.

Will John caught Nina's eye across the heads of the soldiers and porters massed by the gate.

I'll try to save the boy, Will, she thought. I'll try! She raised one hand in farewell. Thu turned his head away, as if checking a nearby pile of bales.

One of the soldiers called an order and the mass of bodies began to move. Even towering over the darker heads around him, Will John soon vanished from sight.

As quickly as he vanished from my car in Saigon, Nina thought. On that awful Fourth of July.

Thu watched the procession, counting bales. When the last mule had gone through the gate, he asked suddenly, 'Do you want to go with him?'

'Are you serious?'

'Do you question my honour or my understanding?'

'Neither,' she said. 'Only your trust.'

'I nearly trusted you once before.' His tone was deceptively level. 'I would rather you went now. . . .'

He means that he won't survive another betrayal, she thought. 'I don't want to go,' she said simply. 'I just don't want to.'

He waited, as if giving her time, still, to change her mind.

'Besides,' she said. 'I can't leave you at the mercy of nothing but chinchooks.'

The relief in his eyes was as great as it had been the night before.

'Then I'm very glad to see the last of him,' said Thu.

Night came abruptly. Nina waited on the rock observation platform as the sound of the light aircraft engine climbed and dwindled in the dark sky. This ending of a possible life caught briefly at her throat.

Go! she willed it. Go! While I am still happy at the way it has all worked out.

Then the faint sound died and the night sounds pressed in again. The rock was still warm beneath her thighs, as warm as Thu's body.

We've made it! she thought. Will John is free. Thu is retrievable. Hien is only a very young general. I have a family and a place in the world. It needs working on still, but I think we may all have made it!

She stretched herself full length on her back on the warm rock and looked up at the astonishing, sagging net of stars. A small creature rustled dryly across the rock and an insect whirred in the tuft of grass on the trail up the Tiger's Head.

I'll invite Ethan to visit us in Thailand, or Burma, or wherever we end up. I wonder what he'll make of Thu. She stretched again sensuously and rolled onto her side to watch for the lights returning up the trail from the airstrip.

All three, Nina, Thu and Hien, went to the hut that night. Thu hung his lantern on a peg under the porch and cleared his throat.

'Hien,' said Thu. 'This woman will be your mother now. It is time you had more to do with women.' He watched his son with a severity which masked a deep fear of making the boy unhappy.

Hien drew in and let out an enormous breath. 'What does that mean?' he asked. His voice wobbled ever so slightly. He looked away from Nina and his father, and his face worked in a way which Nina could not read.

She knelt in front of him, put her mouth near his ear and whispered, 'It means that you can brag about anything you like. And it means that I won't go away.' Please, she implored any listening deity, let me keep that promise!

'Does my real mother mind?' asked Hien. He sounded angry.

Thu started to speak, then closed his lips again.

Nina shook her head. 'No,' she said carefully but firmly. 'She is very happy that someone is here in the world of men to do the things for you that she would like to do herself.'

'How do you know?' Hien asked fiercely. His large eyes were now bright with the threat of tears, but challenging.

Nina drew a shaky breath. 'I know,' she said, 'because I have a daughter in the spirit world with your mother, and *I* am very happy that someone is there to care for her, the way I will care for you in this world.'

Hien turned his face aside.

'Would you like me to do that?'

He shrugged. Then he nodded a quick little jerk with his face still averted.

'Shall we go to the graves together in the morning to tell your mother?' asked Nina. 'And ask her for her blessing?'

Hien nodded once more, with his lips sucked in and his nostrils pinched. He blinked three times. Then he gave Nina a quick, almost furtive smile. She sent back a smile of blazing joy. Hien stared back a moment longer before all his young male dignity and stoicism deserted him.

'Ohh,' he said quietly, and tears ran unchecked down his cheeks from under the dark lashes of his closed eyes, while he stood, arms at his side, neither fighting nor giving in. Nina wanted to embrace him and bury her face in his soft hair. Instead, she took both of his hands in hers and waited, feeling the tight grip of his bony little fingers, kneeling beside him while he allowed eight years of tears to leave him at last.

'We're all agreed then, *mon petit général*.' Thu's voice finally broke the mood. Something in his tone made Nina stand up and turn to face him in the lantern light. In her joy at Hien's acceptance, she took a second or two to register the odd expression in Thu's eyes as he looked at her. Then she realized what she had said, or rather, not said, to Hien.

'I have a daughter . . .' Not 'You have a sister.'

Not now! she thought in despair. Please, not now!

'Thu,' she said. 'Husband. . . .'

He continued to look at her with the same odd detachment, smiling a strange, reflective half-smile. 'Truth. . . !' he said.

She touched his scarred left hand which he had hooked in his belt. With her other hand, she touched his mouth, as if silencing him. 'Our past is as heavy as a fishing net full of rocks,' she said softly.

His eyes seemed frightened of what she might be going to say. She wanted to say, don't worry, I know that there are limits to what a human soul can bear.

'We can set aside anger,' she said, 'but we will always continue to know what we know. We can't erase the past. But we must try to transform it into a future. Otherwise, we will never move, trying to drag all those rocks around with us.' She reached up and kissed him lightly on his unmoving lips. 'Don't search for more rocks.'

Neither of them breathed. Behind her, Hien also seemed to be holding his breath.

'We choose the truth we decide to act on,' said Nina, 'as best we can. My truth, which took me a long time to find, is that I wish to be with you. Please choose to share it.'

Thu lifted his free hand and pressed her fingers hard against his lips. Briefly, he shut his eyes, as if to erase the expression they had carried a few seconds before. When he opened them again, they were clear and tinged with the slightest hint of amusement.

We know each other so well, thought Nina, that we will never need to discuss our complicity. She smiled up at him, sharing both his relief and his amusement.

'We're all agreed, then,' he repeated. 'It would be fitting to mark the occasion by going back to offer gifts at the family tombs in your father's village,' he said. 'Or what's left of them. I shall find out what travel conditions are now like in North Vietnam. In the meantime, you and the boy should by all means go in the morning to let his mother in on the latest domestic gossip.'

Nina felt Hien come to stand close beside them and laid her free arm across his shoulders.

Simpson and McNeill watched eight PAVN take a track away from the village, to the east.

'The caves are the other way,' said McNeill. 'South west.' He was opening and closing his fingers again. They had not heard a second scream.

More villagers slipped away. Then a few more, with more children.

'What would your ancient Chinese general suggest now?' asked Simpson. 'Just how do we descend like a thunderbolt?'

'I been thinking about him,' said McNeill.

'Anybody ever been a farmer?' he demanded when he and Simpson had returned to the group's lie-up position. Lewis and Cucic were on guard, but the rest were huddled anxiously, not talking.

'Yo!' said Bennett, raising his hand as if volunteering to be eraser monitor. 'My pop had a dairy herd . . . Why? Are we going to give up on Jimmy and play "What's My Line?" instead?'

'When it's dark,' said McNeill, 'I want you to see how close you can get to those cows down there.'

'Those aren't cows!' said Bennett. 'And I can tell you now – about sixty feet.'

'But those little kids . . .' began McNeill.

'You can tell a city boy,' said Bennett pityingly. 'Those little kids, yes. Round Eyes end up as human hamburger.'

McNeill thought a moment longer. 'Man, I need some of those kids.'

'No!' said Simpson. 'You can't use children!' He saw Boucher crossing the field, headed for the hut where the baby was crying.

'Kids and fat,' said McNeill to Man. 'Three or four boys who can keep their mouths shut and as much coconut butter or oil or lard as you can find. And try to get as many more people out of the village as you can without raising an alarm.'

'What are you going to do to the village?' asked Simpson.

McNeill's eyes were absent with thought. 'Bennett, Stillwell . . . go cut some bamboo. About a hundred feet of length and 2–3 inches in diameter. Then, dry grass. Really dead, so it will burn nice and easy. A little heap of it, so high.' He held out a hand at waist level. He turned to Spiegel. 'Dig out the biggest bandages you got.' He looked around the group happily. 'The problem is twenty-four PAVN, four *raydoviki*, and no diversion, right?'

'Bill,' repeated Simpson, 'what are you going to do to the village?'

McNeill told them what he had in mind.

Spiegel nodded. Bennett doubled over in mock hysterical laughter.

McNeill turned to Simpson. 'That sound OK to you, Gabe?'

Simpson shrugged helplessly. 'Who can tell?'

'It worked for T'ien Tan in 279 BC.'

Bennett now turned his eyes toward the heavens. 'I knew this guy was nuts from his first phone call! We got nukes, and he talks about 279 BC!'

'Oh, the principle's fine,' said Simpson to McNeill. 'Principles are always fine. It's the practice that screws us up.' He looked at McNeill's face. Bill wanted his approval, for some reason. 'It sounds like a great idea,' said Simpson. 'Great!' He looked around the rest of the group. 'I think it should work,' he said. 'Really.' He looked at Bennett. 'Better than nuclear bombs.'

'Time for me to relieve Lewis out front,' said Spiegel. 'Wish I could see his reaction when you fill him in!'

When Lewis returned, McNeill set him to dropping small stones into the metal canteens and tying them in pairs. Stillwell and Bennett disappeared to cut their bamboo and dry *lalang*. McNeill gave final instructions, then went to relieve Cucic. When Cucic returned, he and Oyama opened their packs and began to sort through their supply of explosives. Spiegel laid out his entire stock of triangular bandages then began to stripe them with night-black camouflage make-up.

Gabriel Simpson found himself removing the sacks from four pack frames, redistributing their contents into the remaining four packs, and tying witches brooms of Stillwell and Bennett's *lalang* onto the frames, like the ear tufts of giant owls. After half an hour, he became totally immersed in the problem of making the pack frames into mammoth masks of grass, leaves, bandages and rattan.

Man returned in two hours with the requested fats, three small boys and confirmation that Putnam was definitely in the second cave in the line of five shown in the photograph, counting from the top. Oyama and Cucic supervised Lewis, Stillwell and Bennett as they made the *lalang* into more witches brooms, and packed them with coconut fat and oil. Man went to cut lengths of flexible, rope-like rattan.

As dusk thickened, the three boys began to herd the buffalo and oxen slowly toward a patch of field partly shielded from the village by a stand of bamboo and *lalang* tussocks. While the boys were gathering the animals, Man passed on information from his two companions about the schedules of the PAVN sentries. The men rehearsed the details of the planned sequence of events.

'How long will it take you to get ready this end?' asked Spiegel.

'The boys think about half an hour, for them,' said Man. 'Maybe a little more.'

'Forty-five for me,' amended Oyama. 'With a guard just inside the main gate.'

'Forty-five it is,' agreed Spiegel. 'You may have to give us a little longer than that to respond. Don't panic.'

'I won't, but the cows might,' said Bennett.

'Is this really going to work?' asked Cucic. He was white around the mouth with nerves.

'It's been tested on the ground,' said McNeill.

They synchronized their watches. McNeill gave Spiegel the Verrey pistol and three flares.

'Remember what I told you at our first meeting,' said McNeill. 'No heroes. I want to see every goddam one of you at the airstrip. Plus one. Jimmy'd hate a trade-off just as much as me.'

Spiegel, Cucic and Lewis set off into the darkness after Man, to the south west, down toward the five caves. Oyama took his pack and crawled away in the direction of the village, followed shortly by Stillwell who had his eye on the newly-changed sentry.

The three boys worked like small, serious demons, tying onto the oxen and two buffalo the objects which they and the men had prepared during the afternoon.

'Leave the canteens and bamboo till last!' whispered McNeill urgently.

The boys lashed the pack-frame masks between the animals' horns. They rigged loose harnesses of rattan rope around the beasts' bellies and attached fluttering strips of white bandage, the paired canteens, and hula skirts of bamboo canes on fine strips of rattan. They tied fat-packed bundles of *lalang* to the tails and horn tips.

The animals began to stamp and low, as their transformation progressed. The new clatter of their own movements began to alarm them.

'Keep the damn things quiet, can't you!' begged McNeill.

495

Two of the boys hung on the neck of one bullock, crooning and soothing it back to relative calm.

'Mahhhooouh!' a cow protested.

'Oh Jesus!' whispered Bennett. 'Can't they shut it up?'

'Come on, Spiegel!' begged McNeill. 'Come on! Any time now. Come *on*!'

'OK,' whispered one of the boys in English. He raised a thumb in the air. 'Ready for take-off!'

The boys began to herd the restless, complaining animals toward the village, with the men close behind. The racket the animals made as they moved sounded deafening.

'Come on, Spiegel!' muttered McNeill again. The rest of the men watched the dark sky to the south west.

'Come on, Spiegel!' they muttered in incantation. 'Come on, Spiegel!' They held their rifles unslung and lighters ready, while the three boys were poised near them with unlit, fat-filled torches.

Lewis caught the sentry by the cave off guard. A blow behind the ear sent him to the ground.

'Didn't see us,' panted Spiegel. 'Leave him. Like Bill wants . . . One, two!'

He and Cucic climbed into the second cave.

'Jimmy Putnam, are you in there?' Cucic called softly. 'We've come to take you home.'

'Come on, Spiegel! Come on Spiegel!'

The animals were becoming more and more agitated. They swung their heads from side to side, trying to throw off the alien weight on their horns. They switched their tails and bucked their hindquarters.

'They're going to knock it all off again, if Spiegel doesn't blow the starting whistle!' muttered Bennett. 'Oh God, Spiegel baby, where the fuck are you?'

'Who's that?' asked a stunned, hoarse voice in the darkness of the cave.

Spiegel and Cucic followed the voice back into the cave to a heavy grilled metal door. Something was scrabbling in the darkness behind the grille.

'Who is that?' croaked the voice again.

'Some old friends from the World,' said Cucic. 'We're gonna look after you now. How far away from this door can you get?'

'Oh, my God!' said the voice. 'Oh, my God!'

Cucic repeated his question.

'Thirty of my feet,' came the immediate reply this time. 'Size eleven.'

'I'm going to turn on a light,' said Spiegel. He turned the beam of his flashlight onto the lock on the grille.

'Get as far as you can, and get down,' said Cucic. 'I'm going to blow this gate to get you out!'

'Gimme time . . . time!'

'All you want of it, once we get you out,' said Spiegel. 'Are you flat on the floor?'

'Yes.'

There was a silence of a few seconds while Cucic worked in the beam of Spiegel's light.

'Count twenty,' said Cucic. He and Spiegel retreated to the mouth of the cave.

After 20 seconds, a blinding flash, brief as lightning, lit the cave. The explosion shook pieces of rock loose from the walls and ceiling.

'Putnam, you OK?' asked Cucic.

There was silence.

'You OK?' repeated Cucic, as he and Spiegel clambered over the hot wreckage of the grille and fallen rubble.

The voice was faint and confused. 'Over here. Over here.'

Spiegel's light found the dazed face of the man raising himself awkwardly from the cave floor. Cucic took his hand to help him stand. Then he embraced the thin shaking body.

'Take it easy, Jimmy. You're going to be OK now. Leave it to us. We're going to take you home.'

Putnam was so weakened he could hardly stand. Spiegel and Cucic supported him between them and dragged him out into the night air.

'I don't believe it!' murmured Putnam. 'I don't believe it!'

Spiegel fired off the red flare.

The red glare lit the sky behind the trees and sank slowly back into darkness.

'They got him!' cried McNeill in exultation. 'Go, Goddammit! They got him! *Go!*'

Small fires ignited in the darkness, lighting larger fires.

'Go, Oyama!' begged McNeill. 'Oyama, where are you?'

The side gate of the palisade exploded. Then the main gate blew out, taking a length of palisade with it and setting the night briefly alight.

The cattle bolted away from the village. Then bolted back again, away from the volley of gunfire behind them.

Voices shouted inside the palisade. A woman began to scream, pumping out a high, continuous wail of terror and despair. McNeill, Bennett and Simpson fired again and the cattle stampeded through the broken palisade into the Avenue St Cyr. Two grenades, thrown wide, sent them careening and wallowing along the avenue. The dangling three-foot lengths of bamboo and the stone-filled metal canteens rattled and clattered along the ground. Behind them swirled the yellow and green clouds of smoke grenades. The flaming witches brooms on their horns and tails set fire to three huts. From their heads, monstrous demonic faces leered through the smoke and growing flames.

The terrified animals galloped and bellowed, trying to dislodge the flames from their horns. They swung long burning tails of bamboo and fat-impregnated *lalang*. In their panic-stricken stampede, they trampled a PAVN soldier who tried to run out through the now-burning gate.

The charging demons reached the Palace and spread up the fan of avenues. Soldiers peered in disbelief and confusion from the front gate of the jail. One had climbed to safety on the shoulders of Major Lucky's statue. Several huts near the main gate were now burning fiercely and others began to catch fire along the avenues. Guns began to fire inside the village. Villagers who had not slipped away took refuge on the raised verandah of the Palace. McNeill threw a last smoke grenade through the side gate and ran. Another charge exploded along the side of the palisade. Simpson threw a final smoke grenade and followed McNeill.

There had been not one, but two sentries at the cave. The second had gone a short way off to relieve himself just before the Americans arrived, leaving his rifle leaning against the cliff face outside the cave. When he heard someone in the darkness, he froze against the rock, trying to figure out what was happening. Then he saw the size of the two men who climbed up into the cave. He heard the explosion and started to run. When he saw Lewis on guard outside the cave, he froze again. Just as Spiegel and Cucic carried Putnam out of the cave, the sentry decided to run for help. He pushed past Lewis, jumped from the rocky ledge outside the cave and disappeared into the black jungle.

Spiegel and Cucic were hampered by Putnam. Lewis, who was closer than Man, leaped after the sentry but lost him.

'Oh hell! Oh hell!' said Spiegel.

'What was that?' came Man's startled whisper from farther up the track. 'I heard something go by me just now!'

'A sentry that got away,' said Spiegel.

Man hissed between his teeth. 'Got Putnam?' he asked.

'Yeah!'

'Let's move!' said Man. 'Better go up the track. We got to cover ground before they come back for us.'

Then pandemonium broke loose above them, in the village.

'Run, you son of a bitch!' Cucic begged Putnam. 'Or we'll all be keeping you company back in there. Just stand up! You'll be OK now. Your friends have got you.'

Cucic and Spiegel half-carried, half-dragged Putnam up the track.

'Listen to that!' said Lewis exultantly. 'Will you just listen to that going on up there!'

Hanging against the door of the drawing room of his palace, Major Lucky had fainted. He was doing his best to burrow deeper into the blessed respite of the faint when the village gate was blown in.

The *spetznatz* leader ran from the drawing room onto the verandah of the palace. He fought his way forward through shouting, screaming villagers and stared down into the Palace. For a few seconds, he was dazed by the smoke and confusion, then he recognized the demons for what they were. He took another moment to consider how they had come to be charging and milling in the streets. Then he sprinted back into the palace to call the other three Russians and the eight PAVN who were in the dining room and on the back verandah respectively. He put his head back into the drawing room.

'Leave the blubber bag!' he told the two PAVN standing beside the Major. 'There's somebody out there we've got to find!'

The sentry from the cave panted up the mountainside to the back gate of the village and stopped dead, staring at the smoke, flames, and charging beasts who had ricocheted off the far end of the village and were beginning to mill about, setting more huts on fire as their torches burned to their last inches. Broad grey and rust-brown backs churned around Major Lucky's statue and across the canna beds. The sentry heard the gunfire. He watched for one brief moment more, then slid back into the trees to find his wife and children where they had hidden for the night with the other villagers.

A few small boys clung to the plinth of the Cenotaph and three others – two of whom had helped prepare the buffalo – leaned over the Pagoda porch, watching the excitement. The third helper, who had been hit by a stray PAVN bullet, would not be found until the morning.

★

Simpson and Lewis took cover just off the beginning of the track to the Tiger's Head.

'Look at that!' Lewis kept saying. 'Will you fucking look at that!'

Organization was beginning to quell the confusion in the village. Tiny dark shapes beat at the flames. Groups were forming. Then the first white phosphorous flare went up. The hot night turned briefly into cold day.

'They're looking for us,' said Lewis, gleefully. 'But they're not going to find us!'

Simpson looked at his watch in the fading white light. The others had nearly a half an hour start. How much distance they had made depended on Putnam.

Maybe we've done it after all, he thought. With no more damage than some burned huts and shell-shocked buffalo. And the sentry I shot yesterday, he reminded himself.

'Beautiful!' said Lewis, as a second flare lit the tree tops and *lalang* tussocks into high relief against black, black shadows. 'Son of a bitch!' he said suddenly. 'There's someone coming!' He raised himself slightly and settled into firing position.

'No!' said Simpson. 'No!'

Lewis fired a single shot. The small silhouetted man spun around and fell.

'You shithead!' said Simpson, as they backed out of their positions. 'You goddam idiot!' Simpson felt like crying. They ran, doubled over, toward the trail to the Tiger's Head. Simpson heard a shot and saw Lewis nose-dive into the rocky ground. Another flare went up, still from the village. Lewis had been hit in the back of the head.

Like Kennedy, thought Simpson. Just like Kennedy. He waited, motionless. Nothing moved between him and the village. Then a man was silhouetted briefly against the flames inside the gate.

Gone for reinforcements, Simpson thought. Now they know which way to look. He dragged Lewis off the track, behind a cairn of rocks.

Maybe Man will keep them busy at the village. Maybe they won't find Lewis, he thought. Maybe they won't be sure we've taken the track. He kept his mind off the reality of Lewis's death. And of having to tell Bill. He sprinted south along the track.

There were at least five men on the track behind Simpson. And they had spotted him. He fired two single shots over their heads. They dropped into cover. Simpson turned and sprinted south again, keeping low. He heard a shout, then a crack. And another. He leaped over the crest of the ridge like a rabbit.

The parachute flare lit the mountain ridge like a floodlight at a football game. Simpson hit the ground, rolled over a hump and into a shallow hollow in the rocky soil.

Just like the Fourth of July, he thought. I may die . . . Fourth of July.

Another flare etched out jet black shadows in the rocks and between the wrinkles of his shirt.

He wondered how close to the Tiger's Head the rest were now, with Putnam and whether they would make the opium flight.

'The flight for Ban Houei Sai, Phayao and Chiang Mai is now boarding at gate number. . . .'

I might be able to take out five, he thought, if I have the right cover. And don't hesitate. Plans always seem so complete until you're in the middle of the reality . . . then all kinds of unexpected details crop up. Like Lewis's decision to shoot someone, then shuffle off this mortal coil when someone, not surprisingly, shot back.

'Come out,' shouted a voice in accented Vietnamese. Another flare floated its deadly glare down from the sky.

Simpson peered cautiously over the hump. As far as he could see, they were no closer. Two of the figures had looked much taller than the others before they hit the ground.

The voice repeated its order in guttural French.

There's always a chance I'm dealing with reasonable men, thought Simpson.

'Hey, *raydoviki*, try English!' he shouted back. He waited for the last flare fired to die away.

There was silence and darkness for a count of six. 'I'm an American!' shouted Simpson. 'With as much right to be here as you have. Think about that for a minute!' He began to crawl backward out of his hollow. 'Think it through very carefully!' He waited again. He could not hear them. The sky remained dark. 'I'll keep your secret, you keep mine!' Cautiously, he eased himself to his feet and began to run.

The flare and the shouts seemed to come together, a fraction of a second before the blow on his shoulder tip. He staggered and kept running south along the track.

I gambled wrong! he thought, and ran and waited for the next blow which would knock him forward to scrabble in the dirt like the sentry he had shot the day before.

But it didn't come. Ten minutes later, he leaned against the rock, gasping at the night air, and trying to listen over the rushing of his blood in his ears and the vibration of his heart against his ribs.

I made it! Oh God, I think I made it! He was filled with ferocious joy. I'm still alive! And we got Jimmy!

Then he heard the faint distant sound of an engine pass overhead in the night sky, in the direction of the Tiger's Head.

The Russian turned on the PAVN soldier. 'I said to let him go, you halfwit!'

The allies returned to the ruined village in hostile silence.

Major Lucky had a heart attack as he hung from his own carved and panelled door. First came the foreboding – a belch of uneasiness and fear – then the terrifying pain which tightened his soft body like a fist. Then he recognized the message of that pain. He felt himself sliding from pain into an ineffable sweetness. With surprise and enormous relief, he greeted that elusive something he had sought for so long.

In the deep darkness beneath the Tiger's Head, McNeill called a halt.

'What for?' demanded Stillwell. 'The airstrip's down there to the left.'

'We have to wait for Gabe and Lewis,' said McNeill.

'Wait at the strip,' said Stillwell. 'At least La will know we made it.'

'Without Gabe and Lewis, we haven't made it,' replied McNeill tiredly. 'How's Jimmy?'

'Semi-conscious,' said Spiegel. 'From shock and exhaustion . . . badly dehydrated and feverish.'

'But he knows what's going on,' said Cucic. 'Doesn't believe it, but he knows!'

Cucic and Spiegel laid Putnam on the ground. The rest squatted down just off the trail. They passed around the remaining canteens but said very little.

'Come on, Jimmy boy, have a drink,' murmured Cucic. He lifted Putnam's head and poured a little water between the dry, cracked lips. He lifted his own head, replaced Putnam's gently on the ground, and froze like the rest of the men.

They all heard the faint droning at the same time. It grew louder and louder, passed nearly above them, then dropped over the ridge.

'Fuck!' said Bennett. 'That's our lift!'

'Only landing,' said McNeill. He dropped his forehead against his arms which rested on his knees.

'Bill. . . ?' said Spiegel. 'We may have to make a choice.'

'Yeah,' said McNeill's muffled voice. 'I know.'

★

Take Jimmy and go! Take Jimmy and go! Simpson tried to get the message through to McNeill. Get the hell out of this place. Get Jimmy out!

At the same time, he stumbled and galloped forward along the trail though his shoulder burned, his breath clawed at his lungs and his eyeballs felt they would burst. Wait for me! another voice clamoured. Oh God! Please wait for me!

'What do you want to do, Bill?' Spiegel's voice was quiet and flat. 'Seven for two? We'll have to decide soon. We don't know how long it will take La to load, or how long he'll wait.'

'Wait a little longer.'

Someone exhaled shakily in the darkness. McNeill turned his head that way. 'I won't let Jimmy down. Or fuck up the rest of you. I just want half an hour.'

'Why don't some of us start down with Jimmy?' said Cucic. 'You, Lewis and Gabe can move fast once they get here.'

McNeill considered it. He nodded angrily. Worry about Gabe was slowing his brain right down. That was the trouble with having friends. Friends confuse the right thing to do. He had meant never to let that happen again. 'OK,' he said. 'Go. I'll stay here.'

'And me,' said Bennett.

'Me,' said Oyama. 'You're married.'

You need someone else, reasoned McNeill. No heroes, remember? Not even Bill McNeill. 'Oyama,' he agreed reluctantly.

Spiegel and Cucic lifted Putnam once more.

'Wait for Gabe!' The voice was strange and hoarse. Putnam lifted his head and peered in confusion into the darkness. 'Where's Gabe. . . ?' Then Putnam's head dropped again to swing loosely against his chest.

In the settlement below the ruined villa on the Tiger's Head, Nina woke in sudden fright soon after falling asleep. The world was out of order. One of Thu's soldiers was in the hut. Thu was not on the bed but by the door with Hien at his hip, talking to the soldier. Lights moved among the huts.

'What is it?' Nina asked breathlessly.

'American soldiers!' said Hien, over his shoulder. 'On the trail from Major Lucky, just below the Tiger's Head.'

The soldier disappeared. Thu pulled on his uniform jacket.

'Soldiers?' asked Nina. 'But the war is over.'

'Only on paper!' said Thu tightly.

503

'What do they want?'

'Is it ever good?' demanded Thu. He buckled on his belt and picked up his rifle.

'How many?' Nina felt a thud of panic for Thu and Hien. She imagined loss. She would die. Simply stop, as her father had done when he had no further interest in the world.

'My sentry saw seven, one of them wounded. And there may be more.'

'Are you sure they mean us ill?' Nina's panic spread like flood water over dike to drown her in a new thought.

'I will not give them a third chance to destroy my home!' Thu vanished onto the porch of the hut. Hien raced after him.

'Can I come?' begged the boy. 'Please!'

'No!' cried Nina, at the same time that Thu said, 'You stay and look after your new mother.'

Hien danced with mixed frustration and pride.

'Be careful!' begged Nina. 'Please be careful!' But Thu had gone.

Exhausted and faint from loss of blood, Simpson staggered into a run, slowed to a walk when his heart kicked like an engine broken loose from its mooring, then pushed himself back into a run again.

McNeill heard him long before he saw him. 'You horse's ass!' he said fiercely as he embraced Simpson. 'You're damn lucky I'm not an NVA patrol!' He looked over Simpson's heaving shoulder at the wet darkness on his own hand. 'You hit?'

'And Lewis!' gasped Simpson.

McNeill looked past Simpson at the stillness of the trail. 'Not coming?'

Simpson shook his head.

McNeill drew a breath. The ants were all over him now. Things were falling apart. 'Tell me about it later. Can you still walk good enough to get down to the airstrip?'

'It just tickled me.' Simpson began to stagger forward on autopilot.

'Down here,' said Oyama. 'Take it easy. It's not far.'

They had moved two hundred yards when they heard the gunshot, just one. Then voices, loud and angry, speaking Vietnamese.

Nina flung her *panung* around her waist and stepped into her sandals. Together, she and Hien ran to the top of the track down to the airfield and stopped to listen.

'Did the plane leave yet? I didn't hear it. It's late!'

'Not yet,' said Hien. 'Maybe the Americans want to attack the plane!'

Nina looked at the boy, hit by a sudden thought about the Americans and the late departure of the opium plane. Then she was shocked by the sound of the distant shot, faint and muffled by the jungle but unmistakeable.

Thu ran across the airstrip to the small, two-engine plane, where Loopy La was visible in the faint greenish glow of the cockpit. La saw him coming and climbed down to meet him.

'What's holding you up?' demanded Thu.

'Passengers didn't arrive.' La looked past Thu at the soldiers massing at the bottom of the trail. 'Excitement?'

'Round Eye soldiers coming down from the ridge,' said Thu. 'Take off if you don't want your plane to get in the way!'

La looked at the luminous dial of his watch. Then he looked at Thu, and again at the soldiers.

'Go now!' said Thu. He shouted to the men waiting by the oildrums. 'Light up for Mr La!' To La, he said, 'I don't want my cargo risked. Do you understand me?'

La and Thu understood each other very well, though they had fought on different sides before the war was ended on paper.

'Mr La,' said Thu quietly. 'Your passengers will not be coming.'

La shrugged. 'Their time – and mine – is running out anyway. My cousin will have to forgive me.' He climbed back into the plane and closed the door. The double lines of flames staggered into life along his exit path.

Thu rejoined his men near the foot of the path to wait for the Round Eye soldiers.

The Round Eye soldiers aren't attacking the plane, thought Nina. They're heading for it! 'Hien, I must go talk to your father! Quickly! He may be making a mistake.'

'Father doesn't make mistakes!'

'Sometimes even he is in danger of it!' She took the boy's hand. 'You stay here!' How many Americans can there be in this area? she asked herself. Up here? At this time? 'Please, Hien!'

'But he ordered me to protect you!' said the boy.

'I'll be safe! You stay here!' Nina started down the trail. Hien followed her.

'Please, Hien. I order you now to stay here!'

'I'll get my gun and protect us both,' said Hien. He darted back toward the huts. In nine seconds, he returned with his rifle. Helplessly, Nina looked up the dark mountain side toward the source of the gunshot, then down toward the airstrip where Thu and his soldiers were waiting for the Americans. 'All right, come!' she said. 'But there will be no fighting! Do you understand me? To fight will dishonour us all!'

McNeill crawled between *lalang* clumps and slid out onto open ground which gave him a view of the trail below. One light . . . a lantern. Dark shapes, armed. Spiegel, Cucic, Stillwell and Bennett. And Jimmy Putnam. Cucic supporting Jimmy. Spiegel kneeling to hold Stillwell by the shoulders. How many dark shapes? How many guns? Five. Six . . . seven . . . Three of us still free and armed, thought McNeill. A man shouting at Spiegel and Spiegel shaking his head. 'Seven' the man said. They must have spotted us before we split up! How long have we got?

'They're talking . . . Any chance those are friendlies?' breathed Oyama in McNeill's ear.

McNeill was still trying to count black uniforms in the dark. 'We didn't leave many friends up in these parts . . . and those aren't 'yards anyway. That's Vietnamese they're talking!'

'We have to get Jimmy back!' muttered Simpson, close behind McNeill and Oyama. 'He can't be held again!'

'Nope,' said McNeill. 'You're right . . . Oh Jesus. . . !'

One of the captors had hit Spiegel on the side of his head with his rifle butt. Two men hauled Stillwell to his feet.

He's conscious. Not hurt too bad . . . Might be able to help out. Jimmy can't. We're eight all together . . . Bennett's got no gun, even if they weren't disarmed . . . Jimmy can't be a prisoner again. . . !

Then the Americans were shoved single file down the track. The dark shapes of both prisoners and captors faded into the shadows of the scrub.

'What are we going to do?' asked Oyama.

'Tag along,' said McNeill between his teeth. 'Play hide and seek. Figure something out. . . .'

As Nina and Hien followed the firefly light of a soldier's lantern down the trail to the airstrip, the airplane's engines revved in alternation, slowed for a short taxi, then leapt to full strength like a race horse from a starting gate.

Please, God, let them be on it! thought Nina. Please!

Even if the Americans were not McNeill's men, Thu would destroy the future if he shot even one of them . . . if he had already shot one of them! Ethan Perry wouldn't be able to wipe the death of Americans from Thu's record. Even unofficial Americans. End of their chances – hers, and Thu's and Hien's – to resettle peacefully in Thailand! Nina would be condemned to live as an outlaw's wife, Hien to his fate as a general-to-be!

She and Hien arrived at the airstrip just as the sound of La's plane dwindled to a mosquito hum beyond the limestone peaks and Thu's soldiers ushered their prisoners out of the scrub into the oily smoke of the extinguished flares.

McNeill listened to the airplane fading into the night.

I should go down and put a bullet into Jimmy's head right now, he thought. And then my own. There'd be time. We'll never get him back out alive the way we came in. Even without all those bastards down there!

'We should have left it alone!' whispered Gabriel Simpson.

'Just shut up, Gabe!' Now what? McNeill begged himself for instruction. What do we do next? His left hand began to smooth his trousers against his thigh.

'We have just come from Major Lucky's village,' said Spiegel, still dizzy from the blow to his head. 'Snatched back a prisoner. La was waiting for us! He said that a Colonel Thu who lives up here knew we were coming!'

The Americans looked helplessly at the ring of dark figures around them.

'Where are the rest of you?' demanded Thu in Vietnamese.

'Does anyone here speak English?' begged Spiegel. '*Je parle un peu français.*'

'*Où sont les autres?*' Thu repeated. 'Come out!' he shouted into the darkness, 'Or I will shoot your comrades!'

'We can't let him!' whispered Gabriel.

Oh sweet Jesus! begged McNeill. What do I do now?

Thu pulled his pistol from his holster. He fired it into the air. The crack echoed faintly from the surrounding ridges. A startled jungle fowl crashed through the scrub above the track near Nina and Hien.

Thu let the silence grow. 'Imagine!' he called at last. 'Think what that would have done to a man's head! Now I will count to twenty and start with the bald one.'

507

'Wait!' cried Nina from the edge of the strip. She stepped forward, followed by Hien. She was sure the bald-headed man was the one she had seen in Chiang Mai by the Moat Gate.

Thu wheeled around, siezed a lantern from a soldier and marched fiercely to meet Nina and Hien. 'I gave an order,' he said in a voice both quiet and deadly. 'How dare you bring the boy into danger? Hien, you have disobeyed!'

Hien looked at Nina for aid in the terrifying task of confronting his father.

'If there's no fighting, we won't be in danger,' said Nina. 'Please, husband! I can speak English to these men. Perhaps I can help!'

'These men are enemies, with friends we haven't found yet. There is risk! Take my son back to the huts!'

'The shiny-headed American said that they took a prisoner from Major Lucky. That can't displease you!' said Nina desperately. She poured her energy onto Thu like the heat of a fire. 'Consider the possibility that they do not mean to fight you! Let me ask them more about their business with Major Lucky!'

'Please, Father,' begged Hien in a shaky voice. 'I think it's good advice.'

'The world has gone mad,' said Thu, 'when women and children presume to advise in battle. Go!' He marched back to his prisoners.

'Now I will begin to count,' he called. 'Even Americans can understand counting in French. I never bluff!' He walked up to the bald-headed man and raised his pistol.

Nina looked at Thu's men. Thu would never bend to a woman in front of his own troops. But she would try the only possible way. 'Honoured husband!' she cried. 'I beg you! Let me speak to these men first in English!' She shoved Hien between the shoulder blades and fell onto her own knees. Thu turned once more.

Nina flung herself prone in the old-style kowtow, long outlawed in Vietnam as decadent. She had forbidden her own employees to make it to herself. She waited with her nose against the dust, trying not to breathe it in and choke. Beside her, she heard Hien's clothing rustle. The night made its usual noises. Thu was silent. Then she heard footsteps near her head.

'I dream,' said Thu's voice in ironic disbelief. 'First, women and children advise on warfare. Then I see a lady dragon rubbing her nose in the dust!'

'Things aren't as they were,' said Nina to the ground. 'With us or with the world. Please, husband, for the sake of our future life together!

508

Treat these men first as friends.' She was going to choke. She pressed
her palms against the earth and raised her head. With the side of her
eye, she saw Hien still prostrate beside her. 'My darling Thu, let me
talk to them. You will never hear me beg like this again!'

'Nor see you disobey?'

She heard the dry edge to his voice and felt danger. 'The truth?' she
asked.

'The truth.'

I have chosen truth, she thought. Please, truth, help me now! 'Oh,
honoured husband,' she said, too softly for his men to hear, 'there must
be reasonable limits to my promises.'

The silence grew.

'Then I will trust you now,' he said. 'Hien, get up!' He turned back to
his prisoners. Nina rose onto unsteady legs and followed him, followed
in turn by Hien.

In the lantern light, Nina recognized only two of the men – the bald-
headed one and the tall, round-faced one who stood beside him. The
rest were lost in the shadows, two supporting a third.

'I think you are in command?' Nina said to Spiegel.

He hesitated, then replied, 'Yes.'

'Do you have Jimmy Putnam?'

Spiegel stiffened. 'I beg your pardon. . . .?'

The tall one's eyes and head jerked toward the dark shape, supported
against another shadow. 'Is he all right?' Nina suddenly had to fight to
control her voice.

'No,' Spiegel burst out. 'He needs food, water and medical attention
urgently. Then he needs to go home!'

'What are you saying?' demanded Thu.

Nina bowed slightly, deferentially, her hands raised apologetically,
begging a little more time. 'Where's Bill McNeill?'

This time, the Americans could not hide their consternation. Nina
raised her voice and called into the darkness. 'My husband knows
you're there. Mr McNeill, it's Nina Desanges! Please come out! It's the
only way you can hope to save your friends!'

'Who's Nina Desanges?' whispered Oyama.

McNeill did not answer. Both he and Simpson stared down the slope
toward the woman's voice, turned to stone by a witch's curse. Then
McNeill's left hand began to smooth the fabric of his trousers against

his thigh again. 'Well now. . . ,' he said. He rubbed his large fingers back and forth across his forehead. 'What about that. . . !'

'The woman from Washington. . . !' whispered Simpson.

'Maybe . . . maybe. I don't know anymore . . . did she say "her husband"?'

'You going to answer?' Simpson's head was still turned, as if listening for echoes of the voice. 'Whose side is she on?'

'Tell him!' Nina begged Spiegel. 'We don't have long. Thu won't wait, with all of his men watching. Please tell that stubborn, idiot bastard to come out!'

Spiegel stared at her in wonder and dismay. 'Who the hell are you?'

'Tell you when we have time . . . if you want to have any time, just get McNeill out here!'

'Are you saying we'll be safe?'

'No,' she said. 'But I promise that otherwise you're guaranteed dead! For God's sake trust me . . . the way McNeill should have done!'

Spiegel looked at Nina and then at Thu's pistol. He raised his head. 'Bill, I think you'd better come down here.'

'Is it a trick?' asked Oyama.

McNeill shook his head dumbly, not listening, thinking hard.

'Do you really think the three of us can get Jimmy out?' asked Simpson.

McNeill stood up and stepped onto the dark trail. 'It's McNeill. We're coming down there,' he called. 'Tell everyone one more time that we're friendlies. Do you ever take "no" for an answer, Miss Desanges?'

'Thank God . . . thank God,' murmured Nina. She bowed slightly toward Thu once more and stepped back humbly, gratefully, away from his prisoners.

Three dark shapes stumbled out of the scrub onto the airstrip.

Thu glared at the Americans. 'Who is in command?' he demanded in French.

'What the hell,' said McNeill. He lifted a hand wearily. 'Me. If you call running this kind of cock-up being "in command".'

'What did he say?' Thu demanded of Nina.

'Speak to him in French,' she told McNeill softly. 'And tell him the truth.'

This time, Nina obeyed when Thu ordered her and Hien back up to the huts. She had done all she could. Now she had to trust Thu. Please, she begged him, as she climbed. Please do the right thing!

Thu's soldiers carried Jimmy Putnam and the two wounded Americans up the trail behind Nina and the boy. Nina called for clean mats for the floor. She helped prop Jimmy Putnam upright against a post of the hut. Then she lit the lantern and knelt in front of him. His eyes were closed.

'Bring rice and tea,' she ordered one of the men. 'Jimmy,' she whispered in English. 'I think it's going to be OK. You've been found!' She wiped roughly at the tears on her cheeks. She lifted her head to listen for sounds from the airstrip. For gunshots. Please, Thu, she begged him. Don't do the wrong thing now!

Putnam opened his eyes and stared at her in confusion. His thin face twisted, like a child caught between nightmare and waking.

'Your father never gave up on you,' Nina said. 'He is real, and he never gave up!'

'How do you know my father?' Putnam asked softly, in a voice hoarse from disuse. 'I don't believe what's going on! . . . How do you know my father?'

Nina's attention was still divided. The night remained silent.

'You're on your way home,' Nina said. 'So help me God, you're on your way home!'

The balding man had followed them up the track, carrying his rucksack. He took the lantern from the peg, crouched beside one of the wounded men, and gently began to examine him. Hien immediately squatted to watch what the medic was doing. Now the man raised his head from his patient and looked at Nina across the hut.

'What are the chances we'll get out?' he asked Nina. 'Realistically?'

'I haven't heard a shot yet,' she replied.

He nodded and took some instruments from his sack.

The girl with the scarred face brought hot tea and a small basket of sticky rice for Putnam. 'He's an American?' she asked in surprise. 'But he's not pink!' She squatted and watched while Nina tenderly scooped up a ball of rice and held it to Putnam's mouth.

'There are many kinds of Americans,' said Nina. 'More than you can imagine!'

'Who are you really, if you don't mind my asking now?' The medic was holding a small silvery blade in the flame of the lantern.

'At the moment, just the boss's wife,' said Nina. 'And here he comes now!' She and Spiegel turned anxious faces to the door of the hut.

Nina saw Thu's teeth, white in the shadows. He was dwarfed by the following bulk of Bill McNeill. McNeill was not under guard. As Nina had deduced at their first meeting, McNeill's French was rough but adequate.

511

'Major Lucky has had a bad night,' Thu said, sounding delighted. 'These men who had the temerity to disturb him are sensible to throw themselves on my mercy . . . How are your patients?' he asked Spiegel. 'Do you have everything you need? I hear you used up your own bandages in a most extraordinary way!'

Nina sank back onto her heels with a deep, deep sigh.

'This one has a bullet in his shoulder,' said Spiegel. 'Can someone give me a hand?' He dug into his medical pack and gave Hien an instrument to hold. Nina left Putnam with the girl with the scarred face and went to the mat where the injured man lay face down.

Thu turned away to let McNeill show him something on a map.

'Can you hold him?' Spiegel asked Nina. 'It won't take long. The bullet's just perched there.'

Nina dropped to her knees at the man's head. She placed one hand on his light brown hair and the other on the nape of his neck. She closed her eyes when Spiegel probed into the torn flesh of the shoulder blade. Hien leaned forward for a better view.

The man's neck stiffened against Nina's hand and vibrated with unreleased sound, like a cat growling in its throat. Nina stroked the head softly while Spiegel sprinkled antibiotic powder into the wound and bandaged it.

The wounded man tried to heave himself over.

'Careful, Gabe,' said the medic. Over his shoulder, he said to Thu, 'I'll leave you the rest of my antibiotics, Colonel. I expect you can find a use for them.'

The injured man turned onto his back with a muffled grunt.

Nina looked down at the thin face on the mat and gasped. He opened his eyes. Even in the lantern light, Nina could see that they were bright blue. They looked up at her in recognition, waiting for her response.

'Gabriel!' she whispered in shock.

'I was pretty sure it was you, down on the airstrip,' he said. 'Even in the dark. So you made it!'

She shook her head in disbelief. 'And so did you.'

'After a fashion.'

'Is there another way?'

He closed his eyes for a moment. Then he opened them and his good hand reached up for her face. 'Are you all right? Here and not in Washington? Do you have what you want?'

Thu was now looking at the envelopes of antibiotic powder the balding man had given him. Nina glanced at Thu, then back at Simpson. 'More than enough,' she whispered. Simpson nodded and pulled back his hand.

512

'I'm very glad you're alive,' said Nina. 'I wished so often I had asked your last name, so I could check.'

'Well, well, well. . . ,' he said.

'Is his shoulder serious?' Nina asked the medic.

'He'll be fine,' said Spiegel. 'We'll get it x-rayed in Chiang Mai when the Colonel helps us get back there. He'll be fine.'

'After a fashion,' murmured Simpson.

'Oh Christ! . . . is that Gabe?'

Everyone in the hut turned to Putnam. Jimmy tried to stand, failed, and pulled himself across the dirt floor to Simpson's mat. 'I think I must have died a while back,' his hoarse voice said. 'None of this makes sense otherwise. You dead too, Gabe?'

Simpson's good hand reached out.

'Oh Jesus!' cried Putnam, lunging for his friend.

'Careful!' Spiegel started to say, then checked himself.

'Yeah!' said Simpson. His good arm pulled Jimmy Putnam down into a fierce embrace. 'Oh yes!'

'Was it interesting enough, Gabe?' asked Jimmy's muffled voice. '. . . Interesting enough?'

Nina slipped out of the hut and leaned against one of its woven walls in the early pre-dawn light. She wiped her cheeks again and shook her head. Too much good and too much bad. Too much change, too fast, she told the trees and the early morning sky. Stop now. I'll settle for this. There are limits even to my desires. This is enough! Stop.

Mrs Junor stood with her ear against the living room door, listening to the sound of Harry listening.

'Oh Jesus!' he said suddenly. 'Oh sweet Jesus!' He sounded like he was maybe going to cry. She put her hand on the wooden door knob, then took it off.

'Uh huh,' she heard him say. 'Yeah, OK . . . Yeah, I think so. Maybe . . . Great! . . . That's really great!'

She tried in vain to construct from these scraps of language whatever news it was that had made his voice go so high, and tight and excited, instead of angry the way it had sounded for such a long time.

She heard him hang up and quickly went to her chair by the kitchen table.

'Did you hear that?' Junor marched into the kitchen and began to circle the table like a racehorse coming down after a gold cup finish.

She started to deny eavesdropping but he cut her off, not noticing.

'They got him out! They fucking got him out!'

'Don't say that word in this house,' she said automatically. 'Who's out?'

Junor flung open the storm door of the kitchen and disappeared down into the yard. Mrs Junor ran into the back bedroom to watch him disappear up the trail as usual. He was throwing wood from the woodpile all over the backyard. One piece smashed the row of icicles hanging from the old garage roof. Another piece hit the side of the house and made it reverberate like a drum.

'Harry!' she cried. He didn't hear. She watched two pieces she had split the day before as they sailed onto the roof of the old garage and lodged in the snow. She lifted the sash window, and the storm window and leaned over the sill. 'Harry! You cut that out!' she yelled.

'Whoooeee!' he yelled back. 'I'll split you some more!' He bounded over and jumped up to catch the window sill. He chinned himself so that the green eyes appeared level with her hands. 'He's out, Mom! Can you fucking believe it! Alive and out!'

He let go and dropped to the ground. 'Here you go, Mom!' He picked up the axe and steadied a section of unsplit log on the tree stump she used. He swung the axe. The log split cleanly at the first go. 'Everybody out!' he shouted. 'Everybody out!'

'You be careful with that axe,' said Mrs Junor fiercely. He didn't hear her. She closed the storm window and then the sash. Then she sat down on the bed beside the sleeping cat and began to cry.

You stupid old cow, she told herself, smiling and shaking her head. You got nothing to cry about. What's wrong with you?

514

Epilogue

Washington D.C. – 1982

People walking on the Mall with their dogs or children pretended the young man wasn't there. It was not so much his long hair and crumpled clothes that alarmed them, as the odd, uneasy glitter of his green eyes and the definite possibility that he was drunk. Carrying a six-pack of beer, he set off purposefully from the trees that separated the Mall from the street. He stopped, wavered, changed direction, walked a few steps in the new direction. Then he crossed abruptly to the nearest tree and sat down with his back against it, looking out into the flat green space of the Mall, tilting his head as if listening, giving little affirmative shakes and then a violent one of disagreement. As further evidence for the prosecution, he carried a tramp's suitcase – a cardboard box of clothing and personal effects.

Harry Junor felt raw, fragile and in need of consideration. There were too many people. He kept losing track of them. They disappeared behind him. Cut past on tangents. Came up out of nowhere. To feel their hostility as well, however slight, was making his heart beat so hard it deafened him. Being out wasn't easy.

He looked at his watch. An hour to go. He had come early on purpose to get the lay of the land. To give himself time to change his mind if he wanted to. He couldn't see the Vietnam Veterans' Memorial from where he was sitting, just grass. But in the distance, to his right and to his left, people kept walking slowly down into the ground.

Down to see the dead, he thought. I never knew they had visiting hours down there!

He shut his eyes and pushed his head back against the tree trunk. Billings exploded again, in front of his eyes. One minute he was there, grinning over his shoulder. The next minute there was just noise, and a red spray in the air and small fragments arcing through the spray. And then Junor himself was hit. Then Billings grinned again over his shoulder and exploded again.

Junor forced his eyes open, and opened his fists. He looked around to see if anybody had noticed. A dog was sniffing at his cardboard box, but its owner was elsewhere.

515

You got this far, he told himself. Keep going!

He made himself leave the tree and move farther out onto the grass, into the open space with nothing at his back. He sat down on the ground again, the box beside him, the six-pack between his legs. He looked around defiantly, as if to say, I have a right to be here, just like everybody else. I'm waiting, that's what I'm doing!

He glanced over both shoulders then focused straight ahead toward the hidden depression into which the visitors to the underworld were still walking.

Some of the men were about his own age. He watched them, trying to decide whether they were vets, or their brothers who got academic deferments and safe jobs in the rear.

A black family slid slowly down an invisible ramp until they sank behind the grass. The little boy walked soberly between his father and mother. They made him think of Jimmy P's family, only this boy was probably too young to remember his big brother, if that's whose name was on the Memorial.

An old lady carrying a bunch of flowers made Junor think of his mother. Dickie was down there somewhere, over that invisible edge.

He looked at his watch again. A half an hour had already gone. Half an hour to go!

You've done harder things, Harry, he told himself. Get going! Get the first part over with.

Not giving himself time to reconsider, he rose smoothly, with the box under one arm and the six-pack under the other and walked toward the left end of the ramp down which people were sinking into the earth. His mouth was dry and his hands were damp. It was worse than going into a dark room as a child. He nearly decided to go back to the truck and think about it a little longer. But Bill McNeill had gone to a lot of trouble for today, even though he was only back in the country for a few weeks. Junor didn't like to think of reporting an aborted mission to Bill McNeill.

From the top of the gentle ramp, he could see one of the two black wings of stone lodged like a giant prehistoric bird in the ten-foot cliff cut out of the flat green grass of the Mall. He decided not to go down the ramp yet. Instead, he circled across the grass until he was opposite the meeting of the two shiny black wings that spread nearly 247 feet, wingtip to wingtip. From here he couldn't see the names, just the separate slabs of polished granite.

They were all there in one place – all the dead, all the fragments and splinters which had been young men and women. And all the missing

516

ones. He tried to take it in – all 58,000, plus or minus a few. He had read about it in the papers when the Memorial had been dedicated, and every name read out loud. Families had travelled from all over America to hear the name of a father or husband or brother or sister read out loud, to hear it made real in public what that father or husband or brother or sister had done, and what it had cost. It made Junor feel a little shaky.

Months after the dedication, people were still coming. Junor watched them for a long time. Most acted a little as if they were in church, walked slowly, talked in low voices, or stood silently and just looked at the thing. The black family had huddled close together, not talking. The man had his arm around the woman's shoulders. Then the little boy reached out and stroked the cold surface.

Junor picked up his box and beer and approached the dark cliff face. Suddenly, all he could see were names – line after line, panel after panel – and his own face, and the Washington Monument reflected in the shiny dark surface. The top date on the panel to the right of the centre angle was 1959, with just two names under it. The date to the left was 1975. He looked one way, then another, confused. There were too many names. He didn't know where to start looking. He didn't know who to look for first. He kept thinking of more and more names he'd like to know about.

'Can I help you?' The man was wearing a Park Ranger's Uniform.

'Richard Junor,' said Harry.

'Do you know when he was killed?'

'Twelve of October, 1970,' he said flatly.

The man consulted a book he was carrying. 'You'll find his name on the second panel on the west end,' he said.

Harry's pulse was settled slightly by the matter-of-factness of their exchange.

'And if there's anyone else you want to find,' said the man, 'There are directories over there . . . alphabetical. They tell you the location of the panel and which column and line to look for.' He pointed to some short posts with miniature shelters on top, like phone booths for the pigeons.

'Thanks,' mumbled Junor.

He walked along the western wing away from the centre, past tiny flags, and flowers and hats and teddy bears, and a pair of boots, which people had left for the dead, moving backward through time along the precipice of death. There were so many names. His own experience, which had occupied such an enormous part of his life, shrank into a minute fraction of time beside all these lives which had been and then ended.

517

'Richard Junor.' There it was, with a diamond in front of it to say that the death had been confirmed. Harry felt calm now. He set down his box and looked at the wall. Without thinking, he reached out and touched his brother's name, as the little boy had done.

'There you are, you son of a bitch,' he said quietly. He stood for a minute, just looking at the name and thinking. 'I guess this is as real as anything gets,' he said to the name. 'You're there and I'm here.'

He waited for tears or a sense of enlightenment to hit him but felt only the new calm and a slight puzzlement. 'Can you make any more sense out of it than me?' he asked his brother's name. 'If you can, I'd like to pass the good news on to Mom.'

With his foot, he nudged the cardboard box with his uniform, medals, and photographs against the wall, between a pot of red-orange plastic geraniums and a San Francisco Giants baseball cap. He suddenly remembered he was in public and looked to see if anyone had noticed him talking to the stone wall, but everyone was absorbed in his or her own private relationship with the black granite. He touched the name once more quickly, then walked away toward the directories the ranger had pointed out, by the western end of the Memorial, with the Lincoln Memorial in the background.

Now came the part that really made him jumpy. He turned to P, then found the name Putnam, James Michael. He memorized the location and began to walk back along the Memorial, up through time, past his brother's name, past the end of the war and into its beginning.

He couldn't see the face clearly. The man had shoved his hands deep into the pockets of his heavy parka and stood staring at the Memorial across the heads of a picnicking couple. Junor saw steam rising from their open thermos.

'Jimmy P!' called Junor cautiously. He was suddenly terrified of getting it wrong. Of finding nothing to say. Of tapping the wrong man. Of Jimmy not coming after all. Of his really being dead, in spite of what everyone was telling Junor now instead of what they used to tell him. How did one know any more when it was the truth?

Putnam turned. The two men looked at each other for a second of incredulous, unambiguous recognition. They approached each other awkwardly, still incredulous. Their hands lifted and touched the other, questioningly, on the arm, the face.

He's a lot thinner, thought Junor. Then he heard himself let out a whoop.

'Son of a bitch!' He grabbed Putnam's head as if tackling him and pulled it down against his own chest. 'Son of a bitch! Back from the fucking dead . . . I don't fucking believe it!' He thumped Putnam between the shoulder blades in time with his words.

'You trying to kill me for real?' demanded Putnam's muffled voice. He twisted free and grabbed Junor with both arms. They embraced hard, with tears now running down both faces.

'I don't believe it!' said Junor again.

'You better believe it!' Putnam said. 'Somebody's got to!'

Unless he saw their tears, a passer-by might have thought they were trying to wrestle each other to the ground, as they rocked first right and then left, still locked in their embrace.

The picnicking couple stopped eating and watched the two men. The man and woman whispered together. Then the man rose and went to stand awkwardly near Putnam and Junor. 'I hope you don't mind my butting in. . . ,' he said.

They looked at him distantly, still lost in disbelief. Junor shook Putnam's arm by the elbow as if testing it and slapped it as if to say that it had passed the test.

'. . . but are you two men vets?'

Now Junor and Putnam focused on him. They nodded in wary alertness.

'I just wanted to say . . .' said the man. 'I've been wanting to find someone to say it to and you two showed up . . . My wife and I were against the war. . . .'

Putnam and Junor exchanged glances, this time without smiling.

'We're still against the war,' the man went on, pink and hurried with self-consciousness. 'And seeing all these names here today makes us feel that more strongly than ever. But we also defined something else today. We disagree with the policy makers, but we're grateful to the individuals who went. The war wasn't your fault. You did something hard and we want to tell you we appreciate what it cost.' He stopped. 'We're sorry it took so long. . . .'

There was a pause.

'So thank you,' he said. There was another, longer pause.

'That's real nice of you,' said Junor.

'Good luck, both of you,' said the man, already retreating.

'Oh man!' said Putnam, shaking his head. 'What's been going on while I was away?'

'I don't really know either,' said Junor. 'But I think it's good we missed it.' He looked sideways at Putnam. 'Are you really OK?'

519

'The shrink thinks I can handle law school next fall,' replied Putnam drily. 'I can probably deal with the stresses, he thinks. I think he really means they trust me now not to blow my mouth off and stir up the student radicals.'

Junor gave a short laugh, then laid his arm over Putnam's shoulders. 'Come on then, let's get this over with!'

They walked slowly across the green, green grass to the black granite wings, Putnam limping slightly.

'There we are,' said Junor suddenly. 'Billings, confirmed; Donaldson, confirmed; Petrie, confirmed; Putnam. . . .' He stopped.

'I still have a diamond by my name!' said Putnam so softly that Junor could barely hear him. 'I'm still dead!'

Junor felt Putnam's shoulders judder under his arm. 'It takes time for the word to get through,' he said reassuringly. 'Give them time.' He patted Putnam's far arm, feeling helpless.

Putnam just kept staring at his own name in the list of the dead. Junor took his arm away.

'They'll do it,' Junor said. 'They'll do it. Don't worry. It's just the office pogues screwing up again. Don't mean a thing.' Junor didn't recognize the eyes Putnam turned toward him.

'How much of my life do they want?' asked Putnam.

Junor shrugged. 'Nobody's counting.' He wished he had thought to check the Memorial beforehand.

They stood silently for a long time, side by side but not quite touching.

'You're back – that's what matters,' said Junor. 'We came here to celebrate . . . and say hello. Right?'

Putnam nodded wordlessly.

'Right!' Junor squatted down and put the six-pack of beer on the ground in front of him. He opened all six cans. One by one, he placed four of them against the wall – one for Billings (confirmed dead), one for Donaldson (confirmed dead), one for Petrie (confirmed dead), and one for Thaddeus, also confirmed dead. He reached one up to Putnam and picked up his own. Putnam squatted beside him. For several minutes, they looked at the names on the wall and their own faces reflecting back from the polished surface.

'Well,' said Junor finally. 'I don't know. . . . Here's to the best bunch of Mike Foxtrots that ever got the shit blown out of them!' They raised their cans to the wall and drank, quietly, shoulder to shoulder, each more pleased than he could ever say that the other was there.

'It's not cold,' said Junor. 'Sorry about that.'

'I never thought you'd get my message about the beer,' said Putnam.

'Well, I sure as hell never thought you'd get out to claim it,' replied Junor. 'To think I could have drunk it all myself!' He raised his can sideways to Putnam, without turning his head. 'We're both out now. It just shows you never can tell . . . thank the Lord!'

'Just as well, sometimes,' said Putnam. 'Falacci couldn't come?' he asked abruptly.

Junor shook his head. 'He won't come near this . . . thinks it's a big con. Too late and too little. He's still one angry man!'

'Here's to him anyway,' said Putnam. He drained his can.

'If you're ready to move on,' said Junor, 'I got two more six-packs in my truck. You still got a long way to go to catch up, but you're in expert hands now, my boy!'

'Sounds good,' said Putnam. He shivered. 'Come on! I want to get out of this place!'

When Nina gave birth to a son, in the new villa northwest of Chiang Mai, Ethan Perry flew to Thailand for Thu's party. In theory, the celebration was for the Festival of Songkran, the Thai New Year. Thu did not wish to alert either the gods or personal enemies to the new object of his intense private joy.

The house was the former residence of a British teak magnate, a series of linked, open-sided pavilions, with swooping tiled roofs. It sat on the ground rather than stilts, as the mountain shoulder where it perched was never threatened by flood. Nina's view from her new verandah was a little less open than that from the Tiger's Head but still as deep as an indrawn breath. On that day, the courtyard heaved with laughing, damp, dishevelled people, who balanced glasses and food as they tried to avoid puddles, kittens, children and the more enthusiastic celebrants. Two cats warily regarded the melee from corners of the curving roofs.

A shrieking nymph in *panung* and bare feet threw a basin of water over Ethan Perry's left arm. His head was beyond her aim. He retaliated by emptying his glass over her small black head from an unfair advantage of height.

'What a waste of gin!' he called up to Nina, just before Hien caught him squarely in the face with a jet from a water pistol.

'Everyone's gone loony!' Perry said to Nina who was watching the ritual pandemonium from the verandah. He wiped his face with a soaking handkerchief, then his bare knees, and climbed the five wooden steps to join her. Her blue silk jacket and long silk skirt were water-splashed and her feet were bare on the sun-bleached teak floor. She wore a garland of pale pink orchids around her neck.

'No more than usual for this day,' said Nina. 'I'm so glad you could come! . . . Hien! Go shoot someone else!'

'I had to do something to raise the tone of your guests,' said Perry. His dignity condescended happily to dishevelment, like a giant forest tree to strings of fairy lights. He gazed across Meos, Americans, Laos, a few French and English, and Thais, toward a large, crew-cut head on the far side of the courtyard. 'What is that McNeill character doing out here? Back home, they're still trying to decide whether to decorate him or to prosecute.'

'He and Thu have been muttering in corners,' said Nina. 'I hope our legal status is confirmed before they do something terrible and get us thrown out of the country! And I hear from the cook that he's thinking of moving in with a local Meo woman. . . . Oh!' She turned suddenly to the *ayah* who had appeared carrying the baby as proudly as if she had produced him herself. 'Here's your godchild, Ethan!'

Perry inclined his length toward the small bundle. 'Oh, my dear!' he said. 'Oh well, yes!' He cleared his throat. 'Well done! Very well done!' He leaned closer to the wrinkled, fierce-eyed bundle. 'A boy. Well. . . !' He glanced at Nina under his bristling brows. 'I expect Thu's quite pleased.'

'So am I, Ethan,' she said contentedly. 'And one day. . . .' She reached for her child. 'Don't glare at Ethan like that, darling piglet. You'll frighten him away!' She raised serious eyes back to Perry. 'I remember the first time I heard Thu use those words, talking about our future, on the Tiger's Head . . . when I was carrying Mouse. They terrified me. Now . . . one day.' She looked down at the child in her arms. 'I still don't quite trust them, but I can say them again.'

Glossary

The following acronyms and the organisations they refer to are real. Any others mentioned in the book may be considered to be entirely fictional.

ARVN   Army of the Republic of Vietnam (South Vietnam).

CIA   US Central Intelligence Agency. Organised after WWII, on foundations of the OSS (qv), using many former OSS personnel.

DIA   US Defense Intelligence Agency. Established in 1961 to consolidate the many different general intelligence-gathering activities of the defense services.

FBIS   Foreign Broadcast Information Service. Monitors foreign language broadcasts.

IDC   Interagency Defector Committee. IDCs are maintained in most major US embassies, to deal with walk-ins and other defectors.

IPWIC   Interagency Prisoner of War Committee. American.

MACThai   US Military Assistance Command, Thailand. Based in Bangkok.

MACV   US Military Assistance Command, Vietnam. Military, naval and airforce HQ. Based in Saigon.

NLHS   Neo Lao Hak Sat. Lao Patriotic Front. Communist-dominated, *de facto* governing body of much of Laos, in conflict with the Royal Lao government.

NPIC   National Photographic Interpretation Center. American.

OSS   Office of Strategic Services. American WWII intelligence organisation. Officers of the OSS trained Ho Chi Minh and his guerrillas as resistance fighters against the Japanese in Indochina.

PL or Pathet Lao	The military arm of the Communist NLHS (qv) which, at the time this book takes place, controlled much of northern Laos.
PAVN	People's Army of Vietnam. North Vietnamese.
PRC	People's Republic of China.
Royal Lao	Basically right-wing, headed by Lao royal family. Pro-American.
RCRRB	Red Cross Refugee Reclamation Bureau.
SDECE	Service de Documentation Exterieure et du Contre-Espionage. French intelligence organisation.
Southeast Asia Publications Bureau	American body for monitoring open source published materials.
Spetznatz	Russian Special Forces.
USAID	United States Agency for International Development.